O♥T:
A Schoolboy's Tale

David Brining

Contents

"May you of a better future, love without a care and remember we loved too. As the shadows closed in, the stars came out."
Derek Jarman, *At Your Own Risk*, 1992.

"Reach for the stars; and when that rainbow's shining over you, that's when your dreams will all come true."
S Club 7, 2000.

About the author
The author has lived and worked in several different countries and has been, variously, a camel jockey, a tennis coach, an underwater photographer, a motivational speaker, a magazine editor, an opera singer, a pantomime dame, a cat-sitter and a ghost-buster. He is the author of *Tombland Fair*, *A Teenage Odyssey*, *J*, *Yo-yo's Weekend*, *Dead Boy Walking* and *Out*, all published as ebooks on Smashwords and Amazon Kindle and in print from Amazon.

For Kate in Bristol who suggested the need for this book and George in Sheffield who needed it most.

1: Feel This Moment

YOU would not *believe* what happened at the tennis club. When I say tennis club, please don't think this is some poshed-up, Pimms-drinking, Panama-wearing, toffee-arsed effort. No, it's like this bunch of scruffy courts tucked into some corner of this park my Dad used to work in? About ten minutes' walk from our house, you know? But the council calls it a club, so they can charge you a quid for playing there, I guess.

Anyway, so I was with Tim Wilson, right? My oldest friend and spit-brother. You know. Where you spit in your palm and then like shake hands? We went back years, you know? I mean, like *years*, man, like all the way to Primary Three, and we'd like moved together aged 11 to the local grammar school when we passed the scholarship exam. His dad was this dentist but his mum, who *my* mum called a social climber 'cos she came from some place in London called Saint Reatham wanted him to go one better and be like an actual *proper* doctor? He was really good at Science and Maths and that kind of stuff and had this caring, compassionate thing which went 'I can see you're unhappy. Why don't you tell me about it?' Unfortunately he would then refer you to Doctor Jesus but I'd known Tim for years and, as I said, he was my spit-brother, so what could I do, eh? Especially as I suspected that once he actually *became* a doctor it might go 'I can see you're unhappy. Take a pill from my latest pharmaceutical supplier.' And I'm not talking Es, right? He'd even got himself this girlfriend during the holiday, for God's sake, some woolly-hatted, tambourine-bashing nitwit with flaxen pigtails and massive round specs called Holly or Hilly, something beginning with H. They went to the same Bible Study, so obviously hadn't even begun to think about approaching Base Minus Gerzillion, right?

A good-looking guy, he was taller than me, about 5' 9, thicker-set (though I was so thin I'd been nicknamed Belsen Boy), with battleship-grey eyes and barley-coloured hair cut short off a wide forehead. We'd done sleepovers when we were younger, kipping on camp-beds in the attic and taking turns to dress and undress so we wouldn't see each other's willies, like when we went swimming at the municipal baths and shared a cubicle then, sitting on a wall, vinegar-soaked chips-and-scraps from a paper bag, we'd changed under our towels for the same reason. Didn't want people to think we were, like, 'funny', you know?

Anyway, there we were at the tennis club, halfway through a set, three-three and going with serve, a nice sunny Tuesday at the start of September, a couple of days before school started again. The pollen-count was low and my tennis was improving. I had good ground-strokes and could hold a baseline rally. My serve was also getting better. It was still not fast but it was, like, accurate, you know? I could generally place the ball where I wanted, and get some sidespin too. I couldn't lob so well, though my passing shots were pretty cool and I did this utterly awesome backhand slice which had so much spin the ball would like literally drop over the net then squirm away at some super-crazy angle. Tim, very much the serve-and-volley player, had these really hard like hammer-shots but no spin so it was just a question of being in the right place to hit the returns, you know?

I had this really cool blue Dunlop racket that I got for my thirteenth birthday and proper Dunlop Green Flash tennis shoes, and I was wearing this like pale yellow T-shirt, white shorts and white sports socks, and this dark blue Adidas baseball cap. Tim, obviously, wore snow-white whites and Rayban mirror-specs. Anyway we were just on this like water-break when two Sixth Formers from our school appeared on the next court. One was Mark Sonning, a tall, friendly blond in blue trackies and this white Lacoste T-shirt who was like captain of cricket, captain of tennis, captain of swimming and head of my house. Dumping his bag of six rackets on the grass and doing some stretching routine, he called "Hi, Jonny."

The second newcomer, in these baggy white shorts and this startling orange T-shirt, was Alistair Rose. Lazily unzipping this like super-awesome red graphite Slazenger, he squirted Lucozade from a squeezy bottle into his mouth then, ever so casually, nodded to me. Something jolted, like I'd been electric-shocked. Pumpkin seeds fell from my hand, scattering in a light patter on the court. Actor, writer, editor of the school magazine, winner of English prize after English prize, prefect, deputy head boy, Alistair Rose was literally a Legend with a capital L. About a head taller than me, his longish, bruise-dark hair tumbled thickly from an untidy parting towards his right eye. He wedged a shock-absorber between the strings and tapped the racket-head three times against the soles of his white Reeboks.

I knew him from *A Midsummer Night's Dream*, last year's school play. He'd been Oberon and I'd been Puck. He'd like utterly over-awed me and I'd literally never managed a conversation without stammering like some village-idiot, especially since he'd played Oberon bare-chested and I hadn't been able to tear my eyes from his pecs. He'd also been Fagin to my Oliver in my first school play back in 3Y, utterly terrifying me with this toasting-fork which he'd jabbed in my ribs and a long wispy beard. Although I'd loved every second, I was so nervous I'd actually thrown up before 'Where is love?' and breathed these like sicky fumes over the poor girl who'd played Nancy. The review said I had sung sweetly but my dancing was shite, or words to that effect. I like literally trip over my own feet, you know?

"Oh boy," groaned Tim. "Alistair Rose. That's all we need."

"Why?" I tried to inject some innocence into my voice.

"Rosie has an eye for the boys, if you know what I mean."

I didn't. Instinctively I touched the little gold cross I wore round my neck, a confirmation gift from my mother.

"Well, you should," said Tim darkly, "After that play you were in."

"He hardly talked to me," I said. "Anyway, what *do* you mean?"

"Rosie's queer," Tim said impatiently, "Like your bumchum Paulus. So I heard."

"Bollocks," I said. "Where did you hear that?"

"Graham Brudenall." Tim bounced a ball on the grass. "And my sister."

Super-reliable sources, then. The bitchiest boy in our form and some gossipy girl.

"Anyway, Paulus isn't queer," I protested. People said nasty things about Andy Paulus because he sang in the Chapel Choir and had curly blond hair, like fresh wood-shavings.

Watching Rosie, poised and alert on the other court, I like kind of wondered, but, to be honest, I didn't really know what it meant anyway, you know? No-one ever talked about it, 'cept in a hushed mumble about this like grubby old geezer who attended our church. Sitting alone in this discreet side-pew, he always wore the same dirty beige mac and had like this lank, greasy hair. Mum didn't know his name. No-one knew his name. He was just 'the queer fellow in the corner' and I was told to stay away from him. When I asked why, Mum said he'd feed me poisoned liquorice allsorts and I'd die, and then where would I be?

In Heaven? I quipped, getting one of Mum's looks.

Anyhow, 'queer', to me, was this like geriatric coffin-dodger with his bag of poisoned sweets? Not Alistair Rose, this exuberant, handsome, charismatic seventeen year old in the Day-Glo shirt, but I didn't want to admit that I wasn't sure what Tim meant. I mean, obviously I'd heard rumours at school that some men like hated football and dressed in their mum's knickers, right?, while others lurked around public toilets peeping at little boys' little willies, but that clearly wasn't Rosie, you know? Confused, I dismissed Tim's statement as bollocks.

Brace up, I muttered, gripping the racket-handle in both hands. Focus. On the game. Not on him. On the game. Tapping the frame against the soles of my Green Flash, I wound myself up to serve. Then Rosie laughed, a silvery, joyful sound which jolted my heart again.

"Long!" called Tim.

The second serve worked but Tim shot a winner down the left-hand tramline that I couldn't reach. As I kind of staggered off the court, Rosie like smiled at me. I mean, smiled.

"Steady there, JP," he said, "Or you'll do yourself an injury."

His eyes were utterly amazing, warm, kind, humorous, deep blue pools I just like literally wanted to lose myself in, you know?

"Thanks," I stammered idiotically, blushing pink as a, well, as a rose.

Shit. What the fuck *was* this? I touched my cross again.

"Come on, Jonny!" cried Tim impatiently.

Shaking myself like a wet otter, I returned to the service-line, tapped the frame against my soles like Rosie and span the handle round. Now my concentration really *was* shot. Rosie the Legend had not only spoken to me, he'd like used my nickname? Man alive.

I lost the game, the set and the match. Bollocks.

As I slugged water from a plastic bottle, trying to ignore Tim's somewhat unchristian celebrations, I watched Rosie stretching to whip the racket-head through this arc, rolling his wrists for the topspin. My God, he was good. He was like *really* good? And the red graphite Slazenger was like *sooo* cool, you know? I *had* to get one.

"Hey!" called Sonning, "You wanna make up a doubles? You two and us two? Ali's winning, so I need some help."

"Sure!" I heard myself saying. "I'll play with Rosie."

"You can play with me any time, baby." He laughed that silvery laugh again.

My heart seemed to like melt, you know? What the hell was wrong with me?

"Alistair!" Sonning warned sternly. "No innuendo in front of the children!"

His serve literally blistered past my ear like some ballistic missile.

"Come on, Jonny," called Tim, "Move about a bit." Not stand there like a rooted tree. "It's like playing against a fruit-bowl, what with a yellow shirt and an orange shirt."

Rosie grinned. "Well, we're a fruity pair, aren't we, Jonathan?"

I blushed strawberry-red.

The game like mixed ecstasy and agony in equal measure. I was so conscious of Him. Every time he high-fived me for a winner, my knees wobbled. Every time he patted my shoulder to console a missed shot, my legs trembled. Every time he smiled, my stomach lurched. And he smiled a lot. But the ecstasy was being with the Legend, being *noticed* by the Legend, being *friends* with the Legend. I wanted the afternoon to like last forever.

We lost 6-4. Only Tim cared, dancing round the court crying "Losers, losers."

Rosie and I shook hands. The contact sent this electric bolt searing through my body.

"We're having a couple of shandies," he said casually, "If you'd care to join us."

"No." Tim kind of glared antagonistically across his bicycle handlebars.

"Yes," I said, gazing at Rosie.

"Right-o," said Sonning. "See you in school, er… Wilkins."

Rosie ignored Tim altogether.

"Yeah," I said. "See you in school."

Tim's face kind of twitched like some out-of-control electric cable but I didn't care. I was rolling with the prefects. I wheeled my bike to the pub and sat outside at a wooden table with Sonning while Rosie went for drinks, Tetley's for them, Foster's for me.

The 'Lake View' had once been the Big House on the estate before that'd become the sprawling suburban park it is now. The terrace, situated between solid, blackened Doric columns, had, surprise surprise, a view of the Boating Lake, not that anyone ever *went* boating. It's about two feet deep and full of prams and shopping trolleys. When I read that the Council was gonna start a rowing club there, I laughed my arse off. It's about fifty meters long. By the time Redgrave and co are breaking sweat, they'll be like crossing the finish-line.

Anyway, the pub had this large, seedy, rundown bar whose staff were like really sketchy about checking your age, you know? and a posh restaurant we saved for special occasions, like Dad's fortieth birthday when the Grunters (aka my grandparents) had complained all evening – Gruntpa said my spaghetti looked like rubber-bands and the Parmesan smelt of sick whilst Gruntma sent all the vegetables back saying they hadn't been properly cooked and could they boil them a while longer otherwise they'd play Hamlet with her dentures. And why was the food served on roof-tiles? Didn't they have any plates? You'd've thought, with such shocking prices, they'd be able to afford like proper plates, right? God. I thought I was like gonna die of embarrassment?

Sonning asked if I'd been away during the summer. Back in July, I'd spent a week literally crammed with the folks in this two-roomed thatched cottage on some wind-swept clifftop in Arse-end, Norfolk, swimming in this bollock-freezing sea, collecting seaweed and razor-fish shells and reading *Thunderball* (I found the part where Bond sucks sea-spines out of Domino's foot so utterly sexy I'd like spurted in my PJs - twice) whilst Dad complained about these strange snuffling noises I apparently make in my sleep.

Popping into Norwich for a day, we'd visited the cathedral and the castle then gone to Great Yarmouth's Pleasure Beach where, amazingly, I somehow persuaded Mum to let me have, like, a hot-dog? Like, with onions? *And* a go on the waltzers and this swinging pirate-ship. I know. Fucking miracle, eh? I even got the folks onto the dodgems for like twenty minutes. Six days, and like a bazillion hours in the back of our silver Sierra watching mile after mile of flat, featureless fields flow by whilst Mum chattered endlessly about knitting, baking and bird-watching ('No, Jonathan, you can*not* have the radio on. We're engaging in conversation, for God's sake') and I buried my head in Kenneth Ulyatt's *Custer's Gold*. I sort of admired General Custer, standing heroically against the enemy and dying in the cause, but this book suggested he was some deranged, gold-greedy glory-hunter and an inept tactician. Maybe so. I'd never divide my forces like he did. The other book I had on the subject, Jeff Jefferies' *Seventh Cavalry*, presented an opposite view, that Major Reno and Captain Benteen had lost the battle by holing up on a ridge and failing to relieve their commander. I liked that book because the central character was a bugler called Peters. I kind of fantasized it was me Custer was ordering to blow 'Reveille'. I was really into Westerns and had tons of little plastic figures, all 1:32 Airfix cowboys, Indians, horses, blue-jacketed 7th cavalrymen, even Mexican bandits with massive hats, droopy moustaches and crossbelts of bullets. I had covered wagons so I could do wagon-trains and some plastic buildings, like a two-storey saloon with swinging doors, a bunk house, a bank, a fort and some brown plastic bars for a corral. I constructed my very own Wild West in the back yard and re-enacted the Gunfight at the OK Corral and the Magnificent Seven and my own stuff, even photographing some for posterity.

I'd spent the rest of the seven-week summer holiday at home. I'd played tennis with Tim, cycled to a local National Trust property in the country with Mark Gray, listened to the Proms on Radio 3, blasted like a bucketload of motorcycles and tanks out of the trees in *Deathchase*, my new favourite video game, enjoyed loads of British athletes winning like a bazillion gold medals at the Olympic Games and endured England v West Indies on TV. I'd even taken a train to Leeds for the first (rained off) day of the Headingley Test and sat under an umbrella nibbling paste sandwiches waiting for something to happen. Nothing did. Also, the Grunters took me to see the Humber Bridge and, later, to Mother Shitbag's Cave in Knaresborough. Nothing happened there either. Sonning, by contrast, had spent a month in Provençe knocking down walls and plastering ceilings in his parents' holiday farmhouse.

"You ever been to Provençe, JP?" I shook my head. "You'd love it. Golden sunlight, olive groves, vineyards, cicadas singing in the dry grass… it's very romantic."

I'd never been abroad. The furthest I'd ever been was Pembrokeshire in Wales and, once, Edinburgh in Scotland. Anyway, for some reason I blushed, especially when Rosie, returning with the drinks, described his trip to Venice. He reckoned I'd love Venice even more, with its sweeping stone-bridges, soft strumming of guitars, canals and gondoliers serenading cuddling lovers with romantic ballads and tossed red roses. I mean, pass the sickbag, eh?

"I saw it in *Moonraker*," I said, "When Bond drives that gondola into St Mark's Square and this pigeon does a double-take."

But it's nothing like the book. That's set in Kent. Now I've never been to Kent, so I kight be wrong, but I don't think it's *much* like Venice, is it Or the Moon. They only kept the title and Hugo Drax, the villain, and they changed him from some red-haired, buck-toothed, one-eyed freak who cheated M out of loads of loot at cards into some boring, bland guy with a slicked black hair, a trim goatee and no personality. Anyhow, it's a really good book which would make a brilliant film and I don't know why they had to change it.

"You'd look really cute in one of those straw boaters," Rosie remarked.

Thanking God once more for Foster's, I hid my burning face in it whilst they chatted about school stuff then drew me in by asking if I would be in the play Rosie was writing.

"I've written a part especially for you," he said. "You'll love it. You're a great actor. You were awesome in *The Dream*." The reviewer had said 'poised and coolly controlled'. "*The king doth keep his revels here tonight*," he quoted, then summarised "And Oberon is angry for his wife has stolen a lovely boy." His eyes seemed to penetrate my soul.

"JP's always been a star," said Sonning. "Broke our hearts as Oliver and made us laugh as Puck. We're lucky to have him. You're going into what form, JP?"

"Upper Five H," I said. "Mr Hutchinson's. 'S OK. I like him."

Rosie, swallowing his beer, stretched out his legs in the late-afternoon sun. Bathed in gold, they kind of hypnotized me then I realised Sonning had like noticed me staring, so downed half my drink in a massive gulp to cover my embarrassment, which made me cough then hic. Suddenly wishing I was wearing baggier shorts, I pulled my cap over my eyes.

"Easy, tiger," Rosie said amiably, "There's no rush."

I hicced a few more times. Sonning suggested I hold my breath.

God Almighty. I was *sooo* lame. I was rolling with the prefects, with Rosie, the Legend, and like matching them pint for pint, and I'd got hiccups. They'd think me such a loser. Then Rosie's eye caught mine and there was another of those sudden, invisible, electrical sparks that made my heart bounce like one of our tennis balls.

The sunshine-stained trees, gold, red and pink, were reflected sharply in the cool, polished-steel mirror of the water's unruffled surface. Somewhere a bird erupted into a joyful melody. We sat in comfortable silence till we had to go. Rosie said he'd see me home.

He lived about half a mile from me. Most afternoons he caught the school bus, sitting at the back with the other Sixth Formers whilst I sat at the front with Maxton and Gray doing our homework. Idly I wondered where his house was, what it was like, what his bedroom was like. After two pints of lager on a sunny afternoon, I felt a little light-headed as I wheeled my bike across the zebra crossing, stepping only on the white bars 'cos step on the black, you'll break your back, then up this leafy hill, Rosie strolling beside me.

"I like your bicycle," he said.

It was this black and orange Raleigh ATB, 22-inch wheels, chunky tyres, 5-speed Sturmey-and-Archer gears.

"Thanks. I got it for my birthday. You got a bike?"

"Yeah, but not as cool as yours. It looks like a tiger." Despite myself, I laughed. "I like your T-shirt," he continued. "The colour really suits you."

"Thanks," I said again. "Yellow's my favourite colour. My toothbrush is yellow. But I also like orange. *Your* T-shirt's awesome. Tim's right. Together we make a total fruit-bowl." God Almighty, what was I babbling about? He'd think me a right twat.

"Yellow makes you open, energetic and cheerful," he said. "My toothbrush is blue. Apparently I'm seeking a quiet life, I'm calm and placid. So I read." Red was passionate, green relaxed, white organised, purple ambitious. God, he was so clever. "You're a Gemini, aren't you? May 30th? *And* you were born in the Year of the Dragon."

How did he know *that? And* my birthday…

"*Super*-cool," I confirmed.

"*Super-flashy*," he corrected. "You're an air-sign, Mercury, quicksilver, light, breezy, endlessly curious, a little mischievous. You wanna be ahead of the crowd. You thirst for knowledge and new experiences, you could be a writer, and you probably talk non-stop..."

"Like a demented jackdaw." I quoted my Dad. *He'd* say the profile was spot-on.

Rosie, born February 23rd, was a Pisces, two fish swimming in opposite directions. Ruled by Neptune, sensitive, often confused, and living most of his life in Fantasy-Land, his greatest desire was to turn his dreams into reality. I wondered what those dreams were, and

8

then we just like started talking, about music and movies and stuff. I learned that he liked Mozart, Mahler and Tchaikovsky and we discussed Monday's prom (no 51), Claudio Abbado and the London Symphony Orchestra doing Debussy's Nocturnes, Stravinsky's Violin Concerto and Tchaikovsky's fabulous, shattering, doom-laden 4th symphony then agreed that the climactic moment of the first movement, when the bloody trombones come in on this descending chord, and the mental third movement of his *Sixth* Symphony, where everything kind of goes mad for a minute, was the most exciting thing in all music, 'cos it like literally pulls your heart inside-out and is the best music written like EVER – I saw Witold Rowicki and the Polish Symphony Orchestra do it in my local town hall when I was like ten and it was so fast and amazing I burst from my seat cheering and clapping like everyone else in the hall 'cos it was so thrilling and like sealed my love of serious music forever (if you don't know it, man, you gotta hear it. It'll blow you away!) '– apart from the last movement of Beethoven's Ninth, or his Fifth; that goes without saying. Each leaves me shaken and stirred, Mr Bond … Then he said he found Bach too dry.

"You must be joking!" I cried. "Have you *heard* the B minor Mass? The Gloria is probably the single most awesome piece of music ever written. Ever! I mean, like EVER!"

"You should sing it for me," he said. "What d'you like that isn't classical?"

"The Beatles, Wings, Genesis, Pink Floyd, good story-tellers." 'Wish You Were Here' was my favourite song and *Dark Side of the Moon* my favourite album ever, 'cos it tells a story with fantastic lyrics and great songs, then films.

"I love James Bond – *Live and Let Die* was like so awesome, especially when he runs across those alligators and drives that bus under this bridge – and I love Clint Eastwood, especially *Josey Wales* and *The Good, the Bad and the Ugly*, you know where there're the three gunslingers facing each other in the cemetery and the eyes and the twitching gun-hands." Pointing my finger at him, I imitated Eastwood's soft drawl: " *'there're two kinds of people in this world, those with loaded guns and those who dig'.*" Those amazing teal-coloured eyes were smiling at me. "I love Laurel and Hardy - *The Music Box* is genius, that bit where they're getting the piano off the cart and Hardy goes *'this requires a little thought – now ease it down on my back'* and it like absolutely fucking flattens him, ha ha, and *Way Out West*, where they do this, like, dance?" I shuffled a couple of steps on the pavement to show him what I meant. Then he said his favourite film was like *The Wizard of Oz*? Oh. My. God.

"You gotta be kidding," I scoffed. "Follow the yellow-brick road, we're off to see the Wizard, caught by the Munchkins, all that 'no place like home' shit? Ha ha. It's like *sooo* lame."

"You're not a friend of Dorothy then," he said drily.

I didn't understand.

"Why do you like it?" I said.

"I like it because, because, because, because…"

"*You're* so lame." But I couldn't help laughing.

"All right," he said, "How about *The Sound of Music*?"

Yikes. Fingers on kittens and whiskers on ribbons and the hills may survive… I mean, what a loser! Someone just shoot me!

Suddenly we were at the crossroads that cut through my street. I could see the white-washed side of my house peeping through its thick ivy shroud and the black wooden gate with the paint peeling off and my heart became this like lump of lead?

"So," I said, "This is me."

"OK," he said.

But something seemed to have literally nailed my Green Flashes to the pavement.

"Better go," I said.

Still I didn't move. The silence seemed to last forever. He glanced at his watch, this really cool, black Casio G-Shock. Man, it was like *sooo* cool, you know? Black rubber with gold writing with this digital display, three dials, depth-gauges, different time-zones and a stop-watch. I just *had* to get one. The only extra on my lamo Timex was this tiny date-counter you literally needed a fucking microscope to read.

"Listen," he said, "Do you want to come back to mine? It's only a few streets away."

"Better not," I said reluctantly. "My Mum'll be expecting me."

Still we didn't move.

"Well," he said.

"Yes," I said.

"See you Wednesday."

We stood for a minute longer. Then he softened into a radiant, affectionate smile that made the whole world shine.

"Get off home then, Fruit-bowl."

He touched my right arm, just above the elbow, and this electric thrill ran through my entire body, like from my fingers to my toes, you know?

When I reached my gate, I turned. He was still standing at the bottom of the street, that vibrant tangerine shirt pasted against the sky of my life like the newly risen sun. I waved enthusiastically then, like, vaulted over the gate and raced to my room, the Gloria from Bach's B Minor Mass bursting joyously from my lungs, from my lips, from my CD player, from the depths of my soul as I stripped off my sweaty T-shirt and, waving it round my head, danced in my bedroom in shorts and socks, ecstatic excitement bubbling through my blood and sending my heart like literally to Heaven.

2: Can't Get You Out of My Head

THE evening passed in a blur. After *Hong Kong Phooey* (Number One Super Guy) and a shower, I shared a spinach quiche with the folks and told them about the tennis with Sonning and Rose, although I omitted the bit about the Foster's. Then I played Beethoven's *Moonlight Sonata*, like all these limpid rising arpeggios in the first movement, a lilting middle movement and this like manic, thunderous finale, whilst Dad organised his stamp albums and Mum did some ironing and asked every polar bear in like Greenland why I never put my clothes away.

"I don't spend hours washing your clothes so you can just chuck them on the carpet again." Technically, of course, she *didn't* spend hours washing the clothes. The washing machine did that but I decided it'd be imprudent to mention it. "And *please* put your socks in the laundry basket. Who else do you think's going to do it? The Sock Fairy?"

Yes, Mum.

"I've told you like a billion times."

Yes, Mum.

"And was it you who put the empty milk-carton back in the fridge?"

"No, Mum, I don't drink milk, remember? I like *hate* milk, you know? Makes me sick?"

"Roy! Honestly, it's like having *two* bloody kids in the house. Roy! Milk-carton?"

Later we watched David Attenborough take a Red River Safari from Mount Kenya to the Indian Ocean on *Wildlife on One* and something about child seatbelts on *Top Gear* but when I went to bed I couldn't sleep. The bamboo wind-chimes hanging from the curtain-rail chinked in the breeze which stole through the window, open behind the yellow curtains. I felt kind of high, you know? Sort of light-headed, and a little confused by the intensity of the feelings I'd experienced that afternoon, the electric shocks, the lurching heart, the wanting to cry, the sheer, utterly overwhelming joy I'd felt in his company. I also kept thinking about *him*. I couldn't even focus on *Deathchase*. Somewhere in Level Four I swerved through the forest, fired a missile to blow up the yellow motorbike to earn $1000, fired another to bring down a helicopter, then smashed my own motorbike into a bloody great tree. GAME like *sooo* OVER, yeah? I wondered if Rosie liked *Deathchase*. It was such a cool game. Of course he did.

He absolutely fascinated me, this talented, confident young man with the world at his feet. His charisma had bewitched me during *The Dream* but I'd been so skittish and he'd been so cool, effortlessly chatting up girls, riffing off Simon Dell, who'd played Bottom, and annoying Big Willie Western, the director, whilst delivering mesmeric performances over four nights. I'd just scampered round the stage like some demented squirrel. Halfway through the run, I'd realised I wanted to *be* him. I'd wanted to *be* Alistair Rose, to like inhabit his body, to live in his mind, just for a day, to find out what it was like to be this awesome, incredible boy. Then the play was over, the term was over, and I immersed myself in music and cricket, but now he was back in my thoughts and I had, like, a zillion questions. What did he read? Did he play a musical instrument? What A Levels was he doing? Where was he born? What was his favourite food? What was he doing now? Was he sleeping? Was he watching TV? Did he like the same programmes as me? What was his room like? What did he wear in bed? Did he wear pyjamas? Or pyjama-shorts like me? Or maybe he slept in his boxers. Did he even wear boxers? Maybe he wore slips, like me. I hoped so. Boxers are *sooo* unsexy. They don't, like, show off your boy's bulge as well as slips, you know?

I fetched the school magazine with the photo of us in *A Midsummer Night's Dream*. We were 'on the bank where the wild thyme grows'. I was kind of crouching, hair spiky and legs bare, 'cos I was wearing shorts. Rosie, standing, had his hand on my shoulder and I was like gazing up at him saying I'd 'put a girdle round the earth in forty minutes,' you know? It was such a cool picture, though my legs looked like twigs and my bare chest was so narrow my ribs stuck out like carvings in marble. God Almighty.

I hated my body. I was 15, short and really like scrawny, about five foot four and six-stone nothing. I had this mole about the size of a 5p coin on my left shoulder, another splashed on the left of my neck and two very close together on my left thigh. My arms were dead straight, thin and very weedy. I seemed to have absolutely no muscle-bumps of any kind and it was said my hips could fit through a coat-hanger, though I had pelvic-bones you could rest a cup on. I had this fine, wispy hair in my armpits and some tufty strands round my willy, this slender three-and-a-half-inch water-spout, four-and-a half when hard (of course I'd measured it. Hasn't every boy?). I mean, compared to my classmates I was this like total weed, you know? Thank Christ my voice had just about broken.

I liked my face though. I thought I had a kind, open face, mostly zit-free, thank fuck. It was quite round, had a few freckles, like I'd been literally spattered with creosote, this nice, small rosebud mouth, and my cheeks kind of dimpled when I smiled, which some people thought cute. My eyes were the colour of conkers, my hair, cut round my ears and in a short fringe across my forehead, was the black-brown colour of Bovril. When I was going out, I'd spike it up with a handful of gel, something Mum really hated, but at least it wasn't greasy, like Maxton's, dappled with dandruff, like Gray's, or massively curly like Burridge's, or, fucking hell, GINGER, like Crooks'. I mean, imagine the teasing.

So that was me, Jonathan David Peters. I didn't *look* queer.

Well, I wouldn't, would I?

'Cos I wasn't.

I re-read Bob Hoare's account, in the second chapter of *Great Escapes of World War Two*, of Charles McCormac's escape from the bestial Japs who, on page 33, bayoneted twelve men to death to like teach the others a lesson, savage bastards. Then to chapter five, 'The Great Escape' and Tom, Dick and Harry, Dad's third favourite film, after *El Cid* and *Zulu*, and one of mine too. I put the light out again at about two, and *still* couldn't sleep. Tomorrow was school and I was gonna see Alistair Rose again, you know? Excitement literally bubbled through my body. How would he greet me? What would I ask him? I would see him in Assembly getting his golden prefect's tie and black gown. I felt so proud of him.

'Hey, Ali,' I would go, all casual and, like, *sooo* relaxed.

'Jonny!' I imagined that dazzling grin breaking out on his face. 'How was Day One?'

'Great. Yours?'

'Fantastic, even better for seeing you. By the way, I really enjoyed playing tennis with you. We should play again.'

'Well, I'm free this Saturday…'

Did he sleep on his stomach with his hand pushed up under the pillow like me, or on his side? And which side? Did he curl his knees up? Did he snore? I bet he did! Hell, I'd tease him about that all right!

'Morning, Ali,' I imagined myself saying, propped up on an elbow and, like, gazing down at his beautiful face. 'Didn't get a wink, thanks to your snoring. Like a pig after a truffle.'

'Ho,' said Fantasy Ali, 'What the hell are those weird snuffling noises *you* make, Badger-Face? Your Dad says they drive him crazy.' And I'd slap his chest with my hand.

I wondered how he got on with his brother Bobby, a year below me and a total pain in the arse. Pushy and mouthy, I hated his lame comments and lamer jokes, most of which were aimed at 'Poorly' Paulus for seemingly dodging rugby like forever.

What did his parents do? What were they called? I wondered where his grandparents lived. Maybe I'd meet them. I'd love it if his grandfather'd been in the war and had some stories for the school magazine. Mine had, but he didn't. As a gunner a gazillion miles behind the front-line pounding the Monte Cassino monastery into dusty rubble, he'd seen nothing. Still, he'd won a couple of medals for like just being there.

'Hi, Granddad,' Fantasy Ali said, leading me by the hand through the day-room of a nursing home where a dozen scary crones were like colouring sketches of Mickey Mouse, doing needlepoint and poring over jigsaws of beribboned kittens unravelling balls of wool.

Old people's homes were utterly, totally terrifying. No way would I *ever* put Ali in one. Ever! You know? Ever. I'd never let him leave our Cotswolds cottage. Amadeus, our cat, would never forgive me if I sent *Ali* away. I could never do it, never… I'd rather like fry and eat my own liver? With fava beans and a nice Chianti, fffff, ffff, fff.

'This is Jonathan,' said Fantasy Ali, 'He's writing an article for the school magazine about war-time experiences.'

Rosie had like written loads for the school magazine? God, he was so clever. He was a brilliant actor, a brilliant speaker, a brilliant writer and a brilliant tennis player and he was my friend. Hugging the magazine to my chest, I rolled onto my front, shoved my right hand under my pillow and smiled. In six hours I was gonna see him again and I couldn't wait.

The alarm literally exploded in my eardrums like this nuclear fucking bomb. 6.45 already. September 10th already. First day back already. I scrambled out of bed, washed my face with Imperial Leather and Clearasil, spiked my hair with a little gel then peeled off these purple pyjama-shorts I wore in bed, dressed in my favourite lemon-coloured slip and the school uniform of ribbed grey socks, grey flannel trousers, white shirt and green-and-navy house-tie I'd been awarded last year. I tended to save the gold-and-navy school-tie for school occasions like Speech Day or concerts and, on a day-to-day basis, usually wore a grey shirt instead of white (these were our choices) because it lasted the whole week whereas the collar of the white was normally filthy by Wednesday. But I wanted to look really good today. For Alistair.

I scampered down to the kitchen where Dad was preparing my favourite breakfast, this massive orange bowl of oats, blueberries, bananas and walnuts in yogurt followed by buttered toast and scrambled eggs with tons of black pepper and this large dash of bright red chilli-powder. Mum was banging on about this yoga-class she was giving somewhere and Terry Wogan was telling us about something recently banjaxing him.

I really liked our kitchen. It was always warm, with brown cork floor-tiles and these units that looked like wood but weren't. By the window was this chunky wooden four-seater table where, back in second-form Geography, I'd spent hours tracing this map of New Zealand's mega-crinkly coastline for Frank Gallagher? I'd often done my homework there, especially like in the winter, 'cos it was warmer than my bedroom? And I'd used it for wargames with Tim, building Airfix models and various birthday parties. This table was part of my schoolboy's tale.

A selection of herbs grew in plastic pots along the window-sill, suffusing the kitchen with the heady aromas of thyme, basil, mint and rosemary. As well as making her own jam and chutneys, Mum also baked bread, so on Saturdays the most tantalising smell in all the world drifted round the house, drawing me from my bedroom to beg a slice, warm from the oven and soaked in melting honey or slathered in home-made strawberry jam. Metal wind-chimes hung from a paper lantern in the centre of a moulded ceiling-rose. They showed the Zodiac signs in browns and reds. The walls were painted this dusky peach, giving the place this soft warm glow. The cork pin-board had a collection of postcards from friends' holidays, a mini-whiteboard for urgent messages and my RNLI lighthouse calendar, a Christmas gift from the Grunters. I particularly liked February's red-and-white pepperpot at Orford Ness and the weird hexagonal North Foreland in Kent on my birth-month of May, though they might've listed a few *Top Trumps* stats. September's was this black-and-yellow hooped job from St John's Point, Northern Ireland. This Wednesday was marked in massive black letters, **SKOOL,** misspelled 'cos I really wanted to go to, like, Grange Hill, you know? 'Cos unlike us, they had *girls*, you know? Girls. I hadn't been in a class with girls for like five years.

Spooning up my home-made cereal, I wondered what Rosie had for breakfast. Did he have fruit and oats like me or did he just have Weetabix? Was he even up? Maybe he was still sleeping. I wondered what shampoo he used, what colour his towel was. What was their bathroom like? He said he had a blue toothbrush. Man, I *had* to get one too. Yellow was *sooo* like for kids? Blue was for… Rosies. Or Roses.

"You OK, son?" Dad dished out the scrambled eggs. "You're a million miles away."

I said I was just thinking about school. Wogan was playing Randy Crawford: "*One day*

I'll fly away, leave your love to yesterday, what more can your love do for me? When will love be through with me? Why live life from dream to dream, and dread the day that dreaming ends?" Yikes. I literally buried my blushing face in the scrambled eggs and listened to the folks outlining their days.

Dad, 41, was this shambling, shapeless bear with fading floppy brown hair and brown Labrador eyes. He had experimented unsuccessfully with this beard a couple of times but had looked 'sinister'. He favoured slacks, checked shirts and these like baggy cardigans, so going out was a trial. Whatever he selected from his admittedly limited wardrobe was always wrong. The three-times-outfit-exchange had become such a ritual I'd joked we should put a catwalk down the hall, you know? Unfortunately it meant we were always late leaving for things. "Honestly," Mum'd huff, "It's like having *two* bloody kids in the house."

Dad had been a bus driver, which was why, according to family legend, I was like conceived on the upstairs back-seat of the number 52 to town. Apparently. Which was like totally bollocks anyway. I think. Anyway, he'd hated it, especially the school-runs. I sympathised. School-kids are generally total bastards, especially to bus-drivers. After some kind of break-down, he was like on the dole for ages before getting this Council job painting white lines on footie pitches in parks. Now he worked as like this gardener, you know? Selecting, cultivating and planting flowers, installing water-features and tending the hanging-baskets that brightened the city centre. He was like really into ponds and knew everything about grasses you never wished to know, though *our* garden, obviously, was like this total tip? It wouldn't do for me. I get hay-fever. Mind you, Mum had something homeopathic for hay-fever. She was a yoga teacher and aromatherapist, whatever the hell *that* is. She made flowers, herbs and spices into oils and potions. 'Like a witch-doctor,' Tim Wilson had once helpfully told everyone at school. Anyway, as far as I could tell, it involved switching pills for smells. If I had a headache, I didn't get Panadols, I got this smear of lavender dabbed on my forehead. If I had indigestion, I didn't get Rennies, I got camomile tea. Even though I thought it a load of old bollocks, there must've been *something* in it. She'd got certificates, for God's sake, and a super-long client-list.

Mum, 39, was dreading the Big 4-0. She thought it was gonna be like literally the end of life itself. I mean, everyone knows *20* is the end of life, eh? Anyway, she was desperate to stay slim, to get into *my* 26-inch jeans, as it were. Why I didn't know. *I* wanted to be bigger. Anyway, her copper-coloured hair was cut in this kind of bob with a lightly feathered fringe. She favoured these long, cable-knit sweaters, cardigans in pale pastel shades like peach, apricot and mango, floaty scarves, blue skinny jeans, brown calf-hugging leather boots, and had this neat brown-gold handbag. She didn't do jewellery, just the wedding-band, the occasional bead necklace, maybe a bracelet, and make-up was generally the subtlest touch of blusher. She'd been a hairdresser. That was how she'd met Dad, cutting his hair once a month on his way to the depot. I found it hard to imagine romance blossoming among the hair-clippings, disinfected combs and cracked lino of *Kurl up and Dye* but hey, romance, I guess, can blossom anywhere. Just look at me. Who'd ever imagine romance in a school?

I liked my school. I liked the buildings, I liked my classmates, I liked my teachers, most of them anyway, I liked the study and I liked the atmosphere. There was this constant buzz of activity, whether it was music or drama, sport or hobby clubs, there was something for everyone, from chess-players to fairground-organ builders, electronics enthusiasts to film-buffs, gliders to cavers, stamp-collectors to war-gamers like me. See? Something for everyone, and even though we inevitably coalesced into like-minded groups, I somehow managed to straddle all of them numbering as I did rugby-playing hearties like Collins, swots like Huxley, skivers like Stewart and keenos like Paulus among my friends. I wasn't really sure *where* I fitted, to be honest. Although I was like fucking brilliant at playing the piano and a brilliant actor, I wasn't really a keeno. I didn't hang around the music rooms, or with Austen and the other Ac-*tors*, and I certainly wasn't a hearty, 'cos I wasn't in any sports team but I liked PE and Games and played break-time footie like everyone else. I definitely wasn't a skiver, 'cos I didn't like getting yelled at, but neither was I a lick, 'cos I occasionally got lines or detention, nor a swot. I mean, when it came to Maths I had the memory of a fucking goldfish. Most of my friends didn't really fit into these groups either. Like Fosbrook. Or Gray. Where the hell did *they* fit? Our school was weird like that. We had our groups (not 'jocks and nerds', because, as Collins frequently reminded us, we were not Americans and didn't need to borrow *their* vocabulary) but few seemed to belong to just one. Chris Morreson and Jamie Arnold, for instance, hearty rugger-buggers both, also belonged to the editorial committee of the school magazine and the Choral Society respectively. It was all about cross-over, making Renaissance Men, excelling at everything.

At half-seven I swallowed a cod liver oil capsule, brushed my teeth and slipped into the navy blue blazer with its gold and blue badge on the breast pocket. The badge showed a golden sheaf of corn under a golden crown and the school motto *'invenire et intelligite'*, ('to discover and understand'). I shoved a couple of tissues, my front-door key and two £1 coins into my trouser pocket, checked my new bus-pass and black comb were in my inside blazer pocket, scooped up my black Adidas backpack and raced downstairs again. Calling "See you," I headed to the bus-stop. It was only when I was on the number 21 to town with my earbuds plugged into Sibelius' melancholic Seventh Symphony, the one where the trombones seem to swell mournfully through the rest of the orchestra at three climactic moments before dying to nothing, that I remembered I'd forgotten my pack-up and would have to get a bloody school lunch, lumpy mashed potato, over-boiled, lifeless cabbage and indescribably leathery meat. It also meant borrowing someone's lunch ticket, queuing up with a load of gimps, finding somewhere to sit and someone to sit with on one of the long wooden benches in the gloomy, wood-panelled refectory, standing whilst a master recited *'Benedictus Benedicat per Jesum Christum Dominum Nostrum'* from the High Table, the reply to which, *'benedicto benedicatur'*, I was just supposed to know, 'you bloody slumdog gimp.' Fucking hell. I'd rather like bake and eat my own heart, you know? With carrots and a nice Shiraz. Someone just shoot me.

My school was this ancient, blackened sandstone pile squatting on a hill near the uni. You could see it for miles 'cos this gold-brown steeple, our supposedly haunted bell-tower, poked up like some finger warning off the town below. Although the school was founded in 1507 by King Henry VII, no Tudor buildings remained. Most of it, St Aidan's Chapel, the Dawnay Library and the Refectory was Victorian Gothic and clustered round this like *totally* out-of-bounds cricket pitch The thousand-seater Beckwith Hall, the art room, the Britten Music Centre and the language labs were housed in some brutalist 1960s concrete construction imaginatively named the New Building whilst the science labs were in the Jessop Wing, this swish new extension to the three-storey Victorian school that housed the form-rooms. English was in this really cool yellow Edwardian townhouse, romantically named Heathcliffe Lodge, with stained-glass windows and creaky floorboards. History was up in that haunted bell-tower, which Bush-head and Hellfire called Eagles' Nest. Our 25-metre swimming pool and Sports Centre dated from the 1970s whilst the Sixth Form Common Room, Staff Room and Admin were in this powder-blue Georgian house called The Lupton Building. There was a kind of wood by the Sports Centre where gimps played hide-and-seek and sword-fights with sticks.

I loved feeling part of this history, like there was some amazing magic connection between me and the thousands of boys who'd like studied here over the last half-millennium, so, once in the Room 31 base of Upper Five H, I was like totally and quickly immersed in the first-day chaos of shouted greetings, handshakes and back-slaps, finally slumping down by Philip Maxton, my gangly, mop-headed, Maths-genius, zit-spattered, horse-faced friend.

"What's up?" he grunted.

"All right?" I grunted back. "Good holiday?"

"So-so. Brittany with the folks. Pretty boring actually. You?"

"Norfolk. Same. Like *sooo* tedious, you know?" But at least he'd been abroad.

Setting his Sizes 12s up on the table, he started picking England's team for tonight's opening World Cup qualifier against Norway at Wembley and on the radio at 8.00 whilst twisting this Rubik's Cube round in his hands. Rubik's Cubes were the latest craze. Everybody had one except me. I couldn't see the point of trying to get a load of coloured squares to conform to a pattern. Life wasn't like that. I preferred the faces mixed up. Diversity was so much more interesting than conformity, you know? As Ian Dury (from The Blockheads) said, there's more to life than just 'fitting in', eh? Like, 'Hit Me with your Rhythm-Stick', ha ha.

"Seen Claire lately?" Andy Collins, the coolest guy in the class 'cos he lived on a farm, drove Landrovers through muddy fields, bottle-fed new-born lambs in his bedroom and had screwed literally millions of girls, had been at *that* party. "She's so into you she'd like fuck you in a heart-beat? Did you call her?" Shit. "Jonny, you *total* twat. She fancies the arse off you, man, and she's bloody gorgeous an' all, *too* gorgeous for a gimpy twat like you."

Sparky, elfin Claire Ashton was the headmaster's daughter. She *wasn't* my girlfriend although everyone kind of wanted her to be? Including her father? I mean, yikes. He's the headmaster, man! Anyway, during the summer term 'cos I helped her with her Grade 6 oboe exam and we just kind of like started hanging out together, you know? We went to the cinema once and held hands through some fuckwitted American teenage 'romcom' which she'd like totally loved and I'd like totally loathed, you know? We'd kind of kissed a bit after but I wasn't really that interested back then? There was like plenty of time for the slushy stuff when I got to uni. Anyhow, in early August, I'd taken her to Michael Crooks' 15th birthday party. Which ended in total, absolute, humiliating disaster. Literally the end of my life, you know?

Gray, who'd also been at the party, filled in the details. "She's like puckering up for this lovely, romantic kiss and you puke pizza up all over her brand-new, sixty-quid Kickers. Ends *your* chance of being head boy. I heard Ash-tray himself had to hose 'em down."

Everyone in earshot laughed and started alternating vomiting noises with loud kisses.

Yikes. I went like Spiderman-red, you know? Someone just shoot me.

Thank fuck for Ian Hutchinson, our 30-something form-master, who arrived with timetables, handbooks, calendars and lectionaries with the Michaelmas Bible readings and I could hide myself in something other than my own embarrassment, except he caught Gray's remark as we all stood up and snapped "*Peters*? Head boy? Over my dead body! Fasten your collar, you scruffy little tramp. You're at school now, not some wild party. Siddown."

Yikes, even *he* knew. From Dr Ashton, no doubt. God Almighty. Who else had he told? Man, life was *sooo* unfair. One little mistake and I was gonna get literally crucified round the fucking school. Fortunately, everyone fell to swapping holiday stories, tales of Provençe, the Dordogne and the Italian lakes. It seemed the whole bloody form had decamped to the continent and every one of them had been bored totally stupid by the foreign girls they'd fancied and totally failed to fuck, ha ha. Better stay in England like me, eh? You're not even gonna get your *hopes* up at home, let alone anything else, ha ha.

Scouring the Calendar for the dates of concerts, music competitions, house drama evenings and the other stuff I did and pretty much ignoring the rugby, squash and cross-country fixtures on the back, I like snorted with total dismay. The bloody music competition *did* clash with my clarinet exam. Thursday November 20th. For fuck's sake. Would you believe it? I circled it bitterly, along with the house play dates of November 6th and 7th, Murray house swimming, October 23rd, and the Christmas charity concert, December 12th. Seemed a long way off, as did the end of term on Wednesday December 17th.

Anyway, back to Hutchinson. Teaching Mathematics, he'd like dismissed me years ago as some total turnip-head. I consistently finished bottom of the class and my best exam ever was a triumphant 33% way back in third form. The brilliant mathematicians like Maxton and Stewart thought he was awesome and, despite his opinion of *me*, so did I. Easily the best Maths teacher in the school, he'd taught me in 2W, where we did like trigonometry, all that sine and cosine shit, and bases and negative numbers, you know? I mean, what the fuck *is* a negative number? It either *is* a number or it isn't, you know? Anyway, seeing me struggling, he gave me this one-to-one lunchtime coaching like twice a week throughout the summer term and I kind of scraped through the exam, though he still thought me this mince-for-brains dunce.

"Have you learned *nothing* since 2W?" he said when he got me back in L5C.

"No, sir," I answered miserably. Algebra had gone like totally over my head, 'cos I'd had some bloody useless twat called Jennings (our Lower School house tutor) and this guy called Robinson who wasn't even a Maths teacher, and returned, as it were, to Base One. Thank God my education was free, otherwise we'd have sued. Thank God too for the timetabling god (Rev Crawford) who returned me to Mr Hutchinson in my GCSE year. Now I might stand a chance of like passing the bloody thing, you know?

Hutchinson's nickname was Bunny, from Hutchinson to Hutch to Rabbit to... you following? I didn't know who'd *originally* coined it. Some said Mr Yates (aka Cedric), a noted fashioner of sobriquets. Some said Bunny himself 'cos he had this blond hair like Hutch out of *Starsky and Hutch*. Some said his tutor at Oxford 'cos he had like these Bugs Bunny teeth yeah? No-one *actually* knew. Like most stuff, it was lost in the mists of school history.

Some nicknames were imaginative, like Harry Langdon was Hellfire 'cos his initials were HEL, others just a connection with someone else, like Mr Perry was Fred, like the tennis player, Mr Gallagher was Frank, like the guy from *Shameless*, Mr McDonald was Ronald the burger king, and others just boringly alliterative adaptations – Jacko Jackson, Millie Milton, Willie Western etc. Some were just rude – Bush-head Bleakley, Leper Leeson, who had this scaly red skin, Wingnut Knight, whose ears stuck out from his head at right angles... we were inducted into this culture pretty much from Day One and gleefully passed on our knowledge to the next lot of gimps, as Lower School newbies were called.

The school, about 800 boys and 50 masters, was divided in two, Lower being the first, second, third and fourth forms, boys aged ten to fourteen (so Years 6 to 9, in your language, I think) - I'd joined the second form (Year 7) - and Upper (Years 10 to 13, maybe?) comprising the GCSE-focused Fifth Form, Lower and Upper, and A-Level focused Sixth Form, Lower and Upper. There were five forms of about 20 in each year, except the Sixth Form which broke down smaller, like groups of 8 to 12, and the First Form which was 40 boys from the prep school. It meant year-groups of 100 and 8 houses of about the same, so you like got to know pretty much everyone eventually.

The houses were named after these local heroes, like the guy who invented stainless steel (Brearley), a deaf-and-dumb astronomer (Goodricke), a lighthouse-builder (Smeaton), a chocolate-making Quaker (Rowntree) etc., and each had its own history, traditions and colours, like, respectively, yellow, purple, dark blue and light blue. Our house, the one me, Paulus and Burridge were in, was named after Matthew Murray who'd invented a steam-engine and our colour was green. We were pretty rubbish. We never won anything. People said we were green with envy, ha ha. But houses were great 'cos you got to work with kids you might not otherwise, like Trent and Sutcliffe (younger) and Rose and Sonning (older).

"I guess," Bunny, who was in Leeman House (lawyer, railwayman, MP, red) with Lamp-post Lewis and Gutbucket Gardiner, drawled as he dished out our locker keys, "That you did absolutely nothing whatsoever during the last seven weeks. Well, that stops now. You're in the top 1% of the country's sixteen year olds, God help us, and you know that a C is as good as a fail." So no pressure then. "This is the most important year of your sad little lives."

Since every year had been the 'most important year of our sad little lives', we coughed sceptically, although ten GCSEs awaited us in May. Happy fucking birthday, Jonny.

Because I was number 17 on the register, I got locker 17, on the bottom row below Paulus's and next to Maxton's. I hated having a bottom-row locker. I'd have to grub around on the floor every time I opened it. I also hated having a locker next to Maxton 'cos he'd like stick these pictures of Debbie Harry and Kate Bush inside the door and leer at them with sly elbow-digs into my ribs. I preferred sports stars like Geoffrey Boycott and Kevin Keegan.

"Bollocks." Maxton was inspecting his timetable. "We got Fred for Music, not Wilfo."

Rarely in class, Fred (Perry) was dull whilst Wilfo Reid, rabbit-toothed and violently bearded, wore spectacularly flowery shirts and crazy bow-ties and did funky stuff like tying Coke tins into the piano and filling drums with dried peas to 'see what happened'. His real name was Geoff. Why he was nicknamed Wilfo I had no idea. I guessed I could ask Cedric. But Music would be okay. The composition stuff was easy. I'd done Grade Eight theory like a billion years ago. The practical exam would also be easy. It was only Grade Five after all. I'd chosen the course partly 'cos my mates were doing it but mainly for the music history part, for Mussorgsky's 'Night on the Bare Mountain', Vivaldi's 'Gloria in D' and a Haydn string quartet 'cos I wanted to be a music journo when I left school, like writing reviews and CD sleeve-notes and stuff. Like Maxton and Gray, I preferred Wilfo to Fred 'cos Fred was stuck in the Dark Ages – he once chucked Jamie Arnold out for just *mentioning* jazz, which was like fair enough, especially since Arnie looked like Zippy off *Rainbow* (a wide-mouthed rugby-ball) - but Wilf had conducted *Oliver* and accompanied me in all my clarinet exams whilst Fred seemed to hate me. I didn't know why, and he never said. It was just this impression I got, you know?

"It's even worser," groaned Gray, "We got Herbidacious for Bio."

Herbidacious (like those magic words in *The Herbs*), Derek Herbert, was a total cunt. He hated *everyone*, his colleagues, his students, maybe even his wife and kids. Strict, pedantic, icily sarcastic, blisteringly tempered, he'd taught us Chemistry in 3Y and Biology in 4M. He *hated* us and the feeling was most definitely mutual. So Herbie-fucking-dacious, eh?

Scouring the timetable for more information, it was already clear that Tuesdays and Fridays would be like my best days, you know? Registration at 8.45, break from 11.20 to 11.40, lunch from 1.00 to 2.10 and school finishing at 3.40, with the buses ten minutes later. That was our day. And this was my U5H timetable:

	Assembly 0855	1 0915	2 0950	3 1035	4 1140	5 1220	6 1415	7 1450
MON	Full school in main hall	Maths ITH 31	Biology DH 46	History HEL 61	Physics CJM 8	Physics CJM 8	English WW 22	French BMG LL2B
TUES	U/School house meeting	German JLP 51	English WW 22	Maths ITH 31	History HEL 61	French BMG 40	Games	Games
WED	5th Form in auditorium	German JLP 51	Biology DH 46	Biology DH 46	Music APP 102	Music APP 102	Chem. MJ 41	English WW 22
THURS	5thForm Chapel	Chem MJ 41	Chem MJ 41	German JLP 51	Maths ITH 31	History HEL 61	RE GDK 7	French BMG 40
FRI	Full house assembly	PE SMV Gym	Maths ITH 31	French BMG 40	English WW 22	History HEL 61	Physics CJM 8	German JLP LL1A

Everyone wanted Cedric for French. He was a brilliant teacher and fabulous form-master who'd taken us on this like totally awesome trip walking the cliff from Robin Hood's Bay to Whitby. He'd shown us these really cool, super-romantic abbey ruins and dragged us round the Dracula Experience, leaping from shadows yelling 'Boo' and totally failing to scare us. It was on *that* trip I discovered this mega-awesome second-hand bookshop in Whitby and bought five James Bond novels for a quid, including *Octopussy*, *Diamonds are Forever* and *Doctor No*, my all-time favourite because of Honey Rider like emerging from the sea wearing, like, nothing but a belt (man, I had some absolutely EPIC dreams then, I can tell you!), Bond's escape through heated pipes and a cage of red-eyed spiders and [**SPOILER ALERT** – **if you haven't read it, look away now**] Doctor No getting literally buried in this massive pile of bird-shit. But we didn't get Cedric. We got Boring Ben Goddard instead.

I loved Hand-Out Hellfire, Head of History, Head of Cricket and barkingly mad, combining demonstrations of forward-defensives and cover-drives with explanations of Bismarck's foreign policy. Like two lessons for the price of one, you know? Though obviously how to hook a short-pitched delivery for a boundary-four would probably not come up on the GCSE, worse luck, 'cos *that* was easy. Anyway, although Hellfire taught by gap-fill worksheet, I was really looking forward to World War One, the Russian Revolution, Nazism and World War Two, all my favourite stuff. We'd done the French Revolution last year with Bush-head and I'd produced this awesome project on the Napoleonic Wars. I thought History might be my 'thing.' I'd loved it since primary and had like tons of history books, you know?

I also liked 'Big Willie' Western, the Head of English, whose classroom on the top floor of Heathcliffe Lodge, had the original 1903 stained glass windows and was plastered with massive posters of Shakespeare and plays from the National Theatre. He had directed *The Dream* and instilled my love of Dickens, Ted Hughes, *Tess of the D'Urbervilles* and *Animal Farm* back in 4M. Although Sarah May, twenty-something, long dark hair, 'come-to-bed' eyes, short skirts and leggings and known as Spam (her initials were SPM), was said to be brilliant, especially with Shakespeare, and half the school like totally lusted after her, I was happy with Willie, and looking forward to *Twelfth Night*, D. H. Lawrence and *The Mayor of Casterbridge*.

Best of all, we had 'Beaky' Phillips for German again. Beaky was my absolute favourite teacher by like a mile. Tall, pencil-thin, scanty hair, beaky nose (still following?), eccentric to the point of like 'somebody take him away', he was one of those old-school teachers who just seemed to understand teenagers and pitch stuff right, you know? He'd helped me during a dreadful first week when I was utterly overwhelmed by 800 massive boy-mountains stomping up and down the stairs. Getting lost several times and late for Assembly, I was yelled at in front of the whole school by Ash-tray (Dr Ashton) himself.

Burning up and squeezing in beside Mark Gray, I'd muttered a 'Hi' which, overheard by my new form-master, Frosty Winters, earned me another public bollocking and a hundred lines for talking in Assembly. Then, haring round a corner 'cos I was late for a house meeting I couldn't find, I had literally collided with Bunny, knocking an armful of exercise-books to the lino and winning a lunchtime detention for running in the corridor, you stupid gimp. All this in my first hour. I'd withdrawn to the window-sill corner with my Walkman and *Hornblower Goes to Sea* from my primary school Puffin Club. I really loved sea stories then, especially Hornblower, 'cos from *that* book I learned how to walk along a pitching yard-arm in a storm, how to heat red-hot shot, how to besiege a Caribbean fort and how to get a ship off a mudflat by firing a broadside to break the suction, all useful skills for a growing boy. In addition, my historical hero back then was Horatio Nelson, shot down by a sniper and dying in battle for his people on the quarterdeck of his ironically-named *Victory*. Despite his dodgy private-life, he seemed the most admirable admiral to me. Anyway, so I was reading about Hornblower losing his prize-ship 'cos its cargo of waterlogged rice swelled to burst the seams when Frosty asked me what I was listening to.

"Wagner, sir," I said. "*Die Walküre*. The first-act finale, you know? Siegmund and Sieglinde's Love Duet." It was like my all-time favourite piece of music back then. He didn't say anything, just looked a bit surprised, you know? It was only later, when I realised none of the other 11 year olds were listening to Wagner that I understood why. He must've bowled back to the Staff Room to tell his colleagues about this weird freak in his form 'cos during our first German lesson, Beaky, grinning cheerfully, said "Oh, Mr Peters. The lad who likes Wagner." I thought he was mocking me, but he wasn't. He asked if I knew *The Ring Cycle*, and which recording I had, and I said Boulez's, and he pulled a face and said it was a little modern for him, but I'd seen it on BBC2 and absolutely loved it.

"Well," he'd said, "Each to his own. I prefer my Brünnhildes with horny hats and flaxen pigtails. They remind me of *Mrs* Phillips."

Water had like literally snorted out of my nose. From that day on, I had a bond with him and consistently came top of the set, I guess because he enthused me so much, especially when he taught us about culture and literature. He played Beethoven and Weill, read us Brecht and Goethe and offered chunks of Yorkie as quiz prizes. He was the kind of utterly inspirational, tuned-in teacher you really wished you had.

Settling in had been difficult for me. I mean, my dad was a bus driver. Everyone else's were doctors, lawyers or academics. My first term seemed to consist entirely of fights, lines and detentions. Kevin Seymour and Graham Brudenall were my biggest tormentors. Both were physically much bigger than me, and much, much richer. It was Seymour who coined the early nickname Rubber, like Rubber-Jonny. I didn't know what it meant, 'cept everyone like pissed themselves when he said it. I thought he meant I was an Eraser, like Arnie in that film. Gray finally told me it meant 'condom'. I didn't know what one of those was either so Gray gave me the old birds-and-bees talk on the bus home. So I punched Seymour out, although he was twice my size and had a face like a baked potato. He kind of respected me after I'd smashed his lip. Then Brudenall like wound me up by asking if I was a virgin. I was 11, let me remind you, and the only virgin I'd ever heard of was called Mary so, assuming 'virgin' was another word for 'girl' said "Of course not. Do I look like a virgin?" Brudenall and the hearties howled with laughter. When I got home, I looked it up in the dictionary and was like totally mortified to learn that I'd told him I'd had sexual intercourse. Aged eleven. Even though I didn't know what it was. Until Gray explained again. Anyway, back I went, said "Met her on holiday and it was fucking brilliant, you tosser," and kicked his leg and ankle so hard that he cried. Like Gray's soppy sister Melissa.

Up to then Gray had seemed really embarrassed to be seen with me. He'd even asked why I kept hanging around him like a lost puppy but afterwards he'd crowed that I would 'keep the bullies at bay.' He was like the first to call me JP and he introduced me to Philip Maxton. All living near each other, we caught the same bus at 3.50 every afternoon. Tim was too busy making friends with the sons of his father's medical friends to be bothered with me but Gray had been friendly. I liked him. He was a good pianist and sang in the Choral Society with me. He had crinkly brown hair, large black-rimmed specs that cut his square face in half, traces of adolescent acne on his forehead and a blazer two sizes too big, the sleeves covering his hands. We played *Top Trumps* every break with Maxton and David Fosbrook. I had these really cool sets, 'Dinosaurs', 'Tanks', 'Space Phenomena' and 'Classic British Cars', with Ford Escorts, Mini Coopers, Triumph Spitfires, Ford Cortinas and super-cool Aston Martin V8. We were like really into *Star Trek* and *Doctor Who*. We particularly loved the Master (in Chapel, 'He who would valiant be/Follow the Master', always made us laugh), and kept saying 'Make it so' like Captain Picard, although we *really* wanted to be Zaphod Beeblebrox, the coolest cat in the Galaxy. Sadly we were more Marvin the Paranoid Android, always like 'so depressed.'

I looked round the class now, at Collins, tall and broad-shouldered, wheat-coloured hair swept sideways from a flat, rectangular face, at Paulus, with his upside-down-triangle features and soft mid-blond curls glowing in the sunlight, at Crooks, the elfin cross-country runner with green eyes and copper-coloured hair... I *did* belong here. I had earned my place in this tribe. They were my friends and I like totally loved them, you know? Like *sooo* TOTALLY.

So when, at break, I ran out to play football, swapping black Clarks for silver-grey Reeboks, and Arnold yelled at me to play up with the others against U5B, and that mop-headed lamp-post Lewis passed me the ball, I felt I was back where I belonged. I slid the ball through Coleman's feet and raced round to chip it to Collins who headed back to my left foot (I'm like really and *totally* left-footed). Ten yards out, with only Robbins, their lardy-arsed, curly-haired keeper to beat, I drew him off his line then lobbed the ball delicately over his head and through the piled-blazer posts making it 3-2 to us. Lewis ruffled my hair. Maxton slapped my back. Even Spud-Face Seymour clapped appreciatively. JP was back, and already scoring.

During the first Assembly, I sat in front of Austen in U5S and behind Robbins in U5B and between Gray and Maxton on the dusty Rises in the aircraft-hangar named after Thomas Beckwith, an eighteenth century artist from York. The 400 Lower Schoolers sat cross-legged on the floor below us. The 200 Sixth Formers sat in chairs behind us. Down on the platform stood the gleaming black Steinway I loved playing so much. Fred was teasing out this Bach prelude in F sharp minor. The twenty new prefects were chattering excitedly in a row along one of the walls. Their names were listed in the Handbook. D.S. Rose, U6L, was sitting beside

S.J. Leverett, U6MS. Under his black prefect's gown, he was wearing this dark grey suit, white shirt and this gold prefect's tie with the school's crown-and-sheaf crest. He looked really happy.

The Headmaster, Senior Master, Chaplain and Head Boy, Tom Redmond, a rugby-playing tree in a stripy blue-and-gold Colours blazer, filed in. The masters were in like full academic dress, not just gowns but also hoods in their different university colours. Standing, I opened *Hymns Ancient and Modern* at number 184, 'Dear Lord and Father of Mankind, forgive our foolish ways'. The hymn-book was battered now and ink-stained from the same accident that had done for my French dictionary and stopped me carrying actual bottles of Quink in my backpack. All my forms (3Y, 4M, L5C, now U5H) were listed on the inside front-cover where I'd once, long, long ago, written J.D. Peters 2W in this blue-black ink. Because I knew the words, I could sing *and* watch Ali helping some teary-eyed gimp find the right page. That's my Ali, I thought, showing kindness to others.

My Ali. Yikes.

Blushing, I returned to breathing through the earthquake, wind and fire.

After we'd mumbled "Our Father, which art in Heaven, hallowed be thy name" and Redmond had dully intoned *Proverbs* Chapter 1, that "*The simple will be endowed with shrewdness and the young with knowledge and prudence,*" Ash-tray gave this like motivational address which went along the lines of 'work hard, play hard and always do your best to discover and understand.' Finally Gallagher called up the prefects two-by-two for a handshake and to sign this book. I felt this surge of excited pride when 'Alistair Rose' was announced. He was my friend, after all. As he left the platform, he kind of glanced up into the hall and, across eight hundred heads, our eyes like locked, you know? and my stomach flipped over like a pancake in a frying pan and Leatherbridge Leatherbridge, our IT-teaching Year Head, bawled that the boys on the Rises should remain where we were to stop U5S shoving us into U5B below, something Leatherface loathed almost as much as he loathed the boys on the Rises. I reckoned it was 'cos he didn't teach like a *proper* subject, you know?

"Leverett's a right bastard," said Gray as we filed out. "Mr Rule-Book or what."

"Rosie's all right though," I ventured.

"Pah," said Gray, "Broody reckons he's a proper poofter, bit of a Paulus, you know?"

"Paulus isn't gay," I said. "Nor's Rosie."

"That's all *you* know," Gray answered darkly.

On the bus home, while Maxton was fiddling with his bloody Rubik's Cube and describing this *Space Invaders* game he and Stewart had played at lunchtime in Sweaty Betty's, Rosie appeared behind me and said "Hi, Jonny."

My reply was so girly it made me blush. I kind of like sighed 'hiiiii.' Gray frowned.

"You still wanna be in the play, don't you?" he said.

"Yeah," I blurted enthusiastically. "I can't wait. But I might not be able to do all the rehearsals. I got Choral Society, Chamber Orchestra, clarinet lesson on Thursdays..."

"It'll be fine," he said. "Will you also join the debating team?"

"Mass-debating team," Maxton sniggered coarsely as nine squares clicked blue.

"Yes, but I've never done it before." I sounded breathlessly excited. God. To be on the same team with him. To sit beside him in the lecture theatre. Me and him together...

"Bet you have," sniggered Maxton. "Mass-debated... ha ha, like every fucking night, eh, Jonny? Over some sizzling hot bird in *Razzle,* eh?" I coloured like a clown's nose.

Babbling thanks, I sounded like some over-eager, rather needy puppy and could feel Gray's eyes literally drilling into the back of my neck like some bloody Black and Decker.

"Yikes," said Rosie, peering over my shoulder. "You got Herbidacious for Biology."

"Yeah," I said. "Already ruing the thyme I'll have to dill with him, ha ha."

"You're *sooo* not funny, Peters," Maxton remarked through Rosie's groaned grin as Gray slapped my hand. "Why do you suppose he hates everyone so much?"

"Miserable childhood," said Rosie, "But you got Hellfire. European history 1789-1914. You'll be in Hand-out Heaven. Hellfire's my form-master this year. Upper Six L."

No way! I'd be in his class-room. I could sit where *he* sat, maybe in the same chair...

"And you got Beaky," he continued enthusiastically. "I'm doing A-Level Literature with him. Man, it's awesome. I love Brecht, *and* Thomas Mann. We're doing *Death in Venice*. You *have* to read it, J. It's about this old man who falls in love with a beautiful young boy..."

Gray snorted. As Rosie reddened like a, well, like a rose, I rescued him by asking him to test my French vocab.

"I hate testing people," he groaned, taking my blue vocab book. "Mum makes me test Bobby. It's so boring. Sheep."

"Un mouton."

"Cow."

"Une vache."

"Rabbit."

"Un lapin."

"Squirrel."

"Un écureuil."

"I never knew that. I never saw that before."

"Get on with it."

Tapping my nose gently with my book, he said teasingly "This time I want you to act them out, so I know you really understand what they mean."

"You're kidding, right?"

"Duck."

"You've *got* to be joking."

Sitting back with this evil grin, he ordered me to be a French duck so I ended up going 'quack quack' on the bus, then 'oink oink' for 'un cochon', and everyone was pissing themselves and Nick Shelton, this hottie from 4D and Firth with a silver brace and smouldering eyes, shouts it sounded like *Old Macdonald's Farm* and Rosie goes "That's genius, Shelters. Sing it in French, JP! With the actions *and* the sound-effects," so me, Rosie, Shelton and Trent, also 4D, are like singing it at the tops of our voices while Gray and Maxton are kind of literally shrinking into the seats pretending they don't know us, you know? Then Warburton from the Upper Sixth yells "You missed out cock!" We all pissed ourselves and Shelton and Trent did these insane rooster impressions and we pissed ourselves again. It was such a laugh, you know? Like the most totally AWESOME first day back ever!

As I got off the bus, Rosie grinned and my heart kind of somersaulted like a gymnast on a trampoline? I leap-frogged this concrete bollard outside Ladbroke's then leapt like a salmon to slap this STOP sign at the top of our street. Utterly elated, I raced down the road like I had yesterday, singing at the top of my lungs, "The Heavens are telling the glory of God" from Haydn's *Creation*. Man, I felt so alive, you know?

3: Walking on Sunshine

SATURDAY. No getting up at seven. No trudging to the bus-stop at 7.40. No school. Just homework and pleasing myself. Waking just after nine to hear the rain pattering on my window, I rolled lazily back into my duvet and curled into a warm, cosy ball. Saturday was the best day ever invented. Soon the folks would be off to Sainsbury's, B & Q and my grandparents, so I would listen to Radio 3's *CD Review* on the black Crown radio I got for passing the 11+, have a wank, take a hot, steamy shower, blast a quick game of *Deathchase* and wrap my head round linear equations, transpiration, gas laws, chapter 1 of *The Mayor of Casterbridge* and the German essay: 'An einem Samstagsmorgen wachten sie frueh auf; es war herrlicher Sonnenschein. Wie war der weitere Verlauf des Tages?' Ha ha, Herr Phillips. If only.

"Jonny?" Mum was shouting up the stairs for all the hippos in Africa to hear.

"What?"

"Mow the lawn, pick some blackberries, some runner beans and some tomatoes, please. I want to make chutney this week."

"Right!"

"And cut back the brambles by the compost-heap and empty the dish-washer."

"Okay!"

It was like half-past nine and I'd already got this massive job-list. What did your last servant die of? I didn't shout. Overwork, came the imagined reply from the African hippos.

"I *have* got homework, you know, *and* music practice!" I called irritably.

"You should've done it last night!"

On a Friday? What does she think I am? Who does their homework on a Friday? Not when there's *It's a Knockout* (Belgians dressed as giant squirrels, man!), *Starsky and Hutch* and the Last-But-One Night of the Proms, James Loughran conducting the Hallé in a mind-blowing Beethoven 1 and 9. Snorting, I listened to Michael Kennedy assessing recordings of Elgar's Introduction and Allegro for strings and read *Bleak House* for another hour as the morning sunlight seeped softly through the butter-coloured curtains. I'd really got into Dickens after *Oliver* and had read that, *Christmas Carol* and *Great Expectations* already. Halfway through, Krook had like spontaneously combusted, Esther had smallpox and Richard had broken with Jarndyce his guardian. It was like *Corrie*, but more believable. Finally, like around eleven, I set aside my book, silenced the radio, stripped off my PJs and threw back my duvet.

Although I absolutely *loved* doing it, and *totally* loved spurting more than *anything*, I didn't masturbate as often as my friends. Though I started when I was about eleven, I hadn't like *spurted* back then, not really. That didn't start till I was like thirteen, you know? And it was the best feeling ever, I mean, like EVER! Anyhow, Gray claimed he did it like twice a day into a tissue, once before he got up then again before he went to sleep. Collins said he did it every night onto his bedsheet. Maxton said he did it only when he had 'the urge' but, being fifteen and packed full of hormones and stuff, that was probably three or four times an hour. I knew for a fact that he once swapped a French class for a toilet cubicle, preferring a five-knuckle shuffle to a vocabulary exercise on sport and leisure. I joked he had made his own sport and leisure *that* morning. Tim Wilson, of course, had read in the Bible that God disapproved so, having got *me* hooked and sent to hell, stopped, saving his spunk, I suppose, for Jesus, while Paulus, we supposed, was far too prissy to put up with the mess.

I usually did it three times a week, every Sunday in the bath - there was something about wanking in hot, soapy water that really turned me on, you know? – and every Saturday when my parents went shopping when I could stretch naked on my bed, stroke my whole body and get totally lost in ten minutes of absolute bliss. I also did it on Wednesdays when Mum went to yoga, locking myself in the bathroom for a quarter of an hour and squirting directly into the toilet. Occasionally, of course, I had to do it at other times too, like when I had a wet-dream or when I'd been reading or watching something really sexy, but I didn't really like doing it while the folks were at home. I mean, if they caught me, mega-embarrassment or what?

My folks *never* talked about sex or body-parts or anything like that, right? So they'd never sat me down for, like, THAT talk, you know? Never explained puberty, adolescence or what this strange wispy hair that floated seaweed-like in the bathwater was all about. I got my sex ed. from Gray in 2W and from Brudenall's *Razzles* in 3Y. It was like during those breaks that I'd really experienced my first real erections and, like everyone else, had occasionally shot my load into a school bog while claiming a gyppy tummy during RE. Nonetheless, if Mum or Dad, I didn't know which would be worse, ever caught me wanking, I just knew I would literally die of shame. Anyway, they weren't in now so I grabbed a tissue, raised my knees, closed my eyes and slicked my right hand sharply down. Seven wonderful minutes and forty-three blissful seconds passed. Spitting into my palm and moaning, I arched my back and spread my legs, heels and bottom digging down into the mattress. My head flopped on the pillow. My heart thumped like it was trying to smash through my ribcage. I was leaking like a half-open tap. Jerking my hand brutally down so I cried out, I closed my eyes, rolled my head sideways, felt my lips part, felt my heart beat faster, my mouth dry, my buttocks clench...

I imagined Claire hugging me, kissing me, touching me, there... there... yes, THERE, kissing me THERE... licking... taking me into her warm, wet mouth... then Alistair's face, Alistair's legs, appeared in my mind, and I imagined him wanking me, sucking me, fucking me... Gasping sharply, I ejaculated with this earthquake force that like totally shattered my entire body. Spunk spurted everywhere, like some epileptic hosepipe was pumping it out, spattering my chest with long, warm ribbons then fat sperm-splashes on my stomach and fingers. I uttered a joyful groan and, as my heart-rate and breathing slowed, wiped my skin with a tissue, staggered weak-kneed to the shower, dried quickly, chucked on a plum-coloured slip, a pair of black knee-length shorts and a plain, dark green T-shirt then danced downstairs two at a time to the kitchen for breakfast, the gold cross bouncing on my chest.

The fridge was packed with salad, fruit, vegetables, the whole-fruit Innocent smoothies I liked, skimmed soya-milk, bottles of wine, several types of low-fat yogurt, organic eggs and a variety of farmhouse cheeses. I know *they* aren't low-fat but Dad won't give them up, whatever the doctor says about his cholesterol, and I could scoff a block of Double Gloucester with chives in like one sitting, so Mum was stuck with it. We avoided processed food, except bacon and ham, and virtually everything containing preservatives. If we couldn't pronounce what was in it, we agreed, we wouldn't eat it. Occasionally, when I needed a high-carbohydrate input, like for sports, a play or a concert, I had pasta with Dad's tomato, garlic and basil sauce. This was so delicious I wished I played rugby every day, though my favourite meal ever was shepherd's pie with baked beans and gravy. *That* made me drool like a dog and on Sundays we usually had a roast. Coming in from church at 12, Mum would do a joint of beef or a leg of pork or a whole chicken with crispy roast potatoes, seasonal veggies and fluffy Yorkshire puddings bathed in gravy so thick you needed a spoon, and we'd share a bottle of wine so they could teach me 'responsible drinking'.

At least once a week we had fish, usually salmon, trout or something like plaice, whatever was fresh in the market. We never bought frozen. Dad said it was all water unless it'd been flash-frozen in nitrogen and would you really want to eat something saturated in nitrogen? Friday night was Curry Night. We usually made it together, me chopping stuff, Dad grinding spices and Mum stirring it all together in a big red Le Creuset pot. It was usually chicken or prawns but we experimented, the three of us poring over this curry encyclopaedia together. Mum baked *na'ans*, I made cucumber and yogurt *raita*, Dad fried black-pepper *poppadums* and there was always a jar of mango chutney on the side. The best one we did was a Sri Lankan black-pork curry. The least successful was a tomato-and-egg curry which made us fart like dogs. We followed the recipe fairly closely but curried eggs? Oh boy. But Fridays were great because it was the three of us working together and also my pocket-money night. I earned this through drying the dishes after dinner, hoovering the carpets, mopping the kitchen and bathroom floors once a week and washing the car every fortnight. I got £5 a week, to save, or spend, on anything I liked, except junk food, comics, sodas or crisps.

I wasn't allowed sugary drinks like Fanta or Pepsi, and I didn't like them anyway. I was more your beetroot juice and lemon in hot water kind of guy. I also hated milk, I mean *seriously* hated it. Just the smell of it made me puke like a cat. We had a zillion types of tea, black, green, white, fruit-flavoured, herbal, and every type of honey you can think of and a few you can't. Coffee was, inevitably, decaffeinated. I couldn't remember the last time a bag of crisps, Cheetos or Monster Munch got into our house. Instead we had dried apricots, pumpkin seeds and soya-nuts, although I had recently discovered banana chips. Fried in coconut oil and shamelessly high in calories, Mum hated them but since I could barely remember chocolate bars either, which was a shame, 'cos I love chocolate and the simplest bar of Galaxy made me drool like a fool and sneeze like a donkey 'cos of an allergy, she accepted the banana chips, at least for now, as my 'teenage rebellion'. As for comics, I'd once bought a *Warlord,* because of Lord Peter Flint (Codename: Warlord), the dandified conscientious objector who was really a crack British spy fighting the Nazis, and such a storm broke I felt like 'Union Jack' Jackson storming the beaches of Guadalcanal with Sergeant Lonnegan and G.I. O'Bannion.

"I haven't signed you into the library so you can read comics," Mum had said, promptly confiscating it for Dad to enjoy later.

So I tended to save my pocket-money, all stuffed inside my piggy bank, a pink plastic pig with a great fat belly, a smiley face and big flappy ears. He had a round red hat with a slot in it for depositing the loot. Mum paid my bus fares and cut my hair whilst Dad paid for clothes and stuff so that fiver a week was for books, CDs and Airfix kits. I didn't care that I was an only child. I had room to be myself. Anyway now I needed to start my homework so took my brain-food, this massive yellow bowl of chopped strawberries, banana slices, blueberries, pumpkin seeds and yogurt, two slices of granary toast with honey and a peach and passion-fruit smoothie, back to my room.

With the little fluffy owl imaginatively called Ozzie who I took to exams for luck, about an inch high and an inch across with a red back and a white front, an orange, carrot-shaped felt beak, little orange feet and black googly eyes, watching me beadily from beside Piggy Bank on the shelf over my desk, I opened my pencil-tin, which was pale blue with a colourful map of the world printed on the lid, the USA in green, Canada in plum, Mexico in orange, Russia in yellow and a minuscule UK in pink, all on a sea-blue background, and rooted around for a fresh blue-black cartridge for my silver Waterman, a yellow pencil-sharpener with Winnie-the-Pooh on the front and a black and yellow HB pencil topped with a yellow rubber banana. This had a smiley face, buck-teeth like Julie Wilson's (I mean, you'd never know her old man was a dentist, would you?), and little arms and legs. I collected these humanised-fruit pencil-ends and had an apple, a plum and an orange in the tin, along with some pencil-shavings, a couple of pencils, two gel-pens, one silver, one gold, a searing yellow highlighter, a small Pritt-Stick, an inky, furry lump of blu-tak and some loose paper-clips which I liked to unbend while I was thinking. Spooning up my home-made Fruit-bowl, I stared at this like head-breaking SMP Maths book and my even more incomprehensible black Casio FX-85 calculator and read

"Draw axes with x and y from 0 to 15, then

a) draw and label the line where $3x + 4y = 12$,

b) draw and label the line where $3x + 4y = 24$,

c) draw and label the line where $3x + 4y = 36$.

d) what do you notice about the lines?

e) Shade the region where $3x + 4y > 36$."

I mean, what the fuck does it mean and who the fuck cares anyway?

I sucked the banana's foot, scribbled some shit, banged Pink Floyd's *The Wall* into the CD player and started writing up last week's Physics experiment in this green book:

"A beaker was filled with water and ice cubes and a thermometer and a capillary tube with oil in it were placed in the beaker. The length of air between the bottom of the tube and the oil was measured and noted down. The water was heated and every 5° C the temperature went up, the length was noted down again. A graph was drawn up to 100° C."

I'd already drawn this on the facing squared-paper page.

"When the Charles Law and Pressure Law are extrapolated back to zero pressure and volume, it is found the lines cut the temperature axis at about the same temperature. Accurate experiments show that this temperature should be nearly 273° C below 0. This is the lowest possible temperature when as thermal motion stops completely. This is called the absolute zero of temperature."

Re-reading it, I realised I had no idea what any of it meant. I carried on regardless.

"The absolute scale has its zero at the absolute zero of temperature and the degree is the same as that on the centigrade scale, e.g.

Freezing point of water = 273K
Boiling point of water =373K
Room temperature = 290K
Air freezes = 70K
CO_2 freezes = 200K"

"Hey you, out there in the cold, getting lonely, getting old, can you feel me?" I sang, *"Hey you, don't help them to bury the light, don't give in without a fight."*

"We can now see that pressure and volume proportional to the absolute temperature and write:

$$\frac{V_1}{T_1} = \frac{V_2}{T_2} \qquad\qquad \frac{P_1}{T_1} = \frac{P_2}{T_2}$$

"Hey you, would you help me to carry the stone?" I warbled as I scrawled an example, *"Open your heart, I'm coming home."* Cue air-guitar.

"A given mass of gas has volume 500 cm³ at 0° C. What will be its volume at 100° C?
$V_1 = 500$,
$T_1 = 0° C \rightarrow 273K$,
$T_2 = 100° C \rightarrow 373K$,
$V_2 = ?$
$$\frac{V_2}{373} = \frac{500}{273}$$

Therefore
$$V_2 = \frac{500 \times 373}{273} \qquad = \qquad 683 \text{ cm}^{3.}"$$

Eccellente. Job done.

I fired a paper pellet at the yellow sun on the wooden part of the wind-chime and hit the curtain instead then chucked a table-tennis ball at the wall for a low catch at first slip to win the Ashes back for England, tossing it up to the ceiling in victorious celebration.

"No matter how he tried, he could not break free, and the worms ate into his brain." I chucked the Physics book aside for the marbled grey Biology hardback book. "Transpiration is a process where water-vapour is lost by the plant to the atmosphere principally by evaporation through the stomata." Blimey. There was even a diagram of a potometer to be drawn. I would have to dig out the Crayolas. This song was so awesome. *"Hey you, standing in the road, always doing what you're told, can you help me?"* - Alistair was so awesome - *"Hey you, out there beyond the wall, breaking bottles in the hall, can you help me?"* – I chucked the table-tennis ball again and dived forward onto my bed to take it one-handed at cover. Everything was awesome. Winning the Ashes was awesome.

"Don't tell me there's no hope at all, together we stand, divided we fall," I sang, slapping the Bio book on top of the others. It might be right. I didn't *really* care. I'd never need to know this stuff ever again in the remaining seventy-odd years of my life. What a waste of fucking time. Still, it kept people in jobs. Otherwise what *was* the point?

As the table-tennis ball bounced back at me, I flung myself full-length on the carpet getting both hands under it, running in from extra cover. I decided to play sock-football next and win the FA Cup for Norwich City. After I'd scored a stunning left-foot volley into the top corner of the curtains from a rebound off the wardrobe, and punched the air, then got into a fight with one of my pillows, who got arsy 'cos I'd nutmegged him for a second goal under the diving body/bed of the goalkeeper, I knelt on my bed, air-guitared *'Now I've got that feeling once again, I can't explain, you would not understand, This is not how I am, I have become comfortably numb...'* then karate-kicked the pillow through the open bedroom door.

I really didn't know what to write for this German essay. How *would* I spend a sunny Saturday morning, given the opportunity? In our earliest German lessons, we learned that Herr Ehler's 'Stopplicht ist kaput' and that he was a Farter and we all obligingly giggled. Beaky had taught us prepositions that took the dative case by setting the list, 'aus, bei, mit, nach, seit, von, zu' to the German National Anthem (the accusative case 'durch, für, gegen, ohne, um' fitting the next part of the tune – go on, sing it. You know you want to!) but all I could remember about my earliest French lessons in primary was that the teacher gave us all French names, like I was Patrice or Patroclus, something beginning with P. I mean, why?

Sucking my pencil-banana again, I like stared at this glowing golden lava flow from Nyamalagera in Zaire depicted on my most awesome Volcano poster and considered the rarity of a sunny Saturday morning where I was free to do what I wanted.

My favourite place in the universe was Malham Cove, this massively awesome, expressionless 260 foot limestone cliff in the Dales that might once have been a waterfall. I also really liked Aysgarth Falls, where the River Ure descends a triple flight of waterfalls over a one-mile stretch but then there are like a million fabulous places in Yorkshire and many of my best days out had been spent cycling round Wharfedale with Gray or Wilson or hiking up Buckden Pike or across the moors with my parents before tucking into a well-earned fireside lunch in some cosy country pub. Then I had this like brainwave, you know? I would go to Scarborough with Alistair, and do what I'd done as a kid when Mum's folks had the B & B overlooking the North Bay. I loved Scarborough. We'd let the train take the strain, like snuggle into each other as the world flashed by, then walk barefoot, hand-in-hand, on the beach. We'd paddle in rock-pools, share an ice-cream, get fish and chips then head to the castle to gaze at the sea and cuddle up to watch some cricket at the best ground in the country. That's a day out, I thought, just like in that song by Fiddler's Dram, 'Didn't we have a lovely time, the day we went to [Scarborough]?' Jeez, that was one of the few singles I'd like actually bought, that, *Rat-Trap, Bohemian Rhapsody, Space Oddity* and Bay City Rollers' tartan-trousered *Bye Bye Baby*. Mum said singles were a waste of money. Wait for the album. More bang for your buck. But what if the other songs were, like, a bit crap, Mum?

I inserted a fresh cartridge into the Waterman and *The Magic Flute* into the CD player, feminized his name to 'Alison', wrote the date, Samstag 13th September, and produced the most romantic story I'd ever written whilst this exhilarating opera about love being tested by fire and water roared around me. I had to look up the word for 'snuggle' in my *Langenscheidt* dictionary and then write an edited fair-copy for Beaky which finished with the words "Und dann, wir küssten..." but I was proud of my work. It was a good story.

I steered the motorbike through the trees and zapped a white helicopter with one of my heat-seeking missiles then veered to the left to loose another off at a pink tank on the horizon. I pressed hard on the Z key and blew the yellow bike out of the forest to raise my score to $4231 and into the night patrol level. The blue sky went black and the trees got thicker. My whole body swayed to the right as I leaned on the arrow keys and guided the handlebars to the left. Eight minutes later - Sector 7. $31,835 and rising. Ha ha. Closing in on new high score. Blue bike, white tank – blown apart, ha ha. $38,750. Sector 8.... Closing in. $15000 bonus if you finish Sector 8.... Come on, come on, come on... SHIIIT. Fucking nerve-shredding jangle of the telephone jolted me out of my world and sent me smashing into a tree for a faceful of bark, no bonus and another gloating GAME OVER. Bollocks.

It was about half-one and the bloody lawn was still awaiting the mower. Mentally preparing my excuses, I answered the phone. It was Alistair Rose. Christ, I'd just been thinking about him. My stomach did this violent somersault and my voice dried to a croak. He wondered if I wanted to meet up. A bazillion thoughts like thundered through my throbbing brain. He wanted to see me. Today. At the weekend. What did it mean?

"You promised to play me the B minor Mass," he said semi-accusingly.

"All right," I kind of squeaked. "Do you want to come to my house?"

"Sure. Half an hour?"

"You know where I live?"

"Black gate." I could hear the grin.

Shit.

Half an hour. Oh. My. God. I had to get ready.

What should I wear? Should I wear jeans? Should I wear shorts? I knew he liked my legs. What about my T-shirt? What colour would he like?

Damn what *he* liked. It was more important to *smell* good.

Pounding to the bathroom, I cut my fingernails, brushed my teeth twice, flossed, sloshed Listerine round my gums, then dived under the shower with the Imperial Leather and this avocado, lime and coconut shower-gel, soaping my boy-bits several times. Just in case.

Fuck. In case of what?

How should I do my hair? Should I do it straight, or spike it with gel?

What would he be wearing?

What should *I* wear? I hadn't settled *that* yet.

What about my hair?

Frantically scooping a handful of gel from the jar, I dragged some through my fringe to lift it a little but it went *too* spiky so I flattened it again, didn't like that either, so dragged my fingers through it again, standing it up like a hedgehog's spikes. Shit and bollocks. I'd have to start again. Worse, I thought I'd seen a couple of spots emerging at the corner of my nose and on my forehead. Fucking hell! I stuck my head under the shower again.

I didn't really have time for this.

Fuck's sake.

I sprayed myself liberally with Dark Temptation, slapped on some of Dad's Old Spice.

Clothes. What clothes?

I was searching my wardrobe manically when the doorbell rang.

He was here.

At my house.

And I wasn't ready. I was naked and sweaty and my hair was a fucking disaster. My palms perspired and the elephant leaping around my guts made me feel sick. I just literally threw the clothes I'd taken off back on, and ran barefoot downstairs to the front door.

He was wearing black jeans and a white open-necked polo-shirt. The thick lock of bruise-black hair fell carelessly towards his right eye. My heart thudded and, as his cool hand shook mine, I felt again that electric tingle.

"You look good," he commented. "That green really suits you. Nice house."

"Thanks." Fucking hell. Get a conversation, you loser.

"So what were you doing when I called?"

"Writing a story for Beaky," I said. About you, I didn't add. "It's a romance."

"I knew you were a romantic," he grinned.

"I was gonna do my piano practice," I said. "Do you wanna listen?"

The music room had once been a small dining-room at the front of the house across the hall from the living-room. Three old sofas in muted autumnal reds and browns were arranged in a U-shape facing the battered brown Bechstein upright piano my teacher had given us. A large, intricately woven, slightly faded rug lay in the centre of the uneven walnut-stained floorboards. One wall bore bookshelves. My parents were not great fiction readers so most of their books were about local history, gardening, flowers and plants, yoga and Pilates, nutrition and child-rearing, titillating titles like *Amateur Astronomy, Get to Know your Local Churchyard, A History of the King's Own Yorkshire Light Infantry (KOYLIs), Pond-Fish for Beginners, Make the Most of Geraniums, Fighting the Flab: Easy Exercises for Weight-Watchers* and *Bringing up Baby: A Guide for New Parents.* There was a Koenig and Meyer music-stand, my clarinet and Dad's guitar. He'd played a lot when I was younger, mainly stuff by Paul Simon and Pete Seeger. I remembered him crooning 'Puff the Magic Dragon lived by the sea' to get me to sleep but he'd given up around the time I'd started the piano. Why he'd stopped I didn't know. I just supposed he'd got bored with it, like so many of his other hobbies.

Sitting at the piano, I played some scales then rolled into the first movement of Mozart's F major sonata K332 I'd played for Grade 8, enjoying the punched dynamics in bars 60-65, the dancing, syncopated, bouncing left-hand and flourishes from bar 84 to the repeat at bar 93. He simply stared at my frowned concentration, then kind of sighed.

"Man, you're *sooo* good. I can't play anything." He looked enviously at the framed certificates with the red crown crest of the Associated Boards of the Royal Schools of Music (in gold) that clustered on top of the piano, the four I had for clarinet, presented for examination by Martin Angus BA, LRSM, and the eight 'to certify that JONATHAN DAVID PETERS was examined in Grade… Piano' and presented for examination by Barbara Lennox OBE, MA, FRSM, D.Mus. (Hon).' Yes, my teacher was that good she had an OBE, and an honorary doctorate from Leeds Uni. So ha.

"Nothing?" I said, slightly disappointed. He shook his head. "Never too late to learn, Alistair. Maybe I'll teach you."

I'd started learning aged six. I don't really know why my parents invested in me. I mean, Dad's record collection consisted mainly of James Last and The Shadows whilst Mum favoured Barry Manilow and The Carpenters. They said I sat down at someone's piano and knocked out a tune by ear and whoever it was said I was really good so my parents talked to the music teacher at primary who got me to play something and the next thing I knew I was off to audition for Barbara Lennox, the most famous teacher in the north. The woman had written books, for God's sake, and taught professional concert-pianists, competition prize-winners and one famous conductor. She rarely took on new pupils, especially children, and she only agreed to hear *me* because my primary teacher was an old college friend. Sitting with her arms folded and her eyes shut, she'd looked both grumpy *and* scary until I played this lovely, lilting Brahms lullaby I'd like learned by heart? I'd been tremendously nervous and made some mistakes but, as I played, her whole expression softened.

"The boy has potential," she'd remarked. "I'll take him."

The rest, as they say, was history, Grades 1 and 2 in the first year, then steady progress through the others, concerts, recitals, festivals, prizes, cups, acclamation in the Press, I had become Mrs Lennox's brightest star and six years later, I passed Grade 8 with distinction and was now preparing for Grade 8 on the clarinet which I'd started because of my asthma. Like swimming and singing, it really helped me control my breathing.

When I started at the grammar school, in the first music lesson, Fred Perry went round the class asking who played an instrument and there were a bunch of kids saying 'piano' and 'violin' and Perry asked what grade and they were all going 'two' or 'three' so he got to Mark Gray who said 'Piano, Grade Five' and there was this kind of whistle of appreciation. Perry said 'play something for us', so Gray played Debussy's *Clair de Lune*. It's kind of slow and languorous, very famous, very beautiful, and at the end, although he made a few mistakes with his fingering, everybody clapped. He looked a little embarrassed while Perry continued round the rest of the class – we sat in alphabetical order – and gets to Andy Paulus, who was a 'cellist, and he also said Grade Five, but he didn't have a 'cello to prove it. I was sitting next to him, so Perry goes 'Who are you?' and I go 'Jonathan Peters, sir,' and he goes 'Do you play an instrument, Peters?' and Tim Wilson shouts 'He plays piano, sir, and he's awesome.' Perry asked what grade I was, and I said 'Distinction in Six, sir, and now doing Seven.' He does this double-take, like he can't believe this 11 year old kid's preparing for Grade 7. Anyway, voice dripping scepticism, he goes 'Play something' and I go to this massive fuck-off Steinway and did 'Farewell to Stromness' by Maxwell Davies, the most beautiful piano piece I ever heard, from memory and without a mistake, rocking through those opening bass crochets and treble triplets into these powerful six-finger chord progressions and back again. You could've heard a feather drop by the time I'd finished. It felt like I'd woven some strange magic spell over them. Perry's ruddy, fat face was rigid with shock as the whole class sat, suspended in time, and I played Debussy's *Golliwog's Cake-Walk* as a perky *encore*, but despite that, and everything else, Perry never really warmed to me. I guess it's hard to teach a prodigy when you haven't like made it yourself, you know? Besides, he never really forgave me for turning down a place in the Chapel Choir. I had a voice like an angel but I didn't want to commit the time. Every Sunday morning (and I had piano lessons in the afternoon), plus Friday after school and Wednesday lunchtime. I had other stuff to do, you know? Also, I didn't fancy the get-up, these floor-length blue cassocks like dresses and frilly white ruffled neck-pieces? Man, ticket to Lamesville, or what?

"You must remember this," I grinned, flowing into Chopin's D flat major nocturne, Opus 27 number 2. I'd won both the individual and the house music contests last year with this and played it in the summer concert. Rosie had totally raved in the reviews about my 'singing right hand,' 'liquid beauty' and 'steely fingers'. What he wrote had utterly thrilled me.

"Oh man," he sighed again, "I *love* hearing you play that. *Sooo* beautiful."

Lost somewhere, he was like gazing at my face now. Shit. The magic spell again. Electricity kind of crackled through my tingling body. There was a sudden singing in the air that might've been angels as I hit that top note that made audiences shiver.

Standing abruptly, I closed the lid and said "Do you wanna see my room?"

4: Laserlight

ACROSS the landing from my parents' soft green under-sea cocoon, my bedroom looked out over the back lawn, which I suddenly remembered I hadn't mowed, Mum's precious rose-bushes, the greenhouse where Dad grew tomatoes, which I hadn't picked (bollocks), the fruit trees, apple and plum, honeysuckle bushes, which exuded this powerful, heady scent from treacle-coloured flowers and the bloody bramble patch waiting like that shark in *Jaws*.

"Nice garden." He was kneeling on my bed watching butterflies through the window.

We hadn't always lived here. We'd started in this like two-up, two-down in some scuzzy part of the city, the kind of place where tattooed ruffians drag unwilling, unmuzzled pit-bulls up and down the kerb, and the front doors are literally caged behind metal grilles of Fort Knox proportions, the kind of place Dad refused to park our battered Fiesta in case the wheels got nicked, the kind of place they hung washing across the cobbled street, the kind of place dodgy substances changed hands of an evening, the kind of place where a nervy, neurotic grammar-school kid whose class-mates despised him became even nervier and even more neurotic. Walking up that street in my 'posho' blazer with its bloody corn-and-crown badge and Latin motto was like yelling 'Mug me, please!' although, to be fair, it never happened. Why, I have no idea. Anyway, four years ago, Mum inherited enough money from selling her parents' Scarborough guest-house to move us up in the world, or at least to a detached house in the suburbs, and, more excitingly, to a silver Ford Sierra. Oh, come on! I was like 11, you know? Silver was like the coolest colour EVER!

"The wind-chimes are cool." The moons and stars were painted blue and yellow.

"Thanks." I felt myself blushing cricket ball-red.

"I like your room," he grinned. "It's like being in a giant fried-egg."

This made me laugh. The walls were painted bright yellow but my bedding was all white, white sheets, white covers, white pillow-cases, everything white. I liked the simplicity.

"Are these your PJs?" Brown cotton shorts and beige T-shirt sprawled on the pillow.

"Yeah, sorry." My face burned like a lava-field. Hoping he hadn't seen the stains on my shorts, I chucked them on the yellow carpet with my yellow dressing-gown, dirty tennis socks, pale yellow T-shirt, damp blue bath-towel, one silver Reebok lying on its side and this single, tan moccasin. "I like shorts in bed. Proper trousers are too hot. What about you?"

Shit. I was babbling.

"Nothing," he said. A thrill tingled through my spine. He slept naked! Oh boy! I *had* to try it. "You've got lots of books." He glanced over my library. Suddenly it seemed absurdly childish, these like Ladybird books about Nelson, Scott of the Antarctic, David Livingstone, Henry V and Richard the Lion-heart, I-Spy 'In the Night Sky' and 'London from Trafalgar Square', The *Observer* Books of Flags, Birds and Wild Animals, *Biggles of 266* and *Biggles of the Interpol*, the Hardy Boys *Viking Symbol Mystery, Five on a Treasure Island, The Castle of Adventure*, all the Tintin books, Treece's *Viking Saga, The Eagle of the Ninth, The Midnight Folk, The Chronicles of Narnia, The Greatest Gresham*, all the James Bond books, then these Westerns I was into, *North Against the Sioux, Custer's Gold, Seventh Cavalry…* thank fuck for the classics, like *Around the World in Eighty Days, Black Beauty, Last of the Mohicans, Grimm's Fairy Tales, Treasure Island* and a load of history, R.J. Unstead's four-volume *Story of Britain, Great Leaders* and *Royal Adventurers, Great Escapes of World War Two, Everyday Life in Ancient Rome, Monsters and Mysterious Beasts*. I had a *Readers' Digest* World Atlas, *Fighting Men and their Uniforms*, a *Question of Sport* quiz book, *Tutankhamen, Dinosaurs*, a bunch of science-fiction like *I Robot, Chocky* and *The Midwich Cuckoos, War of the Worlds* and *The Time Machine*, Sherlock Holmes in *The Hound of the Baskervilles* and my latest craze, the well-thumbed war stories of Sven Hassel.

"It's a very eclectic collection," he commented.

31

I didn't know what he meant. Defensively I said I'd read anything, except like wizards or zombies? Wizards and zombies bored my arse off, you know?

"Who's your favourite poet?"

"Ted Hughes," I said. "I love the Crow poems. 'Where is the Black Beast? Crow roasted the earth to a clinker, he charged into space...' The futility of science. I love it, and 'Crow's Last Stand', "Limpid and black – Crow's eye-pupil, in the tower of its scorched fort" and 'How water began to play' but I like Blake too, 'The Poison Tree' and 'London' with the chartered streets and mind-forg'd manacles. They're such strong images. Who's yours?"

"T. S. Eliot."

I'd never heard of him.

" '*What we call the beginning is often the end, and to make an end is to make a beginning*'," he quoted. I didn't understand. "I like Dickens too" He nodded at *Bleak House* on my bedside table. "What's your favourite?"

"*Christmas Carol*. Utterly, utterly brilliant."

Grinning happily, he said "Snap" then "I like your models."

A Tamiya Stuka, an Airfix Spitfire and an Airfix Messerschmidt ME109, all 1/35, hung suspended from the ceiling on black strings in this like frozen dog-fight near this Airfix Lancaster bouncing bomber. That was 1/72. 1/35 would like fill the room, right?

"Thanks," I repeated. "I'm doing a Tiger tank next and I want to build this like Alpine diorama with German mountain troops?" I showed him the little tins of Humbrol paint on my desk and the edition of *Airfix* magazine with the design-plan. He seemed politely interested.

"Your posters are cool," he said. "You like volcanoes?"

I couldn't remember where I'd got the massive Volcano poster that covered most of the wall behind my bed but I really liked the contrast of black background and orange fire, especially the spectacular picture of Hekla erupting at night. It told me that 'eruptions occur when magma (hot molten rock) and volcanic gases are forced under pressure through weaknesses in the earth's crust', had a diagram to illustrate it and a list of notable eruptions which included Helgafell in 1973, Hekla in 1970 and Krakatoa in 1883. A massively bearded, horny-hatted Viking from 2W's trip to York's Jorvik Museum loomed from the wardrobe door. I also had this awesome framed picture of the Bloody Red Baron's Fokker Triplane over my desk and an absolutely massive gold-and-black Dalek tacked to my bedroom door.

"You like Daleks?" he said unnecessarily.

"Sure," I grinned, "but the Master's the *best* villain."

He liked the Sea-Devils. I said he was lame. The Sea-Devils looked like my Gran, with their tortoise necks and shiny net nighties. Not like the black-bearded Master with his hypnotism and cynical laughter. And *his* TARDIS worked.

"Favourite *Doctor Who*?" he said.

"*Genesis of the Daleks*. Scary Nazi types and real moral dilemmas," I replied. "I mean, would you do it? Could you do it? Exterminate one species to save another?"

"Maybe," he said, "If I had a cool scarf, a floppy hat and jelly babies."

"But if you could go back in time," I persisted, "To kill Baby Hitler or Baby Stalin?"

"They're too recent," said Ali. "The Doctor says 'Out of this great evil some great good may come.' We have a different perspective on evil now, thanks to Hitler and Stalin. In a hundred years, the world may be much better because of them. Why stick to the twentieth century? What about killing Napoleon? Or Buddha? Or even Jesus?" Shit. I touched the gold crucifix round my neck. "It's a futile question," he shrugged. "Good and evil are subjective, relative and contextually determined social constructs. *Pyramids of Mars* is better."

I liked that one too, but I wasn't admitting it.

"So lame – all those phony mummies..." Imitating one, I lumbered across the room, arms outstretched, groaning whilst he flopped back on my pillow laughing. "Urrr, Alistair! I'm going to kill you..." Launching myself forward, I fell into his arms. Chest met chest and I lost myself in those deep teal pools as his arms folded round my back. My breathing changed, my stomach knotted tightly. One of his hands strayed to my bottom. Closing my eyes, I pressed myself into his body. Then he gently rolled me aside and asked what else I had.

Choking back a flare of disappointment, I threw open a cupboard and dug around for the toy Daleks. Unfortunately I only managed to dislodge a box of toy soldiers and the Afrika Korps kind of cascaded over my head in a shower of plastic. Ali said it was Rommel's revenge for saying Sea-Devils were lame. I chucked a couple of soldiers at his chest.

The Grunters had given me several die-cast metal Corgi cars over the years. I kept them on the shelf over my desk next to Ozzie. Ali was admiring this Ferrari Maranello, a Porsche 911, a Lotus Elan, an Aston Martin DB9, and my all-time favourite, the Jaguar XJS, when he spotted my Palitoy Action Men (with realistic hair and gripping hands). Blond-bearded Jim was dressed in a black jumper, blue jeans and black boots, ready to climb mountains or, in actuality, the staircase banisters, with his Special Operations kitbag of dynamite, hand-grenades, Primus-stove, cutlery, knife, binoculars, boxed radio and sub-machine-gun whilst brown-haired Bob, dressed in NATO uniform of khaki trousers, khaki sweater, black boots, black beret, shot at him from behind the potted cactus on the window-sill. As I told this story, I watched this slow grin like light his face and didn't feel stupid because *he* had an Action Man called Rocky, for fuck's sake.

"Man," I said, fishing this book, *Action Man: Antarctic Explorer*, off the shelf, "You are *so* sad." The front cover depicted bearded, blond Jim dressed in this red fur-trimmed parka, white boots and red skis, a wolf, some penguins and a map of the Antarctic. Inside were the stories of Captains Scott and Oates, Shackleton and Hillary, then Action Man's Expedition, with photos and an expedition log, plus make your own Antarctic Station out of a shoe-box *and* make your own penguins out of toilet-rolls. Mega-bonus, right? Of course I'd made them all but had no idea where they were now. I'd even constructed my own adventure, writing a similar log. Couldn't find that either. But Rocky… I mean.

"That's so sad," I repeated, collapsing in a heap of giggles. This time he like chucked Afrika Korps at me until, eyes dancing, he saw the board-games stacked in the cupboard, *Game of Nations*, *Treasure of the Pharaohs*, *Mouse-Trap* and *Escape from Colditz*.

"I haven't played *Colditz* for years," he said excitedly.

"Do you want to play now?" I said. "I'll be the Germans. Tim Wilson always plays as the Germans, 'cos he loves the Shoot to Kill card, being a Christian and all that, or we could play *Mouse-Trap*." I sprang for the cupboard, and trod on the bloody Afrika Korps. "Oww!" I cried, "Fuck it…" Kind of yowling and cradling my foot, I collapsed on my bed. I cursed the tears that flooded my eyes. God. If I cried in front of *him*, I would like *die* of shame. Literally.

"Let me look," he said softly, taking my foot into his hands. Gently he blew on the pink mark. Soothing and tickling in equal measure, it made me shiver.

Kiss it better, I screamed mentally.

Please.

Kiss my foot better.

Laying back on my pillow, I prayed for his lips on my sole like James Bond in *Thunderball*. Instead he noticed the brown moth-eaten teddy-bear with the threadbare nose who had been with me forever and who lived on my pillow.

"Who's this?" he grinned.

"Pickles," I said, suddenly cherry-red embarrassed. "I got him when I was one."

"I love it when you blush," said Ali, dangling the bear by his right ear. "What would you do if I took him hostage?"

"It would depend on what you wanted."

A kiss. Exchange him for kiss, my heart screamed.

"Promises, promises," he said, waving the bear in the air.

I threw myself at him with a laughing cry of "Give him here, Ali!"

Next thing we were wrestling on the bed and laughing and somehow he flipped me on my back so he could tickle me under my ribs. Howling, I gasped "Stop it! Ali… stop!"

33

"Beg me." He pinned my hips with his knees and tickled me more.

Squirming, knees raised, body thrashing under his weight, my willy was hardening.

"Please, Alistair. Please."

"Please what?"

"Please stop tickling me!"

"Say please master."

"Please Master…" Oh God. I was really *really* hard. He must be able to feel it poking against him. And the bulge was so massive, so obvious…

Squeezing my sides with his thighs, he gazed at me with ferocious intensity.

"I love your dimples," he said. "They're really cute."

I grinned. "You think I'm cute? What do you think I am? Five?"

He was suddenly like really serious.

"No. You're fifteen, and you're really, *really* gorgeous."

The atmosphere changed. The blood in my ears hummed like wind through telephone wires. My heart thumped violently, my body seemed to melt. I reached up, put my arms round his back and drew him down onto me, chest against chest. I heard him murmur my name, twice. Now, I urged him. Now.

Kiss me.

The wind-chimes gurgled softly.

My lips parted. My stiff, hard cock strained in my shorts. I felt his, hard and insistent, pressing through his jeans against my stomach. It made me stiffen more. His eyes darkened as he leaned towards me. He cupped my cheek in his palm. His lips moved towards mine.

"Oh Ali… " It came out as this languid, contented sigh.

I put my hand on his bottom and pulled him closer. My lips nuzzled his neck and I felt him writhe, rubbing his cock against mine. I closed my eyes and whispered "I love you." Suddenly he moaned softly, buried his face in my neck and shuddered. Oh man…

The front door slammed and Mum was calling up the stairs that they were home.

"Shit." I scrambled desperately off the bed. "Shit. Fuck. Oh, *fuck*."

Or not.

"Hi Mum," I said from the top of the stairs, straightening my T-shirt and praying she wouldn't notice the tent in my shorts. "Did you have a good day?"

Her shopping bags sagged to the floor as Ali materialised behind me.

"This is Ali from school," I said. "He came round to…"

Kiss me? Seduce me? Fuck me? What *had* he come round for?

"Talk about the play." Ali held out his hand. "Hello, Mrs Peters."

"Ali's going to be directing us," I said dully. "He's written it himself."

Pointedly ignoring the outstretched hand, Mum said "Oh, Alistair Ross. You're in the Sixth Form, aren't you?"

"Rose, and I'm a prefect now," he said cheerfully.

"Well," she said tightly. "Did you mow the lawn and cut the brambles back?"

"No, sorry. My hay-fever played up."

Tutting irritably, she asked why I hadn't taken some lemon-balm and eucalyptus mix.

"I couldn't find any," I said, "But I did loads of piano practice. I'm really getting to grips with the *Berceuse*."

"So long as you weren't getting to grips with anything else. Nice to meet you, Alistair."

Pleading, I asked if he could, like, stay for tea. I wanted desperately to resume our session, you know? He was going to kiss me. I *knew* he was going to kiss me.

"No, he can't," she snapped.

"But *why*?"

Fuck, I sounded so whiny, so bratty.

"For God's sake, Jonathan, just stop arguing." She shoved past us into the kitchen.

"You'd better go," I said as Mum told all the monkeys in like Borneo that I should go help Dad with the shopping.

"That was great, J," he said brightly. "You're such fun. See you Monday."

I felt awkward as he shook my hand. I had so desperately wanted him to kiss me. He must've known, mustn't he? God Almighty. What the hell had happened? I think I said I loved him! Oh fuck. How the hell would I be able to ever face him again? But I *had* loved the physical contact with him, loved being touched by him, loved touching him. That'd been fantastic. This was like the best day ever. And the worst.

I knew what it meant, and I wasn't, I didn't want to be, I couldn't be *that*.

Oh man. Someone just shoot me.

But I had previous. This was history repeating itself, that yearning, that feeling, that need for another boy, for sex with another boy...

So it hadn't been the booze. It'd been me. Oh fuck. It *was* me. Once was an accident, twice was... Someone *please* shoot me. Locking myself in the bathroom, I spurted so hard into the toilet bowl it made my knees shake.

Holed up in my room with this awesome Tamiya 1/35 King Tiger tank and the radio commentary of Liverpool vs WBA, I was vaguely aware that Alistair, like David Fosbrook and Niall Hill, supported Liverpool and would probably be listening to this same commentary. I was happy his team was 2-0 up though Leeds (supported by Dad, Gray, Collins and most of my class-mates, except Maxton who supported West Ham and Crooks who liked Aston Villa) were 0-0 with Spurs and Norwich (vaguely my team) were one up against Southampton. I didn't like Dirty, Dirty Leeds. I prefer my footballers to kick footballs, not other players.

I dabbed the plastic gun-barrel with some poly-cement so I could stick it to the olive, chocolate and red-brown turret whilst the German cross and serial number 113 were peeling off the transfer-sheet in a bowl of warm water. Arsenal (Bunny's team) went 2-0 up against Stoke and Man U scored their 5th when I decided to ask Claire out. I figured my boyish charm and good looks would get me past any lingering embarrassment from *that* party. Man, it was better than furtive fumblings with another boy. Claire could save me, like Mum had done.

We met at five in a café on the parade. My excited mother gave me a fiver so I could treat her. Dad even looked up from his pools coupon to wish me luck.

"Bloody hell, Dad," I muttered, "It's not a date, you know. Just a meet-up."

Consequently I just turned up on my ATB in like blue trackies and green rugby jersey. Claire, however, was in this neat knee-length black-and-silver dress. She even wore lipstick and eye-liner and had clearly done more than drag a wet comb through her hair. This made me feel really awkward, especially when some neighbours who must've like witnessed the building of Stonehenge, you know, asked if this was my girlfriend. Claire kind of radiated at the remark. Mumbling something, I buried my rowanberry-red face in a menu.

"So," she said across the check tablecloth, "What were you doing?"

Making a plastic King Tiger sounded lame. Writing a story in German sounded lamer. Getting off with Alistair Rose sounded... well, you know.

"Nothing much."

Yikes. What a saddo. It sounded like I'd only asked her out for something to do.

"Playing the piano."

You fuckwit. You sound like that gay twat Paulus, totally, like, one-dimensional. But then what *should* I say? Oh, hey, I did like this twenty-five K parachute-jump this morning then a ten-K cycle-ride and then climbed Malham Cove with a piece of string. Oh, and then I did four hours of weights in the gym, *after* my charity marathon-training, of course. Then I'd call her 'babe' and be like a total wanker, like people who say 'K' instead of Kilometre, babe. Alternatively I could say I'd spent the morning assisting at the church soup-kitchen before cleaning and painting the hostel, like Tim and his new best-friend Charlie Rix, but then I'd sound like a pious twat, or someone desperate to impress on a UCAS form. At least I was a *real* boy, Pinocchio.

Claire had gone for a jog round the lake then had this taekwondo class before her midafternoon Arabic lesson at the university. She'd just got back.

"You're learning Arabic?" I said as the food arrived, a mushroom omelette and fries (mine), green salad (hers). "Why?"

"It's fascinating," she said, "Especially the calligraphy. It's so beautiful."

"Would you like a drink?" asked the waitress.

"Coke, please," said Claire.

"Water, please," I said, explaining I didn't do sodas.

"Why?" She had dimples too. I'd never noticed before. "Do they make you burp?"

"It's the chemicals," I said. "If you can't pronounce it, don't consume it."

"And yet you drank so much at that party," she said. "You're so mixed-up."

"It's living on celery, carrots and pumpkin seeds." I speared a chip.

"You have so much talent," she said, "And yet you seem to hate yourself."

I'd gone into this total, booze-fuelled, tear-stained meltdown at that party.

"It's so hard," I replied, "Having to perform to my best all the time. It's so stressful."

"Most people would kill to have an ounce of what you have. You were wonderful as Oliver, brilliant as Puck, and as a musician, well…"

Shrugging, I forked omelette into my mouth and said these things didn't matter.

"So what *do* you want?" she demanded.

"Oh, I want to play scrum-half for the school," I sighed. "I don't want to look like a weedy bag of bones. I want to be taller and bigger. I want some muscles. I don't want freckles, *or* dimples. I want hair that doesn't hang limply over my forehead. I want longer legs. I want to grow a beard. I want hair under my arms. I want, for once in my miserable life, to take off my shirt without someone calling me Belsen Boy."

Smiling slyly, she sucked on her Coke and said "Some people like you as you are, Jonny. Some people think you're really cute."

"I don't *want* to be cute," I said angrily. "Cute is what kittens are. I want to be…"

"Mad, bad and dangerous to know," she finished, quoting something I'd said at the party. "Jonny, we're fifteen. We have a lot of growing to do, you know?"

I pushed ketchup-soggy chips round my plate. "Do you think I'm weird, Claire?"

"Oh *God*, yes," she answered, "You're *seriously* weird. But that's why I like you." Her eyes locked onto mine. "I mean, *like* you, Jonny. *Really* like you."

Fuck. This was like some kind of code I just didn't get.

"Thanks," I mumbled through my omelette. "I like you too."

"Well," She nodded at my clothes, "Next time make an effort, eh?"

Don't try to mould me, I screamed mentally. Ali doesn't. I wondered how the conversation might've gone if it'd been him at this table rather than her. We would've talked about school, music, books and movies, sport and Action Men and had a laugh.

"What's your favourite movie?" I asked her.

"*Titanic*. Yours?"

She'd never heard of *Way out West*, not even when I sang 'Trail of the Lonesome Pine'.

"Favourite play?"

"*Cats*."

Someone just shoot me.

But she seemed to have forgiven me for the shoes and we discovered a mutual love of *The Muppets*. While she enthused about 'Pigs in Space' and we chorused this joint impression of Swedish Chef - 'Puurt thuur chiir-ken airn der bewl, bork bork bork' – I felt myself relax for the first time because the future was suddenly bright. The future *was* Claire. The future was straight. I mean, I had a girlfriend, man, and she was like so hot for me?

She sat on my lap, safe between my outstretched arms, like Katharine Ross and Paul Newman in *Butch Cassidy*, and I let my bike free-wheel down the hill towards her house, the wind rushing through our hair and over our faces, making us both scream with delight. We stopped to kiss under a street-light, and I mean, KISS, man, full tongues and *everything*, yeah?

A proper full-on 10-minute snog, and it was so awesome, you know? AWESOME. I even got my hand on her breast as our lips fused together and my tongue explored her mouth. But when I waved goodbye and was riding the half-mile home, I realised what *hadn't* happened, like, down below, you know? Like NOTHING, right? My body didn't want her. It wanted him.

So here it was. As I settled down for this BBC series about a female police inspector running an all-male station, and The Last Night of the Proms, Mackerras conducting the BBCSO in the usual bollocks + *Sea Drift* and some Percy Grainger, I was kind of like going out with Claire – we'd snogged a bit and Collins reckoned she'd fuck me and I thought so too – but I thought about Alistair more, *much* more. I wanted to know everything about him, every last little detail, and I felt, when he left me, like Henry Hoover had come along and sucked out my heart. Claire had never done that. Ali had, and so had Michael Crooks. Holding Ali, being *held* by Ali had *really* turned me on, I mean so much it had hurt. And now I just wanted to die because I couldn't be *that*, not that. Not me. Not that. I would rather like steam and eat my own stomach, you know? With lentils and a nice dry hock.

5: We Can't Stop

I'D been in the choir like forever, passing the audition in 2W with a piped rendition of 'The head that once was crowned with thorns', and I'd sung in *Messiah*, *St Matthew Passion* and *The Creation*. Now my voice having just about broken but not yet settled, I was like this slightly reedy baritone who couldn't get either the bottom register of the basses or the higher notes of the tenors, but singing was fun and helped my asthma 'cos of the breathing.

Pushing through the massed ranks of gimpy trebles to the back of Perry's massive, marble-floored rehearsal room in the Britten Centre where Zippy Arnold and Bungle Gray were warming up with the *Rainbow* theme: '*Up above the streets and houses rainbow climbing high*' and Paulus was trying to decide if he was a tenor or a baritone, I noticed Ali, on the same row, deep in conversation with a couple of other Sixth Formers, music editor of the school mag, Mike Holt from Rowntree, who had this like massive bush of curly black hair, and Jason Middleton, a tall, bland guy from our House.

"Hey, Rosie," I called, gulping a little, "Didn't know you were a singer."

"Sure," he drawled, "Regular Pavarotti, me."

"Pavarotti was a tenor," I began pedantically then blushed as Rosie laughed, Fred bawled at me to tuck my shirt in and sit down and Stewpot Stewart licked his finger and touched it to his cheek with a loud 'Tssss' to mock my redness. As I collapsed between Zippy and Bungle, who were now reviewing England's 4-0 win over Norway like Terry Venables and Chinny Hill, Paulus handed me the red Novello paperback score of Bach's *St John Passion*. I hadn't known Ali was in the Choral Society. I'd resolved during Sunday that I was just gonna treat him like anyone else, like Max or Gray or Collins. He was just a mate. Also Claire's father, sitting on the row behind with Hellfire, Wingnut and Don Donovan, smiled approvingly so I gulped and blushed again. Yikes. The head was, like, marrying me off to his daughter! In front of the whole damn choir, my mates and my teachers. Stewart was like pissing himself.

As we began the opening chorus, 'Hail, Lord and Master,' and Arnold and I hit the *forte* crotchet B flat 'Hail' exactly on Perry's downbeat into Bar 19 then up a third to D then straining to a note none of us could comfortably reach at a double-ledger-lined E flat we grinned. Being a bass was fabulous. I counted a steady four-four beat through 'Show by thy Cross and Passion' and kept together, though Fred said we sounded 'agricultural.'

"I thought I'd wandered into the National Farmers' Union instead of this school's premier choir," he declared, singing 'boi thoi crorss and paaaashun' in a thick Zummerzet brogue. We laughed. Fred, for all his boringness as a teacher, was a brilliant musician who had persuaded Benjamin Britten to open this music centre. There was even a plaque.

When we moved to chorale number 7 on page 26, 'O mighty love, O love beyond all measure,' I couldn't help it, I swear. I glanced at Alistair and my ears turned red as a fire-truck. Again. Now *everyone* went 'Tssss.' He just laughed, the twat.

St John Passion was dramatic and exciting, with the chorus playing a range of characters, the mob baying for Jesus's blood, the crowd at the fireside confronting Peter, the disciples broken and confused at the foot of the Cross, and us, reflecting on the events from hundreds of years into a future. These restless, surging notes churning around in G minor in the lower strings on page 1, running for eighteen bars of introduction, serve like some prelude to an opera. There's this kind of tension like bubbling under the surface, you know?

Sitting in front of us were three altos from 4D, super-singers with super-rich voices, two off the bus. Leo Trent was in Murray, like me, Ali and Paulus. A rather girly-looking kid, he had this floaty candy-floss butter-coloured hair, startling lilac eyes, a silver-wire brace on his upper teeth and a really cute, lightly freckled, slightly Labrador-shaped face. Very light, with fewer muscle-bumps even than me, he oozed self-confidence. Nick Shelton, the smouldering hottie, had a broad nose, freckles like a Jackson Pollock painting, coal-dark eyes and hair. Philip Brudenall was Graham's spectacularly cute wheat-haired, cornflower-eyed kid-brother, and given that Graham was a spoon-faced wobble-bottom, it was hard to believe they were related. None of them older than 14, they were gloating because they would be joined for the concert, which was in Lent term on March 31st, by the girls' school's contraltos.

"We'll get to know them *really* well," said Brudenall Minor, "Then you losers'll be *begging* us to be friends with you."

He and Shelton got into a belching competition with Holt and Rosie which made us all laugh again, and drove Fred mental. Rosie, leaning forward, flicked Shelton's ears. Shelton responded by sliding his chair backwards into Rosie's knees.

"I was aiming for your balls," he grinned over his shoulder, "But forgot you don't have any, being a woman and all that."

Holt collapsed into uncontrollable laughter. Rosie ruffled Shelton's hair merrily.

"For God's sake," roared Perry, "You missed your entrance, altos."

"Be thankful Rosie missed *your* entrance," Trent told Shelton brightly.

"All deliveries round the rear," cackled Brudenall.

" 'O mighty love' indeed," finished Shelton, and the altos howled again, especially when Brudenall gave us his latest poem while noisily playing slaps with Trent:

> There was a young man from Nantucket,
> Took a pig in a garage to fuck it.
> Said the pig with a sneer,
> 'Get away from my rear,
> Come around to the front and I'll suck it.'

Rosie reckoned they would be a load of fun to sit behind for the next six months. "They're all mentalists," he said. "You know Trent is playing the maid in the house-play? Guess what he says? 'At last I get to wear a frock!' Man, he's such a poof."

"Yeah," I scoffed uncomfortably, "Such a poof."

"Really enjoyed Saturday, by the way. Thanks." He touched my arm.

"Me too." I felt myself redden like some fucking traffic light, and suddenly melt.

Ash-tray, smiling warmly, said how much Claire had enjoyed herself. He even told Hellfire about my mushroom omelette and wicked impression of Kermit the Frog. Blushing so you could like fry an egg on my face, I just like stared totally tongue-tied at my toe-caps while Gray and Arnold, lurking behind the headmaster, grinned like idiots who'd lost their village.

"Maybe you'd like to come over for dinner again," Ash-tray concluded.

"Sure, sir," I mumbled. "Thanks."

"But next time, Jonathan, comb your hair, eh? Girls like that kind of thing, you know?"

Dating tips from the headmaster. Someone just shoot me.

Wingnut and Hellfire chuckled smugly. Gray slapped his forehead with the heel of his hand and mouthed 'loser' at me. Zippy Arnold mimed flicking spit at my face and going 'ssssizzle.' Those twatty little gaybies Trent and Shelton blew silent kisses and smirked. Rosie had gone. Feeling suddenly desolate, I scoured the crowd. He had definitely gone.

"Come on, Casanova," said Gray. "Time for French, the *langue de l'amour*."

"Claire knows all about his lover's tongue," Arnold cackled.

"*Oh Claire, the moment I met you, I swear…*" sang Stewart.

I told them all to sod off but secretly I was like really happy. This affectionate teasing was a sign of acceptance, of being one of the gang. I had a girlfriend and my classmates were happy, like I was happy when Arnold got off with Olivia and Gray with Becky. Although Claire being Ash-tray's daughter would bring extra ribbing, as it were, at least I wasn't a Billy No-Date saddo like Ferrety Fosbrook or a poofter like Poorly Paulus.

"So many careless errors," bawled Benjy. "You're supposed to be the best brains in this poor bloody city, God help us, and yet, during a seven-week break, you appear to have forgotten every word of French you ever crammed into your tiny bird-brains. I am far from satisfied with your performance."

"Bet he hasn't had a satisfying performance for years," whispered Gray.

I stifled a grin.

"Peters! What's so funny?"

"Nothing, sir."

"Hundred lines. 'I must not laugh in class.' Have it tomorrow on my desk. And do your bloody collar up. You look like a tramp."

"What's he gonna have with you on his desk?" whispered Gray.

"That's *two* hundred lines," Benjy bellowed. "You, at least, did tolerably well, pathetic, simpering idiot that you are. *You* scraped nineteen out of twenty."

Fuck. What did I get wrong? It was so easy. Wrestling with the grey shirt's top button, I fixed my eyes on the posters of the Eiffel Tower and Notre Dame that dominated Room 40's walls. As Ben lobbed the blue exercise book at me, he enumerated my classmates' scores bellowing "Pathetic!" each time, Walton 7/20, Fosbrook 9/20, Bainbridge 6/20.

Bollocks. Duck. Double-bollocks. How could I forget 'canard'? Especially after Shelton's fabulous impression on the bus had made me laugh so hard I nearly puked. Even though I had the best mark in the class by miles, even better than Super-Swot Paulus's 15 (ha ha), I was annoyed I'd 'canaille' instead of 'canard'. You bloody fuckwit, I muttered.

While I sat on the bus writing 'I must not laugh in class', I reckoned I'd have to write *all* the lines. Benjy was the kind of pedant who'd count every bloody one. At line 61, the bus braked sharply for some numpty on a zebra-crossing and a blue-black line juddered across the page. I swore bitterly, especially when Maxton jeered 'is it a bird, is it a plane, no, it's Super-Swot,' curled his fingers and thumbs round his eyes like glasses and went 'rrrrrrrrrr' like a fucking aeroplane. Bollocks. I slammed the red rough-book roughly (ha ha) into my backpack. I'd do it in *Blue Peter's* report on their Malaysian expedition and *Paddington Bear*.

I saw Ali Rose *twice* on Tuesday. First was in house assembly. He and the other prefects, Turner, Warburton and Sonning, lurked at the front with Mr Jackson and Rev Knight while I lurked at the back with Paulus and some other Upper Fifth Murray-ites, Kevin Lees, the violist from U5D and my Music set, North and Kemble from U5S, Rhodes, Eltham and Jeremy Whiting from U5B who were arguing about why the bowl of petunias created by the Infinite Improbability Drive had thought 'oh no, not again' as it fell through space (if you don't know, it's in *Hitch-hiker's Guide*). Sonning cut us off by clapping his hands so he could read us seven things the Lord detests, from Proverbs 6, verses 16 to 19, these being, for your information, "*a proud eye, a false tongue, hands that shed innocent blood, a heart that forges thoughts of mischief, and feet that run swiftly to do evil, a false witness telling a pack of lies, and one who stirs up quarrels between brothers.*" Then we stood up while he does this prayer of St Anselm, who I remembered from 3rd form RS had been Archbishop of Canterbury before falling out with King William Rufus, this being way back in 1093 when Wheezy Wally was a boy.

"*O Lord my God,*" goes Sonning while I peered under half-closed eyelids at sallow, lanky North's rumpled grey socks and flat-headed Kemble's scuffed black shoes, "*Teach my heart this day where and how to find you. You have made and re-made me and have bestowed on me all the good things I possess, and still I have not yet done that for which I was made…*"

"Rugby!" I called when Warburton was recording the Games options. The usual jeering of Poorly Paulus and Lazy Lees opting for swimming was drowned by a chorus of catcalls as Whiting presented Sonning with yet another excused note.

"Got an allergy," he goes.

"Yeah, to fucking exercise," says North.

Anyway, after Warburton blasted me for having my top button undone and ink-stains on my fingers (man, when I was in 2W I seemed to have ink-stains everywhere all the time), and I won two chunks of Yorkie by getting all 10 spellings in German right, even remembering the double t in *enttäuschen*, to disappoint, so swivel on that, Brudenall, though it made me sneeze like a mad monkey so everyone laughed and Stewart went 'It's his allergies' in this really wet voice, the melon-faced twat, I saw Ali again in the period before lunch when David Fosbrook and I were climbing the rickety wooden staircase up to the haunted bell-tower in the Eagles' Nest. He was telling me about Villeneuve's spectacular sixth-lap crash at the Italian Grand Prix. The whole back of the Ferrari was ripped off, and wheels went flying all round Imola. Apparently the Canadian Grand Prix on the 28th might decide the title for Williams and their Aussie driver. I wasn't really into motor racing, but thought I might watch that race, if only for Murray Walker's commentary and the possibility of another smash.

"I'd love to be a commentator," said Fosbrook. "Especially on *Test Match Special*. All those cakes. Yum. I love cakes, especially fat choccy ones with coffee cream."

"You could stand to eat a few," I remarked. He was even shorter and weedier than me, with tar-coloured hair, a furtive, ratty, acne-pitted little face, striking blue eyes and occasional eczema. "But you gotta talk about pigeons, and trains, *and* cricket. All right, you know about trains, being a sad little anorak who like lurks around in the dark on station platforms like some pervy old flasher and writes the numbers down in a spazzy little book, but you know fuck all about cricket. I mean, you're like 'which end of the bat do I hold again?' Remember?"

He'd actually asked that once, Fozzie. Hellfire, head of cricket and Fozzie's Brearley House tutor had just made this kind of choked noise, like he was being strangled, you know? Anyhow, we turned to Saturday's climactic episode of *Doctor Who*. For a programme that had started promisingly on Brighton beach with K-9's head blown off by seawater, it had wound up with scaly, green bug-eyed monsters disguised in human skin-suits and some madman attempting to clone an army of selves but getting thousands of identical Doctors instead.

"Imagine having thousands of identical twins," mused Fosbrook. "It'd get so confusing. Mind you, it'd be really handy if no-one could actually tell who the real you was."

"I don't suppose it'd be called a twin," I said, "Not if there's more than two."

"Clones?"

I thought for a second. "Twones! They'd be twones."

"What the hell do we have to come up here for anyway?" puffed Fosbrook.

"Get fit," I said censoriously. Fozzie was a notorious skiver, using his eczema and allergies to avoid most sports, except wanking, to which he was utterly addicted. "Visit the ghosts. You heard about the skeleton they found under the stairs a few years' back? Some ferrety little Fifth Former, his blood sucked dry till his body collapsed like an empty balloon, blood drunk by the evil creatures who live in this old belfry, creatures of darkness that come out at night to spread misery and distress among the gimps…"

"Ha!" Battering me with his backpack, he cried "Herbidacious!" and chased me up the wooden staircase trying to grab the tail of my blazer. Suddenly Rosie clattered towards us, taking the steps two at a time, his golden tie whipping over the black backpack on his shoulder, the bruise-black lock of hair flopping.

"Hey, Alistair!" I cried.

"Hey, Jonny!"

If I hurried, his seat by the radiator at the end of the second row under the massive poster of 'Your country needs you' (you know, the one where the guy with this massive fuck-off moustache points right at your heart) might still be warm but Fosbrook could not, apparently, simultaneously climb stairs *and* do his best Davros line - 'you, Doc-Torrr, the Grrrreat Exterrr-minatorrr, the man who keeps running 'cos he dare not look back' - and we ended up late. Worse, Phil 'Gutbucket' Gardiner had parked his lardy 20-zillion stone arse on Ali's chair and I had to sit at the front next to Poofter Paulus who smugly told me off for stopping to 'chat up' Rosie. This shocked me. Chat up? What did he mean, 'chat up'?

"I just said hi," I muttered.

"It's the *way* you said it," Paulus explained. "There's 'hi', matter-of-fact, manly and butch, and there's 'hiiiiii', all breathy, girly and just a little bit, like, gay, you know?"

Angrily spitting "You mean *you* know, you great poof," I punched his arm so hard he yelped and focussed on filling in gaps in the Stalin Worksheet.

'He was exiled,' I read, 'To Siberia for revolutionary activities and had gained fame writing for _____.' '*Pravda*,' I wrote, meaning 'Truth'. 'He was a member of the Sovnarkom and in 1922 became Secretary of the Communist Party. After Lenin's death there was rivalry between _____ and Stalin for leadership of the Communist Party.'

"JP," hissed Fosbrook, "JP, what's question 2?"

I tutted. It was *sooo* easy. "Trotsky," I mouthed. "Got an ice-axe through the skull in Mexico City," I added for Paulus' benefit. "KGB killed him." In the next section, 'Stalin introduced a series of _____ in each of which the people were set certain targets in order to improve and extend the economy.'

Yesss! 'Five Year Plans.' I knew that too. I grinned at Kitchener's fuck-off moustache.

Paulus, smirking, drew a massive D on the back of my hand with a blue biro and put a little heart in the centre. I smacked him again, on the exact spot I'd bruised earlier, and made him cry, the stupid gay twat. Turned out to be a massive mistake. At lunchtime he produced this like massive plastic box of pasta in tomato sauce. Like bollocks. Gray tucked into this succulent tuna and cucumber baguette, a bag of pickled onion Monster Munch and orange juice. Maxton, the pizza-faced fucker, dug out this bloody great all-day-breakfast butty, Yorkie, bag of Doritos and can of Coke. These lunches made me drool like a starving dog as I nibbled one wholemeal Ryvita, two carrots, celery stick, one apple and some pumpkin seeds and necked a cup of water from the cloakroom tap. As Maxton mumbled through a massive mouthful of sliced egg and crispy bacon, that rabbit diet wouldn't keep anyone together.

"You'd be better off with a school lunch," Gray observed sagely. "At least the custard would be like lagging for your ribs."

I pleaded with Paulus for a forkful. Grinning maliciously, he like made me shuffle on my knees across the dirty floor and bark like a bloody sealion before he forked like this microbe into my open mouth. I told him I hated him very much, and please, Master, could I have some more? What a cunt. Just 'cos he fancied Rosie, the poof. Grumpily, I chucked my sports bag over my shoulder and set off after Crooks and Collins for the Sports Fields a mile up the road. They'd taken their blazers off. I could see through Collins' white shirt the waist-band of these checky tartan boxers, NEXT in bold red letters on the black of the cotton, and through Crooks' a purple TOP MAN. Bollocks. Mine came from M & S. So uncool, right? Thanks, Mum.

"Yeah," Collins was saying, "But his heart had stopped."

"But if his heart had stopped, how was he alive?" said Crooks, not unreasonably.

"He was Undead, you know? Alive but not alive?"

"Who's this?" I said, dancing over a crack in the pavement 'cos step on a crack, you'll break your back, yeah?

"Some German spy they caught at the Cornmarket."

"What?" An answer I didn't expect.

"Yeah, he was like this zombie, right? Dressed in SS uniform and waving a Luger."

"An' he was dead?"

"Yeah, yeah. They found his grave, like this empty coffin, the bloody lot."

"So if he's like dead, right," goes Crooks, "How's he walking about waving a Luger? If he's dead?"

Collins clicked his tongue impatiently. "Cos this virgin swore to marry him and save him from an eternity of being Undead, yeah? That sparked his brain into life."

"But not his heart?" I said.

"Fuck's sake, Jonny, he's a German spy, you know?"

"What's he doing in the Cornmarket?" goes Crooks.

"Having a coffee," says Collins.

"A coffee? He's a dead man, his heart's stopped, he's gonna marry this virgin, he's all dressed up in his SS uniform, and he's having a coffee?" I'm trying to clarify the narrative. "In the Cornmarket? Downtown?"

"Sure. He's *German*. God Almighty, Jonny, don't you know *anything*?"

"What's this film again?"

"Bloody hell, Jonny, it's not a *film*, it was on the *news*. They killed him by prodding him in the spine with a stick. He just crumbled to dust."

"What you just said," Crooks mused, "Made absolutely no sense at all."

Collins just shook his head like we were scarecrows in search of a brain.

The sports grounds were this vast patchwork of twenty green pitches with this massive two-storey, concrete long barn-like changing room which could easily hold a few hundred kids. Upstairs were these rows and rows of wooden benches and pegs on metal frames and some low-pressure showers of the lukewarm dribble variety, down these iron steps on the ground floor, the masters' changing room, all comfy chairs, kettle, telly, electric fire, steamy powershowers, the bloody lot. Sitting on a bench under my uniform, I was screwing a replacement-stud I'd scrounged off Arnold into a red and black Colt Patrick football boot - I'd already changed, navy shorts, green socks and green jersey, but had forgotten about the missing stud - I hadn't used the boots since March, after all – when a noisy burst of obscenities and a chorus of '*I'm having a bit tonight, tonight*' by Jock Strap and his Swinging Ensemble preceded Stewart and Maxton into the changing room. Bob Stewart, a chubby guy with a melon-shaped head, permanently dry, chapped lips and shaggy dark-blond hair hanging to his eyebrows, battered some Lower Fifth kid aside with his holdall as he picked through bags, legs and blazers yelling how much he loved the smell of wintergreen in the afternoon.

"All right, JP?" Maxton, pulling at his black and purple tie, collapsed beside me.

Grunting, I tightened the stud with Arnold's spanner.

"My favourite game, rugby," he said, grumpily unbuttoning his grey shirt.

"Do something else then," I suggested.

"Like what?" The Games options were fairly limited. "Like swimming?" Maxton hated swimming. He hated getting wet, but swimming was a good choice. You could stay at school for the full lunch-hour rather than walk the mile in the drizzle to the playing-fields, often as wind-swept, blasted and muddy as a First World War landscape.

"Swimming's for wimps and woofters," Stewart declared, "Like Paulus and Huxley." Don't drop the soap in the shower, you know?"

"I've got a verruca," said Maxton. "It'll keep me off swimming for weeks."

"You could do cross-country," I said.

"That's a bloody stupid idea, JP." He levered his massive shoes off with his toes. "Pounding through muddy woods in pouring rain is not my idea of fun."

"Well," I pulled on my boot. "You're stuck with rugby then."

"Wish we could play footie," he said for like the gazillionth time.

I'd been friends with Maxton for three years, although, apart from football, the Boomtown Rats and first-desk clarinet in the chamber orchestra, we seemed to have few common interests, though we'd been obsessive *Top Trumpers* in Lower School. He wanted to be an accountant or an actuary, something involving money and beginning with A. Despite living within a mile of each other, I'd never been to his house, or even to his birthday parties (March 21st) though he'd been to mine. His father worked at the uni, in admin or ICT or something. I'd only met *him* once, after a concert. Stewart's dad was a Chemistry professor at the uni. I'd *never* met him. Obviously.

"I'd rather play footie too," I said, "But we can't, and anyway I quite like rugby."

"When the fuck did you become a hearty?" Max was struggling into his purple jersey.

"I like the game."

"You mean you like sticking your head between boys' sweaty thighs," he grunted.

Snarling at him to shut his face, I yanked on my boot-lace, which snapped.

"Fuck it!" I swore, chucking it away. "Bloody bastard laces have rotted." Now I knew, when it was too late, why Mum said I shouldn't keep damp boots in an airless plastic-bag for several months. "I haven't got a bloody spare either." The remaining lace broke again so I was left struggling to tie these ragged, rotten, inch-long strands together. "Fucking hell!"

"No need to snap." Stewart pulled his blue shorts over his chunky thighs.

Maxton hooted again. "I think your patience is a little bit frayed."

"Stringing together so many oaths..." Stewart reached for his yellow rugby shirt.

I told them to sod off and stalked down to the pitch, metal studs clattering on the metal staircase, whilst my friends continued stringing together their rotten puns.

Jim Wade, the Head of PE, divided us into teams according to our shirts, colours or whites. Our house colours were a rainbow assortment of Murray greens like me, Brearley yellows like Stewart, Goodricke purples like Maxton and Crooks, Rowntree pale blues like Gray and Tim Wilson, Leeman reds, Smeaton dark blues, Tetley orange and Firth browns. The white was just a boring training shirt and I'd left mine at home.

"Peters," he called. "Whites."

"I forgot it, sir," I said.

"God above," he said. "Then you'll have to play topless." He had this totally bald, egg-like head, this like really scratchy-looking, chin-hugging black beard and legs that bulged like tree-trunks below his black shorts. Few people answered him back.

"Come on, sir," I said through the sniggers, "Give us a break."

"Like your lace," muttered Stewart.

Elbowing him roughly, I pleaded with Wadey. I was weedy enough *in* the shirt.

"Come on, sir," cried Gray. "It'll be like watching a plucked chicken running about."

"Put you right off your tea, sir," added Maxton merrily.

"Remind you *of* your tea, sir," chortled Wilson.

"You'll confuse him with a post, sir," called Stewart.

Why was I so fucking weedy? Won't someone just shoot me? Heaving this pained sigh, Wade told me to go scrum-half for the colours. Yes! Result! My favourite position! I could control the game from there. If I'd been topless on the Whites' team, I'd have probably shivered to death as full-back. So mega-result!

Stewart's face lit up when he saw Matthew Robbins' portly shape on the other team.

"Oi, Robbins!" he called. "Why are you so fat?"

"Same reason you're so ugly," Robbins returned. "Inherited genes."

This time *I* laughed.

"I think you need to lose some weight," said Stewart.

"I think *you* need a punch in the face," said Robbins.

They were facing each other as opposing tight-head props.

"Cheeky sod," said Stewart. "Did you hear that, JP?" He was actually hopping with fury. "Did you hear what he said? He threatened me. Threatened me! Go over and belt him one." Shaking him off irritably, I told him to go over and belt him himself.

"Stewart!" shouted Wade. "Stop acting like an idiot."

"What makes you think he's acting, sir?" said Robbins cheekily. Stewart's eyes bulged in their sockets.

As the match unfolded and we went three-nil ahead from a penalty-kick, Stewart and Robbins traded insults and, when the first scrum came, seemed to be clawing each other.

"Pack it in," I said, slapping Stewart's back. "Ball coming in... now."

Chucking the ball under the front-row's boots, I scurried round the back as the scrum heaved forward to collect the pick-up. The number eight held it momentarily with his studs then I had it and, twisting sideways, hurled it out to Wilson who raced away up the line.

"Good scrum, Jonny!" cried Wadey, jogging after the backs.

I chased upfield too as Wilson touched down for a try. Yesss! I flung my arms in the air, yelled my congratulations and high-fived him. Unfortunately, Stewart, nominated to kick the conversion, missed. Badly. We watched the ball sail high and wide of the post.

"I could kick myself for that," he snarled furiously.

"Better let me do it," Robbins remarked. "You might miss again."

But for Maxton holding his arm, Stewart would have gone for him there and then.

"You should keep an eye on those two, sir," I advised Wadey. "Could be trouble."

"It's all right, Jonny." Wadey rubbed his scalp. "They're not going to kill each other."

Lining up for the re-start, I shook my head doubtfully whilst Wilson was telling Stewart to leave Robbins alone.

"I can't stand him," Stewart spat viciously, "With his stupid curly hair and his stupid fat face and his stupid bloody glasses. Stupid fat twat."

"It isn't his fault," Wilson explained, "He's got a medical condition."

"Yeah," shouted Stewart, "It's called Being Fat."

"Should stop eating," advised Maxton, "Then he'd get better."

"Scoop his insides out and solve the housing crisis," I suggested through the laughter.

"You're not exactly a heavyweight yourself, are you, Jonathan?" said Wilson.

"More like featherweight," said Stewart. "What's lighter than a feather, Tim? Molecule or something?"

"Supermite," grinned Maxton, "The Bionic Midget. Watch out or he'll bite your knee." Ha bloody ha.

The ball came to me from a ruck and I kicked it upfield as a forward crashed into me, knocking me flying. Winded, I watched Crooks catch the ball on the bounce, swerve round the full-back and touch down for another try. He was awesome. Grinning, he waved at me and called something about the Ginger Ninja striking back. I laughed.

"Concentrate!" bellowed Wade at the opposition. "You're playing like a load of pansies. Who'll take the kick?"

I volunteered. Maxton muttered I'd turned into a keeno. Bollocks to him.

It was about sixty degrees and twenty yards. Digging a hole in the pitch with my heel, I placed the ball and took six strides back and, because I was left-footed, to the right. My team was lined behind me, the white-shirted opposition lined between the posts. I looked up at the target, took a deep breath and, running in, chipped the ball at its base. Rising smoothly and steadily, it sailed dead-centre through the posts, clearing the bar by several yards for my first-ever conversion.

"Good job, Jonathan," said Wade approvingly as Gray and Wilson patted my back.

"Bloody keeno," muttered Maxton.

I was having a great afternoon so I decided to ignore the simmering Stewart-Robbins tension and throw everything into the game. Chucking myself at Coleman's massive thighs, I got my shoulder behind his knee to haul him to the ground.

"Great tackle, Peters!" cried Wadey, blowing his whistle for a scrum.

"Come on, pack!" I smacked Maxton's shoulder. "Down!"

"Touch!" shouted Wadey. "Engage!"

The front rows locked. I slapped Stewart's back.

"Ready? Ready? Ball in … now!" Hurling it into the middle again, I bawled "Push!" at the top of my lungs. Back-heeled out, I seized the ball and charged forward, head down. Someone blocked me. I twisted as another player shouldered me in the ribs. I was trying to set up a rolling maul.

"Bind! Bind!" I cried as Gray arrived to help me out. Another player jumped in and, as I went down, I somehow squirreled the ball to Stewart who set off towards Robbins. He ran right over him. Then Robbins caught him round the neck and jabbed an uppercut into his face.

"Sir! Sir!" Wilson was calling for a foul.

Coleman, kicking for touch, won a line-out.

Crooks chucked the ball, Gray jumped and palmed the ball to Wilson who passed it to me, yelling "Go, Jonny, go!"

I froze for moment, racked with indecision. Should I pass or should I kick it? Or run?

"Don't dither like a fairy, boy!" yelled Wadey. "Run!"

I was off like a hare from a trap, sidestepping one, two, three tackles. Someone crashed into me but I fended them off with my forearm and flung myself across the line. The team went berserk as I got shakily to my feet. My first-ever try.

"Fantastic!" Gray hugged me wildly. "Absolutely fantastic. Jonny, fucking awesome."

Mr Wade smacked my back, saying "Game of your life, Jonny, game of your life."

Then, at the next scrum, the focus shifted back to this stupid Robbins-Stewart feud.

"Crouch!" cried Wadey. "Touch! Engage!"

The punches flew when Stewart collapsed the scrum. As Wadey blew for a penalty, Robbins was up and kicking Stewart in the chest, his face twisted in a rictus of anger. Jumping in, I pushed him away but his swinging arm landed a haymaker under my left eye. Wadey was there now, seizing Robbins and Stewart roughly by the collars, one in each massive ham-shank hand, shaking them angrily like a dog with a chew-toy.

"Bloody kids," he shouted. "Get off the field and don't come back." Gingerly I touched my face. Swelling up, it was stinging like fury. Wadey pulled my hand away. "You'll have a shiner in the morning, Jonny," he said. "Better get some ice on it. Go to the teachers' room."

"Sir..." I started jigging about, really agitated. "I'm all right. I want to play."

"There's some ice-packs wrapped in cloths in the fridge."

"Aw, siiir..."

"Don't argue, Jonathan," he snapped. "Just go."

Tears of fury swelled in my eyes. I'd been playing so well and enjoying it so much and my stupid friends had spoiled it. As I turned to trudge dejectedly back to the changing-room, Wadey dropped a heavy hand on my shoulder.

"That's the best game of rugby I've ever seen you play. Truly outstanding."

"Will I make the Colts, sir?"

"We'll see." Rubbing his beard, he scanned me quickly. "You'd need to bulk up a bit."

Decoded, you're like too skinny to play for the school, yeah? So stop eating Ryvita and carrots and get some carbs inside you.

Tim took my arm. "Jonny, you were like awesome, man, absolutely awesome!"

The grin hurt my swelling face. "So were you, mate," I said, touching his shoulder.

Pressing the ice-pack to my cheek and slumping on a bench, I tugged off my boots and socks and knocked dried mud off the studs by bashing the soles on the concrete floor. Stewart and Robbins were being bawled out by Hellfire. Served 'em right, the childish bastards. Then I heard the hearties, Lewis, Arnold, Brudenall and Seymour:

'Twas on the good ship Venus, you really should have seen us,
The figurehead was a whore in bed, and the mast was a massive penis

Hurriedly I dressed so they wouldn't laugh at my body.

Tim having gone off with Charlie Rix and his mum who'd come to collect him, Maxton and I shared a cigarette on our way to the bus-stop. I didn't really like it. The smell clung to my hair and the smoke curled into my eyes and made them sting. Maxton had started smoking in the summer. When he and Stewart sloped off to Sweaty Betty's to play *Space Invaders*, they also stopped in the park for a smoke. They thought they were adults 'cos they could do smoke-rings. I thought they were twats, but that didn't stop me like taking a couple of drags off his Marlboro Light as we discussed Stewart's spazmoid antics.

"He'll be on running for the rest of term, or swimming," I said.

"With the wimps and the woofters." Maxton passed me the tab-end. He was already a lanky six foot four. I wondered what we looked like standing together on the kerb.

"Do you really think Paulus is a woofter?" I wasn't really sure what one was.

"No doubt about it. Just look at him. Camp as tits. Look at those shoes. He's got buckles, for fuck's sake. Golden fucking buckles. Fucking hell. *And* he plays the 'cello."

"Huh?" I drew on the half-smoked ciggie. God, I *really* hated it.

"Hard woody instrument pinned between his moist, quivering thighs."

"What does that say about us?" I said. "With hard woody instruments in our *mouths*."

"Unlike you," he said, "I don't imagine I'm giving mine a blowjob. 'Oh, Andy, Andy, I just love your hard woody between my lips.' " He snorted with laughter as I smacked him on the arm and told him to shut up. "Come on, Jonny, lighten up. I'm only teasing. If I *really* thought you were gay, I wouldn't be sitting anywhere near you." Flicking the tab-end into the gutter, he flagged down the number 9. "Course," he added as I fished my bus-pass from my inside pocket, "You'll *never* get a bird, not with your greasy hair and orange teeth. Not even my sister likes orange teeth." His sister, Jane, didn't like me anyway. She was in the Sixth Form at the girls' school and apparently thought me 'too cocky by half.' I thought her boring.

Coughing irritably, I hoisted my backpack and followed him through these crumbling grunters to the back where he could put his clown-size 12s on the seats without being seen.

"Let's have a look at this history prep then," he said.

Which meant 'lend me your history book, JP, and I'll do your Maths for you.'

'How did Stalin rule Russia?
1. <u>Dictatorship</u> – head of the Communist Party – only party in Russia.
2. <u>Secret Police</u> – liquidation of enemies and dissenters.
3. <u>Censorship</u> – newspapers, speech, religion
4. <u>Nationalisation</u> – industries and agriculture
5. <u>Military strength</u> – army increased and improved.'

"Christ," yawned Maxton, "This is *sooo* boring. And you wanna do this for A Level?"

At least it makes sense, I grunted. And if I was Stalin, guess what *I'd* do? Yep, same as you, but to different people! I pulled *The Chrysalids* from my backpack.

6: Every time we touch

LEANING weakly against the white-washed wall, the borrowed racket fell towards the sprung-wood floor as I drew a deep, rasping gasp and lifted my drooping head in dumb submission. Ali was in the school squash team, for fuck's sake, and I'd never played before. Fortunately, there was no-one around this lunchtime to see his steady dismemberment of my pride. He'd won the first two games easily though I had somehow got enough lucky ricochets to take the third. We were into the fourth and I was knackered. I was wearing white shorts and socks, the Green Flash and my pale yellow, sweat-soaked T-shirt and wishing it was the zero-gravity squash I'd seen in the last *Doctor Who*.

"Had enough yet, J?" Ali bounced the green rubber ball on his strings.

"What's the score?" I gasped.

"Six-one."

"I never played before."

"I couldn't tell."

"Just serve, will you?"

Grinning merrily, he like battered the ball with all his might towards these two stark, blood-red lines on the white-washed wall. I sprinted forward, soles squeaking, and slammed it back, trying to win with sheer force and speed of rebound. He sent it over my head so I had to jump. My racket swept through thin air. Bollocks. Another point to him. Mega-bollocks.

We fixed the game when he'd phoned to find out about my face.

"All right," I said. "A bit swollen." Despite Mum dousing it with tea-tree oil, it was still a notable bruise and drew comment from teachers and peers alike throughout Wednesday.

"You know what they say? Rugby's a game played by men with funny-shaped balls."

I called him lame.

Beaky, fondly indulgent, said I was becoming the school's East Clintwood as he declared we would have a 'small quiz'. I was going to reply with my favourite *Josey Wales* line, "Don't piss down my back and tell me it's raining," but didn't. Instead I drawled he'd 'made my day.' Explaining he couldn't face any actual teaching, he said he'd brought this special treat for us, in a crumpled paper bag which he withdrew gingerly from his briefcase.

"This," he declared, "Is one of Frau Phillips' specialities. It is, without doubt, the most succulent, mouth-watering, golden-brown, home-made fudge my dog... I mean, *I* have ever tasted." The rough cube he held before us looked really solid, stodgy and dull. "Wouldn't you like a piece? I love it, but I am willing to get rid of it... I mean, share it with you so that you too can... er... experience the lingering taste, the unique texture... Herr Paulus. Could I tempt you with some home-made fudge?"

"Wouldn't want to deprive you of your lunch, sir," Paulus replied.

"Herr Seymour?"

"It would be very selfish of us, sir."

Beaky looked crest-fallen. "Herr Peters? You won't let me down, surely."

"You know what they say, sir," I grinned. "Moment on the lip, lifetime on a drip."

The quiz, on jobs, proceeded, each of us like trying to outdo the other in sheer rubbishness. Sitting on the front row, I could see the answers scrawled across a sheet of paper in Beaky's spidery handwriting, a paper that had been left 'carelessly on purpose' for me and Paulus, but we could also see the fudge, squatting malevolently in its squareness.

We had to match sixteen jobs with their descriptions, like 'eine Sekretärin... arbeitet an einer Schreibmaschine,' if anyone still *had* a Schreibmaschine, and 'ein Friseur... schneidet Haare.' Deliberately fudging (ha ha) questions *j* ('ein Briefträger' who I said made underpants – clever, eh?) and *n* ('eine Verkäuferin' who I claimed mined coal), I finished with twelve out of sixteen. Phew. Somewhere in the middle. I couldn't get zero, that'd be too obvious, but fourteen or better was too risky. No. Twelve was OK, though Paulus, the swotty smug twat, contrived to get ten.

"The lucky winner is," Beaky announced ceremonially, "Is... is... "

God, it was like *Strictly*. Tensely I sucked the rubber orange on the end of my pencil and stared at the massive poster behind Beaky's desk of Neuschwanstein Castle (that fairy-tale one from *Chitty Chitty Bang Bang*, my favourite film EVER when I was like 8, even though the Child-Catcher like scared me to death 'cos he snatched kids from their beds and locked them up in cages 'cos Baron Bomburst didn't want any kids in his kingdom?)

"Herr Collins." A name greeted with massive grins of relief. "You, Herr Collins, alone among your peers, may savour my wife's delightful fudge. I hope you don't feel too ill... I mean, want any more because it's the last piece."

As Collins bit confidently into the cube, twenty people craned forward to watch him turn green, vomit, or simply drop dead. Collins merely glanced at us with a superior look, swept a hand through his thick blond hair and popped the rest into his mouth.

"Lovely, sir," he said, licking his fingertips, "Lovely. Compliments to Frau Phillips, sir."

Beaky's jaw fell as he gaped, then gulped and stage-whispered "Is he all right?"

"Looks it, sir," said Paulus.

"No," hissed Beaky, tapping his forehead. "I mean, is he all right up here?"

"Well," I said, "That's what we ask every day, sir. So difficult to tell these days, what with medication and therapy and that. Marvellous what they can do, isn't it, sir?"

Beaky, clearing his throat, said page 65, an interview with some guy called Lars Richter, protesting through a unison groan that he had to get on with the syllabus.

"Tell us about German fudge, sir," said Paulus. "Aren't there several varieties?"

"Like their chocolate," I added hopefully.

"Ah, well," Beaky settled on the edge of his desk. "I did once visit a chocolate factory in Zurich..." Lars Richter was forgotten as we settled back for a lengthy lesson-killing, work-avoiding anecdote. Result, eh?

Double Biology, on the other hand, started badly but finished well. Herb's lab in the Jessop Wing was this like freak-show of a dozen jars of pickled nasties, lurid diagrams of human innards and stuffed animals glaring bitterly from the shelves. What the fuck was *wrong* with him? No wonder we felt so weirded out when we went to Biology, especially since we'd come from Beaky's cosy world of fudge and Yorkies, posters of Brecht and photos of German landscapes, this mini-bust on his desk of Schiller, who'd written Ode to Joy (you know – 'Freude schoener Götterfunken Tochter aus Elysium' and all that - Beethoven's 9th, yeah?). Anyway, someone had written on the board 'GET STONED. DRINK WET CEMENT.' We thought it witty. Herbidacious did not. Glaring wickedly, he turned on us. "Who wrote that?" We remained silent. His face darkened with suppressed fury. "I am waiting for an answer." His eyes raked us, searchlights scouring a night-sky for enemy bombers. "Look, Upper Five H. I will not tolerate..."

"I think it was probably someone in the Lower Sixth, sir."

Yikes, was that *me* speaking? Or was it just a timid squeak? I stared at Herbie, a terrified rabbit literally hypnotized by the stare of a snake.

"I beg your pardon, *Mister* Peters?" The Mr was heavily stressed. "Who asked *you*?"

"Well, you did, sir, kind of. Ask us. Sir."

Stop talking. For once in your life, just stop.

For some reason that song from *The Herbs*, 'Oi'm Bayleaf oi'm the gardener, oi work from early dawn' popped into my mind, and I giggled. Christ Almighty, I thought he was gonna have, like, this massive stroke, you know? With frothing an' twitching an' stuff?

"So *you* find it funny, do you, you half-witted buffoon?"

"Well, not funny as such, sir. More like witty, clever, you know?"

Please stop.

"Which form is it?"

"Lower Six CR, I think, sir." That fucking bastard song. I struggled not to laugh.

"Tut. Yet another example of the immaturity of the present Sixth Form. Get rid of it, Peters." He chucked a dirty cloth at me. The Lower Sixth or the slogan, sir? Did not tumble out of my mouth. Thank God. My shoulders shook with silent laughter as I wiped the board.

You know, we *tried* to engage with him. Fosbrook, asking if he'd had a nice holiday, was curtly told to mind his own business and when Lewis asked if it'd been a sun-soaked place full of bathing beauties, he was sent out, but the lesson itself was awesome. Me, Maxton, Gray and Fosbrook dissected a sheep's eyeball, smeared the jellied gunge on each other's sleeves then slipped the bits into Stewpot Stewart's pocket. Like *mega*-result, eh?

In Music, we composed and sang a happy birthday song for Jamie Arnold, who was 16 today - we'd given him the traditional class card signed by everyone at Registration - then I got 14/15 on a test on Handel's *Israel in Egypt* – how could I confuse a *cor anglais* with a bloody trombone (question 7)? The bloody trombone hadn't been invented then, you soup-for-brains fuckwit. But then I saved my rep with an awesome presentation on Mussorgsky, illustrated with extracts from *Boris Godunov* (the overblown Coronation Scene and the tsar's desperate, ghost-haunted death on CD) and *Pictures at an Exhibition* (Baba Yaga and Great Gates of Kiev) on the piano. Using Grove and a biography from the City Library, I'd enjoyed researching the life of this alcoholic military officer turned civil servant who loved 'all things Russian' and had drunk himself to death by the age of 42. Man, *there* was a lesson! Dead at 42. From vodka. Shit, man.

"Lesson for *you*, mate," Ali said, tying his laces, "After that party."

Fucking hell. Even *he* knew about it.

Hammering the green squash ball at the wall, he darted aside as I lunged too close and crashed down with a bone-jarring thud, my racket clattering to the floor. Instantly he was beside me, asking if I was all right.

"Just winded," I said, holding my rib-cage together with my fingers. "Get on with it."

The ball, literally blasting into the wall like some mad thunderbolt, shot back past me like a bullet at about a megazillion miles an hour. I like scampered into the far corner, got my racket under it and sort of scooped it back, racing forward for the return, but Alistair, anticipating my move, thwacked it high over my head and back into the wall.

"You should run around a bit more," he advised drily, "Get some weight off."

"There'll be nothing left." I dragged a weary hand through my sweat-soaked hair. "Just a fucking skeleton."

Grunting, he whacked the ball again. Recklessly I dived for it, landed heavily on the court, kind of skidded and literally shredded my knee as I cannoned painfully into the wall.

"You're bleeding," he observed wisely.

I tugged a tissue from my pocket. "No shit, Sherlock."

He promptly declared a draw because I'd retired injured.

"Bollocks, Alistair. You won. You were eight-three up"

"But if you'd been able to continue, who knows?"

"You'd *still* have won. You're like totally brilliant? And I'm like totally shit, you know?"

He helped me limp to the changing room then sat me on a bench, gripped the back of my calf and dabbed the deep, bleeding gash with this water-soaked handkerchief.

"Is that better?" he asked softly.

Man, it was better than brilliant. He was touching my leg. Electricity tingled through me, like when Gray doodled on my hand. Then he like gave me his water-bottle, you know? Where his *lips* had been. Where his mouth had been. Where his... Shit. I almost passed out.

"Does it hurt?"

"No," though it stung like a bazillion wasps were partying in my kneecap.

"Do you think my legs are too thin?" I asked. "I think they're like matchsticks."

"I'll get some TCP from the staff First Aid box."

Fuck no! Not that fucking molten lava sulphuric fucking acid...

"Argggggghhhhhh!" Blinded by tears, I dug my fingernails deep into his shoulder.
"Sorry, J," he whispered. "Does it hurt?
"Fucking fuck you, you fucking fuck-witted fuck-wit. Of course it fucking hurts!"
"Sorry, darling."
Darling? What the fuck?
Abruptly he stood up, flinging the blood-stained hankie at me.
"Anyway," he said gruffly, "You can sort yourself out from here. It's just a cut."
I want *you* to do it! Please, Ali… *you* do it… *you* hold me… *please* hold me. Ali…

He stripped off his T-shirt and dumped it on the bench. His chest was narrow but his shoulders were broad. A thin line of fine black hair connected his waistband to a deep pit of a navel. I saw black hair in his armpits. Fucking hell. Why was I such a little weed? You could like *count* my fucking armpit hairs, you know? I watched enviously as he sprayed himself with Lynx Fever and tossed me the can. I reddened like a winter sunset. God, now he would see just how pathetic my pathetic little body really was.

He was wearing thigh-hugging black hipsters. Not boxers. And black was *sooo* sexy.
Not on him, obviously.
On me.
"Nice pants," I said idiotically, piling my T-shirt on the bench with my shorts.
"Yours too," he grinned. They were a nice apricot colour.

I followed him to the toilet. I like really wanted to *look*, you know? See what *his* was like? If it was bigger? Or nicer than mine, you know? Though I thought mine fairly nice anyway and kind of big for my body, but his looked thicker, a little longer… Darting this furtive glance to my left, I realised with a sort of horrified excitement that he was totally checking mine out too. Shit! Fuck! Shit.

Blushing like a carnation and feeling like really guilty, I fixed my eyes on the straw-coloured liquid trickling along the stainless steel trough. His and mine, two streams merging… I glanced again, deeply ashamed yet unable to stop myself, and met his lazy smile. I gulped. My piss seemed to have frozen in mid-air. My heart threatened to choke me. My cock was swelling. Oh God! Ali. My darling. Look at me. Look at my hardening cock. Touch it. Kiss it. Our eyes met.

Oh Ali.

Oh fuck.

Someone just shoot me.

Then he was gone, looping his gold prefect's tie through the collar of his pale blue shirt and ruffling my sweat-dampened hair, and I slumped on the bench to stick a plaster on my knee and lever off my trainers while my erection subsided. My mood had suddenly shifted from elated excitement to wanting to cry. He had left me, and my life felt so empty.

Moodily I pulled on my grey trousers then the grey shirt and buttoned it, except for the top one, shoved my grey-socked feet into the black Clarks, tied the laces, slung my Adidas backpack over a shoulder and emerged into the soft drizzle and the trees surrounding the Sports Centre where some gimps were playing conkers. The school buildings were on the far side of the cricket pitch. Bollocks. Cutting across the field was punishable by like a gazillion deaths so I'd have to walk round and get wet. Double-bollocks. My hair would be soaked.

The afternoon brought the *mega*-yawnorama of Physics. Mr Milton could be a really entertaining teacher. Yeah, I know that sounds impossible, right, in Physics? But Millie, who sported this beard you could lose a bulldog in and horrendous socks patterned with Simpsons characters, was certifiably insane. Virtually every experiment ended in utter disaster. Our form-master in 4M, he'd blown almost everything up and taken us on this mad day-trip to London, to the Science Museum followed by the National History Museum, chasing us round Kensington at like a million miles an hour 'cos he was afraid we'd miss the train home. He'd started this awesome class project of building a fully working crane out of Lego and an AA battery. It even kept me away from Wargames for a while. He'd done this lesson on weather-patterns and ended up miming the whole bloody thing? flicking the lights on and off for lightning, banging his fists on the board to simulate thunder, tapping his fingers on the desk for rain then blowing hard through his teeth for the wind. He'd followed this up by digging his hands into a box of chalk and hurling the contents into the air with this lung-busting cry of 'VOLCANO!' He wasn't like that today. It was all equations and problem-solving. Still, he was like a trazillion tons better than Dr Moss, who was quite possibly the worst teacher in the school. Bald, boring and drily academic, I learned *nothing* from him except that I should underline stuff in pencil not ink *and* that I was a total waste of carbon atoms.

My mind wandered back to the squash game. What the hell happened there? I'd been overwhelmed by such strong feelings again, like in my bedroom that time when I'd wanted, really *really* wanted him to like hug me, to KISS me. When he'd gripped my knee, my heart had thumped so violently, and my blood had literally caught fire. And when he left me, I'd felt like crying again. Christ, I always felt like crying when he left me.

He had called me 'darling.'

Darling.

What if he was, you know, in *love* with me? And was I like in love with him? Was that what it all meant?

Shit and bollocks.

Boys didn't fall in love with other boys, at least not in *real* life, nor in *my* life. I'd rather fry and eat my own eyeballs with a crisp side-salad and a chilled Sancerre than have some drooling pervert peeping at *my* boys' bits. 'Cos neither Alistair nor me were poofs. We were just curious. Unlike Paulus who was a total poof. He had gold buckles on his shoes. I mean, shut that door, ducky.

The high-pitched, banshee wail of the fire-alarm abruptly shattered my train of thought. Second erection subsiding, I trailed downstairs from the swish Jessop Wing into the drizzle.

"Typical, holding a drill on a day like this," muttered Maxton. "It's bloody freezing."

"Probably Leatherface smoking his pipe under the bloody detector again," grumbled Stewart. Which our leather-faced tosser of a year-head had actually done, twice, the twat.

The rain wet my face as we lined up on the muddy field between U5S and U5B.

"Shut up!" roared Bunny. "Alphabetical order!"

There was a sudden *frisson* of tension.

"I don't think it *is* a drill," I told Paulus. "I think it's for real."

"Peters!" yelled Bunny. "I thought I told you to shut up. For God's sake, boy! Don't you *ever* stop talking? Tuck your bloody shirt in and do your collar up, you lout!" He started barking out the roll – Arnold, Bainbridge, Brudenall, Burridge, Cooke – I grinned at Wilson in the U5S line –Collins, Crooks, Fosbrook, Gardiner, Gray – then waved at Lees in U5D – Harrison, Huxley, Lewis, Maxton – and nodded at Coleman in U5B – Morreson, Paulus, Peters .... PETERS! The 6' 2 spud-faced brick shithouse that was Kevin Seymour standing behind me dug me hard in the spine so I kind of squawked "Here, sir!" like some frightened chicken which North and Rix in U5S imitated till the whole of the fucking Upper Fifth seemed to be taking the piss. Bunny just gave me this utterly withering look and finished the roll with Seymour, Stewart and Walton. God, the man thought I was such a twat.

I wished it would stop raining. For Arnie's birthday. Shit, man. He was 16. I wouldn't be 16 for like ages, like (I worked it out on my fingers) fucking 8 months! Bollocks. And Arnie wasn't the oldest in the form. That was Burridge, on 3rd September. After Arnie was Chris Morreson on 28th then we were into October. At least I wasn't the youngest, though. That was SuperSwot SpecSaver Adrian Huxley on 23rd August. Man, he'd only just turned *15*. But anyway, I'd still have to watch (I counted on my fingers again) 14 others reach the age of consent before me, *and* sign the bloody congrats cards. There were only Stewart (July 14), Crooks, Fosbrook (June 15) and Huxley younger than me, and only Fosbrook was titchier than me and he and Hux were like NEVER getting laid anyway EVER 'cos one had elephant ears and the other a ferrety face so it didn't like matter to them like it did me, you know, young, hot and full of hormones? Life was so unfair, you know? Anyway, as Gallagher appeared with two policemen and a fire-officer, an uneasy silence spread through the 800 boys on the field.

"Away from the buildings!" Gallagher shouted. "Get away from the buildings."

Alistair Rose emerged from the middle door and spoke to the fire-officer then he, Leverett and Chris Crooks started herding us backwards.

"Bloody fire-engine," said Maxton. "Look."

"Dammit," scowled Stewart. "Isn't it gonna burn down after all?"

Beyond the chapel, blue lights blazing, a gleaming red fire-truck was pulling up. Then we noticed a gas cylinder burning outside one of the workshops.

"Not much of a fire," Stewart muttered scathingly. "Bit of spit would put that out."

"Bloody rain'll do it," Maxton concurred.

Several firemen jogged past. Some Sixth Formers cheered ironically. Bush-head, U5B's form-master, chatting with U5S's Soggy Sugden, he of the paunch, receding hairline and cheap tweed jackets, glared at them.

"Shut up!" shouted Alistair, tense and anxious.

"God, what's up with him?" muttered Maxton.

"Time of the month," said Gray.

"Drama-queen, more like," said Maxton.

"*Some* kind of queen," said Gray darkly.

"Peters!" bawled Bunny, "Shut up! One more word, I'll put you in detention."

"But sir…"

Sugden, leaning across, slapped the back of my head. "Stop talking, Peters. It's a *gas* cylinder. It could blow up and take half the school with it. And do your damn collar up."

Fucking hell. I wrestled the grey button through the hole behind the knot of my tie as everyone waited nervously till the cylinder was neutralised by some kind of foam. Our cheers were sharply cut short by Ash-tray himself.

"The fire-officer tells me that half of you might have been killed if that cylinder had exploded. All you stupid little boys who thought it was a jolly jape might have burned to death in screaming agony on the field. You do as you are told and move away from the buildings."

"Blimey," said Stewart behind me. "Laying it on a bit thick, isn't he?"

"When you leave the room, the last one out must shut the doors and windows. Rose and Leverett inspected the school and found most of them open. It is not good enough. You have been told time and time again. So do it. And take it seriously. Fire is not a joke."

Ali, standing beside him, was frowning directly at me. I wondered whether to wave. Just a little one, a discreet flick of the hand. His frown deepened.

Ash-tray made us stand in the rain for a little longer. Fine with me, I thought. Less time in Physics. Mentally I hummed my new favourite song: '*they got a message from the action man, "I'm happy, hope you're happy too…" Ashes to ashes, funk to funky, we know Major Tom's a junkie…*' When he finally dismissed us, and the lines of boys and knots of masters broke up, Ali descended, his expression thunderous.

"What the hell was that?"

"I was just saying hi."

Seizing my shoulder, he propelled me roughly towards the sandstone wall.

"You stupid little boy," he said. It felt like a slap across my cheek. "You don't know, do you? You never stop to think. 2S were in that workshop with Mr Rutherford. He dragged it outside. He burned his hands and tore a muscle. He's gone to hospital. But if that cylinder had exploded, he'd've been killed. *You* might've been killed." He seemed on the verge of tears. "*You*." Gulping, he looked away. "I couldn't bear it if anything happened to *you*."

My heart raced. Suddenly my palms were sweating.

"Why?" I said.

He gulped again, struggling with himself.

"You know why," he said finally, his eyes darkening.

"Peters!" Gallagher was shouting. "Get back to class!"

"Call me," I said breathlessly, squeezing his arm. "Call me tonight!"

"Peters!"

I was about to blurt out the truth. I was about to tell him how I felt.

"Ali... me too...I..."

But Gallagher was striding towards us.

How *did* I feel?

"Call me," I said again, then ran after the others.

He loved me.

He really loved me.

It was in his eyes.

I was so excited I could hardly breathe. Man alive. He loved me. Nothing mattered now, *nothing*. Alistair Rose loved me. He was in love with *me*. With *me*! I could hardly wait for the first play read-through at 3.45. I'd seen in his eyes. He loved me. Alistair *loved* me. Me. Could this be, like, the greatest moment of my life? Like, EVER? All the prizes and concerts were nothing to this. That someone so brilliant could love *me*, someone so stupid and weedy... it made no sense. Then a cold realisation chilled my blood. If Alistair Rose *was* in love with me, that would make him homosexual. Queer. Gay. A poofter. Like Wilson and Gray said.

How the hell could *he* be a poofter? He was so confident, relaxed and clever. I mean, it was like so fucking ridiculous, you know? Poofters mince and wear make-up, don't they?

But he loved me.

God Almighty. How would I face him at the first read-through? Anyway, when I arrived in the Beckwith Hall, he was like sitting in the Headmaster's chair scribbling on a clipboard whilst Bill Laud dished out scripts and rehearsal schedules and Leo Trent hailed me with a piping "Hey, Peters, can you lend me fifty pence? I lost my bus-fare."

"Lost it or spent it?" I demanded.

"I was *sooo* hungry," said Leo, "Like starvingly ravenous. I had to get something."

"Do I look like a bloody bank, Trent?" I dug through the crumpled tissues and chipped, fluff-dusted Polos in my pocket for a coin. "I only bring what I need then I can't waste it on crisps and sweets like you kids. If you ain't got it, you can't spend it. Here."

"Thanks, Dad." Miming a kiss, he scampered away crowing his latest poem:

Mary had a little lamb, she tied it to a pylon.

Ten thousand volts shot up its arse and turned its wool to nylon.

"Dad?" said Sonning. "You sound more like Granddad. You'll be turning into some greybeard, wearing a loincloth and dispensing wisdom from a lotus position under your tree."

"God, JP in a loincloth," said Harry Turner. "Imagine it. Legs like fucking Twiglets."

James Warburton cackled. "Rosie's fantasy, JP in a loincloth. Or less."

Blushing red as a post-box, I told Warburton to shut his face and flicked through the script. I always enjoyed the house plays. Last year I'd been Sean in Ted Hughes' *Sean, the Fool, the Devil and his Cat.* Laud had directed and Ali had played the Devil. It'd been good but Firth House had employed a prostitute, so to speak, which had gone down a storm. Ali had clearly learned that, in an all-boys' school, there is nothing funnier than a prop-forward in a dress and had written no less than four such parts. His play was called *Last Will and Testament.* Turner muttered darkly that he hoped it wasn't an omen for Rosie's career.

My character, Jasper Farthing, was the villain, mad, bad and dangerous to know. The story, such as it was, involved Guy Sharp (Andy Paulus) inheriting a fortune from some dead relative and the attempts of the other characters to get their hands on it. I, Uncle Jasper, and my wife, Penelope, were to adopt Guy as our child. There were two gangsters, brothers called Marco and Giuseppe Sclerotti, played by Harry Turner (Lysander in *The Dream*) and Richard 'Sooty' Sutcliffe, who employed as their henchmen Herr Lakker, a German barber played by Jason Middleton, and Jock Macabre, a drunken Scotsman played by James Warburton. These two infiltrated the country house during a dinner-party to celebrate the inheritance. The guests at the party included deaf Aunt Clarissa (Sonning in a frock), and Lulu, the nymphomaniac played by Leo Trent, who was determined to marry money and didn't care whose. Bobby Rose was playing Perkins the butler. There was a gardener called Arthur McArthur (James 'Jambo' Hartley from 4M), solicitor Kirby Mills (Mark Burridge) and Marco Sclerotti's wife, Nessie, played by this absolutely enormous flanker called Stuart Anderson from U5D whose thighs were like thicker than my chest, you know? Although the Sclerottis got the loot, they were double-crossed by Lakker who was working for Jasper all along. The climax involved me shooting Lakker then opening the briefcase containing the cash as Sclerotti's bomb exploded in my face. When the grandfather clock tolled midnight, Perkins emerged from its interior, Lulu bashed me over the head with Jock's whisky bottle, North and Whiting, playing these dim-witted, flat-footed Plods, PCs Cox and Bull, dragged me away and Sharp got the money.

Despite it having, in Turner's words, more corn than a packet of cornflakes and a story no-one could really follow, we thought it hysterically funny. The gimps kept snorting and spitting sandwiches all over their scripts, Anderson was perfect as the Dame and every time Sonning opened his mouth, we *all* cracked up. Leo, loving his part and the chance to hog the spotlight, put on this super-seductive voice whilst Middleton and Warburton adopted outrageous *'Allo 'Allo* accents. My sides were aching so much I could hardly deliver my lines. Paulus said he thought he was going to be sick. Alistair's face radiated with joy as we brought his words to life. I gazed at him, happy he was happy. God, my boyfriend was so clever.

Huh? My *what*?

After the read-through he asked me and Paulus to join the school magazine's editorial committee. Apparently he and Webbo (Mr Webster) wanted some younger boys on the committee to improve contact between the committee and the school, to develop the Features and Original Contributions sections, to get a wider range of contributors and to stop it being this exclusive Sixth Form clique. Ali thought me and Paulus, and then Shelton, Pippy B and some red-headed gimp called Gittins from 3R might spearhead this, write some stuff ourselves and commission others.

The chance to work with Ali Rose on something *else* was too good to miss. I left on a massive high as Paulus, grinning inanely, blabbered on about these sonnets he was writing and how he could publish them and how ace it was gonna look on our like UCAS forms.

"And Rosie's *sooo* cool," he added enthusiastically.

"I know," I blabbered. "He's fucking awesome. I played squash with him and he like whipped me? but I didn't care 'cos I was like playing with *him*, with Awesome Ali, and I fell and cut my knee and he was so kind and gentle… man, I thought I was gonna like die, and then at the fire alarm… oh Jesus, he's like so fucking awesome, you know?"

I suddenly became aware of Paulus' narrowed blue eyes coolly appraising me. Equally suddenly, I became aware of what my blurting meant. *I* was in love. With Alistair Rose.

Yikes. Someone please just shoot me. I'd rather like fry and eat my own appendix with broccoli and a nice Chardonnay than be, well, *that*, you know?

I hardly slept that night. Even a half-dozen drops of lavender oil on my pillow didn't help and the jingling wind-chimes seemed to be laughing at me. Ali haunted every thought, and every thought alternated between despair and desire.

I loved him. I really *really* loved him, you know? Yet how do you describe this feeling? I just wanted to be with him, to be near him, to hear his voice, to feel his touch, to gaze on his beautiful face, to breathe the same air, to feel those lips against mine…

Oh God, help me. Help me get Ali. Help me get the boy that I love so much and I will do anything you ask, *anything*, just so long as I can have half an hour with kissing him.

What the fuck?

Another boy?

Kissing *him*? Another *boy*? Kissing? Like, with tongues? Like I had with *Claire*? Oh fuck. This could not be happening. Not to me. Other people were gay, Paulus, Trent, even Rosie, but not me, not Jonathan Peters. How *could* he be a homo? He fancied *girls*. A girl. Kind of. Maybe.

Savagely punching my pillow, I rolled miserably onto my front. I shouldn't *want* to kiss him. We're just teens. I'm 15. He's 17. He's another boy. What the hell's wrong with me? Of course I didn't love him. I *couldn't* love him, could I? I mean, he's a guy, right? A guy like me, yeah? And I am NOT a fucking homo, OK? Imagining its screaming sirens, I stared at the Stuka diving towards my bed. It was heading for me. I shoved my right arm under the pillow and drifted into a dream.

I was walking barefoot through mud. It squelched between my toes as I passed through a rundown street populated with ragged people in ragged clothes. Ali Rose emerged from a house and gave me an umbrella. As I opened it, he hissed 'not here' and dragged me round a corner. Then he pushed me up against this roughly plastered white-washed wall and French-kissed me, tongue on tongue, and I put my hand inside his trousers...

7: Live while we're young

MAYBE it *was* that party, Michael Crooks' 15th birthday bash, that started all this. Because it was August 3rd and not dark till 9 or so, we were starting in the garden about 7, sitting on cool, soft grass under these big old trees, mostly limes and planes, before moving through the open French-windows into this like square Edwardian sandstone semi and the dining-room where a buffet waited. Michael's parents, both university lecturers, slipped discreetly away for dinner somewhere leaving older brother Christopher in charge. Because he was in the Upper Sixth, a prefect, head of Goodricke and on the school mag committee, he was therefore responsible. Of course, as soon as their Audi had vanished round the corner, we begged him to get some booze from the Co-Op 'cos absolutely, totally, like nobody fancied a night on Coca-bloody-Cola, so when he returned with several bottles of industrial-strength cider the size of walruses and some bomb-sized bottles of vodka, we got stuck in.

There were perhaps twenty people, a mix of girls and boys, including Mark Gray and Andrew Collins, who was Mikey's then best friend, and some lads from the harriers team, Hood, Tern, some others. To a soundtrack of Elvis Costello, Ian Dury, The Jam and Blondie, we sat on the grass swigging cider with our girlfriends. I had kind of invited Claire. I'd just finished preparing her for Grade 6 oboe, as I said earlier, and had consequently spent hours at her house playing accompaniment to this nice Andantino by Cherubini and Nielsen's Fantasiestück Op 2/1, unfortunately titled 'Romance', I say unfortunately because the way she said it made me blush like a jug of Sangria and her giggle like a, well, like a schoolgirl. She was popular, pretty, clearly worshipped me, and I enjoyed her company. Her father seemed to like me too and I had actually had dinner there a couple of times. Mrs Ash-tray had done a roast chicken once and the other time we sat in their kitchen eating spaghetti and laughing as Dr Ash-tray told risqué stories from Roman plays – he had a Cambridge PhD in the plays of Plautus and kept quoting *The Pot of Gold*'s most famous line, 'Consilium audax habeo', or 'I have a cunning plan' – and Mrs Ash-tray affectionately chided him for corrupting us, and what kind of behaviour was that from a headmaster?

I liked Ash-tray. He had this rugger-bugger's build, iron-grey Brillo-pad hair, a kind, creased face and bright blue eyes that sparkled when he laughed, which that night was often. His son, Toby, Tony, something beginning with T, had left school in July and was waiting to go up to Oxford to read Law. He gave me this 'chat' about 'treating his sister right, or I'd never play the piano again'. I almost laughed. The guy was as weedy as me and wore these massive specs in blue NHS frames that reminded me of a slightly startled barn-owl.

Anyway, when Mikey's party cropped up, I just invited her. I didn't want to be Billy No-Date after all, and she was the only girl I knew apart from Julie Wilson, and there was no way I was getting lucky with her. And, like, yikes! Doing it with frizzy, pug-faced Julie? Man. I could practically hear my own skin crawling. I'd rather, like, sauté and eat my own kidneys, you know? With Borlotti beans and a nice Frascati. Anyway, I collected her from her house near the park at seven-sharp. I'd put on black Levis and a black shirt, open to the third button displaying my gold crucifix. Mum didn't like me wearing black. She said it made me look like a Nazi. Tough titty. Black suited me. Claire wore this really pretty backless dress in a soft plum colour and these new Kickers in a darker, aubergine shade.

"They cost £60," she said, taking my arm, "But I just *had* to have them. I queued till midnight! But they're *sooo* cool, aren't they? And I got another tag for my collection."

"You look fantastic," I said truthfully. She'd painted her nails matching aubergine and wore a little discreet make-up, just a dab here and there.

Mikey's was only half a mile or so but somewhere near the cricket club, she slipped her hand into mine and chattered brightly about this Pierrot duvet cover she was getting. Pierrot, this sad white-faced clown pining with unrequited love for Columbine, his only friend the distant moon, was the latest craze at the girls' high school. Claire had poster-prints by Picasso and Chagall, cushion covers, a fan and even a Pierrot mug. Man alive. Girls, eh?

"Do you know *Pierrot Lunaire*?" I asked. "It's a song cycle by Schoenberg."

She didn't. Bloody hell. What did they teach at that place?

She was older than me, by three or four months. Her birthday was in January. Or was it February? I wasn't really sure. What I *did* know was she'd got a distinction in her exam and I just *knew* she was going to reward me with a shag. This night, I thought, is the night I *finally* lose my virginity. Ha! So when she sat on the grass and put her arm round my waist, I smiled warmly, swigged more cider and put my arm round her shoulders. Collins and Gray exchanged grins. They seemed genuinely happy for me. Soon tonight I'd be men like them.

A couple more girls joined us, a horse-riding, pony-tailed fanatic called Sarah, Sharon, something beginning with S, and Mary, a squat, wall-shaped girl with a mad mop of dyed-black hair and black eyeliner who was trying to be a Goth and was crazy about Mikey, who flopped on the grass with them. He was wearing jeans and a short-sleeved shirt in green, blue and white checks. Under that copper-red hair, his luminous green eyes were alive with enjoyment. Even his freckles seemed to be dancing.

"Happy birthday, mate." I raised my bottle of cider. "Ginger ninja turns fifteen." I'd given him a Madness CD. *One Step Beyond. 'My girl's mad at me'*, etc. He grinned as Mary started up this game of Pass-the-Polo which involved passing a mint round a circle from tongue to tongue. I found myself touching tongue-tips with Mikey and then with Claire and giggling furiously as the litre of cider I'd consumed set my senses spinning. But I was enjoying myself. I'd never been drunk before, and I liked it. I liked feeling relaxed, not caring what people thought, just like chilling, you know? I even snogged Claire a little but the game collapsed into a chorus of boos when Gray and Collins refused to participate.

"Chicken!" I crowed. "What do you think? It's gonna turn you gay?"

Narrowing his eyes, Gray dragged on the spliff he was sharing with this girl, Annie or Angie, and muttered something then Mary started this new game.

"Claire," she said. "Truth or dare?"

"Truth," Claire replied.

"Is there someone at this party you really, *really* fancy?"

Blushing, she nestled against me, kissed the mole on my neck and giggled "Yes."

Everyone in the circle *oohed*. I didn't know why. The answer was blindingly obvious.

"Jonathan," said Mary. "Truth or dare?"

"Truth," I said.

"Is there someone at this party you're hoping to sleep with tonight?"

"Wa-hey!" roared Collins. "JP gets lucky tonight, lucky tonight, lucky tonight."

Red as a Valentine heart, I muttered "Yes" and felt her squeeze my waist.

"Have you brought any condoms?" asked Mary. "I'm sure Doctor Ashton doesn't really want to be a grandfather yet."

"Mary!" shrieked Claire, appalled and delighted.

I blushed even more hotly and prayed for someone to just shoot me.

"Well, Jonathan? *Did* you bring any? Or should Chris go to the chemist for you?"

"No," I muttered, so red you could sizzle a fucking steak on my cheeks.

"JP's not getting lucky tonight, lucky tonight..."

"Shut up, Andy," I snarled as he and Gray dabbed their faces and went 'Tssss.'

"Basic facts of life, Jonathan," said Mary, "But perhaps you're still a virgin?"

Ha ha ha.

"*Are* you still a virgin, Jonathan?" she persisted.

I wanted to slap her. Hard.

"Schoolboy error, JP." Gray passed me the spliff. "You gotta bring protection if you wanna get laid. Birds expect it these days."

Schoolboy error? I thought bitterly as everyone laughed. Funny that...

I sucked from the joint, hating being stoned, hating the smell and the sudden dizziness, hating the situation, especially when Collins casually flicked a foil-wrapped Durex into my lap. "You can have one of mine. I always carry three but guess we can take it easy tonight, eh, babe?" Grinning, he started massaging Suzy or Sadie or whoever's left breast. "Jonny needs to get laid so badly..."

"Just don't flush it down the bog when you've finished," Chris Crooks advised. "I did that once. Couldn't get rid of it. Had to fish the bloody thing out with a Biro."

Howling, Mikey said "I remember that! You were bricking it, man. Who was the girl?"

"Fiona Jenkins."

"*You* had Fiona Jenkins?" said Collins, outraged. "Bollocks. *I* had her. Didn't know she was *your* sloppy seconds."

Chris laughed. "Sloppy's the word, mate. Yuck."

Mary continued round the circle asking really banal questions of everyone else, like 'what's your favourite colour?' and 'what's your favourite film?' until she got back to Claire.

"Truth or dare?"

"Dare."

"OK," said Mary. "I dare you to drink a glass of vodka, down in one."

Smiling, Claire accepted the shot-glass. To wild encouragement, she put the glass to her lips, tipped back her head and swallowed the lot. Everyone cheered as she turned the glass upside-down over her own head. Mary clapped her admiration, then turned to me.

"OK, Jonathan. Truth or dare?"

Truth had been like horribly humiliating but I could do a vodka-shot.

"Dare," I grinned. My head was light and I was a little stoned.

"I dare you to kiss Michael."

Collins whooped "Yeah, go on, Jonny, kiss Mikey. It's his birthday. Give him a kiss."

"Truth," I said lamely, trying to blot out the yells of encouragement.

"What's up, JP?" jeered Gray, "You chicken? Scared you might like it too much?"

I looked desperately at Mikey, who sort of shrugged, as though it didn't bother him.

"OK," I said, draining the bottle of cider and taking another drag from the joint. "OK. I'll kiss Mikey." I searched his luminous green eyes. "If it's OK with him."

"Go on, Mikey!" cried Chris. "Let him do it! Let him kiss you!"

Smiling calmly, Mikey reached for me as I pecked him drily and quickly on the cheek.

"On the lips!" yelled Collins, pounding the grass with the flat of his hand. "Kiss him on the lips! It's his birthday! Kiss him on the lips, Jonny!"

So I did.

I planted my lips on his, closed my eyes and snogged him for a full minute whilst the audience whooped and cheered. I felt his lips moving against mine then his hand stroked my hair, brushed my cheek, and I lost myself in the moment, touching his tongue with mine.

"Fucking magic!" yelled Collins as Mikey and I broke apart for a breather. His eyes were soft with affection, his face easing into a friendly smile.

"Thanks, Jonny," he whispered as Collins whistled. "That's the best present so far."

But I felt really confused. As I was kissing him, I'd had this... well, this massive erection, right? I got a hard-on from kissing this boy. What the FUCK was wrong with me? I'd never had one kissing Claire.

I lurched towards the house with Gray, reeling from the cider, the dope and that kiss, and grabbed some sausage-rolls and two slices of pizza. The Vapours were '*turning Japanese - Everyone around me is a total stranger, everyone avoids me like a psycho-ranger, That's why I'm turning Japanese, I think I'm turning Japanese, I really think so...*'

"You seemed a little too into that, Jonny," Gray said darkly.

"How do you mean? I just kissed him, like you all wanted." My speech slurred a little.

"You got a hard-on, didn't you?"

"Bollocks," I said, cramming pork pie into my mouth. "Why the fuck were looking anyway? You turned into a poof, or something?"

Scraping some coleslaw onto a paper plate, he said "Takes one to know one."

Fucking hell. My best friend thought I was a homo. Someone just shoot me. More drink.

I slugged back a quarter-bottle of vodka, from the neck down the neck, feeling the fire warm my belly, feeling my head lighten then, rooting around in some kitchen cupboards, I found this stash of homemade wine. Ha ha! Victoriously, I seized some orange-coloured stuff and staggered back to the garden holding the bottle aloft like an Oscar statuette. The letters on the label, dancing crazily before my eyes, told me it was plum wine. I growled some lines from The Jam's 'Going Underground', '*what you see is what you get, you made your bed, you got to lie in it,*' or something, and lurched outside to the sounds of Madness. My return was greeted by a laughter. Fuck you guys. I grabbed Claire's arm and tried to kiss her mouth.

"Ow!" she protested, pushing me aside.

"Way to go, Peters," murmured one of the older boys.

"*My girl's mad at me,*" sang Suggs, "*Why can't I explain? Why do I feel this pain? 'Cos everything I say she doesn't understand, she doesn't realise, she takes it all the wrong way.*"

"Let's play something else," I said, unsteadily lighting a ciggie I'd nicked. "Strip spin-the-bottle. Let's see what you're all made of, see what you've *really* got between your fucking legs." Taking a large mouthful of this plum wine, I threw my shirt into the hedge. "Come on, Mary. Get your fucking kit off, you evil fucking cow. What are you so fucking scared of?"

"Jonny." I felt Mikey's hand on my arm. "Calm down."

"He's fucking wasted," one of the older boys observed.

"Looks like a fucking skeleton," Chris said. "Hey kid, do you ever eat anything?"

Claire put her hand between my shoulder-blades. "Settle down, Jonny. It's a party."

"Was kissing me *so* bad?" said Michael.

No. That was the problem. Kissing you, Mikey, was unbelievably wonderful. And I wished you would get your shirt off too, 'cos you're fucking gorgeous…

A wave of nausea rolled through my stomach. Getting up, I staggered a yard or so and threw up in the hedge as Chris's friends cheered. Claire rushed over, solicitously kind, putting her hand on my shoulder to steady me, and that was when I puked on her Kickers. She kind of screamed, I rushed inside to the bathroom and chucked up everything left in my stomach straight into the bidet. Then I slumped to the floor. Next thing I knew, Gray and Collins were detaching me from the pedestal.

"You all right, Jonny?" said Gray. "Jonny? Can you hear me?"

"Mmm fine. Fuck off," I said, collapsing in a jumbled heap on the bathroom floor.

"Christ, Jonny," said Gray. "What the fuck have you been drinking?"

"This!" I said, triumphantly waving the half-empty bottle of plum wine.

"Which you nicked from Dr Crooks' cupboard?" said Collins. "Fuck, Jonny. What the fuck's wrong with you?"

Seizing Gray's shirt, I shook it vigorously and shouted "I'm *not* gay, you bastard. I'm *not* gay, all right? All right? I'm *not* fucking *gay*."

"All right," he said, adjusting his black-framed specs. "Jeez, Jonny. It was just a joke."

"Well," I slurred, "It's not fucking funny, all right? You don't make jokes like that."

"All right. For fuck's sake. Lighten up."

I lurched away, still clutching the bottle. Concern was etched on every face.

"Fucking hell," I heard Collins say. "He's totally out of control."

Somehow, staggering back through the dining-room, I managed to knock half the buffet onto the carpet, then I like crashed into the French windows and finally fell against one of the trees, naked to the waist, bawling Blondie "*Oh, uh-huh make it magnificent, tonight, oh your hair is beautiful, ah, tonight, atomic…*"

Atomic! I am atomic. "Oh, this tree is beautiful, oh tonight," I sang, "I love it."

"Jesus," said Chris, "He's totally fucked. There's no way he's getting home tonight."

"I love you," I murmured to the tree. "Can I shag you? I got protection..."

"He'll have to stay, Chris." Michael was pleading. "He can sleep in *my* bed. He'll be okay. He just needs to sleep."

"Mikey," I murmured, surfacing from my tree to loop my arm round his neck. "I love you, man. You know I love you, don't you?" I kissed him on the cheek. "You're my bestest friend in the whole world."

Then I saw Claire, sitting with Sukie or whatever her name was. She was crying. I could see her shoulders shaking. Swigging more wine, I lurched across the lawn.

"Hey!" I shouted, "Let's dance. I love ABBA. *'Voulez-vous, take it now or leave it, now is all we get, nothing promised, no regrets, Voulez-vous?'* Vous? Voooouuussss?"

I swayed heavily. For some reason my feet were like rooted in the grass, you know? Like I'd literally become this tree? I swayed heavily, then collapsed at her sick-stained feet.

"You're so fucking pretty, Claire," I said. "Will you marry me?"

"Fuck off, Jonathan," she said angrily. "I don't even want to see you right now. I can't believe you're so drunk. I can't believe you just did that. Sixty pounds!"

"Sorry," I slurred, taking another draught from the almost-empty bottle. "Fuck it. Is there any more? It's really good." I smacked my lips.

"Please don't drink any more," she said quietly. "Jonathan. Please just stop."

Suddenly I slumped against her breast and uttered some long, desperate moan.

"I'm *sooo* unhappy," I wailed. "I don't know who I am. I never had a proper childhood, you know? All I ever seemed to do is play the piano and read books. I don't know who I am." I started crying. "Claire, help me. You gotta help me. I'm so unhappy."

Cradling me against her chest, she rocked me gently whilst I sobbed

"I hate my life!" I cried, draining the last of the wine and tossing the bottle into the hedge. "I hate my life so much! My life is so shit." My head was pounding and I felt really sick again. I choked back more vomit then started hiccupping. A circle of steel was squeezing my temples. My vision was so blurred I could hardly see. My guts heaved.

"I'm gonna puke," I groaned.

Claire held me while I sicked up again, spattering my bare chest and the grass with pork pie, pizza and plum wine. Then I started shivering.

I don't remember the next hour or so. It was and still is totally lost to my memory. I guess I carried on talking. I later found a load of scrapes and grazes on my arms and chest - Gray told me I fell into the hedge - but suddenly Chris was there, with Michael and Andy.

"Come on, Jonathan," said Andy. "We're gonna get you to bed."

I protested I was having a good time but I was weak as a new-born kitten so they were able to manhandle me upstairs without much difficulty. Truth was, I was half-asleep anyway. Bundling me into this like purple room, they dropped me like a sack of cabbages onto a bed. Andy levered off my trainers whilst Chris forced some water down my throat. Someone, Michael I think, removed my jeans and socks. Then Chris lay me in a recovery position and covered me with a duvet. I started mumbling "Sorry I ruined your party, Mikey" as my eyelids drooped like someone had attached lead-weights to the lashes.

At some point, his parents returned. I heard Chris explaining to Dr Crooks that I'd had a few too many. Dr Crooks said he would call my parents and tell them I'd be staying over. Then I heard Mrs Crooks shriek "Oh God, someone's been sick in the bidet!"

Why is it always the mothers who don't understand?

When I woke, my head felt as though it were being hammered by a giant with a granite mallet. I could barely see, and I felt like *really* sick. My mouth was so dry I thought it'd been filled with sand. My tongue felt like a rubber shoe-sole and there was this awful, sickly, soapy taste coating the back of my throat. My skin was covered with this light film of sweat. Michael, asleep on the carpet, was curled into a sleeping-bag, a bare freckled shoulder and arm draped outside. I lay still. I was only wearing this peach-coloured slip. Bollocks. Where the hell were my clothes?

Groaning feebly, I rubbed my temples then my eyes, wincing as pain shot through my skull. The early-morning sunlight filtering through the thin purple curtains hurt too, but then *everything* hurt. My shoulder, where I had crashed into the French-windows, was sore. My stomach ached from the constant puking. My knee was grazed from where I had fallen over. I couldn't figure out why I'd like gone so utterly mental. Then I gazed at Michael's naked shoulder and arm, and understood. I had kissed him, and it'd been absolutely amazing.

But *you're* not gay, I told myself. You have Claire.

But, my other brain said, you'd rather kiss Michael than Claire. Come on. Be honest. You'd rather kiss Michael Crooks. If you could get out of bed, you'd crawl across that carpet, across broken glass, to kiss that shoulder, that *naked* shoulder, wouldn't you?

But I'm not like that.

Am I?

You don't really like girls, said a small voice. You only say you do because it's what they *expect* you to say, but you don't really. You remember when you shared that cubicle at the swimming-baths with Tim you were absolutely *desperate* to see what was under his towel? You remember your fascination with his body? You remember how desperately you wanted to see *it*, to *touch* it, to *suck* it on sleepovers and never did? And now Mikey, with the rusty copper hair and the big green eyes and the freckly face. You kissed him, and you went to Heaven. If you'd kissed Claire, do you think you would have felt the same thrill?

But I was going to do it with Claire tonight.

No, you weren't.

You'll never do it with a woman.

Ever.

You'd rather do it with Michael. Or Tim.

Groaning again, I told myself to shut the fuck up.

You're drunk, I said. You're thinking shit. Jonathan Peters is not a bender.

So why did he love kissing Michael so much?

Clambering off the bed, I staggered to the bathroom in my pants, had a piss then studied myself in the wall-cabinet mirror. I looked like Death, you know? My skin was this kind of greeny-grey colour and I had so many lines I looked about a hundred and ten. My face was this like pickled walnut. Yellow sick-dribble was crusted on my chin. My eyes were massive black-holes in a paper-bag, the flesh around them puffily swollen. I splashed cold water over myself then, trying not to lurch into anything breakable, returned to the bedroom where Michael was sitting up and blinking. I could see his ribs, ridged in his scrawny chest. His nipples were small but very dark. Despite my hangover, I found him really attractive.

"Morning," he yawned. "Man, I feel rough, but you must feel like shit. What the hell were you drinking?"

"My mouth tastes like the bottom of a bird-cage." I slumped tiredly onto the bed. "As for what I drank, two litres of cider, about a half-bottle of vodka and a whole bottle of plum-wine. I think there was some more vodka. I can't remember." I groaned loudly. "I think I smoked something. My chest hurts."

"Cannabis," he said, "And a couple of Marlboros."

"Oh fuck."

"I'm slightly surprised you're still alive," he said mildly. "We had to put you to bed, me, Andy and Chris. Mark took Claire home."

"I bet he did," I said. 'I'll be a laughing-stock at school. I'll never recover from this."

Blinking, he shook his head. His eyelashes were long and the colour of sand.

"What happens at the party stays at the party," he said. "Code of honour and that."

"Your parents must think I'm terrible," I said.

"It's nothing they haven't seen before," he said. "Chris had his moments. He was once so drunk Dad had to carry him upstairs and put him to bed."

"I'm sorry, Mikey. I wrecked your birthday."

"Don't be stupid," he replied. "It was a great party. Absolutely awesome."

We lapsed into silence whilst I tried to gather my scattered, pounding thoughts. I had to ask him, *had* to.

"You know when I kissed you? How did you feel?"

He grinned. "You mean was it a good kiss? Jonny, it was the best kiss I ever had. You're a really good kisser." He grinned again. "Even better than my girlfriend."

My heart almost stopped. "You have a girlfriend?" It came out as a moan.

"Katie. She's away with her parents in Spain."

Now I really *was* confused. Mikey was straight. So I *couldn't* fancy him.

"It's not what I mean." I frowned with the effort of articulation. "I mean, did you... were you... turned on by it?"

"A little, I guess," he admitted slowly. "Were you?"

"No," I lied defensively and hating myself for lying, especially since he had told the truth. "Well, maybe a little. But not really."

I could see in his face that he knew I was lying.

"But I liked it," I said hurriedly. "I liked it a lot."

"Me too," he said. There was a pause. He raised his eyes to my face. "Do you want to kiss me again, Jonny? Right now? I won't tell anyone."

"My mouth tastes like bird-shit," I pointed out.

He smiled lazily. "Go clean your teeth. Use my brush. It's the purple one. Get a drink of milk. I'll wait."

Saying milk made me spew, I skipped back to that bathroom. Michael wanted me. Beautiful Michael. I cleaned my teeth thoroughly with his toothbrush, found some mouthwash, splashed my face and chest with soap and hot water, and, with rising, swelling excitement, returned to his bedroom. Michael was going to snog me, and maybe more. Maybe he would actually hug me, you know? Maybe even let me *touch* him...

"Morning, Jonathan," said Dr Crooks. "How do you feel?" Wrapped in an expensive-looking gold-and-green dressing-gown, he was leaning against the edge of Michael's desk. Michael, looking at me, shrugged mildly.

"Terrible," I said, adding crushing disappointment to my hangover. "Like a herd of hippos are jiving in my skull."

Dr Crooks held out my black shirt.

"I imagine this is yours," he said. "I found it in my Yorkshire Glories this morning."

I clasped it to my bare chest. "I'm so sorry." I was really ashamed. Not only had I stolen his wine, I'd puked over his garden and was now trying to seduce his son.

"Not to worry. These things happen. Get dressed and I'll run you home."

"Another time," Michael said evenly, scrambling in his boxers from the sleeping bag.

I wanted to cry. I'd been *sooo* close. I'd nearly had him. It wasn't fucking fair.

Dr Crooks, as he drove me home, misread the strain in my face for he told me he would explain what happened to my parents, but of course it wasn't that. It was what I'd learned about myself. I was more attracted to boys than girls, more attracted to Michael than to Claire, and it ripped me in two. I knew, just *knew* I was gay and I just wanted to die 'cos basically being gay meant the end of my life.

8: War Baby

UNDERSTANDING what had happened over the last few weeks struck me with the force of a ten-ton truck. I knew why I'd not been able to tear myself away, why I felt like so empty when he'd gone – I was in love with him. My chest prickled at the thought.

I had wanted him to hold me in his arms. I had wanted him to kiss me.

To kiss me.

Oh God.

To kiss me.

With his tongue.

Like Claire had kissed me.

And when he hadn't, I'd been so disappointed and that's why I'd felt like crying.

But it was worse.

I wanted to touch his cock. I wanted to *kiss* his cock, to… oh no, no, NO!

And what if he put it *inside* me? You know? Like in my arse? You know?

If he wanted to, he could. He could do *anything* he wanted, *anything*, 'cos I loved him so much… and I would have *him* in me, becoming part of me, *inside* me… oh God… yes.

Wilson and Gray said Ali was 'queer'. My *Concise Oxford Dictionary*, the blue hardback where I'd written my name and form in spidery blue-black writing down the closed pages, *J. Peters 2W*, said on page 1007 *that* meant 'strange, odd, eccentric; of questionable character, shady, suspect.' Well, Ali wasn't any of those. He was perfectly normal. Like me. We even liked the same things. Then I'd seen the **H** word. *You* know the one. It's on page 583. 'HOMOSEXUAL: a. & n. Having a sexual propensity for persons of one's own sex.' What the *fuck* was 'propensity'? I looked up 'GAY' on page 507 and learned it meant, along with 'light-hearted, sportive, airy, offhand,' that it also meant 'dissolute, immoral, living by prostitution.' Well, fuck me, but I wasn't any of those either. This was the Oxford dictionary edited by Fowler and Fowler. I mean, this stuff wasn't anything I understood. What was 'propensity' again? My parents' Collins dictionary told me (page 620) 'sexually attracted.'

I stared, transfixed, at the words on the page.

Sexually attracted.

Meaning you wanted to have sex with them.

Was that I wanted? What *he* wanted? Sex? His cock up my arse, right? 'Cos that was sex, right? Cocks going *in* places. But I didn't have a vagina… so…

No fucking way. I'd flambé and eat my own tonsils with tomato sauce and a nice Beaujolly before I'd let someone bum *me*.

Anyway, it was all, like, total bullshit, yeah? Like I said before, neither of us were 'homosexuals.' Homosexuals I had seen on television. They minced. They had limp wrists, camp voices, effeminate gestures and said 'Have a gay day', 'I'm free', and 'Shut that door.' They wore their mother's dresses and carried handbags. Surely Ali didn't do that. I certainly didn't. Tim Wilson was talking bollocks. Ali wasn't homosexual, and neither was I. I liked sport, for God's sake. Also I wasn't a man yet? I was, like, still a boy. Boys *couldn't* be homosexual. There were laws against that kind of thing. I snuffled into my thick white duvet and switched off the bedside light.

I spent Sunday catching up with the chores I hadn't done on Saturday, like mopping the bathroom floor and washing the car then, pushing my feet into green Dunlop wellies, I followed Dad into the garden where the leaves were turning a buttery yellow. Dad wanted me to hold these four-foot overlapping panels so he could like pin them to the posts but, whilst Gruntpa could literally construct a potting-shed from lollipop-sticks in under an hour *and* creosote it beautifully, without smears, runs, faint patches or leaving bristles from the brush behind, Dad was the least handy handyman in the whole universe. Most of his DIY projects wound up recycled as something radically different from their original purpose. For instance, this bookcase he'd tried to build me became some sort of cold-frame whilst a tiled splash-back over the cooker transmuted into some kind of weird Romanesque mosaic and there were like these strange hand-prints all over the living-room window-sill where he'd painted it? Without his six-inch nails and a hot-glue gun, he would've been lost. As it was, I suspected that without my assistance, he might kind of staple his cardy to the fence-panel? Anyway, the less said about the time he'd change a washer under the sink and flooded the kitchen the better, and when he'd got stuck in the Venetian blinds, Mum and I still got the shudders. Do-It-Yourself? More like Bodge-It-Yourself, we said. Dad claimed his spirit-level 'ran off' at strange angles.

"Did you get these from B & Q?" I asked. AKA Bodge-It-Quickly.

"Wickes, I think," he grunted, firing a nail into the earth and narrowly missing his shoe. "Bugger. I forgot that was loaded."

Of course, as Mum'd pointed out, he wouldn't have to replace the panel at all if I hadn't like kicked the last one to bits by booting my football against it and then scrambling through the holes to retrieve said ball from next door's rockery when it went sailing over. Still, it was better than being in church with Mum, Tim Wilson and that cloth-head Hilly waving my arms in the air to the tambourine-and-maraca version of 'Jesus is my Superhero.' Nonetheless, I remained preoccupied. About The Gay Thing. I did not want to be gay. It was just too hard.

I had, after that party, when I first thought I might be, gone back to the sex ed. notes from school. Not surprisingly, they were shit. Officially, our sex education had been with Mr Chapman, last year's Biology teacher, and set firmly within the context of heterosexual reproduction. My Bio book defined Reproduction, as 'an increase in numbers of one species and of individuals' and classified into sexual and asexual. Since we'd done it at the end of last year, most of us were like fifteen already and masturbating for England. Perhaps Chappers figured there was little to teach us. Anyway, in my angularly rounded blue-black handwriting:

'Sexual Reproduction
This must involve two phases.
a) Reduction divisions (meiosis) to form half cells or gametes
b) Fusion of gametes to form a zygote.
Formation of Gametes
Male
Male gametes or spermatozoa are formed by meiotic divisions of the germinal epithelium lining the seminiferous tubules of the testes. The testes are located in the scrotal sacks-sacs which are extensions of the abdominal cavity.'

So far so unsexy, right? Even the drawing of the male reproductive system I'd done, in coloured pencils and labelled 'prostate gland,' 'sperm duct,' 'penis' etc., was like drily medical. Curiously, we hadn't done a drawing of the *female* reproductive system. Didn't need to. Too racy, yeah? Anyway, Chappers clearly felt the woman was merely a baby-incubator and the less we knew about 'women's issues', as he termed them, the better.

'The spermatozoa are carried passively in the fluid towards the collecting duct or epididymis. They are stored here before being removed via the vas deferens.' Crikey. It wasn't going to give us a stiffy, was it? Maybe that's why he didn't get us to draw vaginas.

The next paragraph in my notebook described what happened 'meanwhile back in the ovary' when the male gamete and female gamete fused into a zygote. There was no mention of how the one actually reached the other. The words 'erection,' 'penetration' and 'ejaculation' were utterly absent. As indeed was any mention of homosexuality. *This* came in the other strand of official sex education, in Lower Fifth RE with Wingnut and in the context of healthy, i.e. heterosexual relationships leading to marriage and the shared blessing of children, because sex was a supremely special expression of romantic love and otherwise was just selfish and evil, like masturbation and oral sex, because you only thought about your own pleasure and sex outside a loving marriage would lead only to disease, loneliness and despair because it was not fulfilling. Homosexuals (cue embarrassed sniggering) were the worst of all because sex was for the procreation of children, and they couldn't. Which was why they were so bitterly angry. They couldn't love. Instead they *groped* children in public toilets and cut off their cocks for revenge and that's why you should NEVER go in one, boys, 'cos they're full of queers who cut off your cock with a breadknife. Anyway, all queers die of AIDS, which you get for defying God and nature and it serves them damned right for being perverts.

"I once saw someone who knew someone who met a fairy," said Wingnut. "He shot his mother then put on her knickers and bra and hanged himself. That's what it's like, boys. Absolute misery." So my school's advice to gay kids was a very simple 'don't be.'

Someone, smirking Seymour, I think, asked about anal sex. Wingnut, scraping his throat in embarrassment, just said "We don't recommend that, boys." And we all laughed, saying how would he know? And could you imagine how much a right bumming would hurt? Getting it up the arse, you know? But maybe it wouldn't... it would depend who was doing it...

I considered talking to Mum. We'd always been close. But then I recalled a recent news item about a gay-bashing downtown. She'd grunted 'serves them right'. Yikes.

Maybe Dad?

No way. He'd simply shift awkwardly, clear his throat, gaze uncomfortably at his slippers and suggest I talk to my mother.

Talking to a teacher was like *totally AND insanely* out of the question. I squirmed with embarrassment at the very idea. Bunny already thought me a turnip-brained twat. If he thought I was a poofter as well... God Almighty... but there was always Wheezy Wally.

I had this real bond with the Chaplain. Exceptionally scary, Reverend Crawford could walk into a roomful of 200 yelling boys and have instant silence just by standing in the doorway. He was ancient, I mean like *super*-ancient. He'd fought in WW2 with some kick-ass regiment like the Paratroopers or the Commandoes or someone and had, like 'Union Jack' Jackson in *Warlord*, literally killed Japs with his bare hands. He'd even won the Military Cross, you know? He had this fine, silver-white hair and spoke in this soft wheeze 'cos he'd taken a slug in the lung somewhere in Burma, hence his nickname Wheezy Wally, but he had degrees from Oxford *and* Cambridge and a doctorate in Divinity from Durham. An exceptional Bible scholar, he had taken me under his wing in those dark, early days.

I got into this fight when 'Blubber-Belly' Brudenall and 'Spud-Face' Seymour called me a 'jumped-up back-street brat' who did not belong at their school. Along with a full scholarship, you see, I got these free school dinners and uniform vouchers, pink papers Mum exchanged in the school shop for two rugby shirts, one green, one white, a green PE vest, white shorts, navy shorts, green socks, blazer, grey trousers, grey sweater and school tie, all plastic-wrapped and brand-new. Mrs Locke, the school secretary, told Mum I'd be fine.

"I've seen his scores on the entrance exam," she'd confided, "*And* I typed the recommendation for the Governors. They love him, Mrs Peters. They love him."

"You fucking leech," Seymour had said. "My Dad pays for you, you fucking leech."

"This is why the school's going to the dogs," Brudenall had sneered, "Letting in charity cases like you."

"And why are you so thin?" Seymour had demanded. "You look like you live in Belsen." Hence the nickname. "What the hell does your mother feed you? Kitchen-scraps?"

"Gruel," Brudenall had suggested. "It's what they eat in the work-houses, unless it's the shit they like scrape off other people's shoes."

I punched him in the face several times, chipping a tooth and bloodying his nose. According to Gray, I went 'absolutely mental'. Crawford was the one who broke it up.

"You're for it now, Belsen Boy," Seymour had hissed. "Nice knowing you. Give our regards to the slums, haw haw."

Sitting me down in his office, Crawford had listened while I poured out my unhappiness, that maybe I *should* leave 'cos I *didn't* fit in, my father being a bus-driver and Seymour's being a bank-manager, that I didn't understand *anything*, and the school was so big and there were so many rules and standing up when the masters came in and Latin grace at lunch and the Latin school-song and *invenire et intelligite* and serve the Sixth Form first and pass the gravy to the *left*, not the right, you ignorant gimp…

He'd steepled his fingers and said "Jonathan," (the first person to use my Christian name), "*You* are here because you passed an exam and an interview and won a scholarship. *They* are here because their fathers have money. Who do *you* think deserves to be here most? The rich and stupid or the clever and talented?" He'd smiled kindly. "Do you remember your interview? I asked where you would go if you had a time-machine."

"And I said Shakespeare's Globe for the world première of *Hamlet*." I couldn't help smiling too. "Sir, you must've thought me so precocious."

"You said your hobby was writing stories," said Crawford, "And you loved cricket but didn't know how to join a club because your parents didn't have the right connections. Jonathan, this school was *founded* for boys like you, with great talent but no opportunities. This school exists to give you those opportunities."

"But it's so confusing," I'd said, "And everyone's so horrible to me."

"They're young," said Crawford, "They're tribal and they fear the outsider. You are new. You're unknown. You've shaken their world. For example, Andrew Paulus and Robin Keighley were the best musicians. You are better than both of them. Adam Austen was the best actor. You are better than *him*, even though his father's the Playhouse director. You are a threat to them and their tribe but just be true to yourself and in time they'll accept you."

And most of them did. So Wheezy was on my side, always had been. He was sympathetic, a good listener, and had been through a War. But he was so *old*. He probably hadn't had sex *since* the War. Same with Frank Gallagher. Like him though I did, I didn't really want my private stuff on a school file. Besides, I reckoned the school would tell my Mum, and my life would be like totally over.

Thing is, I didn't *know* anyone gay. I mean, we all joked about Poorly Paulus getting bummed by Fred Perry, but I didn't really know what it meant, and I really liked Paulus. We'd been friends for years. When I was thirteen I'd melted when he played this Bach Sarabande in the house music competition, just him hugging his 'cello, so beautiful, so limpid, and then he'd sung Purcell's 'I attempt from love's sickness to fly' so meltingly it sent this tingle down my spine. With his soft blond curls and triangular face, he looked like an angel. I guess I kind of fancied him a bit but I didn't want *him* to know in case he tried to bum me in the showers.

After that party, I'd cycled down the city centre to find a book, either in the Central Library or in Waterstone's. I found nothing, no novels, no advice for teenagers, nothing. There were no books for or even *about* gay teenagers. The *X-Y Toolkit for Boys* had three pages on homosexuality from one hundred and forty-one. Dealing with 'coming out' *as* gay rather than finding out if you *are* gay, it implied being homosexual was so disappointing for everyone that you just shouldn't bother. Another (American) book, aimed at parents, also had three pages (out of 158!) which said, in summary, 'just hope your kid grows out of it. It's way too difficult for them. Everyone hates them, they have miserable lives and end up in therapy, with AIDS or killing themselves.' There was more on drugs and body-piercing than on understanding your emotions. Same with *Newsbeat*'s guide to growing up. It was like these writers didn't *want* to deal with the topic or, more sinisterly, didn't want their teenage readers to know about it. I decided the latter. They didn't want us to know about 'it'. Better for all concerned if you just grow out of it, eh? But what if you didn't? Surely there must be someone who wrote about people like us, who published information *for* people like us.

I was wrong. Gay Men's Press had closed down and Waterstone's had scrapped their Gay and Lesbian section altogether.

There weren't even any gay characters for us to identify with, not in any teenage book *I* ever read. Why the hell wasn't there something for *us*? Today. All we had was *Maurice*, *Brideshead Revisited* and *Dorian* Bloody *Gray*. It'd be nice to have something like not set in Oxbridge in the 19-bloody-20s. The Teens section was even worse, crammed with shit about vampires, zombies and X-Men. Yes, I so *got* the metaphor of the outsider? It was *sooo* bloody obvious, you know? But I didn't want metaphors. I wanted books about *me*, not the Walking fucking Dead. I wasn't Walking fucking Dead. I was alive with my difference, so why were there no books about kids like me?

Anyway, in the end and in despair I bought *Biggles and the Plot that Failed*, in which Biggles flew off to the Sahara to rescue an archaeologist and find a Pharaoh's tomb, and *Doctor Who and the Abominable Snowmen*, in which the Doctor and Jamie visit a Buddhist monastery in the Himalayas and battle with fur-covered robot Yeti, and cycled home.

I wondered if I could talk to Michael Crooks. He was kind and generous and we'd shared several intimate moments. But I was terrified he might tell someone else, like Gray or Collins, and I would literally *die* if my best friends found out. Tim, obviously, was a total no-go. Maybe Ali himself? If I worded it properly, perhaps drop a heavy hint or two, he might grasp that it was me. Unfortunately, when I phoned him, the actual conversation went:

"Ali, can I talk to you about something?"

"Course you can. Ask me anything. Is it about the play?"

"I have this friend who thinks he might be... well... you know... possibly... be, well..." My voice vanished into a squeak and my face sizzled like bacon on a grill. "Gay?"

"Oh," said Ali, "Andy Paulus. Anyone can tell he's a bender. Just look at him."

"Yes." I snatched that life-line. "Paulus. Right fucking bender. Anyway, he doesn't know what to do. He thinks he's in love with this Sixth Former... says he can't stop thinking about him. He thinks he's in love."

"Bah," snorted Alistair. "Age-difference is a killer. No-one would allow it. They'd send him to jail, Jonny. Paedos and all that shit? Fuck's sake. You know how hard it is? Being different, I mean? Everyone's against you, and I mean *everyone*."

Yes, I kind of gathered that.

"But should he tell this guy how he feels?" I persisted. Then, taking a chance, added "What would *you* do, Ali? If it were you."

"Keep my bloody mouth shut. Unless he's got a death-wish. Anyway, how's the *Berceuse* coming on?"

In the middle of the night, I woke, sticky, wet and distraught from another sex-dream.

I'd been lying in bed when Paulus came in. He was wearing a white, buttonless, short-sleeved shirt and white Bermuda shorts and was carrying a violin. He sat on the edge of my bed and played Paganini, resting his right ankle on his left knee. I noticed his legs were completely hairless. Reaching out a hand, I stroked his thigh then hugged him, and we kissed as his fingers curled round my cock. His clothes were on the floor and the room was a mess. He licked my cock-tip then slid it between his lips... I woke up spurting.

Sweat dampened my hair and my shorts stuck stickily to my skin. Stiffly I swung my legs from under the white sheet, peeled off the clammily clinging T-shirt then the sperm-soaked shorts and sat in the dark listening to the rain pattering gently against the window-pane. I parted the yellow curtains slightly to see what was happening out in the back garden but everything was still, calm and black and the house behind ours was obscured by a row of thick-trunked elm trees. Everyone was asleep, except the guilty, and I was so bloody guilty. I had wet-dreamed about another boy. Again. Talk about shame. I mean, just fucking shoot me.

The bedside clock told me it was 4.05. When I was younger, I'd found sleeping difficult, especially after a really boring day. My brain never seemed to stop buzzing, and when it wasn't communicating, it was racing away in like hyperdrive, you know? I tended to switch lines of thought, heading off on tangents without proper development. People said my writing was like that. In fact that everything was like that. Creative thinker but not a finisher, a butterfly mind with the attention span of a gnat, Mr Hutchinson had once said. I suppose I get quickly bored with the same-old, same-old. Anyway, now my sleep-patterns were becoming increasingly disrupted by dreams I didn't like, because I'd dreamed about Paulus like tons of times. That's what worried me. Once I'd dreamed that I was shut in an understairs cupboard, gasping with asthma and shouting for help, although my voice wouldn't work. Paulus, in a navy blue sailor suit, had like opened the door, burrowed in beside me, whispered 'shush' and kissed my mouth. I cried after that dream.

Most dreams repaid analysis. They came, I'd read, from your subconscious, about subjects, issues or people in your thoughts or heart. I'd also heard that dreams were a form of wish-fulfilment or a reflection of your fears. Obviously my dream about Paulus was the latter. Obviously. 'Cos he like fancied me and was a poof, and I wasn't, you know?

I wondered if I should write something on dreams for the school magazine, establish myself as an agony-uncle perhaps. After all, I couldn't do worse than the numpties on the radio. They reflected a *very* narrow understanding of humanity. I'd read a letter recently in my mum's *Woman's Weekly,* which, I would point out, I read *only* for Russell Grant's predictions for Gemini's week ahead, hoping I was going to win the lottery and/or meet a tall, dark, sexy lady, but I never managed either. Anyway, the letter basically said "Help, I think my son's a homosexual, what shall I do?" Part of me scoffed dismissively at the unlucky sap and part of me read the reply with a mix of dread, delight, shame, fear and excitement.

"Discovering you're gay can be both frightening and confusing," said the agony-aunt, "And can bring feelings of loneliness, isolation and shame. Many teenagers fear rejection or even punishment, so it's very important that parents provide support, not judgement. Gay children need to feel secure, to know they are still loved despite being different."

Good luck with that, I'd snorted, turning instead to the England football captain's reflections in on yet another early exit from the European Championship in the latest *Shoot!* I reckoned we were bloody lucky to have qualified, given the total bollocks England pretended was football. Boot the ball very hard and run like fuck seemed the tactic. Anyway, that was *before* the dream. And *before* I kissed Michael Crooks.

Miserably I sat on my bed cuddling Pickles, watching the rain in the darkness outside, and croakily singing my new favourite song several times, 'Waterfalls' from Paul's *McCartney II* album I'd got for my birthday: '*And I need love, yeah, I need love, Like a second needs an hour, like a raindrop needs a shower, Yeah, I need love every minute of the day, And it wouldn't be the same if you ever should decide to go away.*'

Drained, I touched the crucifix on its thin gold chain and resolved to put this sickness behind me by avoiding everyone on Monday I'd had sexy dreams about, so I gave Choral Society a miss. They were only doing some chorales, Number 9, 'Thy will, o God, be always done,' Number 20, 'Peter, with his faithless lies, thrice denied the Saviour' and Number 21, which opens Part 2, 'Christ, whose life was as the light, by his friends forsaken,' which were really easy. I also skipped the play rehearsals 'cos I didn't think I could look at Ali, or Leo, or Andy, without like totally burning up with embarrassment, you know? So I marvelled at the Canadian Grand Prix with Maxton and Fosbrook - there'd been this utterly spectacular 7-car pile-up on the first bend of the first lap when Jones and Piquet touched wheels – immersed myself in clarinet practice with Mr Angus, mainly scales and the Lutoslawski, and played *Across Suez*, the Battle of Chinese Farm from the 1973 Arab-Israeli War at Wargames Club with Adam Rubenstein from U5B, my violinist friend with the straight jet-black hair, warm brown eyes, sallow skin and beaky nose, as short as me but stockier. I was the Egyptians trying to cross the Suez Canal and retake the Sinai Peninsula from Adam, playing as the Israelis. I kind of joked that, being Jewish, he should switch and play as the Arabs, just to get a different perspective. He didn't laugh, just loosened his yellow Brearley tie, bombed my amphibious vehicles to bits and whipped my arse back to the desert. Anyway, I kind of got through the next few days unscathed and on Friday, joined a bunch of others flopping around in the park.

While Lower Schoolers weren't allowed out of the school during lunch, we Upper Fifths could go to the park across the road and the parade of shops housing Sweaty Betty's chip shop, and the Sixth, lucky bastards, could go into town so long as they stayed out of the pubs. It was a gorgeous day, sunny, too warm for footie, we just flaked out and watched these scanty white clouds rolling across the high blue sky. Collins was describing this fat lass called Emma who apparently had the hots for him to an appreciative audience of Lewis, Arnold and Brudenall.

Shirt sleeves were rolled up, collars unfastened and tie-knots loosened as I sat cross-legged on the grass watching these Painted Ladies flit round these purple Michaelmas daisies and yellow Rudbekia I thought my dad might have planted.

"She was all over you, man," Lewis was saying, "And she came with that lass Hannah, from the swim-team. God, she was so hammered she could hardly walk."

This was Arnie's birthday party, to which I, not being hearty enough, had not been invited.

"Yeah, but she was a great shag," said Brudenall. "She's just split up with Graeme Vesey. Nothing better than a bird on the rebound. Sucked me dry, man. You should've let Emma jump aboard, Collie. Fat birds go like trains. Image issues or some such bollocks."

"Problem is," Collins mused, "She's so fat you could use her knickers as a hang-glider. She's got a figure like a hippo an' a face like a pickled bloody walnut."

"Plus a fanny like a horse's collar," I chipped in. "Be like fingering a toilet seat."

"Like you'd fucking know, JP," jeered Brudenall. "Bet you've never even *seen* a fanny outside *Razzle*, let alone fingered one."

"Fuck off, Graham," I countered angrily. "I fingered Claire Ashton." There was like this shouted chorus of disbelief. "I fucking have! I fingered her last week, got three right up inside her. Man, she *loved* it. Juice every-fucking-where, man."

"You fingered Claire Ashton?" jeered Lewis. "Where was this?"

"In his head," scoffed Brudenall, "While he was wanking. Right, Peters?"

Cheeks glowing like a workman's brazier, I just tore at some blades of grass while Lewis howled derision and Brudenall licked his fingertip, touched his cheek and went 'Tssss.'

"Emma's mum's all right," Arnold told Collins. "Do her instead."

"Oh aye," said Collins, "But the old man's a nutter. He'd tear my head off and feed it to his dogs. Got these ruddy great Rottweilers to keep the rozzers away from these stolen ciggies he stores in his garage."

"You could do the dogs instead," Arnold suggested. "Put 'em in a good mood."

"*Your* mum's foxy, JP," said Lewis. "I'd like to get my hands on *her* puppies."

"Oh aye," said Collins again. "I'd give *your* mum one any day, Jonny. Great figure for a woman of forty. Tits like fucking grapefruit. Firm but squeezy, eh?"

"Bet she bangs like a door in a storm," added Brudenall. "You'd want her on top, wouldn't you, Andy? Let her ride you like a fucking stallion, eh? Like that girl in the toilet at Cinderella's last week. Woah, she was *bloody* good, though the blowjob was even better."

"Yeah," said Collins dreamily. "I'd love it if your mum blew me, Jonny."

Open-mouthed, I stared at him, at his thick blond hair, blue eyes, arrogantly handsome face with its high, sculpted cheekbones, broad chest and shoulders of a rugby-playing swimmer. God, he wanted my mother to suck his cheesy great knob. My mother! I threw the grass at his head and told him to shut the fuck up.

Collins grunted. "You can do *mine* if you like, if you wanna like do a swap. She's had five kids. Knockers to her knees, man. Like punctured balloons after a fucking party."

I said I'd rather shag the sheep on his farm. He said he guessed that already. The others started baaing in chorus. Jumping on Collins, I wrestled with him on the grass while Lewis chucked torn-up grass blades at us, then Brudenall dived in and we rolled around trying to tickle each other, laughing and calling each other 'sheep-shagger, sheep-shagger' until our sides hurt and the bell rang for afternoon school.

German was in the language-laboratory on the top floor of the New Building. I sat in the front row between Paulus and Gray, headphones round my neck, ready to start.

"A little later we'll listen to this wonderful tape from *Heute Direkt*. It's about sport and leisure, so you'll hear some oom-pah music and plenty of stories about hiking in the mountains." Beaky glanced around uncertainly. "Er, can you switch this infernal machine on, er… Herr Seymour? I can't figure it out." In fact he usually ended up recording his own voice stammering 'how do you turn this thing off?' over some other poor sod's material.

"I am a very keen cyclist, you know, just like Herr Gray, who wrote about it in his essay. Like him, I cycle to school but, unlike him, I must set off very early to be here for half-past eight. I can't oversleep like you boys because I have Upper Six P to register so I wave farewell to Frau Phillips and Fräulein Phillips on the doorstep as the clock strikes eight..."

"Hang on, sir," said Gray. "You live twenty miles away. You'd be pushing it to get here in thirty minutes."

"I once did sixty miles an hour on my rickety old bike when I was living in Switzerland," Beaky said haughtily

"Aye, and uphill too," I added to general laughter.

"I was renowned for my sporting prowess, Herr Peters," he continued, "Especially on skis. Do you know how to get up a mountain on skis, Herr Collins? I'll bet you don't."

"As a matter of fact," said Collins, "I do. You take your skis off and get a cable-car."

I burst out laughing.

"You do no such thing," said Beaky. "You tie sealskins to the underside so the hair acts as a brake and provides some grip. There. Now you've learned something. There's nothing better than standing atop some lofty summit with the landscape sprawling before you, the mountain breezes ruffling your hair... have you ever been in the Alps, Herr Lewis?"

"No, sir."

"Crystal waterfalls cascade into deep green pools of icy nectar. Springs bubble forth from rocks. Heedless of Alpine torrents thundering through ice-built arches radiant with the rainbows of Heaven, I strode across the roof of Europe, Richard Strauss's Alpine Symphony ringing in my ears. Do you know Richard Strauss's Alpine Symphony, Herr Brudenall?"

"No, sir."

"I do," I chirped.

"You would, you lick," scowled Herr Brudenall.

"Is there anything you *don't* know?" growled Herr Lewis. I just waved two fingers.

"In my time, I've done the Matterhorn (snigger from Brudenall) and the Jungfrau (snort from Seymour). In fact, I met Frau Phillips whilst she was a Jungfrau, ha ha."

"Did you wear *lederhosen*, sir?" asked Fosbrook cheekily.

"I certainly did. I still have a pair. I may wear them on Open Day."

"I wouldn't wear them *open* on Open Day, sir," said Collins. "You'll get had up."

I burst out laughing again. Beaky peered over the top of his little wire-framed glasses.

"You're in a merry mood, Herr Peters. Perhaps it's because of your little story. I have to say it was exceptionally good. Frau Phillips and I read it together and both agreed it was worth ten out of ten. You should submit it for the school magazine."

Yay! Result. I preened a little as he passed over a bar of Galaxy and flicked two fingers surreptitiously at Brudenall who was mouthing 'lick.' Of course the first square made me sneeze twice – bloody allergies – but then I almost choked when Beaky said he was gonna read it the class and started "Es war der schönste Tag in meinem Leben, dem Tag, als ich fiel verliebt, Hals über Kopf..."

"No, sir," I cried desperately. "Don't. Please." I felt my face burning like coals in a builder's brazier.

He peered at me again, then back at the paper, then back at me. "But why not, Herr Peters? It's an excellent piece of writing."

"Go on, Jonny," said Arnold. "You're a really good writer."

I had in fact won last year's Lower Fifth creative writing prize for my end-of-year exam essay. The task was to write a story either starting or finishing with the lines 'When I looked up, the beach was empty' so I wrote a story about a private detective, you know the sort, a hard-boiled, fast-talking, mac-wearing gumshoe, and crammed in every fishy pun I could think of, from the relatively simple 'Good Cod' to 'you're a dab hand at this' to 'I'm sorry, I'm hard of herring' to 'you should learn your plaice'. When Willie, grading it forty-eight out of fifty, read it to the class, they laughed, clapped and whistled and Burridge surrendered his crown. Now

71

they were expecting more of the same, and they weren't going to get it.

"It's too... personal," I said.

"Well, now you've *got* to read it," said Collins, "If it's about *Claire*."

There was a chorus of 'oooh,' a raucous yelp from that bloody ferret Fosbrook and 'Claire, the moment I met you I swear...' sung by Lewis and Arnold. My ears glowed crimson. I heard Brudenall go 'Tssss' again. Then the rest of the class sizzled and I shrank unhappily into my shoulders, eyes fixed on the grey Formica table-top, while Beaky silently pondered me for a moment. My life would be so like over if he read that story out, yeah?

"If he doesn't want to, he doesn't have to," said Beaky, handing me the paper with the 10 and 'ausgezeichnet, sehr romantisch' scribbled in red. "I'll read Herr Paulus' instead."

"Oh God," cried Arnold. "It'll just be about how many hours of 'cello practice he did."

"You think I'm so one-dimensional, don't you?" said Paulus indignantly. "You'd be surprised. I don't *just* play the 'cello, you know."

"No, you play the piano too," said Arnold.

Just then there was a light knock on the door and Alistair Rose entered.

"Sorry to disturb you, sir, but I'm showing some prospective parents around and I wondered if I could bring them in here."

As I turned in my seat, he flashed this utterly dazzling smile at me. My blood tingled and my heart melted. Again. Paulus, the gay twat, nudged me suggestively.

"Fuck off, you gay twat," I snarled.

"Just a minute, Rose," hissed Beaky. "You lot, put your headphones on and look like you're working." He let flow this stream of guttural German which I could barely follow concluding with "Und so müssen wir etwas machen."

Resting my chin in my palms, I gazed admiringly at Ali while he introduced the parents to Beaky and explained the facilities. God, he had such long, soft eyelashes, you know? He was so handsome. But after class, when I was packing up my books, Beaky took me to the front of the room, waited till everyone had gone then said, very quietly, "I really did enjoy your story, Jonathan, but it isn't true, is it? It *was* just a fantasy?"

"Of course, sir." The edited version had been romantic, not steamy.

"This Alison." He removed his spectacles. "Would it be, by any chance, Alistair Rose?"

I went cold all over. "Of course not. Whatever gave you that idea?"

"The way you looked at him this afternoon."

Something was blocking my throat.

"It is not uncommon for schoolboys to develop crushes on other schoolboys," he continued, "Especially at an all-boys' school. The hothouse atmosphere and so on. Boys are incredibly romantic creatures. You know that yourself. It's fully expressed in your story. Most of these crushes are perfectly harmless, and may involve some degree of fantasy, but some develop *un*healthily, into inappropriately physical relationships. Do you know what I mean?"

"Yes, sir," I muttered. "You mean sex."

"Enjoy being in love with Rose, if you are," He raised a hand to stem my protest, "But be careful. Don't let things get out of control." He replaced his glasses. "I like you, Jonathan. I respect and admire you. I don't want to see your life ruined because you chose poorly."

Yikes. It was so obvious everyone was beginning to see it. What the hell would I do? How could I conceal it, especially when Ali was around? But what if it wasn't? Love, I meant. What if *was* just a schoolboy crush that I would grow out? I mean, what exactly *is* love? How did you know when you found it?

But I already knew. I touched my cross.

Love is thinking about him all the time. Love is struggling to breathe when he is near. Love is when his smile lights up your entire world. Love is the blood singing in your ears when he looks at you. Love is wanting to cry when he says goodbye. Love is the tingle down your spine when he touches your hand. Love is standing at the edge of forever.

God, I thought. I sounded like a soppy adolescent. But then again, I *was* a soppy adolescent and, sorry, Beaky, I *was* in love, absolutely, totally head-over-heels. I wanted to be with him. I wanted to hold him. I wanted his lips against mine. I wanted his chest pressed to mine. I wanted *him*. I wanted him so much. So I guessed that *did* make me gay, and I'd rather like boil and eat my own intestines, you know? With mashed swede and a nice rosé than be gay? I mean, someone might as well shoot me 'cos my life *was* so, like, over, you know? Hmm. Maybe a life as myself, my *true* self, was about to begin.

9: Bad Romance

AT ten on a drizzly, grey Saturday morning at the start of October and dressed in blue Reeboks with orange stripes, blue jeans and this cosy cobalt-blue woollen sweater over my favourite pale blue polo-shirt (with dark blue and red shoulder-stripes) and the blue Adidas baseball cap, I clambered into the back of a white Volvo estate and headed off to support Michael Crooks and Leo Trent in their first cross-country race of the season. Why? Oh, you know. Leo asked me. Mikey asked me. Leo, in a navy tracksuit and blue Barbour, was very excited and, bouncing about enthusiastically, crashed his sports-bag into my side more than once. He kept thanking me for coming but the truth was I wanted to be close to Michael again. Besides *CD Review* was doing Offenbach. Ticket to Snoozeville, right? 'Cept for the Can Can.

I felt tired. When I finally got to sleep, I had this weird dream in which I was sitting on a ledge halfway up a mountain with Nick Shelton. The mountain overlooked an angry sea. We were watching people of all ages trudging up a stony path. Refugees, they were dressed in rags and clutching cheap suitcases and plastic bags. Behind us, towards the summit of the barren grey peak was a white temple with friezes of scenes from ancient times carved in its walls. The friezes showed farmers driving cattle through water-logged fields. As we watched, the waves rose, raging more furiously under the leaden sky whilst the line of people oozed closer. Shelton was wearing this dark blue T-shirt and white shorts. His bare knees were drawn up to his chest, his bare feet rested on cinders. We were holding hands. Suddenly the sea swelled massively into one gigantic wall and lashed at the people on the path, like a tiger's claw at a mouse. Most of them were swallowed up in the grey-white water. Shelton leaned over and kissed me on the lips. Then we stood up, brushed ash and cinders from our clothes and, still hand-in-hand, walked to the temple. A bell began tolling. My alarm clock. What the hell? Maybe I shouldn't sleep under a poster of lava-spilling volcanoes. But at least I was dry. Painfully hard, but dry, so I spat into my hand and tossed off in under a minute, my body shuddering from top to toe as I squirted into a tissue which I flushed down the bog. But Nick Shelton? He was in 4D. That wasn't good. But he was *sooo* hot...

The match was a triangular against two other schools in some God-forsaken hole in Fuck-knows, Bollock-dale. Leo claimed the course had a near-vertical hill, a stream and a great deal of thick, dense woodland. Perfect for running, he reckoned, smacking his palms together with questionable relish. Now, probably like you, I've never understood why seemingly sane people volunteer to slog through six miles of mud, water and thorn-bushes. Seems the very definition of lunacy to me. And you, I guess.

When we arrived at school, Oggie Ogden, the bulbously nosed, curly-haired master-in-charge, promptly commandeered Mr Trent's Volvo as a 'support-vehicle' for the minibus so I found myself crushed with the rear-door handle jammed into my kidneys as Philip Brudenall and a Sixth Former called Hood piled in the back with captain Gary Dunn in the front. Leo was virtually sitting in my lap. Looping his left arm round my shoulders, he smiled happily and said "This is cosy."

"Loverly," I grunted. "Keep still, for God's sake. You weigh a hell of a lot more than you look. You're crushing my knees."

"Just hope he farts on your bollocks," chirruped Brudenall, who was also squashed against me, thigh to thigh. "Get your cheapies free."

Leo, blushing, giggled like a May Queen. My heart jolted. He was really pretty when he blushed. But what the fuck did Broody Minor mean?

"*There was a young fellow called Smalls,*" he squeaked, "*Who performed magic tricks with his balls...*"

"Are you running too, JP?" asked Hood.

"No chance," I said, glad of the distraction. "What do you take me for?"

"A sadist?" Brudenall suggested.

Leo, giggling again, whispered something about boys' legs which made them *both* giggle and me redden like a robin 'cos Broody Minor had gorgeous legs. It was a bloody long journey, especially when Leo and Broody started describing last night's *Terry and June*, in which June got a job and accidentally poured hot tea over Terry's bollocks. Leo did these wicked impressions of Terry Scott going "*Oh Juuuune*," and ignoring my attempts to shift the focus to a really good *Starsky and Hutch* (some woman had blasted from Starsky's past to kill him) or how the French had snatched *Knockout* from the Yugoslavs on the last game after the Yugoslavs fell into the pool - "*Oh, Juuuune*," goes Trent again, then, thank God, Brudenall chirruped "*There was an old fellow from Harrow, who tried to have sex with a sparrow...*," fished out this Rubik's Cube and started twisting it one way then another whilst the opening movement of Beethoven's Seventh Symphony, this epic, exciting dance, blasted from the CD player. Leo bounced happily on my lap with the last line of the show, "*Juuuune, I'm sitting on my nutcrackers.*" God Almighty. "Piiiip, I'm sitting on *Jonny's* nutcrackers, ha ha ha..."

"*Mary had a little lamb, it had a massive willy...*"

"Bollocks."

Brudenall had dropped the Rubik's Cube and was scrambling round my feet to retrieve it. Somehow his elbow ended up in my face, his hand in my lap. Godder Almightier.

"I like your cap," simpered Leo.

"Didn't we have a loverly time the day we did cross-country?" I sang mentally.

My trusty Timex told me it was nearly eleven. God Almighty. It felt like I'd been here a lifetime. The rolling moors were undulating impressively into the distance, onto the foothills and stark, black crags of Ilkley Moor, the Dales rising majestically beyond. Oh bollocks. This was the Arse-cheek of Fuck-Dale. It reminded me of our Outdoor Centre, some converted, whitewashed farmhouse in Backside, Bollockland where the school scouts went for activity weekends, the Christian Union went for prayer retreats and classes went to 'bond' playing midnight poker in the eight-bed dormitories and hiking over the hills in bracing winter winds. I'd been twice, once in 4M and once with the Christian Union, when sneaking out to the pub was replaced by seemingly endless guitar-strumming and hand-waving over baked beans and bacon delicately charred over a camp-fire. We were due to go again in the new year with Bunny. I couldn't wait.

We crept towards a so-called village, a miserable clump of cottages and farmsteads huddling together for mutual protection under a grim, grit-stone crag. The road, a tortuous, twisting line of grey like a worn-out typewriter-ribbon, wound through a patchwork of fields, the freshly ploughed furrows reminding me of the channels in pieces of corduroy. A clutch of plump black rooks were the only living inhabitants of this landscape, perching cockily on the out-stretched arms of a tatty scarecrow constructed from some rough sticks of wood, a bag of straw and some baggy, faded old clothes. As the Volvo lumbered by, they rose from their slumber, sodden black rags squawking in protest, then settled back in their original positions, spying our progress with beady eyes.

'*Crow laughed* (wrote Ted Hughes)
He bit the Worm, God's only son,
Into two writhing halves...
God went on sleeping.
Crow went on laughing.'

"Oh, Juuuune," said Leo, "*There was a young runner called Rick, who had an enormous...* "

Grumpily, I plugged in my earbuds: 'Didn't we have a lovely time the day we went to Fuck-dale?' On the brow of a hill stood a small, forlornly bedraggled gathering of sick-looking poplar trees, stark, aloof and rigid, guarding the landscape beneath.

Leaving civilisation behind, we jolted painfully up some stone-strewn cart-track through a sparse forest to a tarmacked area just below a wind-swept grassy slope. I could barely feel my legs as the load disgorged from the Volvo, first Hood, then Brudenall, then finally Leo, who like managed to brush his fingers suggestively over my groin. Like, ticket to Yikesville, right?

Crooks, with a green tracksuit top draped round his shoulders, was showing Hugh Stern from U5D these new banana-coloured running-shoes he'd got. His bare, beautifully sculpted legs made my stomach flip over. Again I wondered what might have been if his dad hadn't come in. Nothing, as it transpired. Mikey's news, jabbered into my ear with hot-breathed excitement, was that he had done it at last with Katie, and was consequently a virgin no more.

"Man, it was epic," he whispered, emerald eyes glowing. "We were making out in my room and then she just… well, you know…"

Actually, Michael, I didn't fucking know, thanks for reminding me.

"Twenty minutes, Jonny. Twenty minutes! Oh God… you gotta do it with Claire. You'll love it. It's *sooo* amazing. Sex is the best thing EVER! I mean, like EVER!!!!"

Fucking hell. Mikey was two months younger than me. He'd only just *turned* fifteen, the lucky jammy bastard. Swallowing my searing jealousy, I offered my congratulations.

"One-nil to the Ginger Ninja," grinned Crooks.

Bollocks. Life is *sooo* unfair. I reckoned I was just about the only virgin left in the bloody class apart from saddoes like Fosbrook, who couldn't even get VD off a prozzie, and Huxley, who didn't want it anyway 'cos it would stop him swotting. I mean, I was *such* a loser.

The black clouds obscuring the sky looked very threatening. Mr Trent considered his muddy paintwork ruefully whilst I grumpily volunteered Leo's car-washing skills and eyed the course. It looked the kind some utterly insanely deranged mountaineer might enjoy. Leo touched knuckles with Brudenall, said "*Heghlu'mekh qaq jajvam*," which, apparently, is Klingon for 'Today is a good day to die' and scampered to the minibus. Yikes. At least *they* were still virgins, and, given the Klingon, likely to remain so for a *very* long time.

I was glad not to be running even though I quite liked the inter-house cross-country competition we had to do every February. After two weeks of practice runs, the house-captains would choose the top ten runners for their teams then we'd do another practice run, as a team, before the race itself in the week after half-term. At first, I'd hated pounding grimly past these like moss-shrouded headstones in this creepy Victorian cemetery, trudging through these soggy woods, hurdling this gurgly stream with whippy branches lashing my thighs and arms, mud spattering my legs and face, rain soaking my hair and clothes, sweat stinging my eyes.

I always got this crippling stitch halfway round. Crying off with asthma or some other sick-note only worked for so long. You had to run twice, whatever, even by yourself in April after school. Ultimately there was no escape. Even Fozzie's eczema only worked so long. We joked that even if you only had one leg, they'd expect you to hop round the course. Forget about the end of your crutch sinking into the mud. To add insult to injury, the teachers, snugly wrapped in sheepskin coats and furry hats, huddled together under a selection of massive golf-umbrellas yelling that we all needed good, hard boots up our arses. Anyone caught cheating was sent twice round the pitches and pelted with mud. Character-building, they said. Anyway, it was always freezing and I usually wore black woollen Thinsulate gloves. Twice I'd actually like *walked* the six-mile course with Maxton and Stewart as a kind of protest and finished 202nd out of 224. Result. Got me out of the team and really fucked off Jennings, my idiot Maths teacher and Lower School house-tutor. Anyway, in 4M, Gray, who had to tie his black-framed specs round his head with some twatty piece of elastic to stop 'em falling off, said something like 'you gotta do it, JP, so make the best of it. You'll keep warmer and finish faster and the faster you finish, the sooner you go home.'

Which was true. Once you'd finished and reported your time, you could go home. Boys like Crooks, Hood and Dunn were usually off by three while we were still delicately picking our way across the stream. Me and Maxton weren't getting the bus till like quarter-to-five or something stupid. So I changed my approach and ran with Gray. He made me run through the inevitable stitch, timed my hurdle so I cleared the water, encouraged me to keep going when I collapsed, panting, against a tree, sobbing I couldn't run any more, I could hardly breathe, I'd left my inhaler in the changing room... I came in 51st, my highest placing ever, and won Jacko's approval and Gray's praise. He finished two places ahead of me. Usually he was in the top twenty. I know he got bollocked by Benjy Goddard, his house-tutor, but he didn't care. He'd made me into a runner. I got in the Murray team and finished 47th in the race (7th in the house), impressing myself and delighting Wingnut. Most importantly, I was able to enjoy Maxton and Stewart lumbering home a bazillion hours later and call them losers. Last year, I'd improved to 32nd (5th in Murray), and set myself the target of breaking into the top 30 this year whilst my loser mates blew smoke-rings in the crem.

Whilst the runners loosened up, I chatted with Leo's dad. He'd brought a flask of coffee and several cups, for which I was already grateful. The wind was chilling my fingers. Idly, I twisted Brudenall's Rubik's Cube to line up 3 reds. The Beethoven symphony was in the final frantic *allegro con brio*. I lined up 6 greens. Ha. Piece of piss. I couldn't see why Max thought it so awesome. Then I realised the reds were no longer aligned. Bollocks.

Suddenly Leo, in this gold and navy running-vest and slinky navy blue shorts, trainers dangling from his hand, dashed back to the car wailing that he'd forgotten his socks. Ragging everything from his bag, he said he couldn't run without socks.

"Course you can," his father reassured him.

"I can't! My feet'll blister."

"Oh, for Heaven's sake," I said from the passenger-seat, "You can borrow mine."

His face lit up as I unlaced my trainers and stripped off my socks.

"Thanks so much, Jonny. You're a life-saver," he said breathlessly as he pulled them over his small, pale feet and scampered away.

"They'll come back filthy," remarked Mr Trent.

"Doesn't matter," I shrugged. "They'll wash."

"Still," he said, "It was a kind thing to do." He watched his son warming up with the others, stretching and loosening muscles. "He thinks the world of you, Jonathan, admires you very much. It's a kind of hero-worship, I guess, but you're like his role-model, you know? He wants to be just like you. Actor, musician, cricketer, all those things you excel in. You lending him your socks will be the best thing that's ever happened. Unfortunately he'll talk about it for days." There was genuine affection in his voice. "But you're one of the good guys, Jonny. He could do a lot worse than have you as his role-model."

Yikes. I'd never considered myself a role-model before, you know? I was almost proud, until I remembered the shameful secret buried deep in my soul, the worm of guilt which gnawed at my heart and burrowed into my every waking thought. If you knew, Mr Trent, what I was *really* like, you'd take your pretty little son and run for his life. Embarrassed, I picked up this Spiderman comic and leafed through some confrontation between Spidey and Doc Ock then dug out my Chemistry book. We had this massive fuck-off test coming up, like everything you never wanted to know about lead. Man. Who'd be a schoolboy? It's *sooo* shit. Especially with a Chemistry teacher like Mr Jones, unpredictable and a bit too 'down with the dudes' for someone who resembled Barney Rubble. I mean, come on. We don't even call each *other* 'dudes'. Who the fuck does?

'Lead (Pb)

Occurence   (Bollocks. I'd misspelled it!)

It occurs as 'Galena' (Pb^{2+}S^{2-} - led sulphide). (Oh for God's sake...led?). It is found over most of the earths crust. (Is there an apostrophe here? I wasn't 100% on apostrophes.)

Atomic number is 82. It is a Group IVA element like carbon.

Ion: loses 2 electrons to form Pb^{2+} ion.

The IV oxidation state is also possible i.e. Pb^{4+}O$_2$$^{2-}$.'

What the hell did it mean? I had absolutely no fucking idea, you know?

Anyway

'Physical Properties
Lead is a typical metal; it is very soft and malleable and is a good conductor of heat and electricity.
It gives a blue flame with white streaks in the flame test.
Lead has a bluish-white lustre, but tarnishes quickly.
Lead exposed to moist air tarnishes due to an insoluble white layer of lead hydroxide/lead carbonate mixture forming on the surface...'
There were 14 bloody pages of this stuff, ranging from the formation of lead (II) oxide and the effect of dilute sulphuric and hydrochloric acid (none) to uses
'1. Manufacture of sheets for lead roofing.
2. Manufacture of batteries.
3. Making various alloys e.g. solder and pewter.
4. Lead compounds used to be used in paints but less so now due to the risk of poisoning.'

I wondered if sucking the end of my pencil might poison me. Possibly. Though it wouldn't get me out of the test. Even if my head swelled up like a bloody barrage-balloon.

'Lead (II) nitrate is a soluble; forms an <u>anhydrous</u> white powder. It decrepitates and melts to give yellow lead (II) oxide, nitrogen dioxide and oxygen.
$$2Pb^{2+} (NO_3^-)_2 (s) \rightarrow 2Pb^{2+}O^{2-} (s) + 4NO_2 (g) + O_2 (g)$$
NB This is the best nitrate to use for preparing nitrogen dioxide because there is no water for crystallization.
2. In the test for hydrogen sulphate ide gas, filter paper soaked in lead (II) nitrate solution can be used instead of lead ethanoate solution giving the same black ppt of lead (II) sulphide.'

Mega-yawn-o-bloody-rama! God Almighty. Someone just shoot me. Why hadn't he picked silver? There were only 4 pages on silver. And it was more interesting than bloody lead. I mean, you didn't have a lead jubilee, did you? Or a lead anniversary? You didn't give your bird a lead bracelet for her birthday, did you? The Silver Fox sounded cooler, sexier than the Lead Fox. The FA Cup wasn't made of lead, was it? And him in the Fantastic Four was the Silver Surfer not the Lead Limper. Grinning, I began sketching in the back of my Chemistry book what the Lead Limper might look like in a stand-off with Doctor Octopus and Spiderman. Doc Ock's flailing tentacles reminded me now of the RE project I was supposed to be doing on Hindu Gods. There was this one called Brahma with like four arms and three faces. Bloody hell, he'd be hard to sneak up on, eh? Especially by the Lead Limper who moved at like Nought Miles an Hour 'cos his left leg was like half as long as his right one and he had this really heavy costume and no Super Powers except absorbing X-rays, so he might be all right in The Hulk or against the Silver Fox, who I was gonna do next.
Anyway, I liked projects. They were a chance to spend a month or so with my head buried in a bunch of books then writing a report. The best thing I'd ever done at school was my history project on the Napoleonic Wars for Bush-head Bleakley. I still had it, in two pink folders, 77 pages of foolscap covered in my angularly rounded blue-black script. It was entitled THE REVOLUTIONARY AND NAPOLEONIC WARS and was by Jonathan D. Peters, 4M. It was divided into two sections, the first containing biographies of four significant figures, Napoleon Blownapart (described on page 5 as 'poor, out of favour and often hungry' – in 1795, not when he was Emperor, obviously), Horatio Nelson, Arthur Wellesley and André Massèna, and the second, pages 14 to 76, twelve chapters beginning with 'The War of Inaction' and 'The First Italian Campaign' and concluding with 'The Last Attempt' and 'Peace'. It was illustrated

with nine colour pictures and eighteen maps which I'd traced out of the history books (15 in the Bibliography on page 76!) from the local library or off my own bookshelf. The map of Holland 1793-5, with all the rivers, islands and Zuyder Zee to shade blue, had taken ages, as had Denmark and the Northern Powers. Bloody Skagerrak and Kattegat! Thank God for Russia, just a white page ('cos of all the snow, yeah?) with an orange dot for Smolensk and a red line for the Belorussia-Ukraine border.

I'd particularly enjoyed researching Wellington's battles in Spain and the Retreat from Moscow - 'On September 20th a rain-storm stopped the blaze. Napoleon decided to withdraw to Smolensk for food and supplies but he made a fatal error. He withdrew back the same way that he had come. There was nothing along that route and, when the French were halfway between Moscow and Smolensk, winter closed in. Cossacks and peasants also closed in, cutting off stragglers. The French had left Moscow with 100,000 men but when they reached Smolensk they only 40,000 left. [*Had I really omitted 'had'?*] There were no supplies and the withdrawal continued.

'The temperature fell to thirty degrees of frost and the French retreated as quickly as possible. The Grand Army that had crossed the River Nieman in June, 1812, now re-crossed it but this time a beaten horde of ragged men.'

Bush-head called it 'A highly competent project; carefully researched + well written.' He said I was a good story-teller, but I enjoyed telling those stories. I wasn't so sure about Wingnut's. Sure, the myths behind the gods were interesting, although the gazillion incarnations of Siva confused me, but why worshipping Kali, Vishnu and Ganesh was perfectly OK and worshipping Zeus, Poseidon and Hades was not confused me more. I mean, like if I said I worshipped Odin and Thor, I'd get a) laughed at and b) locked away. But if I worship some god with an elephant's head I don't, right? Or some old psycho-twat who sawed off his own kid's foreskin with a fucking flint-stone (**YIKES AND YOUCH!**) is *not* like child abuse (even though they *still* do it, albeit with a knife not a blunt stone) but fine 'cos it's Jewish, right? But Apollo who loved rather than mutilated a beautiful boy isn't OK 'cos he's Greek, yeah? And Thor with his mighty hammer doesn't like exist but the guy with the elephant head and a zillion flailing Doc Ock arms does? I mean, the world is such a load of old bollocks, you know? Anyway, it's not like any of them are actually *real*, is it? Not like Wellington and Blownapart.

In the back of the Chemistry book, I found where me and Maxton had predicted the Top 10 for 26th February. We'd both correctly named Blondie as Number One and the Ramones at number 8, but he got Elvis Costello new in at five and we both had the Whispers at two instead of three. Honourable draw. Facing page, the predictions for 4th March, and other lists by MWG, PL, GDH, Bob, and AC. For some reason MWG (Gray) had only bothered with the Top Five. Curiously, none of us had reckoned on 'the bravest animals in the land, [that's] Captain Beaky and his Band', leaping twenty-four places to number three, but who the fuck had, except Terry Wogan, who loved it? Though, to be fair, we loved it too and sang it at the tops of our voices in RE to piss off Wingnut. Fozzie did Batty Bat, 'who had a wheeze to fly up into the trees,' Max was Artful Owl, 'that clever fellow,' Gray was Timid Toad, 'his eyes a-popping', Stewart was Reckless Rat, who 'stood there in his reckless hat' and I was Captain Beaky himself, 'who, leaping off, said "follow me" and ran right into a tree'. The class loved it, so much so that when we went to Andy Collins' birthday do, he'd got us all 'HISSING SID IS INNOCENT' T-shirts. Wingnut, inevitably, hated it. With such a passion he made us pick up all the litter from his classroom floor, the nonce.

We'd also guessed the number of new entries to the Top Forty chart, listing by initial the eight of us who had passed the book round the back of Barney's boring lab. AEC had the lowest, at 14, GDH the highest at 27, JDP for 20 and MWG for 22. The correct number was 21, so me and Gray won bragging rights and shared the Mars Bar prize. Then there were four pages covered in Maxton's handwriting listing the Top Ten in reverse-order through May and June, some song called 'I'd do it in a heartbeat' (and I bloody would if I could, and so would you, eh?) entering at 24, and 'Gary Numan (pillock)' added in pencil. Shit. I'd only got 2 that week. Bloody Undertones and their perfect bloody cousin, eh?

I also found Stewart and Gray's epically awesome Pinka's Gang, an entire cast of animal cartoons inscribed in the back of *my* Chemistry book with *my* Waterman, because only *I* used blue-black ink. Mousey, Froggo, Munko, Fat Cat, Herbert Horse, Piggo (my favourite) and Pinka herself, a dog with massive floppy ears and her name on a collar, were arranged around the greeting " 'Hi!' say the Pinka Gang!" They cropped up at various places in all my Science books, mainly because I sat with Gray and Stewart quite a lot. I minded that my Chemistry book had become a graphic novel for the form because brainiacs like Huxley and Bainbridge sniggered at my shit homework. In a way, I preferred Gray doodling on the back on my hand. That was where Pinka had first appeared, a sketch in blue Pentel on my left hand. It'd made me laugh in an especially tedious Geography lesson on the movement of glacial moraine and I'd quite enjoyed having my skin graffitied. Gray had also tried balancing as many pencils as possible on my ears. Many French lessons passed with me sitting statue-still hoping the clatter of another failure would not alert whoever was droning on at the front. Our record, a rather respectable five, held for months, till Martin Cooke managed to get six on one of Huxley's, which wasn't fair, 'cos Huxley had massive elephant-ears, though Huxley was all right really. He had about as much movement as a tree in cement and could never decide whether to do PE with glasses on or glasses off. Glasses on and he was like an uncoordinated bear thrashing through a jug of custard. Glasses *off*, oh boy. It was like 'are those *my* feet?'

Anyway, fun though Pinka's Gang were, they were nothing compared to the characters Maxton and I had created in my music book under our setting of 'Hey diddle diddle, the cat and the fiddle' (G major, with one sharp, 3-4 dance rhythm, an *allegro* tempo, very simple and rather dull). The super-thin pencil-head of Jocelyn Nosepick was telling Mr D. Bimp of Kent that he was a pillock whilst Mr D. Bimp of Kent, a Sponge-Bob lookalike, appeared several times, announcing first "I am bent", then "I hate cheese" and proclaiming my sketched melody for 'If all the world were paper, and all the sea were ink' as "silly." I had no idea where Mr D. Bimp of Kent had come from but *I* had created Miss Jocelyn Nosepick. Maxton had supplied the drawings and the legends LIVERPOOL FC and ZAPHOD BEEBLEBROX, the spaces shaded in pencil.

Bored, I returned to my swotting, wondering if, during the test, I dared insert one of my favourite Laurel and Hardy lines - '*you can lead a horse to water but a pencil must be led*' ha ha ha. Perhaps I should. I was feeling fairly cocky, as Jane Maxton would've said if she'd actually bothered to talk to me, like, ever, like after *Oliver* when Philip had introduced me with a somewhat proud 'JP's my best mate' and she'd gone 'I loved you in 'Consider Yourself' with Adam (Austen who played the Artful Dodger and had a voice like a fucking food-mixer)' and I'd just gone ketchup-red and stammered a bit. Anyway, I'd done this brilliant History test and followed it up with an equally awesome German test. I was so proud of the History test I'd showed it to my folks:

'1. Stalin ruled strictly and ruthlessly yet he introduced voting etc. Industry picked up and the standard of living rose. But his purges were unfair and brutal. He was hated but made progress.' Got a massive red √. Yay!

'2. <u>Industry.</u> More money was put aside for industry but strikes were forbidden. The workers were fed but conditions remained bad. This improved greatly and coal, oil, steel, iron etc was produced, ~~and~~ improved. & increased.' Another red √.

<u>'Agriculture</u>

Excess food was bought from peasants but they still didn't own land. Conditions improved for them but they were still virtually serfs. State farms set up. More food produced. Peasants forced to produce more food.' Running out of time. Ungrammatical sentences. Know what I mean? Probably not. (See? Cocky. Massive √).

<u>'Justice</u>

This was almost non-existent. With Show Trials and sentences before trial in the Media and the newspapers people didn't have much chance in Stalin's courts. There were executions, deportations and tortures carried out by Cheka – the Secret Police. Terror reigned as it tried to combat Terror.'

18 from 20 and an 'intelligent engagement with the issues.' Ha. I knew my Stalin. Maxton got a lukewarm 10 for the list he copied from my book 'cos he just wrote down the list. He didn't add anything new. If I'd been Stalin…
Anyway, to the German quiz:

'1. Ich werde Sie nicht heute Abend am Bahnhof treffen. √
2. Er ablehnte meine Offerte ab. √
3. Ich habe meine Pfeife angezündete. √
4. Die Strasse ist gut anzünden. √
5. Es hat endlich zuregnen aufgehört.' √
Und so weiter for ten out of ten, as Beaky recited his favourite poem:
'As you set out on life's arduous hike,
You want to get what you want to like.
But when you look back with a sense of regret,
You learn to like what you bloody well get. '
And I'd responded with mine:
'If you can laugh when skies are grey,
If you can laugh when grief holds sway,
If you can laugh in the darkest day,
You'll probably laugh when they cart you away.'
Paulus had giggled like a gerbil while the rest of the class fell about and Beaky's craggy face softened as he presented me with another square of chocolate and my volcanic sneeze set Paulus off again.
I was smiling again when a filthy red Fiesta lumbered up the hill to make my life complete. To my surprised delight, Alistair Rose got out of the driver's door. He was dressed in black jeans, a navy blue hoodie and this black Peter Storm anorak. Bollocks, I forgot. Bobby, his twatty little brother, was in the race too. Ha. He'd have to wade through mud and rain, the little twat. Bobby Rose was a first-prize twat. He'd been in *Oliver* too, one of the also-rans in Fagin's gang who had clearly resented every moment I was on that stage intead of him.
Dumping my books, gabbling something to Mr Trent and grabbing my black Regatta parka, the one with the fur-trimmed hood, I left the Volvo and strolled over, this big grin on my face. Ali was here. Despite the angry black clouds blotting out the sky, my world had suddenly and unexpectedly brightened up like Mikey's banana-shaded shoes.

10: I will survive

"HI, Alistair." My voice shook with excitement. "Didn't know you could drive. Is it your car?"

"I *am* seventeen, you know," he said, "And it's Mum's. Didn't expect to see *you* here."

"I'm supporting my friends. What about you? You come to watch the boys too?"

Giving an irritated twitch, he growled "What the hell do you mean by *that*?" and strode after the runners who were climbing the hill to the starting-line. Faltering, I left Mr Trent tugging on his wellies and followed Ali up the path to this five-bar gate, some muddy fields, a stream and a copse. The other schools, already there, were waiting for the whistle.

Gary Dunn set off at a cracking pace, Hood just behind him, Crooks a little further back. I watched them reach the middle of the field then heard the juniors start. Bobby Rose, showing a not-so-clean pair of heels, was already leading, with Leo and Broody chasing him.

"They need to keep a steady pace," grumbled Oggie, "Not take off like a ferret after a rabbit, otherwise they won't have anything left for the hill."

"There's another one?" puffed Mr Trent.

"Oh, aye," said Oggie, "Nearer the farm."

Leaving them talking, I crossed to Alistair.

"*Crow Grinned*," I quoted, "*Crying 'this is my Creation,' flying the black flag of himself.*" He just grunted. "What's the matter with *you*?" I said. "Thought you liked Hughes."

Grabbing my elbow tightly, he steered me away from the adults then span me round. Black with anger, he kind of shook me, like said ferret with rabbit, spitting viciously "What's the matter with *you*, more like."

"Ow! You're hurting me!" I cried out, suddenly scared.

"You wrote a story about us. Some twisted fantasy about a trip to Scarborough." It was not a question. "Beaky Phillips dug me out of English. Thought I should know. You changed my name to Alison. Alison." He laughed abruptly. "Very subtle, I don't think, *Jenny*, you stupid little twat." I tried to interrupt but he was suddenly raging, fingers digging cruelly into my arm. "Phillips thinks you've got some kind of crush on me, like you're some kind of homo. He thought I should know. He asked if I was interested in you. Christ Almighty! If *I* was interested in *you*. Like I'm some kind of fucking kiddy-fiddler." Brutally he flung me away. Staggering backwards, I slumped into a clump of damp nettles.

"Well? Is it true? Do you fancy me? Is that it? You fancy me, you little queer? Eh? Do you fancy me, you queer fucking freak?"

I thought he was going to kick me and scrambled backwards on my bottom. The nettles were stinging like fury. Choking, I stammered "Don't be stupid. What do you think I am?"

"I *know* what you are," he said nastily. "You're a sick little queer who eyes up other boys in the toilets. So do you fancy me, or what?"

Tears were building behind my face. The breath literally died in my lungs.

"N... no," I stuttered, "Of course I don't. I'm not like that. I just thought..."

"You thought wrong," he said flatly.

"I thought you... you... after the fire... you were going to say something... " I said, crying now and gasping to breathe, my chest tightening in the vicious clenched fist of an impending asthma attack. The nettles were setting my skin on fire. "I thought...."

His face distorted again, a mix of emotions struggling for control, pain, anger, deep sadness, despair, everything I was experiencing myself.

"I was telling you to get back to class," he said bluntly. "You're sick, Peters, the way you mince round the school. You disgust me." He spat in my face and stalked away.

For a second, numb with cold, shock and pain, I buried my face in the grass then, sitting up, started crying properly, huge gulping sobs ripped from my soul, each swallowing the other, tears flowing in this utterly endless salt-flood as bleak desperation totally engulfed me.

Inevitably the storm-clouds broke, dumping a torrent of freezing rain on my head, plastering my cap to my skull, pounding off the peak over my nose and dripping down the neck of my sodden parka. My heart had just been totally wasted.

Wordlessly clicking open the car door, Mr Trent handed me the Thermos. I sipped the scalding coffee furiously while the rain battered the roof and hissed off the windscreen. Through the distorting film of pooling, coalescing liquid, I saw Alistair slam into the Fiesta and accelerate sharply away, leaving a deep gash in the mud. Sniffing loudly, I swallowed the tears that were about to explode again. My skin like screamed from the nettle-stings.

Mr Trent said carefully "Has something happened, Jonathan? Between you and Alistair, I mean? You went down the hill together and..." He spread his hands on the wheel.

For a moment I considered telling him everything. He was an adult. I liked him. But then he'd said I was Leo's role-model. He'd surely hate me if he knew the truth.

"No," I said, "Nothing. It's fine. Everything's fine."

The rain hurled itself against the windscreen, drops splattering to shapeless splashes with the steely determination of Kamikaze pilots attacking an American fleet. Streams threaded their way like chains down the glass. I returned to Doc Ock's flailing tentacles and Spiderman's gymnastic gyrations then like broke down, you know? Like *totally*? Slumping forward with my face on my arms on the dashboard, I just howled, every cry dragged from me, my whole body shuddering with their force. Mr Trent put his hands on my shoulders and pulled me into his chest where I clung, a shipwreck-survivor clutching a life-belt, and shook like a zillion volts were passing through me. He said nothing, just held me till it had passed.

"I'm sorry," I mumbled, straightening my clothes. "I got you all wet."

He took a box of Kleenex from the glove compartment. "Without interfering," he said, "If that's what he caused, he doesn't deserve you."

"I love him," I said simply, blowing my nose. "I love him, and he hates me."

He just like patted my arm.

"You don't seem shocked," I observed after a moment.

"Some people are gay," he answered, "Some are straight, and there are millions of others in between. It's the way God's made them."

"But why's he made *me* this way?" I blurted. "If being gay is like *this*..." I sniffed loudly. "I don't want to live like this. I feel so alone. There's no-one like me. Why is it only *me* who's like this?" I started crying again. "I hate myself for being like this. It isn't fair!"

"Listen," he said, "They reckon one in ten people are gay. In your school that means there's about eighty of you. It's quite a lot. There's Leo. There'll be others. You'll find them."

"Leo?" I gaped at him. "*Leo's* gay? How do you know?"

"I'm his father. In a way I love him even more. He's a very sweet, very special boy. We don't think he's sure yet. He's still quite an innocent." Mr Trent gazed through the rain-spattered windscreen. "But when he needs someone..."

"A shoulder to cry on?" I smiled through my tears.

"You can be there for each other."

"But what about Ali? He hates me, and I can't get him out of my head."

"He needs time," said Mr Trent. "I think he loves you but doesn't know how to tell you. Be patient, Jonathan. It'll come right." He smiled encouragingly. "Love finds a way."

"I feel so ashamed," I muttered.

"Of what?"

"Fancying boys." My face was burning. "Wanting... well, boys... you know? 'Cos it's wrong. My mum says it's wrong, everyone says it's wrong."

"It's not wrong for *you*, Jonathan," said Mr Trent. "You gotta be yourself."

The race had finished and the runners were returning. The downpour had eased to a drizzle. Leaving the car, I walked thoughtfully towards the gate.

Crooks, second behind Stern, was exhausted but satisfied as he approached me with a lazy call that the banana-peel shoes had been fantastic. Then he saw my face.

"What the hell happened?" he demanded. "You've been crying!" His luminous green eyes became solemnly funereal. "What happened?"

I told him I'd had a fight with Ali Rose.

"It looks like he's broken your heart," he said, "And not just broken it but torn it from your chest and stamped on it, the fucker."

"He said some horrible things to me." The memory brought that tear-prickle again.

"Fuck him," said Crooks angrily. Then, more calmly, he laid a mud-spattered hand on my arm. "Look, Jonny... it's OK, you know, to be... well...you know... like, different... yeah?"

I shook his hand off like it was the hand of a leper.

"Well, I'm not, all right? I'm not..." Tears sprang back into my eyes. "Not... like that."

He watched my struggle sympathetically then said "When you want to talk, J, I'm here, OK? I don't care what you are. You're still my friend."

That made me cry again. I loved Mikey. If only I could tell him. Could I tell him? Of course I couldn't tell him. There was nothing to tell. I'd rather roast and eat my own tongue with garden peas and a nice Merlot than admit I was gay. God Almighty. Imagine what they'd say. Someone would shoot me.

The juniors were back. Leo, who'd finished fifth, was forlornly wringing muddy water from his blue-gold vest with grim determination while his father wrapped him in a blanket. He'd made a superhuman effort and needed to massage Ralgex into his calves. Bobby Rose, having won, was doing this stupid dance, crowing like a cock on the roof of the henhouse where all his lady-hens are waiting, legs akimbo, for the Great Hen-House Gang-Bang, before he noticed his brother's car had gone.

"Where's Ali?" he shouted. "I want him to see me get my medal."

"He left," I said tiredly.

Bobby, about my height, a little heavier, with shaggy brown hair and eyes like hard grey pebbles, confronted me angrily.

"What did you say to him, Peters, you poof?"

"Nothing."

"Listen." Pushing his face close to mine, he hissed at me. "My brother's going out of his mind because of you. He *tortures* himself because of you. Your miserable fucking existence is screwing him up so do him a favour and get out of his life."

Pip and Leo, drained and wet, slumped against each other in the back with Hood. I travelled in the front, deeply unhappy. Mr Trent turned on the radio for the football commentary but no-one was really interested in Villa against Sunderland.

"Villa are magic," Brudenall quipped. "Watch them vanish from the First Division."

Manchester City and Queen's Park Rangers had both sacked their managers in midweek. Both were losing, City at Liverpool. Newcastle and Leeds had, obviously and inevitably, sacked their managers about three minutes into the new season. In the mournful silence, Mr Trent switched station. Don McClean's voice sang my story: '*I thought that I was over you, but it's true, so true, I love you even more than I did before, but, darling, what can I do? For you don't love me, and I'll always be crying over you, crying over you...*' Fuck it.

It was a terrible journey, especially as it was dark, the rain was heavy, the stuffy car reeked of wintergreen and I had to struggle really hard not to burst into tears. The Volvo crawled back into the gloomy storm-drenched suburbs like a predator, engine raucously growling, yellow eyes groping for the road ahead, for the next bedraggled bend. Despite Mr Trent's sympathetic encouragement, this had become the worst day of my life.

When they dropped me at my house, Leo said in this tiny, pathetic voice that he would wash the socks and return them on Monday. I said OK then thanked Mr Trent.

"It'll work itself out, you'll see," he answered.

If only I could believe him.

Leaving my wet, muddy trainers on the doormat, I popped my head into the kitchen to say I was home. Dad, in a soft ash-grey shirt and navy blue cardigan, was at the table with a bulb catalogue and his Littlewoods pools coupon while Mum, in a soft apricot sweater and jeans and her London Underground apron, was preparing a Delia Smith tomato sauce to go with our cod fillets. James Alexander Gordon was reading the football scores. Middlesbrough had thrashed Norwich 6-1 and Leeds, second from bottom, had drawn 1-1. Dad was pleased.

"You look like a drowned rat," said Mum. "How's your chest?"

"OK," I said tiredly. "I'm going upstairs."

"But what about dinner?" asked Dad, glancing up from the home-wins and the no-score draws. "You must want something after all that rain."

I didn't know which would be worse, forcing Cod Provençal down my throat or listening to the folks discussing where to plant the wildflower garden.

"I'm not hungry," I said. My hands really stung from the nettles.

"*Basil Brush* in a minute." Dad tried again. "Boom Boom, Mr Jonathan. And *The Generation Game*. Oooh, shut that door, Everard." He flapped his wrist campily. Fuck's sake. My dad was about as camp as *Warlord*'s 'Union Jack' Jackson.

Sitting on my bed in damp, mud-caked jeans, I listened to the first movement of Tchaikovsky's 'Pathétique', to those brass chords swelling through the strings, and just like stared at the yellow carpet with my head in my hands. In the space of a few hours, my world had totally crashed around my head. I had come out to a friend's father, learned that that friend might also be gay, and thought Michael Crooks and Bobby Rose had guessed too. But worse, the boy I loved so desperately totally hated *me*, despised me as a 'little queer', and was disgusted by me. Miserably I ran a bath, lacing the cascading, steaming water with jasmine and tea-tree Radox so a huge mattress of foam built up on the surface. I dropped all my clothes and my sopping cap on the cork tiles and eased myself under the suds with a loud 'Youch!' It was bloody hot. My feet were already pink as pot-boiled lobsters.

Totally exhausted, I took off my cross and sank down so the hot water lapped over my stomach and chest. What a fucking awful day. And it had started so brightly with Leo and Broody making me laugh so much. But what the hell had I told Mr Trent? And why? How'd I been so pathetic? I'd cried like a bloody little girl who'd dropped her ice-cream. I glared at the yellow duck bobbing under the taps. I was 15, for Christ's sake. I shouldn't be crying at all. Let alone crying over another boy. Being gay *was* a fucking misery. My teachers and *Newsbeat*'s agony-uncles were damn right. This was no life. I *had* to change. Smearing shampoo into my hair, I considered Claire. Maybe she was just the wrong girl. Maybe I should go after someone else, someone with massive jugs and a fanny like a toilet seat who'd shag my brains out, like this fat bird of Collie's. Forget meaningful relationships and chaste kissing. Mindless fucking sex. That's what I needed. Mindless fucking.

I soaped myself with Imperial Leather, thinking maybe Broody could introduce me to someone who went like a barn door in a hurricane. I'd have to do it doggy-style or she'd snap me in half. Woah. Grip her hips and push it in. Woah again. Like a stick of rock. Shut your eyes and drift away.

But then if she was *really* experienced... Seymour's cock was enormous. I'd seen it once in PE. It was about six inches long and like really really thick? And that was when it was soft! Arnold too was hung like a bloody horse. Lewis's swung when he walked. He was the tallest boy in the class at 6' 4. It was so unfair. *My* three and three-quarters would hardly touch the sides. I slapped the bathwater angrily. I was such a fucking shrimp. No muscles, no hips, no body-hair, just fucking spider-legs under my arms, size 5 feet, 4 inch cock...5 foot 4 and 6 stones of bones. No wonder girls ignored me. Even *queers* ignored me and Rosie Rose actively *hated* me. Jesus. Jonathan Peters was such a fucking loser he'd never get laid. By anyone. Not even a rubber duck. But then there was... Claire... Andy... Leo... Pip... uhhh

Hunching over slightly, I raised my knees from the water, slicked my soapy fist down twice and squirted a jet about two feet, like some bloody Super-Soaker, right into the suds, the globby white ribbons twisting to string in the bath-water. Man, I really *really* needed that.

I gazed round the bathroom. It was mostly pale yellow tiles with this brown cork-tile floor. It had a frosted window facing over the back garden, a deep yellow tub, a low-rise toilet and a pedestal wash-basin. The shower-head I used to wash my hair was attached by a silver hose. A yellow shower-curtain hung limply above the tub.

My toiletries were arranged in this chipped Queen's Silver Jubilee mug on the window-sill. I didn't have much. I was a boy, after all, so just the yellow toothbrush, a yellow flannel, Lynx Dark Temptation (Mum would have got roll-on Old Spice because aerosols kill dolphins or something but Old Spice is *sooo* like for crumblies, yeah?) and a bottle of Clearasil. Stuff like shampoo (Herbal Essence), toothpaste (Colgate), mouthwash (Listerine) and soap was collectively owned. In addition to a blue toothbrush, Dad had this cheap Gillette Blue II razor and a Tesco spray-can of shaving foam. Mum's stuff, on the other hand, could have stocked a small pharmacy. Face-packs, cotton-buds, liquids, lacquers, lotions and potions, tweezers for eyebrows, wax-strips for leg-hair and armpits and, thankfully concealed in a cupboard, the tampons she bought in Sainsbury's, in full view of everyone, and made me like shrivel up with embarrassment, you know? Fucking hell. No wonder I was so gay, surrounded by all this women's stuff, bras in the laundry basket, tampons, that kind of squirmy stuff. I mean, once I'd found these Durex Featherlite condoms? I mean, mega-yikes, right? I mean, my folks like... doing... well, It, you know? Still makes me shudder. Should be banned when you're old and wrinkly, right? I mean, like over 25, yeah? Otherwise it's just sick.

"You *are* gay." I stared into the coal-dark eyes reflected in the bathroom mirror. "You're a queer, a bender, a shirt-lifting pervert. You're a homo, a fairy, a faggot, a woofter, a poof, a mincing, limp-wristed, a cock-sucking, shit-stabbing, fudge-packing, boy-bumming queen."

Fucking hell. There are so many abusive words for boys who fancy other boys.

And now I was angry, I mean, like so fucking angry my asthma came back like some vice crushing my chest while the wind-chimes clanked morosely in my semi-dark bedroom. As I dragged Ventolin from my inhaler, I replayed the scene with Ali over and over in my head. I could scarcely believe he'd said these vicious, spiteful things to me. 'A little queer,' he'd called me. What a cunt. He clearly hated my guts but I didn't cry any more. I was spent with crying.

I replaced my crucifix, put on my dressing-gown, this cheerful yellow towelling job, and went downstairs. I could hear Dad laughing at something on *The Generation Game* as I lashed into the pounding Presto of the *Moonlight Sonata* and hammered my rage, sorrow and frustration out through the keyboard. As I reached the last bars, I became aware of my father standing in the doorway with a mug of hot chocolate and two slices of Cheddar cheese melted on toast, my crisis comfort-food. I blinked back some tears at his thoughtfulness.

"What's the matter, son?" he said softly, putting the mug and plate on the coffee table behind the piano stool.

"Nothing," I said.

"You look wiped out." He settled himself in the red armchair Ali had sat in. "You look as though you've been crying. Has something happened?"

Swallowing hard, I looked at this big, gentle bear with the loyal Labrador eyes, shook my head and hid my face in the hot chocolate. He wouldn't understand.

He waited a few moments then tried again. "You would tell us if anything was wrong, wouldn't you?"

"Sure," I said. "Of course I would."

"I mean, if you were ill or being bullied or... anything... you know?" He sounded really anxious. "I mean, we're your parents and we love you very much. We'd do anything to see you happy, you know? Good job, nice family, nice house, you know? You're our only child. You're very precious to us. Sharing your life has been an endless joy for both me and your mother. You winning that scholarship was the proudest day of my life, and I'm still proud of you, of everything you do. So don't do anything silly, will you, son? Eh?"

Cripes. I'd never heard my father speak for so long.

"I had a fight with Ali." A headache was beginning and I felt kind of shivery.

He seemed genuinely startled. "Ross? Ali Ross? That Sixth Former who was in the play with you?"

"Rose," I said, "He's called Rose, Alistair Rose."

"I thought you were friends with him."

"Me too. Seems I misunderstood."

Now Mum appeared, pissed off 'cos I'd left my muddy trainers on the mat, a tidemark in the bath and my sodden, dirty clothes on my bedroom floor rather than putting them straight into the washing machine. Who did the penguins in Antarctica think was going to do it? The Clothes Fairy?

"And where are your socks? You haven't lost your socks. Honestly, Jonathan, you really are the limit."

"I lent them to Leo Trent," I said tiredly, huddling deep inside my dressing-gown.

"I mean the other one. One of your grey school ones. Any idea where it might be?"

I was puzzled. How could I lose one sock between my bedroom, the bathroom and the washing machine? Maybe the machine ate it. Wrong answer, as the penguins learned.

"I'll have to sew name-tags in again," she grumbled. "Bloody kid. And those pyjamas you put in the laundry are in a right state. What the hell have you been doing in them?" I said nothing. "You seem wiped out," she continued unsympathetically. "Didn't you sleep?"

"Not much," I admitted. "I've got a lot on my mind."

"Well," she said briskly, "If you need to talk, you know we're here for you."

"OK," I began cautiously, "There's someone in my class I think is… well, homosexual."

"Ridiculous," said Mum dismissively.

"Who?" Dad said anxiously.

Me, I didn't say. I think I'm this screaming queen.

"Andrew Paulus."

"Rubbish," snorted Mum. "Andrew isn't gay. My God, just because he sings in the choir and has curly hair. What will you think up next? I suppose Mark said so, did he? Or Philip Maxton?" Shaking her head, she added "This is not some novel, Jonathan. This is *real* life. Boys of your age aren't homosexual in *real* life."

"Jonny," Dad said, "You should tell Mr Hutchinson if you think there's a queer in the class. I mean, you do swimming and PE and stuff, don't you? Better safe than sorry, eh?" Now he understood. "No wonder you've been so moody, worrying about some queer in your class. I mean, it's just not natural, is it?"

"No, Dad," I said miserably, "It isn't."

I felt like someone had shot me.

As I brushed my teeth, Simon and Garfunkel's song eased into my mind: "*I am a rock, I am an island, I have my books and my poetry to protect me, safe within my womb, here within my room, I touch no-one and no-one touches me, if I never loved I never would have cried…*" Damn right. I had to move on from Ali Rose. He was such a fucking twat.

I could still scarcely believe I'd told Mr Trent. And Michael knew too.

But hell… so what? Neither seemed to give a shit.

After *Juliet Bravo*, as I slipped under my duvet with Pickles and *The War of the Worlds*, where I was to learn about the anatomy of the sixteen-tentacled Martian from the narrator hiding in a ruined house with a curate, I felt utterly wrung out but strangely liberated. I thought I might still be gay – I'd fantasized about Mikey *and* Paulus and now Leo, Shelters *and* Broody Minor, but at least I was over that twat Rose. It'd been traumatic but, and here I touched the gold cross on my chest, I felt happier. I could manage this, I knew it now. I could handle it. I had a Cross to bear, as it were, and I would bear it cheerfully. After all, I was a rock, I was an island, and tomorrow I was gonna go to church with Mum and thank God for saving me. Hell, I'd dress in my best clothes, the brown cords and russet sweater, sit dutifully with Mum, smile and be polite to her stupid friends, go up for communion, even raise my hands to Heaven and ' get down' with the woolly-hatted dudes for 'Kumbaya', 'I'm so happy' and 'Jesus is my Fwiend.'

Man, I'd even be nice to Holly, though I knew she'd ask me to the youth-group:

'We don't see enough of you, Jonathan,' she'd say this woolly-headed nitwit. 'There'll be games and songs and then we'll discuss the sermon, share our burdens in the group, because you know what they say, Jonathan? A burden shared is a burden halved.'

'You're all right, Hols,' I'd answer, 'I've got a piano lesson this afternoon.'

'You don't know what you're missing,' she'd tease owlishly.

I *do* know what I'm missing, and that's why I'm missing it, I wouldn't reply, and if the 'queer fellow' was there, that stoop-shouldered, lank-haired mumbling child poisoner in the grubby beige mac, I would smile, say hello and shake his hand and revel in the flurry of fear that would ripple round the clap-happy hypocrites in their Sunday best.

But he wasn't, 'cos Holly told me the church committee had asked him to leave. Apparently he was unsettling the mothers.

11: Sexy Boy

WHERE illness was concerned, Mum believed that everything was just some lame excuse for skiving off work, that 'flu didn't exist and you should simply pull yourself together because colds were all in the mind. Telling her mine was all in my nose, I managed to wangle two days in bed with a hot-water bottle and the thrilling second act of Beethoven's *Fidelio,* where love, giving *'strength to free you from your chains'*, saves a life, and sinking my aching face into the steam rising from a hot eucalyptus/menthol solution, rubbing my chest with Vicks Vaporub, drinking countless mugs of hot lemon and honey and reading *SS General*, which was all about how bloody awful the Siege of Stalingrad was, this *Rattenkrieg* where you captured the kitchen but still had to fight like a fox in a sack for the living-room, where nearly 2 million men, women and children died during 5 months of brutal, desperate combat and where the average life-expectancy of a newly arrived Soviet soldier was less than one day. I mean, *Gott in Himmel und Donner und Blitzen*, as ze Germans say, right?

I'd read nearly all Sven Hassell's novels. My favourite was *Reign of Hell*, about the razing of the Warsaw Ghetto, and my favourite characters were Porta, because he told these like madcap stories, cut dodgy deals and seemed to know just about everyone in the German Army whilst being brave to the point of stupidity, and Sven himself, because he was honest about his feelings towards the brutality and futility of war. Some of the writing was really graphic. I didn't want to picture soldiers with their guts hanging from their stomachs or their faces sliced off. I preferred my soldiers as plastic models or cardboard counters.

I lolled around in navy trackies, white socks and cobalt sweater. Mum, working from home, stoked me with chicken soup and even played *Treasure of the Pharaohs* with me, though I had to suffer *Manilow Magic* over and over again. Man, if he *'came and he gave without taking'* one more time, I thought I'd put my foot through the CD player. Having said that, *'we dreamers have our ways, of facing rainy days, and somehow we survive... I made it through the rain'* had such resonance I wanted to get up and belt it out to an imaginary backing-band on an imaginary Vegas stage. Bazza seemed to be like singing my life-story right now, you know? Unfortunately my Vegas Moment came out as a croak.

Well, anyway, I don't think Mum liked the game much. I had no idea why. I mean, you took like these little explorer figures in pith helmets (I always chose the yellow one) through this pyramid, cross a bridge which had a trap-door into this snake-pit, raise the Great Stone of Cheops, negotiate the Hall of Mummies and hope to avoid the Curse of the Pharaoh, or, as Dad called it, the King Tut Trot, ha ha. I mean, walk like an Egyptian, right? Clench your arse-cheeks tightly and skip to the loo, ha ha. Anyway, there was even this ruddy great picture of Tutankhamen's Mask on the box! What more could you want in a game, eh, Mum? I wondered if Ali would like it then scoffed. Ali who? I'd play it with Tim instead.

Mum seemed happier with 'Space Phenomena' *Top Trumps*. I had Halley's Comet, trying to decide what category to pick. Not speed, for sure. It was only 5 mph, which was like rubbish, slower than an asthmatic tortoise carrying a ton of shopping up Kilimanjaro. Diameter was 16000 miles. Temperature might do. 57 Celsius. I liked this set. With comets, galaxies, black holes and meteorites, every game was an exploration of the Final Frontier.

"Temperature," I said.

"One million," went Mum. She only had the bloody Supernova, 'one of the most explosive and energetic events in the known universe.' I tutted and sniffed.

"Mass," said Mum.

I had the Earth. Ha. The Earth was bloody heavy.

"24.78," I said confidently, laying down the card.

"31.14," said Mum, using the Cygnus XI black hole to swallow up my Earth.

I unclogged my nose into a soggy tissue.

"Jonny," she said suddenly. "You know this fight with Ali Ross?"

"Rose," I snapped. "He's called *Rose*, not Ross, and he's a stuck-up spazmoid twat."

Mum studied me thoughtfully for a moment then asked the question Dad had ducked. I looked up from the M17 Nebula, with the awesome diameter of 380 million billion miles and a temperature of 10000 degrees Celsius and shook my head. No, I said. He hadn't molested me. No-one was molesting me. No. No-one. I wasn't getting fondled by a friend, touched by a teacher or pawed by a prefect. My virginity was totally intact. Unfortunately.

Relief flooded Mum's face as she conjured up the bloody Milky Way with its trumping diameter of 940 billion billion miles. "You promise?"

I promised.

The Sun. 5500 degrees Celsius. I stared at Uranus (shut your face!) and threw in my hand. Everything was fine 'cos my boy's bits were ungroped. Since that's all that matters, I *must* be OK. Grumpily I stomped off to blast some skyscrapers off the New York skyline in *Ground Force Zero*, this new game where you had to pilot a plane that is losing altitude all the time and the only way to land it safely is to basically obliterate any buildings in your way.

The living room was this light airy space with a massive marble fireplace in which, during winter, Dad lit real fires with coal and logs. A fairly knackered TV and video stood in a corner facing this three-piece suite in browns and oranges to match the orange walls and varnished woodwork. Mum and Dad usually took opposite ends of the three-seater, mainly so Mum could sit in her pyjamas, white with lavender cats, with her feet curled up in the middle for Dad, in his thick green dressing-gown and Paisley PJs, to rub absently whilst they contemplated the answers to *Mastermind* or the antiques on the *Roadshow*. I generally sprawled on the two-seater in PJs and dressing gown, legs hanging over one arm, head on the other, swinging one tan-moccasined foot till the slipper dropped off. They didn't mind. They just seemed pleased their teenager wanted to watch telly with them.

There were several pot-plants, a couple of paintings, one a seascape, the other some kind of vaguely yellow forest-scene, and, on the mantelpiece, an expensive ornamental vase Mum'd been left by some aunt. This was surrounded by some framed family-photos, them on their wedding day eighteen years ago, all loud colours, flares and massive hair, me as a baby crawling on a rug on the Grunters' back lawn, the Grunters on their golden anniversary, Mum's parents, me in a tux and black tie performing at the Harrogate Festival two years ago. It was a nice room and I enjoyed spending time in it, especially when I could scoff a bag of banana chips with a classic *Star Trek* with a Klingon war-bird fighting the *Enterprise* and some baby born into a primitive tribe getting named after Kirk and McCoy, a brilliant *Horizon* on BBC2 on time-lapse photography and *Paddington*. I liked *Paddington*. He was a marmalade-sandwich-scoffing bear with a crazy hat. What wasn't to like? Though I preferred *The Wombles*, you know? Underground, overground, Uncle Bulgaria, long furry noses and a cool song called 'Wombling Free' but they weren't on. It was *Paddington*. But *Top Gear* involved turning a Renault Espace into a convertible using power-saws then setting fire to a car-wash. I laughed so hard I almost puked.

Returning to school on Wednesday, Double Biology was its usual rueful (ha), thyme-less (ha ha) dilling (ha ha ha) with the force of darkness that was Herbidacious who said I looked like death warmed up and that if Lamp-post Lewis held out an arm the dogs would come before making us copy this fiendishly detailed diagram of the ear from the board then complaining they were all too small. I mean, what a twat. Why didn't he like tell us first?

I did OK in the Music test, though I got two wrong (a plagal cadence I incorrectly identified as imperfect and a key-change from G major to A minor that I thought was E minor – what a spaz). Perry also hated my latest composition 'cos he had this thing against parallel fifths. I told him I didn't do classical harmony but he said the examiners did, and deducted 5 marks. Meanwhile that swot Paulus got 10/10 for the weird discordant shit he claimed was 'modernist'. Paulus liked Schoenberg, Ligeti, Birtwistle and Reich and was desperate for the school orchestra to tackle that cheery number *Different Trains*, about people going off to be gassed at Auschwitz. After an argument between him and Tredwell about whether minimalism really *was* music, to which Mr D. Bimp of Kent's contribution was 'what a bag of wank', we listened to the dramatic excitement of *Night on the Bare Mountain*, focussing on this massive key-change at bar 256, *sostenuto pesante*, with a lot of pizzicato strings culminating in these triple fortissimo chords in bar 281, just before letter Q in our yellow Eulenberg scores.

At lunch, I went to Wingnut's class-room for the play rehearsal, sat at the back rocking on my chair scoffing Ryvitas, a celery-stick, some raw carrots, a bag of pumpkin seeds and an apple from our garden whilst Rose glared sourly at me, said "Nice of you to show up for once" and ran through Scene 1 with Turner, Sutcliffe, Middleton, Warburton and Anderson. It was no longer funny, not after eight readings.

"Oh man, this is so shit," I whined to North. "Wish we were doing a proper play like Tetley." Austen and Dell were doing *Waiting for Godot*. I was even more fed up when I learned that Rowntree were doing *Toad of Toad Hall*, with Pip Broody as Ratty and Niall Hill as Mole, Collins, for Smeaton, was going to fall through a sideboard, and Leeman, Bunny's house, were doing *Ali Baba* with about thirty kids and loads of singing and dancing.

"Don't worry," muttered North. "Firth's doing a French parable, Goodricke are doing a Noel Coward satire and Brearley something by Sean O' Casey. *We* got off lightly."

Unconvinced, I contributed my half-dozen lines in a hasty gabble, got another scowl from Rosie and legged it. Fuck him. He hadn't phoned me while I was sick and anyway I had a footie game to play.

Waving my arm in the air like some demented budgie and screaming "David! David!" at Fosbrook, I scored one screamer of a goal with a sweetly taken volley from his exquisite cross and then saved a goal with a desperate sliding-tackle on Bainbridge then tipped an absolute scorcher of a shot from Niall Hill round the blazer-pile post. Sure, I ripped most of the tendons in my fingers, but I impressed the hearties. Anyway, the day got even better when Big Willie read out my comprehension answers on how Jerry's swim in *Through the Tunnel* symbolised his rebirth and represented his movement from child to adult and this was reflected in the more grown-up way he spoke to his mother at the end of the story. Apparently it 'shows rare perception.' I didn't think so. I thought it was easy. The story came from *Modern Short Stories in English*, a book me and Willie really liked which contained 'Sunday' by the best poet EVER, a story about a guy called Billy Red who kills rats with his teeth, 'Great Uncle Crow' by the guy who created Ma and Pa Larkin, 'Superman and Paula Brown's New Snowsuit' by the the the late wife of the best poet ever (though the feminists'll cut my balls off with a rusty breadknife for saying that), and this Doris Lessing story I loved so much. It was about a boy who drew on every ounce of courage he had ever possessed to attempt, and succeed at, something utterly impossible, in his case swim through an underwater, under the rocks tunnel, but in our case, a metaphor for anything unbelievably challenging, like being… ~~gay~~ I mean, different.

Man, we'd been set the questions on page 28 for prep: '1. Talk about Jerry's mother. What kind of person is she? Talk about a time when you knew an adult who was similarly concerned about your actions and feelings.'

What the hell to write? I'd copped out by writing about Mrs Lennox, my toad-faced teacher, sweating it out before my rendering of Maxwell Davies' utterly beautiful 'Farewell to Stromness' at the city council's primary schools' star performers gig at that pink and gold candyfloss town hall when I, little Jonny Peters, 10 years old, had blown the competition into the stratosphere because I *felt* this aching, longing music, and brought it to life. Similarly, Willie read my work on my favourite short story and read it to the class to demonstrate how to weave direct quotations into one's own sentences, a skill I'd recently developed.

"Tell me," he finished, "Have you read F.R. Leavis?"

"No, sir."

"Well, do. You'll learn a lot."

"Tell me, Keeno Brainiac," mimicked Maxton sourly as I danced down the parquet corridor, "Have you read every book in the universe yet?"

"Say, Max, you read *any* books yet, or are you still on pictures?"

"Least they're pictures of *women*, not sheep," he said, slapping me round the head and bleating "Baaaaaaa! Jonnyyyyyy Peeeeeeeters shaaaaaaags sheeeeeep."

Yelling joyfully, I flicked two fingers at some prefect banging on about running in the corridor and, jumping down the vast wooden staircase three at a time, chased Max past the stained glass windows and pot plants of Heathcliffe Lodge to the school bus.

When I got home, I got stuck into Chopin's *Berceuse*, playing the opening two bars with my left hand only then hit a treble F with the middle finger of my right hand to begin the top-line melody. I played to the end of Bar 12, noted my fingering in orange pencil on the score then studied the next page. The *Berceuse*, with five flats, was packed with trills, grace-notes, high octave runs and, yikes, in Bar 32, an accidental double E flat. Peering at the black spot, I counted three ledger-lines. Oh, man, there was another in Bar 33, a double B flat... at least the left hand was straightforward.

I moved onto the clarinet, playing some scales and the perky third Lutoslawski Dance Prelude for my exam. Dealing with a succession of grace-notes in the first sixteen bars, I realised that the notes themselves were not that hard to hit, but the rhythm was everything, and fairly tricky. I glanced over the list of 'homework' pieces from Otto Langey's *Practical Tutor for the Clarinet*, 'Sep 22nd, page 125, 121, Oct 20 page 102.' Page 125 was the Adagio from Mozart's concerto, page 121 the slow movement of Weber's first concerto, page 102 more Mozart, the Larghetto from the Quintet. Nice stuff even Dad might appreciate. Then it was prep time. Gazing for inspiration at the red Fokker triplane on my wall, I shoved a cartridge in my Waterman, glanced at Ozzie's googly eyes and wrote

"Rates of reaction. 1) Does the size of particles affect the rate of a reaction?

"A suitable reaction to study is that between lumps of marble (calcium carbonate) and dilute hydrochloric acid."

Whistling 'One for the Vine' from Genesis' *Wind & Wuthering*, I wrote an equation which I hoped was correct. I loved this song, this whole album. I'd had it like forever.

"$Ca^{2+}CO_3^{2-}$ (s) + $2H^+$ (aq) + $2Cl^-$ (aq) $\rightarrow$ Ca^{2+} (aq) + $2Cl^-$ (aq) + H_2O (g) + CO_2 (g)"

"*In his name they could slaughter, for his name they could die, Though many there were believed in him: still more were sure he lied, But they'll fight the battle on,*" I sang, writing "The course of the reaction can be followed by observing the loss in mass of the reactants as the carbon dioxide escapes from the reaction."

There was this massive table which Maxton had recorded whilst I'd called out the elapsing time and mass and Gray had calculated the differences.

"The weight of the vessels containing the reactants," I wrote, "Was noted every half-minute and graphs of loss in weight against time were drawn." Since this wasn't due till Wednesday and I had other stuff, I would do that bit tomorrow.

"*He walked into the valley, all alone,*" Trying to sing like Phil Collins, my voice soared up into a *falsetto* stratosphere that made the wind-chimes hum. "*There he talked with water and then with the vine,*" whistling again and writing "Precautions:- i) saturated the acid with carbon dioxide so that it would not dissolve the marble, ii) wad of cotton wool in flask to prevent acid spraying out."

"*They leave me no choice, I must lead them to glory, or most likely to death...da da da da da, da da da...*" My voice went into the stratosphere. Man, I'd forgotten how good Genesis were. I'd have 'I know what I like (In your wardrobe)' on next.

"Deductions Graph B is steeper showing that reaction B is faster. (In fact the gradient of the graph shows how fast the reaction has proceeded). 2) Both graphs gradually flatten out, (i.e. reaction is slowing down) and eventually become horizontal (i.e. the reaction has stopped)." I'd do the questions tomorrow.

Slapping *that* book shut, I looked at some French: "craindre, to fear, je crains, tu crains, il/elle craint, nous craignons, vous craignez, ils/elles craignent, cueillir, to pick or gather, je cueille, tu cueilles, il/elle cueille, nous cueillons, vous cueillez, ils/elles cueillent." My blue pocket *Collins Gem* French-English dictionary had the blue-black ink-stains from the burst bottle of Quink back in 2W and, scrawled in pencil on the inside-front cover, 'Qu'est-ce que c'est?' which was like crossed through with diagonal pencil-slashes. I had no idea why. It was like my green *Collins Gem* Dictionary of Biography, a pocket-book I'd carried everywhere with me. It had 505 pages of brief life-summaries, from 'Aalto, Alvar (1898-1976), Finnish architect and furniture-designer' to 'Zworykin, Vladimir Kosma (1888-1982), American physicist, b. Russia. Developed scanner from cathode-rays and first practical television camera.' Five supplementary pages listed <u>Sovereigns of the United Kingdom</u>, from William I onwards, <u>Presidents of the United States of America</u>, and <u>Prime Ministers of Australia, New Zealand, Canada and Great Britain</u>. Also inky and well-thumbed, it had my name J. Peters and, again in pencil, 'Spencer Perceval, Tory P.M. Assassinated 1812' and 'Sir Henry Campbell-Bannerman, 1906 Liberal P.M.' Don't ask me why. But I'd also written, on the back page, in blue biro, 'Are you easy to fall in love with?', then scribbled it out with black spirals. Huh?

I scanned the list of random German vocab which Beaky would be testing us on later in the week, "überfahren = to run over, sich schämen = to be ashamed, beschließen = to decide, bestellen = to order (goods), meiner Meinung nach = in my opinion, der Verbrecher = criminal, die Träne = tear, streicheln = to stroke, der Imbiß = snack, leuchten = to glow, gleich = at once," sitting with my back against the radiator so the heat could seep through my jumper.

I kicked some balled-up socks against my bedroom wall, booting them hard with my left foot then diving on the carpet to block the rebound, firing Norwich towards a penalty shoot-out against Bayern Munich in the UEFA Cup Final till Dad yelled something about elephants and what the hell are you doing up there? Man, I got energy to burn at 15, don't you remember? Anyway, although Wednesday was shit for telly, I managed to find *Top Gear* blasting a Robin Reliant into space from their base in the hysterically named Penis-Town and show-jumping on *Sportsnight*. Then I went to bed with a hot-water bottle and lost myself in the *Custer's Gold* prequel, *North Against the Sioux* where [**SPOILER ALERT – if you haven't read it, look away now**] Portugee Phillips breaks out of the besieged fort and rides through the snow with Red Cloud's Indians hot on his tail, arrows whizzing round his head, and revelled in the Boomtown Rats, '*my mind beats time like clockwork, I think in sync, like clockwork*' and 'Rat-Trap', that raucous saxophone and Johnnie Fingers ' *glissando* piano, Bob Geldof's snarling narrative, the powerful lyrics: '*Hope bites the dust behind all the closed doors and pus and grime ooze from its scab-crusted sores.*' Barry Manilow this was not.

As October evolved into darker mornings, darker evenings, central-heating, vests, sweaters, raincoats and drizzle, life settled back into the normal pattern of lessons, homework, break-time football and lunchtime activities presided over by the atmospheric calendar photo of Flamborough Lighthouse at sunset. Mr D. Bimp of Kent said he was bored whilst Miss Jocelyn Nosepick said he was a twat and Pinka and Munko played conkers.

"So," said Collins, "I got up this morning, all tousle-haired and bleary eyed, as you writers say…" He nodded at me. I had never in my life written like that. I would have to be some hack-writer of over-sentimental teen-angst romances to use such clichés.

"All right, all right," he cut me off with an irritable flap of the hand. "Well, my mother had made some porridge, really thin, runny, watery, you know."

"Like workhouse gruel," I suggested brightly.

"I wouldn't know, JP," he scowled pointedly. "Anyway, it looked disgusting. I wasn't sure whether to eat it or pebble-dash the house with it, you know? Then Dad butts in, says it was all I was getting, we couldn't afford to waste good food, well, food, and Mum goes 'what do you mean?' and while they're arguing, I give it to the dog, 'cos he eats anything, even Mum's cooking, he doesn't care. Well, you all know our Max. Greedy little bastard, bit like our Richie. He never stops eating either. Don't know who's greedier, my brother or my dog."

We all laughed appreciatively. Yes, everyone knew Wolfie, a hyperactive but soft-as-butter Alsatian, and everyone knew Collins' equally hyperactive younger brothers. We'd all been out to lambing parties at his family farm, even swots like Huxley and Cooke, because Andy Collins was the most generous, inclusive guy I ever met.

"So I slop this porridge stuff into his bowl and shove off back to the kitchen into this mega-argument between Mum and Dad, and think I ought to fix my own breakfast…"

"Just a sec," I frowned. "The porridge. Did the dog eat the porridge?"

"Yes, but that's not the point of the story," said Collins impatiently. "Bloody hell, JP, you do insist on the details, don't you? God help us if you ever do become a writer. You'll bore the arse off everyone with your digressions and side-tracks and bloody blind avenues. People haven't got time for all the ins and outs. They just want to get to the meaty bits."

"Doesn't sound as though this *has* any meaty bits," Paulus muttered.

"Ha ha!" Collins beamed triumphantly. "That's where you're wrong. I went to the fridge, took a couple of sausage rolls, shoved 'em in my trouser pocket and strolled innocently back to the table. Just then, our Eddie, the one in J5, you know? He's in the choir, and the swimming team, and the footie team. In fact they're going on some tour at Christmas. Can't remember where, Worcester, Gloucester, Leicester, somewhere ending in –ster. He plays in defence, pretty nippy little right back. Last week he goes on this mazy run up the wing…" Risking another glare, I cleared my throat. "Anyway, since JP's got the attention-span of a half-witted goldfish with a learning disability… Eddie comes up to me and goes 'Hi Andy' and smacks me right there, right in the pocket, right where the sausage rolls were. You ever had a pocketful of squashed pastry and sausage-meat?"

"What did you do?" grinned Maxton. He had a cold sore coming on his lip.

"Dug the remains out with my fingers," said Collins, "And I was just about to scoff them, 'cos you shouldn't waste food, when bloody Wolfie comes up, jumping and slavering all over my trousers and licking my hands like I'm some ice-cream. Then Mum's going 'where are my sausage rolls?' And Richie's going 'Andy's got 'em' and Mum's going 'Andrew! Have you eaten my sausage rolls?' and I hold out my hands and shrug, 'cos Wolfie's eaten the bloody evidence, but he's got crumbs on his whiskers and before he knows it, he's out in the yard with Mum's toe-end up his arse, ha ha…"

"Good story," I grinned.

"Ta," said Collins, "Like that geezer you like, Dixon, Dachshund, him."

"Dickens?" I suggested brightly.

"That's the one. Great story-teller. *Gulliver's Twist*, *Tale of Two Kitties*…" Anyway, 'cos I kept laughing on and off all bloody day, I did like the worst Chemistry test in the entire history of the Universe.

'Iron is manufactured by passing a blast of hot air through a mixture of iron ore, coke and limestone.

a) Explain carefully, with equations, the function of 1) air 2) coke 3) limestone

b) Give the reason why pig iron is brittle.

c) State briefly what has to be done to the pig iron to convert it to steel.

d) If you were to build a new factory for making steel from imported iron ore, suggest two factors which would ~~inful~~ influence your choice of ~~sight~~ site.'

Fuck me. Apparently this was revision. We'd done it in May. The 8th to be precise. Well, hello! That was like yonks ago?

Staring at the paper, baffled, I just wrote 'a) breathing, drinking and building, b) 'cos its thin, c) steal the pig and d) nice views; good weather.'

I also got bollocked in Chapel by 'Leatherface' Leatherbridge, the Director of Fifth Forms, for not being ready to sing Hymn 290, 'Through all the changing scenes of life, In trouble and in joy…' and having my top button undone *again* then fidgeting through his fucking boring reading from the Book of Proverbs, Chapter 1, beginning at Verse 20 while Gray doodled Pinka on the back of my left hand with a biro.

Dedicated to St Aidan, the chapel had this polished wood Victorian Gothic interior, a gleaming brass lectern in the shape of an eagle, this marble monument to the dead Head from the 1840s who'd contributed this Chapel, and these richly coloured stained-glass windows including a memorial installed in the 1950s to the old boys and masters who'd died in the two world wars. It was this long, sobering list, especially when you like looked at the ages of the kids. Some were just seventeen when they were gassed at Passchendaele or blown apart at the Somme: Ali's age. Imagine if he got blown apart or gassed... God, I couldn't bear anything happening to *him*. Or anyone actually, 'cos there was nothing special about HIM.

The window contained images of martyrs such as St Bartholomew, St Laurence and St Sebastian. I was fascinated with St Sebastian, the guy who was shot with arrows. This picture had one buried deep in his ribs, and another stuck in his thigh. What a martyrdom. But if I had to pick a way to go, it'd be that. Neither flaying alive, like Bart, nor roasting on a grid, like Larry, held much appeal. No. If I had to go, someone just shoot me with arrows, like Seb. The iron point would pierce my skin, the strong shaft drive into my flesh, skewering me, impaling me, like Jesus and nails through the palms... yikes. Ticket to Screamsville, yeah?

The altar, covered in a green cloth, had this brass crucifix in the centre and two candles burning either side. Above it was some stained-glass depiction, in rich reds, bold blues and glowing golds, of Christ's Ascension into Heaven. These images of the northern saints we'd studied in 2W glared down at us, resplendently red-robed Aidan of Lindisfarne himself, died 651, Bede of Jarrow, with a long white beard, died 735, Wilfrid of York, died 709, and white-robed Cuthbert, died 687. Their ferocious glower seemed to penetrate my soul to the core of its wickedness. When I mentioned this to Maxton, he asked what I was smoking.

"*I in my turn*," roared Leatherface from the pulpit, which had demons and angels carved into its dark wood-panels, "*Will laugh at your doom and deride you when terror comes upon you...*" Three verses from the end of the thirteen, he suddenly stumbled.

"Shame," whispered Gray, drawing Pinka's nose, "He was going so well."

"I'm sorry," said Leatherface, "I'd better start over." And back he went a gazillion pages to Verse 20. My loud groan earned me the bollocking. Smuggling a Polo into my mouth earned me yet *another* bollocking *and* a hundred lines for eating in Chapel. Moodily I leafed through the *Book of Common Prayer.* Easter 2027 was on March 28. Ascension Day in 2019 fell on May 30, my birthday. When I was a kid, I'd gone to Sunday school, drawn pictures of Jesus and acted out parables. I'd not known then how evil I was. Although I believed Jesus forgave people like me, I felt guilty just being there. Through my grey shirt, I touched the crucifix and mumbled the Lord's Prayer, like 'deliver us from evil' was aimed at me personally.

In Choral Society, I sat next to Gray as we tackled number 54, this awesome chorus where the Roman soldiers decide not to divide Jesus' robe but to cast lots for it. Fred wanted us to start *piano*, as in the score, but to whisper it to each other, like we were discussing a rumour, or plotting something in secret. We started high up on C for a bar before the tenors joined in. The music was tremendously exciting as got louder and stronger, increasingly confident in our plan, increasingly powerful, until the trebles hit this climactic top A that sent a shiver through me. Fred said we sounded like a lot of washerwomen. It didn't help that me, Gray and Arnold kept singing the treble line in *falsetto* and making the altos laugh, then tickling Shelton's neck till he squirmed and swore at us in the filthiest language, making me and Leo howl with laughter, then Stewart coughed like Wilfred Owen's 'machine-guns' rapid rattle' and Fred asked if he'd accidentally wandered into a TB ward and *everyone* laughed. Afterwards, high on confidence, I stormed the English lesson like a Roman soldier storming Jerusalem.

After all the stuff in chapters 18 and 19 of the *Mayor of Casterbridge* involving letters, the death of Susan (the wife Henchard sold to a sailor at a fair back in chapter 1), the discovery that Elizabeth Jane is not, in fact, Henchard's daughter despite what he has just told her, and lots of meetings in graveyards (man, it was getting complicated), Donald Farfrae returns to the story [**oh, I forgot the usual spoiler alert! Never mind. If you don't want to know what happens NEXT, look away NOW.**] According to my summary of <u>Chapter 24</u>, 'Lucetta is coquettish. She is preoccupied by appearance. Farfrae's new seed-drill arrives as L decides what to wear. L. and EJ go to see it and, coincidentally, meet H and F. L. winces whenever EJ mentions an event that has a connection with L. She is trying to cover up her past. EJ realises that L is in love with F. L. is said to be an amiable and brilliant companion. EJ is a "discerning, silent witch." She is perceptive.'

"What's 'coquettish'?" Maxton yawned.

"Flirty," I said. "She's obsessed with appearance, how things look on the surface, what she wears. Putting on clothes is a physical symbol of her hiding the truth about herself, covering up the past."

"Brilliant," goes Willie, "Tell us more."

Bollocks.

The seed-drill, I told the class, is new technology and shows Farfrae as far-sighted (ha ha) and embracing the future whilst Henchard consults a weather-prophet (in chapter 26) before he buys corn showing his superstition (don't forget his daughter is described as a 'witch' who meets Lucetta in a graveyard, I added). Yes, I read ahead, and yes, Maxton called me a lick and Stewart called me a swot but frankly I didn't give a shit. I felt God had brought me back from the brink of disaster. That trip to church with Mum had clearly paid off. I skipped as many play rehearsals as I could get away with and dodged the first round of the debating competition so I didn't hear him propose the motion that 'This house believes that the Devil has all the best tunes'. Although we won, Burridge said Rose had performed poorly before a disappointingly small audience of some dozen bored gimps from Brearley, fumbling his jokes and addressing questions uncertainly. Burridge also said rehearsals were going badly. Rosie seemed distracted and irritable and argued with everyone, even Sonning, finally flinging his coffee-cup at the wall and storming out. Turner'd muttered something about 'time of the month.' Tough shit. The twat was lucky I hadn't quit his stupid bloody play altogether.

On the school bus, I saw him looking at me unhappily, heartache written on his face, like he really really missed me, you know? My heart flipped, and I considered talking to him, then remembered I was a fucking rock, you know? An island. And Rose could sod off. The final of *Jeux Sans Frontières* was coming from Portugal, and these people dressed as giant cats were gonna steal lobsters, prawns, clams and stuff from a pot of stew while giant puppet seagulls controlled by the opposing team tried to nick them from a net. Then there was this water-skiing German in a fat-suit dodging Belgians and Yugoslavians dressed up as swordfish who've got to plant a rosette on her arse using their super-long noses. I mean, who thinks of this stuff? And the swordfish have these really lecherous expressions? *Sooo* surreal, and a megabillion times better than Jasper Farthing's frankly feeble jokes. Yes, Rosie Rose could truly sod off.

12: It's a sin

ON Saturday I listened to Radio 3's comparisons of our GCSE set-text, Vivaldi's Gloria in D, on my black Crown portable (I preferred a boys' choir for the purer sound), then accompanied Dad to McColl's the newsagent on the parade for his Lottery ticket and then the Racecourse for a stamp-fair. I liked going to the racecourse. In the close-season, when there weren't thoroughbreds thundering round the grass, they held antique-fairs, car-boot sales, model-railway exhibitions and military-modelling displays and I had, over the years, acquired many books from their monthly second-hand collectors' stalls. The stamp-fair was OK. Once I'd been really keen and still had this blue, hard-backed album from Stanley Gibbons of 391 Strand, London, WC2. This included a red one-penny stamp from Australia of King George V, a red two-cent George Washington (US Post) from 1902, some weird diamond-shaped ones from Mongolia, a set of twelve stamps issued in 1933 in the Deutsches Reich to mark President Hindenburg's birthday (the 10-mark stamp was missing), a nice set of British cathedrals in old money (York Minster 5d, St Paul's 9d, Durham 5d, Canterbury 5d, St Giles Edinburgh 5d and Liverpool Metropolitan 1/6d) and the really colourful Christmas stamps I'd liked, angels from 1972 and scenes from Good King Wenceslas from 1973. I'd also collected foreign stamps from places that had changed their names like East Germany (DDR), Ceylon, Tanganyika, the USSR (CCCP) and the Belgian Congo. The countries were all in alphabetical order and I'd stuck flag-stickers on each page. Stamp-collecting had taught me names of countries in their own languages, like Finland is Suomi, Greece is Hellas and Poland is Polska. Cool, eh?

Dad, collecting stamps from the Empire, tracked down some from India with George VI's head on them, four from 1937 and the two he needed to complete his set of nine from 1940, and some coronation stamps from Canada. Though I'd actually grown out of collecting stuff ages ago, it was still an interesting morning out and, for old time's, I bought a four-stamp set for Winston Churchill's centenary and a five-stamp set of British explorers from 1973, which had Livingstone (3p), Stanley (3p), Drake (5p), Raleigh (7½ p) and Sturt (9p). I marvelled that stamps'd once been so cheap. The dealer who sold me the explorers' set, some white-haired old boy with a purple nose and rheumy eyes, was totally checking out my arse. As I sauntered down the grandstand steps, I felt his eyes undressing me. I couldn't help running a hand through my fringe and smiling at him. Jailbait Jenny had arrived.

We watched a bit of telly when we got back. The adverts included Rowenta Tap-Master, which Mum wanted, Denim 'for men who don't have to try,' which Dad wanted, Monster Munch, which I wanted, then a Western movie shoot-out for Hubba Bubba, ('Big Bubbles, No Troubles,') preceded a massive cat like Kitten Kong from *The Goodies*, stalking a miniaturised Bernard Cribbins round a Hornby railway set. It was all rather disturbing, though I found adverts quite interesting after an English project last year to create our own TV ads and John-Boy Walton, me and Boxhead Harrison (Willie picked the groups) made 'Hob Nobs, the knobby biscuit' and the 1st prize-winning 'eco-friendly shoes – good for the soul,' ha ha.

After lunch, I cycled to Tim's. He'd invited me to tea and to try out this new Battle of Waterloo game he'd got. Although we were still spit-brothers, this, and tennis, was about the only thing we had left in common since he'd exchanged Biggles for the Bible, Kate Bush for Graham Kendrick, pictures of Jimmy Connors for pictures of Jesus and me for that owlishly spectacled tambourine-basher Charlie Rix. He was in a different house, he wasn't in my form any more, or any of my Options groups, having chosen Latin over German, Geography over History, Art over Music. We really had gone our separate ways. He was now about five foot nine, having grown a couple of inches or so since September. God, I was such a titchy little kid, especially now the peachy fuzz on his legs had been matched by some soft down on his cheeks. I didn't envy the moist-looking zits on his forehead or the dandruff flecking his brushed-up centre-parting though. I felt self-conscious enough about this spot in the left corner of my nose but, thank God, at least they weren't spattered all over my face like Maxton's.

At primary, Tim and I had shared a passion for history, especially Big History, leaders, kings and queens, battles and stuff, and mined R. J. Unstead's *Story of Britain* and *Royal Adventurers* for tales of Julius Caesar, Genghis Khan and Frederick the Great (favourites of mine), King Alfred, St Augustine and Edward the Confessor (favourites of Tim) and Napoleon, favoured by both. We'd re-enacted much of the Second World War on various carpets with model soldiers and Action Men. We'd played *Escape from Colditz* over and over, got the wire-cutters, stolen the Staff Car, tunnelled out of the Chapel and collected our Red Cross parcels. We knew every line of *The Battle of Britain*, calling each other Rabbit Leader (me) and Red Leader (him), shouting 'Scramble' and warning each other to beware the Hun in the sun. Once at grammar school, we had to select two after-school activities so I joined the Choral Society, he joined the Christian Union, and we both joined the Wargames Club. I'd collected a few over the years, *Seelöwe*, the German invasion of Britain, *Search and Destroy*, my Vietnam game which involved guerrilla-fighting, laying explosives, digging tunnels and other Viet-Cong stuff, and *Global War*, the game of World War Two, which took months to play. We had to dismantle it every week, writing all the information in notebooks so we could set it up again seven days later. I'd played it last year with Tim, Adam Rubenstein and Martin Cooke. The Axis forces had won. Playing as the Germans, I had, to a massively appreciative cheer, nuked the Pentagon.

Adam was into space-based games so we'd played this really cool *Battlefleet Mars* game for several weeks, space combat in the twenty-first century, zapping star-ships with lasers and the like, whilst Cookie got me interested in older stuff, playing as Hannibal in *The Punic Wars* and as Alexander the Great sweeping through Persia. Although I loved the history, the games I really wanted were *Fulda Gap*, a 'battalion-level game featuring chemical and nuclear warfare, pitting NATO's active defence against the Soviet multi-echelon attack' and *World War Three*, which SPI's catalogue described as 'Hypothetical (hopefully) strategic conventional warfare between the superpowers with multi-scenario, nuclear options.' Playing a nuclear war against Adam and Cookie, who were great wargamers, would be challenging.

Anyway, so Waterloo was set up on this table in the loft near Dentist Wilson's model railway. I thought it was really cool, with little tunnels, fake tufts of grass and miniature phone-boxes with miniature people, minuscule cows, and microscopic milk-churns on the platforms. At six o' clock every evening, Dentist Wilson set a tatty grey cap on his tatty grey hair, played a record called *Sounds of Steam*, sat himself at the console then, pipping an old tin whistle, sent the 1800 from Fuck-Cares-Where chuffing out of the station. Spellbound, I'd watch this green Great Western drag two blood-and-custard carriages through this amazing landscape to a tiny town with thatched cottages, red signal-boxes, skeletal gasometers, butchers' shops, greengrocers and goods yards filled with trucks and shunting engines. It blew my eight-year-old mind. Tim thought it stupid but I envied the awesome railway-set, as I envied the massive tank of brightly coloured tropical fish in his bedroom and his easy, effortless charm with girls.

"How's Holly?" I asked.

"Fine," he answered guardedly. "Wants to know when you're coming back to the youth group. Says you could help with the confirmation class."

"Oh," I said. I always felt Holly dismissed me as a total heathen. "You kissed her yet?" I grinned. "Or maybe gone a bit further, eh? Eh? Tim? You *dog*, eh?"

"Don't be so immature," he frowned. "A kiss is as good as a wedding-ring. And as for any *further*, as you put it, we're still children, you know. And it's Timothy, actually. Holly prefers me to use my full Christian name."

"You must've held hands," I said, "In the pictures or wherever you go. Timothy."

"We go to Prayer Group," he said piously, "Where we *all* hold hands."

An awkward pause. My best friend had turned into a twat.

"Hey," I said, "You seen that Hornby advert with Bernard Cribbins and Kitten Kong?"

"No," he said disinterestedly. "You wanna be Napoleon or Wellington?" He directed me to a beige map marked with green forests, blue rivers and grey buildings and overlaid with a grid of hexagons. Multi-coloured cardboard counters, blue for the French, green for the Prussians and red for the British, were heaped in groups on their starting hexagons. I studied the rulebook, the victory conditions and demoralization levels on page 6 and the combat results table and probability ratios on the board itself.

"What would Charlie choose?"

"Charlie doesn't believe in playing at war," said Timothy. "He says it's not Christian. I might do Bible Study instead. By the way, we had a great time down the soup-kitchen last weekend. You really should come. There's some really interesting people."

"Tramps."

"Don't be so judgmental, Jonny. Just because they're tramps doesn't make them bad people. You have to look for the person within. Now who do you want to be?"

"Napoléon Blownapart, hon hon," I said, adopting an outrageous Inspector Clouseau accent. "Ze Frenchies are coming, Monsewer Teem. 'Ide your flurffy leetle sheep."

Studying the map, I decided to avoid the chateau, concentrate my fire on the flanks and work round Hougomont on the left. Then I could send the cavalry round the right through Papelotte, create a pincer and surround the whole Allied line, with a diversionary excursion to Les Vieux Amis and Waterloo itself. Scribbling the start-time of 1100 hours on 18th June 1815 on a pad, I rolled the dice and sent General Jacquinot's First Cavalry Division over the top whilst the infantry left Plançenoit for the Lasne River. I'd done some preliminary research by consulting last year's history project. Chapter 11, about the Last 100 Days, started on page 72 with my brief summary of Napoleon's escape from Elba and his march into Paris at the head of the very troops sent to arrest him. Now that's what I call leadership.

Anyway, my account of the Battle of Waterloo said that "a sunken road ran nearly all the way along Wellington's front-line. This road was bounded on the right by the Château Hougomont and on the left by the farmhouse of La Haye Sainte and the village of Papelotte. At 11.30 a.m. the French artillery opened fire from the opposite plateau of La Belle Alliance. Then four divisions began moving forward against the British left-centre and the Dutch and Belgian brigade there fled in panic." I was hoping the same would happen on the first game-turn of the simulation. "A fifth division," my project continued, "Took the grounds of La Haye Sainte after Dubois's cuirassiers had ridden down some Hanoverians. Just then, a stunning volley crashed into the French and the British 5th Division charged forward, led by their commander, General Picton."

Timothy, following history, sent two units against Fichermont but the dice fell badly and he had to retreat. Sending an artillery unit into the village, I seized the bridge and cried "Ha ha, ze breedge, c'est moi!"

"You're such a spaz, Jonny," frowned Tim. "You just said you *are* the bridge. You should have said 'Le pont est *à* moi'."

"It was a joke, Timothy." Man, he was so serious these days. He even wore serious clothes, this plain blue shirt with the collar buttoned and a grey crew-neck sweater. He'd never race Space Hoppers down his drive with me again, you know? Fifteen going on fifty.

We totted up the casualty-count. I'd lost 28 of the 60 available. Another 32 and I'd lose the game. Tim'd lost 16 out of a possible 45. It'd been a bloody first Game-Turn, but I'd gained a lot of territory. Unfortunately the battle went from bad to worse. A series of disastrous engagements cost me a further eleven points, with no ground gained at all, save for some tiny farmhouse miles away from the Allied line. Then Tim advanced the Prussians to the Lasne Bridge. This wasn't good. Sucking my pencil, I decided to gamble and dispatched a cavalry unit round the rear of Hougomont to tie up the English infantry and three units to Lasne to delay the Prussians till I could get some proper reinforcements. Then I captured Les Vieux Amis at odds of 16-18. Although the Prussians drove me back from Lasne, there were resounding successes all over the battlefield. The gamble seemed to have paid off. Papelotte, two hexes worth, was in my hands, along with half of Braine L'Alleud on the left flank. In fact, the Allies were being driven steadily back as the French continued their remorseless advance.

Tim unleashed the Prussians on the Couture Marshes then fell into my trap by detaching several cavalry units from LVA to support his infantry at La Haye Sainte where I'd feinted an assault. Everywhere, the French held firm, the Allies collapsed. Immediately I renewed my attack on Braine, moving the Imperial Guard into position for a concentrated assault on Hougomont itself. Massing my troops against the château, I unleashed the dice. The ratio in the book was 36: 18. Two to one. If the Guard failed, I'd lose 'cos the points lost would exceed the Demoralisation Level. It was another huge gamble.

But I did not fail. Hougomont fell and the Grenadiers moved in. Punching the air, I crowed "You lost it, Monsewer Teem. Surrender your tasty 'orses to our fine French chefs."

Abandoning restraint, he hurled the Dornberg cavalry unit over a ridge against my Chasseurs, at odds of 1-5. Inevitably, they were totally destroyed and the Battle of Waterloo collapsed into isolated pockets of desperate fighting. I held all the strategic positions but everything now hinged on my casualties staying below the sixty-point limit.

Tim chipped away, grinding me down, a point here, a point there. I decided to fall back, consolidate my remaining strength but most of my forces were cut off from the centre. I was just 6 points away from defeat, Tim, aided by the Prussians, 16. This was just like the real battle, I realised, and unleashed everything I had against the left-flank and rear of Hougomont in an attempt to eliminate his artillery, which was totally battering the Guards around the château. I lost another 2 points, but took 6 off Tim. It was going to be tight.

Tim retaliated by reinforcing La Haye Sainte and forcing the Clocq Forest. My Imperial Guard cavalry unit was destroyed at a cost of four points, and that was that. Defeat. According to page 74 of my project, "The French faltered and Wellington ordered a charge. Maitland's men lowered their bayonets and charged, the 'Invincibles' fleeing before them. The Prussians swept out from Plançenoit and the British swept over the French battle-stations. Napoleon rode from the field with his army behind him, his Empire finished." Bonaparte was indeed Blownapart. Bollocks.

Disappointed, I surveyed the map while Tim sat back with a self-satisfied smirk. I was still holding Hougomont and Papelotte/Fichermont. I'd also cleared the bend of the river and swept the Allies completely from the Eastern edge of the map. I still held Maransart and the Lasne river crossing, so territorially I was still dominant. I'd lost ultimately 'cos of that disastrous first Game-Turn where none of my attacks had succeeded and nearly half my casualty points had been lost. Only the risky venture against the château had paid off. However, just like in history, if it hadn't been for the Prussians… I wondered if it were actually possible for the French *ever* to win at Waterloo. I'd beaten Tim playing as the Germans on D-Day, pushing his Allies back into the sea. I'd also beaten him in *Seelöwe*, successfully masterminding the German invasion of Britain. But Waterloo? It always came down to the Prussians, and the casualty counts. Bloody Hun in the Sun, yeah?

As we settled in their antiseptically neat living-room with its nest of tables and pastel paper for the end of *Grandstand* and the footie scores, I wondered how Dad had got on with the pools this week as Spurs lost 3-0 to Villa and the Merseyside derby ended 2-2. Nicking Philip Brudenall's joke, I said "Everton are magic. Watch them disappear from the league."

Tim grunted. He wasn't much interested in football. He hadn't watched England lose controversially to Romania in midweek. Mind you, I wished I hadn't either. Diabolical display, as the pundits had said, despite the dodginess of Romania's seventy-fifth minute penalty. Couldn't see us qualifying for the World Cup Finals now, but what's new, eh?

Tim wasn't much interested in *Doctor Who* either. Well, fair enough. This particular story had this cactus for a villain. It was hardly scary. You'd just water it to a soggy death, wouldn't you? It was hardly Sarah Jane facing down Davros the Great Creator, was it? And this was the genius part. What if Davros, the creator-exterminator, was right? That mankind was like *sooo* tiny we didn't actually matter? I for one was desperate for the aliens to come and save us. Anyway, *The Muppets* were like hysterical, you know? They started with Paul Simon duetting 'Scarborough Fair' with Miss Piggy, this brilliant Waldorf-Statler line that they'd seen better 'fairs' on the bus, then Gonzo did this song, 'For You': *"For youuu... I'd wash my hair with stinky glue, I'd fry my legs and eat them too, I'd put a spider in my shoe... for yoouuuu!"* Then his chickens and asparagus (like, WTF?) ran away... man, it was mental, and we laughed like drunken hyenas. Tim and I were slowly re-bonding, especially when I said I liked his drawings.

As I said, he did Art as his option and he was actually pretty good. He'd done this grey pencil-sketch of a leafless tree at the end of a footpath. It was set against an empty sky, and I liked the way he'd used light and shade for contrast. It reminded me of David Hockney. He was also working on some pencil sketch of a Rubik's Cube. This, apparently, was a class project in which everyone had to incorporate or translate the cube into some other image. Tim had distorted his into this squeezed diamond shape with a thorn on the top and a drop of blood oozing from the bottom. A lynx-eye stared from the centre. I said it was cool and asked if I might have it for the school magazine. Now he was so flattered he asked what I was planning to play at the music competition and when I said Chopin, he said I was really good with Chopin. Then his Mum called us for tea into this like brown-and-orange kitchen with these mental Moroccan-style brown ceramic tiles and beige Formica tops – the latest fashion, apparently.

She'd baked lasagne, usually one of my favourites, but too much Parmesan made the whole kitchen reek of sick. A jug of water stood on the table in front of Tim's sullenly glaring sister, Julie, whom I had, of course, known forever.

"Hello, Julie," I said cheerily.

"Would you like some orange squash, Jonathan?" asked Mrs Wilson. "Or milk?"

"No thank you," I said. "It's terrible stuff, all chemicals, E-numbers and Tartrazine and milk makes me spew."

"I'd forgotten what a strange little boy you are," she answered tightly. "I don't suppose you've got a girlfriend yet?"

Flushing, I muttered I was dating Claire Ashton. Mrs Wilson snorted sceptically.

As I pulled out a chair, Julie turned on me. "Why don't you come to church any more? Have you stopped believing?"

"No," I said, "But my piano lesson's on Sunday now so fitting it in's a bit tricky."

"You shouldn't be just 'fitting' Jesus into your life," Julie said disapprovingly.

"Are you still with Barbara Lennox?" asked Mrs Wilson, taking the lasagne out of the oven. She'd been terribly jealous when I was accepted by the best piano teacher in Northern England while Tim was plodding through Grade 1. In Mrs Wilson's mind, Tim could've had the same if he'd had such a break but *he* wasn't invited to audition because, basically, he was shit at music. To Mrs Wilson, though, there was nothing I could do that Tim couldn't do better and I'd clearly blagged or bribed my way onto Mrs Lennox's books. Nothing to do with natural talent, obviously, or being fucking brilliant for my age.

"To be honest," I added, "I don't really enjoy that type of worship any more, guitars and tambourines and stuff. I'd rather have an organ." Realising what I'd just said, I giggled and clapped my hand to my lips. "Gosh, I don't mean..." I went phone-box red. "That sounded *sooo* gay." I giggled again.

"Like your friend Rosie," said Tim sourly.

"*Alistair* Rose?" said Julie curiously. "Gail's got such a crush on him, like from when they did *Midsummer Night's Dream* together."

"She's not the only one," muttered Tim, half under his breath.

Gail, playing Titania, had leched after Alistair's open-shirted Oberon but, now it was crystal-clear, he'd only had eyes for *me*, in my green war-paint, shorts and satin leaves. Fuck. How hadn't I noticed at the time? God, and that photo. It was *so* gay. Fuck.

"I keep telling her," said Julie, "You're wasting your time with that one. King of the Fairies? Talk about type-casting."

"He isn't gay," I said defensively, blushing hotly. "He's just confused."

"Huh," grunted Tim. "Same difference. And you made quite a good fairy yourself."

Fortunately his dad arrived, greeting me with a cheerful "long time, no see, Jon-Jon. Busy with your music and stuff, are you? Got a girlfriend yet? I mean, you're fifteen, aren't you? Timothy's got *loads* of girlfriends. I mean, you're not *bad*-looking, Jon-Jon."

Cheers, you cheeky slap-headed twat.

"He's actually going out with the headmaster's daughter," smirked Tim loudly.

I turned the colour of Superman's pants.

When the food arrived on the table, I dug in merrily, then froze. The others were staring at me, expressions of horror etched on their features.

"Grace, Jonathan, grace!" said Mrs Wilson, shocked at my forgetfulness. "I don't know what you do in *your* house (you bunch of Hell-bound heathens) but in *this* house we give thanks for our food."

Tim thanked the Lord for blessing us with food and companionship, asked Him to save us from sin and invoked His peace on the world, His people and on us. Amen.

"You should pray for Rosie," Julie said sanctimoniously, "That Jesus will enter his heart and heal his sickness."

"It isn't a sickness," I said passionately. "It's a natural state."

"Homosexuality?" Mrs Wilson was incredulous. "Of course it isn't, Jonathan. It's about as unnatural a state as anything could possibly be."

"These people need therapy," added Julie.

"Why?" I protested. "If two people love each other, it doesn't matter, does it?"

The Wilsons' collective look of blank incomprehension and Tim's sad, slow shake of the head and murmured suggestion I read my Bible should've warned me to shut up and eat my dinner but they didn't and I was becoming angry.

"I don't get why you're so bothered by what others do in their bedrooms," I said. "Blimey, Tim, you said *I'm* judgemental."

Mrs Wilson repeated that she'd forgotten what a strange little boy I was. Furiously, I forked up some lasagne. It was stone-cold. I left soon after.

When I got home, Mum and Dad were waiting in the kitchen. Mum had the kind of expression that normally goes with the tapping of a hand against a rolling-pin, you know?

"What's up?" I said. "I'm not late, am I?"

"Pam Wilson phoned," she said. "Apparently you got into a fight about homosexuality."

I shrugged, whilst struggling to believe the mardy cow had rung to complain. "So what? She's a stupid, ignorant woman. You know that. You've said it yourself."

"See?" said Dad. "I told you he was just being provocative. You know what he's like."

"She said *you* said homosexuality was normal," said Mum.

"Well," I said, still standing in the doorway, "It is."

Then there was this like nuclear explosion of what I can only describe as a load of old bollocks about Nature and God and marriage and kids and family and the collapse of civilisation and so on – you can fill it in for yourself – and Dad finishing it off with this kind of strangled 'How can it be normal? Some fat, hairy bloke shoving his cock up your arse?'

"Roy!" gasped Mum.

"Well," said Dad. "Anyway, what do *you* know about it, Jonathan?"

"Nothing," I said bitterly, slumping into a chair. "There aren't any books about it, not for teenagers. There aren't any novels, or characters *in* novels. If you're g...," I changed words, "If you're a teenager, there's nothing out there to help you. There aren't even any magazines. There's only *Gay Times,* that's for adults, and Smith's doesn't stock it any more anyway."

"I should hope not," said Mum. "Filling silly kids' heads with filth."

"Filth?" I protested. "Information, Mum, information, so you know what it's all about."

"I don't *want* you knowing what it's all about," she snapped. "It's that Alistair Ross, teaching you all sorts of rubbish. I don't like you hanging around with him."

"He thinks too much," said Dad censoriously.

"Since when was thinking a crime?" I yelled. "You should try it sometime, Dad. Give your brain a visit like every decade or so. Maybe you'd find something interesting, but I doubt it." His face crumpled like an empty crisp packet. Immediately regretting this cheap shot, I apologised, but the damage was done. "Maybe it's a generational thing," I said placatingly.

"So we're a bunch of dinosaurs," Mum cut in, "Because we have morals and standards?" Suddenly she flashed "I don't want to talk about this any more, Jonathan. Get off your bloody soap-box, please, or leave the room."

"What if *I* am?" I snarled. "What if *I'm* homosexual? What if *I'm* gay, eh? What then?"

"Don't be so bloody ridiculous," said Mum.

"What's ridiculous?" I shot back. "Suppose I *am* gay. What then? Eh? Eh?"

"You're *not* gay," she said with an air of finality. "God Almighty, Jonathan, why do you have to be so bloody melodramatic? You've become an insufferable little brat, you know?"

Christ, why was everyone against me? Tim, Julie, Dad, Mum… everyone. Mum said I wasn't gay. So I wasn't. End of chat.

"Stay away from Alistair Ross," said Dad suddenly.

"Rose!" I screamed. "He's called *Rose*! There *is* no Alistair Ross. He's Alistair *Rose*, for fuck's sake. Get his name right! Ow! Get off, Mum. You're hurting me." Her fingers were digging deeply into my upper arm. She was actually shaking me.

"Whatever," said Dad. "You're not to see him again."

"Bit hard," I said defiantly, "Since we're in the same house and catch the same bus."

"From now on," said Dad, attempting to be decisive, "I'll collect you in the car."

"No!" God, only total losers got picked up by their folks. "What is *wrong* with you?"

"What's wrong with *you,* more like?" Mum fired back.

"You know!" I yelled, storming out of the kitchen.

I heard her scream after me "Don't slam the fucking door!" as I slammed the door so hard the windows rattled. I heard her start pounding upstairs after me, then Dad yelling at her to calm down and her raging that he always took my side and what was wrong with *him*?

I wasn't used to fighting with my parents – I don't think only children are – and I hated it. We got along so well. We hardly ever argued about anything and I didn't do the stereotypical teenage thing, you know, like loafing around in bed all day with super-loud music and a bad attitude. Sure, they told me off about stuff when I was a kid, like sitting up straight and not eating bread-crusts off the bird-table and not chewing my hoodie strings but that's what parents do, isn't it? To tell you *that* kind of stuff? Not that your love for someone else is 'filth'.

I put on The Cure CD Andy Paulus had given me for my birthday and cranked up the volume – "*I try to laugh about it, Cover it all up with lies, I try to laugh about it, hiding the tears in my eyes, 'Cause boys don't cry…*"

My folks were such bloody dinosaurs they ought to be featured in Carey Miller's *Dictionary of Monsters and Mysterious Beasts*, except, if they'd gone alphabetically as The Peters Family, they'd've been between Pegasus the Flying Horse on page 125 and the red-gold fiery Phoenix on page 126, two super-cool beasts, which wouldn't have been right. No, they'd have to go near the ogres or trolls.

"Why's the landing light on?" shouted Dad. "This isn't the bloody Blackpool illuminations, you know! And turn that racket down!"

Furiously waving two fingers at the Dalek on my door, I screamed "Fuck off!"

Sobbing with rage, I slapped my face, then, crying a little, because I knew what I had to do, how much it would hurt, but the blood-sacrifice would save me. I took the compass from my Oxford Maths set, bit my left wrist to stifle the scream and stabbed my left thigh twice.

13: It's Raining Men

THURSDAY 23rd October. I'd committed to going with Paulus to house-swimming after school. The purpose of the session was two-fold. First, we were trying out for the Murray House swim-team then having a life-saving lesson. I really wanted to get that badge. I thought it would be useful though I hadn't yet figured out how. As for Poorly, he wanted to get in the school swimming team.

Willie set our English homework to write a review of tonight's BBC broadcast of *Taming of the Shrew* with John Cleese. Yay. Watching telly. Great homework, right? But Shakespeare? On the *telly*? Give us a break. It was even on the front cover of the Radio Times, Cleese in this beard and Shakespearean costume. Anyway, Barney went ballistic about the 0/10 Chemistry test I'd done, said he'd be writing to my parents about my attitude and put me in detention. Humourless fucking twat. Everyone in the *class* laughed. I told him I couldn't do it. He just said there were a lot of things I couldn't do, weren't there? Well, fuck him. I had a brilliant lunchtime clarinet lesson in the Purcell Music Room sight-reading this B minor study on page 39 of the Demnitz book, this Gade *Humoreske* I'd played for Grade 4 and absolutely nailing the Brahms F minor sonata so that Martin Angus nodded enthusiastically as I let the final, four-beat D fade away. I snoozed through Wingnut blithering on in RE about some loser sitting cross-legged under a tree somewhere in India for like a trazillion years whilst Gray doodled a new version of Piggo on the back of my hand then, discussing Liverpool's 1-0 win over Aberdeen and Bayern Munich's utter trashing of Ajax in the UEFA Champions' Cup with Maxton, beetled off to French.

Benjy seemed tense, tired and strained when he arrived ten minutes late. This grace-period at the end of the day was the perfect cue for a massive paper-fight but Benjy, of course, went absolutely ballistic when he saw his classroom floor littered with balls of screwed-up A4, calling us a bunch of irresponsible louts and yelling we would stay after school to pick up every scrap of rubbish with our teeth. Yeah, yeah. Whatever.

"Thanks," muttered Paulus who, inevitably, had not joined in despite being pelted by me and Gray and being called a saddo by Maxton. "Now we'll be late for swimming."

"Quiet, Paulus," snapped Benjy, "Books open, page 114, get your heads down, get the exercise done, and don't open your smart-alec mouths again." Anticipating, he held up a warning hand. "Breathe through your *nose*, Peters."

I laughed approvingly and shut up. Clever to head that one off. Benjy was usually all right with me, even though he'd once said I mangled the French language like 'a horny, yowling cat desperate for a bunk-up with Mrs Cat (dramatic PAUSE like he's on *Strictly*) in a bag.' The entire class had split their sides, and Broody nicknamed me Horny Cat for a while. So all right, we'd trashed his classroom but he'd really gone off on one. It wasn't like him to yell and scream, and we didn't like or respect teachers who did. We liked teachers who met us on our terms and in our own way, with the kind of world-weary humour judiciously laced with sarcasm that we used with each other. We liked teachers who understood us, enjoyed our company and, when we pissed them off, 'cos we were teenagers and would piss off Jesus, outwitted us mentally because they were older than us and had seen it all before. Those teachers we admired tremendously. Those teachers we'd work for. Those teachers we'd trust and follow as they led us through their courses. Teachers like Beaky and Cedric, Hellfire and Bunny. Teachers who believed in us. Teachers who respected us. Teachers who *liked* us. The bond between us and them became unbreakably strong. Teachers who tried to dominate us, like Barney and Herbie, generally failed. Teachers who tried to work with us generally succeeded.

A sudden, deafening hammering interrupted this idle meditation and I realised with a start I hadn't even started the transposition of the text from present to past. I guess most hearts skipped a shocked beat when Frank Gallagher burst in and whispered something urgently into

Benjy's ear. Benjy's expression hardened. Scrambling to our feet, we glanced at each other, suddenly concerned, as Gallagher, pausing at the door to tell us, calmly and cheerfully, that a prefect would come and in the meantime, get this bloody room tidied up, you little animals, and Peters, you slob, do your top button up, led him away by the elbow. A buzz of speculation erupted as we set to work, Seymour, who'd turned 16 on Tuesday, holding up the waste-bin like a basketball-hoop and inviting us to take turns at getting a paper ball into it.

"I reckon he's been arrested," said Gray.

"Why? What do you think he's done?" said Stewart.

"I caught the words 'hospital' and 'baby'," said Paulus.

"Well, that's it," said Gray. "He's got some silly tart up the duff, hasn't he? Next thing he'll be run out of town by the angry husband."

"*You* said he was gay," I recalled, "Because he wears hair-gel."

"I know," said Gray in disgust. "At *his* age. I mean, he must be *thirty* at least!"

"Well," said Maxton, "Whatever it is, I feel sorry for him. He's got Frank lavishing care and attention on him. That's enough to make *anyone* wish they were banged up."

I wondered who the prefect would be as I popped a paper-ball into the waste-bin and earned a round of applause. Not Rose. *Anyone* but Rose. I aimed another paper-ball, calling 'hold it steady, Kev' as Leverett showed up. Bollocks. I meant anyone but *Leverett*. Less than happy that his free period had been interrupted for a bit of baby-sitting, he chucked this black ring-binder onto the desk and scowled at me.

"Bloody hell, Peters. What're you playing at?"

"Mr Gallagher told us to clear up," I said cheekily, "But he didn't say how." I plopped the paper ball deftly into the bin and smugly acknowledged the applause of my class-mates with a half-bow. Leverett just yelled at me to sit down and do my bloody collar up or he'd slam me in detention, the mardy-arsed twat.

"What happened to Benjy?" asked Maxton.

"I told you," Gray maintained. "Long arm of the law finally caught up with him. Man with hair like that, it was only a matter of time."

"Shut up," growled Leverett, throwing himself into Benjy's chair, "And get on with your work. Page 114, I believe." God, he was a moody bastard.

I settled into my Maths prep so I could get Maxton's help but he was wrestling with the French, which was actually a piece of piss. It was some picture-story called 'La famille Leclerc part en vacances' with three comprehension questions per picture, stuff like 'Est-ce que c'est loin?' under this picture of a ruddy great road-sign reading '115 km.' Still, the road-sign matching exercise on page 110 was fun, like the buying petrol role-play on page 112. You never knew when such info might come in handy in real life. Unlike rearranging these formulae, which wouldn't ever. I mean, like EVER! I felt my brain melt as I stared at the questions:

'1. Re-arrange the formula $d=fhs$ to make f the subject.

2. Re-arrange the formula $A = \underline{\frac{bh}{2}}$ to give h in terms of both A and b.

3. Re-arrange each formula to give the letters in **bold**:

a) $t = \boldsymbol{p}rs$ b) $s = 3r\boldsymbol{t}y$ c) $k = a^2\boldsymbol{b}c$ d) $V = 1/3\pi \, r^2 \, \boldsymbol{h}$.' I mean, why?

"What's up, Peters?" snarled Leverett.

"I can't bloody do it," I snarled back, frustrated.

"I'll help you," Huxley volunteered.

"Blimey, Adie," said Maxton, "It'll turn your hair white. He's got a brain like a Swiss cheese-plant. Full of holes."

Pointing out it was either Swiss cheese *or* cheese-plant but not both, I told him to shut his face then Leverett told me to shut mine and I listened, frowning, whilst the class swot talked the class turnip patiently through these examples. God, it was sooo boring. I was infinitely happier *à la station-service*. At least I knew what they were on about.

When we finally got out, Leverett having retained us whilst he inspected the floor with a like a fucking microscope, I dragged my sports-bags from my bottom-row locker, thanked Huxley for his help and headed off with a still-grumbling Paulus. As we left the main building for the swimming pool, we were joined by Leo Trent and Richard Sutcliffe. I quite liked Sooty. Though he seemed a bit sullen, his nose was too beaky and his eyes too close together, he was a promising cricketer and seemed a decent actor. But a bit too Captain Beaky for me.

Stop, I yelled inside my head. Sooty Sutcliffe? Stop. He's bloody fourteen.

"What's this about Goddard being caught by the Fuzz?" Leo demanded.

"That'd be painful," I joked, "Caught by the fuzz. Not that you gaybies have any yet."

"No," said Sooty excitedly. "Apparently some coppers came for him, tooled up like they're going to bust up a crack-den on a council estate. Apparently he yells 'You'll never take me alive, copper,' smacks one in the nose and legs it down the corridor."

"Gallagher rugby-tackles him." Leo took up the story. "Has to sit on him while the other copper's going 'Eat floor, scumbag, or I'll blow your fackin' knee-caps clean orf, you slag'."

"Then they drag him off to the piggy van," says Sooty, "An' he's swearing to go round their piggy houses, kill their piggy children and eat their piggy livers." He's even acting it out.

"Fuck's sake," I said, pushing open the changing-room door. "Like with fava-beans and a nice Chianti, eh? Where did you hear all this shit?"

"Mark Gray told us," said Sooty, dumping his bag on a bench, pointing his fingers at Leo and crying we'll never take him alive while Leo snorted like said pig and fired back.

Mark Gray. Never one to let the truth stand in the way of a good story. No wonder he wanted to be a lawyer.

"We were there, son." Paulus unlaced his shoes. "Frank came in, spoke to him then led him outside. He said something about 'hospital' and 'baby'. So that's what it's about."

"Son?" I said, hanging my grey shirt on the peg with my sweater and taking off my shoes and socks. "How long did *you* sit under the tree to become a wise old greybeard? Does Wingnut know? He'll drone on about you in some boring lesson, the Endless Enlightenment of Poorly Paulus." Paulus slammed his fist down on my bicep. "Ow, you twat! You've got a fist like a rock." I rubbed my smarting upper arm. It really hurt, the twat.

"Shit!" Leo howled with delight. "So it's true! He *has* got some bird up the duff."

"I always thought he was gay," Sooty remarked, "On account of the hair-gel."

Oh boy.

"Afternoon, lads." Jacko popped his head round the door. "Any more coming?"

There were two skinny second-form gimps and some lardy-arsed third-former changing shyly under their towels in the corner. I half-expected one to dive whimpering into a cubicle. I despised such self-conscious little wimps. I mean, we've all got one, for fuck's sake. Just 'cos *yours* is a Tommy Tiddler…

"I think Alex Hartley's coming, sir," said Sooty.

"Oh God," I muttered, stripping off my vest. "He'll have to partner the Podgemeister." Leo spluttered.

Jacko's blue eyes crinkled a little. "I'll put him with *you*, JP, if I hear any more of *that* talk. He has an eating disorder."

"You mean he can't stop, sir?" I asked innocently, unfastening my belt.

"It's a disease actually, for your information, Mr Peters," said Jacko.

"Yeah, it's called Greedy Bastard-itis." My trousers fell down my thighs.

Leo howled, thumping his knee. Sooty guffawed. Even Paulus cracked a smile.

"Just because *your* ribs look like a garden-rake, Peters," Jacko said, walking away as Sooty, Leo and Paulus laughed some more. I wouldn't care, I scowled, but none of *them* were exactly heavyweights.

"Except," said Leo, nodding at my salmon-pink slip, "In the trouser department."

Paulus, cackling, added "Supermite, eh? The Bionic Maggot, ha ha."

As I slapped his bare shoulder then chased him up the length of the changing room towards the showers, whipping him with my tie, Sonning, in his stripy blue-and-gold blazer, and Rose, in his charcoal suit, appeared in the door and moved towards the pegs.

"Hey, Mark," I cried, Paulus forgotten, "You look like a stick of rock."

"Better than having a brain like a rock, JP," Sonning returned. "Nice knickers."

"Though not much in 'em!" cried Leo, who was now sitting stark naked on the bench rooting in his bag for his trunks. Red as a Man United shirt, I told him to shut up.

"Hope you haven't forgotten them," said Rosie.

"Aye, like you did your socks," I added teasingly.

Ali's eyes met mine across Leo's blond candyfloss hair. Was that a twinkle of humour in those deep teal pools?

"Oh," said Leo, "Soz, JP. I meant to bring them back. I even washed 'em." His voice took on a tone of pride. "In real Fairy Liquid."

I slapped my forehead and called him a spaz as the others laughed. With a ringing Klingon victory-cry, Leo pulled his trunks from his bag. 'They' were this sparkly, spangly pink-purple thong which resembled a cheese-wire.

"What the *fuck* are those?" said Sonning, pausing in his shirt-unbuttoning.

"Yikes," cried Sooty, slipping into blue trunks. "They're *so* gay. Who chose *them*?"

Turning my back and quarter-erection slightly away from the older boys, I slid off the salmon slip, conscious of Ali's eyes boring into my backside, conscious that the tan I had acquired during the summer had now faded from bronze to a faded pale biscuit, like a piece of paper left out in the sun too long. He had his shirt off and I thought I might've been staring at his smooth, hairless chest again.

"I did," said Leo indignantly. "I think they're really cool. Don't you like them?"

"They belong in a stripper's *boudoir*," said Ali drily.

Quivering with laughter, I tugged up my own trunks, red with a white knot-motif.

"Nice trunks, JP!" called Sonning. "Haul on your bow-line, eh?"

Now it was their turn to laugh at me. Merriment bubbled into Alistair's face.

Leo was squeezing himself into his cheese-wire, twerking like said stripper. He had a pale, fragile-looking body, a tight bubble-bottom, absolutely no hips and a dusting of golden pubic hair. His alabaster chest was narrow, his nipples small, and his waist like a wasp's.

Face the colour of a first-class stamp, I turned away. Why the hell was I staring at Leo Trent? Because his dad said he might be gay? Because he was amazingly cute with the body of Cupid? Because otherwise I'd be, like, staring at Ali Rose's boy-bits?

"Shine a light!" Leo exclaimed. "They're really tight and scratchy."

You could also see every bulge and bump.

"Blimey, Leo," said Paulus, "You are *such* a tart."

"Don't get your dive wrong," said Rosie, pulling on these really sleek, black, mid-thigh Speedos, "Or they'll slice your boy-bits off. We'll find your winkie floating on the water."

Everyone laughed again, then Jacko returned to hurry us up. We trooped out, still laughing and teasing each other, enjoying companionship and the blokey banter, until we reached the white-tiled pool and its blood-red surround. Surveying the rolling, unnaturally blue 25 x 10 metre expanse of heavily chlorinated water, we decided it looked very cold. This might not be so much fun after all. Settling my blue goggles and gritting my teeth, I launched into a good, clean racing-dive, and surged upwards near Paulus, who was shivering on the edge in these tight, tiny pine-green Speedos, the soles of his feet just touching the water. Paulus too was skinny and sharp-boned but he was a little taller than me, so seemed stringier, longer-limbed, more coltish, you know? He was also quite hot. I gulped and tried not to look at him.

"What's it like?" He glanced at the gimp hovering indecisively at the top of the steps.

"Well," I said through chattering teeth, "It's warmer than usual. You still have to watch for the icebergs but at least you don't have to break the surface."

"Sarcasm doesn't suit you, JP," said Jacko. "Get going. Two warm-up lengths, favourite stroke."

I couldn't resist the oldest quip in the book, "Well, that'd be breast-stroke, sir," and took off in a steady front-crawl.

"Keep your legs straight!" bawled Jacko. "What're you waiting for, Andy? Christmas? Go." He smacked Paulus on the shoulder. Paulus slid into the water. "Leo! Sooty! Go."

They bumped knuckles, crowed 4D's Klingon war-cry, "*Heghlu'mekh qaq jajvam,*" today is a good day to die, then, one after the other, swallow-dived into the pool.

I was nearing the wall, consciously keeping my hips up and my arms close to my head. Touching the wall with my fingertips, I rolled into a perfect racing-turn, one hand on the wall, feet up for propulsion, and made it back in what I thought was a good time.

"What the hell were you doing with your arms, JP?" barked Jacko. "You're flailing around like some bloody washerwoman."

I heard Leo's familiar hyena-howl of laughter mingle with Rosie's silver-bell tinkle.

"Two lengths' back-stroke. Go."

Getting my feet up on the wall, I launched myself into the air, landing back in the water with a small splash, and was away, staring at the ceiling, arms working like windmill blades, my shoulder muscles beginning to loosen.

"Your hips are still wobbling about like that washerwoman, Jonny!" called Jacko from the side of the pool. I muttered something rude and straightened my body-line.

Leo and Sooty were in this widths relay-race against Sonning and Rose, screaming and shouting at each other, Leo dancing on the pool-edge and yelling encouragement at Sonning, Rose, beside him, urging on Sooty. The three gimps were splashing about in the shallow-end. Paulus was sitting on the top step, shivering violently, stifling a sneeze and scrutinizing the sole of his right foot for possible verrucas.

"I thought you said it was warm. It's freezing. An' I'm coming down with your cold."

"Do something," I suggested, splashing water at his flat, smooth stomach. I actually felt energized. "Move around a bit." Demisting my goggles, I surface-dived to the tiled floor.

Ali and Leo, battling head-to-head, were being screamed at by their team-mates. Jackson, equally animated, was yelling advice. Then he saw me watching.

"Ready for your lengths, JP?"

"I've done 'em, sir."

"Four? You call 'four' lengths?"

Sonning was shrieking Leo's name now. His twiggy arms were thrashing the water, his matchstick legs kicking, slightly ahead of Rosie, whose head, twisting, broke the surface for air. I saw his mouth open for a tremendous gasp, then he plunged under again, but Leo won by a half-metre and promptly went mental, dancing in the water with his arms aloft like a boxer while Sonning bawled 'well done, Lion, well done' and Jacko clapped enthusiastically.

''Well done, all of you,'' he cried. ''I think we found our relay team.''

Sonning hauled Leo's light body out of the pool. It reminded me of apple-bobbing.

"He must weigh next-to-nothing," Paulus muttered.

"Five stone?" I reckoned. "What's lighter than featherweight? Atom-weight?"

"JP! You know that washerwoman I mentioned? Less gossip, more lengths!"

Bollocks. 20 lengths, 440 yards, 500 metres. Jacko had some crazy notion that I would be a decent long-distance swimmer. He thought I had this inner determination, this steely will, this inexhaustible reserve... fuck knows why.

"Andrew! Shouldn't you be doing a length of butterfly or something? Individual medley didn't include shivering on the steps last time I checked the rules."

Swallowing a mouthful of water, I coughed a laugh.

The first ten lengths were fine but by the twelfth I was beginning to tire. Everything seemed to be coming from my shoulders and my arms were starting to feel heavy. I wondered why I was doing this when I could be at home reading a book or watching *Scooby Doo,* anything but this. I forced my leaden arms to move. The cold was starting to seep through my skin. My trunks stuck to my buttocks like clammy cling-film. I shut out my thoughts, that this was pointless lunacy, that I should stop and rest, and instead counted lengths, counting every stroke, sixteen, sixteen, sixteen, sixteen, then seventeen, seventeen, seventeen, seventeen, counting with the rhythm, then this weird mantra-chant broke out in my brain, eighteen, two to go, eighteen, two to go, eighteen, two to go…

Touching the tiled trough for the final time, I clung on grimly, uttered a rattling cough and spat out a load of water. Pushing my goggles up on my forehead, I ducked my head under the surface, floated for a moment then dragged myself up the steps, chest heaving with exertion. Limbs reduced to jelly, I stumbled towards Jacko and the stop-watch.

"Good effort, JP," he said. "23 minutes 16. Come next week, one lunchtime perhaps, or on Tuesday afternoon with Andy and we'll try to get you to a minute a length."

I panted incoherently as he told me to take a break and get a drink. Still gasping, I collapsed on a bench, stripy blue towel round my shoulders, to watch Paulus swim a length of back-stroke and Leo thrash a length of fast front-crawl. In slow-motion, Ali passed, so gracefully, like a dancer, and his legs were so slim, especially in those sleek thigh-hugging shorts. Man, I *had* to get some.

"You look knackered," he said, tossing a black rubber brick into the pool.

"Fucking right," I panted, clutching the towel over the gold cross on my sternum. "Still, personal best." Smiling, he dived after the brick.

For life-saving, we were split into pairs, Sonning and Ali, me and Andy, Leo and Sooty, the two gimps together and Hartley with the chubby kid.

"Yikes," muttered Paulus, "Jambo's gonna drown."

After two minutes of treading water, Jacko got us to swim a width underwater. I got halfway across before my protesting lungs gave out. Still, I made it further than Paulus. Leo swam the whole width without surfacing once and bounced up and down on the other side waving two fingers and calling us losers. Then we had to tow each other a width by getting a hand under our partner's chin, sculling backwards with our free hand and kicking with our legs. I messed it up immediately when Paulus kicked me by accident and I let him go so we switched and Paulus tried towing me. We got halfway when a water-wave slapped my face and made me splutter. Leo and Sooty, obviously, were brilliant. Bloody water-gaybies.

"What a balls-up!" roared Jacko as Paulus yelled I was 'such a spaz'. "Change partners. Andy with Mark, JP with Rosie."

The moment I had been secretly dreading yet secretly wishing for had come.

"Sir," said Ali, "I can't."

"Nor me, sir," I glowered. "I'll go with Sonning."

"You'll go with Rose," snapped Jacko irritably.

"But sir…" said Ali.

"You're a senior prefect, man!" growled Jacko. "Act like one."

Facing him in the water, I adjusted my goggle-strap.

"So, *Alistair*, you gonna drown me then? Like the sick freak I am?"

His eyes narrowed slightly. "Shut up. Just breathe out and let yourself sink."

"I knew it," I said, "You hate me so much…"

Muttering 'shut up' again, he forced my head under the water. As I spluttered a protest, he flipped me onto my back, cupped his left hand under my chin and took my upper body onto his. I could feel his skin against mine and suddenly I couldn't breathe properly and it wasn't from the water but from the touch that had sent the now-familiar tingle of excitement racing through me, set my heart on fire, sapped the strength from my limbs and sent a surge of fire to my groin. I settled back on his chest as he sculled across the pool. His soft stubble scraped my shoulder and I heard him breathing in my ear, warm, rough, rasping gasps. I wondered if that was how it would be when he made love to me. Oh boy. When he made love to me… Closing my eyes, I wallowed in this moment. I wanted to stay like this forever. Suddenly, sadly, we reached the side and he dragged me from the water, lifting me by the hips, touching my hips. I trembled as I flopped onto the blood-red floor and felt him manipulating my limbs like I was a broken Barbie doll.

"Play dead," he said, his voice oddly harsh.

I opened my eyes. "What?"

"Pretend to be dead. I've got to do the A-B-C."

"Like this?" I froze my expression, mimicking *rigor mortis*.

"No," he said, struggling not to smile.

"Oh. Like this?" I let my face fall sideways, mouth hanging open, tongue lolling out.

He didn't reply, then I heard him laugh. I squinted up at him. His eyes were sparkling.

"Stop pissing about," he said, miming compressions on my chest.

"Ow!" I said.

"I'm not even touching you. One. Two. Three. Four. Five."

He pinched my nose and then leaned towards me. Mouth-to-mouth. With Ali.

Oh boy! Best day ever!

His eyes darkened with hunger, desire, love, everything raging together, everything so intense. For a moment, angels hung between us, barely breathing. Time froze. I stared into his soul and saw the truth. I parted my lips for the contact that was coming. It was coming. But instead he flipped me roughly into the recovery-position. I yelled "ow!" again, genuinely this time, and called him a twat as he cried "Finished, sir!" I could see an erection in his trunks.

"Good work, Ali," said Jacko, walking down the line of rescuers and rescued, yelling at Jambo to pound the fat boy's chest.

I heard Jambo saying something about not wanting to lose his hand in the flab as Alistair breathed into my ear that he had to flip me 'cos I had this massive erection.

"So've you," I grinned.

"Shit," he spluttered, and dived over me into the pool.

Everyone was fairly exhausted when we returned to the changing room, even Leo, but, as I peeled away my trunks and stood under the hot, reviving shower with my bottle of supermarket-brand shampoo and felt the circulation returning to my limbs, I felt really happy. We were friends again and, it seemed, he still wanted me.

"Thank God I'm out of those." Leo tossed the spangly Speedos across the showers.

"So 'm I," I murmured hungrily as Ali prowled towards us wrapped only in a towel.

Leo shot me this quizzical glance and splattered camomile and acacia honey Timotei over his butter-coloured curls. "You're glad I'm out of my trunks?"

"What? No." I slapped his shoulder. "You gay or something?"

Leo, laughing, said "Yes. Aren't you?"

"No, you stupid little twat," I snarled, "Of course I'm not."

Leo simply laughed again, swivelled his body in the shower-spray and started warbling in a *falsetto* Sheena Easton's 'Modern Girl': "*She don't build her world round no single man, But she's gettin' by, doin' what she can, She is free to be, what she wants to be, 'N all what she wants to be, is a modern girl.*" Stupid little twat.

"So, Leo," said Alistair, taking the place beside me, "Are your jewels still in the same place or have they migrated north?"

Leo fiddled with himself for a moment and said everything seemed to be there, and did anyone want to double-check?

"Just so long as they're in working order, eh, Jonny?" Ali gave me a wink.

"I'll find out tonight," said Leo chirpily, soaping himself, "In my bedtime wank." He was erecting in front of us and didn't seem to care.

Tearing my eyes away from Leo's thin pencil-stub penis, I watched white steamy foam streaming down Ali's lean frame. He was using Wash 'n' Go. Man, I *had* to get some.

"Look," he said, running a hand through the wet, bruise-black hair. "I'm sorry about that Saturday. I behaved like a jerk."

"Yes you did," said Leo smartly. "You were a total cunt."

"Leo," said Ali impatiently, "Go play with yourself while the grown-ups talk."

Leo's face took on this sly, foxy smirk as he blew us a kiss and paraded through the changing room wiggling his hips to '*I'm sexy and I know it*' and summoning Sutcliffe whilst the showers hissed around my head. Ali seemed so much bigger than me.

"Didn't know you were a Christian," he said, touching the gold cross on my chest.

"Yeah," I said, "But I'm not as serious as I used to be. I got fed up with being told how everything I want to do is a sin."

Alistair grunted. "Like what?"

"Oh, you know," I said airily, "Drinking, sex before marriage… blimey, if I have to wait that long, I'll *never* get it. Have to settle for masturbation, and that's even *more* sinful."

That silvery laugh switched on parts of my body I would rather it hadn't. I so much wanted to gaze at his groin but, knowing what that would do to mine, I kept my eyes fixed on the wall-tiles and tried to think about something else, Maths, rugby, God, God knows what.

"Look," he said, "I *am* sorry. I was upset, confused and scared. It's pretty intense, this stuff, isn't it? I'm not sure what I should feel any more." He sounded so tired. "It's really confusing, don't you think?" I wasn't sure what he meant. Did he mean love? Or realising you fancy another guy? "Anyway," he squeezed my arm. "Can we start over? I really want us to be friends."

"You were so mean to me," I said. "You called me horrible names."

His eyes saddened. "I know, and I'm ashamed of myself. You're the best thing in my life. I didn't mean to hurt you. It just came out badly."

I *had* to give him another chance. His heart was breaking before me. My eyes softened and, returning the squeeze, I felt the last trace of straightness vanish like a soap-bubble. Skipping onto the tiles, I wrapped my towel round my waist and said "Starting over."

"Love that mole." He tapped the side of his neck. "You know you've got one on your left shoulder-blade too?"

I grinned. "You shouldn't be looking!"

Paulus, sitting on the bench in a white slip and vest, jerked his head towards the showers. "So it's true then."

"What is?" I replied defensively.

"You and Rosie." He ran this Adidas speed-stick inside his smooth, hairless armpits.

"Fuck off," I said. "Where did you hear that?"

"Something Wilson said. And Gray. A few people."

"Well," I said, "It's a load of bollocks, Andrew."

Paulus nodded at the tent in my towel. "What's that then?"

"So I get erections in the shower." I hoped a little light laughter would cover my embarrassment. "Don't you?"

"Not when I'm in the shower with other *boys*," he said, narrowing his chilly blue eyes. "I saw the way you were looking at each other in the life-saving class. You were about to kiss."

"Bollocks," I laughed uneasily, "Anyway, why were you looking?" About to add 'you great poof,' the words died in my throat.

"If I saw it, others might see it too." He buttoned his white shirt thoughtfully. "Be careful, J. People see, people talk. People don't know stuff, they make it up. Look at the newspapers. Look at Goddard. His wife just had a baby but that hasn't stopped people inventing stuff. Never let the facts stand in the way of a juicy story." Squinting down at me, he slipped into his blazer and said "You're my best friend. I'd hate to see you in someone else's story."

14: Give me just a little more time

I FINISHED the half-term with mixed mid-term grades, with 5 As (English, History, French, Music and German), two Bs (PE and RE), two Cs (Chemistry and Biology) and two Ds (Maths and Physics), finishing bottom of the class in both. Like no surprise there. Bunny just shook his head sadly, like I was some dribbling mush-head. "Cute," he told Jennings, "But terminally stupid." Jennings, the fucker, had agreed.

"I just can't do it," I told the folks over a mixed-bean curry. "I haven't got the kind of brain for algebra. I mean, what are all those letters for anyway? I can like write about experiments and stuff but I can't do the equations, you know?"

"You'll have to do better than that in June," Mum said.

Bollocks. I was doing my bloody best. I wasn't doing exams in PE or RE, and it wasn't my fault I was a jelly-for-brains scientist. More like the bloody genes, *Mum*!

"Perhaps," she suggested icily, "If you spent more time on your studies and less time on the 'phone?"

Ouch!

I'd, like, started phoning Ali at eight every night, just for a chat, to see how he was, how his studies were going, how the play was going, how the magazine was going, but mainly just to hear his voice. I sat on the second step, the receiver close to my mouth, nervously excited, literally quivering with anticipation as I dialled his number then went through the ritual of "Hi, it's Jonathan Peters. Is Alistair there?", feeling this, like, explosion of intense happiness when he answered "Hi, J, how's it going?"

Hours passed like seconds. Before I knew it, the clock'd be chiming nine, or once ten, and I'd have to go. Hanging up turned my heart to lead. Sometimes we didn't speak for ages, we'd just sit and listen to each other breathing.

I had a pile of work, most of which I left to the end of the week, a decision I came to regret when it all turned out bollocks. There was this English essay on the relationship between Michael Henchard and Donald Farfrae, and one for History on Lenin's contribution to Russian Communism. I had to write about this experiment to measure the growth of plant-seeds for Biology and like some prose piece for German? There were also a shed-load of simultaneous bastard equations to solve. This was our holiday, for fuck's sake! What was it with these teachers? And don't say, like *they* did, 'oh, GCSE is the most important year of your life,' because it bloody isn't! It's just another bloody hoop to jump before university!

On Saturday I stuck the decals on the Tiger, listened to Liverpool play out a 1-1 draw with Arsenal, helped Mum fry onions for our liver-and-bacon dinner and watched tennis and snooker on *Grandstand*, then the new *Doctor Who* story which introduced this new boy-companion but seemed to involve experiments with melons and marshmen. Yeah, I know. Anyway, on Sunday I watched a load of telly. Episode 4 of *A Tale of Two Cities* was followed by *Songs of Praise* from Hartlepool, *Mastermind* from Cambridge, with a taxi-driver answering questions on Henry II and a retired major doing the history of Rome, a sitcom about a posh woman living on a country estate and a serial set in Bristol about a private detective. I also listened to this new opera by Philip Glass called *Einstein on the Beach* with episodes intriguingly titled 'Knee Play 1', 'Train' and 'Dance 1 (Field with spaceship)' which Andrew Paulus raved about. I could hear why. I'd never heard anything like it before. There was also *Biggles of 266*, where wily, sausage-eating, square-headed Huns wore coal-scuttle helmets and Biggles, *Donner und Blitzen*, dropped leaflets from his Sopwith Camel on Brussels to win a gramophone. Unfortunately I got so engrossed that I forgot about the washing on the line and didn't hear the rain over *Steve Wright in the Afternoon* so everything got soaked. Mum snarled 'bloody kid' as she stomped past with the washing-basket. Also, I'd hung it wrongly anyway. She'd've pegged the shirts tail-first at the house-end, then the pyjamas, then the socks, pants and bras. To be honest, I didn't feel comfortable handling either Mum's black frillies or Dad's washed-out Y-fronts so I'd just kind of done it. It wasn't my fault she'd had a bad day at work. I suggested she do some yoga to align her *chakras*. Bad move. I think every parrot in the Amazon rainforest heard the response. Who'd have thought my mother knew such language? She told the parrots she got it off me, bloody cheek. And then there was the usual Gestapo interrogation about why hadn't I made my bed, and who did I *think* was gonna do it, the Bed-Making Fairy? Anyway, by Tuesday I was *more* than ready for our rehearsal.

Leo and I turned up around 11. We'd travelled the three miles on the 21 bus together. He wanted me to accompany him in his Grade 6 flute exam and the music competition. Of course I said yes. I liked Leo. I'd put on white Chinos and a dark blue shirt and dragged a little gel through my hair. Leo had these pale lilac Converse hi-tops, a pale pink, sorry, 'crushed strawberry', Lacoste sweater and pale green, sorry, 'pistachio', jeans.

"Pastel colours are pretty," he said simply, swinging round a lamp-post.

"With my trousers and your shirt, we make a whole ice-cream," I remarked.

"*I scream, you scream, we all scream for ice-cream. What's your favourite flavour?*"

"Lemon," I said. "What's yours?"

"No," he said petulantly, dancing down the kerb. "You've got to *sing* it."

I began to understand why his father thought he was a little bit lavender.

"*I scream, you scream, we all scream for ice-cream. What's your favourite flavour?*"

"Bananas with cream."

It was a long journey, you know?

Unlike some of the others, I didn't mind going into school during the holiday. The play had become fun again. Ali was desperately trying to contain Harry Turner's rather risqué ad-libbing, without much success, so there was always lots of laughter. Now, with one week left, we gathered for our dinner-party scene round the table on the dusty brown floor of the Beckwith Hall where the gimps sat on a Monday morning. Super-cool in these black jeans and a black sweater, he was standing in the hall with a clipboard talking to Peter Dwyer, his stage-manager, whilst Turner, Sutcliffe and Middleton waited on the Rises, these twenty wide wooden steps that spread back from the halfway point to a bank of permanent seating behind a rail but could be pushed in under that bank to create a huge exhibition space for Open Day and, most crucially, for exams, 'cos the Beckwith Hall could accommodate 200 nervous exam candidates and their desks.

"This isn't right." Paulus. "If I were scared of Lulu, I wouldn't sit next to her, would I?"

"No," said Ali, "That's true, very true."

"It says in the script that Clarissa is head of the table," Laud pointed out.

"Doesn't matter," said Ali. "The script's flexible. My master-copy's covered in arrows, deletions, insertions… it's a template not a headstone, Bill, a work in progress."

Sonning, playing Aunt Clarissa, suggested we all move round one place so that Lulu was at the head and he and Paulus were on the corners.

"Right," said Ali. "Everyone move round one."

"But," I said, as I settled into my new seat, "Surely they wouldn't put Lulu at the head of the table. It'd be a man. Jasper, perhaps."

"OK," said Ali, "Move round again."

"Blimey," said Warburton, "It's like musical chairs."

"From the top," said Ali, squatting on his haunches, clipboard dangling.

Sitting on a packing-case later, I listened to the Sixth Formers' conversation.

"I heard he can down a pint in three and a half seconds," said Dwyer.

"That's nothing," said Rice. "I heard he swallowed one in *two* last week."

"Gets plenty of practice," said Turner. "I know for a fact he gets people in the pub to buy him a pint so he can show them."

"Anyway," said Dwyer, "He's got a beer-gut already."

"Some people'll do anything for a free drink," said Sonning.

"You mean like Rosie?" Dwyer made a crude masturbation gesture which drew coarse laughter from the Sixth Formers, except for Sonning. He frowned.

Ali was talking to Sutcliffe, telling him to look at the audience and speak from his stomach so he'd get a more substantial sound and wouldn't strain his voice. Then we did the dinner scene again. Leaving the script, I only needed two prompts. Ali flashed me this brilliant smile and asked me to sit with him while Paulus and Leo went through their seduction-scene, Paulus lying on this sofa with Leo crawling up him. I caught Rice and Dwyer's eyebrow-twitches as I sat down. Fucking hell. They thought this all *very* fruity.

Paulus, unnerved by Leo's public pawing, forgot his lines three times. The third provoked a burst of furious swearing which made Leo yell back and stomp tearfully off.

"Two right little ponces," grunted Rice.

"Little Lion's a bit highly strung," said Dwyer.

"Yes, he should be," Ali riffed effortlessly.

"And you know what Poorly needs, don't you?" said Dwyer.

"No," grinned Ali, "Tell me."

"A good hard kick in the balls," said Dwyer. "Make their voices break at last."

"I thought you were going to say a good hard cock up the arse," said Ali.

"I'll leave that to you, Rosie." Dwyer moved off to reset the stage.

Alistair laughed, and laughed some more when he saw my shocked expression.

"Lads' banter, J," he said, looping his arm round my shoulders and shaking me. "By the way, you look really nice today. That shirt suits you, and I really like your hair spiked up a bit. Leo!" he called, leaving me blushing like an over-ripe tomato on the Rises and striding down to where Paulus was reclining. "You should unbutton his shirt a little more sensually, like this." Perching by Paulus and gazing into his eyes, he reached down and slowly, lovingly, unfastened the second button on Andy's shirt. I felt a sudden pang of jealousy. That should've been me, though when I heard Turner suggest that Rosie and Poorly were obviously bum-chums, I was glad it wasn't and glad when we moved on to the last scene.

"I'll take the deeds." I drew an imaginary gun. "Come on. I haven't got all day." Standing beside the evil Herr Lakker, I covered the others with my double-barrelled fingers.

"We gonna have real guns on the night, Ali?" asked Sonning.

"Sure," grinned Ali, enjoying himself at last, "With a couple of undertakers to clear up the bodies. Add 'em to the stage-crew."

After Lakker had disposed of the gardener with a cackled "I don't need you any more," I yelled "And I don't need *you* either," shooting him with a loud cry of "BANG!" Then Warburton entered, Leo clinging to his chest, a plastic squash-bottle in his hand.

"Whit's all this noise, Jimmy?"

"BONG! BONG!" went Ali, signalling the chiming of a clock.

His brother burst out of a cupboard in a perfect forward-roll. As I turned to cover him, Leo grabbed the bottle and like crashed it down on my head. I crumpled at the knees and collapsed on the floor with a heart-felt "fuck's sake, Lion, no need to kill me."

Leo, grinning maliciously, stuck out his tongue.

"Brilliant, guys, brilliant!" Alistair clapped excitedly. "Go again. 'I'll take the deeds'."

We did it again and again and one more for luck. My hip was bruised, my head was ringing and my immaculate Chinos were smeared with dust. Rubbing my bruises ruefully as the cast dispersed, I remarked "I think you only wrote this play so I could get bashed about."

Alistair, grinning, asked what I was doing now.

"Going home to apply some bruise-lotion," I said sourly. My hip was really sore.

"You wanna come to the theatre supplier downtown? Get some wigs and stuff?"

I *had* been planning to go to the autumn food-fair with Andrew and Leo. Every year you got dozens of stalls selling international food, German, Moroccan, Thai, Chinese, pizzas and a massive paella interspersed with a load of arty-crafty shit, like beads, woolly hats, jewellery and friendship bands. We really wanted this tongue-tingling, lip-livening sweet-sour prawn and lemongrass soup, *tom yum kung,* and then glass-noodles with seaweed.

"You can help me choose, and then *we* could go to the food-fair," said Ali. "I'll buy you a cup of mulled wine."

I'd prefer a hot, thick sausage, I didn't say.

High on his play, he chattered like a demented magpie as we crossed the university campus, me skipping round the cracks 'cos step on a crack, you'll break your back, you know? I tightrope-teetered along the kerb into the red-brick Victorian quarter. We cut behind the children's hospital and down a small alley to the art gallery then slid past the library towards the theatre. Hearing him laugh was thrilling and his excited enthusiasm was contagious as we cracked jokes, quoted lines and swapped impressions all the way to the shop, some dingy, seedy-looking establishment with the legend *Nigel's Theatrical Knick-Knacks* painted in fading gold letters above the dust-caked, bird-shit-spotted window in which sagged a dragon, a zombie and a vampire. A tiny bell tinkled as Alistair pushed at the door and called "Is there anybody here?"

"Knock once for yes, and twice for no," I whispered as Ali shushed me.

Nigel materialised behind this old-fashioned wooden counter. He was tall, thin, with greasy black hair and a long, bony face. A sickly scent of strong perfume wafted our way. He wore this blue pinstriped suit, pink frilly shirt and a bow-tie, blue with pink spots, and sported this pink carnation in his buttonhole. He had long, bony fingers. Suppressing a nose-busting sneeze, I scanned the racks of dusty, moth-eaten costumes whilst Ali said he'd phoned earlier about some wigs and a maid's outfit.

"Oh," said Nigel, winking slyly at me, "And will the maid's outfit be for your little… er… friend here? Or perhaps…" Rocking his head back slightly, he appraised me leeringly. "He's not so little where it counts, eh, ha ha?"

"He's about the right size," grinned Ali.

"Oooh," sighed Nigel, fanning himself with a limp, flapping wrist. "I'll bet he is."

"He'd be a very good, though possibly tight fit."

Nigel's knees seemed to surrender. "Oh my," he said, leaning on the counter, "I've come over all queer, with a bit of luck, if you get my drift."

"Fucking hell, Ali," I muttered. "He's camp as tits."

"Try this on," said Ali, thrusting a wiry ginger bush into my hands. "It's for Jock."

For the next twenty minutes, we tried on various wigs of various hues and laughed ourselves sick whilst Nigel slipped in these not-so-subtle innuendos about his little knick-knacks and hinted even less subtly that he fancied the arse off me. He kept adjusting the wigs, his fingers lingering on my face. The scent of his perfume was quite overpowering.

"Right," said Ali when we'd got six wigs, ''Leo's costume. You'll have to try it on so I can see how it looks."

"Ha ha," I said. "You're joking, right?"

"Certainly not." He grinned again. "Get in touch with your inner Jenny, Jonny."

"Fuck off," I hissed, glancing over to where Nigel was ringing the wigs through the cash-register. "He'll cream in his pants if I dress up as a girl."

Ali grinned an evil, beautiful grin. "Flash your legs, J. You'll get us a discount."

Someone just shoot me.

Snatching the hanger with this bloody black frock and stupid frilly apron, I marched towards the fitting-rooms saying "Alistair Rose, I hate you so much." He merely laughed.

Shaking my head in disbelief, I stripped to my mint-green pants and squeezed into the outfit. Needless to say, I'd never worn anything like it before. The skirt came to mid-thigh. On Leo it'd be up to his arse. But, tying the apron-strings, I couldn't help admiring myself in the mirror. Not bad, actually. Especially my legs. My inner Jenny approved.

"Oh my dear boy," purred Nigel, "You look ravishing. Let me adjust the hem a little."

"You're all right." I backed away. "Leo's mum can do that."

"Well, just the apron then." His fingers closed on the hem around mid-thigh.

Pulling himself together and shaking himself like a wet sheep, Ali cleared his throat. "Great, J. It'll be great. Maybe some fishnets or suspenders, eh, Nigel?"

"I have just the thing," said Nigel, bobbing behind the counter again.

"You're a bastard, and I hate you," I told Alistair.

"You look fantastic," he replied.

"Well, I feel like a twat."

He pulled me closer and whispered "Your legs are gorgeous, you know?" He had that hungry look in his eyes again. "Try it with the wig." This was a long blonde effort made of nylon and shot through with silvery strands. It fell below my shoulder and was incredibly itchy. "*Oo la la*," he said.

Nigel returned, his jaw falling slackly.

"Oh, my dear. You are adorable, utterly adorable. What are you doing this evening?"

"My homework," I said shortly. "I'm still at school."

"Well," said Nigel, "So was I," and he gave me this filthy, lecherous wink.

Someone just shoot me. Again.

"Leo'll love this," said Ali. "He's game for anything."

Nigel popped up again, this time with a packet of lacy black stockings.

"I'm not trying *those* on," I said strongly. "You can both fuck off, you pair of pervs."

Nigel arched an eyebrow.

"Sorry about him," said Ali. "He can't help it. Care in the community and all that. I take him out once a week to give his carer a break."

Nigel instantly switched to 'sincere condolence' mode. "Many apologies. I didn't realise he had..." glance over the shoulder and lowered voice, "Well, learning difficulties. Isn't that what you say these days?"

"He covers it well," said Ali, wincing as I slapped his shoulder.

Nigel bagged up the outfit and, as Ali was handing over the cash, said "I almost forgot. There's a French tickler to go with it. Will you be wanting a French tickler for later?"

Ali erupted into the loudest guffaw I'd ever heard, spluttered "Put one in the bag" and hustled me into the street. Leaning on a lamp-post, he wheezed, tears in his eyes.

"What?" I demanded. "What?"

"French tickler," he coughed, "Is a type of condom."

"What?"

"A rubber, Jonny. A Rubber Johnny, Jonny. Ha ha ha ha."

His knees seemed to be buckling so I kicked them hard and said I hated him.

"Oh, my dear, you look quite ravishing," he spluttered, mincing along the pavement and flapping his wrist. Then suddenly, from nowhere, "What a poof. He's gay as Paulus." He snorted with laughter all the way to the food-fair where he got me a tub of sweet and sour pork, which I love, and a plastic cup of warm spiced wine, all consumed sitting on a wall outside Marks and Spencer. Then we dived into Holland and Barrett for some soya nuts, Next to look at scarves and HMV to look at DVDs, returned to the fair for more spiced wine and these friendship-bands for a pound apiece, yellow, red and brown for me, blue and red for him, and tied them round each other's wrists. Then we caught the 21 to our shopping parade from outside the Cornmarket. I told him about the zombie German spy.

"His heart had stopped," I said, swinging round and round the bus-stop with my left hand, "But he was still walking about, like a regular guy, till someone poked him in the back with a brolly and broke his bones."

"Which film was this?"

"It was on the news," I said, still swinging round the post. "Andy Collins told me."

"Nothing you said made any sense at all," he replied as the bus pulled up. "I like the photo on your bus pass."

I didn't. I'd had it taken at the end of the summer, before Mum had cut my hair for school, so the fringe was really long and over my eyebrows and my ears were totally covered.

Also I had my mouth half-open, like I was about to speak. Mum said I looked 'gormless' and Gray said I looked about ten, but I'd used the last of my coins in the photo-booth and was stuck with it till it expired on 31 July. The pass itself had my name, address and the address of the school and was laminated in hard green plastic. Numbered 52133, it entitled me to two half-fare journeys between home and school during term-time, but I was Roy Peters' lad so none of the drivers looked too closely.

"Listen," said Ali casually, "You wanna come to mine? Bobby's out all afternoon and my folks are at work. We haven't got a piano, but I got Action Men. It's only half-two."

We'd got off the bus outside William Hill, McColls the Newsagent and the fruit and veg shop where we bought our Christmas trees.

"Sure," I said as nonchalantly as I could through a suddenly dry mouth and a croaky throat that seemed to contain my whole swollen, thumping heart and a wish that he would be like *my* Action Man, you know?

His house was this white-washed semi with an open porch and bay-windows set behind cherry trees, a neat, square lawn, well-turned soil borders and a beech hedge, now a blazing coppery gold.

"Spectacular in May," he said, ushering me up the two steps to the porch, through a black front-door and into a hall with a red shag-pile carpet and this like massive cheese-plant in a pot. "All pink and white blossom." The telephone stood in an alcove on a nest of wooden curly-legged tables. "This is where I call you from." He kicked off his shoes. "Want some tea? Or a beer? We got some lager, I think."

"Whatever you're having," I said, noting these sharp, gleaming Kitchen Devils, the vegetable-rack overflowing with potatoes, carrots and onions, the fruit-bowl stacked with apples and oranges, the wooden wine-rack with four bottles of Shiraz, a Monet water-lilies print in a clip-frame on the wall and deciding I liked its mustard-coloured homeliness.

He tugged back the ring-pulls of two cans of Foster's. "Don't tell your Mum. Cheers."

"Oh, my Mum knows I drink a bit," I said, clinking cans. "I'm fifteen already. Everyone does it. Some people in my class drink ten pints a night." Well, Seymour claimed to have drunk ten pints one Saturday. "I would too if I had the chance."

We stood awkwardly for a minute on the lino.

"I love Leo Trent," he said. "He's such a tart and doesn't give a shit."

"His dad thinks he's gay," I said, then clapped my hand to my mouth. "Bollocks. I wasn't supposed to say."

Ali shrugged. "He probably is. Look at his clothes. Whatever. He's a right laugh."

I sipped the lager again. I couldn't work this out. Ali seemed, like, *sooo* attracted to me, you know? His eyes kind of screamed desire but, when he spoke, he seemed so dismissive of the whole gay thing, as though it didn't interest him at all.

"I'm glad *I'm* not," I said cautiously. "Gay, I mean. Like Poorly." Was he bumming Paulus, like Turner suggested? "I mean, I like him, he's nice but…he's such a poof."

"He's OK," said Ali. "Did you watch *The Taming of the Shrew*?"

"Yeah." I wrinkled my nose. I hadn't really got it. I mean, John Cleese was, like, brilliant but it was so sexist, you know? Breaking this woman in to become a good wife. Or was it supposed to be ironic? *I* didn't know. I'm only 15. Anyway, it was on the cover of *Radio Times* so I suppose it must've been all right. "Did you watch *Taxi*?"

"Danny de Vito's so nasty," said Ali, "And Christopher Lloyd's crazy."

"They're my favourite characters," I said. "I'd love to be Louie. Did you see that one the other day, when the old woman's suing him for running her over, and he thinks she's faking so shoves her wheelchair out of the courtroom, and you hear her clattering down the stairs and he finishes '*No further questions, your honour*.' Fucking brilliant. And Jim's talking about being in court. '*Did they get you on drugs?*' '*No,*' he goes, '*I was already on drugs. That's why I was there.*' Ha ha ha. I love the one where he does his driving test and they go '*mental illness or narcotic addiction?*' and Jim goes '*That's a tough choice.*' Ha ha."

"American sitcoms," said Ali, "Are so much better than ours. They've got sharper, snappier scripts and the characters seem more rounded and real, not the stereotypes and clichés we have, though *MASH* isn't so good any more, not since Major Burns left but you can't *get* more sexist than the BBC. Have you seen that one on a Thursday? All about this sappy bloke getting his sappy wife a birthday present. Man, it's *sooo* vanilla, all these bland, boring, middle-class, heterosexual couples doing heterosexual couple things…"

"At least there *are* women on the telly," I said. "*We* don't exist at all, unless we mince round Grace Brothers or ponce round the jungle like Bombardier Beaumont. I wish I had a *proper* role-model on the telly, someone I could relate to. Mind you," I was talking through his quizzical look, "Do you watch that one on Saturdays, the woman police inspector running her own nick in a sexist environment? BBC always tries to do its bit for women's lib."

"Yeah," he said, "But did you see the first episode? The car chase involved an Austin Allegro and a moped and the cops commandeered a vicar's car and the vicar's going at about ten miles an hour. Man, it's so not *Starsky and Hutch*, is it?" I drank some lager. "Shall we go to my room?" he said eventually, "Listen to some music?"

Heart racing, I followed him upstairs to the place where he slept and studied and wrote his play, his stories, his speeches, the place where, possibly, he lay awake, thinking of me, the place where, hopefully, he masturbated, thinking of me…

It was a blue colour-washed square with a soft, deep-pile blue carpet. The single bed, covered in a plain dark-blue duvet, was pushed into a corner near the lead-striped window. A simple wardrobe stood by a desk which was covered with books, files and papers. A massive poster of the Star-Ship *Enterprise* loomed from the wall.

"Didn't know you were a Trekkie," I grinned.

"President of the Sci-Fi Club," he said. "Don't you read the handbook?"

"Favourite episode?"

"The time-travel one with Joan Collins. 'City on the Edge of Forever'. Classic."

I'd never heard of it. "Anything with the Borg," I said, glancing over his bookshelf. "Resistance is futile. Oh God. Roald Dahl. I can't stand Roald Dahl. It's so *fake*. Boring jokes about farting and bratty little kids. I mean, who *gives* a shit?"

"*The Witches* is really good," he said defensively, "And *everyone* likes *Charlie*."

"What? Bloody Oompa-Loompas?" I scoffed, "And those bloody annoying girls?"

In the sepulchral silence that reverberated round the room, I buried my face in the rest of the spines on his shelves. I'd never heard of this stuff. Lenin, Nietzsche, Freud, Marx, Paine, Jung and Dostoevsky nestled cheek-by-jowl with arty books on Turner, Escher, Picasso, Monet and Michelangelo. The CDs included Joan Baez, Joni Mitchell, Bob Dylan, John Lennon, Pete Seeger and Mama Cass. This was a totally new world, you know?

"I'm working on an essay for German," he said. "It's about Brecht. You'd love Brecht, Jonny. Think of everything you know about theatre and tear it up. This guy's out of the box."

Recalling Beaky saying something similar, I noted the pictures pinned over the desk. Marlon Brando in *On the Waterfront*, Brad Pitt, Tom Cruise in *Top Gun*, an almost unrecognizably young Cliff Richard.

"Cliff Richard?" I scoffed. "My mum likes Cliff Richard. What are you? Forty?"

"*Summer Holiday*," he grinned lazily. "Oh boy! Weak at the knees for a month."

There was also the photo of me and him in *The Dream*, the really like gay one from the school magazine? It was the original and stood on his desk in a frame.

"I got it from Simon Ayres," he said shyly. "It's a really nice picture."

He was already mapping out the school magazine. There was a photo of the Head addressing Speech Day, some shots of rugby matches and some more arty pictures of aspects of the school which Ayres had taken, archways, the bell-tower clock, stained-glass windows in the chapel, that kind of thing.

There was a pile of creative writing, poems and stories from all over the school and formal reports of sports fixtures and house events. We agreed on a deadline of December 17th, the last day of term. Ali would badger heads of houses and team captains and I said I'd ask Niall Hill to draw a cartoon about life in the school for the centre pages. We wanted more original art-work, which I suggested Pip Brudenall co-ordinate. Holt would pull together the music section, Dell drama and Sonning sports. Ali would write the editorial with Mr Webster. I said I'd work with Paulus on the creative writing submissions and Shelton on Features. Then Ali showed me his poem. It was called 'Final Rest'.

'A dark and silent wasteland
Calls
Across the sunless sea

Ten thousand thousand people weep,
Ten thousand thousand voices cry
How long, o Lord, how long?
They cry, alas, in vain.

Man is born good.
Man wants to be bad.

I am free, like a bird
I can fly, I can soar,
I can see, I can feel,
I can breathe, I can hear

The sounds of silence
Echo through the pain.'

"It's not finished," he muttered.

Man, I wished I could write poetry. What the hell did it mean? *Sooo* deep. It was like that poem he had recommended, *Little Gidding,* by his favourite poet, Toilets, or someone: *Midwinter spring is its own season*
Semiternal though sodden towards sundown.

I preferred Seamus Heaney. '*All I know is a door into the dark*' sums up my life.

Paulus wrote poetry. He'd done one called 'Sunlight in a Bare Room' and another comparing a marble to a shooting star. I really liked his poems.

I indicated the poster of Liverpool Football Club stuck up on his wall. "Ferrety Fosbrook supports them. I thought you supported Luton, Leicester, something beginning with L."

Telling me to fuck off, he asked who I supported.

"No-one, really," I replied, "Though I quite like Norwich. They play in yellow. Why do you like Liverpool? You're not a Scouser, are you? You haven't got the perm, *or* the shell-suit."

He said they had the cutest players. Then he showed me his collection of Panini football-stickers and Subbuteo teams, his cuddly rabbit (called Rabby – *sooo* lame), a toy fort, a blue velvet bag of marbles and this massive box of Lego which he used to build star-ships and re-enact *Star Trek*, writing scripts about parallel galaxies, time-warps and black holes.

"I love science-fiction," I sighed, "Though I can't understand the science. Max and Gray got me into it, *The Hitch-hiker's Guide to the Galaxy* and stuff. Do you watch *Dr Who*?"

"The new companion's quite cute," he replied. "I love *Blake's Seven* too. Great ship. Avon's a slimy toad but Vila's a great character and Cally's kick-ass fit."

"Not so good since Jenna left." When I was 13, I'd wanked over Jenna. I'd even cut her picture out of the *Radio Times* and kept it under my pillow, till it disintegrated in the bath one afternoon. "Can't get into *Star Wars* though." I'd been to see the most recent instalment at the cinema for my fifteenth birthday with Max, Gray, Paulus, Fosbrook and Tim. They'd all loved it, kept banging on about the Force and imitating Darth Vader in the queue at McDonald's till I'd wanted to exterminate them. I'd thought it mostly bollocks. I mean, little green men with long ears speaking backwards English... I'd much preferred Fozzie's birthday trip to *The Thirty-Nine Steps,* with Robert Powell hanging off the big hand of Big Ben while ze Germans shot at him. That *was* a thriller.

"Still," said Alistair, "Light-sabers are super-cool."

"Super-*lame*," I grunted. "Pan-Galactic Gargle-Blasters are cool."

"Ha," he crowed, "Wish I had a Babelfish for every time someone said that. Wanna listen to some music? Do you like David Bowie?"

I loved David Bowie. *Ashes to ashes, monk to monkey, we know Major Tom's a junkie...* I couldn't help singing it. He chucked some socks and a shirt from the chair to the floor and slid a CD into the player. Holding my can in both hands, I sat on his bed and sang:

"It's a God-awful small affair to the girl with the mousy hair,
But her mummy is yelling no and her daddy has told her to go..."

Swinging in his desk-chair, he grinned happily as we did the next verse together pretending our cans were microphones and holding the 'Life on Maaars' as long as we could. We drank lager, warbled and air-drummed 'The Man Who Sold the World' then bawled "*Goodbye Yellow Brick Road, where the dogs of society howl,*" and, when 'What You're Proposing' came on the radio, we actually danced, swaying a couple of feet apart, thrusting shoulders, playing air-guitar, pretending we were long-haired rockers:

It sounds so nice, what you're proposin', just once or twice, and not disclosin',
And not disclosin' how we're really really feelin', what you're proposin'...

Suddenly the Police replaced Status Quo:

Her friends are so jealous, you know how bad girls get,
Sometimes it's not so easy, to be the teacher's pet,
Temptation, frustration, so bad it makes him cry,
Wet bus stop, she's waiting, his car is warm and dry,
Don't stand, don't stand so, don't stand so close to me...

Ali, jerking away, crushed his can and tossed it into the bin grunting that he needed a slash. Then it was Barbra Streisand: "*I am a woman in love, and I would do anything...*"

Suddenly I was alone in his bedroom.

Quickly I pressed my face into the pillow and inhaled a mixed scent of shampoo, sweat, laundry and Alistair Rose. Then I had a great idea. I'd take a trophy, a souvenir of the day. Jumping from the bed, I scooped a black sock off the carpet and shoved it into my pocket. Then I had another idea. Maybe, if I rummaged in the bin, I might find a... maybe there was a... There was! A crumpled tissue. God Almighty. My heart missed several beats as I sniffed it, touched it with my tongue-tip. Man alive. Was that really... you know? I almost fainted with anticipation. Then, in his top drawer, I saw this photocopy of a picture of myself in *Oliver*, baggy cap, scruffy shirt, raggedy trousers, the lot. This had been in the school magazine too and *I* had the original. He'd xeroxed it and kept it in his bedside drawer. Oh boy.

A mix of emotions swirled through me, pride that he liked me so much, excitement 'cos I guessed he masturbated while looking at my picture, and shame, that I was excited and aroused when I should be creeped out that this older boy was wanking over me. And then I found *my* missing sock. Bollocks. The sock I'd lost at the start of September was here, in Alistair's drawer. My mouth went very dry, scarcely daring to imagine how he might've used it. My God, he was *sooo* crazy for me! Hearing the toilet flush, I shoved the tissue in my pocket with *his* sock, slapped the drawer shut and collapsed in a heap on the carpet.

"*When eyes meet eyes, and the feeling is strong, I turn away from the wall.*" Streisand.

"*I stumble and fall,*" I sang, grinning up at him, "*But I give you it all...*"

He called me an idiot and told me to get up.

"I can't get up," I said, "I'm too drunk," and joined in as Barbra continued "*I am a woman in love, and I would do anything, to get you into my world…"*

Now he knelt beside me, like in the swimming pool, and I locked his eyes on mine. My heart lurched and my breathing changed. His eyes glittered. His lips came closer.

"And hold you within, it's a right I defend, Over and over again…"

Now, please, on this perfect day, on the best day ever. Do it now. Resistance is futile.

His fingers were fiddling with my shirt buttons. I looped my arm round his neck. The world stopped spinning. The stars held their breath. My buttons came undone, down to the waist. He leaned towards me. His breath warmed my lips. His fingers fumbled with my belt-buckle. My fingers touched his zipper. His lips hovered, an inch away. Make it so. His hand burrowed inside my shirt, sweeping over my skin, ribs and side. I sighed, parted my lips, my fingers unzipping his fly as my belt buckle fell away and my trouser button came undone. Then something, I don't know what, broke the spell. Blinking, he switched the radio off.

"Bob Marley all right?"

"Sure," I said, choking down my disappointment.

He put on *Uprising* and returned to his chair. Levering myself from the carpet to 'Redemption Song', I refastened my buttons and belt. He was gazing moodily into nothing.

"What's up?" I said, putting my hand on his shoulder.

"You know what's up," he said in this thick, choking voice, but he didn't shake my hand off. "I nearly kissed you. That's what's up. And it's happened before."

"Oh *that*." I tried to laugh it off. "That doesn't matter."

He swung round, his dark eyes alight with anger, despair, hatred and passion.

"Of *course* it matters, Jonathan. If I kiss you…" He took a long draught of lager. "If I kiss you… oh God." He buried his face in his hands.

"Do you think I'd be such a bad kisser?" I was like trying to lighten things up, you know?

"No," he muttered eventually. "I think you'd be a *great* kisser, but that's just the point. *We* shouldn't *be* kissing, should we?"

"Why not?"

"Don't be a twat, Jonny. Because we're boys, that's why not. Because we're both boys. Because we're not gay." He squeezed the shape from his beer-can. "Because *I'm* not gay. I am *not* gay." Suddenly he started shaking. I could feel these tremors through his shoulders. "I'm not gay." Then he was crying, great sobs dredged up from his soul. "I'm not gay. I'm not. Gay. Oh fuck… what am I going to do? Eh? Jonathan? What am I going to do?"

Trying to comfort him, I hugged his trembling body and stroked his hair but I had no words except "It doesn't matter, Ali. It doesn't matter."

Thinking of the picture in his drawer, of the picture on his desk, I suddenly realised he was creeped out by himself and his own desires. He was scared of himself, and *for* himself, but more, I thought, he was scared of *me*, and *my* desires. I felt my heart shattering for my poor, poor boy, and it made me cry too. How could it not? I loved him.

"Just telling one person helps," I murmured. "Tell *me*, Alistair. Please. Just tell *me*."

"There's nothing to tell," he said. His shoulders suddenly shuddered violently.

Putting my unfinished lager on the floor by his bed, I gazed at him, this boy I admired so much, this boy I *loved* so much, hunched on the edge, arms on his knees, drowning in misery, loneliness and despair. There was nothing I could say. It was something he needed to face alone. Like all of us at some time or other must face the truth of ourselves, confront our demons. All I could do, all any of us can do, was pray for him and for all those we love.

15: Up all night (to get lucky)

EVERY mouthful of Mum's toad-in-the-hole seemed to choke me. Even bananas-in-custard didn't help. All I could think about was Alistair Rose. I hated the thought of him suffering. He'd told me once he couldn't talk to his parents about *anything*. His father, a pension advisor, and his mother, a college administrator, were these total like dinosaurs living in the Dark Ages?

"I don't *want* to do Law at Oxford," he'd said, "I want to do English at Warwick and be a journalist but they don't listen, they're not interested, not in what *I* want. So imagine if they thought I fancied *boys*. They'd have me to a shrink before you could *say* 'shrink'."

My parents would go utterly ballistic. I'd tried to come out several times already and each occasion had resulted in World War Three. Mind you, I guessed I hadn't raised it directly. Not exactly. Well, you don't, do you? It's kind of embarrassing to talk about sex and feelings and stuff with your parents and to say that you don't like what *they* like, that *you* like willies actually. There was no way in hell they'd still love you after that bombshell. It'd be like what kind of freak have we spawned here? Anyway, I gave up with the pie, said I'd reheat it later and fled to my bedroom.

I lay awake for hours. As the night shaded into dawn, the blackness melting into a vague, washed-out greyness, I drifted off, waking an hour later sticky and sweaty from yet another wet-dream. This time I was lying naked on my front on my bed with my right arm under the pillow. In pale green pyjamas, Andy Paulus was sitting beside me, stroking my hair and my naked back and staring into my eyes whilst I unbuttoned his jacket, although I was worried that Ali might come back for the diary he'd left next to Pickles.

Dream-Paulus shushed me, pressed his finger against my lips and unzipped my chest, from throat to navel. I kissed him. Pushing me down on the pillows, he sat astride me.

'Are we gonna do it then?' he asked.

'Ali left his diary,' I said. 'He might come back.'

'Don't care,' said Dream-Paulus. 'Let's do it.' Pushing his hand between my thighs, he fondled my balls then chucked his pyjamas on the floor and slipped his cock into my mouth...

Miserably I sat up and stared at Pickles' glinting tawny eyes, the ME109 and Stuka above me, the fiery orange of the Hekla eruption beside me. My Timex said 3.37.

Andrew Paulus. God Almighty. So many dreams about Andrew Paulus. Jesus Christ. Lying back on my pillows I masturbated rapidly, panting and shuddering and clenching my toes as I spurted twice on my stomach then dribbled the rest over my fingers. As my breathing slowed, I licked my hand. It was thick, kind of gloopy, you know? Slightly sweet? A little salty? Furtively, I lapped the rest off my fingers. The taste was difficult to describe. But I quite liked it. I wondered what Ali's tasted like. Or Andy's. How much did they come? How far could they spurt? If Andy actually *did* spurt in my mouth, like in the dream... what would that be like? Suddenly I was hard again. I rolled onto my side trying to keep my hands off it and my mind off that image. I was not successful.

Leo the Lion lifted my spirits. He was chatty, lively and flirty, dressed again in the pastel-pink Lacoste sweater, pistachio jeans and lilac Converse over pale pink socks, and I, in black Levis and cobalt-blue sweater put my worries aside to enjoy his company.

"We got you a cracking costume," I said, describing from the keyboard the French-maid's outfit while he slotted his flute together.

"*Oo la la*," he breathed, those extraordinary lilac eyes lighting up with excitement. "I *was* planning to wear a bikini, show some skin, you know? Where did you get it?"

"I worry about you sometimes," I said, striking middle C. "A place called Nigel's Knick-Knacks. My God, the man couldn't keep his hands off me. He even patted my bum."

"Where's this shop?" The innocent tone couldn't conceal his excited curiosity.

"I worry about you," I repeated, striking middle C again.

"I got to get it somewhere, J," he said, jigging a little, "Otherwise I'll burst."

Don't look at me, mate, I thought. I got troubles of my own, and you're *so* under-age.

Fauré's Op 78 *Sicilienne* in G minor was a nice piece, two flats, *andantino*, easy arpeggio accompaniment, but he fluffed the B natural entry in Bar 22, playing B flat instead, so we repeated it then I decided his *sforzandos* in bars 28 and 32 didn't work, that bars 33 to 43 weren't *legato* enough and that his *pianissimo* in in bar 55 was too loud, and made him do *everything* again. When he grumbled, I said that if he wanted to make music with me, he had to get it right and that meant focusing on the detail. I got the impression nobody had ever told him that before. I made him play it twice more then let him practise his Grade Three piano pieces, this Reinecke G major Sonatina and 'Clowning' by Kabalevsky whilst I watched his fingering. I showed him how to play the Kabalevsky, wrote some fingering directions on the page, mainly 3 under the bass notes, and advised him on the rhythm, then I dug out *my* old Grade Three book for sight-reading. I hadn't looked at it for years. Mrs Lennox had like written all over the André Sonatina, circling finger numbers in red pencil and scribbling 'wrists up!' in orange. Tchaikovsky's 'March of the Wooden Soldiers' had been divided into thirteen sections with blue pencil-strokes. I remembered playing each one in turn, in endless and tedious isolated-practice sessions. She'd written at the end 'Pay more attent^n to the rests + LH 5 – 7.' The dotted rhythms had challenged this nine year old, but he still got a Distinction (142/150). In my purple Grade II book, we'd cut the tempo of the Le Couppey study on page 4 from one crotchet = 104 to one = 84. She'd written next to the ninth bar '1) F# 2) smooth RH, phrases LH.' The Khachaturian Scherzo on page 12 had 'little faster & more flowing, not heavy' written at the top of the page, then, underneath, in my childish handwriting, 'slower, steady'. I got a Distinction for that one too (144). I bet you hate me now! Not my fault. I was born that way. Or perhaps I just got lucky?

"What mood are you trying to create?" I asked. "When you practise, you must practise with purpose. Think about what you want to improve before you begin." All my teachers had told me that.

We took some coffee up to my room. Mum'd dumped a load of laundry on my bed with an instruction to iron it and put it away. Instead I scooped everything up and deposited it on the carpet. He said my room was like being inside a boiled egg.

"Nice wind-chimes. Very New-Age," he said, flopping on my pillows, "Very hippy."

I played him the opening of *Einstein on the Beach*. He said it was weird. I told him Paulus was obsessed with it and anything with tapes, repeated rhythms, looped voices, electronics. This part was called Knee Play 1 and involved this woman reading out numbers and going 'these are the days my friends' over and over to this electric organ.

"But there's no tune," said Leo crossly.

"Oh my dear," I said, trying to imitate Paulus, "Tunes are *sooo* last century!"

"Bollocks," said Leo, who was into Madness, Mozart and Adam Ant.

"Adam Ant?" I scoffed, "He wears make-up."

"Who doesn't?" grinned Leo, shuffling *Top Trumps* 'Tanks' while I replaced the Glass with Rachmaninov's wonderful second symphony with its heart-breaking adagio and stirring finale. "Treat yourself to some lippy, J, and a decent eyeliner. Do wonders for your looks."

Sprawling on my carpet, the gay little gimp captured my prized Soviet T-54 with his French AMX-30 on horse-power (520 to 720) and then my Chieftain with his General Patton on speed (25 to 31 mph) whilst singing Dennis Waterman's song, "*If you want to, I'll change the situation, right people, right time, just the wrong location, I've got a good idea, just you keep me near, I'd be so goo-ood for you, love ya like ya want me to…*" Gimp.

Kicking his pink-socked feet up in the air, he suddenly blurted "Is Andy Paulus gay?"

"How would I know?" I scowled, my dream like bouncing back into my brain.

"No reason," he shrugged. "Except you're really close friends. I thought he might have said something." He hesitated then added shyly "About me, I mean. I thought he might, well, kind of… like me, you know?" He ran a pink cat's-tongue over his silver brace. My heart bounced and my mouth dried out like a camel's jockstrap.

"Would that bother you?" I asked, feeling this fluttering in my stomach whilst the lush, romantic strings of the Rachmaninov swirled around us.

"No," he admitted. "I like *him*." There was another hesitation. "Do *you* like me?"

Yikes. What to say? Even the Jehovah's Witnesses would be welcome at the front-door right now. How do you tell another, especially younger boy, 'I fancy the arse off you' without actually *saying* it and sounding like totally creepy? That was how I suddenly felt about Leo. My mouth went even drier. The music intensified, wave after wave of heart-stopping, heart-stirring emotion. But how to ask him? 'Cos 'the question wasn't and isn't actually '*do* you like me?' but '*are* you like me?' I was suddenly red as a pepper as the music crashed to a heart-rending climax and began to die away.

"I'm gonna invite him to my Halloween party tomorrow," he said. "You'll come too, won't you? Fancy dress. We're gonna make pumpkin lanterns, watch *The Omen*, have a sleepover with scary stories... it's gonna be spooktacular, ha ha! Bring your PJs and a toothbrush."

Spooktacular? Oh boy. I'd miss *Starsky and Hutch* – some Spanish girl sees her boss commit a murder - and I didn't really fancy a night with 4D giggling and farting like gimps. Besides, I'd just got into this BBC serial about a public school between the wars. It reminded me of our school, all those posh boys with neat hair and cut-glass accents standing up when masters in gowns entered dusty old classrooms. There was this great episode where one of the teachers had dropped dead in the classroom while spouting Latin insults at him out of *Fools and Horses*. I wondered if, by any chance, it might happen to Leatherface, you know? 'Boys on the Rises stay where you.... Aggggh. Peters, fasten your.... coll-arrrghhh...'

"Any girls coming?"

Leo didn't know any girls, except for his sister's friends. They were all in Year Five and having a pyjama-party of their own. Yikes! I could hear my hair literally standing on end. Talk about Halloween nightmare! Ticket to Shrieksville, please.

"It's not at our house," he reassured me. "The folks couldn't cope with a dozen pre-pubescent girls *and* a dozen adolescent lads mixing it up under the same roof."

For my own part, I would rather eat my own testicle kebabs raw with Savoy cabbage and a nice Semillon Blanc, you know? I'd rather eat *yours*, Reader.

I thought about Leo a lot that afternoon, wondering what he might know, what I might be brave enough to ask him. The eighteen-month age-gap didn't matter, not if we *were* two of a kind. When he left, he kissed me on the lips, just the briefest, darted peck, then gone. It promised so much. Not sex necessarily, but something nice, something warm and good.

I stared into the back garden, at a blue-backed, creamy breasted nuthatch flickering round this peanut-dispenser, a bunch of blue-tits squatting on a suet fat-ball and a few red-faced goldfinches squabbling over some nyjer seeds. A female blackbird was splashing about in the pedestal birdbath and a robin was perched on the fence. The trees were beginning to shed their crisp, brown leaves and the red spikes of dogwood blazed with a fiery intensity. In December, these silver-foliaged shrubs in the corner, and these great soft white plumes of Sunningdale Silver pampas, which, as *Woman's Weekly* put it, burst three metres into the air like fountain spouts and, under the pale skies and sharp frosts of winter, made the garden sparkle as though everything were crusted with diamonds. We had different stuff every season. It was great to watch. Dad, I decided, was a genius.

We hadn't had a garden in our last house, just a concrete-covered yard which Mum scrubbed with a hard-bristled brush. When we moved, I'd found the garden fascinating. I'd spent hours logging bullfinches, chaffinches and thrushes, created habitats from bark and wood-chippings under pot-shards for beetles and earwigs to colonise and gazed into the murky depths of the pond for frog-spawn, tadpoles, toads and newts. Dad even tried goldfish till one morning this scary-looking hunch-backed grey heron swooped in and scoffed the lot.

For Dad, the garden was a place for floral experiment, azaleas, wallflowers, sweet-peas, various bamboos and black grass. You name it, he trialled it. For Mum, it was a food supplier, a stockist of apples, cherries, damsons, various berries and a mass of veg, carrots, potatoes, onions, cabbages. You name it, she grew it. For me, it was a microcosm of the world, where life-and-death struggles for survival were played out on a daily basis by a dozen different species competing for the same space and food with our late tabby cat like some nuclear bomb lurking in the background. You name it, I watched it.

Anyway, most of the jobs Dad had delegated involved skimming (leaves from the pond-surface), pruning (the brambles behind the shed) or painting (the black front-gate and the new fence-panels). I fancied the last job most 'cos I loved the head-spinning smell of creosote in the morning. Though now I had a party costume to make too. Draining my coffee cup, I slipped into wellies and black Regatta parka with the fur-trimmed hood, and headed to the shed for some secateurs whilst considering the problem of waste-disposal. I didn't want to leave it in the garden *or* bag it up in the garage, nor chuck it into the street for the council to tackle. Knowing the Council, that'd be sometime in the next month of Sundays, right?

I imagined I was Henry Morton Stanley hacking through the African bush towards a long-lost native village, i.e. the shed, and when I finally broke through the clinging creepers and crawling lianas, I would utter the famous greeting 'Doctor Livingstone, I presume' before settling by a roaring fire to watch the tribal dancing.

I'd always kind of fancied being an explorer, you know? One of my favourite books, given as a Crissy prezzie by the Grunters like a bazillion years ago, was *Great Explorers,* this big hardback describing the adventures of the Polar explorers Peary and Amundsen, the African explorers Livingstone and Stanley, Captain Cook, Eric the Red, this Viking who found North America, and, intriguingly, a Frenchman called Réné Caillé who discovered Timbuktu. I found this book inspirational and recreated these adventures with my Action Men, all the while resolving that one day I too would be an explorer and visit Timbuktu, or at least the raspberry bushes behind the shed, boldly going where no-one had gone before.

Returning with an armful of brambles, I supposed I could like lob 'em over the wall into next door's veggie patch and blame trick-or-treaters. I really wanted to burn them but Mum'd go ballistic if I lit a bonfire unsupervised so they'd simply have to go on the compost. Boring but better than burning down Dad's new fence, I guess. A sudden vision of forest-fire flaring through the garden wasn't encouraging. Fire dropping from the fruit trees would not go down well with either the folks or the neighbours, you know? So I dumped the stuff on the compost and spent half an hour chucking conkers at this tin of Ronseal while I considered painting the gate and saving the creosoting till tomorrow. One more conker ricocheted off the Ronseal into the pond. Some fat frog hopped out with an indignant croak. Yay! Result!

Resting my Crown transistor against a brick, I prised the lid off the old Dulux crow-black and set to work. Steve Wright was playing Cliff Richard, "It's so funny, how we don't talk any more." I was thinking of what I wanted to take to the party, this utterly gorgeous pumpkin-and-chorizo soup I had found in *Woman's Weekly* near the prediction that Gemini should avoid compromising situations this week, a stack of conkers and Mum's home-made parkin.

Then there was my costume. What would I wear?

"Well it really doesn't matter to me, I guess your leaving was meant to be, it's down to you now you wanna be free..."

The broad, flat blade of the paintbrush reminded me of *Busy Bodies,* the Laurel and Hardy film set on a building-site where Laurel dips a paintbrush in glue and jams it onto Hardy's chin. When the glue sets and Laurel finds he can't remove it, he covers the brush-beard with foam and shaves it off with a plane (not a 'plane like Concorde, a *plane*, like in Woodwork, you know?) Hardy's pained glance at the camera still cracked me up. And the numpty critics reckon the fourth wall was broken last year in some lamoid TV show? And it was *sooo* like radical and cutting-edge? Sorry, numpties. Oliver Hardy did it in the 1930s. Like get a history? Anyway, maybe *I'd* look good with a brush-beard. Maybe that could be my costume for Leo's party. Laughing softly, I turned up the radio, then this muttered curse drew my attention away from the paint-pot and silenced my humming. What I saw made me laugh aloud. Mark Gray was carrying what seemed like pieces of a bicycle past the hedge.

"On your bike, mate!" I called merrily. "Why don't you milk it?"

Gray threatened to stick my paintbrush somewhere intimate.

"I just bought it." He shook the frame so angrily everything rattled. Both the chain and the rear-wheel had come off. "Twenty quid from my sister's boyfriend. He lives on the other side of the park so I cycled up Little Switzerland, you know?"

I did. A steeply sloped road through the woods which bore as much resemblance to Switzerland as I did to Arnold Schwarzenegger.

"Changed gear at the top, there's this bloody great bang, and the bloody chain comes off. Bloody pedals spinning round and I'm going bloody nowhere. Tried to fix it, oil all over my bloody fingers, then pushed it round the corner and the bastard bloody chain slips between the wheel and the brake-fork. Totally jammed it. Weighs a bloody ton an' all."

Sticking my paintbrush into a jar of turpentine and wiping my hands on a rag, I said there were some tools in the shed and told him to bring it through the gate but mind the still-wet paint. He yanked the bike up by the handlebars, which promptly escaped from the frame, the bike sliding backwards and leaving Gray holding just the handlebars connected to the rest of the machine by the tenuous threads of brake and gear cables.

I burst into a massive fit of laughter, wiping my eyes with my knuckles as he tried to re-fit the handlebars to a bike which refused to stay still. Eventually, he furiously hurled the bike to the pavement. This proved another mistake 'cos one of the pedals fell off, rattling defiantly into the gutter. As Gray howled, I clutched my stomach and gasped "The world's first fully collapsible bike. I know he said strip it down but he probably meant when you got home? Not on the way… ha ha ha." I thought I was going to puke.

Gray's face darkened like a thundercloud so I manhandled him and his bike-bits into the garden, roaring with laughter again as I sang Pink Floyd's *'I've got a bike, you can ride it if you like, it's got a basket, a bell that rings, and things to make it look good.'*

"Shut your face," he scowled.

Although I spread a load of newspaper on the kitchen table, Mum still went ballistic when she got in and found like a bazillion tons of rusty, oily scrap-metal all over the place. After she yelled so all the fucking pandas in China could hear 'cos I hadn't taken it into the garage and called me a 'bloody kid', she smiled sweetly at Gray, offered him home-made banana-bread, asked after his sister and Becky and wondered if he could find *me* a nice girl.

"Claire Ashton," Gray answered owlishly. "They're made for each other. Everyone thinks so. And she's crazy about him."

Mum seemed to swell with happiness. The bike was suddenly forgiven 'cos Mark was such a *nice* boy, not like Toffee-nosed Timothy (Wilson) or Awkward Andrew (Paulus), although we had a bit of a row about Halloween while she was cutting my hair. She didn't want me to go. She wasn't sure whether to welcome the fact there were no girls allowed or worry about it, especially since I was the oldest going, and my pointing out Paulus was older, albeit by five weeks, didn't help. She didn't approve of Halloween anyway, labelling it 'American trash', even though trick-or-treating had like originated in medieval England, actually, Mum, if you read your history, and was co-hosting a churchy alternative which she *had* hoped I would support. Tim and 'that nice Holly who wears those lovely hand-knitted hats' would be going.

Yikes! An evening discussing wholesome topics like how kids could remain chaste in this sinfully sexualised world was almost as terrifying as being trapped at Emily Trent's Year Five girls-only PJ-and-pony party. I would rather like literally broil and eat my own bladder, you know? With that diced mixed veg that looks like vomit and a nice Vouvray.

"There'll be a film," she said, snipping round my ears so the dark brown hair pattered onto the paper spread over the kitchen tiles. "It's a sing-along version of *Godspell*."

Wow. That sold it. Far better than *The Omen* and a sleepover with some cute boys.

126

"Let him go," said Dad. "There won't be any booze and he's not gonna get pregnant, ha ha." He was staying in with *Zulu* and a Merlot wine-box. "You could go as a wizard."

A wizard! All that magic-spell shit? *Sooo* lame, Dad. But there weren't many options, you know? God, I *hated* Halloween. Just stick a sheet over my head and go as a ghost, eh?

"Can you put in a parting, Mum? On the left? For a change?" Like Ali's. "Or maybe in the centre?"

"I don't think so," said Mum, cutting it in the usual dead-straight line. "You're not old enough for a centre-parting."

Though I hated zombies, I decided to go as one anyway 'cos I could make a pretty spectacular costume fairly easily. I was gonna mix ash from the fire-place with some talcum powder and some of Mum's white foundation and daub it over my face then draw these like massive black rings round my eyes with her liner-pencil and use some red lipstick to highlight my mouth and teeth, you know? I was also going to sprinkle talc in my hair to make it grey. As for clothes, apart from removing the laces from my black shoes, I didn't really have much I could use except my grey school trousers and a white shirt covered in 'blood' made from red food-colouring and chocolate sauce, not ketchup. Ketchup stank, as we'd learned once in a house-play. I'd also add some brown stains to the shirt with used teabags.

Sticking on 'The Time-Warp Song', I slow-danced in a strawberry-coloured slip between bathroom, living-room and bedroom. I scooped a handful of soft grey ash into a cereal bowl then, while I was going upstairs, wiped my hand through my hair. Unfortunately, while I was jumping to the left then stepping to the right, with my hands on my hips and my knees in tight, I spilled some ash on the hall-carpet. Quite a lot of ash actually. In fact, half the fucking bowl. And dropped the red food-colouring from between my teeth. Then a couple of steaming, soggy teabags splatted alarmingly on the stairs as I struggled unsuccessfully to catch them. Fucking bollocks. Ten minutes with a bucket of hot soapy water and a sponge kind of took care of the carpet but the bathroom was a total disaster-zone. Red food-colouring and chocolate sauce streaked the yellow basin and clumps of ash and talc stuck to the tiles. Ah, never mind. Mum'd be home soon and it was almost time for *Yogi Bear.*

"With a bit of a mind-flip, you're there in the time-slip," I shimmied, *"And nothing can be the same..."*

I'd started off with the old Imperial Leather and Clearasil, in case any spots crept out, before smearing lipstick all over my teeth and gums and, for added effect, taking a massive swig of 'blood' into my mouth then tipping back my head and opening my lips so it dribbled over my face and neck. Unfortunately it also dribbled over my chest and onto the cork tiles. But shit. I looked utterly, awesomely cool, especially with these big black eyes and grey skin.

Then Mum came home.

Honestly, you'd think she'd get why there was a bucket of cold grey water behind the front door, but no. I mean, she just sticks in her key, opens the door and yells 'bloody kid' as the bucket upends all over the carpet. Thundering into the bathroom, she freezes to the spot then screams, I mean, literally *screams* so every lion in fucking Kenya can hear "Is that your school-shirt?" then "Is that *my* lipstick?" and finally, ballistically, for the bloody lemurs in Madagascar, her voice rising to this like shriek, like some jet-aircraft zooming overhead, "Assssssh? From the fireplace? In the bathroom?" She actually *smacked* me, like really hard? Slapping my shoulders with her hand like a gazillion times, she made me sit in the hall blow-drying the carpet with a Babyliss Megaturbo. She must've had a *bloody* bad day at work, right? 'Cos she hadn't like smacked me for years. Not since I was ten and the 'playing with yourself in the bath' incident. Anyhow, maybe the *patchouli* hadn't blended or something. Whatever. There was no need to wallop me. And when I asked if she'd had a bad day, she walloped me again, two sharp slaps on the arse with her hairbrush. God, she was so moody. Fucking menopause, eh? Get to yoga and like sort out your *chakra*s, I didn't say.

Leo's house, a newly built three-bedroom detached with white window-frames, no garden to speak of, just a patch of grass between the front and the road, and old gold carpets throughout, was situated on a new development near the park half a mile or so from mine. A pumpkin lantern squatted malevolently on the white window-sill, a candle glowing through triangular eye-holes. Their living-room was dominated by a large TV, a bookcase and a couple of posh grey sofas. A tiny closet huddled under the stairs and the bigger family bathroom, where Paulus and I spiced up our cranberry juices with vodka, was upstairs opposite Leo's room. Leo's parents' room overlooked the road while Emily's room seemed to have been invaded by an assortment of lurid pink ponies, sparkly rainbows and Barbie dolls.

"Thought this was Leo's room," I muttered to Paulus. "Cheers."

I necked some vodka and, coughing slightly, handed him the bottle I'd liberated from Dad's secret supply.

Andrew, being *very* cool, had come as the Wanderer from Wagner's *Siegfried*. Palely barefoot, he wore an oversized black shirt open to his non-existent waist, black trousers and a 'blood-stained' bandage across his right eye. Wish *I'd* thought of it, you know? Anyway, I told him what'd happened at home, like with the ash and Mum and the bucket? He called me a spaz and passed me his Walkman so I could hear his latest craze, *Nixon in China*, this opera by John Adams, another American minimalist, all sprung, driving rhythms and telling the story of Richard Nixon's 1972 meeting with Mao Tse-tung. I'd never thought contemporary politics could be the subject of opera but it was really exciting, this driving motoric aria *'News, news, news has a kind of mystery, and though we spoke quietly, the eyes and ears of history caught every gesture.'* Man, I just stared at Paulus, blown away. Then 'The Chairman Dances' opened with the classic line *'Let's teach these motherfuckers how to dance.'* Who says opera's boring? I mean, have you heard *Tosca*? Where [**SPOILER ALERT – IF YOU HAVEN'T HEARD IT** (*and, let's face it, you haven't, have you?*) **LOOK AWAY NOW**], she stabs and kills the evil police chief Scarpia, who has the most evil laugh in opera, then jumps to her death off the castle battlements, and all for love 'cos her boyfriend painter gets shot? Man. It's fucking epic. Listen to it. It'll change your life.

Leo's room, plastered with posters of Klingons and Spiderman, was done out in lilac and lavender. A small red cage containing four furry gerbils chewing steadily through a mound of straw occupied a corner of his desk. Man, I couldn't believe I envied *Leo*! I had begged Mum for gerbils, and a hamster, especially after the cat got killed. She'd said we didn't live in a zoo. Anyway, he also had this massive toy lion on his bed. Leo's room felt coolly relaxing, even though he'd decorated it for his Hallowe'en Spooktacular (man, I can't believe I used Leo's lamo gag again!) with fake spray-on cobwebs, a couple of inflatable luminous skeletons and some rubber bats. He also had this CD of scary sound effects, like creaky doors and howling wolves, that kind of stuff. He and Sutcliffe were already trading poems as music blasted from the speakers, everyone shouting in unison "*Who you gonna call? GHOSTBUSTERS!*" whilst Paulus chucked the lion about and I poked the gerbil cage with a pencil to get their attention.

"*Mary had a little lamb,*" chirped Sutcliffe, "*She fed it from a bucket...*" He'd come as a devil, slicking his mousy hair into a skull-hugging V and staining his face red. He'd blagged some thick red tights off his sister and even had a pointed tail made from a short length of red-painted rope. "*And after dinner every night she took him home to suck it...*"

"*There was young woman from China,*" countered Leo, "*Who had an astounding vagina...*" *He* had dressed up as a vampire, with long pointy teeth, a frilly white shirt with frilly cuffs, a flowing black cape and very white face-paint, and kept trying to bite our necks. In fact, and unnervingly, he had given me *another* brief, dry peck on the lips when I arrived.

His Marvel comics had been set upon immediately by the others who sprawled on his Spiderman-duveted bed. I had *never* considered Leo cool before, like *ever*? But it seemed like in Gimp-Land, he was ice, ice, baby, you know? He had the much sought-after *Death of Spiderman*, in which Norman Osborn kills Doc Ock and gathers Sandman and all Spidey's enemies together, and Spiderman talks about heroes, and says his definition of a hero is someone who stands for something bigger than themselves. I kind of agreed with that. Like all *my* heroes took risks and made sacrifices to achieve something beyond themselves. Perhaps that's why Spiderman was my favourite superhero too, and perhaps what I most admired in people was risk-taking, sacrifice-making and standing for something bigger than yourself. Paulus, meanwhile, preferred going "Boom Boom Mister Jonathan" with a Basil Brush glove-puppet whilst Sooty and Leo were playing Darth Vader's death-scene with these Palitoy action figures. Where Jean-Luc Picard and Starsky and Hutch's radio-controlled and ultra-ultra-cool red-and-white Gran Torino fitted in I had no idea.

"Man," sighed Paulus, "I'd love a car like that."

Or the Bugatti Veyron I'd seen on *Top Gear* hammering through France at 180 mph. As 'The Time-Warp Song' blasted out again, Andy and I slugged more vodka. I'd been right to bring it. The Halloween theme extended to the buffet, with brains (boiled cauliflower), maggots (sticky rice), worms (noodles), eyeballs (gooseberries), testicles (kiwi fruit), blood (cranberry juice) and pus (mango juice) on the menu.

"*Dochvetlh vISoplaHbe*," said Sutcliffe, Klingon, apparently, for 'I can't eat that.'

"There was a young lady from Ealing," said Leo, "Who pissed all over the ceiling..."

Then he started lobbing us questions from his *Top of the Form Quiz Book*, "What is the federal capital of Australia?", "What is fool's gold?", "What is the usual means of transport at the Cresta Run?" Sutcliffe asked if we spoke Klingon, in Klingon ('*tlhIngan Hol Dajatlh'a'*?'), then Leo bellowed "*It's astounding, time is fleeting, Madness takes its toll...*" and lined everyone up for yet another extraordinarily camp time-warp. As I told Paulus this could be a *very* long night, I blamed the E-numbers in their drinks. All those chemicals *can't* be good for you, especially since they'd got like a kazillion sugar-hits from trick-or-treating round the half-dozen houses of the estate, like these Jelly Tots, Milky Ways and fistfuls of Smarties. Man, they'd be bouncing off the ceiling by bedtime. Fortunately they burned off a load of energy on the dance-floor, well, Leo's carpet, 'cos after we did the Monster Mash, which was '*a graveyard smash*,' Sooty put on his new Meatloaf CD and we all went mental to 'Bat out of Hell,' air-guitars, posing with hankies, miming motorbike-riding, yowling the lyrics, the works.

"*Then like a sinner before the gates of heaven, I'll come crawling on back to you...*"

Leo, slinging his arm round Andy's neck, sang "*We'd better make the most of our one night together...*" Andy's face tensed under the make-up but even he loved the album sleeve, this motorbike roaring from a graveyard into a blazing red sky, as we loved Iron Maiden's artwork – I mean, have you seen *Seventh Son of a Seventh Son*, with a lobotomised head and a hand holding some bloody heart or liver or something? And it's got 'The Clairvoyant' - '*There's a time to live but isn't it strange that as soon as you're born you're dying...*' which is like this totally epic song. Man, you gotta get it. It'll blow your mind *and* your speakers.

After a supper of hot-dogs and the occasional severed foot (plastic, from Tesco), jacket potatoes, barbecue-beans (with plastic eyeballs concealed in the mix), Mum's parkin and like a megazillion photos of us in our costumes, we paraded through this posh avocado-coloured bathroom with pretend gold taps with make-up remover, cold cream, moisturising soap and deodorant, spray-cans of Lynx, Sure underarm speed-sticks, Adidas rollerballs, and prepared for the film. Leo had organised it so he sat on his bed under his Spiderman duvet with Sooty on his right, me on his left and Andy beside me with the half-dozen others in sleeping bags on the floor. The cushions, pillows, bed-rolls and blankets resembled a refugee centre.

I crammed my costume into my backpack and scrambled under the duvet. I'd foregone pyjamas so was wearing just the strawberry slip and a white vest. Andy was in tartan pyjama trousers and a black T-shirt. Leo, in a white slip, his bare chest marble-white, his long legs sapling-smooth, bounced over with some ready-salted crisps. Gulping, I hid my face in the bowl of salted popcorn which Sooty, stripped to his boxers, handed me. As the film began, he killed the lights so the only illumination came from the glowing TV screen and cried "No wanking, right? Not till the porn film." Then he burrowed into the duvet. There was a lot of wriggling and kicking and Leo and Sutcliffe yelling "Gotcha" and me muttering "Kids" and Paulus calling me Grandma and him, Sooty and Leo crooning the bloody song in these bloody soppy voices (you know, '*Grandma, we love you, Grandma, we do, though you may be far away, we think of you...*'). I smacked Sooty with the lion then jumped on Paulus and tickled him in the ribs till, writhing, he screamed for mercy, Leo hit me with a pillow and we settled down for the film.

Now I don't know if you've seen *The Omen*. If you have you'll know what I'm talking about. If you haven't, let me warn you now. It's actually really bloody scary. It's about this kid born at 6 a.m. on the 6th day of the 6th month who's adopted by this American diplomat. As he grows up, people die mysteriously until the diplomat discovers the boy is actually the Son of Satan. So far so dull, yeah? But it's about how evil can lurk behind the most innocent face and the cutest smile, even like little kids, yeah? 'Cos the devil can assume any shape he likes. It was a little slow at first but then [**SPOILER ALERT... OK, you know**] the nanny hanged herself and the priest was impaled by a lightning-rod and Damien the Devil-Kid knocked his pregnant mother off the landing with his tricycle and a wary silence crept over us as we sank inside this creepy story. Leo held my arm while Sutcliffe, mesmerised, scooped up popcorn like some robot. I was really tense, and not just because of the film. I was really conscious of Leo's bare thigh, warm against mine under the duvet. It was all turning me on, you know?

Anyway, in the film, this photographer and the diplomat were now in this classic haunted cemetery at night, you know? Twisted iron gates, blasted trees, crumbling slabs, the works. They're digging up the skeleton of Damien's real mum, which turns out to be [**SPOILER ALERT - bollocks. If you haven't seen it, you should've**] like this dog, yeah? And the diplomat's *real* son's a baby skeleton with a massive hole in his skull where someone's smashed it in.

"Shit!" I sat bolt-upright, spilling popcorn everywhere as suddenly all these savage, snarling devil-dogs like swarmed from the darkness, barking to wake the dead.

Leo's fingers dug into my bicep as the dogs leapt at the diplomat, and he scrambled over the gate, impaling his arm on a spike as the bloody devil-dogs snapped at his legs.

Struggling out of the duvet, I hissed I was off for a piss, though I was really off for a vodka-hit and a bit of space. I crept into the bathroom, where I had left the bottle, unscrewed the red cap and tipped some down my throat. Suddenly Leo, his bare chest seeming unnaturally white in the semi-darkness, appeared in the doorway, making me jump so I spilled vodka over my chin and neck.

"Soz, JP," he said quietly. "Didn't mean to scare you. How do you like the film?"

"Scarier than I expected," I admitted, my voice dying to a semi-whisper as he sat on the edge of the avocado bath beside me. My dreams replayed across my mind.

"Is that vodka? Can I have some?" The gulp he took made him gasp. "I don't think Andy's interested," he said mournfully, "Not in me anyway." He swigged more vodka. The silence was what they call 'pregnant'. I don't know why. Fully laden? Swollen? About to burst? Full of possibilities? All of those perhaps and more... I'm babbling, I know. I held my breath. Leo was coming out.

"Do you love him?" I asked carefully. "Do you... well, *fancy* him, you know, like... think he's sexy and that? I mean do you wanna... well, do it with him?"

Of course he did. *I* did. Whatever Collins or Crooks thought, Andrew Paulus was like the most shaggable guy in our year. Leo was in love with him. So was I. And everyone in the galaxy thought him gay, except for Paulus himself.

Leo gulped another large mouthful of vodka, then, nodding slowly, muttered "I really *really* fancy him," he muttered. "I wank about him, you know? All the time. I wank about him... like doing stuff to me... You know? *Stuff*... like...well..." He locked his eyes on mine. Moving as though underwater, I slid my arm round his waist and kissed his mouth full-on, slowly, once, then twice, leaving my lips on his. I heard his breathing change, felt his body melt in my arm, then his lips parted and his tongue touched mine, exploring gently, tentatively, then more fiercely, more urgently, my blood surging as I ran my tongue over his brace. I moved him from the bath-edge and sat him astride me so I could pull him to me, chest against chest, digging my fingers into that blond candy-floss hair, pressing the flat of my right hand against the small of his back, pushing my fingers under the waistband of his pants so I could touch his bottom, his hip, his straining cock, pressing him closer as he squirmed and moaned through his nose and moved against my erection. He peeled off my vest and kissed my chest. My head arced back and my eyes slowly closed. He tasted of strawberries and sweet white wine.

After what seemed a lifetime, we came up for air, grinning and kissing, kissing and grinning, and hugging each other like crazy. I cupped his face in my palms and told him he was beautiful. He kissed me again. I didn't really need to ask, but I did anyway.

"As a spangly pink high-heeled shoe," he sighed.

"Me too," I said unnecessarily. "Did you tell your folks yet?"

"God, no. They'd have a bazillion fits." He shifted in my lap so he could rest his chin against my shoulder, his right hand high on my chest as I stroked his hair.

"You have no worries there, honey. I told your dad about me, and he was so kind. I think he guesses about you anyway. Unlike *my* folks who just keep saying it isn't true. Like I'd lie about *that*. I mean, who the fuck would lie about *that*?"

Leo shifted again. "You're in love with Rosie, aren't you? Everyone can see it." Shit. "I mean, the way you look at each other. You wear your heart on your face, darling." We kissed.

"He can't make his mind up." I told Leo what had happened at Alistair's house. As I talked I realised I still loved him, very much. I couldn't help it. He had captured my heart.

"Huh," Leo grunted. "I can't make my mind up either, but not like that load of bollocks. I know what I am. No, *I* can't choose between Paulus and Shelton." He kissed me on the nose. "Or *you*, Jonny." I rubbed his bare back and snogged him again, more gently this time. "I never talked about this before, never actually *told* anyone, you know?"

"Nor me," I replied. "I never told anyone I fancy boys, no-one. I mean, I kind of told your dad but not directly. He kind of guessed and I didn't deny it. You're the first, Leo."

He kissed my chest. "Feels good, doesn't it?" he sighed. "Telling just one person you trust. Like a massive weight's lifted. Knowing we can be there for each other, you know?"

As he padded barefoot back to his bedroom and a chorus of wolf-howls, I got dressed, finished the vodka then took from the laundry one of his pink-and-yellow socks as a trophy. I felt exhilarated, my blood on fire. Leo was awesome. I mean, Henry the Hoover or what? And he had a tongue like a fucking hummingbird's, you know? Man, if Ali really wasn't interested, I could have an amazing time with the Lion. God, he'd be *sooo* good in bed.

Paulus, smirking, whispered something breathily into my ear which I ignored. I had the strawberry-taste of Leo Trent on my lips, and I loved it. For the first time, I was beginning to think being gay wasn't so bad after all. As the gerbils scuffled in their straw, maybe, just maybe, I'd actually, like, got lucky?

16: We found love (in a hopeless place)

CERTAIN now of my emotional and sexual orientation, the possibilities it brought excited me even though Ali's teen-angst confusion was exhausting. He hadn't phoned me since that afternoon. Anyway, the spooktacularly lovely Leo (ha ha) was now in the frame, so, as well as the upcoming play and music competition *and* Christmas, I returned to school in a fairly bright mood, you know?

I didn't see Ali on Monday. He missed Choral Society and *"Away with him, away, cru-u-u-cify…"*, which Fred dismissed as "exciting as a bucket of cold sick," but on Tuesday, smart in his charcoal suit, he took house assembly, reading from *Proverbs* 15: *"A soft answer turns away anger, but a sharp word makes tempers hot. A wise man's tongue spreads knowledge, stupid men talk nonsense. The eyes of the Lord are everywhere, surveying evil and good men alike."* Then he recited St Augustine's Prayer, *"Watch, dear Lord, with those who cannot sleep and those who weep this night,"* led the usual mumbled Lord's Prayer, *"Our Father, who art in Heaven,"* recorded our Games choices, snapped at North for mocking Paulus' usual swimming choice and reminded us of Wednesday's rehearsal. He seemed tired and didn't speak to me at all, just gave me this like curt nod. Shit. Was I *really* that unsettling? "Watch, dear Lord, with those who cannot sleep." Anyhow, me and Leo went to a cubicle in the Sports Centre toilets and kissed till the bell went. Man, it was like having some epileptic eel in your mouth. Best of all, Games was cancelled – thick fog, ha ha – so I got to slack off in the lecture theatre with 100 other Fifth Formers while Wade and Ogden showed some video of the Rugby World Cup and Maxton and me did our homework and played Slaps, which was great till, getting a five-slap penalty, he smacked my hands red-raw and made me yelp so Oggie caught us, moved us to the front and made us write 'Rugby is game for men, slaps is a game for kids' 100 times, the bulbous-nosed twat.

So we reached Thursday's Double Chemistry. I was on the back bench with Maxton, Stewart and Gray. Next to us were Lewis, Collins, Arnold and Burridge, doing an experiment with acid and carbonates whilst Barney was writing 'The Rise of Freon' on the board.

"What's that, sir?" I called.

"Nothing for you, Mr Peters," he replied. "It's for Lower Sixth Chemistry in Context."

"Sounds like a film, sir," I said. *"Rise of Freon, The Decline and Fall of Freon, Son of Freon, Freon and the Freon Empire…* you could get a franchise out of it."

Barney grunted like a constipated frog whilst Maxton called me a twat and Stewpot Stewart, deciding on another experiment, tipped a ton of calcium carbonate into the concentrated sulphuric acid.

"It just fizzes a bit and lets off gas," he explained, replacing the glass stopper.

Sure enough, it began to fizz, releasing this thin white gas.

"That's that, then," I said, giving the stopper a brisk, hard smack.

"What did you do that for?" said Stewart, pushing his stool away in alarm. "Get the stopper out, you spaz. If the gas builds up, it'll explode."

Muttering 'oh shit', I kind of heaved at the stopper. It was stuck fast.

"Give it here, you wimp." Maxton, grabbing it from me, tried to screw it out whilst Stewart chose to coax it with obscenities. Lewis and Arnold were struggling not to laugh.

"Oh, Peters," choked Lamp-post Lewis, "You're such a spastic."

Behind Barney's back, Stewart stealthily returned the bottle to its shelf. "Don't worry," he whispered, "I've hidden it among the others."

I broke into this silent fit of laughter, cramming my fist in my mouth. Behind me, the others started too. Paulus, Harrison and Crooks were staring at us so Gray slipped over to appraise them. Pretty soon the whole class was shaking quietly. The situation only cooled when Lewis took a hand in things.

Stewart had moved to the bench-end so he could see the board better. Behind him, Lewis took a squeezy bottle of distilled water, slid the nozzle into Stewart's blazer-pocket and started filling it up. I collapsed into another fit of giggles and nudged Maxton, who spluttered into his handkerchief. Lewis squeezed the bottle again. Arnold and Collins were purple-faced whilst Gray was wiping tears away. I was laughing so hard I could feel my bacon sandwich breakfast returning.

"What the hell's wrong with you?" Barney demanded.

"Nothing, sir," spluttered Gray.

"Write down the equations then. Buck up, for God's sake!"

As Barney turned away, Collins aimed *his* bottle at Stewart's head and fired.

Me, Gray and Maxton erupted as Stewart leapt up, indignation inscribed on his melon face, water leaking from his blazer, his wooden stool clattering to the floor. Putting his hand in his pocket, he cursed. The whole class, having repressed its mirth for like 15 minutes, kind of howled hysterically, like someone had pumped laughing-gas into a roomful of hyenas. Barney, however, went totally ballistic, lecturing us about irresponsible behaviour and setting two sides on safety in the lab - "On my desk at nine a.m. sharp, or you're all in detention." Then he found the bottle in the cupboard and, although it hadn't exploded, it had kind of reacted sufficiently to create this like milky liquid, yeah? He went absolutely ballistic again.

"God, you're pathetic!" he bawled. "Who did this?" The bell shrilled for break. "No-one's going anywhere. Who did this?" There was a sullen silence. Then, furiously, he pointed at me, Maxton, Gray, Lewis and Collins. "You five, stay here. The rest of you, get out." Lining us up, he bellowed about wasting school resources and put us in a thirty-minute detention with a hundred extra lines for me because my top button was undone 'AGAIN!' Well, fuck off, you uptight non-fucker, I didn't say as we went to play break-time football.

'Blubber-Belly' Brudenall, who always seemed to be our captain, stuck me in goal, which was okay 'cos I quite liked playing in goal. It's the most heroic position but, since we played like on concrete, I couldn't dive without literally breaking a shoulder or two, and fuck that, eh? I did charge off the line for a couple of clearances and, following my dictum 'if in doubt, boot it/him out', whacked the ball into the stratosphere and booted Boxhead Harrison's knee. Then I saw Ali, playing in another space with a bunch of Sixth Formers, dribbling past a couple of defenders and scoring with ease. My game collapsed and I let two soft shots under my flapping hand. Broody switched me for Lamp-post Lewis and I got out for a run, sliding the ball through Maxton's bandy legs for the equaliser. I hoped Ali was watching.

At 3.40, though, when everyone else was packing for home, the five of us headed to Hellfire's classroom in the Eagles' Nest. Bunny had doubled the detention to an hour. I didn't really care. I could sit in Ali's seat by the radiator. Bollocks. Some bloody scholarship tyke who was always getting into scraps and cheeking the teachers had got there first.

"He might as well live here," said Lewis, dumping his bag on the table.

"Make friends with the ghosts," grinned Collins, "Especially that boy they say starved to death up here. He spent so long in detention the masters forgot about him. When they returned they found nothing but a bag of bones, blood sucked out by the resident vampires."

The second-form gimp simply scowled.

I was dragging out my notebook and pencil-tin to start the essay on lab-safety when Mark Sonning arrived. His colours blazer was all blue and yellow stripes.

"Hey, Mark," I called, "Better not wear that on a beach. Someone'll mistake you for a deckchair and sit on you."

"Funny, Peters," he said. "What are *you* doing here?"

Gray and Collins told him the story. He didn't laugh, just shook his head, although it made all of us split our sides again. Perhaps you had to have been there.

Then Ali arrived, black gown over charcoal suit.

"Hi, Batman," I called cheerfully.

He told me to shut up and get on with my work. As I wrote, I glanced at him through my eyelashes. He was reading T. S. Eliot's *Collected Poems,* frowning with concentration, chewing his lower lip, the lock of bruise-black hair falling over his right eyebrow. My blood raced. I didn't think he'd ever looked so sexy. He must've sensed something because he looked up suddenly and caught my eye. I smiled hopefully. He gave a sort of soft sigh and half-smiled back. My heart kind of jumped as I returned to work.

At 4.15 he let most of the others go. Only us five remained, and the second-form tyke who was kicking the table-leg. The wall-clock ticked loudly in the silence, echoing in the high, vaulted ceiling of the classroom. Somewhere near the fire-escape was the little door that led into the steeple itself, into the actual bell-chamber. It was strictly out of bounds, some said because of the ghosts of boys walled up by a mad master in the 1850s, which, David Fosbrook claimed, would eat your brains if they caught you.

"With butter beans and a nice Liebfraumilch," I'd scoffed, but I still wouldn't go up the bell-tower alone in the dark, you know? Finishing the imposition, I sucked the end of my Waterman and started on the homework. Bollocks. I was stumped on question one.

"What's a proton-donor, Max?" I hissed.

"An acid," said Maxton.

"Shut up, Peters," growled Ali.

"But I don't understand the question," I protested.

"Do I look as if I care? Just be quiet. Some of us are trying to learn something."

"What's it about?" I asked.

Sighing heavily, he said "Be *quiet,* Peters. I won't tell you again."

Being ordered around by him was like utterly thrilling, you know?

I struggled with the definitions and, wishing I had stayed with the Rise of Freon idea, gave up. Resting my chin in my hands, I gazed at Ali again. He really had the longest, softest eyelashes I'd ever seen.

Maxton nudged me out of my reverie.

"What you doing?"

He was watching me suspiciously.

"Nothing," I muttered.

"Ten minutes overtime, Peters," said Ali. "Talking in detention."

"Ali…" I wailed, "That's so unfair."

"I've warned you a million times," he said, "And its Mr Rose to you."

Now *I* slumped in my chair and kicked the table-leg.

"Stop kicking the table-leg." He sounded really cross now. "And stop sulking. It makes you look like a whiny little brat."

Even the tyke laughed. Someone just shoot me.

When the hour was up, he dismissed all the others and kept me behind.

"See you in the morning, Whiny Brat," grinned Lewis, "If you ever get out of detention."

I stuck two fingers up, which made them laugh more, and shifted truculently in the hard plastic chair. Ali kept his eyes on the clock.

"How was your holiday?" I asked.

No answer.

The clock ticked loudly.

"Did you have a good time?"

No answer.

"Hello, Ali! Hi! Earth to Ali!"

"If you keep on talking, Peters, you'll never get out of here," he said simply.

I gave this loud, irritated exhalation and flicked a paper-pellet at General Kitchener's unfeasibly bushy moustache. And another at that bulldog-faced fucker Churchill. The minutes dragged on and on. I'd never been so bored. I kicked the table-leg again so the bastard added another minute. I huffed angrily but, at the same time, I was thrilled to be so totally in his power. The clock ticked solemnly. Finally, at last, he stood up.

"Right," he said, "That's it. You can go."

"Thank fuck for that." I scrambled to my feet.

"Five more minutes," he grinned, "Swearing at a prefect."

"Alistair!" I threw myself back into the chair. "This is sooo unfair."

Walking down to me, at last he dropped his hand on my shoulder.

"I missed you terribly," he murmured.

"I missed you more." I gazed up into his beautiful eyes.

"That was a great goal you scored."

I shivered. "You saw it?"

He kind of passed a hand over his face. "I see everything you do, and I think I know why. I figured some stuff out, you know, an' I got you something, if you want it."

Digging in his backpack, he produced a purple paper-bag. Inside was a very soft, very cute, dark brown teddy-bear.

"His eyes are really brown and shiny," said Ali, "Like yours. I thought he'd be company for Pickles. They can sit together on your pillow and when you go to bed you can see him and he'll remind you of me."

"I love him," I said, giving the bear a hug, "And *you*. But I don't need a reminder. I think about you all the time already." Impulsively I hugged him hard. "Thank you."

As he held me against his chest, my whole body seemed to transcend physical time and space. I rested my head against the knot of his tie and closed my eyes as he folded me into his gown. The sleeves were massive and it reached to the middle of my calves. Not to worry. Surely I'd be taller in two years' time when I inherited it.

"Do you ever want to run down the corridor going 'na-na-na-na-na BATMAN!'?"

"No," he said, hugging me closer.

"Bet you do," I said as he wrapped the cloth round my back. "I bet you do it all the time when no-one's looking." His hands cupped my bottom. My voice died to a squeaky sigh and I melted like ice on a hot coal. I lifted my face and murmured his name, then I heard this throat clearing and Sonning was in the doorway. Ali and I sprang apart. I could feel the blood rushing into my face, turning it like water-melon pink?

"You ready, Ali?"

"Yep," he answered, swinging his bag nonchalantly onto his shoulder. Smiling kindly, he ruffled my hair. "See you, Jen."

When I rang him later in the evening, I felt like crying again. He was chatty, bright and sounded really happy. I just sat on the stairs, starry-eyed, and listened. An hour drifted past, then he had to go.

"You hang up," he said.

"I don't want to," I said. "You hang up."

There was a long silence. I could hear him breathing.

"Are you still there?" he asked eventually.

"Yes," I said simply.

"Hang up," he said.

"*You* hang up."

"We'll do it together. After three. One. Two."

"Wait."

"What?"

"Are you going to the bonfire tomorrow? You know. Down in the park?"

"Probably. My brother likes to go. Why? Are you going?"

"Yes, with Mark Gray and some of his friends."

Dad, emerging from the living-room, glared his special 'are you on the phone *again*?' glare. I was still in the doghouse for last week's argument and for leaving lights on all over the house, prompting the observation that 'we don't live in Blackpool Tower, you know.'

"I gotta go," I told him, "But look, I'll meet you at the bandstand at seven, OK?"

"OK."

Dad huffed on the doormat.

"At seven, yeah?"

I ended the call.

"Who was that?"

"Have a guess."

Uttering this noise that crossed a groan with a sigh, he returned to *Question Time* and a load of politicians paid to shout at each other over nothing very important. The spokesman paid by the new Tory government was banging on about austerity budgets, making cuts and saving money because Labour had fucked up the economy, let in loads of immigrants and wanted to sell us to the Russians. So nothing new, eh? In 40 years. Makes you wonder...

Anyway, now I was *seriously* excited. It was Bonfire Night and I was going to the fireworks with Alistair Rose. We were together again, we'd talked, and I knew, I just *knew* he was in love with me. Sitting on my bed listening to Rachmaninov's super-romantic Second Piano Concerto, I reached a momentous decision. I was going to tell him how I felt. I was going to tell him I was in love with him. I was going to tell him I was gay. I was going to tell him *everything*. I was fed up with the uncertainty and the confusion. When he'd held me in his arms, I'd known that was where I wanted to be more than anything, right? My body had turned to water and the imprint of his chest was seared on mine. I *knew* he felt the same, just knew. I'd read it in his eyes. Now I asked God to strengthen me, to help me find the words to express myself lucidly and, most of all, to let Alistair tell me the same, that he loved me too, that he wanted me too, that he wanted to possess me, totally, utterly, like I did him. Forever.

I had our lives all mapped out. He'd write plays, I'd be the music critic for *The Times* and give recitals on the side to specially invited friends. We'd live in London, in a Bayswater flat full of music and books, and go to National Theatre premières and Covent Garden previews and then, when Ali was Artistic Director of the Royal Shakespeare Company and I was presenting *CD Review* on Radio 3 and devising the Proms programme, we'd buy this pretty weekend cottage in the Cotswolds, with a thatched roof and pink sweet-peas round the door, and have a slinky ginger tom-cat called Amadeus who despised us, because cats are superior in every way except for opening the Whiskas tin, and we'd be together sixty years and I'd die at home in Ali's arms, like Benjamin Britten with Peter Pears. I felt utterly ecstatic as I curled into my duvet with his bear. My life was going to be so awesome.

At half-past six the next evening, after a shower, a tuna pizza and *Crackerjack*, and dressed in white ankle-socks, a banana-yellow slip, dark blue 501s and green Dash hoodie, and doused in Dark Temptation, I wandered down to the park gates where I'd agreed to meet Gray. Now I didn't give a shit about Delderfield's rather starchy World War veterans or *Spastic and Crutch*. They were all *sooo* childish, you know?

It was a crisp evening, cold enough for a blue-and-red ski-hat and a navy blue scarf, cold enough to see my breath in the air but not yet cold enough for gloves. Rotting red-brown leaves and warm, glowing conkers crunched under my blue-and-orange Reeboks. I lazily booted a couple into the road then teetered along the edge of the kerb.

I was bruised and sore from football at school. I was on Arnold's side, his fourth pick, I'm pleased to say, and playing well in my usual left-wing slot. Martin Cooke, in defence, played a longish ball down the left for me to chase ahead of Gray haring down for the opposition. I had to dodge a Second Former who scurried like a hamster across my path from another game, which meant Gray, reaching the ball before me, was able to breeze by. Ignoring the anguished howls from my team-mates, I tore back after Gray who turned Maxton inside-out to play square across our back-line to Seymour on the penalty-spot. Fortunately Seymour failed to control the pass and the ball bobbled up his shin and away to Walton who simply booted it as far as he could. The ensuing scramble resulted in Crooks, on our side, somehow getting his chest under the arc of the ball, dashing towards the rugby field and slipping the ball inside to Harrison who managed to shoot straight into Lewis' hands. He bowled the ball overarm into Collins' path. Collins chipped it towards Brudenall. He and I rose together, elbows digging ribs, the ball glancing randomly off my forehead towards Cooke, who hoofed it upfield, literally straight into my face. Brudenall, whooping, collected the loose ball and, spinning on a pinprick, battered it past a static Arnold to score. My smarting elbows had borne the brunt of my fall and my head rang. Cooke was kneeling next to me, like holding my hand, for fuck's sake, his blue eyes shining with tears, apologising over and over whilst Arnold grumbled that it was like having the Chuckle Brothers on his team. Others gathered, concerned and anxious.

"I'm all right," I growled, reclaiming my hand from Cooke's cold fingers.

"It was an accident, JP," he kept saying.

"To me, to you, to me, to you," Arnold was saying.

"God Almighty," I muttered, to everyone's merriment, "I wish you *could* do that on purpose. Then you wouldn't be such a bloody liability."

Gray brought a bottle of cider, a 'teenth of pot and *two* girls, including Claire. Bollocks. I suppose I should've asked her myself. Truth was, I'd forgotten all about her. Double-bollocks. The other girl, taller, pretty, with long chestnut-brown hair tumbling over her shoulders and a ready smile, was Becky, Betty, something beginning with B. She smiled warmly and looped her arm round Gray's waist. Claire took my arm and led me down the path towards the arena.

"I haven't seen you for a while, " she said. "Thought you'd forgotten about me."

Triple-bollocks.

"I'm fine," I mumbled. "Working hard, as usual. House plays next week, then my clarinet exam and the music competition. Same day, worse luck."

"What's *your* play?" she said.

"It's really funny," I said. "You know Ali Rose? Rosie? *He* wrote it."

She wrinkled her nose. "Oh, Rosie. Mad, bad and dangerous to know."

"That's funny," I grinned. "That's what *he* said about *me*."

Down in the bowl-shaped arena, an enormous fire was already blazing. The heat was extraordinary. Orange flames leapt round the dry timber, crackling and spitting like fat in a frying-pan and casting weird, twisting patterns against the indigo sky while they licked at the guy in the centre, worming through the material to devour whatever he was made from. There was some kind of pop music playing. Behind the fire was a large rig buckling under the weight of several thousand pounds-worth of fireworks. Every year the council organised this free event, with hot-dog stands, a beer tent, an ice-cream van and stalls selling parkin, gingerbread, fresh lemonade and hot chocolate with mini-marshmallows. It was great.

Claire's face was flushed from the heat and her dark eyes danced with excitement. I was excited too, but for very different reasons. My Timex said 6.55. I could see the old bandstand up on the hill. Very soon I would be up there with *him*.

Then I panicked.

What if he didn't come?

What if he'd changed his mind? The disappointment would kill me.

"I'm off for some hot chocolate," I told Claire casually.

"Bring me some back as well, will you?" she said. "And some parkin."

"Okay. Mark? Betty?"

"*Becky*," said Becky, smoking Gray's joint. "Lemonade, please."

"Hot-dog, ta." Gray's arm was snaked round Becky's waist. Fire glowed in his glasses.

Sloping off, I pulled my ski-hat further down over my ears and wished I'd worn gloves after all, like Mum had suggested. The stars seemed bright pinpricks in the black velvet of the Universe and the moon, full and round, shone like a pressed-silver coin. The smell of wood-smoke curled into my nostrils. My heart beating quickly and my stomach knotted, I moved towards the bandstand. I suddenly felt incredibly nervous, more nervous than I'd ever felt about anything. Going on-stage, playing in concerts, exams, all of them made my stomach lurch and layered a perspiration-film over my skin, but this, this was something else. I was going to say 'I love you' to someone for the first time ever. I thought I was going to be sick.

He wasn't there.

Fuck.

He wasn't there.

It was 7 on the dot and he wasn't there. The top of my nose prickled with tears. I stared at the Timex's luminous hands. One minute past seven.

He wasn't there. He'd stood me up.

Choking down a sob, I flinched as the first firework went off with a fizz, a bang and long shower of golden sparks.

Fuck. Fuck. Fuck.

He'd stood me up. He wasn't bloody there.

Another firework exploded in a red-green storm. The first tear slid from my eye.

"Hi, Jonathan. I like your hat."

He was standing behind me.

17: On a night like this

HE was standing behind me in black jeans and black Peter Storm jacket. Another firework, purple and orange, illuminated the sky. Down in the arena the fire was merrily burning, some two hundred people warming their hands by it. Up at the bandstand, in the dark, there was, at last and face to face, just Alistair Stephen Rose and Jonathan David Peters.

"Ill met by moonlight, proud Alistair," I misquoted smilingly.

"Wanna a drink?" He held out this silver hip-flask. "Warm you up."

"What is it?" I said, sniffing the open mouth suspiciously.

"Vodka."

It burned the back of my throat and made me cough but yes, it warmed me up.

"You here alone?" I asked.

"With my brother. I'm kind of baby-sitting but he's taken off with his mates to the hot-dog van. I'll scoop him up later. You?"

"Mark Gray brought two girls with him," I said, gulping back a nervous laugh. "I think he thinks it's some kind of double-date. Some bird called Betsy and Claire Ashton."

"The Headmaster's daughter?"

"Yes. We're kind of… friends?"

His face seemed to close. "Meaning what, exactly?"

"She plays the oboe. I've accompanied her a few times. I think she fancies me a bit."

"And that would be a problem?"

Looking directly into his eyes, I said simply "You know it would."

"Why?" Now his face transmuted into amusement.

"Because," I said, "I don't fancy *her*."

I fancy *you*.

I love *you*.

I couldn't say it.

The words choked in my throat. What the hell was wrong with me?

Taking the hip-flask, I swigged another mouthful of vodka.

Then he made it easy for me.

"Who *do* you fancy, Jonathan Peters?"

Another swig of vodka.

"No-one," I said carelessly, "Young, free and single, that's me," and felt a little part of me die as another firework blasted into the air, smearing streaks of gold on the black backcloth, and a series of sparking Catherine wheels whizzed and hissed.

Ali looked over the top of my head towards the bonfire. Resolving something in his mind, he changed the subject. "Good bonfire."

"Yep. It's always good here."

"You don't do anything at home?"

"Nah. Dad's too mean to buy fireworks. Says it's like setting fire to money."

"Huh. Mine too. He's like 'why would I spend money burning stuff in my back garden and getting black smuts everywhere when the council does it for free?' Christ, they're so stingy. When I have kids, they'll get the lot."

I leaned my back against the rickety wooden wall of the bandstand and, shoving my hands miserably into my jeans pockets, jangled the half-dozen coins and keys in the left, crumpled the tissues in the right, and watched the white breath drift from my lungs away into the dark night-sky along with my hopes and excitement. I felt thoroughly wretched. Ali, although he was two feet from me, seemed a bazillion miles away.

"You want kids?" I asked.

"Course." He gazed into the blackness. "Don't you?"

"Fuck, no! I hate kids!"

"Shame," he said quietly, a hint of regret in his tone. "What will Claire say?"

"I'm not going to marry Claire," I said.

"But she's your girlfriend."

"She's *not* my girlfriend," I said strongly. "I don't have a girlfriend."

"What?" he teased. "A cute boy like you? Why not?"

Because I'm, like, gay? You know? You know.

"Dunno," I said. "Just never seemed to happen." Miserably I scuffed the muddy grass with my toecap. "Anyway, I don't want a girlfriend."

I want *you*.

"Really? Why not?"

God, he was feeding me opportunities and I was blowing them all.

"I don't have time." Like then. "Besides, I'm too young for all that romantic stuff."

Oh fuck. His face closed again.

To the crowd's collective gasp, a rocket burst into blue and silver globs.

"Give us another drink," I said miserably. This was such a fucking disaster.

Wordlessly he handed me the hip-flask.

Help me, God. Please help me.

"Do you want to go for a walk?" he said. We wandered off down the slope towards the lake. It was dull, black and very still. "I like this park."

"My Dad worked here for a bit," I said, "He designed the Monet Garden."

"Really? My parents really like that one. I'll tell them your father did it."

And now conversation died in my throat. What could I say? I knew what I *wanted* to say. I *wanted* to tell him I loved him. But how? I'd played this scene so often in my mind, rehearsed the lines, but what if I was wrong? What if I'd misread him? What if the timing was wrong? We'd come close to this moment several times before, and it'd all turned to like shit. What if I declared my actual feelings and it all went wrong again? What if, though he liked me, he wasn't actually *like* me, you know? My hands were like shaking, man, like with fever?

What if he hit me again, or spat at me, or rejected me, said I was sick, or mad, or both, like at the harriers meeting? I couldn't go through that again. Fear, shame, guilt and loneliness were better than seeing the face I loved twisted with hatred, scorn and contempt.

Christ, someone just shoot me and spare me this bullshit pain.

Passing round the top of the lake, we drifted down a path into the woods.

"You chosen your A Levels yet?" he asked.

"English, German, History, like you." My voice squeaked a little.

"German's hard," he frowned. "The advanced grammar particularly. History's boring. It's the same syllabus as GCSE. But English is brilliant. Get SPAM. She's utterly awesome."

"Do you fancy her?" I grinned, then realised what a bloody stupid question it was. I was coming across as this really thick, really immature little kid. Then I seized a possible chance for recovery. "So who do *you* fancy?" I teased. "There must be someone close to Ali Rose's heart."

"I don't have time for girls," he muttered hoarsely, echoing my own words.

"What about boys?" I whispered, touching his hand. "What about *me*? Is it me, Ali? Is it? Is it *me* you love?" Then it all just tumbled out like something had burst. " 'Cos I love *you*, Alistair. I *love* you. I really really love you. So much, you know?"

And suddenly I was crying. Far behind us more fireworks exploded their colours. My heart thumped like a jack-hammer. My throat dried out. My life slowed to nothing. Turning to face me, he touched my cheek gently with his fingers. My hand dropped onto his hip. My lips yearned for his. I went up on tip-toe, and the whole world froze,

Time froze,

Heaven froze,

Hell froze,

Everything froze
because
at that moment
he
KISSED
me.

He swept me up in his arms and kissed me, strong, hard and long on the lips. A soft whimper slipped through my nose. I closed my eyes, opened my mouth and let his tongue in, and I held him so tightly, so very tightly, as my tongue twined with his. Oh God. If I died right now, I wouldn't care. I was kissing Ali Rose.

"Come on," he said, seizing my hand. "I know somewhere."

"A bank where the wild thyme grows?" I said breathlessly.

"Shush." He dragged me from the path and into the woods. Branches scratched us, especially when we stopped to kiss again, but we ploughed on, shoulders down, heads down, hand-in-hand, till we burst into a clearing carpeted in rusty leaves. There he threw me down, following so he was on top of me, and kissed me again, and again, and again. We struggled out of our coats and kissed some more. Sweeping off my hat, he kissed my hair, then returned to my mouth. When he broke off to plaster my face with more kisses, he breathed passionately into my ear that he loved me so much. They were the best words anyone ever said to me.

"I love you too," I breathed back, thinking how *lame* it sounded. But what else was there? Language is so limited. Locking my lips to his once more, I ran my hand over his back then felt his fingers fumbling at the buttons on my jeans and almost melted. I heard some long-stifled moan escape me and stretched as my passion rose and our breathing rasped, a gasp from *me*, a groan from *him*, my whole being swept by a hurricane, shaking me to my core whilst he held me so tightly, so very tightly and buried my face in his neck and cried his name as my body tingled and shuddered… I LOVE YOU, JONNY! I LOVE YOU, and, as I spurted wildly through his fingers, he jerked, swelled and pulsed and I felt it, warm on my hand…

When the storm had passed, I rolled aside on the bed of leaves and tentatively licked my fingers. It tasted weird, kind of sweet and salty together, you know? And it was his, his sperm, his life, his. I grinned happily, but Ali looked anxious, upset and tense.

"That was fucking awesome." I couldn't *stop* grinning. "*You* are fucking awesome."

"I'm sorry," he said. "I shouldn't have…"

"Fuck off," I said strongly. "I'm not sorry. It was amazing." I kissed his cheek. "*You* are amazing, and I love you so very much." I stroked his face. "My Awesome Alistair."

"You don't know how long I've wanted to kiss you," he said, tears welling up in those teal-coloured eyes. "I've loved you for years. First you were Oliver, then you were Puck and we acted together and I worshipped you, but couldn't tell you. I don't know. I just fell in love with you and I've been in love with you ever since, an' it's been so difficult, being near you and loving you and not daring to tell you." He sighed. "I never thought this day would come. I never thought you might…well…" His voice tailed away. Stroking his hair, I kissed him again. "I dreamed of this night. I dreamed of it for two years. I've loved you that long, and you were always so far away from me, so brilliant, so perfect, so utterly, utterly wonderful. I used to cry myself to sleep over you because you never noticed me or really spoke to me." He laid his hand on mine. "Oh, Jonathan. You were my world long before now. You have directed my entire life. Everything I ever did, the play-writing, the school magazine, everything was for you. It was all for you, so you might notice me, so you might… love me." Choking, he turned his tear-wettened eyes to me. "I never thought you might… well…"

"Well, I *do*," I said, "And I am and I will. I am yours, Alistair, yours. I will always be yours. You are everything to me, and now I've got you, I'm not ever going to let you go."

"Why didn't you tell me? What was all that crap at the band-stand?"

Kissing him gently, I stroked his face. "Same reason you didn't tell *me*. It's such a risky thing to say to another boy, isn't it? I thought you might hate me. You *did* hate me."

Somewhere, far far away, another firework streaked across the night-sky and exploded in a shower of silver. Alistair, laying back on the leaves, stared at the stars.

"I fought this for so long. I fought *you* for so long. We nearly kissed a few times. At your house, at the pool, at school, and each time I stopped because I wasn't sure you wanted it, and I was scared of hurting you, or upsetting you, or something. But now it seems so right, so natural, doesn't it?"

I kissed him yet again. "That's because it *is* right and natural. You and me. Ali and Jonny, Alison and Jenny, utterly, unquestioningly, together forever, for the rest of my life. I so much want you to love me. I so much want you to be proud of me, proud to be with me, proud to be *loved* by me, and I'm so scared I'll let you down, embarrass you in some way, make you think I'm some silly little kid after all. You have this picture in your mind of Jonathan Peters, this perfect, wonderful prodigy who can do anything, play anything, act anything, and that isn't *me*, not the *real* me. I *am* a silly little kid. I laugh at jokes about fat women. I fight with my parents. I leave my socks on the floor. I don't do my homework and get yelled at by Bunny. Yes, I can play Chopin like an angel and I know every note of *The Ring of the Nibelungs* by heart, *and* in German, but inside I'm this fifteen year old kid who suddenly learned he might be…" I paused, then plunged on "He *is* homosexual because he's fallen in love with this older boy he worships, but he doesn't know if it's just a crush, like his German teacher says, or real, true, lasting love like they have in books and *Casablanca*, and he can't talk about it, not to anyone, in case they tell him he's sick, or dirty, or some kind of freak, and the only person he's got in the whole world is the guy he loves, and *he* is a fucking genius who writes plays. For this guy he'd give his life, sacrifice everything, I mean *everything,* and he *thinks* he likes him, but he's older, and smarter, and does he really love me, or is he just saying it 'cos he just wants to fuck me, like the German teacher says? And what *he* believes is love, forever and eternal, his parents and friends trash as garbage, worthless, sick, some insignificant crush, and that hurts him so much…"

My shoulders started shaking violently as a lifetime-buried sob surged through me.

"He can't tell his parents 'cos he's scared they'll stop loving him. He can't tell his friends in case they beat him up. He can't tell *anyone*. He has it locked in his heart, burning, rotting, dying, decomposing, like a wound that can't be healed, and the best day of his life is when this guy tells him he loves him, and the fireworks go off over the lake. Suddenly his life makes sense. *Everything* makes sense, because he knows he and this guy belong together, they *belong* together, they were born for each other, but no-one else, not his family, not his friends, will believe that… but it's true, Ali, it's all true, I swear on my life." Crying properly now, I flung myself at him. "I can't live without you. I can't. You are everything to me. I love you. You are my life. You *give* me life, and I love you."

Reeling from my outburst, he held me tightly, kissed my hair. "What happened, J? What the hell happened?"

"*You* happened," I wailed, breaking down completely. "*You*, Alistair. *You* happened." Silently overwhelmed by my emotional declaration, he stroked my hair as I cried "I'd *never* let you down. You'll think I'm some backstreet-brat like everyone else thinks, and if you thought that, Ali, if *you* thought that, I couldn't bear it, I couldn't. I'd kill myself if I thought you hated me. I'd kill myself if I let you down, my darling…" Hysterically, I clung to him like a siege-survivor clings to his rescuer. "I'm in *love* with you. People will hate me. They'll try to change me. They may try to kill me. Because I love *you*. And I'm only fifteen and a little gay-boy so who the fuck cares? They say I don't know my heart, I don't know what I want, I'm still a child, but I know I want *you*, Ali, *you*. I'm not ashamed of it. I love you and I want the world to know it but they won't let me say it, they won't let me say 'This is Alistair, and I love him.' My love for you counts for shit, because I can't *tell* anyone I love you, and no-one takes it seriously and I'm not allowed to be with you and…" That was all.

Slowly detaching my sobbing body from his, he kissed my tears thoughtfully as I snatched up a handful of shiny evergreen leaves and gazed deep into his beautiful eyes. "I,

Jonathan David, take you, Alistair Stephen, to be my boyfriend, lover, companion and husband, from this day forward, for richer, for poorer, in sickness and in health, in good times and bad times, for all of my life. I love you. I worship you. I will honour and obey you. You are everything in the world that is good to me. My body is yours. My soul is yours. My life is yours. All I own is yours. I, Jonathan David, am yours, for all time, till the end of time, till the day I die. *I* am yours, my lovely, darling, beautiful Ali, Alistair, my lovely Rose."

He held me for a second while I sobbed then, with a fierce expression, said

"I, Alistair Stephen, take you, my lovely, darling Jonathan David, as my boyfriend, lover, companion and husband, from this day forward, for richer, for poorer, in sickness and in health, in good times and bad times, forsaking all others, till the end of my life. Darling Jonny, I love you with all my heart, my soul and my being. My life without you is nothing. My happiness without you is impossible. You are my light, my life, my love and my soul. Everything I have is yours. Everything I will *ever* have is yours. You are my world and my universe. I adore you, I worship you, and I will love, honour and obey you, my darling, *darling* Jonathan David Peters, till the end of my life, till the end of time."

Tears were trickling down his face too. Gently I kissed them dry.

"My dear, my love," I murmured, taking him in my arms. "Don't cry, please don't cry."

"I can't help it." He buried his face in my neck. "I love you so much and I'm so, so lucky to have found you, my Jonathan, my wonderful boy."

"Not as lucky as me," I said and pressed a holly-leaf into his hand. "It's not a ring, but it'll do. This leaf is a token of my love for you and a reminder of the promises I just made. I promise to love you for the rest of my life."

With a radiant smile that turned my blood to fire and my knees to water, he gave me one in return and said "With this leaf I thee wed."

Laughing now, I said "You may kiss the bride."

And he did, slowly and lovingly, and suddenly it was half-past nine.

"Oh fuck," I moaned. "I've got to be home by ten, and Claire, Mark and Bessie haven't had their drinks yet."

"I'd better pick up Bobby," he said.

"I don't want to go," I said miserably. "I want to stay here with you."

"Do you really love me?" asked Alistair tentatively.

I kissed his nose, then his forehead.

"I really love you." I resettled my hat. "I love you with all my heart. I never felt anything like this before, never. I never thought I would, well, not for another guy. The strength, the depth, the speed... man, I fell for you so totally. I'm still falling."

"But now I've caught you," he murmured.

"Mmm. You've caught me." I kissed his nose again. "Please don't ever let me go."

We kissed yet again then, holding hands, struggled back through the trees. When we reached the road, I was floating with this idiotic smile plastered over my face. As we neared the arena, we let each other go. Bobby, standing with Claire, shot me a look of pure poison.

"I've been waiting ages," he complained.

"Where are Mark and Betty?" I said.

"They left," said Claire, her face thunderous. "You're lucky *I* waited. What happened to my hot chocolate? And she's called *Becky*, for God's sake. Why do you always do that? Forget people's names? You just don't give a shit about anyone but yourself, do you?"

"Sorry," I said. "I got distracted."

Firing me another glare, Bobby grabbed his brother's sleeve and said he wanted to go. Ali and I exchanged a secret smile but I had like this lead lump in my throat as I watched him head up the path to the gates.

"You can at least walk me home." Claire thumped my shoulder. "Come on. It's cold."

I hadn't noticed. I was still warm from Ali, you know? Looping her arm through mine, we set off. I think I still had this fucking great smile on my face, which Claire thought was for her, yeah? Inwardly, I was dancing, but not for her. I felt alive, *sooo* alive. I was gay, free and so very happy 'cos now, at last, after a nightmare, I had the boy of my dreams.

Up in my room, I undressed, slammed the *Grease* soundtrack and, chucking my clothes all over the room, danced naked on the carpet, high on happiness, high on love, high on him. For every dream had just come true. He loved me. He really loved me, and I was hopelessly devoted to him. More than that, I did have chills, they were multiplying, and I was losing control. I did need a man, and my heart was set on him – he was the one that I want, oo-oo-oo, honey… and I had him. I was Ali's boy at last, and I was ecstatic. It really was the best feeling ever. Like, EVER!!!!

18: Edge of Glory

EVEN an experienced performer like me gets nervous before a show. You never know quite how it's going to go, how the audience will respond, whether there will even *be* an audience, so for the *in*experienced, stepping on-stage before five hundred people can be terrifying. Mark Burridge looked sick, Jambo Hartley's face was green and Jason Middleton was reading his lines, anxiety etched on his brow. I sprayed some Bach Rescue Remedy under my tongue and offered the bottle to Burridge. Our play was fast approaching. The show opened at 7.30 with us on second at 8.15. It was now 6.15. Curtain-up was getting close.

I was sitting on the wide wooden window-sill of our house-room, staring through my reflection at the darkened rugby-pitch beyond, breathing on the glass and writing *'JP woz 'ere'* in the mist, the J and P joined at the stems. The backs of my hands were red and stinging from the vicious slaps game I'd played with Sooty. Man, the parrot-faced little twat had absolutely *battered* my hands, you know? His reflexes were so sharp I'd hardly landed a slap and he'd timed his twitches so perfectly I'd conceded penalty after penalty till he made me scream. Anyway, as I blew on the smarting red skin and vowed revenge, I thought our play would go well. It provided all the groans, boos, cheers and laughs a house play should. It had a great mix of characters, a fast-moving plot, corny jokes and lots of slapstick. What was there not to like?

Since we'd been told to assemble at 6 for make-up at half-past, I'd stayed after school and done some Physics prep with Joe Bainbridge, who was doing the lighting for Firth. Thank God he'd been around. I hadn't understood a damn thing. I mean, I had a GCSE on this in six months' time. Depressed, I stared at the questions and my scribbled efforts:

'Speed of truck retards ~~to~~ from 10 km/h to 5 km/h moving a distance of 30m. How far before it stops will it go?

'It will have gone 60m.'

"No," said Bainbridge, *"Ten* metres."

"What?" The sum was there. "10 to 5 = 30, 5 to 0 = 30+30 = 60."

"It's slowing down," said Bainbridge. "The average velocity is 2.5. It's going three times slower, so a third of thirty is ten. Didn't you read the question?"

"A train, 90 metres long, stops in station, buffers (front) in line with lampost on platform. Starts with average acceleration of 0.45 m/s^2. What will its speed be in km/h, when tail-buffers pass lamp-post? $v^2 = u^2 + 2ax$," I said, although I had opted for ~~v = u + at.~~

$$'v = \theta \ ? \ u^2 = ?^2$$
$$u = 0, \ u^2 = 0$$
$$a = 0.45 \text{ m/s}^2$$
$$x = 90 \text{ m.}$$
$$v = 0 + 2 \times .45 \times 90$$
$$= v^2 = 0 + .90 \times 90$$
$$= v^2 = 0 + 81.00$$
$$= v = \sqrt{81} = 9 \quad =\text{v} = \sqrt{89181 \times 1000} = 9\times1000 = 9000$$

.45	.90
2 x	90 x
.90	81.00

Therefore speed = ~~9.000 km/h~~   ~~9 km/h~~   9 x 3600 / 1000

$= \underline{32.4 \text{ km/h.}}'$

"Hooray," went Bainbridge. "You got one right! But do you know why?"

I stared at him. Blank incomprehension.

"Why did you use that equation?" He flipped over a page to where Millie had written the same question over another disastrous prep with another load of crossings out. In red, 'Way too short and parts of it don't seem to mean anything', Millie had given my Charles Law prep 10/20. Bainbridge just shook his head like I was some retarded, stew for-brains spaz.

"Dunno," I said, "But I wrote you a limerick."

'There was A young student called Joe,
Who fell down and broke his toe,
Whilst covered in pot
It became rather hot,
And his whole leg started to glow.'

"Blimey," said Burridge, "You're helping him with his Physics? Your hair'll turn white."

I got my own back, though, with Chapter 31 of *Casterbridge* [**SPOILER etc.**]:

'The furmity seller's revelation [that H. sold his wife and child in an auction for five guineas] has been the final turning-point in Henchard's decline. The creditors let H. down and H. corn is now bankrupt. He moves out to Jopp's cottage. He hates Jopp but goes as a form of self-punishment. His bankruptcy is precipitated by two events i.e. i) the failure of someone to pay him back ii) scandal over his past. Farfrae buys H's business and his house and F's name obliterates H's.'

"Everyone lies about their past lives and about their true feelings," I said, "And it brings disaster – Henchard, Lucetta, Susan… and even though there's so much bad luck and that, Henchard makes a series of bad decisions and loses everything, including his name, and that's the significance of Farfrae painting *his* over Henchard's."

"He's being punished by the Gods for selling his wife and child," said Burridge.

"Yeah," I agreed, skimming through the novel for a quote and found this, the last line, on page 326: 'Happiness is but an occasional episode in a general drama of pain.' Now you see why I wrote THOMAS HARDY RULES OK? on the back of my exercise book. He had summed up life in a sentence.

The dress rehearsal had been a total disaster. Everything that could've gone wrong went wrong. The lighting-crew missed nearly every cue. The cap-guns hadn't fired. The whole cast'd seemed nervous and ill-at-ease, you know? Turner and Rosie had yelled at each other, Turner declaring the play was 'crap anyway'. Sutcliffe'd tripped over a box, bruising his shin. Dwyer mislaid the props. Even Leo missed an entrance. As for me, I forgot my lines. Ali had alternated between fury and despair, yelling "We're going on tomorrow and you're still pissing about! Get serious, please! We get one shot, one." He'd jabbed a finger at Middleton. "I couldn't hear a bloody word and I was in the front row." Then Paulus got the hair-dryer. "You've got as much charisma as a piece of wood." And me. "You, Jonny, you've got the memory of a fucking goldfish. You've done those lines like a billion times."

We hung our heads, except the Sixth Form, who made wanking gestures behind his back and said he needed to 'go get shagged'. Anderson had suggested Paulus offer up *his* arse. Paulus had thrown this box of plastic guns at Anderson's head. The whole thing had collapsed into tetchy bickering and vicious name-calling. Worse, I'd really *wanted* Ali, to kiss him again, to hold him again, but there was nowhere, no place and no time to be alone.

As the clock ticked round to 6.30 and Bunny barked a brisk 'Right, you lot,' the Sixth Formers packed up their poker, we gathered our stuff and moved to the Grimshaw Art Room where Mrs Locke, Mrs May and two Sixth Formers called Palmer and Liddell were applying the slap. Firth were ready so Harry Turner slipped into a vacant chair where Palmer began daubing his face with foundation.

"Where's Rosie?" demanded Bill Laud. "He should be here by now."

"You got my costume, Jonny?" Sooty was borrowing my black trench-coat for his gangster look. I tossed him a Morrison's bag. It'd serve the vicious, beaky twat right if I'd 'forgotten' it after that Slaps game. He kept chewing his lower lip and frowning. Funny, but when *I* wore the trench-coat, I started *thinking* like a gangster. Maybe that's why Mum didn't like me wearing it. I kind of swaggered through town going 'you want a favour from me? Isss OK, but one day I might need a favour from you' and 'Leatherface is sleeping with the fishes tonight' till Bunny Hutchinson came in and cuffed me round the head saying "For God's sake, boy, don't you *ever* stop talking?"

We started changing. This should've been exciting but I felt anxious for Ali, for the play, for the cast. I desperately wanted it to be successful. I stripped to my vest and, waiting my turn, watched Paulus in the chair between Sooty and Jambo having powder dabbed across his broad nose. There was little conversation. Usually the air was thick with banter.

I'd sat in that very same chair during *Midsummer Night's Dream*, Palmer streaking my bare legs green, Liddell powdering my gel-spiked hair green and Mrs Locke painting my face, guess what? Well done. Ali had been next to me, running through his lines with Mrs May as she made up his face. I was in total awe of him, gulping when he smiled, stammering when he told me I was great to work with and wishing me luck. Now, preparing to star in Ali's own play, I felt exhilarated, 'cos he was my boyfriend now, and now I knew what he'd meant when he said he loved what I did. I remembered in *Oliver* when I'd been shy and nervy, while Mrs Locke was gluing this beard to Ali's chin, he'd suddenly turned and gone 'Jonathan, I love your voice' and in our farewell scene, when he's in jail and waiting to hang, he'd actually, on the last night, grabbed me into an improvised hug. It had made the audience cry, but I hadn't really understood *why* he'd done it till now. I was glad.

Dwyer passed with a cardboard box of cap-guns, asking who needed a gun.

"Me!" I yelled excitedly. Rummaging in the box, I grabbed a long-barrelled toy Colt and a red plastic ring of six caps. I like twirled it round my index-finger in a kind of impression of East Clintwood, and aimed the barrel at the back of Paulus' head. "Hey, punk! Do you feel lucky? Well? Do you? Punk?" Then I span it again, *diddle-diddle-deeing* the theme from *The Good, the Bad and the Ugly*, told Sooty there were 'two kinds of people, those with loaded guns and those who dig – you dig' then cried "Ouch" as the gun wrenched my finger.

"Pack it in, Peters," said Middleton irritably. "I'm trying to focus."

"Get back in line," I growled, quoting *The Outlaw Josey Wales*, "Before I kick you so hard you'll be wearing your ass for a hat."

Paulus chucked a make-up stained cotton-wool ball at my head. I chucked it back, hoping for a cotton-wool ball fight, but Turner slapped my head and told me to sit still.

"JP, you're next," said Liddell, squinting at the hand-written instructions he had been given by Ali, then passing them to Mrs Locke.

"What's this say, Miss? I can't read Rose's childish scrawl."

"Moustache," Mrs Locke decided. "Get the Copydex."

Palmer slapped the cold, clammy cream on my face and started smoothing it in whilst Liddell coloured my hair grey with some kind of powder. My nerves were starting to jangle. I glanced sideways at Burridge whose bird's-nest curls were being powdered white. He looked very sick, his blue eyes dull. Dwyer and Rice started moving boxes of props to the tables in the wings. I heard Paulus mutter something, Sutcliffe reply by saying he thought he might faint, and Bobby Rose call them both 'a couple of knicker-wetting poofs'. Middleton, wearing a black trilby and mac, was pacing again, eyes fixed on his script. Warburton was fiddling with his kilt and sporran. God, it was like *sooo* tense, you know? Like a stretched rubber band, or the *Strictly* final. So thank God for Sonning, thank God for Laud, thank God for Anderson and thank God for Trent. The arrival of our men-in-drag brought us out in hysterics. They had decided to dress together in what Anderson dubbed 'a bit of girly-bonding', and made a grand, Grand entrance together.

Sonning was like wearing this frizzy grey wig, dowdy yellow frock, moth-eaten fox-fur and, bizarrely, grey trainers. A yellow handbag dangled from his arm.

Laud was wearing this royal-blue skirt and matching jacket, and a twin-set in pearls. He had somehow squashed his feet into this pair of blue high-heeled shoes and his head into a huge brown wig which resembled a loaf of bread and added like a foot to his height.

Anderson had crammed his massive, flabby bulk into a ridiculously short, red leather skirt, enclosed his massive tree-trunk legs in fishnet tights and squeezed his gigantic torsos, complete now with enormous balloons, into a tight yellow halter-top. Mrs May had already done his make-up. He had like these massive red lips, huge patches of green eye-shadow and a long curly brown wig. He split our sides.

And then there was Leo.

Our lovely lion scampered in wearing the French-maid's outfit, the long blonde wig, the frilly apron and a pink garter around his right thigh. He'd like pushed these balled-up socks down the dress to give himself breasts, you know? He stood in the centre of the room hoisting them into position with his forearm blaring "I feel fantastic!"

"You *look* fantastic," cried Ali, appearing behind him. "*All* of you look fantastic. You guys will bring the roof down." Laying a hand on Leo's shoulder, he beamed at us. He was wearing a yellow shirt and seemed really hyper. My heart melted.

"Christ," said Turner, "The sun just walked in."

"Some say it matches my personality," said Ali. "Bold and outgoing."

"Or vile and revolting," said Warburton. "Are you trying to lose a bet or something?"

"That's exactly what Leatherface asked me," he answered. "'Is that a canary yellow shirt?' he goes. And I go, 'Oh, no, sir. It's a *canary* yellow shirt'." We laughed. "Then I said 'Where's my team, sir?' He said 'Walk this way' and I said, 'If I could walk that way... ',"

And we chorused "I'd be in a circus!" ha ha.

"You been in the pub?" growled Turner, leaning over to smell his breath.

"Unfortunately not," Ali replied. "I've been meeting the punters. Full house. Six hundred people, waiting for *you*."

My stomach lurched sickly as Palmer daubed this jelly-like stuff on my top-lip.

"Here," Ali told some gimp. "Give these cues to Gregory and tell him if he messes them up, I'll string him from the nearest telegraph-pole by his great hairy bollocks."

"Alistair!" chided Mrs May, "Under-sixteens present, thank you very much. We don't want great hairy bollocks all over the place, do we?"

Everyone bellowed with laughter. Mrs May simply raised an 'honestly, boys' eyebrow at a grinning Mrs Locke and returned to Bobby's nose. Please, God, let me get her for A-Level English. She's *sooo* cool.

Palmer finished my moustache and turfed me out of the chair.

"Very suave," said Alistair, "Very rakish. Mad, bad and dangerous to know."

I slipped into my white shirt and tux and looped my black bow-tie round my collar.

"Can you tie that yourself?" asked Warburton, adjusting his sporran suggestively.

"Course," I said, demonstrating slickly. "Licensed to thrill, me."

"Shaken, not stirred," he grunted sourly.

Ali jerked his head towards the corridor, a mix of emotions, hope, excitement, nerves, pride, anxiety, anticipation, an entire emotional life playing out on his face.

"You look great," he said warmly. "You *will* be great. I hope you enjoy it."

"Me too." I touched his hand. "It's your play. I really hope we do it well for you."

"I wore this shirt especially for you, 'cos I know yellow's your favourite colour."

"It's nice," I said. "Break a leg, Alistair."

The corridor was empty. He touched the crucifix inside my shirt. "I love you so much," he said, and kissed me. Just as I was melting into his arms, applause from the hall alerted us to Bunny's bad-tempered, red-faced return.

"You lot, get out. Get to the Green Room. My house is coming in. Peters, move yourself, will you? Just because you can tie a bow-tie." Then he crashed out again.

I was starting to think he had it in for me.

"Before you go," said Alistair, "Just have a laugh, right? If it goes wrong, it goes wrong, but it won't. You are a brilliant cast. Good luck to you all, enjoy yourselves and," he smiled,

"Break a leg. If not your own, someone else's, eh Stu?" He winked at Anderson.

Anderson grinned. "Yes, boss."

And then we were gone, filing down the corridor on the endless but too-short walk to the school hall and to Room 51, our waiting room for the next thirty minutes.

Excitement was spreading. I felt something gnawing at my intestines. Paulus ran off for a leak. Everyone else was frowning, focussing, getting into The Zone. Ali was whispering fiercely to his brother who suddenly looked up at him with a gaze of total adoration. God. He lived with him. I had forgotten. I was suddenly so jealous!

Sweating inside the dinner-jacket, I was now worrying the perspiration would ruin my moustache. I rubbed my palms on my trousers as another bead of sweat welled slowly through my left temple. Polite applause burst from the hall.

Bunny appeared in the wings and looked at us. "You ready?"

"Are we ready?" bawled Turner. "Are we ready?"

"Ready!" we yelled, tension, anxiety and excitement exploding from our bodies.

"Let's do it!" cried Turner while Bunny hissed feebly for us to be quiet.

Firth House trailed dejectedly past. Their show, directed by Adrian Shelton, Nick's brother, had not gone so well. They'd done Proper Drama, like some serious French piece, and depressed the audience to hell. Simon Ayres' head-shake said it all. If the school mag's official photographer hadn't found something to snap, it must've been shit.

I perched next to Paulus on the prop-table in the wings as the lights came up to reveal Harry Turner, who shall now be referred to as Marco Sclerotti, wrapped in a blue silk dressing-gown, feet propped on a desk, speaking into a telephone. Although I knew it by heart, I followed my highlighted script.

"Yes... yes... yes... yes..." He paused. "Yes... yes... yes..." He paused again and, looking directly at the audience, leaned forward as though about to address them, then he leaned back again and said "Yes ... yes... yes..." There was a murmured chuckle.

Ali, pacing about in the wings, seemed incredibly jumpy, incredibly nervous. All his brash, motivating confidence had melted away. This was *his* script. These were *his* words. And he had delivered them over to a bunch of schoolboys. He was only seventeen himself. I suddenly appreciated, as his brother clearly did, how stressful this was for him.

"So how much has he left?" said Marco. "Two million? Man, that's a lot of bread, as my baker would say." He paused. "It's a joke, Jacko, a joke? Know what one is?" He glared at the audience, dark and silent behind the spotlights, and said "Do *you* know what one is?"

A few people laughed. Someone shouted "Not sure *you* do, Hazza!"

Ali looked sick. He muttered "They hate it" to Anderson, who laid a meaty hand on his shoulder and murmured a consoling reply. I felt so sad for him, and then Sooty Sutcliffe, trench-coat hanging open, black trilby pulled towards black Ray-bans, sauntered casually on-stage saying "Everyone knows what a joke is, Marco, and yours wasn't one." Now he addressed the audience, totally off-script. "Our director has a strange sense of humour. We're not sure *he* knows what a joke is either. *You* don't like it? Spare a thought for us. *We've* had to put up with him for like two months. I've aged ten years. When I started this, I looked like some Junior School gimp. Now I look like Dr Crawford."

That burst of laughter saved the play. This skinny no-hipped fourth-former, fourteen years old, with the beaky nose, the nondescript mousy hair and the eyes too close together, had saved the day so when Jason Middleton delivered his line "I am Herr Lakker, ze German barber," and there was more laughter, I muttered "are they drunk?" to Paulus.

Marco and Giuseppe now laid their plans, that Herr Lakker would make contact with the gardener Arthur MacArthur, con his way into the household, rob the safe and scuttle off to the Sclerottis with the loot, otherwise, said Marco "It's a paira di olda concreta galoshes." Then Stuart Anderson, having added curlers and a Union Jack headscarf to his ensemble, lumbered on-stage and the audience was ours. Heaving up his balloons in best pantomime-style, he received a guttural roar and launched into a nagging, innuendo-riddled attack on Marco's poor bedroom performances and disappointingly microscopic 'equipment'.

"How did you two meet?" asked Giuseppe. "I forget, and anyway, I think the ladies and gentlemen would like to hear the tale."

"I was sitting in my car one evening," said Marco, "When a tree, coming towards me at high-speed, crashed into my radiator. I walked along the road till I came to a pub, the George and Dragon. I knocked on the door. Nessie opened it. 'Excuse me,' I said, 'Is George here?' She invited me in, took her teeth out of a glass, and poured two cognacs. There she stood, cognac dripping from her moustache. Honestly, the last time I saw a mouth like that, there was a hook in it. I took her to a disco that night. She wore a split-skirt. Have you ever seen a hippopotamus in a split-skirt? The bouncer asked me why I had brought a burst sofa to the club. Her knickers didn't have elastic in them. They were on a curtain-rail. I asked her why she'd brought her sister. She said there was only her." Les Dawson lives on, right?

Laughter rolled round the hall. My heart soared.

"After her morning wallow," said Marco, "She proposed and I accepted."

"You sure she didn't twist your arm?" said Giuseppe.

"She couldn't. She'd already broken it in three places with her rubber truncheon."

Herr Lakker then encountered kilted, sporraned Jock Macabre, whisky-bottle in hand.

"Och the noo and hoots mon, Jimmy. Whit's your game?"

"Vot ein vundervoll day," said Lakker, in his bowler hat and furled umbrella disguise.

"Willna last, Jimmy, willna last. The sun rarely shines south of the border." Jocko slugged some whisky, in reality four-day-old cold tea. Me and Paulus had swigged some earlier. It was revolting and made Paulus spew up yet Jocko seemed to like it, especially when he suddenly goes off on one about how everything's so much better in Scotland, and how much Scotland's given to the UK, and how his country's ripped off by public school poofters. It was like listening to one of those bloody tea-towels listing Scottish inventions, you know? Rubber by Dunlop McCondom, TV by Baird, penicillin by Fleming, the Macintosh by Angus McMacintosh, burgers by Fergus Macdonald, electricity by Jocko McPower, water by Jimmy McWater – I mean, McYawnsville, right? Like listening to the bloody Scottish Nationalists and their tedious devolution debate, eh? Ha ha. One small nothingness wants to cecede from another small nothingness. I mean, who cares? There's more important freedoms to fight for.

"Ow!" My bloody wife booted me hard in the shin 'cos the stage-crew were setting the dinner scene, Paulus, as Sharp, and Burridge, as Kirby Mills, were on, greeting the guests and seating them at the table and I was just staring into space, 'like some spaced-out mong.' We had no scenery and we'd not been allowed to paint anything so the audience just had to imagine the plush velvet sofa, the rich shag-pile carpet, the sparkling crystal chandelier, the ancient fading tapestries, the blazing log-fire rather than the old black plastic chairs from the music centre and the Headmaster's table. Nonetheless, when Mark Sonning tottered on-stage, it was to another, almost animal, roar from the crowd.

"Hello, Aunt Clarissa," said Sharp, adding in a loud aside to Mills "She's a little bit deaf, so you'll have to speak up."

"Who can't keep it up?" said Clarissa. "Him? Looks the sort."

"This is my solicitor, Mr Mills," said Sharp. "He's helping with the will. He's been very generous with his time."

"Half-past six," answered Clarissa.

With a sudden lurch of the stomach, I was on, linking arms with Bill and telling Paulus/Sharp how tired and upset he looked and introducing my wife, Lady Penelope Farthing, with the well-upholstered frame and a string of 'leg-over into the saddle' gags when Herr Lakker arrived, seiling, well, Hair Lacquer. Ha ha.

"Somesink to make your hair stay vere you vant it in, Donner und Blitzen und Gott in Himmel. I am Herr Lakker, ze chairman barber. Ve haff vays of making it stop." Clenching his fists, he jigged a little on the spot. "Englischer piggen-dogger und grrrrr."

"Perkins." Sharp ordered. "Be a good chap and chuck the gentleman into the gutter."

As Sharp took me and my wife away to see his etchings (hur hur), Perkins turned towards Lakker. Quick as a flash, Lakker knocked him over the head with the bottle of hair-tonic and gagged him, firing out the immortal line "Shut your faces. This is the best gag in the play." There was this loud unison guffaw from the hall. Feeling Paulus quiver with suppressed hysteria, I choked back a laugh of my own.

"Stop corpsing," hissed Laud. "Stay focussed."

We stumbled into the wings whilst Lakker was shoving Perkins into the grandfather clock, disguising himself in half-mast trousers and a too-small jacket and telling the audience he was a master of concealment, and erupted into fits of giggles. This play was hilarious. We'd forgotten, during the endless, angry hours of rehearsal, just how much it made us laugh. The question was, could we get through the next half-hour without losing it completely?

Our dinner party was a triumph of timing and intonation. It began with Mills, Sharp, Jasper (me) and Penny enjoying pre-dinner sherries (more revolting four-day-old cold tea which made us gag), meeting Arthur MacArthur who suffered, inevitably, from arthritis and being interrupted, at last, by Lulu the Maid. Flying across the stage wailing "Oh, Guy, my *dear*, you must be so upset," Leo flung himself bodily at Paulus, who caught him neatly in his arms. The audience cheered. Leo kicked up his legs coquettishly, batted his eyelids flirtatiously and said "Is there anything I can do to *relieve* you, Guy? Perhaps you need someone to look after you, someone to care for you, someone..." He walked his fingers up a chest then down towards a waist. "To reach those parts other, less *courageous* maids cannot reach."

"This isn't in the script," I hissed to Bill, suddenly jealous. Leo had done this to *me*, and in *real* life, not some poxy play. But the audience was cheering and stamping.

"Dinner, sir," said Lakker pretending to be Perkins, "Is served."

He'd skipped several lines 'cos Ali'd sent him on early to stop Leo stealing the scene. Nevertheless we made our way to the long table.

"I wonder," I said to Clarissa, "If you'd kindly pass the bread."

"Of course he's dead," said Clarissa. "I hope he's dead. If he isn't, he'll have a nasty shock when he wakes up in a coffin."

"What happened to him, nephew?" I asked. "It seemed so sudden."

"Well," came the answer, "He hadn't felt well for ages so he went to the doctor, nose running, head aching, eyes streaming. The doctor said 'flu?'"

"And he said 'No, I came on my bike'," interjected Penelope.

I giggled, which set Paulus off, which set Leo off.

"These crackers," said Jock Macabre, "Are a little hard."

"What's like a knacker's yard?" said Clarissa.

"Switch your hearing-aid on," I said.

"I *haven't* been laid on," Clarissa said crossly, "Not for years, and even then it was over all too quickly. Come as you are, I said... what a disappointment."

Paulus giggled again as the Sixth Form guffawed.

"SWITCH YOUR HEARING AID ON!" I bellowed into her ear.

"I know," said Clarissa, "I'll switch my hearing-aid on. That'll help." She passed her cup to Jock. "Would you put some sugar in please?"

"Let me," I said. "When I went to his house, he had a fork in the sugar-bowl. He turns the gas off when he flips the bacon over."

"Watch your lip, Jimmy," growled Jock.

I stuck out my lower lip. "Can't see it from here," I said, and felt the fake moustache detach itself and float towards the table. Several people laughed then everyone else joined in as I grabbed it, stuffed it into my breast pocket and said "Phew, that was a close shave." There was a round of applause. I gave a mini-bow.

"Excuse me, sir," said Lakker/Perkins, "Mr Mills is on the telephone."

"That's odd," said Penelope. "Wouldn't he fall orf?"

"Off what?" Clarissa had skipped several lines.

151

"The telephone," I said loudly, trying to retrieve the script.

Stewart, confused by the missed lines, killed the lights, plunging us all into darkness.

"Come off," hissed Dwyer urgently from the wings, "Get off."

"Is there a power-cut?" ad-libbed Penelope as we stumbled off. "Damn unions."

"Who sat on your onions?" Clarissa asked. "I haven't had my onions so much as peeled for about a hundred years..."

"Made your eyes water, no doubt," Sharp added, well, sharply. Sorry. I just read the lines I'm given, you know?

Another gale of laughter as Gregory restored the lights whilst Dwyer was marshalling his people to set up the much anticipated bedroom-scene and caught Rice in full-beam. Now there were a few jeers, but when Lulu returned with her line, "Oooh, I really enjoyed that", the jeers turned to cheers and applause.

"Oh Guy," Lulu sighed, clambering up his body as it reclined on the battered, flowery sofa we'd 'liberated' from Smeaton House and Graham Vesey, their SM, "Please, please say you love me. Now we are alone, well, apart from these six hundred people, but just pretend they're not listening, you can speak your true feelings for me. Tell me that you love me."

"Well." Sharp shifted up the sofa uncomfortably. "Do you think it's wise? Just think what the neighbours would say, or the family? My God. The family! If they found us together... on a sofa... and alone? I mean, you're a man and I'm a woman... no, no," he flustered, trying to recover, "I'm a man and you're a woman."

"Wanna bet, Poorly?" yelled someone from the audience.

Back-stage, me and Sooty collapsed against each other, braying like donkeys.

"Then it's *perfectly* natural," said Lulu. "We're *perfectly* suited. We belong together like bacon and eggs." S/he dabbed Sharp's nose with the feather-duster. "Bread and butter." S/he tickled him under the chin. "Coffee and cream," and, turning to the audience with this almighty 'oo-er', repeated the word 'cream' with as much innuendo as s/he could force into it.

The hall erupted.

"Crikey," said Sooty, awe-struck, "He's fucking brilliant."

Lulu dabbed Sharp's nose again, saying, with a glance at the crowd, "How do you like my French-tickler? Big, fluffy and, *oo la la,* so handy for getting into those awkward cracks..."

A loud 'Wa-hey' burst from the Sixth Form and, apparently, from some of the Staff.

"I have something to show you," s/he said slyly. "It's hidden in my apron."

Another loud roar.

"Put your hand in and you'll feel something warm."

Bloody hell. I looked at the others, standing in the wings. Everyone had just dissolved into total hysteria. Sooty, choking, was pounding my shoulder. Ali had buried his face in the script. Anderson seemed about to explode. Even Bunny, leaning red-faced in the wings, seemed to be weeping. Leo unpeeled himself from Paulus, looked directly into the audience and said "My *heart,* you perverts, my *heart.* What d'you think I meant? Honestly! Men!"

Someone, maybe his Dad, maybe Hellfire, started chanting "Le-o, Le-o, Le-o, Le-o."

"Get on," hissed Ali, smacking me on the shoulder. "He's totally off-script."

"Hello, Guy, I wondered if you... Oh. Lulu. I didn't expect to find you here. You defy the laws of gravity. Easier to pick up than to drop."

S/he turned on me, draping himself round my waist, off-script again.

"Oh, *Jas*per. My hunky hero. Mad, bad and dangerous to know. We *belong* together, like bread and butter, like bacon and eggs, like ..."

"Don't say it!" I cried desperately. "Don't even *think* it! Not peaches and *cream...*"

Arching his eyebrow, he twined his right leg, resplendent in the fishnets and garter, round my waist like it was some stripper's pole, flicked his wig and, flirting outrageously with a six-hundred-strong audience, batted his lashes and said in a small, hurt, piping voice, "I was actually... as a matter of fact... going to say... bananas..." *MASSIVE* fuck-off pause whilst he licks his lips suggestively and the audience collapses in tears, "And thick, *THICK* custard."

I turned helplessly away, sobbing with laughter so Sooty had to lead me off. Leo extended his open palms to the crowd with a puzzled shrug, like 'what have *I* said?'

"Get back to the bloody script," gasped Ali, wiping tears from his face. "Stop pissing about and get back to the script." Paulus, Sooty and I clung together, trying to calm down for the final scene where Kirby Mills read the last will and testament of Sharp's uncle and handed over a briefcase of loot, saying "I'll give you the two million now."

"No!" yelled Lakker, "You vill giff it to me." He faltered. "Bollocks. I don't have a gun."

I had a gun but I needed it for my twist-in-the-tale double-cross.

"You're not Perkins," cried Penelope Farthing.

"No! Ich bin Herr Lakker und if you don't giff me ze the money, I vill shoot you dead, every single von off you." Then he hissed to me "Give me your gun."

"What?"

"Give me your gun."

"No," I said. "I need it. Where's yours?"

"I forgot it." The audience started laughing again. Looking round the set, his eyes alighted on the umbrella. "But I do haff zis, and so, Englischer piggendoggers, vill shoot you vis zis poisoned-dart-firing umbrella and you vill die horrible agonizing deaths."

"Brilliant, Jase," I muttered, pulling the cap-gun from my jacket. "I'll take the money, thank you very much."

"Oh Jasper," said Penny, "What are you doing?"

"Shut up, Penny. You tire me. One more word and I'll shoot you."

"But you'll make a hole in my dress, and it was only new this morning."

Arthur MacArthur appeared to tell us the car was ready.

"So ve don't need him any more!" Lakker pulled the trigger of his dart-firing brolly.

"And I don't need you any more," I yelled, leaping about and shooting wildly around the set. "Go ahead, punk. Make my day!"

'BANG, BANG.' Staggering Lakker crashed into this ten-foot tall plywood backdrop so hard it swayed. The audience emitted this 'woooo' sound as he slid to the floor beside Arthur.

"Whit's all this noise?" said Jock from the doorway, Lulu stroking his sporran and mewing something about it being so soft and furry.

"Don't move!" I shouted, jumping sideways to cover them.

As the clock bonged one, Perkins burst out, rolled across the floor and crashed into my legs. Seizing Jock's toffee-glass whisky-bottle, Lulu crashed it down on my head and I crumpled into a heap, the bottle shattered around me, the plywood panel swaying again. Shit, I thought, joining the heap of bodies sprawled on the floor, if that comes down, it'll flatten us like ferrets. Then, as the booby-trapped bag blew up in Sooty's beaky face, he decided to hurl himself bodily backwards into the already swaying set for a spectacular death, the fucking idiot. I watched it swoop, heard another 'woooo,' felt Sooty collapse across me as, backstage, Ali, Bunny, Dwyer and the rest of the cast braced up the scenery. I swore at Sooty who just kissed my cheek, then, while I was recovering, North and Whiting were giving it " 'ello 'ello 'ello" and it was over. Amid the cheers, the lights cut to black.

19: Tears on my pillow

CLAMBERING to my feet, I took my place between Sooty and Paulus, revelled in the echoing cheers, the clapping, whistling and stamping of our peers, and enjoyed the eruption of wolf-whistles for Leo from the Sixth Form and some of the staff. Did he milk it? You bet he did. Blowing kisses to the audience, he mouthed "Oh, thank you, thank you," gripped his hem between finger and thumb, and dipped into a couple of curtsies.

"He's *sooo* gay," muttered Paulus.

"So what?" I returned, high, excited, high-fiving everyone, even Turner, who'd openly hated the play, and Ali, who was firing off the remaining caps and yelling "Fucking awesome! Fucking epic!" He'd written this thing after all and we'd delivered it for him. "So am I. So are you, and we love you." I planted a kiss on his cheek and one on Sooty's. *He* had been a revelation, the beaky, boss-eyed beauty.

Leaving my parents chatting with the Trents and the Pauluses over the so-called surrogate coffee served up under the glowering oil paintings of our founders and benefactors in the Refectory, I scampered into the darkness to find Ali sitting alone on a bench under an oak tree staring at the shadows on the field. He turned his head as I slid into the space beside him and slipped my arm through his. He'd draped a black sweater round his shoulders. I said he looked like a bumble-bee then kissed him tenderly, experimentally, enjoying the taste of him. When we broke for a breath, I asked if he was happy with the play.

"It was extraordinary," he said thoughtfully, "Better than I ever expected, and so exciting, watching characters you created and lines you wrote coming to life. You write next year's, honey. See how great it is."

"What was your favourite bit?"

"When the lights went wrong," he said, "Your moustache coming off. The poisoned-dart umbrella. Sooty at the start. Loads. What was yours?"

"Bananas… and thick, thick custard," I laughed, slapping the bench with my hand.

Ali laughed. "That Leo. Whatever is he like."

"He's wonderful," I said emotionally, "Absolutely wonderful."

"You did like it, didn't you, J?" he asked tentatively.

"I loved it," I said. "It was the most fun thing I ever did on a stage."

We lapsed into silence. I curled my legs up on the bench and snuggled into his shoulder against his chest. Bats were circling in the darkness, wheeling above the cricket pavilion, perhaps the very bats I'd told Fosbrook lived in the belfry. I had never felt so happy, especially when we went into the trees and made a fantastic night into the best night ever.

The post-performance flatness kicked in next morning. There was always a feeling of desperate boredom, an aching empty hole in my life. After the four-day run of *Oliver*, for instance, I'd moped around the house for two days, permanently on the verge of tears, exhausted and listless, and missing the buzz, the camaraderie, the energy, the excitement of doing something amazing. Gray and Paulus had been in the Chorus, doing *'Food, Glorious Food'* and although Paulus was jealous that I'd got the star part instead of him, we'd had such a laugh, especially with Yates directing, and then suddenly it was all over.

The *Dream* had been worse because I'd known I wouldn't be acting with Ali again. Even as I'd delivered the final lines of the play for the final time, *'If we shadows have offended, Think but this, and all is mended, That you have but slumber'd here While these visions did appear'*, I'd struggled to contain my distress and cleaning off the make-up, changing out of my costume and going for pizza with my proud parents had been horrible, you know? My heart'd sunk into my socks, the pizza'd tasted like cardboard and tears prickled my eyes because ten thrilling weeks of rehearsal and four days of fantastic chemistry between me and my Oberon had abruptly stopped. It felt like something had died, a dread of returning to reality bringing choking tears of exhaustion, frustration and fury.

Our play was the talk of the town. Leo's ad-lib of "bananas... [PAUSE, look at the audience, lick your lips] and thick, thick custard" was being repeated everywhere. My lovely boy with the lilac eyes and candyfloss hair had stolen the night. Leeman's *Ali Baba* was a total disaster. The song-and-dance routine had fallen apart in the middle, two actors had got into a scuffle and Bunny went ballistic, ha ha. Rowntree's *Toad of Toad Hall*, on the other hand, was awesome, side-splitting and great fun, with Pip Brudenall and Nicolas Hill underpinning a superb performance from a Sixth Former called Greaves who'd played Toad. The make-up was awesome and the props even better. Gray, Tim and the other Rowntree-ites were very smug on Friday morning.

Anyway, during the house meeting, we celebrated our success. Jacko, fists above his head, called each of us in turn so we could get a cheer from the others. Standing with Burridge, I grinned, red as a cranberry, when Jacko praised me. Laud, Turner, Anderson, Warburton basked at the front then Sonning thanked Jacko for his support and encouragement and for having faith in our writer/director. Home-grown plays were unfashionable. Our rivals opted for tried-and-tested one-act plays by famous writers but we had taken a risk with one of our own and we'd shown *everyone* what we could do, as a team, as a house, when we trusted each other and believed in each other. Tears welled in my eyes. Ali stood with his head bowed as we chanted his name, a hundred boys in unison going "A-li, A-li, A-li", and when he spoke, it was in a halting, quiet voice. My own emotions were quivering like a volcano on the edge of eruption. Choking down a sob of sheer bloody pride, I just wanted to chuck my arms round him and love him.

"I want to thank every single one of you for trusting me to put this show on. I know it wasn't easy at times, and I know we had our moments..." Turner, grinning, nodded agreement. Ali's voice gathered strength. "But I never lost faith in our wonderful cast, in our *team*, in our friends. Thanks to you all. Next stop, the Debating Cup!"

PE today was water-polo. The swimming pool was its usual warm, welcoming self. It seemed remarkable to us that the school heated the staff changing-rooms to sauna-levels yet left the water in much the same state as when it left those mountain tarns. In fact, it was only heated for visiting parents on Open Day. Morreson muttered something about the *Titanic* being at the bottom of the pool. Lewis wondered about polar bears. Suddenly Maxton's verruca and Fosbrook's eczema played up. I considered having an asthma attack and sitting out the lesson on a bench watching Paulus in his dinky green Speedos for half an hour. But I liked PE so unbuttoned my shirt (celebration white today) and hung it on a peg with my house-tie while Mr Vickers, in dark blue tracksuit and white trainers, told us not to be so cynical and detailed the excused to mop the changing-room floors, ha ha, the skiving bastards. Though he was new, we'd come to like Vicarage's brisk, 'man up' approach. As I wriggled into my red-and-white trunks and dashed through the icy shower with Gray, I recalled the fun I'd had here with Ali and Leo, the fun I'd had with Ali last night, Paulus in his Speedos...

"Peters!" bawled Vicarage, "Get your head out of the clouds and back to the game."

"Yes, sir," I said dreamily, but things were already beginning to unravel.

"Hey, Poorly," Seymour jeered at Paulus, "Keep your eyes off JP's packet this week."

"For Claire's eyes only, eh, JP?" Brudenall added. I gave this kind of sickly grin.

I was on Gray's team, with Huxley, Paulus and some others. Adjusting my goggles and wading out to the middle of the shallow-end, I called "All-out attack then, skipper?"

"What else?" grinned Gray as Vicarage lobbed this orange ball into the midst. We all piled in on top of each other.

"This isn't rugby!" yelled Vicarage, as Roy Walton tossed the ball to Brudenall, a good swimmer who set off immediately for the other end, offloading to Morreson. Noting my team had taken 'all-out attack' to mean 'abandon all defence', I swam back to the goals as Morreson fired in a shot, leapt out of the water and got a full-stretch hand to deflect it wide.

"Great save, Jonny!" cried Gray. "Stay in goal!"

"Poorly's the goalie!" I shouted. "Hux, get in the centre."

Burridge flicked the ball over Harrison's head. Walton caught it, slipped it to Cooke.

"Someone tackle him!" I screamed. "Poorly, tackle him!"

Too late. Cookie passed to Brudenall, leaving Paulus splashing about like a wounded walrus. I lunged out of the goal but tangled with Huxley so Brudenall scored.

"Bloody hell, Peters," grumbled Gray, "What you doing fox-trotting with Hux when you should be keeping goal?"

"Hux, you spaz, get stuck in!" shouted Stewart.

"I haven't got my glasses on," said Huxley. "I can't see a bloody thing."

"You can't see a bloody thing when you got your glasses *on*!" I shouted back.

"Just get stuck in!" bawled Stewart again as Huxley fumbled the ball to Walton who lobbed over my head to make it two-nil.

"Bloody hell!" I shouted as Gray splashed a wave of freezing water into my face. "*You* go in," I said, chucking him the ball.

Walton dived forward, wrestling with Huxley, stealing possession, slipping it to Cooke who passed high over my head into Collins' hands. Three-nil. As the opposition high-fived each other, I bawled at Huxley to move about a bit, block the shot. "After all, one of you makes two of me!"

"Bloody HB pencil makes two of *you*, JP," roared Collins to general merriment.

Sighing deeply, Huxley heaved himself out of the pool to retrieve the ball from its resting place against the stone-cold, blood-red radiator.

"Ho bloody ho," I muttered. "Give us the ball!"

Huxley did so, with devastating effect. He didn't throw it especially hard, but it caught me full in the face, and since I was treading water, it knocked me backwards so I swallowed a mouthful of cold, chlorinated water. Coughing madly, rising like an angry kraken and bawling that Huxley was the twattiest spazmoid in the whole spazmoid universe, I sent a tidal-wave slopping towards him as he hovered hesitantly on the edge. Unfortunately I missed and the whole lot cascaded over Mr Vickers instead. His lopsided grin switched to a tight, white-lipped mask of anger as, sopping wet, he glared at me then at Huxley then back at me. The whole form was laughing. Vicarage's face seemed almost black with fury. Crimson and choking, I stammered an apology and awaited nuclear destruction.

"It's like being with the Chuckle Brothers, isn't it, sir?" Collins called. "To me, to you – you should see 'em on the footie pitch. Makes grown men weep."

Vicarage suddenly grinned, said I was not only a prize pillock but King Pillock of Pillockland, which made my friends roar, and that Huxley was Crown Prince Pratt. The tension evaporated into appreciative laughter and five minutes' free time for splashing, ducking and general horseplay. Gray and me sang The Rainbow Song ('*Up above the streets and houses, rainbow climbing high*') in the showers and Gray did this hilarious double-impression of George and Zippy arguing over the bar of soap while I vigorously shampooed chlorine out of my hair.

"No, George, you can't eat it. But it's called a cake, Zippy. Oh, George you're so stupid."

As we got dressed, someone shouted 'The bravest animals in the land' and we were off with our song, all twenty of us, marching out, double-file, into the drizzle under Morreson's supervision and my conducting at the head of the crocodile while Vicarage grinned from the door-frame, shaking his head.

"Welcome to King Henry's, sir!" I called over Lewis and Arnold's tooted theme. Our new PE teacher simply waved and shook his head again. He'd do well with us, we figured. Anyway, U5H left that PE lesson hyper, high and happy. So obviously Maths, coming next, was a total bloody disaster.

's is given by the formula $s = \dfrac{vyz.}{af}$

a) Calculate s when $v = 1.5$, $y=0.9$, $z= 2.4$, $a= 16$ and $f=0.02$.'

OK. Piece of piss. 3.24 divided by 0.32 = 10.125. So s = 10.125.

I think.

'The volume of a cone is given by the formula $V = \dfrac{\pi r^2 h}{3}$

V is the volume in cubic cm. r is the radius of the base, in cm. Calculate the height of a cone who base radius is 5.3 cm and whose volume is 435 cubic cm.'

Right. 5.3 squared is 28.09. 28.09 x 3.14 = 88.2026.... shit. What next? Do I divide 435 by 3? That's... I tapped the keys of my Casio calculator.

145.

Fuck knows. Do I have to move h?

My shoulders dropped despondently. Surely I should know this. Everyone else did. I could see them beavering away whilst I sucked the rubber orange on the end of my pencil and stared uncomprehendingly at the graph-paper. I scribbled something down, moved to the next set of gibberish, peered over Paulus' shoulder but realised he had even less idea what he was doing than I did, exchanged a grimace of despair with him, and focused on the last page of the orange exercise-book where I had recorded, in pencil, this game of *Search and Destroy*:

7 Mar 1966 Phu Yen Province

1̲ US 2nd Platoon fr S to rd.

1st P NW towards village & river

Co. down rd. Gds to L & R of ridge.

discover Peasants

NLF Wound Co. Cmr (US).

2̲ US 2 find ammo.

3̲ US 2P Co finds rice. US Co Cmr – rice

NLF sniper at bridge. pins US unit (2 Plat)

VC unit D. US Air strike – fails. 1 US P cmr WIA

4̲ P US rush to help cmr. 1st Rice   B

NLF turn to fight US nr far E forest with lower River. Air strike hits small wood

5̲

NLF cadre leader K. in battle nr E. for. Last rice found. 2nd Rice. D. AS→d sniper

&   bridge   2P int. peasant.

1st attempt = 0   2nd attempt = 0   ~~r3teas~~exd.

6̲   US 150   NLF 30

√

I'd played this game with Martin Cooke some time last year. I sought him out from the bowed U5H heads in Room 31. His blond hair hung round his head like a bell. I glanced sideways at Paulus. He'd got the hang of the Maths and was furiously scribbling down a load of meaningless shit. He saw me looking, grinned like Zippy and covered his book with his arm. While I fancied him like fury and loved him almost as much as I loved Ali, I hated him too. He was such a swotty little lick.

At break, I bought a red poppy for Remembrance Day and promptly lost it playing football so had to get another one. Adding insult to injury, the footie wasn't good anyway. I got stuck in goal because Maxton wanted to play out for a change and, when Seymour was charging towards me, I couldn't decide whether to come out and tackle him or stand my ground and hope to block his shot. In the end I did neither and let the ball through my legs. Then I kind of flapped at a shot from Collins and, as the opposition celebrated two goals in as many minutes, had to endure Lewis calling me a 'big girl' and Maxton saying it looked like I was trying to hit it with my handbag. Worse, my holiday homework turned out to be total bollocks. The music I'd written came back with 'DIDN'T UNDERSTAND THIS' printed underneath and a load of corrections in red to the parallel fifths I was not supposed to use. The German story came back scored at 26/50, with just 9/20 for the content, a ton of mistakes and the comment 'Another daft story.' Dammit. I thought it would amuse him. I'd written about cycling to a castle where 'Der Herzog war geizig und unglücklich, weil seine Frau neulich tot war.' To compound his misfortune, I managed to set fire to his house and roll his car into a stream but it didn't matter 'weil es herrlicher Sonnenschein war' (the line we were supposed to incorporate into the tale). Well, bollocks to you, Beaky. *I* liked it.

The history essay assessing Lenin's contribution to Russian Communism and covering seven pages of pink exercise-book got just 10/20, despite a mass of red ticks in the margins, and drew the comment 'You haven't answered the question. Russia didn't become Communist overnight. Instead of describing Lenin's takeover you should have spent more time on his activities after 1917, i.e. War Communism, Civil War, NEP and efforts to retain power.' When I re-read the essay, I noticed a load of stuff: "In 1915, the Tsar took command of the army but this made no difference. The Tsarina Alexandra ruled the country but she was only interested in preserving the throne for her son Alexis. Also a so-called monk, Grigory Rasputin, was 'helping' the Tsarina look after the country. He looked after Alexis, who was a haemophilliac," which, being a total fuckwit, I'd misspelt, "The people knew Rasputin to be a drunkard and liar. In December 1916 he was murdered by Prince Yusupov." Yes, it was a fantastic story, Ra-Ra-Rasputin, lover of the Russian Queen, and I found Alexis, the sickly, teenage Crown Prince bleeding internally every time he fell over, a fascinating figure. What kind of Tsar might he have made? Would he have survived the war? Had he ever masturbated? Could haemophiliacs masturbate? What if, like the bleeding, they couldn't stop coming? Just spurt after spurt, like till you died. Man. Death by Orgasm. I never heard of anyone dying of an orgasm. What a way to go. Beats fucking lung cancer any day. Still, great story though it was, Hellfire had a point. It wasn't strictly relevant, was it? But I was more fucked off that he'd deducted a mark 'cos I hadn't used a fucking ruler to like underline the title, you know?

The English essay, a six-page 'account of the relationship between Henchard and Farfrae' in *Mayor of Casterbridge,* got a 'good in parts' 15/30 - 'too generalized, and inadequate and inaccurate at the end.' "Driven to desperation," I'd written, "Henchard meets Farfrae in the granary loft and they have a fight. After several near misses, the 'infuriated Prince of Darkness' forces his opponent's head over the precipice. Farfrae submits and prepares to die but Henchard cannot deliver the knock-out blow." Willie had underlined the last phrase twice in red. "He lets Farfrae live and throws himself into a corner saying 'I care nothing for what comes of me!' Farfrae thus wins due to Henchard retiring form the fight to be counted out in the corner." Willie had written 'Don't be stupid!' in the margin.

The Biology was even crappier. 8/20 and 'very poorly answered.'

"Bacteria in the sewage needs to respire and takes in the oxygen from the river, replacing it with carbon dioxide. This is why the oxygen content drops" got two marks - 'do you really think 2 sentences qualify for 5 marks at this level?'

Er... I don't actually, like, know, Herbie? I'm not the fucking examiner, am I?

'Note: "bacterium" = singular; "bacteria" = plural!'

Well, fuck me! That is *sooo* useful to my life.

"The ammonium is in the sewage at first but then bacteria gets to work on it and converts it to nitrate ions" attracted a big red NO! and a 'read N_2 cycle notes' and the last answer "Algae feeds on bacteria and as there is a high bacteria content, algae will flourish and grow larger" was scribbled out altogether, with a big fat 0 and another massive 'NO! Algae are plants!' Blimey. Herbidacious must've enjoyed marking that lot. *I* didn't know algae were plants. Mr D. Bimp of Kent said I must be a quote total muppet unquote.

Even Chamber Orchestra was grim. We were preparing for this charity concert on December 12th, Save the Children, Save the Aged, Save the Aged Children, something beginning with Save. It was a nice programme. We were starting with this overture by Cimarosa (*The Secret Marriage*), then the woodwind section was doing the first movement of Mozart's C major Serenade K388, me and Max on clarinet, Dell and Keighley on oboe, Brooke on French horn and Nick Shelton on bassoon. We'd already rehearsed once and it was a lot of fun. The strings were doing Corelli's Christmas Concerto with Woodward and Rubenstein on violin, Paulus on 'cello and Williams on harpsichord. Then we all came together for Haydn's Symphony 103 in E flat major, the so-called 'Drum Roll'. During the interval we were gonna sell mince-pies and mulled wine then, in the second half, the jazz band were doing some Duke Ellington and the Lower School Choir was doing *Captain Noah and his Floating Zoo*. The Handbell Ringers were playing some seasonal pieces before we got the audience up for Christmas carols. The chamber orchestra was small, some twenty-four players, the jazz band smaller, with eight, the Lower School Choir had about twenty singers, so it was quite an intimate group, and we hoped to create an intimate atmosphere, even in that acoustically dry barn of the Beckwith Hall.

"Have you got the Haydn?" shouted Maxton over the cacophonous racket of tuning instruments. He was fitting his clarinet together whilst I adjusted the shared music-stand, bantered gently with Shelton, sitting to Maxton's left, and set this thick white ring-binder on the stand. The cover was adorned with a marvellous drawing of Munko from Pinka's Gang, proclaiming in a speech bubble 'JDP's Music Folder', the remains of four games of noughts and crosses in blue biro I'd drawn with Max during some rehearsal long ago, my proposed England XI to play in the upcoming Ashes tour, stickers of Barcelona and AC Milan and Gray's scrawled declaration that 'Madness Rule'.

Wilf said we'd start with the Haydn. Flicking at the folder, I watched in despair as the rings sprang open to send the contents tumbling over the shiny black-marble floor of the Britten Room. Grade 8 theory papers, letters from school about concerts going back three years, copies of music, Grade 3 piano pieces, clarinet solos, songs, notes... some of the sheets had not been hole-punched anyway, but at least they hadn't fallen out on the bus.

As Wilf swept up his arm to bring in Arnold's opening timpani-roll and then the lower register instruments, Finch's double-bass, the 'cellos and Shelton's bassoon, which were playing the same notes, I stretched out my left leg to trap and drag *Five Romantic Pieces for B-flat Clarinet* back from under Kevin Lees' chair. It was OK. We didn't play till Bar 46, so Maxton and the two oboists, Keighley and Dell, scrabbled up Mozart's *Litaniae Laurentanae*, Chopin's D flat major nocturne and Saint-Saens' clarinet sonata whilst Trent, sitting with Mark Williams, principal flute, genius pianist and the squarest square in the universe, doubled over with laughter. Williams just shook his head. He hated me anyway. Of course, missing their Bar 6 entry, they got savaged by Wilf for not paying attention. It was just the clarinets who had this long, ciggie-break-length rest. Whilst Maxton stuffed everything back into the binder, I stretched further for the orange-coloured *Five Romantic Pieces* so far I fell off my chair, clattering my clarinet on the polished floor, bruising my backside and propelling Lees, viola-bow flailing, into his music-stand. Trent erupted into a volcano of laughter (or lava-ter?). Shelton sputtered into his bassoon. Lees, seriously pissed off, called me a spaz. Rubenstein exchanged grins with Paulus.

"What the hell are you doing, Peters?" Wilfo yelled, chucking his baton on the floor.

Maxton set the Haydn on the music-stand. I hadn't fastened the butterfly-grip properly so the stand crashed down, sending all the papers cascading to the floor once again. Trent and Shelton were almost dying by now. Paulus was yelping like an incontinent Chihuahua.

"Just get out, Peters!" Wilfo yelled furiously.

Mr D. Bimp of Kent said I was a twat as I packed up my clarinet and left for the Upper Fifth footie match. Most of me didn't give a shit. I could pretty much sight-read the concert and I was planning this awesome Thai prawn curry for my folks tonight. For my class-mates, I crashed into their football game, attaching myself to Collins' team with a yell of "what's the score?" and a crunching tackle on Cooke, who tearfully called me a 'spazmoid twat.' Whatever.

"No idea. 8-6 or something," said Collins.

"Thought you weren't playing," grumbled Gray.

"Heads up!" called Walton, our goalkeeper, as Hill floated a dangerous cross in from the right towards Crooks. I roughly shouldered him aside, charged down the cross and whacked the ball back upfield towards Bainbridge. Not very subtle, but effective.

"Wilf chucked me out," I said.

"You got chucked out of an orchestra rehearsal?" Collins stared at me. "How?"

"I kept dropping my stuff on the floor. It's not my fault I can't work the music-stands."

Collins, sighing heavily, said I was a total spaz and put me in goal.

As I took the class's sweaty communal goalkeeping gloves off Walton, Lardy Gardiner thumped the ball a gazillion miles into the air but I had time to position myself to catch it as it re-entered Earth's gravitational field and nestle it into my chest. Dropping the ball onto my Reebok, I booted it clear. Unfortunately it bounced over Bainbridge's shoulder and Burridge picked it up, sliding it through Cooke's feet to Crooks. Now I yelled for the defence to protect me. No-one appeared. The Ginger Ninja, shimmying past Collins, flicked the ball to his right and unleashed a ferocious shot which I could only palm feebly into my own goal. As Crooks whooped, Collins told me I should've dived, not wafted it past with my skirt.

"I'm not so good at going down," I protested, then clapped my hand to my mouth as Graham Harrison drawled in the campest voice ever "That's not what I've heard, darling" and everyone else fell about in hysterics. "Ali Rose calls you Henry the Hoover, dear."

I told him to shut his face. He didn't. The others laughed. Boxheaded twat. Suddenly furious, I booted the football as hard as I could onto the rugby field and, ignoring the angry protests of the others, stalked back to the school. And then Mark Sonning intercepted me, steering me down to the woods where the gimps were playing hide-and-seek.

"So, Jonathan," he started, "What's the story?"

Blushing, I squinted up into his face and said defensively "What d'you mean?"

Ali's school mag meeting had gone to shit when Chris Crooks accused him of fucking me. In front of Mr Webster, Mrs May and Chris Morreson. Apparently he'd been explaining how me and Paulus, Brudenall and Shelton were going to form the core of the next committee when Williams snorted the gayboys were taking over the school.

"Fuck me! " I blurted. "He can talk, Fred's little bumchum."

Sonning just looked at me contemptuously then resumed his account. Morreson demanded to know why *I* was going to be Deputy Editor, not him. Ali said something about merit and winning the Writing Prize but the committee apparently laughed scornfully, and that's when Crooks Major said 'is it because he's sucking your cock?'

While Ali was reeling, Jamie Arnold's brother said "You're infatuated with the bloody kid, Rosie, but you can't see it. He's completely turned your head."

"He was always a manipulative bastard," said Crooks Major. "Are you fucking him? Mikey says Peters is bent as a thirteen-bob note and will suck anyone's cock for a vodka shot."

I stared unseeing across the playing field to the yellow brick of the Sports Centre.

"Then there's Leo," Sonning said gently. "Jason Middleton saw you kissing him." Now, cold as ice, I found a bench to sit on. "Listen, what you are is what you are, and you and Leo..." He shrugged. "I don't understand it, Jonny, but I like you *and* Leo, and I love Ali like my brother. He seems so confident and in control but it's all an act. Inside he's really scared."

Shit, Mark. So am I, *now!*

"Promise me you won't do anything stupid," Sonning was saying, "Promise."

I promised then, dazed, confused and fairly angry, I wandered off to Period 6.

20: Red Letter Day

AS the notes of The Last Post swelled and died from Luke Tredwell's bugle, drifting on the still morning air into the two-minute silence, I stood to attention between Paulus and Seymour on the damp grass and watched the Chaplain, the starched white surplice and purple stole flapping in the chill November breeze. He, Dr Crawford, had fought in a war. He had conducted burials out in the trenches. He had seen men die. He, like my grandfather and thousands of others, had been lucky. The bullet and the bomb had missed them and got someone else. Who knew why life was such a lottery?

Monday morning's traditional Remembrance Day event was always more reflection than celebration, but we missed pretty much the whole of first period, yay! Usually we did this on Armistice Day itself, but this year that was tomorrow, and tomorrow, the second Tuesday in November, was Speech Day, and *always* Speech Day. Since the Dawn of Time itself. Even a T-Rex invasion wouldn't change the School Calendar. Set in Stone since the Stone Age. That's my school. Anyhow, I'd rather stand in the drizzle listening to Wheezy wheezing on than bend my brain round quadratic equations, so thank God for the War, eh?

The Headmaster always did this meditation thing, where he'd read some memoir, diary or letter written by one of the school's Old Boys. About 800 had served in the First World War – the same number who stood here right now on the grass – and 129 had died. That was the whole of our year + L5G and half of L5W. There was a brightly coloured memorial window in the Chapel, a brass plaque in the Lupton Building and atop three steps in a corner near the woods a stone cross simply inscribed 'For the Fallen.' It was this we were facing whilst Dr Ashton read this letter written by 20 year old Captain Richard Herbert who'd been a company commander in the ninth battalion of the West Yorkshire Regiment and stuck out in the hell that became the Third Battle of Ypres in October 1917. Captain Herbert had left our school in 1915. Dammit, he had played rugby on the field behind us. He had probably fidgeted in the Chapel, like us, wondering if his Latin prep was any good and bored stupid by some early version of Leatherface intoning the Lord's Prayer. He might well have carved his initials in the wood panelling of the Refectory wall. I thought I'd search for it, scratched among the hundreds of others, next time I was in there, shivering under the vast hammer-beamed vault of that dark Victorian ceiling and avoiding the stony gaze of the oil-painted, gilt-framed grey-whiskered patrons and benefactors who hung suspended between the tall Gothic windows. Man, suddenly I could like sense the ghostly presence of Old Boys past, you know? Prickles on my neck, or maybe that was Seymour's bog-breath.

Anyway, on November 10 (shit, that's, like, today, man!) Captain Herbert had peeped his little tin whistle and led his company up to Passchendaele Ridge where they had, of course, been gassed then mown down by machine guns concealed in the trees within three minutes of entering No Man's Land. The letter, written from a field hospital in Ypres, told his sweetheart Grace that an exploding shell had not only shredded his left leg but also embedded shards of cast iron in his abdomen and groin. I mean. He'd sat in a mud-filled, water-logged hole with five wounded men for a day and a half, listening to the sounds of war, the screams of horses, the shrieking squeal of shells, and the snarls and sputters as all five died. Some private's guts had been spilled all over the mud and a corporal had his face shot away. I tried to imagine what that looked like, a face shot away, and couldn't. Anyway, Herbert, the sole survivor, was finally found by a stretcher team two days after the failed attack. Shipped home to Blighty, he won a Military Cross (I think 80 Old Boys got MCs in World War I), married Grace and become a one-legged bank clerk in Heckmondwike, married Grace, had four kids and went mad with shell-shock. Shit, man. Corner of a foreign field preferable to the hetty-norm, right? Right.

Sonning and Leverett laid this massive poppy wreath on the top step, Tom Redmond launched into that Binyon poem about not growing old while we that were left grew old then

Tredwell played Reveille and Wheezy said some prayers, one for the Queen, one for the Royal Air Force.

"*Let us remember before God,*" intoned Wheezy, "*And commend to his sure keeping those who have died for their country in war.*"

Shit, man. He'd fought in it. He *knew* men who'd died.

"*Grant, O Lord, that our people may devote themselves unselfishly to the common good, giving much and taking little...*"

What *is* the common good? Am *I*, a little queer boy? Would you devote yourselves to me? As the chapel choir, grouped behind the stone cross, sang Tallis's Nunc Dimittis, and I watched Fred and Williams, Leo Trent and Andrew Paulus, their starched white surplices flapping in the breeze, Dr Ashton and Mr Gallagher in their gowns and hoods, Redmond and Sonning standing with Ali, then my class-mates, macho rugger-buggers Seymour, Brudenall, Arnold and Lewis, swotty spods Huxley, Burridge and Bainbridge, cool cross-overs Collins, Crooksy and Stewart, my best friends Gray, Fosbrook and Maxton, I wondered how many would fight for me, for *us*, for me and Alistair, if we were dragged off to Pol Pot's Killing Fields or Adolf Hitler's concentration camps or Josef Stalin's Siberian gulags or by any nutbag loony who wants to kill people who are different from them? How many of the thousands who died at the Somme or the Marne or Alamein or on D-Day would have died for me? For my freedom to be me? For my freedom to be GAY? I wonder.

Remembrance Day was fairly cool, but, even better, tomorrow was Speech Day and we had the morning off. Yay again! It started at 3, and I had to be there around 1.30 (bollocks for being a prize-winner! Losers showed up an hour later!), so I thought I'd head off at half-twelve. This was the day the school displayed itself to the city, it was always spectacular and I was looking forward not just to getting my own prizes but seeing Ali getting his.

I was receiving the Lower Fifth Writing prize, a book-voucher which I'd spent on *The Complete Works of William Shakespeare* (my bookshelf, according to Ali, was naked without one), the Upper School Piano Prize and the Lawrence Harvey Cup for Best Individual Performance in the Music Competition. That one brought with it a solo recital in spring, a generous music voucher and a shiny silver cup. Although I'd won music prizes every year, this was different. It was a *proper* cup, like the one I'd secured in Harrogate two years ago with Schumann's Arabeske in C Op 18. I still knew that piece by heart, this two-part rondo with an opening I liked to make pensive and lilting, especially into the E minor passage where I forced each right-hand note rigidly to the left-hand's rolling triplets, never resting, then into A minor and a haunting, spell-binding coda which I always let just fade into silence. Magical music.

"If he gives you the wrong book," Gallagher had said in Monday's post-Assembly briefing, "Don't grab his collar and shout 'you've given me the wrong book, you dozy old fart' or you'll lose us the half-holiday which means you won't just get your tender little bottoms birched by me, you'll get something far, far worse – your friends will hate you for all eternity. Just smile and say thanks and Mrs Locke will sort it out later."

"Try not to get in the wrong order," Yates advised. "I know it's hard for bird-brains like you to remember when to stand up so I'll have a list but it's helpful if you stay in the order you're seated in. Be there at 1.30. I know it's a 90 minute wait but we'll get Rosie to put on a show, or maybe JP can play something on the organ..."

A ripple of ribald laughter ran through the Sixth Form. I coloured hotly and looked at my shoes. What the hell did *he* know? What did *they* know? Maybe it reeked from me. Maybe my gayness screamed out for all to hear and see. But Cedric smiled affectionately at me. He'd told me several times how talented he thought I was. Now I wondered if he fancied me. I stared at his saturnine features, the dark hair, the piercing blue eyes, the slim build, then shook myself. Man alive, I muttered. He's so old he must be *at least* 30!

"Don't fall off the platform," Gallagher said. "It narrows. Don't knock the books over because you've turned up pissed – yes, Mr Rice, I'm looking at you – and don't trip over the amplifiers. Pick your feet up, stand up straight, and be proud of yourselves. You're the best of this city, shown off *to* this city." So no pressure then.

I got Seat 6 in Row G, between Andrew Paulus and Geography prize-winner Graeme Vesey from U5B. Ali would be on the front row with the other prefects.

"Finally," said Frank, "Try to look happy. You're receiving prizes, not a report from the clap-clinic." The Sixth Form guffawed. I could see why they loved him. "But don't grin like village-idiots, Mr Lister. If he asks you why you chose that book, tell him intelligently. Don't say, Mr Fenton, that it was the cheapest. It may be excruciatingly boring, and the seats in the Town Hall will numb your peachy little bums but the Headmaster is not a comedian, at least not a professional one, and remember, do *not*, repeat *not*, laugh at the Lady Mayoress's hat. Now sod off, and remember, 1.30 sharp, or you'll find yourselves swinging from the Town Hall clock by your short-and-curlies, if you've grown any yet." We would follow this man through fire if he asked.

Lying in bed on Tuesday morning listening to Radio 3's Composer of the Week (Aaron Copland) on the old Crown radio, I read more *Viking Dawn* - Harald Sigurdsson, 15 and savagely whipped in the market-place, was escaping through a tunnel to [**SPOILER ALERT – if you haven't read it, yeah yeah...**] steal a ship which would later break up in the icy seas leaving everyone to drown but him – had a soapy squirt in a steamy shower then fixed scrambled eggs with bacon and this pea-and-mint soup from *Delia Smith's Cookery Course*. Swotting French vocab for a test, I learned that 'appuyer sur' meant 'to press down', 'à peine' meant 'scarcely', 'se rassurer' meant 'to reassure oneself', 'un témoin' was 'a witness' and 'un choc' was 'a bump' then settled into a description of Casterbridge. The last test had been dodgy – 15/30. Willie had clearly hated answer (iv) 'The first detail says that bits of bodies were despatched around the country like "butcher's meat." Jints means joints and this suggests that limbs were treated like joints for shops. It is effective because it shows that Casterbridge was used as an execution place (perhaps the Roman amphitheatre).

'The second phrase means that they do not think about flowers and faces and looks unless they are cauliflowers or meat. This shows that the locals are not really bothered about people, only food and their way of life.'

He'd written 'poor answer' in the margin. So I really wanted *this* essay to be an A.

'The town of Casterbridge,' I wrote, 'is in Wessex. It is a country town, based on the corn industry. To the east there are moors and meadows, where water runs, playing "singular symphonies." This agricultural town is almost totally confined within the Walks.'

Two hours and five pages later I'd covered the streets, the church with a "massive square tower" that rises "unbroken into the darkening sky," the inn built of "mellow sandstone," the fairground, the Mayor's house and Mixen Lane, 'the Soho of Casterbridge, where all the bad characters meet.'

I liked it. I thought it a good essay with a ton of quotation woven through my own sentences, the way Willie preferred. I splashed Clearasil and Old Spice over my face, sprayed myself with Dark Temptation, gelled my hair and ironed my grey trousers and white shirt. A button about halfway down was missing. It'd disappeared last week in some playground football match. Not to worry. No-one'd notice. I polished my Clarks into an oil-black shine and tied my school tie, for a school occasion, then slid into my blazer. Straightening the red poppy in my buttonhole, I checked my pockets for my comb, keys and Calendar and some tissues, shook a handful of coins from Piggy Piggy-bank into my palm, wrapped myself in the black trench-coat Sooty had worn for the play and stepped into the soft November air muttering something about putting a horse's head in Herbie's bed as the bloody *Rainbow* theme-song lodged in my brain: *'up above the streets and houses rainbow climbing high...la la la la la.'*

The branches of rust-brown beeches and chestnut trees seemed to droop under their burden of moisture. The faces of the houses, usually stark-white in the sun, appeared wan and ghostly through gaps in dull green hedges. In the soft mist, delicate, silky spider-webs glistening with silvery dew-drops were strung vaguely between twigs and fence-posts. The fallen leaves provided a crinkly, russet carpet under my shoe-soles. Other leaves, dead and dying, had been gathered into piles at the side of the road like route-markers for a race. The soft moss on the tree-trunks was a damp dark-green, sopping sponges glued to the rough, scaly bark. A dirty paper-bag, blowing lazily by, appeared to vanish into the hazy fog. There was a pungent smell of rotting vegetation and a sharper scent of burning leaves. Thick, black bonfire smoke billowing over a wall added another aroma to the heady mix. As I dribbled a conker along the kerb and kicked some rusty leaves out of the gutter, '*rainbow climbing high*,' I realised I loved autumn very much even though I had to run, coat-tails flapping, for the bus.

"Captain's Log, Stardate 101180020914," I told my Walkman. "Have teleported down to the surface to rendezvous with the Cardassian spy who is posing as a German zombie behind the old Cornmarket. Am hoping he will hand me the phials containing the rejuvenating potion in exchange for the passwords he needs to access the Romulan star-bird's command computers and take control of the ship before it destroys the *Enterprise*." I skipped across the pavement, dodging the cracks, 'cos I *still* didn't want a broken back then passed the soot-stained war memorial, the tattered red-poppy wreaths laid at the feet of the Unknown Warrior, and bowed my head to read lines inscribed on my memory, that '*they shall not grow old as we that are left grow old.*' I didn't care what Mum or Alistair said. Soldiers who'd died fighting for freedom should be remembered, '*at the going down of the sun and in the morning.*' Then I found myself wondering about the gay soldiers. There must've been *some* in the Somme, as it were. No-one talked about *them*. All the letters home we read in History were to *female* sweethearts. Not to men. And if Ali was right and they'd been jailed when they came home, what was the point? Whose freedom had *they* been defending? Not theirs. Nor mine. Nor anyone like me. As Alistair said, the regime whose victory we were celebrating locked the very people who'd helped win the war up in jail or drove them to suicide for being gay, just like Hitler did. Although, unlike *our* leaders, Hitler didn't lie about it. Our hypocrisy unsettled me hugely so I moved away, past the art gallery and library and arrived at the town hall, this hubristic statement of civic pride, a massive, vainglorious Victorian sandstone wedding-cake confection. Springing up the wide stone steps, I breezed past a huge bronze lion and between the thick Corinthian columns like the regular visitor I guess I was and met Tom Redmond striding through the foyer, black gown swelling away from his blue and gold blazer like a malevolent thunder-cloud. He was the Cardassian spy come to hand over the secret of life, the Universe and everything, I muttered to the tricorder's 'Don't Like Mondays' (ho ho).

"Hey Tom, last time I saw something that stripy was on a kitchen floor."

"You're so not funny, Peters," he said, checking his clipboard for my seat number. "G6. Up the stairs. Report to Mr Yates."

Shit, Cedric was the secret of life, the Universe and everything? Not fair. He wasn't having the Romulan codes for that. Not unless he was 42. I flung myself up the carpeted steps, three at a time. Entering at the top of the choir, I was, as usual, overwhelmed by this vast bowl of an auditorium. It comfortably seated three thousand people and was saturated with pink marble and gold-leaf. Massive pink and crimson pillars supported a domed, vaulted ceiling which was covered in cherubs and other angels, like some Michelangelo frieze. The Lower School would sit in the bow-shaped balcony whilst the Upper School would sit on the Rises, the Sixth Form grouped around the huge organ-pipes, the Fifth to the right. The staff would sit in the orchestra. A long table stood on the stage. Here Mrs Locke and Mr Donovan, Leo's form-master, were setting out books, cups and certificates. The Board of Governors would sit here, with the Headmaster and the Guest of Honour, this year some minor industrialist called Riverdene or Riverdale or something. A microphone to the right was where Mr Gallagher would call our names. A mike to the left was where Redmond would move a Vote of Thanks and ask the honoured guest to grant the school a half-day holiday. No-one had yet refused. I wondered who'd lynch him first, the kids or the staff.

Cedric nodded warmly as I moved to the seats on the left where the contraltos and the 'cellos play and now reserved for our prize-winners. I knew this stage so well. Four times I'd played on it, in the Primary Schools' Music Festival then in two recitals of promising pianists

Mrs Lennox had arranged, and then in the city-wide competition which I'd won aged eleven with 'Farewell to Stromness.' The melody wormed through my brain and I found myself moving my fingers, unconsciously stroking out those limpid, melting, heart-breaking notes.

Settling beside Paulus on a red cushion, I half-listened to a brief appraisal of the other house-plays. Brearley's Sean O'Casey had been a disaster, half the cast forgetting half the lines and the other half their cues. Goodricke's Noel Coward was shit (so fuck you, Christopher Crooks!) Andy Collins' collapse through a sideboard had failed to save Smeaton's effort and Tetley's *Waiting for Godot* had bored the arse off everyone, even Adam Austen, who was in it, for God's sake. I was glad I'd stayed home with *Shoestring*. From my pocket, I fished Asimov's *Mysteries*, this book of sci-fi short stories like 'Dust of Death' where [**spoiler alert**] the murderer uses a dust made from platinum coated on a gas cylinder to cause a massive explosion. I was always struck, in sci-fi, how Earth'd moved beyond its present tribal feudalism, nation-states and ethnic groupings to become a mature, stable, planet-wide integrated confederation. Not for the first time, I lamented living in such a retarded era, where people kill each other for waving the wrong little flag or singing the wrong little song. In *Jeux Sans Frontières*, nobody really cared about your flag. It was all just a laugh, yeah? It's why Europe was so good. They safeguarded our freedoms in spite of our governments.

As the Town Hall slowly filled up, I watched my parents walk up the central aisle to their seats in the third row of the stalls, Mum in a cashmere sweater in peaches and cream stripes and matching silk scarf, a brown skirt and long brown boots, Dad in a smart black blazer with shiny gold buttons, white shirt and a nice red tie. They'd not let me down. I shot them a tiny wave, which made them smile. They seemed bursting with pride. Though I'd won prizes before, I think they still got a thrill. So, if I'm honest, did I.

Mr Perry was playing a Bach prelude on the organ, the music swelling from the pipes rolling hugely through the auditorium. Mr Yates reappeared at the top of the Choir, a black gown and red Oxford hood over his suit. I was getting excited now.

"See that hat?" said Vesey. "Looks like a game-reserve. And that one? The fruit-bowl in the second row?"

It was Mrs Wilson. Paulus and I laughed a lot. Niall Hill (U5B), winner of the Pollock Art Prize, spotted an enormously fat woman wearing what looked like a massive floral tent.

"Who's she with?" I hissed.

"No-one," whispered Hill. "That's all her!"

"You think she's watching her figure?"

"She'll be the only one who is," whispered Hill.

"Some men climb mountains," I quoted Louie from *Taxi*, "Others date them."

We giggled until Cedric hissed 'behave' so we teased Paulus instead, reaching behind his back and over his shoulder to snatch the poppy from his blazer buttonhole. He got really mad with us, which made us giggle even more, so Cedric told us off again. Wilson, meanwhile, sat smugly by muttering something to Vesey about sitting with the children.

"Oh," sneered Hill, "You're *sooo* mature, aren't you?" Like Tim, he was in Rowntree House and like Tim did Art and Latin so I didn't really know Hill, except from break-time football. He was slightly taller than me, had a round, pleasant face, soft butterscotch hair cut over his ears, and pale grey eyes. I knew he was a brilliant artist, hence the prize, that he was good at football and was hoping, like me, to break into the cricket team this year. He had lovely, soft-looking lips. He would probably give me a great blowjob.

The music morphed into Karg-Elert's 'March Triomphale' as the prefects, led by Redmond and Sonning, appeared at the door, and I stood with the others, buttoning my blazer, adjusting my poppy and hoping my semi-erection wasn't noticeable. I loved this spectacle. I loved this school. And most of all, I loved the boy who, head bowed, hands clasped, was walking slowly, solemnly towards me, the boy with the bruise-black hair and deep teal eyes, the boy in the charcoal suit, gold tie and black gown, the boy who raised his eyes to mine, the boy who made me smile as he climbed the steps to the A2 in the front row. Hill quietly raised an eyebrow. Blushing, I stared at my shiny black toecaps. Behind the twenty prefects came the staff in full academic dress. This was the School displaying its intellectual power to the world. This was a school where A was the benchmark, where C was an 'also-ran', where GCSE was like the *start* of our education, you know? Not the end.

The colourful rainbow was dazzling, Gallagher with a white fur hood, Crawford in this scarlet silk robe with purple trimmings, fifty others flowing behind in golds and greens, reds and whites. Dr Ashton, in scarlet Cambridge gown, came last with Lord Riverdale, plain dowdy in a dark pin-striped suit. In the battle of appearances between intellectual and industrialist, the intellectual won hands-down.

Now the Governors entered, eight men in suits, but our local bishop, the chairman, wore purple and white silk with gold facings. He was a lean man with dark hair and a hawk's face, but I really liked him. When I was 12, he'd confirmed me in the Cathedral (consecrated in 1914) and done my first communion, then, of course, awarded me this scholarship. He'd been at that Harrogate Festival, with Dr Ashton and Wheezy Wally, and been really nice to my folks. Now he walked with the Lady Mayoress, resplendent in scarlet, a white ruffled neck-cloth and heavy gold chain. OK, fine. Bishops and Mayors outdid even academics.

Our school had been a religious foundation, by a notoriously stingy Tudor King, no less, and a bloody Lancastrian/Welshman, in Yorkshire, for God's sake, and underpinned by charitable donations and local philanthropists throughout its nearly five centuries. They gave the school its traditions, history and heritage, of which this annual display was a celebration, and of which, and I never forgot this, I was an integral part. I had a scholarship, after all.

As the Bishop delivered the School Prayer, "*We bless thee for our creation, preservation, and all the blessings of this life; but above all, for thine inestimable love in the redemption of the world by our Lord Jesus Christ; for the means of grace, and for the hope of glory,*" I remembered, with a jolt, I was supposed to be reporting on this for the magazine, not gazing at Ali or reading *Foundation* inside the programme. So I focussed on Dr Ashton's craggy, lined face, iron-grey hair, bushy, unkempt eyebrows, and recalled the evenings I'd spent round his house with his family, evenings of laughter and learning, how he'd never patronised or talked down to me or made me feel anything other than his equal. This Dr Ashton was different, dry, meticulous and very, very boring. I recalled Gallagher's warning that the Headmaster wasn't a comedian, at least not a professional one, and decided to use the line in my article. Into the microphone he droned numbers, investments, endowments, bursaries, scholarships, charitable donations, A-Level pass-rate (90.3%), GCSE (89.3%), a record year of Oxbridge entry successes (30), other university admissions (173), meaning 95% of last year's Upper Sixth went into higher education but mere statistics, he said, did not convey the type of education the school delivered.

"Alongside our Oxbridge successes, we celebrate the growth of multifarious artistic activity, of musical events, of drama, of areas like design and art and creative metalwork in Technical Studies. We are a day-school with short working hours but we do what we can." The school, he declared, valued diversity, celebrated difference, allowed boys' talents room to blossom and flower, wherever those talents lay. Every boy was an individual and given the space to be so. There was some applause, then he changed his tone.

The times, he said, seemed anxious and depressed. "The educational scene seems perpetually in turmoil. Recession means a hard time for us all, and it is no fault of the state-school sector that they are suffering cuts and changes yet again. They have our sympathy. But, at least for the moment, things look better at our end. Through the generosity and self-sacrifice of parents we are able to preserve a full range of subjects taught by specialist staff and a vast range of out-of-school activities voluntarily organised by this same hard-pressed staff, who do it because they want to, not because their contract tells them to."

As we applauded our teachers for helping us develop into diverse individuals, I wondered how I'd have fitted into Thornbury Comp, like the kids from primary I'd lost touch with. Not well, I thought. I didn't think anything connected with the state welcomed diversity let alone difference, at least not *this* state, which wanted to put me in therapy, jail or both.

At last, it was time for the presentations. Gallagher, programme in hand, moved to the microphone as Mrs Locke and Mr Donovan moved to the table to hand the prizes to Lord Riverdale and Mr Yates moved to the steps with his clipboard.

"The Longford English Prize, the T.J. O' Brien History Prize and the Younger Prize for Best Contribution to the School Magazine," read Gallagher, "A.S. Rose."

Ali, glowing and radiant, left his seat. He was so clever. He'd won 3 prizes. God, he was such a genius. Tears pricked the top of my nose. My Ali was so clever and I loved him. I saw him searching for his parents, applauding proudly in the fifth row. His Dad, short, slightly rotund, had a bald, egg-shaped head framed with some feathery grey tufts, like a nest built by a blind bird, and glasses on a silver chain. His Mum had a fairly long face, a chin that tapered into a sharp point and nut-brown hair tightly curled into an unfashionable perm. His Dad looked kind, his Mum perpetually disappointed. They reminded me of Sir Basil and Lady Rosemary from *The* 'Herbidacious' *Herbs*.

As he shook hands with Lord Riverdale and the Headmaster, he gave me a small, shy smile, then Mr Yates was marshalling us from Row G to the steps. Austen (History) and Driver (Mathematics) had already gone. Waiting in front of Vesey, who, being a six-foot blond hulk, towered over me, and feeling suddenly self-conscious, I wondered what to do with the hands dangling uselessly at my sides. I fingered the hem of my blazer, fiddled with the buttons, smoothed my trousers, then folded them in front of me. Feeling like a priest, if you know what I mean, I clasped them behind my back, then felt like PC Plod (oh, men in uniform!) so shoved them into my trouser pockets and gazed at the hundreds of Lower School gimps massed in the balcony. God. To think I'd once sat up there. Once. In 2W. Before I conquered the world from a keyboard.

"Peters. Get your hands out of your pockets, for God's sake," Yates whispered fiercely. "And stand up straight. You're not leaning on a lamp-post at the corner of the street in case a certain little lady walks by, you know."

Struggling not to laugh and embarrass myself further, I complied, then suddenly, providentially, Gallagher left the microphone and strode to the sound-crew at the edge of the stage. Their speakers and amplifiers narrowed the space so much that boys'd been teetering and wobbling along the rim. The Sixth Form were laying bets as to who might fall off and their grudging applause for the prize-winners was punctuated by cheers, catcalls and disappointed groans. Frank had evidently decided to stop the sport.

"Come on," he snapped, "Shift that stuff unless you want it kicking onto the floor." Angrily he toe-ended thousands of pounds of electrical gadgetry. A massive cheer went up from the Sixth Form, clearly hoping he was going to boot it all off. The dismay when he allowed the crew to rock the speaker into a different position was palpable. A hushed boo swelled.

"The Sixth are in high spirits today," I whispered to Paulus.

"Probably been *drinking* high spirits," he whispered back.

"Peters," went Yates, "Stop grinning like an imbecilic baboon. You're on."

"Pollock Prize for Art, N.W. Hill," Gallagher was saying, "Upper School Music Prize for Strings and Lower Fifth Prize for Modern Languages, A.G. Paulus, Upper School Music Prize for Piano, Wellington Prize for Creative Writing and the Lawrence Harvey Cup for Outstanding Musical Performance, J.D. Peters, Lower Fifth Prize for Geography, G.J. Vesey, Lower Fifth Prize for Chemistry and Littlejohn Prize for Biology, T. N. J. Wilson."

I wondered what the W. in N.W. Hill was. I knew the G. in A. G. Paulus was Gavin, and Tim's N.J. was Nicholas James. What if it were William? He'd be William Hill, like the bookie.

Vesey like prodded me in the spine so I bumped into Paulus who scowled almost as severely as Yates. We moved off to generous applause. Hill blushed when he received his prize. Paulus seemed almost indifferent. Then it was gulping me. My right hand was briefly gripped by a warm, dry piece of wood. Glancing up, I caught a glimpse of impassive grey eyes buried on either side of a hooked nose then heard a murmur of congratulation as he loaded me up with red-covered Oxford Shakespeare, Bach's blue-covered Henle Verlag *Inventions and Sinfonias* and this massive silver cup with a gilded inside. The year and my name, *J.D. Peters,* was inscribed on the plate in elegant, flowing script. The Head muttered something.

"Is that so? Prodigy, are you?"

I was really embarrassed now, beetroot-red and stammering. Everyone was staring.

"Scholarship boy too." He took my hand again. "Great to meet a young man who is making the best of his talents. Congratulations, son. Enjoy the Shakespeare."

"I will, sir," I stumbled. "Thank you, sir."

Ash-tray smiled affectionately then the Bishop caught my sleeve.

"Very proud of you, Jonathan," he said. "You repay that scholarship every day."

Several Governors nodded approvingly. One or two even smiled, these sombre men in sombre suits who'd pledged their faith, and their cash, in *me*, an 11 year old boy, out of my depth but a fighter who'd do his best for them, and for myself.

I muttered another 'thanks' but really I just wanted to get off. Hill and Paulus had vanished up the steps long ago and Vesey was hard on my heels. Riverdale hadn't exchanged words with him nor, I noted happily, with Wilson. Clutching my prizes, I hurried past a twinkling Gallagher, past the snide jibes of my fellow Fifth-Formers to the Sixth Form who looked resolutely bored and past Mr Perry, picking his fingernails at the organ.

"Thanks, sir," I said. After all, the Lawrence Harvey Cup was his award and he'd chosen me over his super-talented Sixth Form favourite Williams. His shrug suggested he didn't care. I was the best musician in the school so why did he dislike me so much? Just 'cos I'd turned down his bloody Chapel Choir.

Collapsing back into G6 with Paulus banging on about cosy chats with the Bishop, I clapped the gimps getting their piddly little prizes then tuned into Lord Riverdale saying what a pleasure and privilege it had been to meet so many talented and personable young men. We were, he said, a credit to our school, a credit to our families and a credit to the city.

"I am not going to say what many speakers say on these occasions, that it isn't the winning but the taking part that counts. I am not going to say that I never won a prize and just look at me now, a self-made millionaire with a multi-million pound business and a seat in the Lords, because I recall one man who *did* say that at one of *my* earliest speech days, and I *did* look at him and resolved there and then to win as many prizes as I could."

The Sixth Form hooted like monkeys, aping Mr Rogerson, who had this distinctive laugh. Gallagher scowled. Rogerson himself added his own echoing hoot to the rest.

"So today," Riverdale continued, "Is a day to congratulate the prize-winners. It is their day and we celebrate their achievement."

Yeah, you bloody losers! The label pasted inside the Shakespeare's front cover bore the name of the school, the corn-and-crown crest and 1507, then PRIZE in the centre surrounded by a laurel wreath for victory and *For* Creative Writing, Awarded to J.D. Peters, Form U.5.H. signed A.A. Ashton, Headmaster below, and today's date.

I glared at Seymour, Brudenall and the other fuckers who teased me and put me down, then along the line at Tim. For all your bloody Maths and Science, you will never, in a gazillion lifetimes, be able to play the piano like me, and you will *never*, because you're too fucking scared, fall in love with someone awesome like Alistair Rose. I glanced at my watch then at Paulus then at Hill and sighed heavily. I wanted it to be over so I could talk to Alistair.

I leafed through the programme for like the trazillionth time, blue print on white, school crest and Latin motto *'invenire et intelligite'* on the cover, 3 p.m. 11th November, the order of events, our names listed alphabetically, A.S. ROSE L.VI on page 1, J.D. PETERS L.V on page 2. Did he get the same thrill as me from reading our names? The middle pages contained the stats Ash-tray had relayed. But of the 825 boys in the school, how many were like me? Mr Trent had reckoned 10%. That'd mean 82. Who the hell were they? I scanned the crowd for signs and found none. *'La la la la la la la la rainbow climbing high…'*

The rest of the programme covered Staff News (leavers like Burnden and joiners like Vicarage), concert dates, drama ('The school play this year was 'A Midsummer Night's Dream' by William Shakespeare and was a joint production with the Girls' High School. It was directed by Mr W. Western – man, is that all? No 'awesome performance' by A. Rose (or J. Peters for that matter)? Just 'The House Plays provided their usual varied entertainment and were co-ordinated by Mr I.T. Hutchinson and Mrs S.P. May.'), Voluntary Service, the Locomotive Society (the what?), Scout Group activities, expeditions ('8th July, nearly 700 boys went as far afield as Winchester, London, Edinburgh, the Yorkshire coast and the Dales and included visits to the Stock Exchange, museums, a zoo, a research farm, an assault course and a brewery.' Who went to the brewery? It certainly wasn't L5C!) and sporting achievements (I noted with a thrill that 'M. Crooks came third in the Northern Schools Harriers Championship').

Wondering how I should describe this for the school magazine, I began composing the piece in my head then got distracted by some chewing gum smeared blackly on the carpet between my feet. Could I scuff it away with the edge of my shoe? Hill seemed to be asleep. Paulus was reading the blurb on the back of the collected poems of some Frenchie called Baudelaire. Blond hulk Vesey was staring at his massive hands. Even Tim Wilson seemed restless. Ali was listening politely, head cocked on one side, but it was too late. I had tuned out of Riverdale and *Rainbow* and into 'Don't Like Mondays.' Before *the silicon chip inside [my] head was switched to overload*, Redmond was moving a dull vote of thanks which Ali would've done a billion times better 'cos he was a genius who'd've made people laugh.

"In closing," Redmond said, "I wonder if your Lordship might prevail upon the Headmaster and the Chair of Governors, on behalf of the assembled school, to grant us and our hard-working teachers, a half-day holiday as a mark of your visit."

"I believe," Riverdale replied, "The Headmaster should grant you, *and* your teachers, a *full*-day holiday, and will prevail upon him, as you put it, to do so this very afternoon."

"Very well," grinned Dr Ashton. "A full-day holiday it is, date to be confirmed."

The teachers cheered louder than the boys. Suddenly we loved Lord Riverdale. Boring old fossil he might've been, but he'd delivered us a whole day off sometime in May.

We stood to sing the School Song, something in Latin from 1897 I'd never fully mastered going "*Floreat per saecula, salus sit fidelibus*." I mean, what? The National Anthem was much easier. Emotions swelled as I bawled "*Send her victorious, happy and glorious,*" although the queens I meant were not living in Buckingham Palace. They were sitting on Rows A and G and up in the balcony. Then Perry clattered into Widor's joyous Toccata, famous for launching a mazillion marriages. If only I could marry Ali. Then I'd be happy. Clawing open my collar-button, I struggled into the street with Paulus and Hill.

"Your play was great." Hill flashed me a knee-weakening grin. "No idea what it was about but young Trent was awesome." He licked his lips. "Especially in that frock. Man, I'd taste his bananas and custard any time, eh, Jonny?" Then he was gone, leaving me confused on the red carpet. Niall Hill? Was Niall Hill gay too? What was he trying to tell me? And why *me*? Why was he telling *me*? What the hell did *he* know? Surely he wasn't telepathic.

Dad shyly shook my hand. Mum proudly hugged me. In front of *everyone*. Yikes. Someone just shoot me. I'd rather steam and eat my own spleen, you know? With green beans and a nice *Sauvignon Blanc* than be kissed by my *mother* in public! As I was muttering 'get off, Mum,' Mrs Wilson bundled by, T.N.J. in tow.

"Well done, Jonathan," said Mrs W, "Though you didn't get any *academic* prizes."

"Nice cup, though," T.N.J. said graciously.

"It'll look good with the others he's won," said Mum smugly.

Then the Roses appeared, Mr Rose beaming, Mrs Rose frowning, and Ali was radiating love and saying how brilliant I was, and everyone was shaking hands and meeting each other and I was just gazing adoringly at him. I *sooo* wanted to kiss him. He was so utterly beautiful. Then suddenly he was asking me out to a concert and dinner on Saturday.

"It's the first concert of the season," he said, waving a flyer he'd picked up in the foyer,

"Here at the Town Hall. City of Birmingham Symphony Orchestra, doing Mahler 2 and Szymanowski. They're bringing their new conductor. He's really young and dynamic, really exciting. It's gonna be fantastic. We gotta go, J, got to. Review it for the school mag."

Mum and Dad were kind of like staring at each other, like cannot compute, right? And I'm kind of going 'please let me go, please... it's gonna be great' and Mum's going 'why?' and Ali's kind of shrugging uncomfortably as though he's said too much, and Dad's going 'it's only a concert' and Mr Rose is going 'what a great idea, you can take him to *Adriano's*, I'll book you a table' and Mum's kind of twitching and Dad looks confused, upset and irritated, all at the same time and I'm like almost on my bloody knees with my hands clasped, like *begging* to go.

"OK," says Dad finally. Man, right there in the Town Hall, in front of like a grazillion people, teachers, class-mates, parents, I chucked my arms round my father's neck and hugged him exultantly, gratitude like tumbling out of me like some bloody emotional Niagara had broken loose. Ignoring Mum's snort, I rejoiced. I was going on a date with Ali! At last! A proper date! With my lovely boyfriend! I was so like totally hyper-excited, you know? 'Cos suddenly my life was like totally *totally* fantastic!

21: Take me to the other side

NERVOUS all day, I was unable to settle to anything, not to Edward Greenfield's comparison of Sibelius' Violin Concerto recordings, nor to kicking my football against the garage wall, nor to sloshing steaming hot water over the silver Sierra, not even to helping Dad scarify the lawn, tidy the flowerbeds and rake up rust-coloured leaves for a bonfire, although I loved the smell of wood-smoke, and I guessed every fucking tiger in India heard Mum yelling at me for treading mud into the kitchen. Bloody hell, Mum! I didn't want to go gardening in the first place.

The week had been tense, Mum making these like snarky remarks about Ali and then, imagine this, said I should take a cork (for my bum) when I went out on Saturday and did I want some extra-thick reinforced pants? Just in case. Yes, my *mum*. I shit you not. I just sighed tiredly and kept my trap shut. I didn't want to give them any excuse to ground me.

Locking myself in the bathroom, I scrutinized my face in the mirror and decided the downy peach-fluff on my chin had to go so I stripped off my T-shirt and reached for Dad's Gillette. I'd never shaved before but I'd seen it on the telly, so how hard could it be? Lathering my face with foam from this spray-can, I carefully scraped the blade across my face praying I wouldn't cut myself or nick the tiny pink pimple that'd sprouted overnight in the crease of my chin then soused my face in Clearasil and patted my cheeks dry. Looking good, I told myself. Clean and fresh. Except for that fucking spot on my chin.

I had a dump, cut my fingernails, showered, washed my hair twice and soaped my boy-bits with Imperial Leather several times just in case. I brushed and flossed my teeth, sloshed Listerine round my mouth then sprayed myself liberally with Dark Temptation and splashed some of Dad's Old Spice over my cheeks. It stung like fury and my face contorted into a scream, like Kevin's in *Home Alone*. Then I danced in my towel from bathroom to bedroom and stuck Bach on the CD player. *Gloria in excelsis Deo. Glory to God in the highest.* Yeah.

What to wear? What to wear.

My favourite white Chinos and dark blue shirt?

He'd seen that outfit before.

Black jeans and black shirt? Black socks.

I thought he'd seen that too.

White shirt and a tie? Grey socks?

Possibly.

I examined my rather paltry collection of ties. The plain red one might be good with a clean white shirt and black trousers. But then a tie might be too formal.

I could always take it off. Or ring him and find out.

Dark blue tie? Gold tie? Bow-tie.

No way. The red one.

Unless it was too formal.

Chinos and dark blue shirt. White socks. No, black. No, white. Yes. Trainer liners.

Again. He'd seen it before.

Bollocks. I really needed to refresh my wardrobe.

I went to the kitchen in a peach-coloured slip, ironed my clothes and dressed, turning up the collar of the shirt. I looked really cool, especially when I gelled my hair into a spiky centre-parting. But I still had like ninety fucking minutes to kill, Goddammit, and I didn't really want to get stuck into the rugby cup final between Hull KR and Leeds on the telly so I hit the piano, playing the whole of the *Moonlight Sonata* then Debussy then Chopin then Bach's D minor invention then, before I knew it, 6.00 had come and, with butterflies in my stomach and a thousand things to say rampaging through my brain, it was time to go and I was tying the laces of my best blue-and-orange Reeboks. Rattling fat, pink, plastic Mr Piggy piggybank, I found last week's fiver and £2.38 in change. The bus-fare was £1.75. £5 would cover a Big Mac, fries, and a milk-shake maybe? The last bus back, £1.75 too. Should just stretch.

Somewhat lukewarmly, Mum said I looked nice but thought I might've worn a tie then asked all the yaks in Tibet why, when I'd finished the toilet paper, I hadn't put a new roll on the holder. Who did I think was going to do it, the Toilet-Paper Fairy? Dad told me to have a good time and not to be later than midnight and if I came home pissed again, he'd ground me like for a bazillion years. I wondered if he'd give me another fiver. He didn't. Not to worry. I was still going to have the time of my life. Settling the gold cross in the V of my shirt, I crossed my fingers, muttered a prayer for a fabulous evening and closed the front-door.

Ali was waiting in the bus-shelter. He looked utterly gorgeous, in the black trousers and black open-necked shirt he'd worn to the half-term rehearsal.

"I guess we both wore our favourite clothes." Smiling, he looped his arm round my waist and gave me a gentle squeeze. "You smell fantastic. And you shaved."

"First time," I said. "I wanted to look good for you."

"Oh, honey," he sighed, "You always look good to *me*."

Why couldn't we just *kiss* 'hello', like straight couples?

"Where are we going?" I said, trying not to bounce excitedly on the upstairs front-seat like some hyperactive little brat.

"Do you like Italian?" he asked. "There's a bistro that does this fabulous *penne arrabiata,* or you could have veal in lemon. That's to die for."

I thrilled to be with him. I scorned everyone else on the bus and pitied everyone in the street beyond the big convex window because they didn't have *him* and *I* did, all to myself, for one evening, and although I still felt nervous, I also felt seriously exultant. I'd *got* him and he'd got *me*, and these people in their little vanilla worlds would never experience love like me. Overflowing with happiness, I pushed my hand into his and asked him about Open Day. He'd spent the morning showing people round the language labs, the model railway Mr Rutherford had built in the engineering workshop, some Sixth Formers doing some dull-arse Science experiments with Dr Moss, a display in the Sports Centre from the judo team (I didn't even know we *had* a judo team) and Oggie's School Scouts doing endless knot displays. Joe Bainbridge was in the School Scouts, a patrol leader or something. Trent, Paulus and the Chapel Choir had sung like a billion hymns while Driver and Rubenstein played a bazillion chess games and Ash-tray had given the same speech six times. There had been a massive photo exhibition in the Beckwith Hall, mainly of boys on expeditions in exciting places like Scotland and Iceland. I'd thought of going but in the end even the lure of free 'coffee' in the Refectory hadn't been enough to get me out of bed on a Saturday morning.

Tucked away in a side-street near the Cornmarket where I'd zapped the Cardassian spy, *Adriano's* looked cosily romantic, candles burning in every recess and alcove, tables covered in red-and-white checked cloths, waiters in black waistcoats and white shirts, long bar stocked with shiny, gleaming bottles of every conceivable colour. Ali looked radiantly happy as a waiter showed us to a round table for two tucked away in a discreet corner.

"I feel like my whole life has been building to this." He lay his hand over mine while the waiter lit the candle in the table centre. "You don't know how long I've waited for you, Jonathan. It feels like forever."

Smiling through this sudden, hard lump in my throat, I accepted a burgundy-coloured leather-bound menu but when I opened it, my spirits sank through the thickly varnished floorboards. My £7.38 would buy me virtually nothing. The cheapest dish was a green-salad starter, and that was £3.20. Worse, everything was in Italian. I had no idea what any of it meant. I only figured out *salsa verde* because of Verdi the composer, you know? His name I knew meant 'green' from Fred's music class.

I could have a spaghetti bolognaise for £6, a glass of water for nothing and like walk home? It was only five miles. Or keep a last 20p to ring Dad for a lift. I shifted uncomfortably. Ali said his parents came here all the time. My parents probably wouldn't know a bistro from

Bisto, ha ha. Why had we always been so bloody poor? I flashed back to Belsen Boy, the backstreet-brat who lived on gruel. They weren't so wrong after all.

"The *scaloppino* is to die for," Ali said enthusiastically.

"Mm-mm," I mused intelligently, wondering what on God's earth *scaloppino* was.

"And we must have a *gelato* to finish."

Indeed we must.

Craning over my shoulder, I noticed three other couples in the bistro, all straight, holding hands and gazing romantically at each other through the smoky candle-flicker. I wondered where the nearest McDonald's was.

"Are you ready to order, *signor*?" A tall guy too bald for his age had materialised at my shoulder, pen hovering over his pad.

"J?" said Ali gently. "What would you like?"

Suddenly I didn't fancy either the five-mile walk *or* phoning Dad so I said in my worst Italian accent "I'll have the *salsa verde*, please."

"Very good, sir, and for your *entrée*?"

Staring at him in confusion, I stammered "My entry?"

"Your main course," said Ali softly. "*That's* a starter."

Someone just shoot me. I couldn't read the menu and, even if I could, there was nothing on it I could afford to eat.

"Give us a minute, will you, Mario?" said Ali.

As the waiter melted away, Ali leaned forward. I tensed myself for the 'you're embarrassing me' lecture but instead got 'you don't eat in bistros very often, do you, honey?'

The last time I'd eaten out, apart from fish and chips on Marine Drive in Scarborough, had been my 15th birthday when we'd gone really posh and eaten prawn cocktail, steak and chips and Black Forest Gateau at the local Beefeater, all washed down with a nice Blue Nun. Thinking about it now, I wasn't sure I'd *ever* been in a *proper* restaurant. Unless you counted Harry Ramsden's. But Ali spoke Italian and even knew the waiter's name. I was so out of my depth I was drowning.

Scraping the bow-legged chair backwards, I gasped that I needed some air and stumbled onto the pavement choking back tears and glancing wildly around for the quickest way to the bus-stop. The sooner I was home the better. This was not my world. Ali and me were so different. It could never work. This date was a disaster already and we'd only been here like half an hour. He'd think me a total yokel, some ignorant backstreet brat.

I leaned against the brick wall, sucking the cold night-air deeply into my lungs. Get a grip, I told myself. Go back in, cancel the salad, order the spaghetti – at least I know what it is – enjoy his company, and catch the ten o'clock home. Put it down to experience and see him at school. Apologise. Say you got cold feet. But then he might think I didn't want to be with him, and I did. So go back in, say you just want a burger. Keep it simple. Take control. He'll follow you. 'Cos he loves you.

But *Adriano's* was so cosy, so romantic. It was the perfect venue. The waiter, Marius, Mario, something like that, didn't seem to care that we were this like obviously very gay couple, and nor did anyone else. They were as wrapped up in each other as Ali and me.

Dragging in another lungful of air, I kicked the wall angrily with my heel. Why had I come? Who was I kidding? This is what you get, said God, for disappointing your parents.

"Cigarette?" Ali appeared beside me with a pack of Marlboro Lights.

Gratefully, desperately, I scrabbled one, leaned into the acrid lighter-flame, sucked in the nicotine feebly saying "I don't smoke" before dragging down another deep lungful.

"Nor do I." Ali placed his left sole against the wall. "But we're on a night out and I thought you seemed tense, so what the hell?"

We smoked together silently for a minute then he said "Is this going too fast for you? 'Cos we can slow it down. We can just go for a walk and go home, if that's what you want." The concern in his voice melted my heart. "Just tell me what you want, Jonathan, and you can have it." Now his voice became urgent. "I'd do *anything* to make you happy."

I smoked the rest of the cigarette and flicked the butt into the street, thoughts and feelings churning in my heart and mind. Slowly I said "I so much want you to love me. I so much want you to be proud of me, proud to be with me, proud to be *seen* with me, and I'm so scared I'll embarrass you." My shoulders started shaking violently as a sob surged through me. "I can't read the menu and I haven't got any money and I've let you down."

Slowly detaching my body from his, he kissed my tears tenderly.

"You will *never* embarrass me," he replied fiercely. "I *am* proud of you, proud you're my boyfriend and so happy you love me." Lifting my chin, he locked eyes with me then kissed me gently, my face, my eyes, my nose, my lips. "I love you, Jonathan, and I will never let *you* down. Don't worry about the menu. Don't worry about the waiter. Don't worry about the money. I want to treat you like the prince you are. You can have whatever you want, my little prince."

"But I don't know what anything is," I muttered.

"So trust me." Smiling, he took my hand. "I will choose for us."

"I like that," I murmured happily. "You choose for us, Ali. Always and forever."

When we returned to our table, Marinus or Martin or whatever he was called simply smiled, murmured something in Italian and poured two shots of grappa, on the house, he said, for young love. It set my blood on fire and I felt myself relaxing at last whilst Ali ordered veal in lemon with fondant potatoes twice and a bottle of chilled *Pinot Grigio*.

"I've only got a few pounds," I said mournfully. "I don't like not paying my share."

"Money left from my summer job," he said, "And I want to treat you. If you feel so strongly, you can get the next one." He raised his glass. "To our first date, and our future."

"'Our first date, and our future." I touched his glass with mine.

As the veal arrived, a delicate pale pink in a clear juice speckled with the green of herbs, he said he wanted to be a political correspondent so he could hold the Government to account for trampling over people's lives.

"Or you could be a politician, change things yourself," I suggested, taking a mouthful of veal. I'd never tasted it before. It blew my taste-buds apart. "This is awesome, Ali."

"Told you," he smiled, "But I wouldn't be a politician. Your private life gets turned into cheap pornography for the masses. Wouldn't want *you* on the front page of *The Scum.*"

He spooned the fluffiest potatoes I'd ever eaten onto my plate. Lapsing into silence, we savoured the food, the wine, the candles and the atmosphere, soaking it all up, gathering every detail into our memories. After two glasses of wine and a grappa, I felt nicely mellow. Alistair ordered a lemon-flavoured ice to share. There was only one spoon so we shared that too. His warm gaze never left my face and the dreamy, romantic expression that told anyone with eyes how deeply in love I was. The waiter brought another grappa and a complimentary *biscotti* with the coffee whilst Ali and I held hands across the tablecloth.

"When did you first think you were gay?" I asked.

"Thirteen," he replied. "I got this massive crush on Mark Sonning. I just wanted to be with him all the time, but *more*, you know? I wanted to kiss him and every time he touched me, it set me alight. I'd get these weird electric tingles all over my body."

"I get those with Mark Gray," I said excitedly. "And you. Did you tell him?"

"Yes." His chuckle was tender. "He was so polite about it. He thanked me very much but, and he didn't want me to take it personally, he really liked *me*, but not like *that*, just as a friend, and he was flattered but he wasn't like that..."

I was smiling tenderly too. I could just imagine him saying it.

"I fancied the arse off Michael Crooks," I confessed. "I actually *did* kiss him, at *that* party. He said he liked it, but I loved it."

"He's very cute," said Alistair, "But is he gay?"

"I don't know," I said. "He's got a girlfriend called Katie. But there must be others in the school. Out of eight hundred boys, we can't possibly be the only two."

Our eyes met, we laughed and burst out together "Leo!"

"What about Paulus?" he asked.

"Don't know," I said.

"But you wouldn't kick him out of bed."

"No," I said, squirming. "I'd do him in a heartbeat. Any in the Sixth Form?"

"A few," he said, stirring his coffee. "Simon Ayres is gay. I had a fling with him last year. It was fun but..." The spoon clinked the china. "You were always in the background."

Ayres was a nice guy. He had this curly brown hair and a pleasantly freckled face.

"Did you sleep with him?" I asked, not sure what answer I wanted.

"Yes," Ali said simply. "But he's the only one. So far."

I twined my fingers in his. "You can sleep with *me* tonight if you want."

"Maybe," he said. "I want to, but..."

"But what?"

He covered his face with a hand. "You're too beautiful for someone like me."

When the bill came, he just slipped something from his wallet into the folder. I felt really low again 'cos I couldn't pay but the concert, man, the concert like blew me away.

Sitting in that pink and gold Town Hall auditorium once again, this time in the seats where our folks had sat, this Szymanowski *Stabat Mater* had these weird, unpredictable progressions, distant rumbling percussion and unearthly unaccompanied voices. The second movement rose to this massive, deafening climax culminating in big bass drum, cymbals and a gong! Parts of it were thrilling, parts of it were strange, but Szymanowski was gay, so I decided I liked it and wanted to hear more of his music. Anyway, this was just the warm-up for the Mahler. The Birmingham orchestra's awesome young conductor coaxed the most amazing performance of anything I had ever heard, even Rowicki's Tchaikovsky 6. The idea of the symphony is that [**SPOILER ALERT – really? Hopefully...**] we go on a journey from death to resurrection, so the first movement is this funeral march with brass fanfares, menacing lower strings and blood-chilling downward scales. It's about 20 minutes long, and after it, when you're breathless and shattered, Mahler said there should be like this massive pause for reflection, 'cos what he'd depicted was Death itself, right? Anyway, I'd been gripping Ali's hand so tight it was a relief when the second movement, this lilting, gentle but somehow sinister dance on *pizzicato* plucked strings came in. Then there's this *crazy* dance based on one of Mahler's songs, St Antony preaching to the fish (huh? Yeah. Fish. Right? Weird, see? Who says music's boring?) with this fabulous perky clarinet solo and it's just kind of jogging along before it goes into this like mental blast of noise and before you know it everything's absolutely still and this woman's voice comes quietly from the wreckage singing *'O Röschen rot! Der Mensch liegt in größter Not! Der Mensch liegt in größter Pein! (O little red rose, Mankind lies in greatest need, Mankind lies in greatest pain)* before an angel from God leads us to the finale, the massive, awe-inspiring fifth movement. This time the floor under my Reeboks actually shook with the timpani and cymbals. *Dies Irae, dies illa*, day of wrath and doom impending... I squeezed Ali's hand again as the mayhem crashed round our ears and under our feet and the choir, sitting where I and he had sat just five days earlier, hushed, reverent, awestruck, came from the wilderness, the desperate lashing of brass and strings and death and grief to whisper Klopstock's' poem, that *'Auferstehn, ja auferstehn, Wirst du, Mein Staub, Nach kurzer Ruh'! (Rise again, yes, rise again, will you, my dust, after a short rest)*. By the time the choir swelled into the final lines, that *I die to live, and my heart, which has suffered, will soar to God*, I was actually crying. Crying? Crying. Holding Ali's hand and crying. What is to say? Music can do extraordinary things in the hands of a genius. That's why I loved making it, listening to it, writing about it. Music is God's greatest gift to His children.

Outside, next to one of those bloody great bronze lions, Ali wordlessly looped his arm round my waist. There was nothing to say. We kissed. It was quarter to ten.

"All right," he said cautiously, "There's a bar behind the Cornmarket that's really popular with people like us. I went with Simon a few times. You can get in but you'll have to keep a low profile."

Floating down this old cobbled street past this swell-bellied building and towards the grimy canal, we smoked another cigarette and reached **LEGENDS**. The name was picked out in pink and gold over a large, brick-edged double-door through which loud dance-music was blasting. A tatty rainbow-flag drooped limply overhead. The bouncer, a shaven-headed guy with cricket-ball biceps and some type of tribal tattoo, gave me a quick glance and demanded £2 each. I kept behind Ali and kind of looked nonchalantly away, like I went there *every* Saturday, while he secured orange bands round our wrists and wished us 'a good one.'

The noise was deafening, all heavy beats and thumping bass, and the light-show was an intense array of multi-coloured lines zig-zagging round a black-painted dance-floor. There was a mix of people, mostly men, with an even distribution of ages ranging from the white-haired man in his early sixties propping up the bar through couples in their forties to single students in their twenties, all dancing and kissing each other. I, of course, was the youngest by far. As I approached the bar, someone wolf-whistled. Another sang "*I feel like chicken tonight, chicken tonight*" while others laughed.

"Chicken's gay-slang for a virgin," Ali explained, "Especially one who's *very* young."

I hauled myself onto a bar-stool, tapped my foot to the rhythm and, drinking in the atmosphere along with the Foster's, reflected that nearly everyone in this bar, and there were about sixty, was just like me. We fancied people of the same gender. Out there, *no-one* was like me. No wonder I felt I didn't belong in their world. It was because I didn't. When 'Titanium' came on, I grabbed Ali's hand yelling "I love this. Let's dance."

We went utterly mental, jumping with our arms in the air, roaring "*shoot me down, but I won't fall, I am Titanium, you shoot me down, but I won't fall, I am Titanium...*" Then we went up up up with Euphoria, walked like Rihanna, found Love in a Hopeless Place, Felt the Moment and ran to the Edge of Glory, singing Born That Way into each other's grinning faces. Sweaty and panting, I collapsed into his arms and, in that safe, safe place, pushed my hands into the back pockets of his jeans and gave him a kiss that lasted forever. I didn't care what we looked like. Here we were free. Here we could express ourselves. Here we could show our love for each other and nobody cared and nobody judged 'cos nobody thought it weird at all that two guys were snogging each other. Everyone was doing the same, or wishing they were doing the same. They were like us, *just* like us. We had found our tribe.

Some drinks arrived, two small glasses brimful with clear liquid, a salt-shaker and some lemon slices on a saucer, compliments of the gentlemen in the corner, four middle-aged men who said my arse was fabulous. I grinned at them, seriously flattered, and ran a hand through my sweaty hair.

"This is tequila," said Ali. "There's a thing about drinking this stuff. Hold out your hand. No, not like that, like this." Crooking my hand into a claw, he sprinkled salt on the mound between my thumb and index finger, then did the same to himself. "Now," he ordered, "Pick up your glass." I obeyed. "We lick the salt off each other's hands, down the shot and suck the lemon. Ready? Three, two, one, go!"

I licked the salt from Ali's hand, threw the tequila down my throat and shoved a lemon slice into my mouth before gasping "Oh, fuck. That was *horrible*."

The men in the corner cheered. Everyone in the bar seemed to cheer.

"You two," said this well-muscled gym-hound in red jeans and a white vest, "Are so into each other it's painful," and sent for two more shots so we could do it again.

It was still horrible but everyone in the bar cheered as I snogged Ali, my head reeling and my heart soaring as someone gave me poppers, a small brown bottle of amyl nitrate liquid I sniffed deeply, like Ali, and my head kind of exploded, you know? Then 'Dancing Queen' came on, and we just had to return to the dance-floor, for this was us: "*You can dance, you can jive, having the time of your life, oooh, see that girl, watch that scene, digging the Dancing Queen...*" Poppers, tequila and lager made my heart race faster. Raising my arms above my head and clasping my own wrists, I sang loudly "*See the sexy look in your eye... so tonight... kiss me like it's do or die... Take me to the other side... We're going all the way... tonight take me to the other side…*" I was like surrounded by all these men who wanted to fuck me but hey, I was gay, I was sexy and I was fifteen. Of *course* they wanted to fuck me. I defy anyone in Legends that night to say they *didn't* want to fuck me. I felt utterly fantastic and so sexy it hurt. Maybe tonight I was gonna get fucked. Tonight. At last. I was gonna get fucked. If not by Ali, by someone, and suddenly I didn't care. As I danced with my arms in the air, I just wanted someone to do it with me. Tonight, as The Weather Girls rained men on my head, I would come of age, you know?

Ali smiled as I sashayed towards him at the bar, looped my arm round his waist, yelled "This is awesome. Thanks so much, my darling, darling Ali," kissed his lips then, slumping on the next stool, shouted "Man, this is so fucking wonderful! Jaegerbombs for me and my boyfriend!" I reworded 'Chicken Tonight', to an appreciative crowd "*I feel like fucking tonight, fucking tonight, fucking tonight…* Jaegerbombs! Please!"

The barman squirted Red Bull into the tumblers then dropped shot-glasses of Jaegermeister into the Red Bull. Clinking glasses, top-and-tail, we drained them in one go.

Ali was sitting with a nice-looking couple in their twenties. Slipping in next to him, I nuzzled his neck. The guys, Patrick and Dominic, were art students, both twenty-one, both a little bland, mousy-haired, sporting ear-studs, both sipping vodkas and black. They'd met at university, had been going out for a year, were living together in a flat near the campus and had rescued Ali from disaster. They were the guys with the poppers.

"He looked so miserable," said Dominic. "His little face was all weepy and pouty."

"Broke our hearts," said Patrick, "And when we saw that gym-hound Rufus sidling over, well, we just had to jump in and save him."

"My heroes," said Ali, kissing them both on the cheeks. He too was on vodka and black and clearly scorning my sharp-tasting Foster's as childishly unsophisticated.

"But," said Dominic, "We didn't know you'd brought your gayby."

"Which kindergarten did you steal him from?" asked Patrick.

Glowering, I fired at Dominic "Where did you get your clothes? Marks and Spencer?"

"Where did you get yours? Mothercare?"

I was seriously annoyed when Ali laughed. "You should be wearing beige slacks and a cardy at your age," I snapped back, "Not green jeans."

"At least I'm not still in Pampers," he returned. "Say, Ali, is your gayby a dribbler?"

Ali cuddled me. "Shooter, definitely. Like a Yellowstone geyser."

"I didn't mean when he comes," grinned Dominic maliciously. "I meant when he eats. Do you have to mash it up or is he still on Cow and Gate? Don't worry, honey. Your baby-teeth'll soon break through. Do you have to burp him before you take him to bed?"

"Spit or swallow?" asked Patrick.

"Swallow, every time," choked Ali. The bastard was almost crying.

Just as I was about to tell Dominic to go get shagged, he kissed my cheek and said I was really cute then wrecked it by adding I probably looked cuter in a knitted bonnet and matching bootees. Whilst I sulked, the other twats started discussing some article they'd read in *Attitude* magazine about gay sports-stars and why there weren't any, this new boy-band I had never heard of, then this new orange-blossom moisturiser they all loved.

"I didn't know you used moisturiser," I sulked.

"I suppose *you* still use Johnson's baby lotion," said Dominic. He was such a twat.

We went out to this courtyard, a concrete rectangle with four wooden tables and some scruffy, plastic chairs. The muffled thump of music carried through the windows. Leaning against the wall in a light drizzle, I smoked one of Dominic's Menthol cigarettes.

"Menthol?" I said, trying to sound like an expert. "What? Like mint?"

"So?" he shrugged, lighting it for me. "I'm gay. I smoke menthols."

"I got footie boots called Patrick," I told Patrick. "They're really cool."

He blew a condescending smoke-ring at me.

"The England footie captain wears them. Well, not mine obviously, but *like* mine. *Your*

177

shoes are *sooo* cool!" Red Converse hi-tops. I *had* to get some.

"Thanks," Patrick replied. "How old are you anyway, Jenny?"

"JONNY! JONATHAN! Eighteen! Like Ali!"

"He said *he* was *nine*teen," said Dominic.

Ali rescued me. "Does anyone know if Liverpool won?"

Patrick affected a yawn and blew another condescending smoke-ring. "What's this?"

"I gather there was a football match today," said Dominic, making 'football' sound like 'a dose of the clap.'

"Which one's football?" Patrick asked. Man, the smoke-ring thing was *sooo* cool.

"The one with the wickets," said Dominic.

"You," Patrick said to me, "I got you sussed. You'd be the bar-bike if you could. You've just learned about yourself, you're madly excited by it all, so you're trying out different roles, the flirt, the tramp, the brat, the helpless little girl..."

"The Kindergarten Kid," added Dominic to general laughter. "Man, you are *sooo* under-age it's untrue."

Before he could tease me further, Patrick passed over the little brown poppers bottle and my head burst again.

"Is it true," asked Ali, sniffing the aroma deeply into his nostrils, "That poppers make your anus bigger so getting fucked doesn't hurt so much?"

"Yeah," said Patrick. "Makes the muscles relax."

Man, I took another deep, deep sniff, made my way to the Gents and pissed long and hard into the metal trough. What a fantastic night! But, to make it perfect, I wanted sex with Ali. I wanted him to fuck me, you know? I spotted some packs of lubricating jelly and some bowls of condoms on the wash-basin counter. Ha! Some of the condoms were flavoured, like strawberry, cola and pineapple, so you could do oral sex and not get sperm in your mouth. Like what??? I *wanted* his sperm in my mouth. More than anything in the world. But anyway, maybe he didn't want mine. Though he'd had mine. Twice. But anyway, now we had proper protection, like grown-ups, yeah? Ha! Free condoms! Ha! No excuse now. He would *have* to do it with me. I mean, really, properly do IT with me. Yay. Ticket to Heavensville, right? Anyhow, as I was pocketing a fistful, he slipped into the Gents behind me.

"Hey, honey. You OK? You seem a bit pissed."

"I'm great, my love." I snuggled into him, left hand on his right shoulder, left cheek on his chest, as he wrapped his arms round me protectively. "I really want you, Ali. Thank you, my love, for the greatest night of my life. I will never be happier than I am right now. At least..." I clambered up him a little, blushing like a Ferrari. "Until the night you make love to me. Then my life will be perfect."

"Do you really want that?" he said.

"More than anything in the world," I answered. "God, I love you so much, you know? So much, my darling, darling Ali. Please fuck me, *please*. I'll do anything. *Anything*. I want to know what it's like, and I want to be *your* boy, *yours*..." I kneaded the hardness of his cock. I heard the breath catch in his throat. Ha. I manoeuvred him towards a cubicle and, grinning, waved a sachet of lube in his face. "Come on, Alistair. We can't stay virgins forever."

Kicking the door shut, I unfastened his belt and followed him down onto the seat.

178

22: I don't care

MORE deeply in love than ever, I now entered this crazy week where I was doing my clarinet exam on the same Thursday as the Individual Music Competition in which I was playing the Chopin *Berceuse and* the Brahms clarinet sonata *and* accompanying Leo in the Fauré in the 12-14 woodwind class *and* Paulus in Saint-Saens' *Allegro Appassionato* Op 43 *and* Ben Finch, the fourth-form double-bassist in more Saint-Saens, this time from *The Carnival of Animals* AND a bunch of Lower School scrapers and tooters that Fred couldn't be bothered with, mainly because they were shit. I mean, have you heard a 12 year old play the violin? Talk about cat-strangling. Anyway, by Thursday, anticipating cramming a dozen performances into a few hours on two different instruments and in several different roles, I was like a caged tiger, especially since I'd sacrificed every break and lunchtime to rehearse these pieces and was now bored stupid by them.

When I got to school at 8.30, Gardiner was playing table-tennis with Stewart. Watching disinterestedly from a desk, I practised scales on an invisible clarinet. F sharp minor, especially the harmonic version, had given me problems. I was pretty secure on the pieces but scales were boring on any instrument. Gray and Maxton were chewing over last night's England victory over Switzerland. We'd won 2-1 but it'd taken a Swiss own-goal to edge it and we'd been hanging on desperately by the end. I'd listened on the radio after *The Goodies* freaked me out with bearded Bill Oddie dressed as a baby sitting in a pram. I mean, ticket to Creepsville, or what?

"Fuck it!" Stewart, losing yet another point, hurled the bat across the room. I dived sideways as it clattered into the lockers.

"Fuck's sake, Bob," I stormed. "You just missed my head, you spaz."

"See what a bad shot I am," he joked.

"It's not bloody funny!" I yelled, leaping from the table to grab his sleeve.

"Take it easy, Jonny," said Maxton but, incensed, I twisted Stewart's arm behind him and smacked his head with the heel of my hand. Suddenly we were being pulled apart.

"Stop it," Lewis ordered sharply.

"We don't fight in *this* class," said Collins angrily. "*We* stick together."

"*We* settle our differences through dialogue," added Seymour, a trifle pompously.

"You, Stewpot, apologise," said Arnold, "And you, JP, shake his hand."

Stewart, wringing his wrist, was glaring at me sulkily.

"I didn't do it on purpose," he muttered defiantly.

"Well, fuck off then," I spat, flouncing out of the room.

"Time of the month, Jenny?" he called. "Cock-sucking little queer."

Stopping in my tracks, I turned, my temper rising again.

"What did you say, you fucking bastard? What did you say?" Arnold and Collins were hustling me into the corridor and I was struggling against them shouting "What the fuck does he mean? Fucking cunt. I'll rip his fucking throat out, the cunt!"

Somehow I hit Arnold in his zippy face and got an elbow into Collins's stomach but they wouldn't release me, despite my oaths and threats, not till the anger had passed, and even after, while Bunny was doing the register, I felt it seething and surging through me. Robert 'Stewpot' Stewart was a dead man walking. I'd bust his chapped, scabby lips for him, the melon-headed spaz.

Double Chemistry was my only lesson today. Leaving school at half-ten for the City Music College with Wilf, I'd miss German and most of Maths then, with the competition starting at about twelve, I'd miss History playing for the gimps and then be involved all afternoon with the Upper School classes missing both RE and French. Most teachers simply accepted it. Not Bunny. He remarked that school wasn't some part-time hobby and that I, of all people, could ill-afford to miss *any* Maths lessons.

"I can do the last twenty minutes, sir," I said helpfully.

"Don't bother, Peters, just don't bother," he said wearily. "You do what you like. That's what you do best."

In Barney's lab, I sat with Crooks and Paulus, ignoring Stewart, who, having joined forces with Maxton, was still winding me up with hilarious cracks like 'What does Peters shout at the football? Up my Arse-nal, ha ha' and 'Backs to the wall, boys. Poofter Peters is coming.' It didn't help that Paulus kept telling me to 'lighten up.'

"How would you like it if he was saying that about *you*?" I snapped.

"He *does* say it about me," he answered icily, "And so do *you*, and I'm straight."

"Like fuck you are," I replied angrily. "You're as bent as me. Even benter."

We were doing something with Bunsen burners and boiling water and, in my fury, I managed to knock the asbestos mat so the water slopped over my hand. Swearing viciously, I screamed with frustration. Stewart said loudly that I should be used to hot liquid splashing my hand and half the class laughed, though Collins shook his head disapprovingly.

"Fucking queers," Fosbrook said suddenly, scratching the eczema outbreak on the inside of his wrist. "Shoot the bloody lot, eh, sir?"

"I've got an exam in an hour," I yelled. "I should be practising, not pissing about in some fucking Chemistry lab with you losers."

Crooks knocked the test-tube rack off the bench. Flash of lightning, I caught it in my left hand, an inch off the floor, without dislodging any of the six or spilling any of the liquid. I earned an appreciative round of applause and a comment from Collins that I should field at slip in the summer. Snarling something rude, I slammed the rack back on the bench.

"I'm going to see Mr Reid," I said brusquely, ripping off the lab-coat and stomping out to a chorus of 'oooohs' and Barney's feeble 'Come back, Peters. I demand you come back.'

Fuck *off*, you Barney Rubble lookalike twat *and* all you arse-wipes in Upper Five H.

I stormed out of the Jessup Wing and dived into the toilets to splash cold water on my face, comb my hair, and kick the waste-bin so hard it bounced off the urinal and bent out of shape. Rescue Remedy under my tongue, lavender oil on my lapel, calm calm calm. Regular breathing OK.

I felt the familiar tightness in my chest that signalled an oncoming asthma attack. I'd done a clarinet exam with asthma before. It was no fun, I can tell you. Staring myself in the eye, I told myself I'd done this like a zillion times before, it was a piece of piss and Stewart was a wanker then, suffering under Bunny's withering glare and his Sixth Form Maths set's collective snigger, I collected my clarinet from locker 17 and headed for the powder-blue Lupton Building as Bunny cracked some lame joke about my tooting someone else's flute. Now I *was* worried. Who was talking about me? Who knew? No-one, except Crooks and Paulus. And Leo. Blabbermouth fucking Trent. Oh shit.

Wilf bounced enthusiastically out of the second-floor Staff Room, clapped me hard on the shoulder and led me down the fire escape to the car park and this battered blue Escort. He had this mad yellow and brown bow-tie on which reminded me of a banoffee pie. It clashed wildly with his blue velveteen jacket and pink shirt. His beard seemed more piratical than ever.

"You'll have to shift the baby-seat," he said, tossing a rattle, a pale pink sock, a bag of mangled sweets and a dog-eared copy of *The Very Hungry Caterpillar* into the back.

Somewhat gingerly, I got in the passenger-seat. I'd noticed some sick-stains on the upholstery and the dashboard was plastered with sticky finger-marks.

"How old's your baby?" I asked, as he eased the car into the traffic.

"Fifteen months," he said. She was called Helen, Ellen, something involving a 'len'.

I told him about Stewart and the table-tennis bat.

"Stewart's an idiot," he remarked. "You're bound to be nervous. Even you, with all your experience, must *occasionally* get stage-fright. You're only human." Teeth flashed in his bushy beard as he added "I think." Peering over his blue-rimmed specs at the gunmetal stream of traffic crawling sluggishly along like a lethargic snake, he let the silence seep in as I lost myself in mental preparation but, despite the traffic, we were ten minutes early. I hated waiting. It stretched my nerves to such a pitch of tension it left a hollow, sick feeling in the pit of my stomach and an ache in my chest. I puffed twice on my Ventolin inhaler.

Arriving at the music college (founded 1873), we entered a vast, light, airy hallway with a sea-green marble floor, busts of Brahms, Beethoven, Schubert and Bach, huge potted plants and a massive marble staircase in the centre under an immense crystal chandelier. We were shown into this dingy room with several wooden chairs, a brightly glowing gas-fire and a view through a grubby window of a moth-eaten rose-bush and a patch of overlong, untended grass. It was far too hot. I found myself sweating and removed my grey jumper whilst Wilf turned the fire down. My white shirt was damp already. First greasing the corks, I assembled the clarinet and, rolling it in my hands, held it to the fire to warm the polished wood whilst soaking the *Barre Mec* reed in a mouthful of spit. I wanted it damp all the way through so it was flexible but not so wet I couldn't control the tone. The logo of Boosey and Hawkes of London, stamped in gold on the black bell, revolved in my perspiring fingers.

Four minutes to eleven.

The silence was broken by the soft ticking of a clock on the window-sill. It matched the metronomic beats of my heart.

Three and half minutes to go.

I glanced at the music in my lap, at Martin Angus's blue and red pencil-marks, at my own notes, flexed my fingers, wiggling them in the air.

Three minutes to go.

The door opened. My heart jumped into my mouth.

It was a pig-tailed, brace-wearing girl of about thirteen and her plain, dowdy mother.

Flashing them a grim smile, I tried to relax. It reminded me of the dentist's.

Two minutes.

This must be what awaiting execution felt like.

One and a half minutes.

This was ridiculous. I'd done this a dozen times before.

One minute to go.

Next time the door opened, it was for me.

I was now very nervous indeed. Wishing I could stop sweating, I wiped my palms down my trousers, took the clarinet and music and followed the usher to a large white door.

"Good luck," said the girl's mother.

"Thanks," I said in a strangled squeak. "You too." I wished Ali were here.

The examination room was dominated by this grand piano with the lid up and a large window which commanded a view of the street beyond. In the corner, seated behind a desk, was this white-haired lady whose half-moon specs perched on an ice-cream cone-like nose.

"Jonathan Peters? Clarinet Grade Eight?" She glanced up from her papers, "Hello, Geoff. How are you? How's Eleanor?"

That was a good start, Wilf and the examiner knowing each other.

"I'm Mrs Jessop," she said. "You're Martin Angus's pupil, I think."

You think right.

Wilf struck B flat and I played C, all four fingers and the thumb of my left hand covering holes. I twisted the clarinet slightly to ease the joints, unscrewing the reed a little to get more play, tuned again, listening to the tone with a frown as I played a couple of C major arpeggios and a quick A minor scale, flicking all the keys to open each hole. Mrs Jessop watched with interest, smiling slightly as I placed fluffy red-and-white Ozzie the Owl on the music-stand.

"Do you play in an orchestra, Jonathan?" she asked.

"What?" I jumped. My mind was focussed on the sound of the clarinet. "Sorry. Yes. Mr Reid's chamber orchestra. First clarinet. And I'm in the choir. Baritone."

"When he turns up," Wilf said kindly. "He's very busy. I know Mr Perry wants him as the Choral Society's *répétiteur* next year when Mark Williams leaves."

"Oh," said Mrs Jessop, "You play the piano too? What grade are you?"

"I finished," I said. "I did Grade Eight last year. Got a distinction."

Now she *was* impressed, especially when I added that I was Barbara Lennox's pupil.

"*That's* where I've seen you before," she said, face softening into warm affection. "I've seen you play at her musical evenings. Didn't you play Debussy in July?"

"Yes," I said, "The two arabesques."

"Marvellous," she said, "Especially the first. You gave it this really dreamy quality. My husband lectures on twentieth century French music and he said it was a beautiful interpretation." My nervousness had dissipated altogether. "You must have done Grade Five Theory." She ticked a box.

"I've done Grade *Eight* Theory," I said, frowning at the memory. In the exam, I had filled in the oboe and violin parts of a Handel trio sonata, completed the outline of a Webern piano piece, composed a 12-bar melody for unaccompanied trombone, where you're given the first 3 bars and asked to continue in the same style – the one I picked was in 3 flats and 3/2 time, *forte, maestoso*. The fourth task was a series of questions on the structure of a printed extract from the first movement of Debussy's String Quartet. I had to identify root-position chords, melodic intervals (diatonic semitone followed by chromatic semitone), and keys, and translate the directions ('un peu retenu', *doux* and '1er Mouv^{t}') from French into English. Finally facing Weber's Overture to *Der Freischütz,* more identification ('chord of the supertonic 7th in first inversion', and, also in the string parts, 'a diminished 7th chord which resolves onto a dominant 7th'), then transposition of clarinet parts from bars 9-15 and the French horns (bars 1-4) into concert pitch and some questions about how Weber had created 'a mysterious atmosphere' (pizzicato, muted timps and horns, *tremolando* effects). Challenging was an understatement.

"And yet he's wasting his time with GCSE," said Wilf.

"I want the music history," I said. "Besides, from the other options, Art or Materials, I can't draw and I'm rubbish at Woodwork. My tea-tray warped into something more like a skateboard and the veneer peeled off like an old scab, and in Metalwork I kept imagining I was Siegfried re-forging Notung." I'd even sung '*Hey, Mime, du Schmied... so schneidet Siegfried's Schwert!*' at poor Mark Gray for hours, till Mr Rutherford shut me up.

"Wagnerian, eh?" said Mrs Jessop.

"Love it," I smiled, "Especially *The Ring.*"

"Well, what are you going to play for *me*?" She pushed her glasses up her nose.

"I'm going to start with the Brahms," I said, nodding at Wilf. I licked my lips nervously, touched the cross under my shirt, placed my fingers over the holes, counted the 3-4 time of the opening four bars, listening to the parallel octaves Fred said *I* couldn't write, then hit the minim D in the fifth as *forte* as I dared. I was away, and blitzing the triplet arpeggios in bar 28 and the bar 100 key-change into C sharp minor. I counted furiously in my head, especially the rests (6 bars from 225 to 231), but I was ecstatic about my control of the dynamics. This Brahms movement, in 7 ½ minutes, went from *pp* to *ff*, with hairpin crescendo/diminuendo in single bars, and a really quiet, *sotto voce* ending in F major. *Allegro appassionato* indeed. I loved playing it. The two Lutoslawski dance preludes were so much shorter and less intense than the Brahms, but No 3 had all these tied grace-notes, staccato markings, fortissimo trills and changes in tempo and, though perky, was quite difficult. *Allegro giocoso*, with crotchet = 180, Wilf and I had agreed to take down to 140 in a lunchtime practice. It was still good fun and Wilf beamed through his beard.

The B minor étude from page 39 of the Demnitz book was a tricky *allegro con fuoco* with a load of runs, accents and *sforzandos* and a change into B major (like five bloody sharps, you know?) for this nice, slow central passage. It wasn't *too* bad, though it could've been better. Annoyingly I lost the rhythm slightly somewhere among the mass of black spots.

Harmonic scale of E major, legato, 3 octaves, then F sharp major, tongued, 2 octaves, then a chromatic scale starting on F, 3 octaves of arpeggios of the dominant 7th of A flat, and diminished 7th starting on F (3 octaves), as on page 23 of the purple Associated Board syllabus booklet, a near-perfect sight-reading and it was finished.

Mrs Jessop peered over her notes. "Will you be playing in today's music competition?" She seemed remarkably well informed.

"I'm playing the Brahms again," I said, "And Chopin's *Berceuse*."

I'd had such trouble with this. In the last lesson I'd strayed off into wrong notes, wrong fingering and rhythmic meltdown and, at Bar 36 where I needed to play triplet semiquaver triads in 5 flats, I'd crashed out several frustrated discords yelling "I can't play it. I just can't play it! My hands aren't big enough!" and lost these running trills in Bar 43, shouting "It's bloody impossible!" until Mrs Lennox calmed me down, helped me regroup.

"I'm also doing a load of accompaniments, Fauré's *Sicilienne* with a flautist and two Saint-Saens' pieces with a 'cellist and a double-bassist. Also, anyone Fred and Wilf, sorry, Mr Perry and Mr Reid don't want gets dumped on me." She laughed aloud and asked why Mr Reid was called Wilf. I said I'd heard someone said he talked like Wilfred Pickles, some Yorkshireman from the war I'd actually never heard of but the Grunters liked.

Smiling warmly now, she wished me luck and said she looked forward to meeting me again at Barbara's next soirée. I thought it'd gone well, and so did Wilf, who said it'd been a privilege to play for me. Although he drove back in like record time, I decided to skip the last half-hour of Maths. I couldn't face Bunny's jibes, Stewart's wind-ups or any other immature bullshit. I'd just spent 40 minutes doing what I do best, playing great music and playing it well, and that's what I was gonna do for the rest of the day, so fuck 'em, eh? Fucking losers.

I went to the Purcell Practice Room to play Debussy on some rubbish upright, ate my lunch, a wholegrain Ryvita, a chunk of Cheddar, a celery stick, 2 carrots and an apple then went with a so-called hot chocolate from a machine in the Lupton Building to the Beckwith Hall where some bespectacled gimp was murdering a Tchaikovsky waltz.

Ali, writing notes, was sitting on the Rises, one row below the balcony rail and conferring with Mike Holt, the magazine's music editor. Stalking up the wooden steps two at a time, I nodded at Fred behind the Headmaster's table with the adjudicator, a kind, creased man in his mid-fifties from Bristol, Brighton, somewhere Down South beginning with 'B'. Fred gave me this weak half-smile. The gimps, bunched together in the front row, were a knot of green faces and fear. But fear not, ye gimps and Mr Oakes. Jonathan Peters had arrived.

Ali had a plastic lunchbox on the seat beside him. As well as a film-wrapped luncheon meat sandwich and a can of orange Fanta, there was a bag of prawn cocktail crisps and a Mint Aero. Yay! Result! As he moved the lunchbox so I could sit down, I scooped up the crisps, popped open the bag, took a fistful which I crammed into my mouth, then offered him the open packet saying "Hey, Alistair, wanna crisp?" Crunching them up, I added "I don't like prawn cocktail. Couldn't you get cheese and onion instead? Can I have some Fanta?" I slurped a mouthful out of the can, feeling the fizz on my tongue. Ali's slap, hard on my thigh, made me yelp and brought a fierce 'hush' from Fred. God, I wanted to kiss him. Ali, I mean. I whispered that into his ear. He hissed back we'd find somewhere later. The Purcell Practice Room, I whispered back, where, during the break he could shag me ragged. He turned the colour of a cricket ball and stared at his luncheon meat sandwich.

"Hey," I whispered, "What do policemen have in their sandwiches?" Pause. "Truncheon meat, ha ha."

"Shhhhh," goes Fred.

"You're *sooo* lame," goes Ali.

"Where are we?" I whispered when the tiny kid finally ground to a halt.

"Gimp-Class Piano," said Holt, putting his finger halfway down the programme. "You're lucky you missed the brass. Two French horns and five trumpets. Boy, it's going to be hard to write something positive about those lads."

"Birthing hippo springs to mind," Ali suggested.

I snorted hot chocolate through my nose.

"Shh." Perry flapped a hand at us.

"How was the exam?"

"Great," I said, adding "Grade Eight clarinet" for Holt's benefit. "Reckon I'll pass."

"Of course you'll pass. You're a genius," said Ali.

"So are you," I said, looping my arm round his waist. He'd been awesome in yesterday's debating semi-final against Tetley House. Rising to his feet, arm aloft like a gladiator to salute his Sixth and Fourth Form fan-base, he had carefully, sorrowfully declared the 'sudden, tragic death of a dear friend and companion, brutally, ruthlessly murdered, bludgeoned to death by something thick, blunt and heavy. Madame Chair, I see the murder weapon... Mr Simon Dell, the proposer of this ridiculous motion, that television is destructive of family life' and reached the peak of his popularity.

"Remember the programmes of yesteryear?" he'd said, "*Andy Pandy, The Woodentops,*" waving a hand over the Tetley team, "*Bill and Ben the Flowerpot Men,* whose dialogue makes as much sense as that of the honourable gentlemen opposite, because these gentlemen believe Little Weed is destructive of family life..." He had to wave down the laughter. "What they would make of *The Herbs*, with its delicate use of *pot*-plants...or *The Magic Roundabout* with its addictions to huge piles of white sugar and large, smokable carrots, and weird tomato-faced, moustachioed colonel ordering little girls 'to bed' I cannot conceive... they'll be telling us there's something dodgy about Captain Pugwash and his friends Master Bates, Seaman Staines and Roger the Cabin-Boy. Honestly, Madam Chair, these people are sick! Nothing is so *descriptive* of family life!" He had swept into quiz shows: "The English Department's favourite, *QI*, the Maths Department's favourite, *3-2-1,* the History Department's favourite, *Blankety Blank*... these are designed to provide hard-working families, yes, *families*, with relaxation, and how we need relaxation at the end of a long, hard day on our bikes looking for work. I have heard it said, Madam Chairman, that *Match of the Day* is to blame for falling birth-rates. I'm sorry, but can one really hold Gary Lineker and Alan Hansen responsible for a lack of bed-action on the part of straight English couples? Slow-motion wrist-action maybe... but if *Match of the Day* were banned, if Gazza, Alan and Lawro were banished to the outer reaches of the imagination, would there be a sudden and massive population explosion, a sudden increase in sex, more broken bed-springs, copulation in the very streets?"

As he swept us into the final for the first time in a hundred years, he was riding a heroic wave. This afternoon I would join him in the pantheon of school gods and icons. Again.

The four squares of Aero he gave me made me sneeze. I mean, chocolate *and* mint? With *my* allergies? He laughed affectionately and told Holt I always sneezed when I had chocolate. Holt grinned. Fred hissed at me. The adjudicator frowned. His face kind of said 'who's this loser?' Rest easy, Mr Voakes. Very soon I'm gonna blow you away.

Kevin Seymour's little brother (Gary? George? George) won the class with a spirited performance of Anthony Hedges' *Concert Piece* which earned him 93 points from 100. He seemed overwhelmed to see us applauding him generously. Grinning, I gave him a thumbs-up which flustered him completely, especially when we said how much we'd enjoyed it.

"But," I said, "Keep your wrists up. You've a tendency to let them drop."

"That's what my teacher says," he replied mournfully, resembling a very sad bulldog.

"You don't want to play with limp wrists," I added, then blushed as Alistair, the cheeky sod, sputtered out laughing and said I should know all about limp wrists.

For the Lower School Strings, followed by the Woodwind, the piano accompaniments were evenly distributed between Fred, Wilf and me, although Beaky Phillips showed up to accompany this honking oboist called Livesey. Gravely he noted me sitting with Ali but didn't say anything. I felt a keen rivalry with the music teachers. If I could get all my people to win, it'd be a satisfying statement, especially since Perry was an excellent accompanist. The light gleamed off his shiny pink scalp as he trotted through another mangled Grade 3 piece. No wonder he got so bored. He'd worked with Benjamin Britten, for God's sake.

The swarthy clarinettist I accompanied in Gordon Jacob's *Valse Ingénue*, a Grade 4 piece, played very sensitively. I hadn't ever really got his name, Simpson, Stimpson, Timpson or something including an 'imp'. Now I thought I should've. He was good, winning with a score of 92. Grinning excitedly, he pumped my hand. Turned out his name was Sumner. Whatever. Unfortunately my violinist strangled his Telemann Gavotte completely and, despite my efforts to bring him back to the score, his nerve broke and he was placed last.

"Bad luck," I murmured sympathetically as he gulped back some tears. Perry shot me a fiendish victory-grin as *his* fiddler took first place with a Corelli Sonata.

So that's how it was gonna be. Game on then, Mr P. I twisted the knobs on the piano-stool to raise the height so he'd have to lower it again to accommodate his great big backside more comfortably. I told Ali, whose laugh sounded like an exploding bomb.

"Shhh," said Perry irritably.

Strings 14-16 featured Ben Finch who was really small with wild curly hair and a face like a startled hamster. He was dwarfed by the double-bass. Holt and Ali thought it hilarious as he struggled on-stage with it.

"Imagine him trying to get that on a bus," chortled Ali.

"I bet he would fit in the case," chuckled Holt.

"He could use it *instead* of the bus," chirruped Ali, "*Slide* down those hills."

"Give him a break," I muttered, trotting down to give him a hand.

Sitting at the piano again, and noting Perry had lowered the stool again, I shot him a cocky grin - his 'cellist had been pretty rubbish – and waited for Ben to give me a nod, then played the lumbering opening bars of Saint-Saens' parody of Berlioz's 'Dance of the Sylphs' known as *L'éléphante*, from his *Carnival of the Animals*. Ben's entry was spot-on perfect and the humour of the piece drew appreciative laughs from the dozen or so spectators and a wry grin from the adjudicator. I allowed the final cadence to resound slightly then hit the damper, raised the stool really high and acknowledged Ben's grateful smile with one of my own.

"Very good," I said, shaking his hand. "That was really *very* good. Well done."

Beat that, Fred.

He couldn't. Paul *'Goes Like A'* Train had a nightmare with Elgar's *Chanson de Matin* which he just couldn't get singing (ha ha) so Finch won with 95, and warm words from the adjudicator. Two-one to me, I chalked up mentally, with one to Wilf.

"Train's really good," I said. "I've heard him play that before. He'll be devastated."

"Perry's protégé goes down again," Holt laughed merrily.

"I have no idea what you mean, Mike," grinned Ali.

"Can I write it in the review, Ali? Can I? Go on. It'd be so funny."

"You'd get me sued," said Ali.

When he whispered what it meant, I slapped his shoulder in mock-disgust, then said, round-eyed, "Perry and Train? You're joking. Perry? And *Train*? Train's fourteen. But Perry! Ew! He's so *old*! And *bald*."

"Get it where you can, eh, Jailbait?" Ali remarked.

"I love you two together," said Holt. "You crack me up."

"Oh, honey," Ali squeezed my hand. "Mike's one of us, aren't you, Mike?"

"Oh, regular dancing queen, me," said Holt. "Welcome to the Good Ship Suck My Lollipop, Jen."

"Ali," I said suddenly, "I think someone knows about us. Bunny made this awful joke."

"About you tooting somebody else's flute," said Holt. "I was there. Man, so funny I thought I was gonna puke."

"Course he doesn't know," Ali scoffed. "*Nobody* knows. Except Sonning, Mike and Simon Ayres and none of *them's* going to tell anyone. Why should they?"

"But Bunny's joke! And Chris Crooks in your meeting, and Bob Stewart called me a cock-sucking queer!" I was getting agitated. "What about *Leo*? What if Leo said something? You know what *he's* like."

"*Screaming* queen," said Holt.

"No, a fucking blabbermouth. Can't keep a secret."

"He's one seriously pretty little airhead," sighed Ali.

"Shut up," I said jealously.

"It isn't him," said Ali, "I don't think it's anyone. Just playground banter. Chill out, Jenny. It doesn't matter."

"Stop calling me Jenny," I said petulantly, "*And* Jailbait. I don't like it."

Thankfully Andrew Paulus slid into the seat beside me with some luscious gossip from the so-called real world. Apparently Stewart, Maxton and Fosbrook had been set upon in Sweaty Betty's by a gang of 'hoolies' from a nearby estate.

"They'd gone to play *Space Invaders*." he explained ghoulishly, "And were just settling into a game when these yobbos came up."

Yobbos? I almost pissed myself. Public schoolboys' definitions of 'yobbo' usually did.

Maxton had won this free game and was about to play when half a dozen 'big lads' pushed them aside and took over the machine. When Stewart protested, the hoolies threatened to 'duff him up' and, to reinforce the point, shoved Fosbrook up against one grease-smeared wall. Some reports said there were three, others five, still others eight, but all agreed they were each 7 feet tall and 3 feet wide, with legs like tree-trunks, biceps like girders and chests like brick outhouses. 18 years old, possibly 20, real Borstal boys with punky haircuts, leather jackets, razor blades up their sleeves and knuckle-dusters in their pockets. The leader's name was Chopper, though whether that referred to his choice of weapon or to its size, ha ha, no-one was sure, though, in my experience, the bigger the boy, the smaller the lad, if you like get my point, ha ha.

"What did Betty say?" I interrupted. "They should've complained to her. She's big enough to face down a couple of weedy retards from the estate. I mean, instead of a christening, she had a launch-party. She has two watches, one for each time-zone she's in."

Ali smiled softly. "She wouldn't put herself out for any of us. All our guys do is use her *Space Invaders* machine. They never actually buy anything."

I clicked my tongue irritably. "So what happened in this non-event of the year?"

"Nothing," said Paulus. "Max and the others just left them to it."

"Pathetic," I said. "They should've stood up for themselves. I would've."

"Yeah, right," said Ali.

"I would!" I started screwing my clarinet together again.

"You'd've drawn yourself up to your full height," said Ali, "And head-butted the leader in the knee. Supermite, the Bionic Midget."

"You could've hit them with your handbag," said Paulus.

"Fuck off, both of you," I said, smoothing grease onto one corked end. "I would've played the free game while the others fought them off. That way it wouldn't have been wasted." I placed the reed on my tongue. "So shut your faces." It sounded so weird.

"You're *sooo* gay, Jonathan," giggled Paulus, "A proper little poofter."

"That is so un-PC," I huffed.

"Yes, but it's true," he giggled again, "Henry Hoover."

And then Leo minced in.

"Afternoon, ladies." He plumped down beside Paulus complaining that I hadn't played with him since the weekend.

"I made you a tape of the piano part," I said indignantly. "Didn't you use it?" It'd had taken ages on some portable Tandy machine with this TDK C-60 cassette.

"I'd rather *you* played with me," he said archly. "You finger my keyboard so tenderly."

Holt spurted coffee out of his nose. Again. Queen's Fucking Corner, this, I thought. Might as well hang a massive sign round our necks reading HOMO BOYZ 'Я' US and prove Bunny, Stewart and the others right.

A bustling rustle told us Fred and Oakes were back in the hall along with a bunch of boys somewhere behind the rail, several teachers opting for an easy last period by bringing their classes to see their friends. Wheezy brought U5S and Wingnut U5H, Phillips brought his German class, Willie brought some third formers, Benjy a bunch of second formers and pretty soon the hall contained about 300 people. Ash-tray, Frank and Hellfire also arrived. Arnold, Lewis, Gray, Keighley, Maxton, Driver, Lees, others, gathered around us, united in music.

"They've come to hear you, darling." Ali pecked my cheek. " 'Cos you're the best there's ever been."

So no pressure then.

I kissed Alistair, then Leo, who whooped and sang '*I don't build my world round one single man*', and stood up.

Adrenaline pumped through my blood-stream again and my stomach kind of swooped. I loved this moment. Let them think what they liked. Let them say what they would. *This* was when I came alive. Now, in this moment.

Flicking open the keys, I took a deep breath, touched my cross and stepped down into the spotlight.

23: Haven't you heard?

SCORING 95, I came first in the Woodwind 14-16 with the Brahms clarinet sonata. Robin Keighley came second, again, ha ha, Paul Driver third, playing Finzi's 'Forlana' which I'd won with like a gazillion years ago, and Maxton a lowly fourth. Max was doing Grade 5 on Tuesday. I mean, Driver was Grade 6. Only Keighley, Grade 8, ever offered a contest. Confidence riding sky-high, I stormed the Piano 14-16 class with the Chopin *Berceuse*, scoring 98 out of 100. Arnold's Brahms was good (92), Gray's Schumann passable (88), Driver's 'Country Gardens' lumpy (85), Tredwell's Mozart characterless (83), Lewis's Bach stodgy (81), Lees' Tchaikovsky pleasant (80) and, for the fourth year in a row, I blew them all away. The adjudicator praised my pedalling, my singing right-hand and control of tone which called 'limpidly, translucently, heart-breakingly beautiful.' It was 'a very musical and highly impressive performance.' Hissing out all the air I'd been holding back, I grinned self-consciously. Although I was expected to win, I felt a little sorry for Arnold, second again, and Gray, with his Grade 7 next week, third again, and there was *always* a crackle of tension when the results were read out, just in case. Anyway, when the final notes had drifted away into the spell-bound audience, and the adjudicator had said his piece, the teachers descended on me in a pack.

"That," Ashton declared to 300 people, "Was the most beautiful performance I have ever heard a schoolboy give. Jonathan, you are a shining light in our school. You have played for other boys and helped them win prizes. You have shared your talent for the benefit of others, and *your* talent is supreme. We take pride in your gifts and pride in your willingness to share them." There was loud, warm applause. I wished my parents had been there to hear it, but they were busy, Mum with yoga and *ylang ylang*, and Dad with sweet peas and manure. Besides, they'd heard it every day for ten weeks. Dad claimed he knew every note by now. Ali, awe-struck, just gazed at me. I'd played it for him, and he knew it.

"My God," he muttered softly, "You are so good 'good' seems inadequate. I don't know what word I could use."

"That's my problem," said Holt. "I'll use 'satisfactory' like in Wheezy's reports."

I called him a cheeky sod through this massive hug from my Lion, 'cos even more importantly, *he* had won his first music prize ever, and Paulus had won his first in 3 years.

Leo's G minor *Sicilienne* was ravishingly gorgeous, like the flautist himself. He was utterly, wonderfully superb, with a lovely, floating tone and the long G he had to hold and sustain at the end for three and half bars and which he'd consistently, annoyingly shortened in rehearsal was excellent, especially as he actually did manage to drop to *ppp* after all. I just kept playing the harp-like left hand arpeggios to hold him steady. He scored 96 marks, the adjudicator calling our performance 'beautifully, heart-achingly tender.' If only he knew, eh? Leo kissed my lips. He didn't seem to care any more. He said it was time to stop pretending. His exam was on Wednesday 26th at the college at 10.30. I had already booked Double Biology off. Ha fucking ha. Herbidacious was spitting blood apparently, but Gallagher basically told him to live with it.

Paulus' *Allegro Appassionato*, 'driving and furious', also scored 96. We'd only practised it twice because the piano part was fairly easy and, unlike the 'cellist, I had bars of rests. Poorly was slashing scales almost non-stop but it was fun and actually, at last, he beat Adam Rubenstein who, with Perry, played the Allegro from Bach's A minor concerto, and played it superbly for 95. The Saint-Saens, though, had brought a deep-seated anger to the surface, and displayed it, burning brightly, to the school. Andy was doing this piece in his Grade 8 on Wednesday at 2, so that was Physics out for us both, ha ha again. As I hugged him, I told him he was gonna storm it and arranged a massive practice at my house on Sunday afternoon for him and Leo, and even promised Leo more coaching for his piano Grade 3 on December 1st. I invited Ali to turn the pages.

Yet even in our moment of triumph, we sensed we had reached our apotheosis. The muttered comments and nasty jibes were becoming more barbed. Bunny had apparently made another crack about 'Peters blowing like an expert' with U5H pissing themselves and Crooks going 'That's so out of order, sir' and Bunny going 'Didn't know you'd joined the Queen's Club too, Michael,' and Crooks going 'That isn't *me*, sir, that's Peters.' I suppose it couldn't remain secret forever. What I'd done at that party was fairly common knowledge, Sooty knew I'd got off with Leo a couple of times and God only knew who might have seen me and Ali at the town hall concert. When I arrived in my form-room on Friday morning, someone had inscribed, with a key, like a cliché from a bad coming-out movie, the word 'GAY' on my locker. Bunny, brushing it off as boys' banter, said I should 'get over myself' but I was angry and anxious. Anyway, the storm broke in PE.

It started, inevitably, in the changing room. I was sitting on a bench tying the Green Flash laces when Arnold bashed my shoulder with his bag and Morreson 'accidentally' kicked one of my shoes away. Glaring murderously, I followed the others into the gym where Vickers was organising basketball. I hated basketball at the best of times. I thought it a stupid game that only the freakishly tall could be good at. Dark vests went on one team, so green, dark blue, brown and purple, and bright vests on the other, so light blue, yellow, red and orange. The house-system provided the only rainbow in the school.

Seymour, on my team, charged me into the wall, grazing my bare shoulder. When I protested, he shrugged and said I got in his way. No-one passed me the ball. OK, I wasn't very good, but it was supposed to be a team-game, wasn't it? At one point, the ball span loose and I managed to get it, bouncing it once, twice, considering who to pass to, when Brudenall elbowed me viciously in the ribs and I cried out.

"You're *sooo* gay," Lewis muttered, scraping me down the wall again.

Fosbrook, the runty little twat, said something to Gardiner about my being 'a wet fish.'

Behind me, Brudenall started singing "*Oh Ali's boy, his arse, his arse is aching.*"

Everyone laughed. Except Vickers. *He* went nuts, cancelling the basketball and making everyone run laps of the field instead. It was pouring with rain and everyone got soaked, hair plastered to skulls like it'd been painted on. Maxton barged me aside, muttering roughly it was my fault for being a fairy and Lewis tripped me so I fell headlong into a puddle. This made *everyone* laugh, except Vickers again, who put the whole class in detention, and Paulus, who looked upset and troubled. Gardiner growled I was 'so dead' as I mournfully picked myself up, water running down my shins, and Fosbrook smeared mud in my hair.

Things got worse in French when Fosbrook and Stewart made these stupid slurping noises every time I answered a question. When Goddard yelled at them to pack it in, they flicked spit-balls at me instead. Then someone emptied my bag onto the floor and kicked my books and pencil-tin round the room. It took me ages to gather everything up again, and while I was on my hands and knees, Stewart kicked me up the arse and sent me sprawling.

"What the fuck is going on?" I screamed.

"We don't want poofs in our class," said Stewart, gobbing on my sleeve.

"Who says I'm a poof?" I demanded.

"Everyone," said Maxton coldly, looking more like a donkey than ever. "Beaky Phillips reckons Ali Rose is bumming you. I heard him telling Wilf Reid."

"Yeah," said Stewart, "And Pete Dwyer reckons Leo Trent gave you a blowjob. Sooty Sutcliffe said you and Leo disappeared for ages into the bathroom..."

"Bollocks," I retorted.

"You snogged Mikey," said Gray quietly.

"That was a dare!" I yelled. "You were there. You saw it."

"Yeah," he said ominously, "I saw it, and I saw you going into the woods with Rosie on Bonfire Night. What did you do? Suck his cock? Fuck's sake, J. You hang around with him all the time, like some bloody little puppy, and *everyone* knows *he's* queer."

"Michael said you *told* him you're queer," added Maxton. "You fancy him, *and* Rosie.

189

Mikey said so. He said you were gonna suck him off but his Dad came in."

Fucking Judas.

I raged off to the toilet to rinse Stewart's spit from my blazer. There I confronted, with an overwhelming sense of desperation, a crude cartoon scribbled on the wall with a black board-marker. It showed a fat, bloated penis and blobs of semen dripping into a gaping mouth. Next to the mouth was scribbled *JENNY PETERS (SUX COCKS).* I drifted, half-dazed, out to the playground football game, not really sure what was happening, or why.

"Bugger off, Peters," said Lewis. "No-one wants you looking at their arse."

Seymour kicked the ball at my chest then Tim Wilson launched this ferocious assault.

"They're saying you're gay. Is it true? Are you gay? Eh, Peters? Are you? Gay?" He stabbed at me with his index-finger.

I was about to say 'No, don't be so stupid' when I realised that if I said that, *I* would be the stupid one.

"What if I am?" I said. "Who cares?"

"Who *cares*?" Tim booted the ball viciously into my thigh. "*I* fucking care, Peters." He was actually crying with rage. "I've done sleepovers with you. I've shared fucking changing cubicles with you. You were my best friend, you know? Best friend, and all the time you were drooling over my arse, you fucking, *fucking* pervert."

"I wasn't," I said mildly. "I don't fancy you, Tim." I hadn't known I was queer then.

"You're all the same, you fucking benders!" he raged, pushing furiously through Driver and Rix to grab my sweater. "Eyeing us up, wanking over us." Spraying spittle, he shook me like a dog might a cat. "I hope you die of AIDS, you little poof! It's all you deserve!"

Rix, solemnly adjusting his specs, started banging on about demons, like I was possessed or something. Gayness, he reckoned, was caused by the Devil.

"Like in *The Omen*?" I scoffed. "The number of the beast is sex sex sex?"

He said I could get cured. I could have aversion therapy which, I gathered, involved watching hard-core man-on-man ass-fucking and, if I had an erection, getting my brain electric-shocked till I vomited. Or there was exorcism. Wingnut could, in the name of Jesus, cast the spirits out, 'cos Satan was living in my loins. He even offered to pray for me at the Christian Union meeting that afternoon. Then I heard someone mutter they should rape it out of me and, feeling sick, I went inside. Christians, eh? Jesus wept.

Chamber orchestra was just shit. Maxton kept turning pages at the wrong time, Keighley just kept sniggering, Williams muttered I made his skin crawl and Lees slid his chair backwards into my knees. Finch just glared at me stonily. Trent, Paulus and Shelton, the cowards, just kept their eyes fixed on the music or on Wilf, who avoided my desperate gaze altogether. Later I heard him tell Fred "He's been in my car, Alan, my car! Where my baby daughter sits! Christ Almighty. The wife'd kill me. A queer in the car? I could lose my job!"

In Physics, Millie, handing back some homework, told me my description of the last experiment was too flowery, which brought forth howls of laughter from the others and a delighted yell from Fosbrook "You mean like a pansy, sir?"

Irritably, Millie called me, Bainbridge and Walton to help him carry these cardboard boxes of equipment from his store-room. Bainbridge dumped one box unceremoniously on the bench and got told off for treating the equipment so roughly.

"We're doing an experiment involving lights and a stroboscope. Usual groups. One to record the results, the rest to carry the stuff. One stroboscope per group of four. We haven't any more, and don't break them. The Department's not *made* of money." Millie tossed over a handful of electric leads. "Right, get started."

"Fuck off, Peters," said Maxton. "Go find another group."

"Yeah," Stewart said spitefully. "Go finger the other bummers, Peters."

Paulus, presumably, who was in a group with Cooke and Huxley.

"Fine," I said, snatching up the cardboard box of stroboscopes and lamps. "I'll take the fucking box an' all. Go get your own fucking lamps."

I waltzed sideways to dodge Stewart's lunge and collided with Collins. The bottom fell out of the box and stroboscope and lamps crashed to the floor. Millie went ballistic.

"Didn't you hear what I said about the equipment, you bloody fool?"

"Wasn't my fault, sir!" I yelled back. "It was an accident!"

"*You're* a bloody accident, Peters," said Maxton.

"Fuck off, you stupid twat!"

"PETERS, you imbecile! Get out!"

"Don't worry, you bunch of tossers! I'm going!"

As I crashed the door of the lab behind me, and Millie bellowed at the class for laughing, I felt like crying then, overwhelmed with anger, booted a hole in this plasterboard wall. Millie went mental again, saying he'd tell Mr Gallagher.

"Whatever." Folding my arms defiantly, I slumped sulkily against the doorframe for the next twenty minutes then flounced off to German.

"Have you brought any fudge today, sir?" asked Brudenall innocently.

"Peters likes fudge, sir," called Seymour.

"I expect he does," said Beaky. "Would you like some fudge, Herr Peters?"

Howls of hysterical laughter accompanied Brudenall's cry "he prefers *packing* fudge, sir." Then for the next fifteen minutes, he, Lewis and Morreson threw more bits of spit-soaked paper at me while Beaky wore this kind of 'told-you-so' look on his parrot face and made deadpan remarks about fudge and chocolate fingers which brought the class to tears of laughter. Fucking parrot-nosed cunt. My tears were something different.

Stewart stuck a Post-It on my back which read 'KICK ME, I'M GAY.' All these gimps, even that cunt Sumner ran up, booted my shins, screeched 'faggot' and scooted away again. Sutcliffe and Hartley ducked away in embarrassment. The Sixth Formers were even worse, shooting me looks of scorn and hatred. Pete Dwyer, Harry Turner, Chris Crooks, Palmer and Liddell, just scowled at me, or made stupid kissy-kissy noises.

The bus-ride home was hell. There were no teachers to protect me and no Ali to cling to. It was just me and Leo, and Leo was as useful as a chocolate teapot. He just sat there, rhubarb-red face buried in some Latin vocab. Maxton and Gray studiously ignored me whilst some of the younger boys sniggered and whispered, and Bobby Rose flew furiously down the top deck towards me.

"Hey, Peters! Is it true you're bumming my brother?"

"No," I said wearily, "It isn't."

Bobby punched me really hard on the cheekbone. The exploding pain momentarily blacked my vision. I really *could* see stars.

"Go on, Bobby. Batter the bender," cried someone from the back of the bus.

He hit me again, really hard, in the same place then in the centre of my forehead and then on the jaw before Maxton caught him by the shoulders and pushed him away.

"Thanks, Phil," I gasped, touching the bruise already swelling under my left eye.

Maxton, glaring at me stonily, returned to his seat as Warburton started singing:

Four and twenty virgins came down from Inverness,
And when they went home again there were four and twenty less.
Singing balls to your partner, arse against the wall,
If you've never been fucked on a Saturday night, you've never been fucked at all.
Jonny Peters he was there, sucking Ali Rose,
And when the paedo came, well, the spunk shot out his nose...

Maxton, face set like concrete, joined in the chorus. I shrank into my trench-coat.

Jonny Peters, queer as fuck, shagging Leo Trent,
Who'd have ever thought that the bastards were so bent?
Jonny Peters, sucking cock, getting fucked by Fred,
Wanking over every gimp and giving Paulus head...

It was a fucking long journey, cheered only when Leo gently touched my arm.

"Oh, Jonny. If I could be as brave as you…" He choked, then added through some tears "You're so brave." I gathered his life had turned to shit too with boys in the Fourth Form kicking him, spitting at him and, in the case of some bastard from the Lower Fifth, trying to headlock him into a blowjob.

Curry Night was depressing, even though Dad was doing his black-pork special and even though I got my £5 pocket money. I was exhausted and actually a little frightened. I'd never been scared of school before. Now I was. The level of hatred was something I'd never, ever imagined, and it was all because I preferred kissing boys, not girls. How mental is that?

I rang Ali, got his father, who refused to let me speak to him, and basically yelled at me for getting him into trouble. Mum too was angry when she saw yet another bruised face and lectured me, over poppadums and dabs of tea-tree oil, about the perils of fighting.

"Who was it?" she kept demanding.

"Bobby Rose," I finally yelled. "It was Bobby Rose."

Another storm erupted along the lines of 'we told you to stay away from the Rosses. Didn't we tell you? Honestly, Jonathan, you must have mango chutney for brains.' I decided now was not the time to tell them about my *real* problems and turned wearily to Terry Wig-on and Esther Rants-on doing *Children in Need* on BBC1. Bollocks. I was a child in need, but nothing was coming *my* way, was it? I thought of phoning in after *It Ain't Half Hot, Mum* to say 'yes, it *was* hot, thanks to my Mum' and could someone please help me? I'm getting bullied at school, because I'm gay, and then realised they'd probably send the pigs round to Ali's and tell me to sod off. I mean, our lovely new Government had just decreed that me and Ali were illegal and had no rights whatsoever. Angered by the hypocrisy of 'Children in Need (that we like)', I went to bed to finish the *Dr Who* book, switching off the light at ten as the autumn rain lashed my window and then had the worst asthma attack I'd had in years. I sat upright with my bare back against the hard wooden headboard gasping shallowly, dragging Ventolin out of my inhaler and breathing into a brown paper bag. My chest felt like Hissing Sid was crushing me to death in his coils while Artful Owl was smothering my face with his feathers. But I didn't tell Mum. Hissing Sid may have been innocent, but Ali Rose? No way.

When Saturday came, I didn't turn on my radio for *CD Review*'s comparison of Berlioz' *Symphonie Fantastique,* though I love it, just cuddled into my yellow duvet with another hot-water bottle, Pickles and New Bear, and Ali's and Leo's socks and listened to the rain. The wind-chimes hung lifelessly behind the curtains. I didn't even have a wank. Even when Mum and Dad returned from Sainsbury's, I didn't get up. I just wanted to stay where I was forever.

"You all right, Jonny?" Dad, setting down a cup of camomile tea, put his hand on my bruised forehead. "Are you coming down with something?"

"Can I have some toast and honey?" I asked in this really small, pathetic voice.

He begged me to talk to them.

"I'm just coming down with a cold," I muttered.

Though he wasn't fooled, he had the wisdom to drop it. I imagined the kitchen conference, the folks seeing my distress, powerless to help, becoming stressed themselves.

I spent Saturday in this weird state of suspended animation. Hangng about the house in blue trackies and white rugby shirt, I couldn't read, I couldn't study, I couldn't focus on my homework, I couldn't even play the piano. I felt sick a lot of the time and scared *all* of the time. My breathing was coarse and rattly and my chest felt like it was caught in a gigantic steel hand. It was a waking nightmare but it was worse for Ali, I knew that, and I thought about him all the time. I phoned him again but this time his mother snapped at me to leave him alone. I read *Dead Ned* by John Masefield, the story of a young doctor wrongly accused of the murder of his benefactor, a crusty old Admiral who had fought with pirates and intriguingly subtitled 'Autobiography of a Corpse', tried to do some homework, a bit of Biology and this English essay on the relationship between Henchard and Mary-Jane.

I watched a film from happier times, *Watership Down*, about a bunch of rabbits trying to save their doomed burrow from developers and fight off some despotic Fascist rabbit called

Woundwort and cried a lot when [**SPOILER…. Yeah**] Hazel died and that song came on: *'There's a fog along the horizon, a strange glow in the sky, and nobody seems to know where it goes, and what does it mean? Oh, is it a dream? Bright eyes, burning like fire,'* and cried some more. I played *Frogger* (you have to get frogs across a busy road without trucks and stuff splatting them) and *Ground Force Zero,* taking out New York twice before I got fried, then dug out *Search and Destroy* so I could nuke Charley and his Gooks. I found some instructions written in cyan felt-tip on a page from an exercise book which I no longer understood:

US		NLF
1 US Coy		1 NVA Bn.
1 ARVN Platoon		1 VC Platoon.
1 APC/Tank Platoon		
(1 Artillery Battery)		
6 Peasants	{4 Mines}	
5 Porters	{4 Ambush}	
1 Arms	(3 Dummies)	
1 Ammo		

'NVA Stationed around road and bridge. US must capture all territory beyond bridge. NVA must hold bridge and beyond.

Length 15 turns.

US enter 2nd on W. side.

NVA "   1st on Rd side.

The Battle of Kien Phuong

Standard Game Rules for Combat/Movement. Variable NLF Battle Order. OPTIONAL RULES INC. are. AMBUSH, CASUALTY POINTS, MEDEVAC, HE FIRE for TANKS and ARTILLERY, and INTERROGATION.

TANKS = 12 strength Pts   1 Hex 32 pts

ARTILLARY = 8 strength Pts   1 Hex 32 pts

( ) optional { } needed.'

Hey, Charley. Colonel Kurtz, he dead. Ride of the Valkyries and the smell of napalm in the morning… I laid the counters out then couldn't find the damn dice. I think they were under my bed with half a jigsaw of Tower Bridge, a tennis ball, Action Man's gold-coloured deep-sea diving helmet, the Slinky (again) and a green and white hooped rugby sock. Instead, I raced a Dinky Lotus, a Corgi Ferrari, a Matchbox Cortina and a chunky Tonka Tipper-truck up and down the landing in the WORLD MOTOR RACING Championship. I even invented some drivers and scribbled their names on a scrap of paper so I could keep a score of the points – Ferdy Diaghilev from Russia for the Lotus, Carlo Feroda from Italy in the Ferrari, Fred Garrison of Australia in the Cortina and Jan Ølsĕn of Norway in the Tipper. The Ferrari won, so I added Dougie Sexton of the US in a Playmobil SUV but he had a dodgy front axle from an encounter with a Lego castle wall and ended up going over the edge and bouncing down the stairs. Then Ølsĕn, the moose-eating tosser, crashed the Tonka Tipper into the skirting board by the bathroom just as Mum came up with a load of laundry. Obviously she went absolutely mental, made me clear them away and help her fold the bedsheets. Inevitably I kept turning them the wrong way. When she told all the kangaroos in Australia that I was a stupid bloody kid with the brains of a rice pudding, I actually cried. I stood on the landing and cried. She just tutted contemptuously and flung the pillow-cases at my head. Christ, I had never felt so unhappy. I switched on my bedroom light and started a story.

'Depression by Jon. D. Peters.

'He walked along the deserted street, head sunk between his shoulders, feet dragging as he trod the steps that brought him nearer and nearer the river. There was a sort of reluctant compulsion inside him. He did not want to go but he had to. He felt he must go to the river. There was just a hesitancy in his step, a sadness, an aura of finality.

'A newspaper, yellowed by age and exposure to sun, fluttered across the path before him. Bus tickets, cigarette ends and sweet wrappers were tossed in the air and settled to rest a few yards away in the gutter. Dead, dying leaves whirled round his ankles like brown fog.'

As I put down the Waterman, the 'phone rang. I hoped it was Ali. It wasn't.

"Hey, Peters, you poof, you know what we're gonna do next week? We're gonna shove a broomstick up your arse and melt your cock and balls in sulphuric acid."

I recognized neither the voice nor the giggling. I didn't think it was anyone in U5H.

"Hey, Peters, you poof, we're gonna shit all over you, then stamp on your balls till they burst. We're gonna set fire to your pubes and piss on you to put the flames out."

Was it someone from the Sixth Form?

"Hey, Peters, you poof, we're gonna gang-rape you with bottles then get your cock..."

Scared and angry, I turned off the 'phone and went to rake up leaves in the dusk with Dad, anything to escape from that house for a while. We burned them all in a big bonfire. Wondering how much burning pubes would hurt made me feel sick. Then Mum screamed at me again for leaving my bedroom light on. I told Dad it was the wood-smoke making my eyes smart but really it wasn't.

I watched racing from Newbury then *Final Score,* but even Man United's four-goal win at Brighton and Norwich beating Sunderland 1-0 failed to move me. I couldn't even bear *The Muppets.* It was so bloody stupid, Swedish Chef going bloody 'bork bork'. I mean, what the fuck? And Basil fucking 'boom-boom' Brush, a glove-puppet talking fox? Like get a fucking life! Even the new *Doctor Who,* some mediaeval vampire story with a phallic spaceship and fuel-tanks brimful of blood, and Ronnie Barker wearing a frock *and* a moustache was bloody stupid. I picked up my pen.

'The sun made a brief, fleeting appearance from behind the thick grey clouds and then appeared to vanish again, plunging the sky into darkness. As it did so, his mind went the same way, thoughts receding into morbidity, the sun of life being extinguished by the gloom of death, the despair of dark evil, the emptiness of loneliness...'

On Sunday, Mum, having phoned Leo and Andrew to cancel our music practice because I was sick, ha ha, returned from church white-lipped with anger. Marching into my room, where I was still in my navy PJs huddled under the duvet with Pickles and fending off another asthma attack, she launched a Polaris missile at my head.

"Pam Wilson says you're homosexual and the whole school knows." I pulled the duvet protectively round my chest. "I told her she was a liar and you were just sensitive because of your music, then Timothy said you'd admitted it to him at break."

"Admitted?" I gasped. "You make it sound like some crime."

"It *is* a crime!" yelled Mum for every wolf in Siberia. "You're *fifteen*! You're a *child*!"

"At 15," I yelled back, "Andy Collins, Mark Gray, Michael Crooks, *everyone* in my class, is having regular sex." Which they weren't, but what the hell?

"That's OK," she returned icily. "That's normal. That's with *girls*." Shit. "This infatuation with Alistair Ross has left you confused."

"I'm not confused, and it's not an infatuation," I protested, "And he's called *Rose* for Christ's sake! Why can't you get his bloody name right?"

"Because he's filling your head with all sorts of nonsense!" she shouted. "He's *grooming* you, Jonathan! God Almighty, he could *do* things to you, you know? Grope you, even *rape* you, you stupid little kid!"

"Well, he won't," I retorted, "Because he loves me. We're gay, and he loves me."

"I hate that word, 'gay'," Mum bristled. "A perfectly good word corrupted by brainwashing perverts. It means happy, Jonathan! Happy! How are *you* happy? You've spent the weekend crying in bed with your bloody teddy-bear."

"I'm happy when I'm with Ali," I said simply.

"Ali, Ali, Ali!" she exploded. "It's all we ever hear from you! You're like some soppy girl."

"You think I *chose* to be gay?" I suddenly shouted. "You think I *want* this? You think I want people calling me names and hitting me and spitting at me? You think I *want* this? I *know* how hard this is. I know I hard this is going to be. But it's who I am! It's who I was born to be. I was made this way, Mum. I was *born* gay. Why, I don't know yet. But I was."

"So it's *our* fault!" She looked at Dad, hovering anxiously in the doorway. "*We* made you, Jonathan. If you were *born* that way, it must be *our* fault?"

"It's nobody's *fault*," I said wearily. "God decided."

"So it's *God's* fault?" she screamed. "Don't talk about God. You're not fit to speak His name." She ripped the gold crucifix from my neck and told me to get dressed. "After your piano lesson, we're going to your grandparents for tea."

"I don't feel like it," I muttered mutinously. I was not gonna miss the climax of *Tale of Two Cities*, denuniciations, executions, guillotines galore and 'far far better thing than anything I've done before' as he sacrifices himself for his friends for the *People's Friend* puzzle page, some limp lettuce leaves, half a tomato and the bloody Royal Variety Show on BBC1. I mean, ticket to Snoresville, or what? A load of dancers, prancers and has-beens doing 'Roll out the barrel,' 'White cliffs of Dover' and telling jokes about washboards and outdoor lavvies. Man, I think there was gonna be a ventriloquist with a talking dog, like on *That's Life*, going 'Sausages' and 'gottle of gear,' and the Grunters giving it like '*this* is entertainment, Jon-Jon, not that stuff *you're* in (Shakespeare and Dickens, presumably).' Someone just shoot me.

"I'm not paying £20 an hour for you not to 'feel like it'." She flung my jeans at me. "You bloody well go. And get off your *fucking* soapbox, Jonathan. I don't want to hear your *fucking* opinions, you obnoxious little brat, not till you're an adult with kids of your own."

"Fucking hell, it's like being in prison!" She slapped me really hard across the cheek. "I hate you!" I screamed through the tears, "I fucking hate you, you bitch!"

"Guess what, you insufferable pig?" shouted Mum, face twisted with fury, "I hate you too! So get out of bed and just for once shut your fucking mouth, you fucking little fairy."

Screaming another obscenity, I scrabbled through my Oxford Maths set for the compass. Last time it had hurt *sooo* much, despite tea-tree oil and a bandage. I'd eventually got a pain-killing jab in my arse from the hatchet-faced school nurse. This time I'd make it hurt so much she'd be like *really* sorry. And to follow it up I'd slash my arms with a pencil sharpener blade. Biting my duvet, I stabbed my thigh till the blood flowed and I passed out.

24: Who wants to live forever?

GULPING and trying to squelch my fast-flipping guts, I called "Morning" as cheerfully as I could and limped into the room. A few heads turned but no-one replied. A hostile, wounded silence crushed me as I went to Locker 17. The word 'GAY' was still on the door and now someone had scrawled 'PEEDO PETERS IS A POOF' on the board.

"For fuck's sake, grow up," I said irritably.

"Oooh," said Seymour, camply flapping his wrist, "Shut that door."

My thigh ached. Mum had just said I was 'so immature.' Dad had cried. It was he who had cleaned the several stab-points with tea-tree and Savlon, applied the plasters, given me Panadols for the pain. He had sat on my bed, cradled me and shushed me and pleaded with me not to hurt myself again.

"Mum hates me," I'd wept. "Everyone hates me. I might as well be dead."

Michael Crooks didn't speak to me and I wasn't speaking to him. The titchy ginger cunt had betrayed me. I just hoped he'd like DIE, you know? Fucking bastard. As Jamie Arnold called him over, I could see our formerly united class fragmenting into factions.

Inside my locker I found a note, scribbled in blue biro on a torn scrap of graph-paper. It read 'you're gonna hurt today, you bent bastard.' My stomach lurched sickly.

Christ, I really hadn't wanted to come today. It was one of those dark, filthy, rain-soaked mornings when you just really want to batter that bloody alarm clock as it bangs in your ear. I'd dragged myself from my duvet at half-past six, dressed in the dark, couldn't find my slippers so stumbled downstairs in my socks for half a slice of granary toast with peanut butter, a banana-and-strawberry smoothie and a cod liver oil capsule and trod painfully on a Lego brick which made me yelp then, shivering inside my school sweater and trench-coat, trudged miserably through the dark drizzle to the bus-stop. Neither parent wanted to turn out for the *gay* son did they? Because the bus was full, I had to stand all the way into town, crushed beneath the sweat-stinky armpits of a massive black bloke in overalls and the jutting mountain-mammaries of a woman who reeked of cheap perfume. My ten-ton backpack dragged at my shoulder and my Walkman faded to static as the battery dwindled to empty. Over the university cityscape, the darkness paled into a scummy grey, dishwater dawn.

When Bunny arrived for 8.45 Registration, he glanced at the slogan and said "I believe 'paedo' is spelled with an 'a'? Nice shiner, Jenny. Bobby Rose, I believe."

Jenny! Did my form-master actually just really like call me Jenny?

"Don't blame Olly, eh, sir?" called Brudenall. "Finding out your brother's a sausage jockey can't be easy."

On the way to Assembly, Lewis, muttering 'cock-sucker,' jarred my shoulder by barging me roughly into the wall. I couldn't find anywhere to sit. No-one made room for me. Some Sixth Former screamed 'filthy faggot' across the Rises.

"Silence!" roared Willie.

"Just sit there, Peters," said Hellfire, pointing at a space beside Fosbrook.

"Sir!" protested Fosbrook, "I don't want *him* next to me."

"Don't be stupid, Fosbrook," growled Hellfire. "It's not a disease."

"That's a matter of opinion, sir," said Fosbrook.

"Just sit down, Peters," said Hellfire impatiently.

"Keep your *fucking* hands to yourself, you *fucking* queer," hissed Fosbrook as Fred started the hymn. "So much as look at me, you're fucking *dead*."

Yikes. As if. Fozzie was the ugliest plug-faced kid in the class.

"Ah, go get shagged, you pizza-faced little virgin," I scowled, trying to locate Alistair on the prefects' row. He wasn't there. Unable to face sitting at the front under two thousand hostile eyes, he'd put himself on late-duty. As it was, Sonning, standing in for Redmond, shared with us some words from Ephesians 1, verses18 to 23 (we'd finished our exploration of Proverbs and were back to the Lectionary): "*I pray that your inward eyes may be illumined so that you may know what is the hope to which he calls you, what the wealth and glory of the share he offers you among his people in their heritage, and how vast the resources of his power open to us who trust him.*" Then we did the usual mumble of the Lord's Prayer - '*forgive us our sins as we forgive those who sin against us*' – and Wheezy did this prayer of St Aidan, '*Leave me alone with God, make me an island, set apart, alone with God*' and then Hymn 442:

> "*All things bright and beautiful, all creatures great and small,*
> *All things wise and wonderful, the Lord God made them all.*"

'All.' I laughed bitterly. *Satan* had made *me*, according to Wilson, Rix and the Christian Union. I was Antichrist, 'cos gay and God were apparently incompatible. While I saw listening to Gallagher and Redmond reading notices, Keighley and Tredwell, sitting behind me with U5S, kept kicking me in the back and making foot-prints on my blazer. Then, when we were waiting for Leatherbridge to dismiss us, Tredwell gave me a push in the back that sent me sprawling into Coleman and Robbins in U5B on the row below. Everyone laughed. Leatherbridge went absolutely bonkers, screaming my name at the top of his lungs, then he spotted my top button unfastened. Honestly, I thought he was gonna have a stroke, like the guy in *To Serve Them All My Days*. Anyway, the tosser waved away my protest that I'd been pushed *and* ignored my complaint that I was being bullied. I even showed him the note I'd found in my locker. He just grunted, told me to grow a pair, if I could, and gave me a one-hour detention for 'disruptive behaviour.' Man, I booted the bin all the way round the bogs then slammed a cubicle door on my hand so I could go back to the nurse for a jab. She just jammed the damn needle in and told me to sod off back to class.

Throughout Monday I was like a rat in a microwave. Vicious comments from all sides, no-one wanting to sit with me, everyone avoiding me, some kids spitting at me, fucking Sumner kicking me hard under the right knee, and this was just getting back to Room 31. Hunched over, I sat alone, staring at the back of my left hand swelling a livid, angry purple, then Bunny swept in, gown black as night, slammed down a pile of orange exercise-books and let rip as we stood up. I knew my homework'd been rubbish. How the hell he expected me to solve equations with all the shit going on in my head, I had no idea. Normally I'd've got someone to help me but that particular avenue appeared closed. Keeping us standing, he tore into Morreson then launched a ballistic missile at Collins for careless mistakes. Shrouded in misery, I braced myself as he told all the others to sit.

"Peters, you half-witted dunce!" he snapped. "What is the square root of 5?"

"Er..." I thought I ought to know this. It was somewhere between two and three, around two and half. "Two and a half, sir?" Someone laughed aloud.

"No, you imbecile," came the icy retort. "How the hell can it be two and a half?"

"I don't know, sir," I admitted unhappily.

"Peters," drawled Bunny, "You're so bloody thick it makes me weep. What do you keep in that turnip you call a head?" Maxton and Stewart laughed appreciatively. "I suggest you clear out the clutter of music and boys and look in the tables!" His voice rose to a scream. "They're right in front of you, boy! Look it up, you imbecile, for God's sake."

Scrabbling through the small booklet on my desk, I blurted "Two point two four, sir."

"So why did you not put that in your utterly wretched prep?"

"I must have misread it, sir."

"I must have misread it, sir," he mimicked. "Are you blind? Or just truly *truly* stupid?" Squirming uncomfortably, I fixed my teary eyes on the grey table-top and bit my lip. "Good God Almighty, you're sitting GCSE soon and you don't even have the brains to look the answer up in the tables. You just guess and hope for the best. You're a bloody idiot, Peters. You always were."

"We can't all be good at Maths, sir," Bainbridge said suddenly.

"But it isn't just Maths, is it, Joe? He swans through life doing what he pleases, breaking the rules, breaking the *law*, because he can play the piano."

It was uttered in the most scathing, contemptuous tone I'd ever heard.

"He's pretty good though, sir," said Cooke. "That Chopin was really beautiful, Jonny."

"Yeah," added Huxley, "You've got a real gift, Jonny."

The tears brimmed over. My class-mates were coming to my defence.

"Perhaps if he stopped eyeing up boys, he'd develop a gift in Maths too," said Bunny.

"Sir," said Andrew Collins suddenly, "You shouldn't talk to him like that. It isn't right. You're being mean and spiteful and besides, it might not even be true. It might just be a rumour, you know? Gossip, a misunderstanding. Eh? Jonny? It might not be true."

I heard the desperate pleading in his voice.

"Well, Jonathan?" said Bunny, glorying in his moment. "Is it true? Are you queer? Are you a homosexual? Or is it just a rumour?"

I felt the whole class, all nineteen of them, tense expectantly, mentally fusing with Collins in begging for it not to be true. Paulus's blue eyes screamed 'Deny it, Jonathan, deny it. We want you back. Just say it isn't true and make us happy again.'

This was my lifeline. All I had to do was say 'Of course it's not true. I'm straight as a pole-dancer's pole. I kissed Mikey for a dare. There was nothing in it, was there, Mikey? And as for Rosie, well, he's got the hots for me but sod *him*, the great poof. *I'm* not interested in a bummer-boy like him. How could I be? I got Claire. I'm just like you guys, you know? I like footie, beer and birds. Grrrrr. And I am definitely *not* a poof.' There'd be this massive cheer and I'd be welcomed back with love. U5H would be happy again, my teachers would be happy again, my parents would be happy again and life would return to normal.

Just three little words.

'It isn't true.'

Three more little words.

'I'm not gay.'

So easy to say.

I could spare myself a world of pain. I could retreat from the battlefield and hide in the closet. Had I learned nothing from wargaming? Tactical withdrawal from superior enemy-fire. I'd get my friends back. I'd get Tim back. I'd get Mark and Max back. I'd get my life back.

But I'd lose Leo, and Andy, and Ali, and Shelton and Hill. More, I'd lose myself. I'd condemn myself to a life of lies and pretence. God had created me this way for a reason. I might not know that reason now but one day I would, and to deny myself, to deny what I was, was denying both God and his plan for me.

"Tell them it isn't true," drawled Bunny.

Drawing a deep breath, I raised my eyes, straightened my back, dragged myself out of the slump and declared "No, sir. It *is* true." I turned to my class and repeated "It's true. I know you don't like it but you're my friends and I don't want to lie to you. So yes, sir, I'm gay. I *am* homosexual. I can't help it. It's the way I was made."

Amid a collective, moaned sigh, Bunny looked vindicated, Gray's head smacked into his palms, Collins collapsed into his seat in despair, Crooks crowed "I told you he was an arse-bandit" and Stewart gobbed in my hair.

"Right," said Bunny. "So now you know. Peters, sit down. Page 21, exercise 3."

Miserable and lonely, I stared at the desk till the bell rang then I went to see him.

"Sir," I said nervously as everyone else was leaving, "Can we like talk, sir? About… what's been happening, sir, you know?"

"I don't have time for cosy chats," he said testily. "2S are coming. Can't it wait?"

"No, sir, it can't," I flared angrily. "It's important!"

He sighed this *heavy* sigh, made some crack to these giggling gimps about drama-queens, shoved me into the corridor and snapped "Well?"

Looking into his clear blue eyes, I said "I don't like the way you talk to me, sir."

Dropping his hand onto the door-knob, he uttered this guttural laugh. "Get off to

Biology, Peters, and stop wasting mine and 2S's time."

"No, sir, I won't, sir," I ploughed on. "It's wrong, sir. It makes me unhappy and none of my friends want to know me any more." Tears were swelling.

"That's nothing to do with *me*," he said shortly. "They don't want to know you because you're a fairy-cake."

"You see?" I said indignantly. "You shouldn't say these things to me."

"Why not?" he shrugged. "It's true. You said so yourself. Now get off to Biology, you filthy little queer." The loathing in his voice was just unbearable. I ran to the toilets, slammed myself in a cubicle and cried.

When I reached Herbie's freak-show, Stewart, Maxton and the other fuckwits made slurpy sucking noises and mooed 'Gaaaay' whilst Herbie demanded to know why I was late.

"I was talking to Mr Hutchinson, sir," I said.

"Jerking off over 1R's swimming class you mean," cried Lewis.

"Sucking off Fred in the bogs," added Gardiner.

"Bumming Trent," called Brudenall.

"He called me a filthy little queer, sir," I said, dazed.

"Well, you are!" shouted Morreson.

"You should've got a note." Herbie tossed my homework book to me. "This book is a disgrace, Peters. It looks as though you've been using it as a doormat."

"He called me a filthy little queer." I was scarcely able to grasp it.

"Sir," said Brudenall slyly, "Why *do* queers exist? I mean, it's against all the laws of nature, isn't it? I mean, your anus is for expelling stuff, isn't it, not taking cocks and that *in*, right? An' what about reproduction and that? Rosie's spunk just mixes up with Peedo's poo. I mean, that can't be right, can it, sir?"

"Can they be cured, sir?" said Stewart, "If you fry their brains or something?"

"Don't be ridiculous," snapped Herbie as others piled in with their questions, didn't gays cause AIDS and if gays caused AIDs, shouldn't they be locked up so other people didn't get it? And shouldn't they be locked up anyway because they were sick and out to grope small boys' bits? So shouldn't gays be castrated, just in case? If they got their nuts chopped off, they wouldn't fiddle kiddies any more. Herbie went ballistic.

"Where did you hear *that*, you moron?"

"In the papers, sir," said Seymour. "It's not like they *need* their balls, is it, sir? I mean, *their* sperm's not for making babies, is it? It's just a drink, like a milk-shake, eh, Peedo?"

They got into this tremendous row as I shrank inside my blazer and Brudenall said castration was right and threw a scissor-cutting gesture in my direction. I felt sick again but what really freaked me out was something I read in a note someone had shoved into my blazer pocket. It said 'We are going to rape you, soak you in petrol and set you on fire.'

Crying aloud, I clapped my hand to my mouth. Who the hell was this? And why did they want to do it anyway? How could they hate me so much? I sleep-walked to Choral Society where some of the trebles started hissing, imitating the gas of a Nazi gas-chamber. Mark Williams, seated at the Steinway, looked at me coldly whilst Fred Perry's fat, round face bore an expression of mingled sympathy and disgust. Hellfire, from the back row of the basses, bawled at the trebles and told me to sit with him.

"It's hard being different in a place like this," he began conversationally.

"I know," I said bitterly. "I've always been different here. First my dad was a bus driver, secondly I had free school-meals and uniform vouchers and now everyone who's always *hated* me for being poor has come out to attack me for being gay."

"So you *are* gay," said Hellfire gently. "I thought so. What about Alistair?"

"I love him," I said simply, "And they hate our love even more."

"Peters, shut up, and fasten your collar," called Perry. "Page 91, number 36 two bars before. '*When the Chief Priests and the officers saw Him, they all crie-ye-d out...*'"

The Choral Society hit the D as one - "*Cru---ci--fy, crucify, crucify, crucify...*" for five pages. "*We have a sacred law* (number 38) *and by this same law He should die…*"

The score drooped in my hands as I slumped back into my chair. Then, whilst Perry was yelling that the trebles sounded more like a bunch of farmyard chickens than a baying bloodthirsty mob, the altos saved me.

"This is so awful," said Leo tearfully. "I love you both so much and I *hate* this school for what they're doing to you."

"My brother's a total cunt," Pip declared. "He's been crowing all weekend, saying you're gonna get what you deserve, and my parents agreed with him! Mother said there's no place for boys like you in a respectable school." He choked on his emotions. "She rang Ash-tray to get you kicked out." He punched his thigh. "It's so shit! I can't believe it's so shit! Like they'd kick people out for being gay." Pip looked wildly at Leo. "I would fire-bomb the fucking school if they kicked *you* out, Lion, or you, Shelters."

Shelton just sat there, frozen numb.

After the practice, Ali was waiting, his face this mask of angry anxiety.

"You look like a hundred year old panda," he said. I didn't laugh. "How are you?"

"Not so good," I replied. "I've been spat at, kicked, slapped and pushed into walls, there's graffiti on my locker and someone's sent me a note saying they're going to rape me and set me on fire. Leatherface put me in detention when I complained and Bunny's been a total bastard." I told him what had happened in Maths. Shocked and scared, we held each other, shaking with a shared fear and distress, then returned to Hell.

Mum wasn't speaking to me either. She just slammed this ham salad in front of me, lips so tight they seemed welded together. When I tried to talk, she bit my head off with 'I'm too tired for your melodramas, Jonathan. Just grow up, will you?' then asked all the moose in Canada why I'd left skid-marks in the toilet. My leg hurt. My hand ached. I couldn't focus on my prep, or on *Star Trek's* search for the Ryetalyn antidote to an on-board epidemic of Rigellan fever or the Captain's encounter with an immortal human and his robot mate, and the news brought the usual bullshit, war in Afghanistan, terrorist alerts at London airports, the American President threatening Iran, our Prime Minister slagging off Europe... man, *nothing* changes, does it? I was miserable, lonely, frightened and in pain. If it hadn't been for Ali, and Leo, I might've killed myself that night. I counted 21 Panadols in the bathroom cabinet and wondered if they'd be enough. I didn't want to fuck it up after all. If I was gonna kill myself, I was gonna do it right, you know? So I fashioned my house tie into a noose and knotted it firmly round a coat-hook on the back of my bedroom door. I would hang myself. It wouldn't hurt and I'd be doing everyone a favour. Mum hated me so much. Everyone at school hated me more. I was just gonna get more of the same tomorrow, and it would never end, never, 'cos, as Chappers and the agony uncles said, everyone hates queers, and everyone knew now that I was one... I stuck my head through the loop and tightened the slipknot. No way choking to death could be worse than my life right now. '*Suicide*,' the MASH theme song claimed, '*Is painless, it brings on many changes... the game of life is hard to play, I'm gonna lose it anyway…*' Damn right. I said goodbye to Pickles, New Bear and my bedroom then, just as I was wondering whether my whole miserable life really would flash before my eyes, I changed my mind. I saw the photo from the school mag of me and Ali as the fairies, greened-up, bare-chested and crowned with flowers. Sure, as Lysander said, "the course of true love never did run smooth." And this was true love. I knew it was. Ali, and Leo, needed me to be strong and just get through it. And besides, why should I kill myself because the world was run by twats? As Puck had said, "Lord, what fools these mortals be." And Lord, they *were* fools, such thick-headed fuckwits it made you weep. Anyhow, I knew that as my life progressed, I would find a way of playing a *different* game of life, you know? I would create my own game, with my own rules, and nuke the lot of them.

Tuesday's weather was even worse than Monday's, thick black clouds and driving rain which, even though I turned up my trench-coat collar, somehow squirmed inside. Brudenall, Stewart and Seymour continued their homophobic drivel whilst everyone else just seemed uncomfortable. I really hoped Games would be cancelled. I couldn't face ploughing up and down a field with a rugby ball, not today. I'd rather stay in school, hole up in whatever room I was allocated to, do my homework and shove off home. Games cancellations were signalled by a triple ring of the school bell at 12, so halfway through French, I was utterly dismayed by the silently mocking non-ringing of the bell. Shit. I'd have to go to rugby. Shit.

Miserably chewing a Ryvita and apple, I added another paragraph to my story: *'He leaned against the bastion of the stone bridge and gazed down into the murky depths. The river bed and surrounding scenery merged in with the rest of the picture, the shades and edges blurred and confused, almost indistinguishable. The lack of colour seemed to accentuate the despondency he felt, and that he felt the whole world was experiencing with him.'* Then I walked to the playing fields in the pouring rain by myself, though Tredwell and Keighley kicked a puddle on to my trousers and threatened to push me in front of a bus.

I felt so fed up as I drifted back into the rain in blue shorts and green shirt to the muddy pitch where Wadey, rubbing his beard impatiently, was waiting to organize the teams.

"Can I play in another group, sir?" said Stewart, licking his chapped lips. "I don't want Peters looking at my arse all afternoon."

"Your arse is way too fat and spotty for me, Bob," I snarled, to some muted laughter.

Pale blue-shirted Timothy Wilson, on the opposing team, stabbed the air before his own eyes with his index and middle finger then flung the gesture furiously towards me.

"JP," called Wadey, "Go scrum-half. I want to see what you're made of."

"He's made of sugar and spice and all things nice," minced Wilson to general laughter. "That's what little girls are made of."

"He'll be fine," Maxton added maliciously. "He likes handling oval balls."

"Bloody knob-jockey!" shouted Stewart.

Wouldn't you know it? Wadey asked Tim to be the opposing scrum-half.

At the first opportunity, from the first scrum, I crashed into him as hard as I could and exulted as he fell heavily into the mud. Feeding Stewart the ball, I yelled "Go!" He just stood there, got tackled by a bunch of people, dragged into this maul and lost possession. Grinning fiercely, Wilson kicked for touch.

"Fuck's sake, Bob," I stormed, "What are you doing?"

"Don't want to get AIDS off the ball," he said, trotting back to his position.

What a twat.

From the line-out, I got the ball myself and dodged past Robbins and some other wheezers before Wilson brutally shoulder-barged me off the pitch. I appealed for a foul.

"Can't take it, Jonny, don't play the game," shrugged Wadey.

Wiping mud and rain from my eyes, I organized the pack and watched the spider-web strands of the backs radiating from the knot. Behind the flankers and the number 8, I eyeballed Wilson angrily as we waited for Wadey's "Ready? Touch. Engage."

"Ball in now!" yelled Wilson, but our pack was stronger and, with an almighty forward-heave, the number 8 back-heeled the ball to me.

Stewart having let me down earlier, I decided to go on a mazy run of my own. No-one cried encouragement as I headed for the try-line, dodging Robbins, dodging Coleman, then Wilson erupted from nowhere, bashing into my chest and knocking me sideways. The ball spilled from my hands. I sat up in the mud, screaming "High tackle!" at Wadey.

"Play on," said Wadey.

Then, in a ruck, Wilson scraped down my shin with his studs.

"He could have broken my leg, sir," I protested, blinking back tears.

"Play on," said Wadey, "And play the game."

"Having a good time, Jenny?" snarled Wilson. "Every time you get the ball, I'm gonna make you bleed, you fucking queer."

He was as good as his word. He shoulder-charged me hard in the ribs then, in another ruck, dug his fingernails into my face to scrape off some skin. It stung like fury.

"Blood injury," said Wade, tossing me his handkerchief. "Clean yourself up."

I stood on the 22 in the hammering rain, my soaked shirt clinging to my chest, my legs and face smeared with mud, my hair plastered to my head, my face sluiced with rainwater, this manky white cloth pressed to my face, yelling at Walton to run or fling it wide to Gray. Then, in a co-ordinated action, Wilson, Robbins, Stewart and some others jumped on me. I didn't even have the ball. Wilson stamped hard on my back and I cried out in agony as his boot landed just under my rib-cage. Then he kicked me hard in the thigh and dead-legged me.

"Penalty-try," said Wade. "Do that again, Wilson, you're off."

As I lay in the mud trying to catch my breath, Stewart twisted my hair and muttered into my ear that tomorrow, after school, he and his mates were going to 'do' me.

"We're gonna break your fucking legs, Peters. We're gonna smash your fucking ankles with baseball bats then we're gonna set fire to you and watch you burn to death."

Suddenly I lost it, you know? Like totally *totally* lost it. There was this kind of wet smack as my right fist crashed into his cheek, then a left-hand jab knocked him backwards, a knuckle-bruising straight right arm, a punch in his fat, flabby gut and an uppercut to the jaw which lifted him off his feet as the other boys yelled 'Fight fight fight fight' and Wadey feebly blew his feeble little whistle. Furious beyond thought, acting on animal instinct, I leapt at him, kicking him hard in the balls and smashing my fist twice against his skull. "Come on, you cunt! You wanna a piece of me? Eh? A piece of me?" Then, as Stewart writhed and squirmed in the mud, I charged after Timothy Wilson, my once-best friend. What the fuck was wrong with him? We'd known each other like forever.

Dancing in fury, I hammered my right fist against his cheek then against his jaw then into his sick fucking mouth. I felt blood on my knuckles. I didn't care. His nose was mine. I just wanted to break it, break it forever, and drove my fist into it with a liberating yell of absolute Victory. As it burst, and his blood spattered my face, he collapsed groaning on the grass and a red mist obscured my vision. I jumped on his chest, screaming and hitting him over and over again, tasting his blood on my lips, pounding his face, pounding his nose, mashing the bastard's face to tiny little pieces.

As Wilson's nose broke again under my knuckles, a million people seemed to dive in, Gray, Walton, Robbins, Wadey... I elbowed Mr Wade violently in the ribs as he tried to contain me against his chest then smacked Gray on the side of the head.

"Fuck off!" I screamed, wriggling after Wilson again. He was crawling backwards, blood pouring from his massively mega-busted nose, absolute terror etched on his face. Stewart lay groaning in the mud. Then Hellfire appeared, rugby-tackling me round the knees, sending me crashing to the grass. As I struggled up, he slapped my face. Shocked, I blurted "You can't *do* that, sir." He slapped me again, then sat on me with Gray while Wadey went ballistic and Stewart and Wilson crawled away, grateful for the intervention. Maxton had run away. The others, a massive ring of about fifty boys, were white with terror. Gray kept muttering for me to stay calm while Hellfire said nothing. Gray, I think, was crying.

Eventually they let me up but I sat on the grass, breathing hard, a snorting bull in a ring demanding Wilson's brains with braised leeks and a nice Pinot Noir, still furious, still clenching my fists angrily, still wanting that blood wet and warm on my knuckles.

"What the hell, Peters?" shouted Wade.

"You saw what was happening!" I shouted back. "You saw it all, you bastard. And you did nothing to stop it. Nothing! Because I'm gay, you let them knock me about. You're a fucking disgrace, sir."

Choking down my anger, I stalked to the changing-room, feeling the blood drying on my face and a searing ache in my seemingly completely crushed knuckles compete with every other area of pain in my body. I sat on the bench, dejected and angry, and peeled off my sopping, mud-splattered, blood-spattered rugby-shirt then prised off my boots and stripped off my socks and shorts as the First XV hearties gathered around me in a semi-circle and the other kids, the swots, the licks, the keenos, the slackers melted away into the recessed shadows of the changing-room. I squinted up at familiar faces made brutally hard with loathing. My heart turned to lead and the metallic aluminium tang of fear tainted my tongue. This had been years in the making and perhaps, for a million reasons, it had to happen.

As they beat me and kicked me and lashed me to the metal peg-frame with their ties, like they were crucifying me, the last movement of Mahler 2, which I'd heard with my lovely Alistair, who'd never hurt anyone, ever, resounded in my aching head – rise again, I shall rise again. Though my stomach felt hollowed out and sickness fluttered in the base of my throat, I just prayed they wouldn't break any bones or burn me. Blood trickled from my nose. I heard people laughing, especially when someone pulled down my shorts and someone else took a photo. My mouth was dry as an overheated sand-tray. I squirmed, naked, vulnerable, nausea rising through my throat, my heart thumping like a crazy child banging a tin drum and my stomach floating somewhere in the empty, dead, sucking vacuum of outer space. I could hear the roar of blood in my ears. Some Sixth Former waved his locker key in front of me, said he was going to carve me up, then slashed across my bare chest, drawing an angry red diagonal over my ribs and making me wince. Then he dragged the key down my left thigh. Boys were filming this. My knees wobbled like a windsock in a hurricane. My muscles turned to water. I felt urine dribbling down the inside of my thigh, pooling round my bare foot. I began to cry properly, bloody snot bubbling out of my nose. My chest heaved. I pulled at my bonds, sobbing "Please please please let me go. I won't tell anyone. Please." The metal frame rattled, like the hollow derision of laughing skeletons. Beyond the grins, my class-mates watched in a mixture of curiosity, loathing and anger. "Someone…" I whispered thickly, "Help me… please… help me…" I rattled the frame weakly as someone returned with a shout of triumph and a plastic cup brimful to overflowing with straw-coloured piss.

"Are you thirsty, Jenny? You must be thirsty. Several of us contributed to your afternoon drink, so there's plenty for you."

The faces, shiny with sweat and bright with excitement, closed in. Someone chanted 'Drink the piss, drink the piss.' As I tightened my lips and clenched my jaw, someone's bony fingers burrowed into my skull, thumb pressing into my eyeball, and another kneed my balls so I *had* to open my mouth. The first boy twisted his fingers in my hair and yanked my face upwards so his mate could tip the piss into my mouth. It splashed over my teeth and chin but I couldn't spit it all out. I had to swallow some, or drown. I sobbed frantically, the musty, salty taste clinging to my tongue like fur, then the rest was poured slowly over my head. It dripped down my face as I writhed against my bonds

Someone slapped my face. "Say it, you queer. Say 'I'm a fucking little queer'." He slapped me again, spat in my face.

I was almost unconscious now. Every part of me throbbed with an indescribably white-hot intensity. Blood trickled from a dozen cuts. Drunk on pain, I mumbled "I'm a fucking little queer." Another punch burst my nose. "I'm a cock-sucking, shit-stabbing, shirt-lifting poof."

I could feel blood in my mouth, feel it flowing over my face and chin. I heard some of the others telling him to leave me and him screaming "Say it! Say it!" My vision dimmed so I could only see him through some hazy fog. My knees buckled. But for the ties lashing me to the metal -frame, I would have collapsed in a heap on the floor.

"Say it!" he bawled, kneeing me viciously in the balls. I felt really sick as another *tsunami* of agony sweep through my poor, battered frame, and I knew what I had to say. I knew what Leo needed me to say. I knew what Paulus needed to me say, what Shelton and Ali and Niall Hill, what every 'fucking little queer' in the whole wide bigoted world needed me to say, what *you*, my reader, need me to say. Gathering blood into my swollen mouth, I sprayed it in his face.

"Go get a life," I said contemptuously, "You sad, twisted loser."

Everyone seemed to go totally mental, slashing me with their locker keys, scoring my skin with angry red lines and someone filming my pain, misery and the terror shining from my eyes. I screamed till I was hoarse and somewhere, sometime, I moaned like a calf on a barbed wire fence and, to a chorus of boos and 'ews,' threw up down my chest.

A firestorm raged through my body. My face was swelling, my eyes puffing, my thighs blackening, my chest purpling. I could feel blood, wet and sticky, on my lips, on my gums, on my cheeks, on the places where they had stamped with their studs, and I forgave them. They didn't understand. They were simply following the lead their parents had given them, the lead their teachers had given them, the lead the straight, heteronormative, adult world had given them, the lead their law-makers and media had given them. They were products of their contexts, prisoners of their culture, trapped in a swamp of bile, hatred, vitriol and viciousness. However much money their parents earned, their parents had failed because their sons were frightened, bigoted bullies. It wasn't their fault. They didn't know what they were doing. They didn't understand. They were not allowed to.

Someone reached up to my blazer, hanging on the hook above my bleeding head.

"You don't belong here, you queer little fuck. You never did. You never will."

He ripped the badge with the golden wheatsheaf-and-crown from the breast pocket, flung it contemptuously into the urine pooled round my feet and wrote **'QUEER'** on my chest in massive letters with a thick black board-marker. I vomited again then closed my eyes while the pain rolled over me like ocean waves.

25: I am what I am

I WAS strolling casually across a lush, green meadow dotted with buttercups. Somewhere a thrush was singing. The sun was warm on my head. I was wearing pink Bermuda shorts, a white cricket-sweater and Ray-bans. The grass was cool against my bare feet. The houses of the small village behind me were modern bungalows built from mellow ochre bricks. Ahead of me was my school. As I reached the green side-door, a bunch of field-mice scampered over my feet. Then Niall Hill, kissing my cheek, opened the door and let me in. The school had become a shopping mall with cafés, boutiques and bars where classrooms and labs had once been. Herbie's Lab of Evil was now a Mediterranean-style beach bar with little tables under brightly coloured umbrellas, a well-stocked bar and a well-muscled barman, Andy Paulus sexily hot in a black, pink and gold vest mixing up Jaegerbombs for Leo, who, in a Hawaiian grass-skirt and yellow feathery boa, was slow-dancing on a table with Pip Brudenall who wore a lilac hoodie, yellow Bermudas and day-glo pink ankle socks.

Needing a piss, I headed down a glass-walled escalator and past a stall selling banana ice-cream and chocolate custard to the Lower School toilets, dingy and stinky as always. I had somehow lost my clothes and entered the toilet naked. The cubicle opened back into the field. This time there was a row of beds, like in a boarding-school dormitory or a hospital ward, and every bed contained a sick or injured child. Some had bandages round their heads. Others had limbs in plaster. Nick Shelton lay in the nearest, his leg and chest wrapped in bandages. I started towards him, reaching out my hand, but I sank into the grass up to my knees so I couldn't move. I tried to cry out but my voice-box froze, so I stretched up, and up, and up but all I could hear was this harsh hissing sound, like gas mixed with the bird-song... I blinked in the stark, sickly, fish-belly paleness of dawn, and opened my eyes.

Slowly I pieced together the events of last night. It was Graham Brudenall and Kevin Seymour who found me, hanging from the peg-frame, rambling, delirious, covered in blood and snot. Broody had yelled something and Seymour untied me, gently lowering my battered body to the concrete floor and going 'who did this, Jonny?' when Andy Collins arrived, crying, to cradle me in his arms and Brudenall fetched Wade and Langdon while Seymour dressed me. I remember my white vest was soaked in blood. I said I'd felt dizzy and fallen down the stairs. My class-mates kind of glanced at each other but didn't contradict me. Nonetheless, it was clear that the teachers didn't believe me either. The word **'QUEER'** written in black ink on my chest was a bit of a clue, I suppose. Anyway, Hellfire, looking at me sitting on the bench, nose bleeding a little, face bruised and swelling, lips split and torn, blazer and shirt ripped, wet and stained, offered to drive me home. As I lurched drunkenly after him, I heard Wadey speaking to Seymour, and saw Collins crying again, Brudenall trying to comfort him.

I was in a lot of pain, so thank God for Hellfire's Mini. The ride only took 15 minutes. A ten-minute wait at a bus-stop then standing up on the packed number 8 for half an hour followed by a twenty-minute walk up the hill from the Ring Road might well have killed me. As it was, his car was like a fucking freezer 'cos he banged the air-con to like Mega-Zero-Brass-Monkey-Ball-Freezer and blasted it right in my face. He also played AC-DC:

'I'm rolling thunder, pouring rain, I'm coming on like a hurricane, My lightning's flashing across the sky, You're only young but you're gonna die, I won't take no prisoners won't spare no lives, Nobody's putting up a fight, I got my bell I'm gonna take you to hell... hell's bells...'

"You have rubbish taste in music, sir," I muttered as he fired questions about Stalin at me, like 'how did Stalin rule Russia?'

What the fuck was this? I wanted to sleep and Hellfire was like asking me for an essay-plan? And why was he poking his fingers into my ribs? They were already sore.

"Ow!" I cried. "You're hurting me, sir!"

"Don't fall asleep, Jonathan," he ordered anxiously, "Just don't fall asleep."

"Dictatorship," I sighed, "through one-party rule, secret police liquidating enemies and dissenters, censorship of newspapers, speech and religion... it's how anyone rules a country. Squash your enemies through witch-hunts and show-trials and only publish stuff that you want people to hear – lock us all up, keep our books off the shelves."

"Stalin," said Hellfire.

"It is difficult to assess his contribution to the world," I'd written, "As much of the evidence is not available, the rest being biased, distorted and some fabricated."

Hell's Bells.

As he dropped me at my gate, he stared at me quizzically and said "Fell down the stairs, Jonathan? Really?"

Wincing, I replied "Fell down the stairs, sir. Promise."

"Jonathan, you *can* talk to me, you know. In confidence."

"Thanks" I wiped blood from my nose. "But there's nothing to say, sir, is there?"

My folks were still at work, thank God. I slugged a tumbler of Dad's best Glenfiddich, crawled upstairs to the bathroom, ran a hot bath liberally laced with Radox, sloughed off all my clothes – even my socks and pants were soaked in blood - and stuck them in the washing machine then inspected the damage in the mirror. I looked a total fright. Great grape-purple bruises had appeared all over my chest, shoulders and thighs. Thin red stripes were scored all over my skin. My cut lower-lip was swollen. A deep gash ran down my left shin. Red marks glared angrily from my face. At least they didn't hurt any more, though my ribs still ached like a gazillion elephants had jived on my chest. The stencilled **'QUEER'** was livid against the marble white skin. I had to scrub it with a pumice stone that left my chest red-raw. The blood-stained vest was totally ruined. I shoved it in a Sainsbury's bag and pushed it into the bin. Biting my lip hard against the sting, I sank into the suds with a choking sob of pain. I was supposed to be playing in Leo's flute exam tomorrow and my fingers were like sausages.

Blondie on the radio: '*Every girl wants you to be her man, but I'll wait, my dear, 'till it's my turn. I'm not the kinda girl who gives up just like that, oh, no. The tide is high but I'm holding on. I'm gonna be your number one, number one.*'

"Jonny?" Mum was shouting up the stairs. I blinked awake and shouted that I was in the bath after Games. God Almighty. I couldn't face either a fight or the Spanish Inquisition right now, neither a tight-lipped 'serves you right, you faggoty little poof' nor an 'it's all that Ali Ross's fault.'

Sitting on the edge of the bath as the mud, blood and water swirled down the plughole, I daubed every cut and graze I could reach with tea-tree oil, screaming into my towel, then bathed the bruises in this evil-smelling embrocation, put on clean, dark green pyjamas, my warm yellow dressing-gown and tan moccasins and went to my room. My head hurt. I could hear rain pattering on the window behind the closed curtains. Because I was shivering, I think with shock, I wrapped my duvet round me, and sat with my back to the radiator listening to Beethoven's final string quartet, in F, Op 135, where everything is reconciled in a peaceful statement of resignation. Cuddling Pickles, I leafed through *Tintin in Tibet*, where Tintin risks his life to rescue his friend Chang from the aftermath of an aircrash and everything is so white, the white that apparently signified the writer's depression. My favourite Tintin was *The Secret of the Unicorn* because it was a really clever mystery, although I also loved *The Shooting Star*, with Decimus Phostle and Philippulus the Astronomer of Doom who declares Tintin the son of the Devil and ends up in an asylum. Well, challenging journalists just *proves* you're mad.

When Mum called me for tea and I finally limped down to the kitchen for chicken and leek pie and roast potatoes, she and Dad went nuts. I told them I'd been mugged on the way home from Games. I reckoned this would gain enough sympathy to get me a day off school so I could figure out what to do and head off the enquiry 'cos, although Dad was all for calling the cops, I just said it happened so quickly I couldn't remember their faces. Anyway, they let me watch James Herriot put a dying dog to sleep on BBC2 and *Arthur C. Clarke's Mysterious*

World on ITV, about the sailing stones of Death Valley (last week's had been about the Martian canals!) until several phone calls unravelled my tale and they interrupted my favourite advert just as I was breaking into song:

Way down deep in the middle of the Congo,
A hippo took an apricot, a guava and a mango....
He stuck it with the others, and he danced a dainty tango.
The rhino said, "I know, we'll call it Um Bongo"

Best advert ever, except, obviously, for *'We all adore a Kia-Ora'* ('too orangey for crows!'). I even barked *"I'll be your dog, woof woof woof,"* like the lead crow. Was he like Ted Hughes' crow, I wondered? Was he the Black Beast bleached white by the sun? Was *I*? Perhaps…

"Mr Langdon phoned," said Dad carefully, sitting with Mum on the edge of the sofa. "He said he gave you a lift home because you fell down the stairs."

I tried to focus on the comedy robots singing *'For mash get Smash.'*

"Mr Gallagher also phoned," said Mum, taking Dad's hand. "He wants us to go to a meeting. About *you*." She suppressed a sob. "He says you shouldn't go to school for the next few days. Oh Jonathan, what have you done?"

"Nothing," I said wearily. "I just told them I'm gay. They can't handle it. It's their problem. They need to get over it."

Mum's face hardened. Parents say their love is unconditional. It isn't. You have to follow their plan, their expectations, a lovely church wedding for the family album, a bunch of babies they can spoil... if what *you* give 'em is a boy and a cat, forget it. They want their day in the sun. Hence same-gender marriage. It's really to make the parents feel happy.

Happier.

I rang Leo and told him I was sick and couldn't do his exam. He cried. Perhaps he'd heard. He didn't say. Anyway, I spent Wednesday in bed but, despite a stack of painkillers, slept badly. I was worried about Leo, and Alistair. My eyes were swollen like waterlogged sponges and my whole body seemed to have become an Elastoplast Mummy, except my head which felt as though it'd been replaced by a much-kicked leather football. Dad over-cooked the porridge so it was like spooning through that weird shit you pebble-dash houses with. He said he'd listen to what the school said then discuss it with me before he did anything.

"Don't worry," he promised, "We'll hear your side of the story first."

Mum's expression somehow hinted otherwise. Steve Wright was playing this Madness song: *'They say stay away, don't want you home today, keep away from our door, don't come round here no more. Our dad don't wanna know he says, this is a serious matter, too late to reconsider, no one's gonna wanna know ya, Our mum says she don't wanna know you, she says I'm feeling twice as older… you're an embarrassment.'*

Every day made that twice as clearer, and there seemed no way out.

Listlessly I listened to *The World at One*, with 'the latest news headlines this Wednesday lunchtime,' then *The Archers*, with posh Nigel Pargetter getting conned by Joe Grundy - 'Oak afoooore aaaaash, we be in for a splaaaaash, aaaash afooore oak we be in for a soak…. Oo ar, oo ar.' Delia Smith showed me how to cook winter vegetables and I was just settling in with some cheese on toast and a cup of cocoa for *Camberwick Green,* where Mickey Murphy baked a cake for Doctor Mopp (Though these guys are puppets, I love it 'cos although *Camberwick Green* might claim to be just a representation of a small Sussex village with types and stereotypes, what they *really* show is that *everyone* in this sad little country is basically just another fucking puppet), when Andy Paulus phoned to tell me how awful it was at school. Leo, with him, kept interjecting tearfully. Apparently, someone had drawn a hangman's noose on Nick Shelton's locker, Paul Train had his head flushed in a toilet by some Fifth Formers, someone had poured white paint over Simon Ayres, someone had hidden a dead rat in Paulus' bag whilst 'ALI ROSE FUCKS BOYS' had been Tipp-exed on the house noticeboard and Niall Hill found a dog turd in his lunch-box. Wilson, Rix and the Christian Union had made posters saying gays spread AIDS and would burn in Hell. As for poor Leo, some Sixth Formers had stripped him, chucked his clothes in the urinal and taken photos. He said his dad had complained, as had Niall Hill's, and been told there was no bullying in school, that these stories were invented, or exaggerated, and the situation would be resolved soon.

God, it was so depressing. All this because we were homosexual. It seemed ridiculous that other people could care so much, could *hate* so much... and they said *we* were sick! Man alive, what the hell was wrong with *them*?

"I'm gonna burn every single one of them," I swore. "When I get back, I'm gonna fry the school. I'm gonna put a nuclear bomb up their arses." Tomorrow I was going to war. I was gonna like grill and eat their lungs, you know? With braised leeks and a nice Pinot Noir.

Climbing that carpeted Georgian staircase in the Lupton Building to Gallagher's office was nerve-jangling. My heart pounded like a jack-hammer, my mouth was dry as a desert and my palms damp as a dishcloth, and yet I was propelled by this really cold, deep fury.

Mum looked as though she'd been crying for a bazillion years. Her face was the colour of dead ash, black rings swelled round her puffy red eyes and the ploughed furrows scored on her skin looked like scars. Dad was more composed but his eyes spoke the deep sadness of a dog denied the gravy-jug. He'd chosen his smart black blazer. I had opted for silver Adidas trainers, white sports socks, black jeans, pale blue polo shirt and green hoodie.

Mrs Locke, trying not to cry, gave Mum this massive hug and said if they chucked me out she'd resign. Then she hugged me and restated her line. Chuck *me* out? I hadn't even considered *that* possibility.

Gasping from a sudden burst of asthma, I realised I didn't care. This fucking school and everyone in it had always been against me. I didn't fit in. I never had. It was only idealistic fools like Ash-tray, Wheezy and the Governors who bucked the trend and awarded misfits like me scholarships, and I *was* a misfit, not just because my dad was a gardener, my mother a hippy (I mean, yoga *and* aromatherapy?), my grandma a biscuit-maker, my granddad a janitor. I was a misfit because I fancied other boys.

"Peters," called the Senior Master, "Get in here, you little thug."

Gallagher, wearing a pale blue long-sleeved shirt and a dark blue tie, and Crawford, in his usual pale grey suit and dog-collar, were sitting in armchairs on either side of the fire-place. Crawford smiled sympathetically whilst Gallagher sternly indicated the hard, plastic chair facing them. I looked at his coarse, rectangular face, at the stony-blue eyes, at the wavy grey hair, and waited.

"Must say you've looked better, Jonathan," he said, noting my split, swollen lip and the grape-purple marks on my face. "How do you feel?"

"Bruised." I touched my cheek as Crawford surrendered his armchair to Mum and brought Gallagher's desk-chair for Dad. "And fucking angry, actually."

Gallagher's ice-blue eyes narrowed coldly as he explained he wanted to discuss certain complaints made against me by some boys, some masters and some parents, to establish what had happened at Games on Tuesday and to investigate the nature of my relationship with Alistair Rose, Leo Trent and other boys.

"The nature of my relationship with Alistair Rose," I snarled, "Is none of your damned business. Sir."

His face sort of twitched, like he'd sat on a cattle-prod, but he soldiered on to say he was on my side, always had been, "even when you produced that utter pig's ear of a drawing of the New Zealand coastline." My laugh made him feel he'd broken the ice. "You can come to us with anything, you know." I said nothing. "Rose is two years older than you."

I shrugged 'so what?'

Gallagher fixed me with his cold blue eyes whilst I shifted irritably in the chair.

"You busted Stewart's nose," he said, "And Wilson's face is pretty smashed up."

"So's mine," I pointed out as Mum blurted 'Tim Wilson? You attacked Tim *Wilson*?' I rolled up the leg of my jeans to display the weeping scabbed scrape his boot-studs had made on my shin and said angrily "He started it!"

But that, Gallagher claimed, was the whole problem. Tim shouldn't have been put in a position to start anything, right?

"So it's *my* fault I got beaten up?" I could scarcely believe what I was hearing. Apparently I had become a 'malign influence.' Leatherbridge had apparently said my relationship with my teachers and the rest of the form was 'troubled' and that this was badly affecting my work. Gallagher, marshalling his evidence, started with the pale green Biology prep book and this rubbish about kidneys.

"Amino acids," I'd written, "Are deamminated in the liver after some go into the circulation as protein. The excess are deaminated into glycogen which the body makes into proteins for body cells."

Herbie had written UREA? in massive red letters right across the paragraph and drawn attention with a big fuck-off circle to the inconsistent spelling of 'deaminate' or 'deamminate'. I didn't know. I didn't care. I wasn't gonna be a fucking kidney doctor, right?

Gallagher silently turned the page.

"a) If a lot of water is drunk the blood becomes too dilute. Therefore, when less water is reabsorbed in the uriniferous tubule and therefore the urine is dilute. There will be more water than urea, salts etc. …

b) Not much urine will be passed due to profuse sweating."

'Not very scientific,' was Herb's comment. He had circled 'passed' and underscored 'not much', about eight billion times.

"This disease is called diabetes. If insulin is not produced, the blood glucose concentration rises."

'Not enough facts,' underlined four times, 6 (out of 20).

"So I'm rubbish at Biology," I shrugged.

And, apparently, at Chemistry.

Here was a recent classwork exercise on writing equations for ten reactions. These were the low-lights –

'Magnesium + oxygen. $Mg (s) + O_2 (g) = Mg^{2+}O^{2-} (s)$.' Massive red cross.

'Copper (II) carbonate + dilute hydrochloric acid.

$Cu^{2+}CO_3^{2-} (s) + 2H^+ (aq) + 2Cl^- (aq) \rightarrow Cu^{2+}(aq) + 2Cl^- (aq) + HCO_3^-(g)$' Massiver red cross.

'Zinc carbonate (heating). $CO_2 (g) + Zn (s)$.' Massivest red cross imaginable.

3 ½ /10. V. poor work.'

What the hell did it all mean anyway? Who knows? Who cares?

"This is third-form stuff," said Gallagher.

"So I'm not going to be a scientist," I shrugged as a German quiz appeared in his fingers, and shrugged again when I saw my preferred England XI for the last European Championships listed on the cover and a bunch of sums in ink that meant nothing to me:

```
 ⁶28        ⁵27
  8 x        8 x
 224        216
             12
            228
```

I mean, huh? What did *that* mean?

Anyway, the test went

'1. Der Zug fährt um 10 Uhr ab. √

2. Die Stunde hat _____ . X

3. Wir haben in die Stadt gekommen. X

4. Er hat die Jacke angezogen. √

5. Die Sonne hat aufgegangen. X (ist)

6. Er Vorschlag, daß wir nach Hause gehen mußten. X

7. Er hat mich eingeladen. √
8. Ich habe aufgestanden. √'

Gallagher pushed the dark green pocketbook aside and placed my blue English book in front of me. Mum had kind of shrunk into her brown coat.

"This is your best subject," Gallagher said quietly.

'Write an account of the relationship between Farfrae and Elizabeth Jane.
'The first encounter between the two occurs in the 'Three Mariners'. Elizabeth Jane is a servant there and Farfrae is a guest. Farfrae sings to the entire pub and Elizabeth is attracted to him. Later she passes him on the stairs. He sings what appears to be a love song. Elizabeth is "rather disconcerted" but likes him. She say that she "didn't mind waiting" upon him.'

Willie had circled the non-existent –s on 'say.' God. *Now* I was embarrassed.

'Elizabeth's mother Susan wants to see Farfrae marry Elizabeth so she arranges a meeting between them by sending out a couple of anonymous letters.... Henchard is now drifting away' (wiggly line and marginal comment 'hardly drifting') from Farfrae and writes to the latter, asking him to stop seeing Elizabeth Jane. When Elizabeth discovers that Henchard hates Farfrae, she goes to warn him. This is through love.'

Yes. Love. I thought it a great gesture. Willie thought it 'too simple'.

'The relationship between Farfrae, now a widower, and Elizabeth Jane hots up towards the end of the novel' (underscore 'hots up', marginal comment 'don't'.) 'On Martin's Day Farfrae and Elizabeth Jane get married. When the wife finds Henchard's present, she begins to like him more. She asks Donald to look for him and they find him dead.'

'C,' wrote Willie. 'Disappointing. Your style comes across as naïve in places and there is no depth here. Avoid slang: add more comment.'

"I've got nice hand-writing," I said, trying to avoid the hurt disappointment in Dad's Labrador eyes. "Don't you think my hand-writing's nice?"

"We were wondering if you'd be happier in another school," said Gallagher.

No way! Despite everything, I didn't want to leave. Sure, they were picky about top-buttons and tucked-in shirts and obsessed with writing in ink not biro and not chewing gum and tying your shoe-laces and a gazillion tiny little rules, and the range of A Level options was pretty shit, like we couldn't do Theatre Studies or Drama, or Media, or Sociology, Politics, Philosophy, Psychology, History of Art, or any *cool* subjects that told you how people think, and we had to do cross-country running and swim in an ice-bath, and stand up when masters entered the room, and everyone was vaguely bored and frustrated but too apathetic to challenge anything, even their career aspirations to be doctors, lawyers and businessmen, but that, I figured was life in Britain today. A ton of petty restrictions that fuelled a real sense of grievance and dissatisfaction but no-one could be arsed to fight for change, so school truly *was* preparing us for adulthood. Besides, until this week, I had felt comfortable there, I suppose because I felt the same vague frustration as everyone else. 'The majority of men,' said Henry David Thoreau, 'Live lives of quiet desperation.' Too fucking right.

"There are plenty of kids with worse grades than me," I protested. "I'm just going through a bad patch. Mostly my grades are OK."

Gallagher sighed. The Venetian blinds in his window cast thin black bars on his face. "Tell us," he said, "About Tuesday's incident at the sports ground. Exactly what happened?"

"Nothing, sir," I said firmly. "I fell down the stairs. I hadn't had any lunch. I felt dizzy and fell down the stairs. Seymour and the others carried me up to the changing-room."

Irritably Gallagher leafed through some papers. "The statements from Mr Wade and Mr Langdon say something rather different."

"With respect, sir, they arrived late and didn't see what happened."

This was my strategy. I had decided that, despite everything they'd done to me, the spitting, the kicking, the humiliating, the name-calling, the beating, the pissing, *everything*, I wasn't going to betray them 'cos I didn't actually hate them. I pitied them. Besides, I suspected the police cuntstables would simply lock *Ali* up if I reported it to them.

"I'm not protecting anyone," I said firmly.

Gallagher emitted this impatient sigh. "Very well. So to Monday. I believe you had an incident with your form-master, Mr Hutchinson. Could you tell us about *that*?"

Here was my chance to hang Bunny out to dry. The lousy bastard had persecuted me for weeks, had started everything rolling. I could fry him if I wanted.

"I'd had a difficult few days, sir, and I was off-loading to Mr Hutchinson and I kind of broke down with the stress, you know? It won't happen again. I'm totally in control now."

Those words, carefully chosen, carefully spoken, summarized the whole situation. I *had* taken control, though they didn't yet know it.

"You told Mr Herbert that Mr Hutchinson had used abusive language."

"I was overwrought, sir," I said. "I was really upset because of everything that had happened, the graffiti, the teasing and everything, that I exaggerated. I just wanted some attention. I'm sorry, sir. I'll apologise to Mr Hutchinson."

"Mr Herbert said that *you* said Mr Hutchinson called you a quote 'filthy little queer' unquote," said Gallagher.

"Ah," I said, as though a dawn had broken, "No. He asked if I liked drinking *beer*. Mr Herbert must've misheard, sir."

Gallagher, sighing unhappily, unfolded a sheet of A3 paper. The school magazine photo of me and Ali in *Midsummer Night's Dream* stared from the centre. Around it, in large colourful letters, were the words DON'T LET THE QUEERS GIVE YOU AIDS. It was an advert for a Christian Union meeting, to discuss how to fight "the poison in our school." I heard Mum sob and Dad mutter something. Crawford's eyes never left my face.

"That's you, Jonathan," Gallagher stated flatly. "The poison in our school."

I shrugged indifferently. "I'm gay. So what? Ignorant twats like these wreck lives and poison communities, not people like me. We have our own communities, thanks very much."

"So the rumours are true?" Crawford asked. "You are homosexual?"

Defiantly I raised my chin. "Yes, sir, I am."

Mum sniffed again. I tried to ignore her.

"Which brings us to your relationship with Alistair Rose."

Now I prickled defensively. I did not want to talk about *that*. *That* was special. It was private. It was intimate. It was mine.

"We are *all* in relationships, sir," I said. "I have a relationship with you as Senior Master, a relationship with Dr Crawford, a relationship with my friends… humankind is defined by its relationships." I looked at Crawford. "You taught us that back in 2W."

Crawford smiled affectionately. Gallagher scowled irritably.

"Don't be obtuse, Jonathan. You know *exactly* what I mean."

"Ali is the best thing that ever happened to me, sir," I said simply. "I love him."

Mum stiffened. Dad stared at his hands, dangling uselessly between his knees.

"A romantic relationship is one thing, a *physical* relationship something else. I need to ask some questions you may find uncomfortable."

Not as uncomfortable as you, I thought, noting his clenched jaw and deep frown.

"Has Alistair ever made… er… advances to you?"

"Advances?"

"Put his arm round you, tried to kiss you, suggested you do things together?"

"I love it when he holds me," I murmured. "And when we kiss, I hear angels singing."

Seemingly staggering in his chair, Gallagher passed a hand over his face.

Mum interrupted suddenly, saying basically this was all bollocks and blaming Ali.

"Before your infatuation with Ross," she snapped, "You were perfectly normal. You were going out with Claire Ashton, for God's sake. He *groomed* you, Jonathan, he *abused* you. You're the *victim*. No-one will condemn you. No-one will judge you. It isn't your fault. He's a prefect. He abused his position. He should go to jail."

I stared at her, dumbstruck by the violence of her ignorance. Then I said coldly "If you send him to jail, I will kill you, OK? Kill you."

Dad's jaw fell. Mum looked like she'd been slapped. Gallagher cleared his throat.

"Has he ever touched you inappropriately? In places he shouldn't?"

"*Never*, sir," I said fiercely. "He has *never* touched me inappropriately, whatever *that* means. He *has* touched me appropriately, though, in places I *wanted* him to."

"Jonathan, this is serious. You are under the age of consent. According to the law…"

"Because I'm fifteen, I don't know my own mind?" I exclaimed. "Because I'm fifteen, I need *you* to decide who I am? Because I'm fifteen, I'm some kind of moron, open to manipulation, I can't figure out what sex involves, what love is? What if it's *me* who's the manipulator, eh? What if I know *exactly* what I want, and then go get it? What if *I* groomed Ali? Who's the abuser then, eh? What does the law say then, eh? Eh?"

"You can't *give* consent, Jonathan, not at fifteen," said Gallagher impatiently.

"Why?" I demanded. "Because *you* say so? Because the *cops* say so? Because some fuckwit politicians say so? It's my body and it's my choice. I choose to give consent."

"Has he…?" Desperately uncomfortable, he cleared his throat. "Has he… er… touched… er… touched your… your private parts?"

"With what, sir?" I said innocently. Dad was staring at me, shocked and impressed. Gallagher's face reddened like a Remembrance Day poppy.

"With his hands," he snapped. "Has he touched your… you… with his hands?"

"Oh *no*, sir," I said, beginning to enjoy myself. "He used his tongue."

Dad and Crawford laughed but Mum was crying. Gallagher seemed completely lost.

"We are simply trying to protect you, Jonathan. We simply want to keep you safe."

"By insulting my intelligence? By not respecting my freedom to choose? By telling me that my love is not important, that it doesn't matter because some tossers in Parliament want to control my life? *I* control my life." Sitting up straight, I said "I love Alistair, Ali loves me, and I just don't understand why anyone else, frankly, would care."

"Have you had… er … sexual intercourse?" asked Gallagher unhappily.

"You working down a check-list or something?" I said contemptuously.

"Have you had anal intercourse? Has he… you know…?" His voice dried up.

I shook my head. This was such shit. "It isn't about sex," I said angrily. "I don't know why you people think it is. Maybe because you can't believe two men can love each other like you love your wives… I love Ali. What's wrong with that?"

Tears were trickling down my bruised face. This was no longer fun. It was wringing me out. This was where words are not enough, when you're trying to persuade someone and they simply disbelieve you, like Mum and Gallagher, because they don't *want* to believe and nothing you say can convince them, because they've like closed their ears and closed their minds to the truth of you, you know?

"My life is what *I* want it to be, not what *you* want it to be. I will *not* let you dictate what that life should be. So I'm gay. So I'm fifteen. I don't care. I *love* Alistair. Just get over it, and if you can't get over it, get out of my fucking life and leave me alone."

As the silence reverberated around the office, Gallagher reached for a pencil and a sheet of paper. "I want you to write down *everything* you and Alistair have done," he said quietly, "And everything *you* have done with Leo Trent."

"You have got to be joking." I stared at him, cold with fury. "I'm not turning my love-life into some pornographic novel. I won't do it."

"I'm not asking, Peters," Gallagher snapped, "I'm telling you. Write the statement."

Folding my arms defiantly, I said "I will not." My eyes locked with his. "There are loads of us, not just in this school, but *everywhere*. We are everywhere, and the future belongs to us and those who love us. One day we will be free. One day we will be able to marry each other. One day we will even run the country. You can't expel us all, not you, nor the government nor MumsNet nor even the readers of the *Daily* fucking *Mail*. We are here, and here to stay. Now

I'm going to meet my boyfriend and *then* I'm going home. You can do what you will."

"Jonathan," Mum began, but I interrupted, feeling my lips quivering, my tears building again as I struggled with my emotions and my words fell like bursting hand-grenades.

"I would die for him in a heart-beat. Alistair is my world. He is my world, and my life. Everything I am is because of him. Everything I will be is for him. Without him I am nothing. With him I am everything and I can *do* anything." Tears spilled down my face again. "He is my entire existence, my Ali, and I *love* him. Love. Remember, sir? Remember, Mum? Love?"

My father put his arm round my shoulders.

"Jonathan," he said slowly, "Of all the things I've seen and heard you do in your amazing life, *this* is the best. You're my wonderful, brave, brilliant son, I love you so much and right now I know why I love you and am always so proud of you, Jonathan, my son."

I turned and, crying now, buried myself in my father's chest. I felt him stroking my hair. I don't know what Crawford and Gallagher or Mum did. All I knew was a door in the dark had just opened into the light.

26: Beautiful Ones

OVER the next few tedious, frustrating and miserable days my cuts and scrapes slowly healed. I got bored with *Pebble Mill, Fingerbobs* and seemingly endless snooker. I continued writing 'Depression.', tried my hand at a poem, listened to Wagner over and over, the Prelude to *Parsifal* where a naïve simpleton rejects the world of sex and women to stay pure and win the Grail to save a kingdom, finished *Dead Ned* and re-read Gillian Avery's *Greatest Gresham*, about three Victorian children with a fiercely strict father and how their friends next door tried to get them to 'broaden their horizons.' The initiation ceremony in the cellar [**SPOILER ALERT – if you haven't read it, blah blah blah**] which made Henry scream always made me shiver a little – ghostly, faceless monks in cowls and so forth – but I always enjoyed the chapter where Aunt B the dressmaker tells this nosy old bag to bugger off and mind her own business. I wished I had an aunt or even a parent like that. Anyway, I lived off banana smoothies, cheese on toast, *Battle of the Planets* and *Crackerjack*. Unfortunately, neither G-Force slamming Styron nor 'Double or Drop' could raise a smile, even though I knew the holy book of Islam was The Qur'an, the capital of Turkey was Istanbul and picadors were found in the sport of bull-fighting and therefore would have won a damn sight more than a cabbage. Even firing rockets at America, blasting motorbikes with missiles or splatting frogs with lorries bored me.

The weekend was horrid. The folks saw my misery. They could hardly not. Living in my blue trackies and cobalt sweater, I spent most of the time staring out of the kitchen window into the foggy garden or sitting on the swing gently kicking my trainers through neat piles of fallen leaves, wavy-edged oak leaves the colour of brass, oval beech leaves like golden toffee, wet, tar-spotted sycamore leaves, pale yellow heart-shaped lime leaves, crunchy like crisp packets and all rotting together in a heap.

Mum, skipping yoga, tried to lift me by asking me to choose some cards from the Traidcraft Christmas catalogue. I picked a set of cartoons called 'Village Christmas' which included a dog sitting in the snow outside a warm yellow and orange brick house and looking up at a ginger cat perched on a red telephone-box. I also selected a nice hand-painted wooden Noah's Ark from Sri Lanka, with blue elephants, green crocodiles, and a curiously pink, blonde Mrs Noah. We also went through the Christian Aid present catalogue deciding whether to spend my Christmas money on a goat for a Kenyan family or mosquito nets for a Bangladeshi orphanage. I wanted to give it to The Terence Higgins Trust for AIDS research, but settled for the goat. It was a nice picture, and I liked goats. Goats were cool. Anyway, Mum made some red lentil soup with this special home-baked cheese and sun-dried tomato bread while I filled in the order forms. Dad, coming in from the compost, had heartbreak all over his face.

"Jonny," he began carefully, glancing anxiously at Mum, "We've been talking and we think you should leave the grammar school. After all this trouble, you might be better somewhere else. I know it's your GCSE year and that, but... well, we can get you in at Thornbury High after Christmas. We can go look round next week if you like."

Most of the kids from Primary had gone to Thornbury. It was OK. No uniform, just these bottle-green sweatshirts, you could wear trainers and it was only a ten-minute walk away. But the buildings were falling down and they didn't do German. Or rugby. But they did cooking and had girls. Some of them went to our church. I could ask them what it was like. I knew nothing about state schools, except what I'd seen on *Grange Hill*, and that simply confirmed my parents' wisdom in taking me out of the state sector when they did.

"Whatever you think, Dad." I was just so tired I no longer cared. "I'll go to Thornbury. I can leave in June anyway, get a job."

"What job?" Mum's shoulders tensed.

"Dunno," I said. "Stacking shelves in Sainsbury's. Or work at the Halifax." I shredded bread into the lentil soup. "I might join the army." I knew *that* would set her off.

On Sunday, Mum spent the afternoon mixing the Christmas pudding to the radio broadcast of an Advent Carol Service - '*Disperse the gloomy clouds of night and death's dark shadows put to flight. Rejoice! Rejoice! Emmanuel Shall come to thee...*' The Collect for the last Sunday before Advent exhorted God to '*Stir up, we beseech thee, O Lord, the wills of thy faithful people; that they, plenteously bringing forth the fruit of good works, may of thee be plenteously rewarded; through Jesus Christ our Lord. Amen.*'

Mum exhorted *us* to stir the pudding. It was a family tradition. We each took a turn with the wooden spoon whilst making a wish. Looking at Mum's closed eyes and tense expression, I guessed she was wishing I'd wake on Christmas Day heterosexual. I guessed Dad, sloping in from the greenhouse in his wellies and overalls and hoping to sample the freshly baked sausage-rolls, was wishing for peace, at least in his home if not in the wider world. Muttering that she'd've stirred it clockwise, Mum handed the wooden spoon to me as the organist on the radio started Bach's 'Wachet auf' (Sleepers Awake).

What to wish for. In the old days, I wished that, like the Famous Five, we lived in Kirrin Cottage overlooking a sandy bay, a shining blue sea and a rocky island with a ruined castle rather than a scruffy inner-city street marred by dog-turds and chip-papers. Escapism was everything. Back then I often wished for brothers like Julian and Dick and a dog like Timmy to chase rabbits and scoff sandwiches with. *Five on Kirrin Island Again* had an oafish, ill-mannered villain called Peters, which I found quite exciting. Those days were over.

I stared into the batter, the red glacé cherries, the fat black raisins and soft brown sultanas, swollen now with brandy, and thought peace would be nice. I was fed up with fighting. It felt that was all I'd done since September. I wished people would stop being mean to me, stop insulting me, stop hitting me, stop spitting at me. That'd be good. I wished people would be nice to me again, smile at me, say hello, include me in their football teams, basically treat me like they wanted me to treat them, you know? That would also be good.

Sleepers Awake. Please.

I closed my eyes and dug the spoon deeply into the batter. "I wish," I said silently, "For my mother to love me again, not wish I was somebody else, and love me as I am." Mentally crossing my fingers for extra luck, I turned the spoon over and drifted back to *Go with Noakes* and the *Mastermind* semi-final (two teachers, an architect and a taxi-driver on Wellington, Nabokov and John Clare, and Westminster Abbey). Then it was Monday. My RNLI calendar showed Longships Lighthouse off Land's End, the most isolated structure in the UK, poking straight up from a rock little wider than its own base and accessible only by helicopter. Maybe I could be a lighthouse-keeper. It was certainly no lonelier than this.

Mrs Locke had called to say I could return to school if I wanted. I didn't. Mum did. After porridge, beetroot juice and bacon and beans, and the ceremonial opening of the first square (a yellow teddy-bear with a red bow-tie) on this year's Advent calendar, a silver glitter-daubed red-and-white Santa house, she drove me in the Sierra whilst Dad phoned Thornbury High School. Wogan welcomed December with 'Manley Barrilow' singing 'Lonely Together', '*your eyes are sad eyes, mine are too, it doesn't take too much to see what we've been through...*'

"It's a positive sign," said Mum brightly. "They asked you back. If anyone picks on you, go to Dr Crawford. Dad'll collect you at quarter-to-four." She kissed my cheek, brushed my parting back into a fringe and, struggling not to cry, wished me luck. Man, it was like my first day again, 'cept I'd gone on the bus by myself 'cos they were like working? Seemed like I'd always had to face the difficult stuff on my own.

As the Sierra vanished round the bend, I tightened the belt of my trench-coat, hoisted up my backpack and dived onto the university campus. I didn't even try to avoid the pavement cracks 'cos a broken back was the least of my worries. There was no way I was going into school. The giggling, the whispering, the insults – and that was just the teachers. Also I didn't fancy getting like kicked about again, you know? I knew it was cowardly. I knew Leo and the others were having a bad time. Fuck it. I'd done my bit. Self-preservation now.

I walked through the soft mist into the city. The black sandstone was oppressive.

Crossing the main square outside the cathedral, I passed these two massive statues, the Black Prince on a horse, sword aloft, and the squat, porky figure of Queen Victoria glaring from a throne, and wandered through these lovely Victorian shopping-arcades, potted ferns, gently splashing fountains, stained-glass ceilings, fashionable boutiques and shoe-shops then went into the Castlegate Shopping Centre, HMV, Marks and Spencer, Top Man, even the Early Learning Centre. I went to the art gallery for an hour then into Westgate Market for hot Bovril. I was cold, my feet ached, and it was only half-eleven. I hadn't realised playing truant would be so boring. Later I sat on a bench outside City Hall with a Greggs' steak-bake then went to the library to warm up and read *The Greatest Gresham*, till this nosey-parker librarian asked why I wasn't in school. I said I was doing a project. He said he'd ring and check so I cleared out, though first I went to the toilet and pissed all over the mardy bastard's floor.

I found myself drifting towards the canal. God, I was living my own story, though there was no way *I* was going to like kill myself, not for these pig-ignorant fuckwits. I watched like this thick black treacle ooze past a redbrick warehouse towards an angled weir then scrounged a ciggie from some guy who was fishing and, while I smoked it, saw a wet, bedraggled rat scurry along the pavement. I hated smoking, but I had nothing else to do. God, I was so bored. Eventually I just went home and watched the *Blue Peter* presenters make an Advent crown out of two coat-hangers, some gold tinsel, four red candles and some baubles. It looked pretty but I figured Mum would see naked flame next to flammable tinsel as a massive fire-risk. Then Mark Sonning phoned to ask me to speak in Wednesday's debating final against Firth. As I sank to the stairs, shocked, nervous, flattered, surprised, he said Mrs May had changed the motion from something on nuclear disarmament to 'This House believes that prejudice is a result of ignorance'.

"She's giving you both a chance to speak about your experiences, to confront these bigots," Sonning said. "I want you to replace Burridge. Ali will open, I will close, you speak second. You get three minutes. We are opposing."

Now I'd done a lot of acting and an awful lot of music but I'd never ever *spoken* to an audience, not as myself. I knew from the semi how many people crammed into the lecture theatre. There could, for the final, be as many as five hundred. But Sonning was right, you know? It was an opportunity to tackle the school head-on and a chance to be with Ali, perhaps for the very last time. Once I moved to Thornbury, I'd probably never see him again, especially since he'd be off to uni. Dammit, I didn't wanna go to Thornbury, but I didn't fancy my own school right now either. Then, in the night, I had the most horrible dream.

I was sitting on a wall with Bob Stewart, for God's sake, when a bunch of gimps from our school came by in full uniform. Stewart and I were sharing a cigarette. Then one of the smallest gimps stopped right in front of us and asked for a light. He was about twelve and skinny as a skeleton. His black hair was really greasy and his face so filthy you could write your name on his skin with your fingertip. His blazer was so knackered it was almost in pieces. He had no shirt, so the navy blue blazer was buttoned across a bare chest. In the V I noticed a puckered, pink burn. He was wearing grey flannel shorts and long grey woollen socks. His shoes were falling apart. His left knee was stitched with white wool stitches. They looked like maggots. I stared into the boy's eyes. They were flecked pink. He was clearly desperately unwell and extremely poor. As Stewart handed him a cigarette, I noticed, with a jolt of alarm, that the twelve year old beggar was me! Me. I cried.

Was it really how I saw myself, really, deep down, as this poor beggar-boy? Maybe I *was* better off at Thornbury. Shit. The boy in my dream had looked so poorly.

Skipping school again on Tuesday, I sat in the park, hung around the university then went to the cinema for *Flash Gordon*, Ming the Merciless and all that shit. It *was* shit, with a bland, blond Flash, dodgy special effects and an overbearing, overshouty Vultan in wings and leather hot-pants. However, I enjoyed the colour and the visualisation (all reds, golds and pastels), the gold-masked Klytus (ripped off from C3PO?) and the bit where Ming's daughter got tied to a table and whipped was surprisingly erotic. Dale Arden's immortal line, though,

'Flash, I love you, but we only have fourteen hours to save the Earth', was as good an argument for returning to school as the sleet and boredom.

Grange Hill depressed the hell out of me too. They'd been running this story-line about kids daring each other to do stuff and it culminated in this hilarious scene where Bullet Baxter followed some lads into the shopping-centre toilets and was peeping under the cubicle doors when this traffic warden comes in and Baxter goes 'It's OK, I'm just looking for some boys.' Bloody funny, thought I'd puke, though these days it'd be all over *The Scum* about paedophile teachers and all that shit, but then this boy, Anthony, walked around the parapet of a multi-storey car park, lost his footing and fell to his death. Fuck's sake. It made me cry. What if one of *my* friends died? What if Leo, or Paulus, or Gray died? What if...? No no no. *That* would kill me. I *had* to go back to school. It was where the people I loved were.

On Wednesday, when Dad dropped me at 8.15, and Mr Wogan had played ELO's 'Confusion' (ho ho Mr Wogan), I swallowed some Rescue Remedy, tightened my belt and this time stepped onto the zebra-crossing that led to the school gate. A few boys glanced at me curiously. Others actually smiled. One or two even like spoke to me? Something seemed to have changed. Collins, Arnold and Lewis welcomed me warmly. Brudenall, visibly upset, shook my hand. Gray even hugged me. I stood awkwardly in front of my locker. The word 'GAY' had been erased. Roy Walton had burned it off with a cigarette lighter.

"You may be a queer, Jonny," Collins said, "But you're *our* queer, we love you and we're gonna look after you." He, Arnold and Lewis had apparently decided the others were bastards, or sheep, and threatened to grass them up if they hurt me again.

And, quite simply, it felt so much better than nuking the bastards. Forgiveness really was the best revenge. One could be a martyr or one could be a Mandela. I had chosen to be a Mandela, and that was why I was now in control.

I noticed Stewart was missing, which disappointed me 'cos I wanted to see what his fucking fat nose looked like plastered across his stupid melon face. But then Seymour was absent too, withdrawn by his father till 'the queers' were expelled. Said he didn't want to expose his sons to the danger of molestation. Everyone, he said, knew that 'queers' couldn't keep their hands to themselves, and that they were on a mission to corrupt the world. For fuck's sake, eh? I mean, what a twat, and the man was the chair of the PTA. Brudenall said *his* parents had taken the same line until Pip had screamed that he'd never abandon his friends, like Leo and Shelters and Jonny Peters, especially when they were in trouble. Broody then said his super-cool kid-brother had confessed to having a massive crush on me.

"He begged me not to hurt him like we'd hurt you." Brudenall said awkwardly. "He was like on his knees with his hands clasped and kind of crying, for fuck's sake. He kept asking how I could hurt you for being in love and would I hurt him if *he* was in love?" He sniffed. "I don't know if Pip *is* like you, and he said *he* doesn't know yet anyway, but if he is, I'd want him to be like you. If you see what I mean." He brushed a sleeve across his face.

I did, and was flattered. That the gorgeous Pip held me as a role-model. Like, wow!

Facing Michael Crooks was more difficult. I asked why he'd told everyone.

"I don't know." He avoided my eyes. "I was really pissed off. They were all going on about you and Ali, and saying shit, and it just sort of came out. I didn't know they'd go so mental about it. I thought they'd be cool, not arseholes."

I forgave him.

Of course.

I loved him.

In Chapel, now decorated with a purple altar-cloth and a warmly winking Advent candle, I sat between Lewis and Collins, my head hunched into my shoulders, trying to ignore the whispers and sniggers. Arnold slapped some kid in the Lower Fifth. Bunny, who'd welcomed me back with this weird half-smile, lashed out a couple of detentions. Tim Wilson, face still bruised, just shook his head as we started Hymn 51, 'Lo, he comes with clouds descending, once for favoured sinners slain.' I wondered what he'd told his mother. Nothing

217

about me, I guessed. First, she'd have been round our house with the pigs like a ferret up a trouser-leg. Secondly, he would never admit to his mum that I, little weedy thicko Jon-Jon, had beaten him at *anything*, let alone in a fight.

Leatherface read Romans, chapter 13, verse 8: "*Owe no man any thing, but to love one another: for he that loveth another hath fulfilled the law. For this, Thou shalt not commit adultery, Thou shalt not kill, Thou shalt not steal, Thou shalt not bear false witness, Thou shalt not covet; and if there be any other commandment, it is briefly summed up in this saying, namely, Thou shalt love thy neighbour as thyself.*"

Wonderful sentiments, but did he believe it? Did *they* believe it? I'd heard Archbishop Tutu say God wasn't homophobic but Tim's Christian Union posters proclaiming 'Gays go to Hell' and 'Adam and Eve, not Adam and Steve' suggested the Bible-bashers thought otherwise. God made *me*, I'd tell them, and *He* made me gay.

Too jittery for dry Ryvitas, apples and carrots, and lunching instead on Rescue Remedy and my asthma inhaler, I went to meet Sonning and Ali in the prefects' common room. I hadn't seen Ali since Thursday. Sonning thoughtfully left us for a few minutes.

"I missed you, J," he murmured, stroking my hair.

"Not as much as I missed you," I said, kissing his lips. "Let's go win this cup."

As we walked downstairs hand-in hand, one or two twats did double-takes. One or two twats made stupid kissy noises. I merely flicked two fingers at them. Something had changed inside me. I'd reached a moment of destiny which I could either embrace or deny. Whatever I chose, my life would change forever 'cos I was ready now to fight the world, for him, for me and for every gay teen.

The lecture theatre was packed and very noisy, every seat taken, every window-sill and most of the steps too. I guessed about 400, so around half the school? The front benches were occupied by masters, Perry and Reid, Langdon and Western, Yates and Donovan, Jones and Goddard, Phillips, Milton, Herbert and Hutchinson. U5H was squeezed into the middle. Most of the house was clustered on the right. Sooty and Leo unfurled a banner with MURRAY painted in green across a white background and started chanting 'Mu-rray, Mu-rray'. The house tutors, Wingnut Knight, Gorton-Smith and Jacko, sat among their boys. On the left, Firth House, including Finch, Shelton, Morreson and Bainbridge sat with Wadey and Chappers. In the middle sat the neutrals, Philip Brudenall, Niall Hill, Rix, Rubenstein, Driver, Train, and, praise God, Timothy Wilson. Please, I prayed, let me touch my friend's heart today. I missed him. I missed him a lot.

Mrs May, fiddling with her glasses, was sitting at the centre of the long work-bench, long dark hair tumbling over her shoulders. To her right, Leverett, Willoughby and Shelton Major were conferring in whispers. As we took the three stools on her left, she smiled encouragingly, especially when someone yelled "Go, Ali, go!"

Perched between the two prefects, I regarded the excited, rowdy audience and felt my nervousness melt into calm self-confidence as Ashton, Gallagher and Crawford arrived, Mrs May called the house to order and invited Mr Leverett to move the motion.

Leverett was a clear, logical speaker who defined both 'prejudice' and 'ignorance' with dictionarily forensic focus then explained that people disliked what they didn't understand giving examples from history, but he was very dry and academic, and received polite applause.

"There's a famous poem," Ali began, "By Martin Niemöller, a Lutheran priest who was imprisoned by the very Nazis the honourable gentleman mentioned. It goes like this:

'*First they came for the communists, but I did not speak out because I was not a communist. Then they came for the trade unionists, but I did not speak out because I was not a trade unionist. Next they came for the Jews, but I did not speak out because I was not a Jew. Finally they came for me, and there was no-one left to speak for me.*'

"My honourable friend talked about Nazis, about their hatred for what they didn't understand but, Madam Chair, I disagree. I believe the Nazis understood everything. These people were not stupid, nor were they ignorant. They were motivated by the need for a scapegoat. They wanted someone to blame for their economic decline and they chose their minorities, the weak, the vulnerable and the isolated, and created a climate of fear, fear of the outsider, fear of the other, fear of those who are different. And what happened in Nazi Germany, where those who *were* different, the Jews, the communists, the gypsies, the homosexuals, were gassed in the concentration camps, was not a result of ignorance but of evil and cowardice. Homosexuals. Gay people. Gassed for being gay. People like me. People like Jonathan." He fixed his eyes on Mr Gallagher then on Dr Ashton. "There are people in this room who would gas the pair of us right now and all those in the audience who are like us." He looked at Leo. "Not because they are ignorant, because they aren't. They are people with degrees and doctorates. They may be *wilfully* ignorant because they choose *not* to understand. They may also be evil but I doubt it. I have always found them kind, courteous and caring. Perhaps they are afraid of us, because we are different from them, and that makes them uneasy. Maybe they can tell us. But what happened in Nazi Germany happened mainly because *good* people, *thinking* people, *kind* people like *you* stood back and did nothing. They closed their eyes, they closed their ears and they pretended it wasn't happening. They marched, they sang, they saluted their leader, they betrayed their neighbours and millions died. Prejudice there was a deliberate choice. Prejudice there was a result of cowardice. Prejudice there was because no-one stood up and said 'this is wrong.' *'When good people do nothing, evil triumphs.'* Edmund Burke. We have seen, recently, in *this* community what happens when good people do nothing. Prejudice reigns and evil triumphs. Metaphorically, the gassing started again. Metaphorically, Auschwitz was reopened. You may think I am being melodramatic, but I ask you to put yourselves in our positions, just for a minute, and consider how it *felt* to be us."

He paused. You could hear four hundred people holding their breaths, the hum of the strip-light glowing from the ceiling, the light patter of rain on the window-pane.

"Was this persecution a result of ignorance?" he asked, "Or was it simply an opportunity to even a score or two? Perhaps it was boredom. Perhaps it was all just a bit of a laugh. But did you see Jonathan laughing when you kicked his face in?"

The guilt and shame were palpable now.

"Where did your prejudice come from? Your parents? Your friends? The media? Or maybe you just followed the crowd, followed the sheep, baa baa. But you know where the sheep go. They go into the slaughterhouse to be made into chops."

Someone laughed, breaking the tension, which is what he'd wanted. Waving a sheet of newspaper cuttings, he read them aloud.

"These are genuine headlines from *The Sun, the Mail, the Express*, and others. 'Pulpit poofs can stay', 'Lesbian teacher horror', 'I'd shoot my son if he had AIDS, says vicar', 'Secret of newsboy killer's gay pal', 'Poll verdict on gay vicars: kick 'em out', 'AIDS menace: he carries killer virus yet works with sick kids', 'AIDS blood in M & S pies plot', 'AIDS kills *innocent* man', meaning the others who died weren't innocent? Innocent of what? Of being gay? So if you aren't innocent, you're guilty… what is this language the papers use? What are they trying to do? What are they trying to make people *feel*?

"The language is emotive, the stories centre on vicars and teachers, child-molesters lurking in bushes, AIDS, conspiracies, plots. This isn't news, it's scare-mongering, designed to stoke prejudice and fuel fear. They want you to believe that we're looking to corrupt you, molest your children and give you all AIDS. And when we complain, *we* are being intolerant and hysterical and getting things out of proportion. This is not ignorance. This is just hatred.

"Tackling prejudice, confronting hatred, protecting your friends rather than betraying them, standing up to your friends when they are persecuting others, takes courage. It takes a *lot* of courage but actually it's pretty easy. All you have to do is say 'this is wrong'. All you have to do is say 'stop'. *You* can close down the gas-chambers. This time could be different. I urge you to reject this motion, as I urge you to reject intolerance and hatred. Those paths lead only to destruction. Choose life. Choose love."

He sat down and, in front of four hundred boys and teachers, kissed my lips. I put my hand on his shoulder and for a moment, as I gazed into the deep pools of his eyes, the universe melted away like we'd been sucked into a timeless black-hole.

There was an absolute and profound silence then someone started clapping, and someone else and someone else, and the audience surged to its feet, roaring and stamping.

"Thank you, Mr Rose," said Mrs May, her voice oddly muffled. "Now Mr Willoughby will second the motion."

Willoughby was a nervy kid who struggled. *Anyone* would struggle to follow that. Sonning destroyed him by interrupting every few words with points of order and points of information. He never got going and slumped back into his seat, exhausted and defeated. Under the bench, Ali squeezed my hand. I was on.

"Look at my face," I said, throwing away my notes. "Look at my body." I unbuttoned my shirt. "Look at these bruises. Look at these marks. These, Madam Chair, are the results of prejudice." I could see the shocked faces as I displayed my injuries, now fading but still, after a week, visible. "This is what happens when evil triumphs. This is not ignorance. They are not ill-informed. They may not understand, but that is not ignorance. It is a choice. Prejudice, Madam Chair, is a choice. Homophobia is a choice. Racism is a choice. Sexism is a choice. Any form of discrimination is a choice. The words you use to describe me are a choice. You can call me Jonathan, or you can call me Queer. You can call me Jonny, or you can call me Faggot. You can call me JP, or you can call me Fairy. It's up to you. The choice is yours. But know this. If I were black, would you call me a nigger? If I were Jewish, would you call me a Yid? If I were a Muslim, would you call me a Pakkie? Of course you wouldn't. And yet you casually use 'gay' as an insult." I shook my head sadly. "Know that I am Jonathan Peters, I am gay and I am not ashamed of who I am, or of who I love. You accept me, or you reject me. The choice is yours. Prejudice is not a result of ignorance. You are no longer ignorant about me. So if you are still prejudiced against me, it must be for some other reason, mustn't it? I mean, look at me. I'm not exactly scary, am I?"

I was emotionally exhausted as I sat down. Everyone in that room felt the same. We had come on an incredible journey in those forty minutes. Adrian Shelton didn't have anything to say really. He just kind of looked at his younger brother and shrugged. Even as Mrs May conferred with the other two judges and declared the motion lost, handed Sonning the Debating Cup to a wild eruption of cheering from our house and awarded Ali the prize for best speaker, and Leverett, grinning like a baboon, stood to applaud us with the others, I could hardly raise a smile. Everything inside was just churning around. We'd never won the Debating Cup, not in a hundred years. Bunny smiled warmly, clapped my shoulder and said I wasn't such an airhead after all while Fred shook my hand saying "At last, Jonathan, you've impressed me." Christ. He'd *never* used my first name before. And yet these moments were bettered by one further remarkable twist when Dr Ashton called an assembly for Period 7.

"From today," he announced, "this school is adopting a zero-tolerance policy on bullying of all kinds, physical, verbal *and* emotional. Anyone abusing or harassing others, making offensive remarks or using abusive language, will be expelled immediately. This policy applies to staff as well as students and it includes homophobic bullying. A school must be a place of safety for *all* its members, straight *and* gay. No-one should come here scared, anxious or afraid. Homophobia is an unacceptable choice in a civilised community."

I laughed aloud. I felt as though a crushing weight had finally lifted from my chest.

"After close consultation between the Governors, the Parent-Teacher Association and the staff," he added, "we have agreed that, just as we welcome boys of any race or religion, so we welcome boys who are homosexual. This is a school for *everyone*."

Andrew Paulus, sitting next to me, squeezed my hand. Although I smiled, I felt sad that our society was so primitive that tolerance and acceptance had to be written into law. Anyway, afterwards, with Leatherface bawling "Boys on the Rises, stay where you are," Bush-head yelling "Peters, do your collar up," and Fosbrook, scratching the rash on his wrist, trying to shove me off the step into U5B below, everything seemed to be normal again. But when we emerged from the hall, we realised it wasn't. Things *had* changed. The rain had turned to snow. Together, Ali and I, hand in hand, watched these large, white flakes fluttering against the darkness, swirling in a crazily-spinning dance and covering our bare heads like giant dandruff. I stuck out my tongue to catch some.

"I love snow," I said. "Reminds of that Laurel and Hardy film, *Below Zero*, you know? From 1930? Where they're busking in the snow outside a deaf institute and then some old woman gives them a dollar to move down a couple of streets and then this street-sweeper chucks a snowball at them 'cos they're singing this song, 'In the Good Ole Summertime,' in a snowstorm, ha ha - '*Hold her hand and she'll hold yours and that's a very good sign...*' ha ha."

"Shush," he said, gently kissing the back of my hand. "For once, my darling, just stop. Stop talking." Through the softly falling snow, I noticed Niall Hill approaching.

"Evening, girls," Hill grinned lazily. "Mind if I join you?"

Others. There were others, from all over the school, coming out to stand with us, side by side, all out together under the canopy of Heaven and the pinpricks of early-evening stars emerging through the swirling snow. In that moment, I knew, as Doctor Who remarked at the end of *Genesis of the Daleks*, that "*from great evil great good must come.*"

The snow inscribed eerie swirls on the inky black sheet of the sky. I shoved in my Walkman earbuds, nestled into Ali's chest and let Siegfried and Brünnhilde's 'resplendent, radiant love' and 'victorious light', the 'siegendes Licht und strahlendes Leben' from the ecstatic finale of the *Götterdämmerung* prologue soar us both to heaven.

27: Chain Reaction

WE all got distinctions in our exams, me 147, Leo 143 in the flute and 140 in his piano, and Paulus 145, and the school quietly buried the whole 'unpleasant business'. My detention was quietly cancelled and a letter from the Bishop stated that the Governors, considering the 'recent developments and misunderstandings', had decided no action should be taken. Whilst there was no explicit condemnation of my sexual orientation, there was no apology either and the tone of the letter was coldly neutral. I guessed they were only on my side when I was poor.

Some boys still couldn't deal with it. Stewart, for instance, ignored me, as did Tim Wilson. Some, like Maxton, just seemed uncomfortable being near me. I joked that gayness wasn't catching but he frowned and moved away. He even withdrew from the Chamber Orchestra. I felt sad for him. Gray, who was glad I was gay 'cos it left more 'skirt' for him, said they felt deeply betrayed. This kind of spilled out at on Sunday afternoon during Martin Cooke's 16th birthday party, which was at his house, one of those typical Thirties three-bedroomed semis with bay windows that you get all over this country. There weren't many of us, just enough to trial this *Diplomacy* game he'd got from his folks. It's set at a European conference in 1901. There aren't any dice, so nothing's left to luck. Players make alliances, break them, move their fleets and armies about the map, occupying space and building spheres of influence in neutral countries. Everyone plays simultaneously, writing orders in secret, then executing them. Cookie thought I might be the Ottoman Sultan.

"Can I wear curly slippers and a massive moustache?" I asked.

"So long as you wear a silk turban," he answered.

In the event, I didn't, I wore my brown jumper, red and white check shirt, black jeans and blue-orange Reeboks, though I still played as Turkey because the plastic pieces, little bullets for armies, tiny ships for fleets, were yellow. The board, a map of Europe, was set out on a table in his dining room and surrounded by pizza slices, salty snacks and giant plastic bottles of Fanta, Pepsi and Corona.

"I don't drink sodas," I said plaintively, hoping for a beer or three, "And milk makes me spew." Instead I got tonic water. With a slice of lemon. What the hell? Sober? On a sixteenth birthday? I mean, who *were* these people?

Cooke played as Russia (purple), Huxley France (blue), Rubenstein Italy (green), Paulus Austria-Hungary (red), Fosbrook Germany (black) and Cooke's brother Gareth from the Lower Sixth was England (pink). The game began in Spring 1901 with a diplomacy phase. I took my tonic water off into a huddle with Fosbrook whilst Cooke and Paulus stitched up a deal to guard each other's borders and keep me out of the Balkans. I had to get my fleet into the Black Sea. I didn't trust Cooke for a second. Bloody Russians. So I invaded Bulgaria and Armenia and persuaded David to get Adam on side, promising them both a share of the Austrian Empire. So I set a Triple Alliance of Turkey, Germany and Italy to carve up Paulus, ha ha, despite his shabby little deal with the Russkies. In the meantime, Fozzie was reaching an agreement with England and France to guarantee Swedish neutrality along the lines of 'if the Russkies invade, we'll go to war.' Belligerent little bastard, David Fosbrook. I wrote out my orders on a scrap of paper, *F Ank→Black, A Con→Bul, A Smyrna→Arm*, folded it and tossed it into the middle of the table. I was going into Bulgaria because Paulus/Austria was going to attack Serbia. I knew that. His Italian ally told me. Unfortunately, my grand design fell apart when France attacked Italy in Piedmont and seized Belgium, England invaded Holland and Austria marched into Rumania, right on my borders, while Russia charged the Germans. I got Fosbrook back into the huddle, then took Cooke out to the kitchen to persuade him to dump Paulus, let my fleet into the Black Sea so I could trap the Austrians in Greece and join me, Adam and David in dismembering Paulus's Empire. There, crimson with embarrassment and with tears in his eyes, he blurted out the truth, that he, too, was homosexual, and terrified his parents would find out. I hugged him, then Rubenstein, who confessed an obsession with Paul Train. It was becoming insane. Boys were coming out left, right and centre. We'd already had Simon Ayres and Mike Holt from the Sixth Form, and gay-curious gimps like Shelton, Brudenall and, in the Third Form, this scatter-brained hyper kid called Gittins coming out in Chemistry.

The game was suspended while Martin cried a little with his brother, and I said to Paulus something like "so what about you, Andrew?" and he shook his head and I said Leo was head over heels and Paulus shuffled uncomfortably, then Fosbrook, scratching his neck, told us he reckoned it didn't matter so long as we were happy and we should ignore the throwbacks and Neanderthals and just get on with it. I gave him a kiss on the cheek, which made him squirm and squawk like a wounded ferret. Huxley pushed his thick-rimmed specs up his nose and smiled encouragement at his friend, before returning us gently to the unfolding disaster of Fall 1904 on the map.

The Cooke brothers sealed their new Anglo-Russian alliance by declaring war on France and seizing Holland, Belgium and Sweden respectively, then drawing Germany in from the East and Italy from the South, and Austria declared war on Turkey, with Russian support.
ENG A Lon→Hol, F Nth C A Lon→Hol, F Nth→Bel,
FRA A Spa→Mar, A Pic→Par, A Por→Spa, F Bel is destroyed.
AUS F Ionian→Aegean, A Vienna→Tyrol, A Rum→Bul, A Budapest→Rum, A Bul→Greece
ITA A Venice→Piedmont, A Trieste→Venice IT F Tyrrhenian s Austrian F Ionian→Aegean
GER A Munich→Burgundy, A Berlin→Munich
RUS A Warsaw→Silesia, A St. P→Finland, A Sevastopol→Armenia, A Mos→Ukr
TUR A Smyrna→Con, F Aegean s A Smyrna. F Aegean destroyed.

I was out the next turn, overrun by Paulus' red Austrians and Cooke's purple Russians. Rubenstein, sensing the end, also declared war and sent his green Italians in. As Cooke took Smyrna and Paulus took Ankara and Constantinople and Rubenstein eliminated my last unit, in Greece, I surrendered. Meanwhile the English and the Germans carved up France, landing armies in Brest and Picardy and leaving Huxley fighting for his life in Paris.I told them they were mean for ganging up on me.

Then Martin blew out the candles on his birthday chocolate cake, we sang 'Happy birthday to you' and I sneezed a lot, which made Fosbrook talk about how awful his eczema was sometimes, and how he felt such a freak when people called him Itchy and Scratchy, or Ferret-Face. Hux hated Elephant Ears. Paulus hated Poorly. God, we were so mean to each other. I hugged all of them, and apologised. We, I told them, had to set an example.

Back at school, Choral Society settled down, especially when I had to sit in for Mark Williams at the keyboard for the first time. Fred got me off the second half of some utterly dreary Physics lesson so we could run through the final chorus, Number 67, *'Sleep well, sleep well, and rest in God's safe-keeping,'* a gentle, peaceful 3:4 lullaby for the burial of Jesus. It was fairly easy, but he wanted me to play the voice parts as well as the four lines of accompaniment and be ready to stop and start, play single lines and give starting notes and chords. Anyway, when I sat at the Steinway and saw Ali sitting with Holt and Middleton, and Gray with Arnold and Paulus, I felt really really nervous, especially when Fred thanked me for stepping in at the last minute and the basses clapped. George Seymour, Kevin's kid brother, offered to turn the pages for me. Thankfully, the Super-Altos, being twats, tried to distract me. As I teased out the opening quaver chords of E flat-C-G then C-G-E flat, I saw Trent thumb his nose and poke out his tongue, Brudenall stick his thumbs in his ears and waggle his fingers and Shelton drag his eyes down with a finger and thumb whilst simultaneously pushing his nose up with his right forefinger. Grinning, I stuck my tongue out and played the G-D-B natural minim while Fred counted 1-2, and… 'Sleep well, sleep well.' Seymour, standing, turned the page.

"The G is not an optional extra, trebles," goes Fred, "Bach wrote it because he wants you to sing it. Altos, bars 40 and 43, your D is a minim. Count it out, and don't breathe.

Jonathan, can you play the tenor line from Bar 60, the scale up to E flat? And by the way, *piano* means quietly, basses? Not thump it out like a rugby crowd. Jonathan, play the closing chord in Bar 72, will you? You're going flat, trebles."

I grinned at Seymour, who was watching my hands like a hawk after a mouse, and mouthed 'flat as farts' which made him laugh on and off for the rest of the hour, shaking silently, cheeks puffed and purple. When I finally banged out the closing cadence of the closing chorale and the choir sang a sustained *fortissimo* 'O Jesus when I come to die, let angels bear my soul on high,' I was elated and deeply moved. The choral society applauded again and Fred nodded his approval. After, he let me play the harpsichord in his office. No-one played the harpsichord, 'cept Fred and Williams. It was *verboten* to the point of instant extermination.

"Sir," I began idly, my fingers running over the keys in this D major fugue, "You know this recital? For the Lawrence Harvey Cup?"

"First week of March," he said. "It'll be in next term's calendar."

"Do I have to do it all by myself, or can I get some of my friends involved?"

I'd had this idea to form a trio with Rubenstein and Paulus, and I wanted to play duets with them both. And Leo. Making music with others was just more fun than by yourself.

"It's your recital, Jonathan," Fred replied. "You can do what you like."

Excellent. I swigged the rest of my cold hot chocolate and belted off to English and a quiet reading lesson where I read and wrote summaries of Chapters 43 and 44 (the last-but-two-and-one) of *Casterbridge*. [**SPOILER... why bother?**] 'H becomes a hay trusser and hears that F and EJ are getting married. H goes back to see them. He buys news clothes and a caged goldfinch as a present. He goes to F's house and hears the party inside, knowing that they are finally man and wife.

'EJ comes out and sees H. He says that he hates himself. EJ says that she hates him too because he deceived her and H goes away.'

Then I sketched out my programme - I would play Mozart with Adam Rubenstein (K380 in E flat major), and Haydn with him and Andy Paulus, the Trio in G with the Gypsy Rondo finale, and Beethoven, but what? The *Appassionata* Op 57? The *Waldstein*? Or Schumann. There were so many things I wanted to play. I'd ask Mrs Lennox. She'd be delighted. Like Martin Angus, she had been on at me for ages about starting a chamber group. If we added Leo, and I could persuade Fred to let me loose on the harpsichord again, we could do some Baroque flute sonatas, Telemann or CPE Bach or someone.

Then it was all after-school rehearsals for Thursday's charity concert, which was great, except the gimps in *Captain Noah's Floating Zoo* were so excited they chattered like mental monkeys while we were waiting in the ante-room and got yelled at by that sour-faced git Williams. Leo and Shelters just shook their heads and said "Kids" so contemptuously that me and Driver, Maxton's replacement, pissed ourselves.

"When did you two turn into greybeards?" I scoffed. "You'll be daubing ash on your foreheads and going around barefoot dispensing lentils next."

Which made Brooke and Dell piss *them*selves.

"Fifth Formers!" Dell scoffed. "Driver isn't shaving and Peters' balls haven't dropped."

Paulus had a cold. I found him in a practice-room hugging his 'cello and blowing his nose miserably into a raggedy tissue. He had a navy sleeveless jumper over his white shirt.

"Haven't seen much of *you* lately," I remarked. "You avoiding me or something?"

"Don't be stupid," he said, snorting some snot back up his nose.

"Could've done with your support," I said mildly. "God knows I needed you."

"You think I wanted to go through what you went through?" He blew his nose again. "I don't know how you can breathe the same air as those bastards."

I shrugged. "Their problem, Andy, not mine, and not yours. You can't let other people's hang-ups wreck your life." His tissue disintegrated into a sodden mass. He was the picture of misery. "You know, telling just one person really does help. I told *you*, yeah?"

"There's nothing to tell." Twisting a tuning-key, he bounced the bow off the 'cello strings. "Sorry, J. Unless you got Vicks Vaporub in your clarinet case, just leave me alone."

It was time to go. White shirts, school ties, grey trousers, black shoes, neatly combed hair, the twenty boys of the chamber orchestra looked smart and felt smart as we filed into the hall behind Rubenstein to our seats. Train, second violin, looked nervous and I saw Rubenstein say something to soothe him. Leo and Shelters squeezed each other's hands. I settled into the grey plastic chair, tightening the screws of the clarinet's mouthpiece and scanning the audience for my parents away to my left, Mum in a navy blue coat, Dad in slacks, a checked shirt and a thick roll-neck sweater, probably the third outfit he'd modelled that evening. I smiled at them and at Ali, sitting in the middle with *his* Mum and Dad.

As Ben Finch clambered onto his bar-stool, we tuned to Simon Dell's oboe then waited for Wilf, resplendent in a blue velvet jacket, ruffled white shirt and flashing Santa bow-tie. All the music was arranged in playing order on the music-stand. Driver opened the Cimarosa at page 1. I'd got to like this piece but the first three *tutti* chords were so ragged they made me wince, especially as my first F was sharp and my third note, a top C, sounded like a mouse being gutted by a cat, and was a beat late anyway. The strings sounded scratchy and Shelton's grunting bassoon like a farting elephant. Lees, in front of me, missed his entry. Train fluffed a note and stopped playing for a couple of bars while he regrouped. It sounded as though we were unsure whether to play or not. We could hear Wilfo humming the tune desperately, trying to bring us together again. The rhythm faltered, then Jamie Arnold punched in on the timpani and restored some order. Unfortunately Driver, carried away, flicked the page so hard the score fell off the stand. There was no time to wait. I tried to ignore the horrified expression in Wilf's beard and made something up. Then Wilf's baton came away from its cork handle and shot across the players like an arrow. Dell, ducking sideways, collided with Keighley who collided with me as the stick struck Paulus' right thigh. Now the orchestra collapsed into a string of ragged finishes and suppressed laughter. Paulus, blowing his nose again, looked ready to cry. Finch seemed to be toppling off his stool. The audience, dismayed, seemed torn between pretending nothing was happening and roaring disapproval. Then Nicholas Shelton set down his bassoon, picked up the stick and offered it back to Wilf with a beatific smile.

"I know we're rubbish, sir," he piped, "But there's no need to kill us."

Driver grinned and pushed his gold-rimmed specs up his beaky nose. Returning the grin, I wiped my lips with the back of my hand as the tension broke and Wilf re-set us to page 1. This time we played the overture with some swagger and much *élan* (Ali's review).

The Mozart was fabulous, this dark C minor opening rising in thirds, the oboes playing C, us playing B-flat, me and Driver absolutely together despite playing different notes, my first clarinet sustaining a high B-flat in Bar 11 while he played four crotchets, then, two bars later, just the two of us over Shelton's bassoon and then just me again, with Dell's oboe and Brooke's French horn. What professional musicians said was true. The woodwind drove an orchestra. We all had to be able to play solos in a way most string players didn't. It was tremendous fun and Shelters was brilliant, perky, commanding and confident, and so hot he sizzled.

Rubenstein, Woodward and Paulus hit Corelli's Christmas Concerto superbly, balancing their solos with the rest of the strings and Williams' harpsichord very effectively. Then Driver was opening the Haydn score and Arnold was rolling that E-flat on the timpani and Shelton, Paulus and Finch, *piano* and sostenuto, were playing the *adagio* introduction, joined by the intertwined flutes. I wiped my hands down my trousers. We had three pages of rests before the tempo quickened, from 3/4 to 6/8, *allegro con spirito,* and even then it was another eight bars till our entry with the full orchestra in a blaze of clean, dancing sound. This was wonderful, life-affirming music and I loved all thirty minutes of it.

Arriving at the interval, the mince-pies, mulled wine and apology for coffee in the ante-room, I breathed excited relief. I was done now, except for the carol-singing at the end, and, after we'd cleared our music-stands, moved some chairs and set the stage for the second half, could settle back to enjoy the rest of the evening. This featured the jazz band, with Rubenstein on electric violin, Walton on drums, Toby Robinson on trombone and some sax players tackling Duke Ellington, 'It don't mean a thing if it ain't got that swing', and the Lower School choir's enthusiastic rendering of *Captain Noah*, the animals going in two by two by two by two and the Super-Altos from the Choral Society doing a trio version of 'O what a wonderful scene, the rainbow overhead...' Finally Lees, Holt, Williams and Wilfo would ring out 'Hark the Herald', 'Silent Night' and 'O Come all ye faithful' on these hand-bells. We, the players from the first half, simply had to sit on the front row of the audience, read the programme and applaud where appropriate, just as the Lower School Choir and the Jazz Band had done when we were on. At the end, as an encore, we all returned to the floor to 'Wish You a Merry Christmas'.

Lots of back-slapping, handshakes and quite a few hugs were exchanged in the ante-room afterwards. *Captain Noah* was wonderful. Who could fail to love our Super-Altos? I loved them all. The tinsel-ringed plastic buckets jangled by prefects in the doorway seemed full of notes, coins and occasional cheques and we were high and excited as we left, except for an utterly miserable Paulus, who kept wiping his nose on these soggy, sodden tissues. I'd tried, I told Ali. He must know we'd all support him and Leo was a ready-made boyfriend who adored him. Still, if he was too stubborn to come out, there wasn't much we could do. Then Claire Ashton appeared, in a knee-length black dress. Mum looked delighted, especially when Mrs Ashton invited me to tea again.

Woah. Ticket to Yikesville. I could think of nothing worse. Her father had considered expelling me and getting my boyfriend jailed for like a bazillion years. Anyway, surely she knew about me. *Everyone* knew about me. Hesitantly, I said dinner might be difficult.

"Afraid I won't be able to resist your boyish charms?" she teased gently, "Or that I'll entrap my feminine wiles?"

"Er, partly," I cavilled. "Look. Has your father said anything? About me, I mean?"

"He was cross when you puked on my Kickers," she chirped cheerfully, dark eyes dancing mischievously.

"No." I squirmed uncomfortably, cheeks burning red as Santa's hat. God Almighty, why was it so difficult to tell people the truth? I glanced desperately across the wood-panelled Refectory at Ali. "There's something about me you need to know."

"You can tell me on our sleepover," she said. "We'll eat ice cream in our PJs, braid each other's hair, try out new lippy and gossip about boys." She must've seen my expression for she suddenly giggled and said "Oh, Jonny, I'm just teasing. I always thought you might be gay. You never seemed to fancy me that much, even though you knew I had the hots for you, and when you kissed me, I could tell you didn't really *want* to, and that night, at the party, you were so unhappy and I figured it was because kissing Mikey confused you. Then on Bonfire Night you disappeared with Ali Rose for absolutely ages, and when you came back you both had this kind of glow... it *is* Rosie, isn't it?"

"Yeah," I said weakly, wanting someone to shoot me as Claire waved at Ali.

"That's fantastic," she thrilled. "I just *knew* you were gay. Does my dad know?"

"Yeah."

"God," she said, "Wait till I tell Becky. She said you weren't, though she said you were weird, which you *are*. Weird *and* gay. It's fantastic! Now you *must* come to dinner and tell me all about the luscious Alistair. Is he a good kisser? I bet he is. You're a *great* kisser, Jonny. He's so lucky. Wait till I tell Becky. *And* Mary. She said you were gay ages ago."

I couldn't help grinning. Hanging out with the girls, even Becky and Mary, might be good for me. It would provide a different perspective. Besides, I *wanted* to see Claire now she knew who I really was. I thought we could become proper friends.

"Sorry, Claire," I said. "You'll find someone else, someone straight, I mean."

Turned out she was already seeing Mark Gray. Everyone knew except me. For some reason, I felt a strong pang of jealousy. Then I noticed this stunning blonde girl lay her hand on Paulus' arm, and Paulus, Poorly Paulus, kissed her cheek. I almost dropped my cup.

"Who's that girl?" I hissed.

"Jessica Marsden. She's in my house. She's really nice. Plays the flute, writes poetry, in the hockey team..." Claire's impish eyes twinkled. "She's Andy's girlfriend." Now I *did* drop my cup. "Surprised you didn't know."

Fucking hell. My best mate was shagging my ex and Poorly Paulus had a girlfriend. What'd happened while I'd been away? The world no longer made sense. And then Wheezy, a mischievous glint in his pale blue eyes, asked me to read at the School Carol Service on Sunday 14th. Me *and* Alistair. He spent his whole life fighting Fascism, he wheezed, and this was another opportunity to make a stand. Bloody hell.

I returned to Episode 9 of my serial and some really cute boys in cricket whites in the nets. One of them was even called Trent, ha ha. But the bloody headmaster with the Kitchener moustache had spotted 'a number of older boys consorting with younger boys' or something. I mean, WHAT? He apparently 'regarded them with disquiet and intended to put a stop to them.' He even wrote a letter asking for housemasters to 'furnish him' with a list of boys they thought were 'indulging in unhealthy friendships.' Lolling back on the two-seater sofa in my purple PJs and yellow dressing gown, I barked a humourless laugh and glanced at my folks. Man, this was set in 1918 or something, and this mortar-boarded arse is leading a witch-hunt against queers. It felt *VERY* contemporary to me. I mean, hasn't Britain moved on since World War One? It's nearly a hundred years ago, for God's sake, and *we're* still fighting *our* war.

Anyway, I lost my Saturday lie-in and wank to our annual Christmas shopping trip. This meant battling into the grotty semi-darkness in Regatta parka, school scarf, black woolly gloves and my red and blue ski-hat instead of cosying up in bed for *CD Review* on Britten's seasonal *Ceremony of Carols*. The weather'd turned bitterly cold and it was a dingy, sleet-splashed day where the windscreen-wipers never ceased, the streets were grimy, slippery and miserable, somehow worsened by the council's tawdry coloured lights, and the wind was sickeningly icy. I shivered as I tossed a 50p piece into a busker's yellow bucket, applauded the Salvation Army's 'Silent Night' and dodged through overcoated beardies selling *Socialist Worker* outside W. H. Smith's into the Castlegate Centre.

I'd emptied every coin and note out of Mr Pink Piggy Piggy-Bank 'cos I wanted to buy Alistair Bach's B Minor Mass and, from H & M, a charcoal-grey cashmere scarf, the softest thing I'd ever stroked, softer even than our late cat. I also needed his card. There was this one with an angel that I really liked, yeah? Since he was my angel, I bought it. (Stop vomiting! I'm 15 and like super-romantic?) I got this really nice lilac ski-hat for Leo, the usual chocolates and aftershave for my grandparents, uncle and aunt, and CDs for my folks, Johnny Mathis for Mum, The Shadows for Dad.

Whilst Mum disappeared into this perfume store, Dad and I ducked into Beattie's Model Shop and like drooled over this awesome railway set displayed in the window. The bright maroon-and-yellow livery of EWS, a station made from transparent plastic and lit inside with tiny yellow bulbs, neat three-bar fences, two smart green engines, little bridges of box-girders and red-brick arches, stone-pebbled cottages... they made Dentist Wilson's set look seriously tatty. Then we spotted this red radio-controlled Ferrari, a fab *Scalextric* set, scale models of the Starship *Enterprise*, the *Scharnhorst* and HMS *Victory* and a new Tamiya set of World War Two German Alpine troops. There were loads of wargames, including *War in the East*, the Sino-Soviet War and SPI's award-winning American Civil War game, *Terrible Swift Sword*. I quite fancied playing Gettysburg as the Confederates and changing history, though Rubenstein said it took longer to play the game than to fight the actual battle. *Strategy and Tactics* magazine apparently dubbed it *Terrible Slow Sword*.

"Say," Dad began, "Why don't we build something together? You're always making models and we always wanted a railway. It'd be a good project." He gestured at this large cardboard box with a bright picture of the West Highland line on it.

"Where would we put it?" I said. "My room's full of stuff already."

"Spare room," he said. "We can build anything you like. If you don't want trains, we can do Scalextric or a battle diorama, whatever you like. Let's get some catalogues."

"Can I have that wargame?" I indicated the brown-grey Gettysburg box with a man charging out of the picture waving a massive Confederate flag.

"American Civil War? You'll start talking like East Clintwood again."

I grinned. "There are two kinds of people in the world, my friend, those who get prezzies and those who pay. You pay."

Dad, grunting "Don't I know it," shoved Hornby and Tamiya catalogues into a yellow plastic bag. "I suppose Alistair thinks you're smart."

My stomach somersaulted. This was a first. "Of course he does. He thinks I'm awesome." I grinned again. "Always said the boy was a genius."

Dad grunted again, this time amused. "Does he like your models? The aeroplanes and stuff? Does he make models himself?"

"No," I said, exchanging the £5 pocket money I'd earned by washing the car for this Tamiya Military Miniature 1/35 tent with Afrika Korps radio operator sitting on a petrol can for a Desert War diorama I'd just decided to make. "Not yet anyway. This is cool. I can do a desert scene with those Afrika Korps I got for my birthday."

"Maybe he could help us," said Dad hesitantly, "Make it a project for all three of us."

That was a really kind thought.

"Dad," I said suddenly. "Why did you stop playing the guitar?"

He stared past me at the tiny tins of Humbrol paint. "I realised I'd never be any good."

"But you *were* good," I said. "You *are* good."

"I'm not." He ushered me into the sleet. "I'm no good at anything really. Not like you."

"I remember you playing Paul Simon and singing folk songs and all sorts."

"It was just a bit of fun," he said defensively. "I never did it seriously."

"But what about the evening classes you used to go to? Why did you stop?" He'd been to car-maintenance, plumbing, wine-making, Beginners' Italian, water-colour painting, church architecture, Basic Book-Keeping, I mean, loads of stuff, and had generally dropped out after two or three weeks. He hadn't finished *any* of them. Because he wasn't any good.

It all tumbled out, there on a bench by a Christmas tree in the Castlegate Centre, how his ambitions had been thwarted, his dreams frustrated, first by his parents, then by his brother, then by my mother, finally by me. I listened, horrified, as he told me he'd wanted to be an engineer and build bridges but had been told he wasn't clever enough, not by his teachers but by his family, who wanted him out of school and into a job aged fifteen. He'd been my age when he'd been apprenticed to an electrician.

"But I liked your guitar-playing," I said. "It's what got *me* interested in music."

"Like if he can do it, so can I," said Dad.

"No, not like that," I said. "More to be *like* you, to be good at something like you."

I'd never realised before how little self-confidence my Dad possessed, how the people in his life had consistently talked him down, undermined him at every turn. He had never undermined *me*. In fact, he'd always boosted my confidence, made me believe in myself, and he was standing by me now, albeit in his own quiet, understated way.

I remembered asking him once about the 'born on the bus' story, put about by his brother, and the family joke that Mum had bought one ticket into town but two coming back. The story upset him quite a lot. He'd actually been watching the Monaco Grand Prix and following Yorkshire v Northants in the Sunday League on the telly in the pub next to the hospital. Then he'd sat in the waiting room listening to Charlie Chester's *Sunday Soapbox*, *Sing Something Simple* then *Semprini Serenade*, (God Almighty, the stuff your folks have to do!) and finally I'd arrived in the middle of 'The head that once was crowned with thorns' on *Sunday Half-Hour*, from Dumfries for Ascension Day the previous Thursday, 27th. He'd cuddled all 7 pounds 9 of me then scuttled off home for a glass of whisky, *A Hundred Best Tunes* and *Ice Station Zebra*. Curiously, *Tale of Two Cities*, the Sunday serial gripping me now, had also been the Sunday Serial the day I was born. Weird, huh? And that hymn, yeah? The one I was born in? Well, I sang it at my audition for the Choral Society. I know. Even weirder, and Yorkshire lost by 7 wickets. Anyway, the point is that Dad had always supported me in everything I did, I mean, everything. When he said he loved me and was proud of me, I believed him. I'd *always* believed him. 'Cos he'd, like, always been there, you know?

"There *is* something you're good at," I said, "Something you're the best in the world at, and that's being my father. No-one else could do the job." I hugged him affectionately.

"Not even Alistair?"

"Especially not Alistair." I hugged him again.

It got dark around 3. Mum dropped us at home and took off to a yoga party with one of her hippy friends. I stashed my prezzies in the wardrobe and settled down for *Horace and the Spiders* on the computer, a Psion game in which Horace has to "rid the Spider Mountains of the deadly octopeds which inhabit them." First he has to travel through the hills by jumping up levels of platforms and over spiders using the Q and P keys, for up and right, and Z and I for down and left, then he has to cross the Spider Bridge by swinging over on a spider thread. Finally he has to destroy the Giant Web by stamping holes in it (using Keys V, B, N or M). The spiders try to repair the web by sitting in the holes, and there Horace can jump on them and kill them. It has these mad psychedelic colours, like backdrops of violent yellow and flashing titles, and this squawky electronic soundtrack. I had a high score of 3100 and, with Mum out and my homework done, plenty of time to beat it. Of course I got cocky, and bitten, and one life left, one spider left, 1100 points – yay! Killed him! Extra life and back to Level 1. Run, jump, run, jump, leap and grab a thread, swing, swing, swing, jump, ha, back in the cave, Spideys. I'll soon stamp a few holes in your web, you eight-limbed bugs. Bollocks. Two spiders, two lives, 300 points to go and stuck... YAY! 3300, extra life, back to the sky blue start. I finally expired on level 2, against the yellow sky of the bridge with 4600 points, a new record score.

Dad lit a fire and together we watched *Final Score* with his pools coupon – Man U drew with Stoke, the Arse lost to Sunderland, Spurs beat Man City and Wolves drew with Southampton - then settled down for *Basil Brush* ('Boom boom') and the last *Doctor Who* episode in which the Doctor, quoting liberally from Shakespeare's *Henry V*, recruited this bunch of rebels to storm the Dark Tower and overthrow this regenerated vampiric 'Great One'. Turned out to be a hand in a green rubber-glove. Still, one companion, in a fabulous display of TARDISial loyalty, shrugged to the other 'You said yourself you're on their menu. No sense in *two* of us getting the chop.' Well, quite.

The Generation Game was the usual parade of sad acts shouting 'cuddly toy' but *The Two Ronnies* did this brilliant parody of *Mastermind* where 'Charlie Smithers' answered the question before, so 'what's the name of the directory that lists members of the peerage?' elicited the answer 'a study of old fossils' because 'what is palaeontology?' was the previous question. You follow? So 'what's the difference between a donkey and an ass?' was 'one's a trade union leader and the other is a member of the cabinet.' They also did this 'Space Wars' sketch which started with a light-sabre fight between Luke and Darth Vader and morphed into Ronnie Barker (RB-PO) and Ronnie Corbett (RC-TAR-C) singing songs before being exterminated by 'Duluks' paint-pots. Nursing bowls of home-made chilli con carne, we had a nice evening, even though we didn't win the Lottery again. After Palace battered Norwich 4-1 and Leeds beat Forest 1-0 on *Match of the Day*, I filled a red rubber hot-water bottle to take the chill off the sheets while I continued Hornblower's journey through a storm in the Channel to land *Hotspur*'s crew on the French coast. As I was leaving Dad to *Three Days of the Condor*, he said "I'm glad you're not going to Thornbury, son, and I'm glad you found Ali."

I stopped in the doorway. "Why doesn't Mum like him?"

"Oh, Jonny, it's complicated."

"You've accepted it."

He stared into the glowing coals. "I've accepted *you*," he said slowly. "You're fifteen. You're in love with Ali. You think you're gay. You might change, you might not, I don't know, but whatever you are and whoever you love, you're my son, nothing changes *that*. Besides, he's a nice boy. I get why you love him, and if you're gay, I'll support you, if you're straight, I will support you. You're my son. I will *always* support you."

"But Mum won't."

"Course she will. She's your Mum. It's just..." He hesitated. "She'll get used to it, I suppose. In time. Not having a wedding, or a daughter, or... grandchildren..."

My parents' plans for me, for them, had been suddenly and totally smashed. Everything they had expected from me had been turned upside down. If adjusting to the new reality had been hard for me, it'd been hard for them too, but when Mum returned from her party and I tried to tell her I understood, she just snapped she was tired and didn't want to talk about it. I just practised my reading for tomorrow afternoon and went to bed with my Walkman and book.

St Aidan's Chapel was especially atmospheric at Christmas when hazy yellow candle-flames glowed smokily from the carved pew-ends, coloured lights flickered in a large Christmas tree and Mark Williams played improvisations on Christmas carols. The Chapel was packed to its old wooden rafters. The Pauluses, the Trents, the Collins Clan, the Arnolds, the Sheltons, the Grays, including Moany Melissa, and a bunch of others I only knew by sight. I wondered if any of the people who'd beaten me up were here in church.

I waved at Ali, who was wearing his dark grey suit, school tie and black gown. Dad also raised a tentative hand, mainly, I think, to Mr and Mrs Rose. Mum kind of sniffed. Claire Ashton, sitting with her mother and brother, flashed me a smile. Mum noticed, waved, nudged me, said what a nice girl she was etc. etc. while I read the Order of Service. I was the 'Member of the Upper School' doing the Fifth Reading, and Ali was the 'School Prefect' following.

The service began with Paul Train singing 'Once in Royal David's City' from the door, then the choir, resplendent in blue cassocks and snow-white surplices, processed through the Nave. I had never really noticed Train before. He was short, had a snubby nose and curly mud-coloured hair. To be honest, I wasn't really sure what either Rubenstein or Fred saw in him. He must have had a tongue like an electric-eel or something. Though Paulus, in the tenor section, looked so sensational my knees wobbled a little, and Leo Trent looked like an angel.

"*O God,*" wheezed Wally, "*Who makest us glad with the yearly remembrance of the birth of thine only Son Jesus Christ; grant that as we joyfully receive him for our Redeemer, so we may with sure confidence behold him when he shall come to be our Judge, who liveth and reigneth with thee and the Holy Ghost, one God, world without end. Amen.*"

Eddie Collins, the 'Chorister', squeaked his way through the Fall of Man (Genesis chapter 3), from the highest step, and even then you could only just see the top of his head. One of the tenors dropped his hymnal with an echoing thud during the reading by the new Chair of the PTA, Mr Seymour having resigned, which provoked an angry glare from Dr Ashton and a lot of giggling in the choir. I was a little nervous when it came to my turn but I had practised it twice in front of my bedroom mirror. As I walked slowly up the Nave between the parallel lines of flickering candles towards the massive eagle-winged lectern, trying to avoid the cracks between the slabs 'cos I definitely didn't want to break my back there in the chapel, I felt every eye on me, saw the choir nudging each other, heard the whispers, 'is that him? Is he the one? *He's* the queer, is he?' and some mutters of disapproval – how could he have the nerve to be in a *church*? I mean, did these people have no shame or sense of propriety? I had polished my shoes to a crow-black shine, ironed my shirt and trousers, put on clean socks, washed and brushed my hair, tied and re-tied my school tie (for a school occasion) so I looked as smart as a soldier on parade. Dammit, I'd even fastened the top button. As I took my place behind the lectern and found the right page in the massive green *New English Bible*, I unconsciously touched the sheaf-and-crown school crest over my heart, glanced at Wheezy, then Bunny, then fixed my eyes on Alistair's deep teal pools.

"*The people who walked in darkness have seen a great light. Light has dawned upon them, dwellers in a land as dark as death. Thou hast increased their joy and given them great gladness... for a boy has been born for us, a son given for us, to bear the symbol of dominion on his shoulder; and he shall be called Wonderful Counsellor, Prince of Peace.*"

Prince of Peace.

I returned to my seat for that little town of Bethlehem and waited with proud excitement for him to replace me at the lectern to recount the story of Jesus' birth and the angels' visitation to the shepherds. The muttering returned - 'that's the boyfriend, I think. He's a *prefect*? What does Ashton think he's playing at? God, he's so much older...do you suppose they're doing it?' Eyes bored into my back once again. 'Their poor parents must be going through hell.'

"*Now in this same district,*" read Ali, "*There were shepherds abiding in the fields, keeping watch through the night over their flock, when suddenly there stood before them an angel of the Lord, and the glory of the Lord shone round about them and they were sore afraid, but the angel said unto them 'Fear not, for I have good news for you and for all people. Today in the city of David a boy has been born to you, the saviour who is Christ, the Lord'.*" Then I was getting the usual thrilling tingle from "*Hark the Herald Angels Sing, Glory to the new-born King, Peace on Earth, and Mercy Mild, God and Sinners Reconciled.*"

Christmas was coming. Yay! But it wasn't a reconciliation with God that worried me. That had been achieved by Jesus. No. As I scurried home to watch two explorers fighthing prehistoric half-humans in a giant cavern *At the Earth's Core*, the Mastermind semi-final from Stirling with questions on Napoleon's Russian campaign and the life of Richard III and Eddie Shoestring working with a psychiatrist to resore someone's memory, it was Mum that worried me. She seemed more remote than ever.

Whilst Mrs Paulus had blithered on about how well I'd read, and how strong I'd become, and Mr Trent had patted my shoulder and praised my leadership, thanking me for coming out, making a stand, challenging biogotry and changing the rules, Mum had stared at the wood panelled walls and the portraits of long-dead headmasters, no doubt wondering if Dr Flogger would have been able to thrash the demon out of me.

When Leo and Andy both hugged me, Mum's lips kind of twisted like she was being force-fed a nitric acid/dog-shit cocktail. She didn't even look at Alistair, and when Dad actually congratulated my boyfriend on his reading, I thought she was gonna puke. This was gonna be a challenging Christmas.

28: Everybody's Free

SNOW, to me, was romantic, cleansing and purifying. It made the familiar different, concealed and disguised the world, obliterated everything. There's a certain silence that comes with a heavy snowfall. The normal noise of the world is muffled as Nature, suspended, holds its breath in expectation of something new. By 6.45 that morning, when my alarm went off, the back lawn was buried under three feet of the stuff. Local radio was churning out lists of cancellations, closures and transport issues on a 'Snow Special', along with updates from the Met Office, the AA, the City Council and the bus companies, but there was no mention of *my* school. We *never* cancelled. After porridge, beetroot juice and beans on toast, I emptied my hot-water bottle and opened the fifteenth window on the Advent calendar for a yellow toy trumpet.

"Come on, son." Dad tossed me my parka. "We'd better dig the car out."

Wrapping myself in my gold and navy school scarf, I put on my gloves and wellies and plunged into the weather armed with a spade and moaning bitterly 'cos I hadn't doubled my socks. Anyway, 15 minutes later we were skidding and sliding away to Terry Wogan's seasonal selection '*Simply having a wonderful Christmas time.*'

As I said, I liked the snow. I fantasized I was Captain Peters VC, Antarctic explorer, nearing the depot which housed food, warmth and the vital supplies that'd fortify me for Base-Camp where Lieutenant Rose was waiting in a howling blizzard for relief (ha ha). Since the huskies and sledge had vanished through the ice into a crevasse, I'd carried all the equipment and charts on my back with the precious scientific surveys for Professor Trent and the Royal Society contained in a special case in my gloved hand. When the glare of sun on snow blinded me, I wished I'd taken Dr Paulus' goggles before he'd valiantly sacrificed himself in the swirling snowfall saying he might be some time. *Sinfonia Antarctica* swelled in my mind as a couple of penguins dodged into a bus-shelter and I reported into my Walkman that, on Stardate 80151.2, the Rigellan fever had worsened, the Ryetalyn antidote was in my briefcase but the Borg were on my tail. I needed immediate beam-up but the snow was interfering with the transporter. I might have to fight my way past the penguins.

The blanket covered everything, flattened everything, a never-ending, unbroken plain studded every so often by semi-igloos. Things looked desperate for our hero as he struggled on, gasping for breath, frostbite nipping his fingers, cold worming into his bones, staggering forward, on his last legs... he scooped up a handful of clean, cleansing purity and felt it burst on his tongue, broke off an icicle, better than any ice cream... we all scream for ice cream...

"Have a good day, darling," said Dad over *Slade's* shrieked '*so here it is, merry Christmas, everybody's having fun...*' Ho bloody ho bloody ho. The Sierra's rear wheel span as Dad slewed away through melting orange grit.

Just five of us made it in, me, Arnold, Burridge, Collins and Fosbrook. Even those who lived within easy strolling distance like Stewart and Morreson had opted to stay in bed, which was particularly galling for Collins, who lived in the depths of the country in the Arse-Cheek of Buttwipe and had had to leave at six in a Land Rover. "Well," he said, "My folks don't want us lot hanging around the farm all day. Alfie'll wrap his presents, get covered in glue and stick his arse *to* his elbow and Eddie'll tease the chickens..."

Knocking the snow off my wellies and taking my shoes from a Sainsbury's bag, I foolishly asked how one teased chickens and was given an impression, slightly hilarious, actually, of young Eddie Collins stalking round a hen-house making fox noises.

"Blimey, JP," said Arnold, "Why didn't you bring your snow-shoes as well?"

Action Man had snowshoes. They were like bloody great tennis rackets. Not cool.

'Don't mock, mate," I muttered darkly, "Do you know how deep it is where I live? You might just wish you had more than those fancy tasselled pumps by this afternoon."

Could've been worse, mind. Collins had these green Hunter wellies with buckles, which were cool enough, but Fosbrook, the loser, had these bloody great red and silver Moon Boots from the Stardust range, ha ha. They had red drawstrings round the top and a picture of an astronaut on the side. Ha ha. One small step for Man, I told him, one giant leap for Ferret-Kind.

The bell rang for Registration. Bunny didn't appear. Hurrah. No Maths. Instead we played table-football with coins, Collins, Arnold and Burridge played poker, Fosbrook read a profile of the incoming new Doctor in *Doctor Who Magazine* and I finished two pieces for the school magazine, my story 'Depression' and the report for the Wargames Society. I also got this fabulous pencil-drawing off Niall Hill which showed a melting Rubik's Cube. I loved it. The upper face resembled churned-up battlefield-mud, some of which dripped down the other two visible faces. He said he'd melted one with a blowtorch and copied the effect. Seemed the best thing to do with the bloody things.

'Depression', I'd decided, would finish optimistically. I had left my protagonist staring despondently into the gloomy waters of the treacly canal. Now I flitted a bright yellow bird before his eyes, '*one that had appeared from nowhere. It perched on the stonework near him, watching him suspiciously. It made a remarkable contrast with the darkness and misery. Just then, the clouds parted and the rays of the sun streamed down.*' It needed a last line.

Sucking the end of my Waterman, I moved onto the Wargames report and scribbled '*Firstly I should thank the cleaners for their patience, trying to do their job without overturning Martian battle-fleets or Hitler's Russian campaign. I should also like to thank our President Mr Bleakley for the use of his room. This is the perfect club for finding out who one's friends really are. Is the quiet, polite Mr X opposite really as he seems or is there a megalomaniacal Caesar lurking beneath that cool façade? Is Mr Z next to you a second Napoleon who will stab you in the back without another thought? And, as in all things, are you good enough and ruthless enough to win? Do the ends justify the means? In Wargames Club, they do!*'

I shoved the top back on my pen and retrieved *Mr Corbett's Ghost* from my backpack. In this Leon Garfield story, a teenage apprentice murders his apothecary master by having a mysterious man tie a black ribbon round something the target has touched, in this case a jar. **[SPOILER ALERT – why bother? You haven't read it anyway]**. The man had, in his house, like a gazillion pigeon-holes containing personal items, a fan, a comb, a hat, all wrapped round with black ribbons, and all representing someone who cursed to die.

"Bloody hell," said Fosbrook, "Imagine if you could *really* do that. Who would *you* do in? Bob Stewart? Or Herbidacious."

"Herbie's all right," I said.

"Herbie's a cunt," Fosbrook responded sourly. And indeed, when we arrived at his lab to find him absent, our rejoicings were cut short by Oggie Ogden handing out a bunch of questions. Although we groaned and said it was the last week of term and pointed out there were only five of us and the other fifteen lazy sods were skiving off and why were we being punished, Oggie told us to stop moaning and get it done. "Told you," said Fosbrook.

'a) More glucose is taken in as food and the glucose concentration therefore rises. To compensate for this adrenaline production is cut down and insulin production is raised. The insulin causes the blood glucose concentration to return to the normal level.' (Herb wrote 'how? Give reasons!' after this, underlining the opening phrase and scrawling 'in what form?'

'The concentration of blood glucose goes down when a person fasts. Adrenaline increases the respiratory rate and causes glucose to be taken in in respiration. It also converts liver glycogen to glucose. Therefore [blood glucose] rises. Adrenaline leads to raised blood glucose for increased body activity. Also thyroxine is secreted converting more glycogen to glucose.' ('Wrong end of the stick!' wrote Herbie.)

"Got a black ribbon?" scowled Fosbrook. "I'd cheerfully tie one round his neck."

Herbi-fucking-dacious indeed.

In History Hellfire actually attempted to teach us, which was foolish since U6L, his tutor-group, Ali's tutor-group, had already marked the festive season with paper-chains, balloons, streamers and 'Merry Xmas' sprayed on the windows with this vile-looking fake snow. At last, I managed to get into Ali's seat near the blue-painted radiator which, as usual in winter, was off. Freezing to death was, apparently, character-building.

"Where *is* Catarro anyway?" Hellfire was scouring a map. "Montenegro, maybe?"

"Where's that?" called Collins.

"Near Serbia." Hellfire clicked his tongue. "I thought you did Geography, Andrew."

"We did Russia, not the Balkans," Collins rejoined.

"That's why you wrote in your exam that Georgia was in South-East USA," said Burridge. "I mean, have you ever heard of an American town called Tbilisi?"

"Always thought Geography was a load of old Balkans anyway," said Collins.

"Aha!" Hellfire's painstaking search had finally paid off. "Found it. Catarro."

"Sir, do you suppose they speak Flemish there?" I said.

Before Hellfire could respond, Arnold cut in saying it was a sickening joke.

Hellfire shook his head in mock-despair and chucked some papers at us.

"You guys are so funny you should be gagged. Here, have a worksheet."

Fosbrook groaned. "Not another one."

"You've only had five on the Balkan Question," said Hellfire.

"I fear a 'so far' lurking behind that statement," said Collins. "How many to come?"

"Wait and see," said Hellfire. "A few, if you must know."

"Like twenty?" said Fosbrook, "So not too many this time."

"Three, actually," said Hellfire haughtily.

"What happened?" said Arnold. "Did your hand seize up or something?"

"Let's have 'sir' tagged on the end, if you don't mind, Mr Arnold," said Hellfire.

"Blimey." Fosbrook was squinting at the faint print. "I can hardly read this. When did you photocopy these, sir? 1935?"

"Nothing wrong with the 1930s, David," Hellfire countered cheerily. "Trams, trolley-buses, early days of cinema, the emergence of jazz and swing, wireless radio…"

"You forget the other attractions, sir," I said, "All the other things that cheered people up, recession, depression, mass unemployment, Hitler, Stalin… great days, the Thirties."

Hellfire grinned. "You should get out more, Jonny. Pipe down and do the questions."

Despite the snow, or possibly because of it, we elected to play our usual break-time football on the field, the five of us plus Vesey, Coleman and Lloyd from U5B and Austen from U5S. It was absolutely mental. The snow was about a foot deep and, having changed back into wellies, I had no ball-control whatsoever but I was better off than Arnold. Not only his shoes but his trousers too were soon soaked through. The ball, accumulating inches of snow, became so heavy it hardly shifted, except to smack Fozzie in the face. Laughing, I settled my scarf round my neck and inside the V of my grey sweater and straightened my Thinsulate gloves. I'd chucked my parka down as a goal-post so just had my blazer, lapels turned up. The cold nipped my nose and my breath clouded in the air. Struggling upfield, I tried to cross over Austen for Collins, who was showered in snow. The ball plopped a yard in front of me.

"Bloody hell, Peters!" he grumbled. "Call that a cross?"

Coleman swung at the ball and fell on his arse then, with a drunken-sounding bellow of '*I put my finger in the woodpecker's hole and the woodpecker said 'Gawd bless my soul…*' by Swinging Dick and the Rudeboys, the staff arrived, in tracksuits, scarves, gloves and proper footie boots, though when I say 'staff', I mean Hellfire, Cedric, Don Donovan, Bush-head, Oggie and Frank. A crowd was gathering on the sidelines. Well, Collins' brothers and some Sixth Formers, including Leverett and a smirking Alistair Rose.

"Fozzie, Fozzie, give us a game, Fozzie, give us a game!" chanted Frank.

"Collie, Collie, give us a game, Collie, give us a game!" roared Hellfire.

"Jenny, Jenny, give us a game, Jenny, give us a game!" bellowed Bush-head, much to the others' amusement.

"Don't call me Jenny!" I barked angrily.

"Oooh," cried a chorus of staff and class-mates, "Shut that door." But it was warm.

Ali kissed my frozen cheek and said "Learn when you're loved, love." So, in Frank's phrase, the Super Staff played the Feeble Fifth whilst my boyfriend wrote notes for a review.

The staff were predictably vicious, sliding tackles, barging off the ball and shoving snow down the backs of our necks. Finally someone, and I was never sure who, got so fed up a snowball caught Frank squarely on the shoulder. Frank's eyes gleamed joyfully and before we knew it we were engaged in this full-on snowball fight involving everyone, and I mean everyone, about sixty men and boys. I laughed as Frank was battered so much he looked like a walking snowman. Then Cedric got me like right in the side of my head, you know? Don and Bush-head yelled congratulations, even though they were fending off full-frontal assaults by Fosbrook, Austen and Burridge whilst Arnold and Lloyd were targeting the prefects and Collins was pelting Oggie. I flung a snowball at Don, got him in the chest, uttered a whoop of delight then suddenly screamed as Hellfire rubbed a handful of snow in my face and shoved some down my collar. Shrieking, laughing and yelling for him to get off 'cos he was cheating, I collapsed in the snow. Then Cedric grabbed my ankles.

"Jenny Peters for the snow-drift, did you say, Mr Langdon?"

"Certainly did, Mr Yates," Hellfire confirmed, seizing my wrists. Together they lifted me bodily from the ground and carried me across the field towards the cricket pavilion and this four-foot deep snow-bank.

"Crikey, Mr Yates," said Hellfire, "It's like carrying a feather."

"He'll hardly make a dent in the snow-drift, Mr Langdon," said Cedric.

"May even bounce off. We'll have to chuck him extra-hard," said Hellfire.

"Noooo!" I shrieked, struggling and laughing like a hysterical hyena.

Now everyone stopped. Frank and Oggie started chanting 'Snow-drift, snow-drift' and pursued us in procession with my class-mates, the prefects and a load of gimps.

"ALI!" I shrieked. "HELP ME!"

"One," went Cedric, swinging me backwards.

"SIR! Mr Gallagher! SIR!"

"Two," went Hellfire, swaying me forwards.

I wriggled again, screaming "Ali! ALI!"

"Three!" cried Ali.

Arms and legs flailing, I flew through the air to a loud cheer and flumped into the snow. Cedric, grin plastered over his face, helped me up. I looked like I'd been dipped in a vat of icing-sugar. Ali and Hellfire, whooping like kids, were hurling snowballs at each other. Oh God, I loved him. Following my gaze, Cedric gently brushed snow from my hair.

"You and Alistair," he said, "I knew it would happen one day. Ever since *Oliver*, there was like this… sizzle between you?"

"I know. I felt it. But I never thought we'd be together." I sighed. "He's so amazing."

Cedric smiled. "You're *both* amazing, Jonathan. *Stay* with him, yeah? You fought demons, monsters and the world for him. You fought your friends, your folks and yourself. And he's worth it, yeah? So you keep him. For those of us who love you." He waved at Hellfire, Bush-head and Frank, Collins, Fosbrook and Arnold. "For us, yes? For all of us?"

Then we were off, closed at lunchtime with buses at one, and clapping 'cos we'd be home in time for *Bagpuss*. The driver somehow managed to move off up the hill without stalling, slipping or crashing his gears, and won a burst of applause from the lads downstairs.

The bus ploughed steadily through the grey slush that had replaced the virgin-white snow, slipping several times on the ungritted road and wheezing like an asthmatic old woman carrying four insanely heavy Carlton Shoppers up Pen-y-Ghent. Cars crawled up the inside as the bus paused, gears grinding, engine whirring as the driver tried to get it moving. Then Ali appeared behind me. I threw my head back.

"You look funny upside-down," I grinned, dragging his school scarf off him.

"*You* look cute." He plonked himself next to me. "Can't wait for tomorrow. What *are* you doing?" he added impatiently as I tied a knot in his scarf.

"A forget-me-knot," I said, hitting him with it.

"You're feisty today, Supermite," he said, "Let's see how you are when you're wrapped up in this," and he tugged my fur-trimmed hood over my face.

I laughed and wriggled, kicking and flailing his scarf in the air as he pinned me to the seat and started tickling me. When he finally let me up for air, I scampered away yelling at him to come get me then I smacked some gimp with the scarf and lobbed it down the stairs. Eyes shining, he stomped off to retrieve it. While he was gone, I hid his bag under a seat and stared out of the window, arms folded, innocently whistling. Slapping my arm, he scrambled on the floor to recover it before wrapping me in my hood again. Then, as the bus lurched forward again, he gave me like this gentle squeeze and said "This is going to be the best Christmas ever." I lost myself in him once again. Breathing on the glass, I wrote **I LOVE YOU** with my finger. He enclosed it in a heart.

The last half-day of term was always exciting. We got our reports, played games, exchanged exchange cards and chilled out. Those who'd been in yesterday teased the others for skiving while we decorated our classroom like U6L and U5B, with tinsel, streamers and cotton-wool spelling Happy Christmas glued to the windows. *We* admired our handiwork, even if Bunny was less impressed. He told us to strip it all down.

"Oh, sir," we groaned, "Sir, Christmas, sir, Christmas," until he relented.

I didn't get as many cards as usual. Maxton, Stewart and obviously Wilson had cut me from their lists but Gray, Paulus, Fosbrook and Collins stumped up. I was also pleased to get cards from Cooke, Hill and Pip Brudenall and one, rather touchingly, from Mark Sonning wishing me every happiness. Nick Shelton sent one with a robin on the front and the message *'You really helped me'* whilst Leo's was predictably pink and glittery. *'To my very own superhero,'* it read, *'Roses are red, violets are blue, faces like yours belong in the zoo! With love and thanks.'* It was signed *'your loving lion, xxxx.'* It brought a tear to my eye. I hadn't written anything like that, just *'Happy Christmas, Love Jonathan x.'*

"Crikey, J," said Paulus, "For such a romantic, you're a cold-blooded bastard."

"So are you," I retorted. "Who's Jessica? Like Jessica Rabbit, right?" His face took on this stupid dreamy expression. "Oh man! You're in love! Poorly's in love! Fuck me!"

Apparently she was amazing. Her eyes were amazing. Her laugh was amazing. Paulus, the gayest kid in Christendom, had a girlfriend. I listened politely as he banged on about her then interrupted with questions, like how long had it been going on?

"Halloween?" I shouted, battering Paulus round the head with his Christmas card. "Why didn't you tell me?"

"Because," he said haughtily, "Unlike you, Jonathan, my love-life isn't a soap opera. Besides, I didn't want you gayboys sobbing your hearts out. I know how much you fancy me…"

Yelling and laughing, I chased him up the stairs two at a time then down the passage to Jacko's room and a wild, rambunctious house-meeting full of whooping and stamping.

"You guys made history this term," said Jacko, "Mark, Mark, Jonny and Ali, our fabulous debating team, the brilliant cast of our play, Stuart, Harry, Bill, Sooty, Jason," Each name got a cheer, "Andy, and, *oo la la,* our very own, wonderful Leo the Lion."

The cheer for him split my ears, especially when the Sixth Formers chorused in unison "Bananas… with thick, thick custard!"

"And Jonathan Peters," Jacko indicated me, "Actor, speaker and yet again, winner of the individual music competition in two classes. You had your own troubles to contend with but you came through them and we're very proud of you."

Zero to hero. Thunderous applause and stamping, except from Stewart and one or two others. Sonning stuck his fingers in his mouth and emitted a piercing whistle which Warburton echoed. This time it seemed affectionate. Even Bobby Rose was grinning.

Leo and Sooty were presented with their green and blue house-ties and we cheered some more, shaking hands and smacking shoulders. Earning your tie in Murray was notoriously difficult, unlike Rowntree and Leeman, which seemed to chuck them around like confetti at a wedding. We joked they got theirs for just showing up on Tuesdays.

"Best day ever!" crowed Leo, proudly tying his. I gathered him in and kissed his mouth then handed him to Ali who did the same. Sooty got a handshake and a hug.

Back in the classroom, I played bridge with Cooke, Paulus and Huxley whilst Bunny talked us individually through our reports. Partnering Paulus, I'd bid us into three spades, holding in my hand the ace, king, jack, eight, seven, four and three, with the aces of clubs and hearts and a singleton diamond. I'd thought of no-trumps but it felt too risky, you know? Whatever, I needed to keep the lead.

Huxley, pushing his glasses up his nose, laid a nine of clubs on the table. Paulus set out his thirteen cards and my spirits rose considerably. He had five diamonds which I could cross-rough with so I pulled his three of clubs, watched Cooke toss down a two and took the trick with my ten. I played my lone diamond, the ten. Huxley, tabling the Queen, won the trick. 1-1. I frowned, reviewed my options as Huxley led the ace of diamonds. To trump or not to trump, that was the question. Then Cooke was called up about his report.

"You gonna watch *The Merchant of Venice* tonight?" asked Paulus. "I'll think of you."

"Me? Why?"

" '*The quality of mercy is not strained, it droppeth as the gentle rain from heaven upon the place beneath*'," quoted Huxley. "Honestly, Jonny, you're *such* a barbarian."

I was actually planning to watch *The Goodies and the Bean-stalk* on BBC1, you know? Where this goose looses a bouncing bomb/golden egg at the Goodies while they're shinnin down the beanstalk and the giant is a dwarf in a massive boot shouting 'fee-fi-fo-fum' through a mega-megaphone. Man, insane! Much funnier than old Shakey an' all. Anyway, ' Huxley said I could watch both. *The Goodies* started at 7.25 and finished at 8.10, when the Shakespeare started. I scowled he was a walking *Radio Times*.

"You forgive very easily," said Paulus. "They beat the crap out of you yet you send them Christmas cards and lie to protect them and I *know* it's not because you're scared of them. It's something else. It's as though nothing ever happened. No-one talks about it, about what they did to you. Brushed under the carpet, brushed out of history. It's a fucking disgrace, Jonathan, a fucking disgrace." His lips were quivering with sudden rage. "They said they were your friends, yet they cut you and burned you, they made you drink piss, they really hurt you…" He glared at Maxton, Stewart, Seymour, Brudenall, "And you let them go."

"Every day they see me," I said carefully, "They'll remember what they did. Every time I smile and say hello, they'll remember how they tortured me. Every day I'm still here will remind them of the savage within."

Huxley grunted. "Blimey, Jonathan, when did you become such a greybeard? You'll be wearing flowers in your caftan and beading your hair next."

"I can't be bothered, Adrian," I said. "Anger and hatred, they're exhausting. Some people choose to be bigots. That's up to them." I smiled at Paulus, rested my hand on his. "And even though you basically dumped me for Jessica Rabbit, I still love you very much."

Huxley asked me to pass him a sick-bag as Cooke returned with a stack of As, Bs and glowing comments. I said he was a swot. He replied that I was a *clot*. I wondered why I'd never been friends with these guys before. They were really nice, you know? So if I'd lost friends like Maxton and Wilson, I'd gained friends like Cooke and Huxley. It was weird.

Fortunately, the break had broken Cooke's concentration and he led out the queen of clubs. Restraining a whoop, I won it with the ace, seized the lead and played out all the spades in my hand, all the diamonds in the dummy, declaring with two over-tricks, sixty points over the line, and ninety under, and reducing our deficit to ten.

Then Bunny was calling me and I was laying my cards face-down on the table, scraping back my chair, wondering if he'd look me in the eye. Despite everything, I'd chipped in a quid for his bottle of whisky and even signed his Christmas card with my trademark JP signature, the two stems merged into one, and a smiley face in the loop of the P.

Our reports came in these blue plastic-covered, hard-backed books. They covered our entire school careers. Mine was a little dog-eared now, the legend *PETERS, Jonathan David* and my date of birth, 30 May, under the crown-and-corn crest and *'invenire et intelligite'*, my current age, 15.7, on the open page.

The positives were English: *'He has considerable ability and works keenly but sometimes fails to prepare his ideas in sufficient depth. His essays need to be fuller,'* History: *'He continues to produce impressive work and should do very well in the summer'* (cheers, Hellfire), and French: *'His approach this term has been most encouraging and he is a careful, conscientious worker.'* That'll do, Benj.

The negatives were Physics: *'He is still floundering. He finds the work difficult and must make a greater effort to get to grips with it,'* Chemistry: *'His work is not good enough and he is still not trying. He must make an effort to learn the subject-matter'* (tell it how it isn't, you Barney-faced pillock) and Biology, *'Very disappointing work all term. He seems to be satisfied always with the minimum,'* (thanks a bunch, Herb).

German was ambivalent - *'He has ability in the subject but his work is rather erratic, at times of good quality, at other times surprisingly careless and some pieces recently have been most disappointing.'* Wingnut said I was quiet in class. Vicarage had written *'A good term's work.'* Perry, the fat-faced twat, had just written *'satisfactory'* but Maths was interesting: *'I think he tries hard but his results are sometimes poor. He seems to be coping better, but needs to ask for help when he doesn't understand.'*

"By which," said Bunny, "I mean ask *me*, not Maxton."

"I'm embarrassed when I don't understand and everyone else does," I admitted, "I feel so stupid."

"You *are* stupid," said Bunny, "Because you sit there pretending to understand when *everyone* knows you haven't got a clue what's going on. What's happened to your German?"

"I had some stuff on my mind, sir," I said drily, noticing no-one'd commented on *that*. Jacko merely stated I'd taken part in the individual music competition, the play, the debating and swimming, and noted that I *'continued to support the Choral Society, the Chamber Orchestra and the Wargames Society,'* all of which I kind of knew already? The Headmaster had simply written *'I don't suppose he will ever find Sciences easy; but as long as he continues to try we can have no real complaints about his attitude.'* See? No mention.

"Not gonna do Sciences, sir," I said smugly. "I'm gonna be a writer."

Bunny sighed. "Come on, Jonathan. Get your feet on the ground, eh? Head out of the clouds, back down to earth, you know? Yes, you're a talented musician but this school's a very small pond. You may find that, out in the big ocean, you're just another minnow. Get your GCSEs, solid A-Levels, good degree... focus that butterfly brain of yours." He slapped the blue book shut. "The way you dealt with the events of the last few weeks... well, if you approach your exams with the same determination, you'll be fine. Happy Christmas."

Final Assembly. 'O Come All Ye Faithful' was bellowed enthusiastically by nine hundred people, more rugby song than Christmas carol. Redmond read the opening lines of John's Gospel in his usual monotonous tree-like drone: *'In the beginning was the Word and the Word was with God and the Word was God. All that came to be was alive with his life and that light was the life of men. The light shines in the darkness and the darkness has never mastered it.'* That Light was Love and it radiated all around me, especially when the Headmaster, in his black gown and a scarlet hood, reviewing the Michaelmas term, awarded trophies to the winners of the inter-house squash cup, the City Cup for rugby, won by the First XV for the fourth year in succession, a magnificent shield to a guy called Linfield who'd won the county Under-19 squash title and the Montgomery Inter-House Debating Cup to Sonning and the Dunlop Drama Cup to Alistair. I swelled to bursting-point. I loved these guys. I loved *all* these guys. Paulus, on my left, nudged me and grinned.

The Chaplain read the Prayer of St Teresa of Avila: *'Let nothing disturb you, Let nothing frighten you. All things pass away; God never changes. Patience obtains all things. The one*

238

who has God lacks nothing. God alone will suffice.' I thought he'd picked it for me.

We launched into a boisterous 'Hark the Herald Angels, Sing,' and my eyes prickled with emotion. School would resume on Wednesday January 7th and I couldn't wait. This truly *was* my home. These people *were* my family, whatever our past, and I was so happy to be staying, even if Leo, in this lurid pink and orange ski-jacket and silver Moon Boots (was this another trend I'd missed out on?), and Shelton, in a black Superdry windcheater and snow-caked black Kickers, bawled 'Ant Music' for the half-hour duration of the bus journey.

Don't tread on an ant he's done nothing to you,
There might come a day when he's treading on you,
Don't tread on an ant you'll end up black and blue,
You cut off his head, Legs come looking for you,
Ant Ant Ant Ant music...

Next, 'Good King Wenceslas', 'I'm a wanker' by Ivor Biggun and The Red-Nosed Burglars, 'We wish you a Merry Christmas', and Ivor Biggun's version of 'Down by the Riverside':

My massive dump made a great big clump, down by the riverside,
It drifted with the tide, "Ahoy!" a sailor cried,
"Would that be shite or the Isle of Wight I see on my port side?"

Bobby draped his arm round my neck and asked if I was coming sledging with him and Ali. "My brother loves you very much, and I love my brother very much, so I guess I should love you too." Then, answering my expression, "We talk, Jonny, we talk all the time. You are his world and I know now you'll never hurt him." He seemed quite emotional. "After all, you bled for him, you died for him, and you saved him."

"That's because I love him," I said simply, and told Bobby of the Cotswold cottage and Amadeus our marmalade cat, and said he could come any time. "You see? I wanna be with him all the time, forever, till the day I die."

Guess what? Bobby hugged me. What did Huey Lewis sing about the power of love?

The park resounded with the raucous cries of excited children. The steep slope that connected the Lake View pub to the lake itself, now half-covered with a thick sheet of black ice, was packed with sledges. Ali pulled Santa hats from his pocket and passed one to me with a "Merry Christmas, sweetheart" and one to Bobby then we charged up and down the slope, yelling and whooping, me on this clunky wooden red thing my Dad had kind of nail-gunned together and the Rose boys on this sleek, state-of-the-art, superlight silver-black aluminium job that would've been perfect for the Winter Olympics. Man, it was so flashy, you know? I was pleased I had something honest. Steaming breath, red cheeks, tingling fingers, sunlight glaring off the endless white wasteland, this is what everyone loves about winter.

When we finished sledging, we chucked a few snowballs about then headed back to my house to make a massive snowman in the front garden using coal for eyes, nose and buttons, sticks for arms and a curved line of bright scarlet rowanberries for a mouth. Standing back, we warbled *"We're walking in the air, floating in the moonlit sky, I'm finding I can fly so high above with you."*

"That's how I feel," I told Ali, hugging him round the waist, "When I'm with you."

Bobby, smiling, said we should get a room and that he was off home. I said he didn't have to. He said he did. He needed to pack for the school ski-ing trip, a week in Austria with Jennings and Leatherface. I mean, no-one deserves that. Even worser, Leverett was going, as captain of the ski team, along with the Seymour Brothers and Matt Robbins, who went every year. Sorry but no amount of *glühwein* would be enough. Besides, this Christmas me and Ali were making a magazine.

"You can feed my hamster while I'm away," Bobby told me, "Give you an excuse to come round." He jerked his head at his brother. "He still hasn't told Mum and Dad about you."

Ali shuffled unhappily and muttered something at Bobby's back. I didn't know how to feel, angry, upset, anxious, relieved? Whatever he thought best, I guess. His parents, I knew, had totally freaked out about him being gay as it was. They'd sat up all night screaming at each other and crying and when his Dad asked if he was seeing anyone, Ali said no. Then his Mum had confronted him over a rumour that he was seeing *me*, and if it was true, she would tell the police I had seduced him. In fact, he only said he was gay to be like me, 'cos for some reason I had bewitched him. I mean. No-one seduced anyone, you know? We kind of fell in love? What's so wrong with that?

The front door opened and Dad, framed in light from the hallway, was peering uncertainly into the murky gloom where Ali and I were kissing.

"Oh," I said stupidly, "I didn't know you were home."

"Not much gardening I can do in this," he replied drily. "I've come home to sort out the ice on the pond. It's frozen right over. How was school?"

"All right," I said. "*We* could do the pond, lob a couple of bricks at it, you know?"

"The shock-waves would kill the fish," said Dad. "You need to melt it slowly. I'm going to use a blowtorch. Hello Alistair. Happy Christmas. Nice hats. How are your reports?"

"All right," I said again, conscious I was still wrapped in Ali's arms.

A momentary pause, then Dad said "Do you want some hot chocolate? There's some banana-bread in the tin. Maybe stay for tea, Alistair? I'm gonna do my famous beef goulash. The secret is loads of paprika and a marbling swirl of sour cream. Melts in the mouth."

I squeezed Ali's hand. "You'll love it. It's the best dinner ever." I smiled winningly at my father. "Can we have marshmallows in the chocolate?"

Dad smiled. "You can have *anything*, my prince. And so can *you*, Alistair, my prince's prince. It's Christmas."

So we stepped into the warmth of the hall and he closed the door behind us.

29: Forever and Always

CHRISTMAS Eve is the most exciting day on the (Advent) calendar - a stableful of animals and a mangerful of hay peer through the double-window marked 24. Full of anticipation, the smells of last-minute baking in the kitchen suffuse the whole house, the now-appropriate Christmas music blares from every radio station, blinking tree-lights reflect enticingly in silver baubles. It's a magical time when all things are possible.

Mum, seemingly glued inside her Christmas apron, had spent the week seemingly working through *Delia's Christmas*, steaming the pudding, stuffing the turkey, smothering chocolate over a Yule-log and baking like a billion mince-pies, sausage-rolls and cheese-straws. Dad was confined to the music-room to wrap presents and finish the cards ("and write more than 'Best wishes, Roy, Beth and Jonathan' this year," said Mum. "Like what?" said Dad. "Honestly," said Mum, "Men! It's like having two bloody kids in the house.") Meanwhile I, once I'd finished blending this gorgeous celery and blue cheese soup from page 87 of Delia and glazing the ham with orange marmalade and English mustard (page 126 of Delia) and peeling like the entire Irish potato crop, was directed to decorating the tree.

"What's the point?" I said lethargically. "We'll only have to take them down again."

It was the same every year, nagging to get the tree u

p then complaining about pine needles in the carpet, arguing about the paganism of holly and mistletoe and 'putting the Christ back into Christmas', moaning it started too early but always rushing to be ready.

Ah, Christmas. I loved it.

Wearing the Santa hat to get me in the mood, I helped Dad drag a six-foot pine tree down the icy hill from the greengrocer on the parade then fetched several dusty cardboard boxes down from the loft.

"*Dub-a-dub-a-dum dum, dub-a-dub-a-dum.*" I draped silver tinsel round the picture-frames and placed the snowhouse I'd made in primary three, a shoe-box covered in cotton-wool, in the centre of the mantelpiece. "*Dub-a-dum-dum-dub-a-dum dub-a-dub-a-dum...*"

Jonah Lewie. My new favourite song.

The tree, obviously, was too short and too bushy. Mum would've got something another foot taller and with less foliage. Dad pointed out this seven-foot giant wouldn't fit in the living-room. Mum would've sawn a foot off the bottom.

"So what's the bloody point...?" Dad began, then gave up and shoved it in a plastic bucket which I'd covered in red crêpe-paper, for that 'seasonal look.'

"I have had to fight almost every night, down throughout these centuries.
That is when I say, oh yes yet again, Can you stop the cavalry?
Dub-a-dub-a-dub-a-dum-dum..."

Sticking this gold star on the top, I stood back to assess my work. No minimalist single-coloured job with just white or just blue or even just two colours for me. No chance. I went for a multi-coloured rainbow riot of orange, red, yellow and blue lanterns, gold, silver and red baubles, green tinsel – man, I wanted the tree to *scream* variety. Ha. Now it really *was* like Blackpool Illuminations, Dad! Mistletoe went up over the front door, the holly wreath on the outside, then I started on my bedroom, stringing fairy-lights round the window and tinsel from my bookshelves and the wind-chimes as another favourite song came on:

So, this is Christmas, and what have you done?
Another year over and a new one just begun,
A very merry Christmas, and a happy New Year,
Let's hope it's a good one, without any fear.

I even made Pickles, New Bear and Ozzie little wreaths of silver tinsel and placed them ceremoniously on their heads, like Olympic athletes back in the day, or The Coronation of

Napoleon Blownapart in that famous painting. Like there was no need for them to miss out on the Xmas Atmos just 'cos they were stuffed. I mean, so was the turkey, ha ha.

What to write in Ali's card? I'd wrapped all the presents in shiny red-gold paper and deposited them under the tree *and* written cards for the folks and the Grunters – the usual bald seasonal greeting ('Merry Xmas and Happy New Year, Love Jonathan') – but what to write for my darling Alistair? 'To my angel' no longer seemed adequate, you know? He'd become so much more. He'd become my entire life. Laughing, I thought of writing a joke card, like Laurel and Hardy's in *The Fixer-Upper*:

> *Jingle Bells, Jingle Bells, Coming Through the Rye,*
> *I Wish You a Merry Christmas, Even as You and I.*

Maybe not. As John and Yoko sang that 'war is over, if you want it,' I decided to write him a letter. I set Ozzie on the shelf and poured my feelings through that silver Waterman onto two sides of pale blue Basildon Bond before the song reached

> *And so this is Christmas, for weak and for strong,*
> *For rich and the poor ones, the world is so wrong...*

I told him how he'd changed my life, how much I loved him, how much he meant to me, how I couldn't live without him, how mere words seemed so inadequate. I punctuated it with endearments and drew love-hearts round the margins. I wrote how it felt when I was with him (walking in the air). I wrote how it felt when he touched me (like stars colliding). I wrote how it felt when he kissed me (like the universe melting away). I wrote how it felt when he told me he loved me (the most precious creature on earth) and I wrote how it felt when we had sex (like time and space were suspended). It was like the most passionate thing I'd ever committed to paper, you know?

Dad called me down to the kitchen where he'd sculpted the white icing on the Christmas cake into something resembling Antarctica, with drifts, dunes and glaciers, and now wanted advice on populating this snowscape. My suggestion that German mountain troops fight a battle with British commandoes was met with a frosty (ho ho) refusal so instead, I selected this miniature Santa, minuscule sleigh and mini skating penguins and arranged them neatly round a tiny igloo and red plastic 'Merry Xmas'. We studded the cake with silver balls then rewarded ourselves with a glass of sherry each and a warm mince-pie from the cooling-rack. Somewhere on Radio 4 'Nine Lessons and Carols' was starting. Now Christmas was *really* here. Bagging another mince-pie, I scampered back upstairs to finish the letter and froze in the doorway. Mum sat, sagging, on the edge of my bed, letter in hand, a confusion of shock, anger and affection swirling across her face.

"MUM!" Screaming in fury, I tore it away. "That's *sooo* private! You can't read that!"

She didn't move and I didn't know what else to say so I flumped angrily into my desk-chair, folding the letter, wanting to destroy it 'cos everything in it, so personal, so intimate and for his eyes only was now exposed to someone else.

"It's the most beautiful thing I've ever read," she murmured. "*Sooo* romantic. You really love him, don't you?"

"Yes," I muttered, swinging in the chair. "I really love him."

"When did it start?" she asked in this surprisingly soft voice.

"In the summer," I said. "I fell in love with him then but we didn't get together till Bonfire Night. That's when we kissed for the first time. Oh, Mum, it feels so right, being with him, you know? If you could only see, if you could only give him a chance, you'd like him, you'd see why I love him, and you'd see how much he loves me. We even exchanged leaves, like wedding rings?" I showed her the evergreen in my drawer. "I want him, Mum, forever and always. Like you and Dad."

She squeezed my hand. Somewhere in the background, far far away, a congregation was listening to St Matthew's story of God coming to Earth as a baby boy. She said nothing for a while, just gazed at Pickles. Eventually she sighed and said "We love you so much, you know. We just want you to be happy."

Seeming to choke momentarily, she kissed my forehead and left me alone. I stared at Ozzie's googly eyes and orange felt beak and wondered if another Christmas miracle was coming. I finished the letter then, high on pure joy, cycled round to stick it through Ali's door singing *'God rest ye merry, gentlemen, let nothing you dismay... o tidings of comfort and joy'* at the top of my voice.

After a delicious dinner of roast salmon with green pesto, sautéed potatoes, green salad, a dill-and-cucumber yogurt dressing and half a Sainsbury's white wine-box, we slumped in front of the telly. It was woefully bad. The *Radio Times* had a nice bright cover - three children, two girls and a boy in the middle were looking out of a window which had blue curtains. They were wearing brightly coloured red and yellow sweaters and were clutching some toys, a teddy, a yellow camel, a robot, and there was a brown dog with a yellow bow round his neck in the foreground. It looked very jolly. Unfortunately, *Val Doonican's Christmas Special* followed by *Big Jake*, a John Wayne film, and *Placido Domingo's Christmas Choice* didn't do it for me. I lobbied hard for Ian Dury and the Blockheads on *The Old Grey Whistle Test*. I fancied a bit of 'Rhythm Stick', as it were. But I lost. So thank you Lord for *The Turn of the Screw*, that creepy ghost story of adult Quint haunting schoolboy Miles and the Governess, über-hysterical symbol of socially moral propriety, destroying the boy whilst trying to 'save' him from himself.

As Mum passed round the Turkish delight, I was reminded of *The Lion, The Witch and The Wardrobe*, where Edmund eats The White Witch's sweets and falls under her spell to such a degree he betrays his brother and sisters. Edmund was my favourite character in the Narnia books, I guess because he seemed more complex than his siblings, and also 'cos he was redeemed, brought over from the Dark Side, as it were, but also 'cos I couldn't help thinking what if Aslan actually *were* the villain, as the White Witch claimed? I loved all the Narnia books, especially the weird underworld of *The Silver Chair*, but I'd spent the last few weeks being told *I* was evil, treated as some kind of wicked witch, and I wasn't. I was just living in an alien environment defined by others. Like Edmund.

Once, long ago, I thought my love of reading came from a desire to learn, or escape from my loneliness, and it was all of those. I *was* lonely and I *did* want to escape from the world I was imprisoned in, but my reading was really, deep down, an endless, as yet unfulfilled quest to find a story like mine, a character like me, a world I might belong to, a book I could relate to...

It's why I wrote this one.

'Cos no-one else did.

At eleven, we left for church. Mum changed into this long grey cardigan and lighter pink shirt, a pink woolly hat and grey gloves and I put on my brown cords and rust-brown jumper. Dad, even though he was told he could wear what he liked and take whatever route he wanted, decided to stay by the fire with Midnight Eucharist from Carlisle Cathedral, *Die Hard* and a large Scotch. I *begged* to stay with him but Mum muttered something about not falling into his heathen ways so I slunk to the Sierra and clambered into the passenger seat. Bloody Rix and Wilson would be there. My heart hit the floor-mat.

Midnight Eucharist brought its usual influx of new faces and drunkards turfed out of pubs. Perhaps they all developed a sense of guilt at Christmas or were praying in advance for forgiveness for the excesses to come. Unlikely, I thought, as they slurred the first hymn. They'd come for a jolly good knees-up. Twice in their lives they'd go to church, first in a pram and then in a hearse. Did they care about the Christmas message of peace, forgiveness and reconciliation or were they too busy gorging themselves and selling their organs to buy their kids the latest toy to cast on the Boxing Day garbage-heap with the tinsel, turkey-bones and tree? And what about the starving kids in the developing world? What about them? I'd once told Mum to stick the sprouts in an envelope and post them to Africa if she felt so strongly about it. Wrong answer. I'd spent Boxing Day scrubbing pans in the church soup-kitchen.

"Happy Christmas, Elizabeth," Mrs Wilson said. "How did Jonathan do with his grades in the end? I remember they weren't so good at half-term. Timothy did ever so well again, ten

A stars. We may as well choose his Cambridge college now. And what about you, Jon-Jon? What are you planning to do?"

Tim glared at me balefully. A strip of plaster was still stuck over the bridge of his nose and I thought I could discern a fading bruise on his left cheekbone. Holly, wrapped in a colourful scarf and matching woolly bobble-hat, clung to his arm, blinking somewhat nervously through her massive owl-like specs. Had he told her what I'd done?

"I can do anything I like," I shrugged. "Tim may have brilliant grades in frankly useless subjects but I play two musical instruments and I sing. I win competitions. I act in plays. I win debating cups. I edit and write stories for magazines. I can do anything I like."

"Oh," said Mrs Wilson spitefully, "We know all about *your* achievements, don't we, *Jenny*? *Everyone* knows about Jailbait Jenny's adventures behind the cricket pavilion. To think you came for *sleepovers*. I'll have to burn the bedding, you perverted little sodomite."

Mum, drawing herself up to her full five-foot six, said in this steady, steely voice "How dare you speak to my son like that, you jumped-up no-one from nowhere who married the dentist after he knocked her up. Oh, no-one else would have you, would they? So you set out to trap yourself a wealthy husband..."

"At least my husband can hold down a job," replied Mrs Wilson. "*Yours* has hopped from one lame occupation to another."

The hope of a cat-fight cheered me up mightily.

"At least *my* husband isn't a hen-pecked wimp," said Mum.

"At least *I* haven't bred a *queer*."

A deafening silence boomed loudly round the vaulted ceiling. Looking Mrs Wilson straight in the eye, Mum laid her hand on my shoulder.

"That he may be," she said firmly, "But my son, my lovely *gay* son, has more courage, honour, integrity and beauty than all you hypocrites bundled together. Come on, darling. Let's go home."

As we reached the car and I was like dragging my jaw off the pavement, I blurted that Mum so *fucking* awesome, you know? She slapped my shoulder and told me to stop swearing. I didn't like care, you know? I just felt excited, proud and happy.

When I was in bed, reading *A Christmas Carol* under the comforting chuckle of the wind-chimes, at the part where the Ghost of Christmas Present throws Scrooge's 'are there no prisons?' remark back in his face, Mum, in pale yellow pyjamas, came to say goodnight. I asked her what'd changed.

"Do you know how precious you are to us?" She stroked my hair gently. "How much we *wanted* you, me and your father? We were married three years before I got pregnant. It took three years for me to *get* pregnant. We had tests and all sorts, Jonny, and it happened really when we'd given up and started thinking about adopting. It was like you were some miracle. It's why we called you Jonathan. It means Gift from God, and David is 'blessed' and you were, you are our blessed gift from God." Sighing, she picked up New Bear. "I hated being pregnant, Jonny, hated it. I was sick all the time, my ankles were swollen like balloons, I had constipation for days then diarrhoea for a week, I needed the toilet every ten minutes... once, in Castlegate, I didn't get there in time and wet myself, in the street! Being pregnant was the worst nine months of my life, apart from actually giving birth. Six hours of sheer bloody agony, stuck on my back with my feet in the air with people peering and poking me. They shaved me, gave me an enema and left me to shit in a bucket. Then they slit me open with scissors so your shoulders could come out. Jonny, I've never EVER felt such pain as when I was giving birth to *you*. But we loved you so much. When you got asthma, you were so tiny. We sat by your bedside in the hospital. You were in an oxygen tent for five days, Jonny. We thought we were going to lose you." Her eyes filled with tears. I was holding my breath. "That's how I felt about this, that we were going to lose you, that we *had* lost you, that Alistair had somehow, well, stolen you from us. You were always such a boyish boy, with your models and wargames and sport. You even play the piano like a boy, Mrs Lennox says. He changed you from the boy we thought we knew into something else, something we didn't understand, and we were scared, *I* was scared – your dad, he dealt with it – because we didn't know you any more. Your dad said *you* were scared, and when you got hurt at school..." Her eyes seemed very bright. "Oh, Jon-Jon, they beat you up, didn't they?" I just nodded. "And the school did nothing." I shook my head. "I found your vest. It was..." Mum gathered strength.

"When that Wilson woman said those awful things to you," she said, "I realised how terrible those weeks must've been for you and how *we* must've hurt you too. When you needed us most, we left you. Like the school, we did nothing, and we swore, when you were small and in that oxygen tent, that we would never leave you, never. We'd fight everything with you, like you fought the asthma." She was crying. "But I didn't. I fought against you and I'm so sorry."

"Mum." She *had* to know. She had to know I'd been injured and so very frightened. She had to know how *she'd* made me hate myself, made me hurt myself, because she feared my love for Alistair so much. She *had* to know. Didn't she?

"I love you, Mum. Happy Christmas."

We cried a little then she replaced the gold crucifix round my neck. At peace, at last, I turned off the light and listened to the wind-chimes gurgling happily above my head.

When I was little, the wait for Christmas Day was quite unbearable. I'd figured out there was no Santa when I was eight. I mean, the whole thing was so implausible, right? A fat old man squeezing down a narrow chimney with a sackful of stuff and flying through the air from Norway on a sleigh pulled by reindeer was bad enough but visiting every house in the world in one short night was utterly ludicrous. There were also the three million tons of mince-pies and one-and-a-half million gallons of sherry he had to scoff. No wonder he only worked once a year! Yet those were the Action Man Years, and they were exciting. Now I was excited for a different reason. I had Love in my life. I had Alistair Rose.

Waking at ten to the wonderful smell of frying bacon and the joyful sound of Bach's 'Jauchzet frohlocket', I hugged Pickles happy Christmas, kissed New Bear, chucked on the pale yellow T-shirt with my dark blue shorts, my yellow dressing-gown and the Santa hat and joined the family for a merry Christmas breakfast of bacon, eggs and porridge. Then we sat in the living-room with fresh coffee and warm mince-pies and exchanged presents to BBC1's backdrop of carols from romantic, medieval Warwick Castle.

Dad seemed pleased with The Shadows and Old Spice, Mum with Mathis and Milk Tray, while I got the red Converse high-tops, a Gillette razor - "so you don't keep borrowing mine," said Dad - Christopher Hogwood's ground-breaking period-instrument *Messiah*, an Airfix Mosquito bomber to paint and build and Susan Cooper's five-book sequence *The Dark is Rising*, which pitted three ordinary kids called Simon, Jane and Barney into a struggle between Light and Dark, the Old Ones like Merlin and the boy Will Stanton against Great Lords like The Black Rider, with a backdrop of Celtic mythology and Arthurian legend and King Arthur's son. I'd been wanting to read it for ages. I also had the annual satsuma and a Terry's chocolate-orange. My grandparents gave me this super-cool red Alfa Romeo 4C in a box, a lifeboats calendar from the RNLI and this really cool black-and-grey Adidas hoodie. Uncle Gordon and Aunty Linda had sent a Cadbury's selection-box and a £5 gift-voucher. Leo gave me a stuffed pink lion and Andy Paulus John Lennon's *Double Fantasy*. He'd marked Track 7, 'Beautiful Boy,' and quoted it in his card –

Before you go to sleep say a little prayer.
Every day in every way it's getting better and better, beautiful boy.

I smiled wistfully. I still loved him, my Andrew. Then I unwrapped the two gifts from Alistair, peeling the Sellotape carefully away from the gold paper to reveal a bottle of CK One Red and this beautiful dark blue scarf.

"I got *him* a scarf," I said, opening his card. Then I stopped. Everything stopped. My heart stopped. I sat on the floor by the Christmas tree reading his words through a sudden tidal wave of tears. He'd written a poem. Wordlessly, I handed it to my mother. He said he knew the Meaning of Life, the answer to the question Life, the Universe and Everything. The answer was me.

"Ring him," said Mum, returning the card. "Ring him now."

That dear, dear voice wished me the happiest Christmas ever and thanked me for the gifts and I told him what'd happened in the last few hours, from church to now.

"I don't get it," I said. "Suddenly they're all 'ring Ali, get Alistair over.' I don't get it."

"Christmas miracle, honey," he said. "Just shows. Never stop believing in magic."

"I loved your poem," I said. "It made me cry."

"Your letter did the same to me," he said. "God, Jonathan, I'm so lucky."

"*We're* lucky," I corrected him. "Not many people find their soul-mates."

Dad appeared in the hall. "Invite him to tea. Go on, ask him."

"Go away," I hissed, flapping a hand. "Not you. Dad wants to know if you'd like to come to our party tomorrow. Please say 'I do' my darling."

He did.

Over the turkey, parsnips, sprouts and potatoes, it was like a dam'd been blown up by a bouncing-bomb. I talked non-stop about him and when the Christmas pudding, doused in dancing blue flames, arrived on the table with a jug of thick brandy-butter, I remembered my wish for acceptance on Stir-Up Sunday. My eyes filled with tears again. Wishes *did* come true, but you had to believe, especially when times got hard. All things pass, except the truth.

"What do you get," went Dad, "If you eat the Christmas decorations? Tinsillitis."

Oh boy. I gathered up the cracker-toys, a bouncy rubber-ball, a mini yoyo, a yellow heart-shaped key-ring, as Mum read "Why are fish easy to weigh? Because they have their own scales" and I had "What do vampires sing on New Year's Eve? Auld Fang Syne." Actually, I thought the last one was really funny. How lame had I become? Considerably, I reflected, adding the trinkets to my presents piled neatly in a corner by the Christmas tree.

Absolutely stuffed, with a large glass of port, a yellow paper-crown pulled over my forehead, the washing-up done, the fire burning nicely in the hearth, I leafed through the lifeboat calendar thinking the facts would make a great *Top Trumps* game, like February (Ali's birth-month) was a Severn class with a crew of 6-7 and a maximum speed of 25 knots, and May (my birth-month) was a Mersey class with a crew of 6 and a maximum speed of 17 knots. I was quite glad his beat mine, though the best was this B-Class Atlantic 75 Inshore Lifeboat, for September. Crew of 3-4, maximum speed of 32-35 knots and a really cool, sleek design. Then we settled back for the Queen's Christmas Message, *Twenty Thousand Leagues under the Sea* and, hurrah, James Bond on ITV, *The Man with the Golden Gun*, Scaramanga, revolving cars, the lot.

"We know," said Her Majesty, "That the world can never be free from conflict and pain, but Christmas also draws our attention to all that is hopeful and good in this changing world; it speaks of values and qualities that are true and permanent and it reminds us that the world we would like to see can only come from the goodness of the heart."

And yet the world *could* be 'free from conflict and pain', if we *really* wanted it so. I popped a segment of chocolate orange into my mouth and sneezed loudly. See? Free.

Normally people arrived for our Boxing Day 'do' around half-one, just in the middle of *Racing from Wincanton* and just before the Bank Holiday footie. This year Boxing Day was a Friday which meant two matches in two days because there was a full programme today and a full programme on Saturday. Seemed barking mad to me, you know? Anyway, I was kind of looking forward to the Manchester United-Liverpool match, especially since Man U had lost 2-1 to Arsenal the previous week (Bunny would be pleased), and figured I might be able to smuggle Ali up to my room to listen to the radio commentary, especially if the locals were distracted by their team's efforts against the powerhouse of Birmingham City.

Dressed in sexy black slip, favourite white Chinos, white socks, new hoodie and Christmas Converse, I tied Ali's friendship-band behind my trusty Timex and settled the gold crucifix round my neck but I was so skittish I couldn't settle into explaining how I'd won the big silver cup on the mantelpiece, keeping glasses full and directing people to the food in the kitchen, especially as Mum kept asking where Ali was, and was he still coming, and maybe he'd forgotten... I got so wound up I went into the street to see if I could spot him. I couldn't. God Almighty. Maybe he *wasn't* coming. Maybe I should ring him. Yes. I'd ring him. But then he might think I was nagging him... oh bollocks. What should I do? Standing on the doorstep, I was in a froth of indecision. I should wait, of course. I straightened the front-door wreath, holly and ivy twined with berries red as wine-splashes, and returned to the excited buzz, the humdrum conversation, the anxiety...

I knew what the horoscopes said. Gemini would experience uncertainty over a friend. Pisces needed to think carefully before making a major decision. Cheers, Russell.

Downing a large vodka-shot, I wondered what to do. Should I phone him? I didn't want to sound needy or clingy. I sank another vodka-shot and picked up the phone. Put it down again. Picked it up. Dialled the first two digits. Put it down. Fucking hell. Grabbing my new scarf and Santa hat, I went into the garden again and, leaning over the frost-crusted gate, scoured the street, up and down. Nothing. No-one. Which way would he come? Would he come? Maybe he'd chickened out. I looked at the snowman we'd built together. His coal eyes glinted blackly back. His grin seemed evil. Suddenly I hated him. If he came alive, like the one in the film, and took me to the North Pole to meet Santa, walking in the air and all that bollocks, I'd feed him to the fucking reindeer.

I opened the gate and, my breath forming white clouds in the freezing air, set off down the pavement, the snow packed hard under my rubber soles. I kept looking at my Timex. It was ten past two, like the last time I'd looked. Where the hell was he?

I reached the crossroads. Should I go home? Maybe he'd come a different way? If I went left, and he was coming the other way, I'd miss him. What if he like arrived and found I'd gone out? What then? My teeth were chattering and my hands were really cold. I wished I'd brought a coat, but then I'd only intended to go to the garden-gate, you know?

Then I saw him, heading up the hill, dressed in a white-and-charcoal jumper and black jeans and the scarf I'd given him, a bunch of red and pink flowers in one gloved hand, a bottle of Chardonnay in the other. God, he was so beautiful he took my breath away.

"I love this scarf," he said, "And I love those shoes. I want some." We kissed under a street-light. "Your face is frozen."

"I came to find you." I wished I'd worn more clothes but better sexy than warm, eh?

He blew on my hands, rubbing them between his, then handed me the flowers while he kept the bottle, linked arms with me and sang *'Follow the yellow-brick road, follow the yellow-brick road...we're off to see the wizard, the wonderful wizard of Oz.'* Friends of Dorothy, we skipped together up the hill. The snowman smiled warmly.

"I love him," said Alistair. "I never want him to melt."

"If he came alive," I said, "Like in the film..."

"I'd want him to fly you to me," we chorused, and laughed.

We kicked snow off our shoes and entered the warmth of the house. Under the mistletoe, I held him for a moment so I could kiss him properly, then the scent of cloves and cinnamon drew us to the kitchen where Dad was ladelling spiced mulled wine into mugs.

"Alistair!" cried Mum, gathering him into this massive hug, "You must be half-frozen. Come and sit by the fire and Jonathan can get you some food."

I arranged ham, chicken-wings, sausage-rolls, apple-and-potato salad on two plates and went to sit with him on the rug by the fire, warming our hands on the mulled wine and listening to stories about my childhood. I twined my arm round his waist and snuggled in against him. Ali said, to appreciative 'ahhhs', "I think he's amazing. I love him so much."

Then we gathered in the music-room for a Christmas sing-song, me at the piano and Dad on his guitar. Mum looped her arm through Ali's and led us into "*The first Nowell the angel did say, was to certain poor shepherds in fields where they lay...*" and everyone joined together, "*Nowell, nowell, nowell, nowell, born in the king of Israel.*" Then Mum said Ali was lovely. Everyone knew he was my boyfriend and everyone seemed happy for me. I sank into his arms and kissed him slowly, and then we danced, heads on shoulders, to ABBA's 'Happy New Year' while Mum and Dad held hands and smiled and their friends chattered warmly and Ali and I held each other and sang "*May we all have a vision now and then of a world where every neighbour is a friend...*"

So that was Christmas, and what had we done? One life over, another just begun. In some ways, nothing had changed but, at the same time, *everything* had. I lost friends, and made friends. My understanding of myself changed, totally and forever. My relationship with those around me, with the *world* around me, would never be the same again. Life would be viewed through the rainbow-prism of my homosexuality. Yet I still had the same hobbies, interests and ambitions, I still wanted to be a music-reviewer and I still wanted to write. Only now I wanted a boy to share my life, not a girl. No-one in the entire Universe could be as lucky as me. I was gay, queer, homosexual, whatever. I knew it and embraced it 'cos someone somewhere had decided that was what I should be. And not only that, I had been given a boy I could love and he was beautiful and loved me too, and that was the best feeling ever.

Dad explained that he *could* put Ali in the spare room but knew I'd just sneak down there in the middle of the night so Ali could choose where he slept, but of course if he slept with me, there were two things he should know.

"First," says Dad, "He makes really weird snuffling noises in his sleep, like a truffling badger or something. Just roll him onto his side and he'll stop. Second, you're under our roof for the first time. We're light sleepers. He's under-age. We're still getting our heads round this, so *please*, Alistair, don't screw him, all right? I understand you might want to, and you've probably done *some* stuff already but he *is* only fifteen and he's still our little boy. He'll beg and plead and wheedle, he can be very persuasive, but don't give in to him, OK?"

Mildly drunk on spiced rum, Ali and I went to sit on the wall to enjoy the bright, sharp cold and the thousands of stars strewn across the universal blackness. Snuggling into my usual place in his shoulder and watching our breath mingle in misty cloudbursts, I had never felt so utterly, blissfully happy. We were going to have a New Year party and invite all the others. I wanted Leo, obviously, and Andy, Niall, Shelters, Ayres, Holt, Ruby, Cookie, all the gays we loved. We'd play ABBA and dance topless and drink Jaegerbombs but I also wanted Claire, Mark and Becky, Mikey and Katie. *We* wouldn't be exclusive.

"You, my darling," Ali began as the glowing full moon beamed fatly down, "Are the best thing that ever happened to me. You make my life so wonderful. Your beauty, your energy, your very soul make this boring world worth living in. I love you so very much. I love every cell of your being and I swear on my life I will never leave you, not ever."

"I love you with every beat of my heart and every breath in my body," I murmured. "My light, my life, my world, my all. Loving you makes me so happy, so complete. I will never leave you, not till the breath leaves my lungs and the light leaves my eyes. You are my radiant light, my shining sun, my guiding star. You are every dream come true, and I adore you. So take me upstairs, my darling, darling boy, take me to bed and do whatever you want with me because I am yours, unconditionally, forever and always."

Finishing the warming, fiery rum, we held hands together under the stars, then I kissed him once more and let him carry me up to my bed for the best Christmas ever.

THE END

Other titles currently available

Tombland Fair

Norwich 1272. Nicolas de Bromholm lives with his parents and baby sister in 'The Mischief Tavern'. When his father's best friend is murdered by a monk, Nicolas' life is turned upside down. Under siege, their world in flames, Nick and his friends must choose which side they are on, that of the rulers, or that of the people.

A Teenage Odyssey

This epic for a new millennium describes teenager Adam Lycett's journey from comfortable home to cardboard box when he flees his violent stepfather to find his real father somewhere in contemporary London, a Dickensian cityscape populated by gin-swilling, pill-popping juveniles bent on burglary, mugging and sex, by fat-cat lawyers and bankers swindling their clients, by an idle aristocracy abusing the poor, and by people living, and dying, in doorways.

Dead Boy Walking

When Iraqi teenager Ali Al-Amin's parents are killed by a terrorist bomb, he is recruited by Arab Intelligence to infiltrate a school for suicide bombers in Syria. There he is turned into a human bomb, a dead boy walking, and sent to murder 3000 people with sarin nerve gas. Ali has just three days to save himself and the world from total destruction.

J.

A Veritable Jackdaw's nest of a book containing secret societies, conspiracies and counter-conspiracies, Jacobites, Inquisitors, artists and dramatists, jays and jackdaws, velcro jumping, Jewish Zen Buddhist blues, mathematical opera, Jacobean theatre, folk and jazz, kings and popes, Jason and JASON, Bedekeepers and Beadkeepers, tarboys and jumbucks, curious ceremonies, arcane rituals, bizarre coincidences, eccentric characters, lots of fascinating but utterly useless information, plenty of ovophiles and the quest to crown a King.

Out: A Schoolboy's Tale

When 15 year old Jonathan Peters falls in love for the first time, it is as unwelcome as it is unexpected because he falls in love with another boy. As his love deepens, his internal struggle with being homosexual spills into the open, impacting on his relationships with family, friends and teachers, who must all adjust their ambitions for him and the way they relate to him.

Yo-yo's Weekend

While spending a weekend in York, schoolboy Yo-yo's ring is stolen by Mr Vanilla, a forty stone jewel thief so he gathers together, among others, Lily Gusset, the reverse drag-artist, Mrs Lollipop, bed-ridden these forty years, Baby the talking blackbird, the custard-pie flinging Lettuce Brother clowns, an angry ichthyosaur, a weed and a pebble, a copper named Kipper, a professional Scotchman named Wee Jocko McTavish and the severed head of the Ninth Earl of Northumberland in a quest to retrieve it.

All titles available in paperback from Amazon and as ebook downloads from Kindle, iTunes and Smashwords.

Printed in Great Britain
by Amazon